Marching Through Culpeper

Marching Through Culpeper

A Novel of
Culpeper, Virginia
Crossroads of the Civil War

Virginia B. Morton

Virginia Beard Morton

Edgehill Books, Orange, Virginia

Edgehill Books

P. O. Box 1342
Orange, Virginia 22960
540-825-9147
vbmorton@edgehillbooks.com
www.edgehillbooks.com

Sincere thanks to the following for allowing the reprintal of quotes or maps from their books:
Judy Brown Brickman and Barbara Brown Hootman for *Stringfellow of the Fourth by Riley Shepard Brown.* © 1960
Dr. Daniel Sutherland, maps and quotes from *Seasons of War* © 1995.
H. E. Howard, Inc. for maps from *The Road to Bristoe Station* © 1987.
Robert K. Krick and The University of North Carolina Press for maps from *Stonewall Jackson at Cedar Mountain,* © 1990.
Specified excerpts from *Diary of a Union Lady 1861-1865* by Harold Earl Hammond ©1962 by Funk & Wagnalls Co., Inc. Reprinted by permission of HarperCollins Publishers, Inc.

Library of Congress Card Number 00-103914

Civil War Fiction

ISBN 0-615-11642-6

Cover art by
Michelle M. Powell

Fax 540-987-8914

Ninth Printing

PRINTED IN THE UNITED STATES OF AMERICA

In memory of

Captain Benjamin Franklin Stringfellow, C. S. A.

Daring Scout and Spy for

General J. E. B. Stuart, C. S. A.

and

Riley Shephard Brown

Author of *Stringfellow of the Fourth*

Acknowledgements

I owe my deepest gratitude to Judy Brown Brickner and Barbara Brown Hootman, daughters of the late Riley Shepard Brown, for generously allowing me to incorporate excerpts from *Stringfellow of the Fourth* into this book. Only by using ideas and selections from their father's marvelous book, could I bring the unforgettable character of Frank Stringfellow vividly to life for you. These portions have been duly noted by endnotes.

Clark B. "Bud" Hall's contagious enthusiasm for Culpeper's Civil War history inspired me to attempt to tell Culpeper's story through the eyes of the people who lived it. I am most appreciative of the extensive research he has shared with me. Dr. Daniel Sutherland's outstanding book, *Seasons of War,* has also been an inestimable resource for me, and I thank him for allowing me to reprint three maps from his book.

To the many friends who have offered kind words of encouragement, I am deeply grateful. The input and support of my good friend, Sherall Dementi, have been invaluable to me. Aruna Ratnavibhushana has given countless hours helping me format the book. I could not have done it without her help and technical knowledge. She is a special lady, indeed. Martha Mothersead has taken time to advise me and has pointed me in the right direction on many occasions. I also appreciate the exhaustive efforts of Virginia Costello, who has spent countless hours working on the cover layout. It is wonderful to live in a community as supportive as Culpeper.

I appreciate the timely efforts of my editor, Lorraine Maslow, and her prompt answers to my questions. Michelle M. Powell went the extra mile while researching and drawing the artwork for the cover. Her creative energy and artistic talent have given me a truly special cover, and I cannot sing her praises enough.

Lastly, thanks go to my husband, Roger, who has endured almost four years of my obsession with this book, and has allowed me thousands of hours on the computer. He was always there to troubleshoot my endless technical problems, and I never could have persevered without him.

Contents

Madison County

Robinson River

To Sperryville

Crooked Run

Griffinsburg

Amisville

Waterloo

Jeffersonton

To Warrenton

Cedar mt.

Rapidan Station

Culpeper Court House

9

2 Rixeyville

1

3

10

Mt. Pony

Welford's Ford

4 Hazel River

Oak Shade

Little Fork

Rappahannock River

6 Orange & Alexandria RR

7

Brandy Station

5

Beverly's Ford

Freeman's Ford

Mitchell's Station

The Flats

16 Stevensburg

14

15

17

Kellysville

Rappahannock Station

Barnett's Ford

Kelly's Ford

12

Somerville Ford

Raccoon Ford

Morton's Ford

Rapidan River

13

Germanna Ford

Richardsville

Chinquapin Neck

Ely Ford

To Fredericksburg

Clark's Mt.

Orange County

Fauquier County

IMPORTANT BUILDINGS

1. Panorama - Charles Armstrong
2. Rose Dale - James and Martha Rixey
3. Pleasant Hill - Charles Rixey
4. Little Fork Episcopal Church
5. Beauregard - James & Fannie Barbour
6. Afton - Taylor Bradford
7. Auburn - James Beckam to J.M. Botts
8. Clover Dale - Catherine Crittenden
9. Val Verde - Thomas & Columbia Nalle
10. Greenwood - John Green
11. The Retreat - Anne Stringfellow
12. Summerduck - Rev. Thornton Stringfellow
13. Salubria - Robert Grayson
14. Clover Hill - John Barbour (Custer)
15. Rose Hill - Alfred Ashby (Kilpatrick)
16. Ashland - Coleman Beckam
17. Madden's Tavern - Willis Madden

Courtesy Dr. Daniel Sutherland from *Seasons of War*

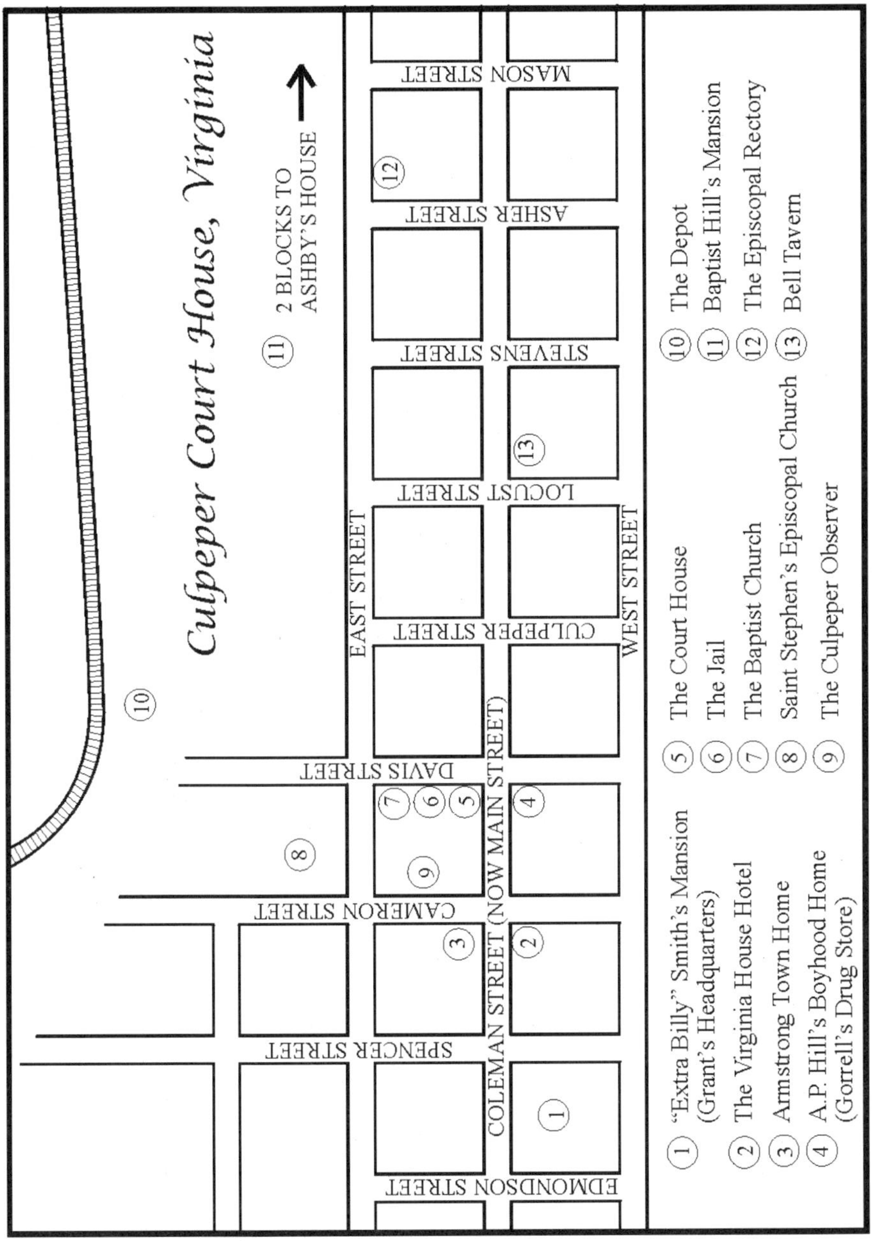
Culpeper Court House, Virginia
2 BLOCKS TO ASHBY'S HOUSE
EAST STREET
WEST STREET
COLEMAN STREET (NOW MAIN STREET)
EDMONDSON STREET
SPENCER STREET
CAMERON STREET
DAVIS STREET
CULPEPER STREET
LOCUST STREET
STEVENS STREET
ASHER STREET
MASON STREET
1 "Extra Billy" Smith's Mansion (Grant's Headquarters)
2 The Virginia House Hotel
3 Armstrong Town Home
4 A.P. Hill's Boyhood Home (Gorrell's Drug Store)
5 The Court House
6 The Jail
7 The Baptist Church
8 Saint Stephen's Episcopal Church
9 The Culpeper Observer
10 The Depot
11 Baptist Hill's Mansion
12 The Episcopal Rectory
13 Bell Tavern

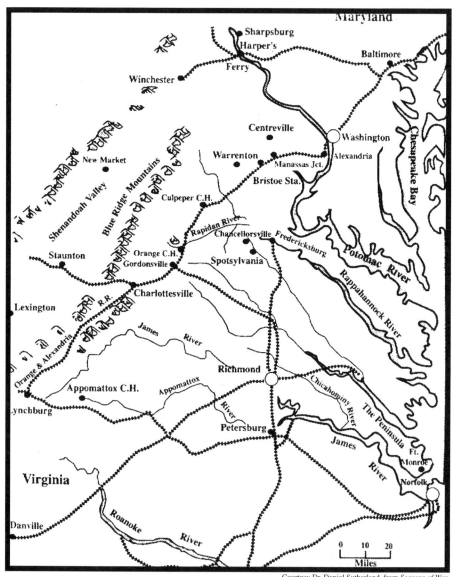

Courtesy Dr. Daniel Sutherland, from *Seasons of War*

12

To the Reader

There was no better vantage point to observe America's deadliest war than Culpeper, Virginia. Strategically located between the Rappahannock and Rapidan Rivers and on the vital Orange and Alexandria Railroad, the county witnessed the movement of more troops than any other locale in the nation. It was a natural point of invasion for the Union army en route to Richmond. Robert E. Lee also considered it an ideal camping ground for the Confederate army. From Culpeper, he could move quickly to the defense of Richmond or the Shenandoah Valley. One army or the other occupied the county much of the war, culminating in the Winter Encampment of more than one hundred thousand Union soldiers in 1863-64. The county witnessed the bloody Battle of Cedar Mountain and the largest cavalry engagement of the war, the Battle of Brandy Station. Countless smaller engagements took place and the major battles of First and Second Manassas, Fredericksburg, Chancellorsville, Spotsylvania and the Wilderness occurred within forty miles of its borders. The majority of the action of this book takes place in the county, with several incidents reported within that forty-mile radius.

This is the story of the lives and experiences of Culpeper's people as they witnessed four years of bloodshed and endured inconceivable privations and hardships. Determined to defend their state and their rights, they entered the War for Southern Independence confident that their cause was just. Although they lost everything material that they owned, they endured the ordeal with a high courage that their adversary could not destroy. The northern perspective is related through the Union soldiers who fought, camped, and died in Culpeper to put down the Great Rebellion.

Although this is a work of fiction, every effort has been made to relate historical and political events as the residents of Culpeper would have witnessed them. Before them passed the now-famous leaders of both great armies, and an attempt has been made to acquaint the reader intimately with four of Culpeper's native sons: General "Extra Billy" Smith (two-time Governor of Virginia), General A. P. Hill (Corps Commander for Robert E. Lee), Captain Frank Stringfellow (scout for Jeb Stuart), and Major Robert F. Beckam (Commander of the Stuart Horse Artillery). Because Culpeper witnessed countless cavalry engagements, fun-loving Jeb Stuart and gallant John Pelham are prominent characters, as are colorful Union generals Judson Kilpatrick and George Armstrong Custer.

Since this is a work of fiction, all conversations are presumed to be fictional unless indicated otherwise. In order to portray accurately the thoughts and feelings of the characters, primary sources such as letters, journals, and diaries have been used. At times, the words from these sources have been put into the mouths of fictional characters.[1] To make the book relevant to modern readers, the rhetoric used is simpler and less flowery than normal conversation of the 1860s.

Constance Armstrong, her family and servants are all fictional, as are Aaron Ames, Granny Ashby, George McDonald, and Major and Mrs. Bennett. All other characters in the book are real people. However, Constance Armstrong was inspired by and modeled after Bessie Shackelford. Bessie's father, a judge, owned the house across the street from the Virginia House Hotel and a farm in the country. Jeb Stuart and John Pelham were frequent visitors, and according to local lore she had a romantic relationship with John Pelham.

To purists who wish to separate fact from fiction, use this simple rule of thumb: most romance is fiction whereas troop movements, battles, politics and news of the day follow the facts as closely as possible.

Culpeper's story is that of a nation embroiled in a fratricidal war that we still grope to understand. The magnitude of the death and destruction are incomprehensible to us. It is my hope that as you live the years 1860-65 with the book's characters, some insight may be gained.

Virginia B. Morton

---

[1] Endnotes (denoted by Arabic Numerals) gives sources for such conversations as well as direct quotes from real characters. Historical and explanatory footnotes (denoted by Roman Numerals) have been placed at the bottoms of pages.

1

Storm Clouds on the Horizon

July 3-5, 1860

"Fanaticism never stops to reason."

President James Buchanan, 1860

July 3, 1860: Rixeyville, Virginia

A feeling of exhilaration engulfed Constance Rixey Armstrong as she spurred her chestnut filly, Queen Elizabeth, to gallop faster. They flew through the lush emerald fields of rolling farmland framed by the Blue Ridge Mountains, twenty-five miles to the west. With the breeze rippling through her curly ebony hair, she turned to see her father rapidly approaching on her left. "Head down to the run," he shouted when his horse galloped past her. With a nod of agreement, she spurred Liz forward and they raced down the hill, swiftly gaining speed. Several minutes later she watched her father and his black stallion sail over the two-foot-wide gurgling brook. Leaning forward, she and her filly likewise flew across as if they were one.

Enjoying the sweet aroma of honeysuckle, Constance slowed her mount to a trot and rode beside Charles Hudson Armstrong III. "Father, did you see how beautifully she jumped the creek? She seems to know my every wish. She's the most wonderful birthday present you could have given me!" The eighteenth birthday surprise had been an extravagant gift, but Charles Armstrong adored Constance, and their mutual love of riding strengthened the deep bond of affection between them.

"Indeed," he said with a laugh. "The two of you appear to be made for each other. Frisky, spirited, and strong-willed."

A vivacious smile lit her face. "Liz and I certainly think alike. Should we start back for dinner?"

"Yes. We don't want to keep Sadie waiting, and I'm famished." He headed his horse across the small wooden bridge and onto the path back to their house, Panorama.

Constance absorbed the tranquil serenity of her surroundings. Her gaze to the north revealed Rose Dale, the three story yellow frame house of her great aunt and uncle, Martha and James Rixey. Far on the horizon to the south, she scanned the silhouette of Pleasant Hill, an imposing brick home built by another relative, Charles Rixey. The rich undulating farmland encircled her like a rumpled patchwork quilt. Alternating strips of wheat, corn, tobacco, and beans intermixed with pastures where sheep, cattle, and horses grazed lazily. Panorama, the two-story white frame house built by her grandfather, crowned the hill before her. He had married Katherine Rixey, daughter of a wealthy landowner in the area. Katherine's father bestowed five hundred acres of land on the newlyweds. The young lovers hiked every inch of the property in order to select a building site with the most expansive view. The high ridge on which they constructed their home encompassed a 360-degree panoramic view with the mountains to the west and the Hazel River meandering below to the north. Hence, they named their home Panorama.

They rode up to the stable where Abraham Jordan greeted them with a big grin. "Y'all have a good ride, Miss Constance?"

"It couldn't have been more marvelous, Abraham. Liz performed like a champ. Walk her until she cools down." Abraham took the reins of the two sweating horses. Soon they would be stabled with Charles Armstrong's ten other horses, some of the finest thoroughbreds in Virginia.

Father and daughter walked arm in arm up the hill. Constance stared intently at the 5-foot, 9-inch, fit seventy-year-old man beside her. Gray haired with a curling mustache, he epitomized a distinguished Virginia gentleman. His blue eyes sparkled with merriment.

The aroma of freshly baked bread drifting from the detached kitchen drew them forward. Judge Armstrong's grandson, Hudson, dashed down the hill towards the two of them, with Isaac Jordan, Abraham's grandson, in close pursuit. "Grandpa, look what I found!" Hudson said.

"What exciting discovery have you made today?" Charles stooped down to peer into Hudson's cupped hands.

"It's an empty bug," the blonde-haired boy said.

"No," said Isaac, a year older and wiser. "Mista Armstrong, ain't that a locust's shell?"

On closer examination, Charles chuckled. "You're absolutely right, Isaac. The locust sheds its shell when it becomes an adult. That loud noise we've been hearing at night is the locust's mating call. Unfortunately, they're eating all the leaves off the trees in the orchard."

"Grandpa, can I keep this locust shell?" Hudson pleaded.

"Certainly, but I don't know why you'd want to remember anything as destructive as the locust. They're stripping our lands."

"Come on, Hudson." Constance took his hand. "We need to get you washed up for dinner." They stepped on the porch that stretched across the back of the house, and Constance's older sister, Amanda, appeared at the door.

"I'll take him, Connie." She peeked into his cupped hands. "What have we here?"

"A locust shell," Hudson said.

"Oh my, what next?"said his tall, slender mother.

The sweet scent of her mother's roses greeted Constance in the center hall with its eleven-foot ceilings. Harriet Taylor Armstrong breezed by while father and daughter washed their hands in the bowl of water on the mahogany dry sink. "Good heavens, Constance, don't tell me you were riding in pants again."

"You know I prefer to ride astride. Don't worry, Mother, I didn't scandalize the neighborhood. We stayed on the farm."

The stately lady stared down her sophisticated nose at her contrary daughter. "You're not coming to dinner in those riding pants. That's inappropriate for a young lady."

Constance folded her arms. "Father's wearing his riding pants. We're only family, so what difference does it make?" Harriet threw up her arms in a hopeless gesture.

Charles rolled his eyes at Harriet as the family gathered around the large rectangular mahogany dining table. Harriet took the seat at the far end of the table. At fifty eight she possessed a grace and aristocratic beauty that attracted attention wherever she went. Large boned and standing 5 feet 8 inches, at first glance she appeared larger than her husband. A native of Fredericksburg, forty-five miles to the east, she was the daughter of a wealthy shipping tycoon. Nothing had been denied her. Marriage and family were postponed until she had traveled to Europe, studied art and music, and fully absorbed European culture. At age thirty three she finally returned to Fredericksburg, knowing that the time had come to settle down. Her brother introduced her to Charles Armstrong, a widower and fellow member of the Virginia Legislature. Immediately attracted to his intellect and gentleness, she accepted his proposal without giving a second thought to leaving the social life of Fredericksburg to live in rural Culpeper County. Their marriage was a strong and happy one.

On Harriet's left sat Alex Yager, Amanda's husband. Tall, muscular, and attractive, he had grown up in the German community of Jeffersonton, five miles to the north. His father owned a prosperous mercantile and was proud that he could send his only son to the University of Virginia, Mr. Jefferson's university. Alex and Amanda, childhood sweethearts, had met when they attended the Jeffersonton Academy. Proud of snaring Amanda, Alex considered his marriage an upward social move. After finishing the university he began practicing law with his father-in-law. He had framed in a house for his growing family over the crest of the hill from Panorama and eagerly looked forward to moving into their own home.

Seated between Alex and Amanda, David Hans Yager cooed, blew bubbles, and played with the piece of toast on his wooden high chair tray. A healthy, cheerful baby this first year of his life, each day he grew to look more like his father with his brown eyes and auburn hair.

Amanda watched him, smiling. Her three pregnancies, including a miscarriage between the boys, had sapped her strength. Beginning to feel stronger, she prayed for the day when she could give Alex a daughter. Sophisticated like her mother, Amanda possessed a slender engaging face. Well read and musically talented, she played the flute, harp, and piano, and possessed a beautiful, well-trained soprano voice. Soft spoken, she never sought attention. However, when she performed musically, her shyness melted away as all eyes focused on her. She had been in love with Alex ever since she could remember and had not hesitated to marry him at age eighteen. Now, at twenty three, her life revolved around her family.

Constance studied her sister. She had watched Amanda become consumed with child-bearing and family responsibilities. Constance knew one thing for certain: she was not ready for married life now and perhaps never would be. She wanted freedom to be creative. Independent and highly intellectual, she devoured books. She had helped her father with legal and political research and constantly stayed abreast of current events. She knew she wanted to write, so perhaps her calling was in the newspaper business. A bitter anger welled up inside of her when she was told these professions were not open to women. Times were changing. Numerous women had written successful novels, and she refused to let her gender alter her dreams. She preferred discussions of important matters over flirtations and social prattle. Although she enjoyed a circle of interested suitors, none attracted her enough to make her consider giving up her freedom. She dreamed of a husband who would accept her as an equal.

Leaning up against his aunt, sandy-haired, round-faced Charles Hudson Yager looked hungrily at the chicken Sadie placed on the table. The four-year-old had carefully saved his locust shell in a jar before coming to dinner.

Charles Armstrong, seated at the opposite end of the table, looked lovingly over his brood. He had been blessed. After losing his first wife and newborn son in childbirth, life did not seem worth living. To overcome his grief, he had thrown himself into politics and later became extremely influential in the Virginia Legislature and the Democratic Party. Then Harriet Taylor's sophistication and intelligence had captured his heart. At age forty five he embarked on marriage and raising a family for the second time. Harriet had lost a stillborn son prior to Amanda's birth and then suffered a miscarriage between the girls. Her difficult pregnancy with Constance determined that she would be the last child. However, even though Charles never uttered one word of disappointment when his second daughter was born, he proceeded to raise her as he would a son. She fished and rode with him and shared his love of politics. Her intellect pleased him, and he realized she had far more legal potential than Alex did. It pained him that this profession was not open to her.

The salary of a judge was not large; Charles spent and gambled too much on horses, his weakness and passion. When his father died, he was forced to sell three hundred acres to divide the estate with his younger brother in California. Charles had retained his grandfather's house in Culpeper Court House, where the family spent the winters. He used two rooms for his law offices and leased one room to a bookstore owner. Forced to sell another fifty acres to pay taxes last year, he possessed little savings.

He reached out his hands and the family joined hands around the table. "Let us pray," he said. They bowed their heads. "Most gracious and loving heavenly Father, bless this food to the nourishment of our bodies. Thank you for the bounty of nature, which we enjoy, and the beauty of your world around us. Let the voice of reason keep our nation from being torn asunder. We know that force and violence cannot solve problems and yet we wonder how our liberties and rights can be guaranteed. In these perilous times, we pray for the leaders of our nation. Grant them wisdom and compassion. Let diplomacy rule over fanaticism. Forgive us of our sins, and show us how to model our lives after Jesus Christ, our precious Lord and Savior. In His name we pray."

"Amen," they said in unison.

Constance noticed the lines of tension on her father's face. "You sound very concerned, Father."

"James Barbour returned today from the Democratic Convention in Baltimore," he said. "He confirmed that the convention had split with the northern delegates nominating Douglas and the southern delegates walking out and later selecting Breckinridge. There's also rumor that a fourth political party is being formed and hopes to nominate Bell as a compromise candidate."

"Since the Republicans have already nominated Lincoln, that means we'll have at least four presidential candidates on the ballot," Alex said.

The judge shook his head. "This split in the Democratic Party practically assures that Mr. Lincoln will be elected."

Shock registered on every face. "Heaven forbid," Alex cried. "The South would never stand for having that uncouth Black Republican in the White House."

Constance leaned forward. "Do you really think he can win?"

"It's inevitable," Charles replied in a troubled voice. "Although more people will vote against him than for him, he will still receive the most votes of the four candidates. The anti-Republican vote will be split three ways."

"That's enough talk of politics at the dinner table," Harriet said. She passed the green beans to Alex. "What time will we leave tomorrow for the party?"

"Around 9:00, but I wonder what kind of a Fourth celebration this will be." Charles took one of Sadie's huge rolls. "You're taking your famous fried chicken to the picnic, aren't you Sadie?"

"Yas'r, Mista Armstrong, ya know it wouldn't be no picnic without mah chicken!" Sadie said. "Me an' Abraham was wonderin' if we could ride over an' see Mary while y'all is at Salubria?" She served the potatoes.

"Certainly," Charles said. "How is she?"

"She's fine. Lookin' forward to bein' a momma." Sadie's wide grin showed her even pearly teeth.

After dinner, Harriet and Amanda went into Harriet's sewing room while Constance followed her father and Alex into the study. She loved the aroma of the leather on the chairs, sofa, and the bindings for the hundreds of books lining the walls. Charles and Alex relaxed into the two worn, tawny chairs and lit their pipes. In most households, it was considered improper for a woman to accompany the men into the study. However, Constance traipsed in and plopped on the couch. Charles always allowed her to participate in political discussions.

"Father." She looked at him intently. "Do you think that Mr. Lincoln's election could lead to war?"

Charles Armstrong puffed thoughtfully on his pipe. His gray eyebrows drew together. "I hope not with all my heart, but the southern states will most likely secede rather than be subjected to the rule of an abolitionist president. If that happens, the question remains, will Mr. Lincoln declare war?"

"The states have the legal right to secede," Alex said. "Our constitutional rights have been violated. For years, we've had to pay the unfair tariff on imports. Millions of dollars have been transferred from the South to the North through the tariff. It has protected their manufacturing interests and built new roads in the Northwest Territories. Meanwhile, they throw insults at us."

"They made a martyr out of that fanatic John Brown," Charles said. "He broke the law, yet the Yankees proclaim him a hero and try to incite the slaves against us. I think they're determined to destroy us."

Constance pondered her father's words. Brown's raid at Harper's Ferry had stunned the citizens of Culpeper County. One of the four innocent, unarmed civilians killed, Fontaine Beckam, the mayor, had been born in Culpeper, and many of his close relatives lived in the county. "Mr. Lincoln's election could be disastrous," she said. "The people will feel that they've been wronged if a president is elected by only the New England states. I'm afraid our founding fathers didn't foresee this type of situation when they wrote the Constitution. No president should be elected who doesn't receive the majority of the popular vote."

Alex inhaled on his pipe. "Are you espousing the theory of one man, one vote?"

"Yes," Constance said. "Only of course I'd prefer one man, one woman, one vote. It's the only true form of democracy. If no candidate receives a majority of the vote, then there should be a run-off election between the top two. That way the country would never have a president who didn't win the majority of the votes. Such a system could avert the impending calamity."

Charles Armstrong looked at his daughter with admiration. "Constance, my dear, in theory, you're absolutely right. However, only a Constitutional Amendment could make that change. Obviously, it's impossible for that to happen before the election, or even at any other time. Meanwhile, we must deal with the situation that confronts us....but enough worrying about politics. I'll ride Liz tomorrow so you'll have her with you when we spend a few days at the Stringfellows. I bet she can outrun any horse on the Stringfellow farm."

Constance perked up and tossed her raven locks over her shoulder. "I know she can, Father. I'll show that Frank Stringfellow a thing or two. I imagine he thinks he knows everything now that he's a graduate of the Episcopal High School in Alexandria." She bounced off the sofa. "I'd better get my clothes packed."

Sadie Jordan wiped the sweat from her brow after she set the tray of dishes and leftovers on the pine trestle table in the brick kitchen. A tall, large-boned black woman, she conveyed strength and energy in her every movement. With a cheerful smile, she addressed her family, "Y'all ready to eat supper?"

"I'm starvin'," shouted her grandson, Isaac.

"Calm down, boy." Abraham pulled the boy down on the bench. "Let's say the blessin' first." Abraham's son Joseph and his wife Selene pulled Hope up to the table and they all bowed their heads.

After the prayer Sadie said, "Mista Armstrong seemed pow'ful upset at dinner. Seems he thinks some man named Lincoln might be elected president an' that could make our people very unhappy. They even talkin' about fightin' an' war."

"We're pretty happy. Sure don't want no fightin' round here." Abraham passed the collards.

"I heard at Monumental Mills that some of the northern folks wanna free the slaves," Joseph said. He piled hog and hominy on his plate. "But nobody knows what they gonna do with 'em after they free 'em. Folks don't like havin' free blacks 'round here. Ya know how it was for us when Mista Armstrong's daddy freed us in his will. Mista Armstrong had to say we'd be taken care of or they'd of made us leave. Who wants to leave their home?"

"Humph!" Abraham snorted. Two of his sons, Noah and John, had gone north and worked for the railroad. Noah had been killed in a dynamite accident and John couldn't tolerate the hard work and the harassment of the Irishmen. He now worked as a cook at a local hotel. "John's glad to be back in Culpeper. He say this is where he wants to be."

"I'm jist thankful Mista Armstrong let me be his overseer," Joseph said. "He's a good man to work for." Judge Armstrong used hired labor and paid Joseph a percentage of the profit on the farm.

"Mah grandma was born on this farm," Sadie said. "This is mah home. Ain't nobody goin' to make this chile leave her home an' her people." She pointed her finger at her chest.

"That's easy for y'all to say," said Selene, a small woman of twenty four with fine features. "Even when y'all was slaves, y'all had a good massa. But I had to put up with mean ol' Mista Kelly. If any slave did the least little thing, he'd chain 'em inside the

20

gristmill overnight an' whip 'em." She stared into Joseph's eyes. "The happiest day of mah life was when Mista Armstrong bought me so I could be your wife. But, I'm still a slave, an' so is mah kids."

"Selene," Joseph said. "Ya know Mista Armstrong had to pay a big price for ya, $1500.[i] He only bought ya to keep me happy. Soon as I finish payin' him back, you'll be free. He says if the kids work for him 'til they're twenty five, he'll set 'em free then. Ya don't know how lucky ya are."

"You right, Joseph." She wiped off three-year-old Hope's face. "I'm jist tired. I'll be glad when this baby comes." She patted her stomach.

"Hurry up an' finish your dinner, Abraham." Sadie stood and collected the dishes. "We's got a lotta work to do to get ready for this trip tomorrow. "

"Yas'um." Abraham grinned, then stood up and headed to the stable.

Constance held the azure cotton sateen dress up in front of her and gazed at herself in the mirror. She whirled around to face Sadie. "What do you think, Sadie? Should I wear this one to the picnic tomorrow? At least these ruffles over the bodice make me look bigger. Why can't slenderness be the fashion?"

"Oh, Miss Constance." Sadie laughed heartily. "You's somethin'. That dress looks gorgeous on ya. It matches your blue eyes. Don't ya fret none 'bout your figure. You'll fill out in all the right places. Jist give it some time. Ya know I ain't never told ya no lie. Trust Sadie."

Constance laid the dress on her bed. "I suppose. These hoops and corsets must be the invention of the devil." She tossed them into the open trunk on the floor. "Why do we let ourselves be enslaved to such discomfort?"

Sadie slowly poured the hot water into the large wash bowl. "I suppose it's 'cause ya wanna look pretty an' attract the gen'men." She pulled Constance's silky hair up in a ribbon to keep it from getting wet. "Ya need anything else, Miss Constance?"

"I'm not sure I see the logic in that argument. But no, Sadie, I'm fine. Good night."

Sadie kissed her on the forehead and closed the door. Constance smiled inwardly. She loved the old Negress like a member of the family.

When Constance crawled into bed, she gazed out of her upstairs window at the last rays of pink light fading behind the dark blue peaks. Fingers of red glowed on the clouds floating above the shimmering Hazel River as nature's kaleidoscope unfolded before her. This was her little corner of the world, this hamlet called Rixeyville, seven miles northwest of Culpeper Court House. She sighed with contentment and well being. If only those locusts would quit making that pulsating racket she could sleep. She flung the pillow over her head, trying to drown out the grinding whir. Damn the locusts and damn Abrahma Lincoln for invading her peaceful world!

Next day, July 4, 1860: En route to Salubria

Constance fanned herself while the carriage creaked eastward along the dusty road past the tiny village of Georgetown, nestled at the foot of Pony Mountain. The trip would go faster now, because the land flattened out eastward towards the Rapidan

---

[i] $30,000 in today's money.

River. Fields of golden wheat rippling in the breeze waved back at her. The wheat crop, the county's biggest money crop, looked bumper this year.

Her mother, seated beside her, dabbed her face with a handkerchief. "I see Ashland." She pointed to the frame farmhouse in the distance. "It'll be good to see the Beckams today. I always love this Fourth celebration because it gives us an opportunity to see all our friends."

Amanda, seated across from them, shifted the napping boys leaning against her. "Come now, Mother," she said. "We know you're the most excited about spending a few days with your dear friend Anne Stringfellow."

Harriet laughed softly. She and Anne had grown up next door to each other in Fredericksburg and were as close as sisters. "You know me well, my darling. One of the reasons I agreed to marry your father and move to Culpeper is that I knew Anne was here." Her almond eyes crinkled at the corners when she smiled. "I'm joking, of course. I would have married your father anyway. But Anne's friendship has been a source of joy to me."

"And you've been a blessing and strength to her since Rittenhouse died," Constance said. "I still can't understand why she's never remarried."

Her mother paused to reflect. "I suppose no one has measured up to him. She's doted on her three boys and has fortunately had Thornton and other relatives to look after her. She's content." Harriet tilted her head to look Constance in the eye. She worried that her strong-willed daughter did not seek enough female friends. "Now tell me Constance, who is your best friend?"

Constance wrinkled her face in deep concentration. "Well, the person who knows me the best, and always makes me laugh is Frank. He's my adopted big brother, and I believe he's my best friend. There's no one else I would confide in or trust like Frank."

"Are you sure, little sister, that he's just a friend?" Amanda stroked David's hair. "You know that Mother and Anne would be ecstatic if you and Frank would marry!"

Constance leaned forward. "Mandy, don't be ridiculous. That would be like incest. I think of Frank as a brother, and that's all. Besides I'm not in any hurry to get married. Why is everybody trying to push me down the aisle?"

"Now girls, calm down or you'll wake the boys," Harriet said with arched eyebrows. "Constance, I'm delighted Frank is a good friend to you, and I'm not trying to hurry you into marriage. Look how long it took me."

"Sorry Constance," Amanda mumbled. "I didn't mean to rile you." She looked out the window thoughtfully. "I think of Fannie Barbour as my best friend. She's always concerned about my feelings, and oh, how we do laugh when we're together."

Constance sulked with her head against the window and stared across the acres of fertile farmland towards Clover Hill, the home of her father's good friend, John Barbour. The frame house, built in 1775, fascinated her. The steeply pitched shake roof was adorned with narrow, double-arched windows topped with fake peaked dormers, almost giving the structure the appearance of an English cottage.

Charles and Alex rode up close to the carriage, and Charles called, "We'll stop at Stevensburg to water the horses."

Stevensburg, the oldest and once the largest town in the county, nestled at the inter-section of Kirtley's Trail, the primary road to Fredericksburg, and the Carolina Road, the main north–south artery originally used by the Indians. Inns and taverns were interspersed among numerous houses at this popular stopping place for travelers. Notorious pastimes such as horseracing, cock fighting, and all forms of gambling, had thrived in the early village. Many of the Quaker families, no longer able to condone these rowdy activities or slavery, migrated to Ohio around 1820. The completion of the Orange and Alexandria railroad in 1854 made growth move to Culpeper Court House, centrally located and now the most populous town in the county. Stevensburg reverted to a sleepy little village. Perhaps things would have been different if Thomas Jefferson had selected it as the location of the University of Virginia. Local legend said the town was seriously considered but was ruled out because of an insufficient water supply.

"Look," exclaimed Amanda when the carriage pulled into Zimmerman's Cross Keys Tavern, "There are Fannie and James."

Everyone piled out of the carriage. David and Hudson rubbed their eyes, and Amanda rushed over to embrace Fannie. "Amanda," said Fannie Beckam Barbour, shifting her baby daughter on her hip, "How wonderful to see you. I've missed our visits. Please ride the rest of the way to Salubria with us so that we can visit."

"I'd love to." Amanda pulled baby Ellen's nose. "How she's grown!"

"Momma," whined Hudson, "I don't wanna ride with those babies."

"Well, of course not young man. You're much too old for that." His grandmother chuckled, then bent over and took him by the hand. "I'd be honored if you'd ride with me." She turned to Amanda and winked.

James Barbour, influential member of the Virginia House of Delegates, shook hands with Charles and Alex. "Looks like all roads lead to Salubria today."

"Indeed," Alex answered. "But this year's celebration may be more subdued than usual."

"Perhaps you're right." James, thirty seven, wiped beads of sweat from his brow. "But we must work to ensure that next year we'll still be celebrating the Fourth of July."

Constance caressed Liz's nose and rubbed the horse's long muscular neck while the filly drank from the trough. "I know it's hot, baby, but we're almost there," she whispered. She moved to the shade cast by the tavern building dating from 1800 and wondered if the simple two-story frame structure with a porch across the front had changed much since Thomas Jefferson stopped there en route to his inauguration. Constance strolled over to the well to join the others for a drink of cool water.

After the short stop, the carriage slowly wound up the steady incline where Stevensburg Baptist Church became visible on the left. The relatively new brick structure with a beautiful steeple sat perched on a high knoll with a commanding view. "I understand that church has grown rapidly during Thornton Stringfellow's ministry," Harriet commented. "The new church has a balcony where the servants sit."

Constance leaned her head against the window, contemplating Reverend Stringfellow, Frank's uncle. Convinced that Africans had benefitted physically and spiritually from bondage, he had a reputation for preaching stirring sermons defending slavery based on Biblical references. It's true; slavery had existed since recorded time and local slaves were some of the best cared for laborers in the world. Still, she wondered how the slaves really felt when they heard his sermons.

Salubria: Benjamin Franklin Stringfellow strolled past the seemingly endless line of tables laden with every imaginable delicacy. The twenty-year-old was hungry as usual, but no matter how much he ate, he could not spread more than a hundred and twenty pounds over his 5-foot, 8-inch frame. He would wait for Constance to arrive so he could enjoy her company while he feasted. He pushed the blonde curly hair back from his high forehead and turned to gaze up at Salubria. The stately mid-Georgian home, built in 1742, was the oldest brick structure in the county and an appropriate location for the Fourth of July celebration. Two lofty chimneys centered on each end of the house crowned the mansard roof. Perfectly proportional with two windows flanking each side of the front door, the otherwise plain two-story façade gained an elegant rhythm by the use of brick arches above each opening. Frank had seen numerous beautiful homes while in Alexandria and Washington, but in his opinion, none of them outshone Salubria. Perhaps his friend, architect Jeremiah Morton, was right. He believed it to be one of the best examples of Georgian architecture in America.

His eyes swept over hundreds of acres of gently rolling farmland. The flocks of sheep looked like cotton puffs contrasted against the verdant fields framing the terraced gardens behind the house. Dark green mounds of boxwood enclosed the gardens where roses perfumed the air. At least two hundred friends and relatives mingled around him. American flags waved in the breeze while red, white, and blue tablecloths adorned the food tables; picnickers sat on blankets or plank benches. His stomach growled. He looked hopefully towards the latest carriage to arrive. The sun glistened on Constance's long hair as she disembarked. Always a prankster, he would surprise her.

Abraham helped the ladies step down from the carriage. "Give our regards to the Maddens." Charles handed him Liz's reins. "Willis Madden is a fine man."

"'Deed I will, Mista Armstrong. Ten o'clock soon enuff for us to be back?"

"I'm sure we won't be ready before then. The dancing won't start until dark." Charles took Harriet's arm and guided her towards the festivities.

Robert Grayson, owner of Salubria, greeted the family at the garden entrance. "It's always a pleasure to see you."

"We appreciate your generous hospitality," Charles said.

Grayson's two unmarried sons, Robert and John, approached Constance with smiles on their faces. "Miss Constance," John, a medical student, said, "I would be most honored if you would save me a dance."

With a low bow, Robert, eighteen, added, "I, too, would like to request the pleasure of a dance."

"Gentlemen," Constance said with an inviting smile, "it would be my pleasure."

The Armstrongs threaded through the crowd to the food tables, smiling and greeting friends en route. Amanda and Constance placed two large trays of fried chicken on the table, then Amanda spied Frank Stringfellow silently stalking up behind Constance. He put his finger to his lips signaling her to remain quiet and threw his hands over Constance's eyes. "Guess who?" he asked in a high squeaky voice.

Constance giggled. "It has to be Frank!" She spun around to look into his deep-set blue eyes. Smooth faced with an impish grin, he still didn't look a day over fifteen. "I've missed you."

Frank hugged her and gave her a kiss on the cheek. "And I, you, my dearest sister. I believe you grow more ravishing every day."

"We haven't been together two minutes and you're teasing me already." She stuck her lip out in a little pout.

"That's what big brothers are for," he chuckled. "And since you don't have one, I've accepted that responsibility. I'm glad you finally arrived. I've been waiting for you so that we could dine together. I'm famished."

The two of them walked along the food tables, piling their plates with ham, chicken, potatoes, strawberries, biscuits, pie, and numerous other delicacies. They planted themselves in the shade on one of the improvised benches.

"Looks delicious." Constance spread the red napkin in her lap. "Sadie says if I eat more, my figure will fill out."

"Don't think I have the answer to that question." Frank took a big chunk out of a chicken leg. "It doesn't matter how much I eat, I still don't gain any weight."

Abraham gave the horses free rein as the carriage jostled over the rutted dirt road towards Madden's Tavern. Sadie smiled at the thought of her Mary being married to Jack Madden, son of Willis Madden, wealthiest black man in the county. One hard-working man, Willis owned a big farm, livestock, the tavern, blacksmith shop, and hauled produce and building materials. She considered him a lot more prosperous than some white folk, especially that riffraff over in The Flats.

Willis Madden, one of 429 free blacks in Culpeper County, came from a family that had always been free, never slaves. His grandmother, an Irish servant, conceived a daughter by a Negro. The status of the mother determined whether a child was free or slave. The free daughter served as an indentured servant on the estate of President James Madison in adjacent Orange County. After fulfilling her years of indenture, she moved to Culpeper and made a living as a seamstress. Willis, one of her thirteen children, was industrious, successful, and respected in the community. Although he could not read, he had built a tavern and thriving business located a day's travel from Fredericksburg on the road west. Teamsters and drovers camped around his tavern with the livestock they were driving to market. Known for good food and spirits, Madden's Tavern was frequented by most of the whites in the county. Madden's two youngest sons, Jack, twenty, and Nathaniel, eighteen, still worked with him. Not owning slaves himself, he hired slaves from adjacent farms when he needed additional labor.

The outline of Maddens's Tavern appeared when the carriage made a turn in the road and creaked up the incline. Several drovers with their pigs already surrounded the L-shaped two-story building with dormers, situated in a grove of trees. Abraham tied the horses to the hitching post and Willis Madden strolled out the front door to greet them. A tall, attractive, dark mulatto, he held his hand out to help Sadie down from the carriage. "Mary said y'all would probably show up today. We've been lookin' for ya."

"Ya know we wouldn't pass up a chance to see our Mary while we was in the neighborhood." Abraham shook his hand.

Petite Mary bounded through the door. "Momma! Daddy!" She hugged them both. "I jist knew y'all was comin'. I made some apple pies an' cooked a roast."

"Lawd, chile, look at ya," Sadie said patting her stomach. "There's more of ya than the last time we seen ya. Ya feelin' well?"

"I'm feelin' fine Momma." She led them into the main room of the tavern. Polished pine chairs and tables filled the room where several customers enjoyed dinner. "This baby sure can kick. Y'all come on back to the family quarters."

They entered the back wing of the house, where upholstered chairs and a sofa sat atop a colorful wool rug before a large stone fireplace. "Y'all sit down," Willis said. "Jack'll be up from feedin' the horses in a minute."

Sadie glanced up at the mantel to see two symbols of Willis Madden's prosperity, a clock with metal works and a photograph of himself.

Willis relaxed into one of the chairs. "I have to tell y'all, havin' Mary here since mah Kitty died has been a Godsend. I don't know what I'd of done without her." He glanced at his daughter-in-law affectionately.

Mary clasped his hand. "Ya know how happy I am to be here. But tell me, Momma, how's everythin' at home?"

Sadie's bushy eyebrows furrowed together. "Mista Armstrong sent y'all his regards. He seems kinda upset 'bout this Lincoln might be elected president. Might be a war or somethin'. Seems Mr. Lincoln wants to free all the slaves. That's good, but what's he's goin' to do with them after he frees 'em?"

"Keep hearin' talk 'bout sendin' all the slaves back to Africa," Willis said with disgust. "Who wants to leave their homes to go to Africa? Still our people have to be freed so we can all have more rights." He paused reflecting on his situation. "I can own property, but I have to pay taxes an' can't vote. Guess I shouldn't complain 'bout that; white women in the same boat. Can't own no weapons. I 'member when I had to use a wooden pole to kill a rabid dog that was 'bout to attack the kids. Can't learn how to read...hate that the most."

"I've got a secret," Sadie said, beaming. "I told Miss Constance I wanted to be able to read the Good Book mahself. She said, no reason I shouldn't, an' she's been teachin' me to read. Y'all jist wait. Then I'll teach all of y'all."

Muscular, stocky Jack Madden came through the back door dressed in coveralls. "Well look here. If it ain't Ma an' Pa Jordan. Ain't seen y'all in a coon's age." He hugged Sadie and shook hands with Abraham. "Is dinner 'bout ready Mary? I've worked up a pow'ful appetite."

"Yes indeed, honey." Mary took Sadie by the arm. "Come on Momma, an' help me get the food on the table. Then we're all gonna have us a nice long visit."

The air grew cooler when the sun dropped behind the western tree line at Salubria. This traditional signal to begin the festivities caused the members of the band to tune their instruments. Robert Grayson walked forward, followed by several members of the local militia carrying the American flag and the flag of Virginia. "Let everybody stand," he announced loudly, "while Amanda Yager and Fannie Barbour lead us in singing the national anthem."

Amanda and Fannie walked front and center while everyone stood and faced the flag. Some saluted; others placed their hands over their hearts, while many others looked bored. Amanda and Fannie sang out lustily, but the crowd sang much less enthusiastically than in years past. Amanda's eyes scanned the group and she noticed many simply mouthed the words, while others made no attempt to sing. The same question haunted every mind...would they be here again next Fourth of July? At the conclusion of the anthem the color guard fired thirteen shots into the air, causing babies to cry and dogs to howl. The band broke into a foot-tapping version of the Virginia Reel and couples quickly lined up to dance. John Grayson pulled Constance forward to join the festivities.

Fannie and Amanda walked to the side of the garden to watch the dancers. "I felt like we were singing alone," Amanda whispered.

A tall young man in an army uniform walked towards them with a military gait and bowed. "Cousin Robert," Fannie said. "Allow me to introduce Amanda Yager. You haven't seen her in many years. She's the daughter of Charles Armstrong."

"Mrs. Yager," he said in a smooth low voice, "I'm Robert Beckam, son of John Beckam of Warrenton."

"Oh, yes," Amanda said recognizing him. "We've met before. My father thinks highly of your father. Are you home on leave?"

"Yes." He glanced at the dancers. "I graduated from West Point last summer and have been serving as an engineer at Detroit where I'm doing survey work on the Great Lakes. This is my first leave in a year and I decided to spend some time with my Culpeper relatives." Constance and John whirled by. "Tell me," he asked while his eyes followed them, "who is the young lady in the blue dress?"

Amanda and Fannie laughed. "That's my younger sister, Constance. Would you like me to introduce you?"

Robert Beckam shifted his weight on his feet and looked down. Clearly blushing, he replied, "She seems to be busy at the moment. However, I'll be certain to introduce myself to her before the night is over. Mrs. Yager, it was a pleasure seeing you." He bowed and strolled away.

Flickering lanterns cast a soft shadowy light on the gardens. Thousands of fireflies twinkled, adding enchantment to the evening while laughing children chased them with glee. Overheated by the dancing, Constance joined a group of her friends. Lucy Ashby, who lived several blocks from the Armstrongs' town home, greeted her. "It's about time you stopped to talk to us, Constance. Perhaps you can help us solve a mystery. Who's that tall, dark, handsome young man in the uniform?"

"None of us have ever seen him before," said Jane, Lucy's sister.

"Heaven forbid there should be an eligible man here and we don't know who it is," giggled Annie Crittenden.

"I'm afraid I can't help you," Constance replied. "I haven't seen anyone in a uniform yet."

"Doesn't my cousin, Daniel Grimsley, look mature and sophisticated tonight? I must admit, I'm smitten," Bettie Browning said with a sigh.

Finding this idle prattle uninteresting, Constance said, "I'm parched. I must get some punch."

Constance wove through the crowd carrying her cup of punch, then noticed her father and several of his cronies talking in front of a cluster of boxwoods. Anxious to overhear their comments on the current political situation, she circled around behind the boxwoods where she would be hidden. Leaning forward, she listened intently.

Coleman Beckam, Fannie's father, said, "The hypocrisy of the North on the slavery issue is more than we can tolerate. The seafaring people of New England have made fortunes transporting slaves from Africa, and then making and trading rum back to the Africans. Now they're getting rich using child labor in their factories to make our cotton into cloth."

"This woman, this Harriet Beecher Stowe, who's never been on a plantation, writes a book of fiction, and suddenly the northerners are convinced we all abuse our slaves," said Reverend Stringfellow. "Our people are well taken care of. Those who mistreat their slaves, like John Kelly, are social outcasts."

"But the real issue is state's rights," argued Baptist Hill. "Our constitutional rights are being violated. My brother, A. P., who's stationed in Washington, says tension is mounting there."

"You all know that I'm an ardent Unionist," James Barbour said with conviction. "Virginia gave birth to this nation, and to leave it would be a tragedy. We grow little cotton here. In many ways our farms have more in common with those of Pennsylvania than the cotton and indigo plantations of the Deep South. I believe Virginia must step forth and be a peacemaker between the two regions."

"James is right. We must explore every means for a peaceful solution," added his brother John, president of the Orange and Alexandria Railroad. "If war should come, the railroad would be prized by both sides. Because of our location, we'd be in the center of the strife."

Robert Beckam edged his way around the boxwoods towards Constance. "Miss Armstrong, are you so bored with the party that you must resort to eavesdropping on a bunch of old men?" he asked in a low voice.

She jumped, spilling punch on her dress. "Oh! You startled me!" She twirled around to look up into the attractive face of the dark-haired young man in a uniform.

"I apologize," he said. "I didn't mean to frighten you. I'm Robert Beckam from Warrenton. You may not remember me, but I met you years ago while visiting my relatives here, but, you were only a girl then. I was hoping to entice you away from the old men, and get you to dance with me."

Dumbfounded, Constance muttered, "Of course," while she struggled to make out his features in the shadows.

He took her arm and guided her out to the garden where they began moving to a slow waltz. Able to see him better now, she admired his long, slender face with its perfectly proportioned nose and features. She gazed up into his dark eyes. "I'm sure you're wondering why I was trying to overhear that conversation," she said with a demure smile. "I'm quite interested in politics. However, since it would have been improper for me to join the gentlemen in conversation, my only alternative was to eavesdrop. Tell me, what's your assessment of the state of our nation?"

"That, Miss Armstrong, is a difficult question. I'm now stationed at Detroit. Those of us in the army try to proceed with business as usual. There are no real hostilities amongst us." He stared into the dancing depths of her azure eyes. "However, each of us knows that if war comes, our loyalties will go to our states." He watched her long lush lashes cast shadows on her china white cheeks. "I do have difficulty controlling myself when I hear the Yanks making a martyr of that lunatic John Brown and condemning Virginia for hanging him. My Uncle Fontaine was murdered in Brown's raid."

They moved in unison, circling with the music. "Yes, I know. It's frustrating that women have no voice in the situation. Our lives would be totally changed by a war, and our hardships would be great."

"You're absolutely correct; all of our lives would be changed. If Mr. Lincoln is elected, we must at least give him a chance." His strong hand guided her around another couple as his gentle eyes caught and held hers.

She studied his lean bronze face and decided to change the subject. "How long will you be here?"

The even whiteness of her vivacious smile dazzled him. "Unfortunately, I must leave tomorrow. I'm spending tonight with Uncle James at Auburn. Then I'll have next week to visit my parents before I return to Detroit. My greatest regret is that I didn't meet you sooner." His smile matched hers with enthusiasm. "So tell me everything there is to know about Constance Armstrong."

Constance laughed and felt her face flushing. When the music ended they continued their conversation under one of the flickering lanterns. Engrossed, she lost track of time before her father joined them, but realized she had done most of the talking.

"I hate to interrupt the two of you," the judge said. "But the hour is late and we must be going to the Retreat. Lieutenant Beckam, it's been a pleasure to see you. Please give my best regards to your father."

"I will certainly do that, Judge Armstrong." He turned to Constance with a smile and kissed her hand. "Miss Armstrong, it's been a pleasure indeed. I've enjoyed our lively conversation." His gaze traveled over her face and searched her eyes. "I hope that if this lonely soldier writes to you, you will be kind enough to respond."

She felt a certain sadness that their time together was ending as she sensed an invisible web of attraction building between them. His quiet maturity fascinated her. "You may be sure that I will, Lieutenant Beckam." Her eyes sparkled with anticipation. "I've enjoyed your company. Good night."

Next day, July 5, 1860: The Retreat, near Raccoon Ford

The aroma of bacon, coffee, and biscuits finally aroused Constance from a deep sleep. At nearly 10 o'clock, she joined the others in the dining room of The Retreat.

"Ah, the fair damsel has arisen," Frank announced dramatically, then heaped apple butter on a steaming biscuit.

"Don't let him tease you, Constance. We all slept late," Anne Stringfellow chuckled with a smile that showed the lines around her eyes. A petite woman with wrinkles that reflected strength, she carried herself like an aristocrat. "None of us has been up long. Get a plate and help yourself to everything on the sideboard."

Constance piled fried apples on her plate. "It smells delicious. It was so kind of you to invite us to stay so we wouldn't have to make the long ride back to town."

"You know Mother tries to lure you here as frequently as possible," commented Frank's oldest brother, Robert, seated beside his wife, Eliza Green Stringfellow.

Constance sat down, devoured her breakfast, and listened to the conversation around the table. Frank's middle brother, Martin, and his bride of two months, Nellie Madison Stringfellow, confessed to being blissfully happy, and Anne told how wonderful it was to have both families there to help with the thousand-acre plantation. She said that in honor of the Armstrongs' visit, she had invited Thornton Stringfellow and his brood to join them for dinner. She hoped to enlist Amanda's musical talents for the entertainment. Flattered, Amanda agreed.

Eager for action, Constance waited for a lull in the conversation and then tossed out her challenge. "You know, Father gave me a beautiful horse for my birthday. I believe she's faster than any of the Stringfellow horses."

"Young lady." Frank stood up and threw his napkin on the table. "I consider that a challenge! I'll protect the good name of our stable."

Constance stood and addressed the others. "Would anyone else like to join us?"

"No," her father replied. "It's a bit too warm today for me to ride. I believe I'll while away the afternoon fishing."

"Let's take our two girls and your boys down to the river to swim," Eliza said to Amanda and Alex.

"That sounds like a refreshing way to spend the hot afternoon," Amanda said. "It's not every day that we get to enjoy the shade beside the Rapidan River."

Frank enjoyed the view from the front porch while he waited for Constance. The Retreat, a two-story rambling frame house, sat in a grove of birch trees on a slight knoll overlooking the Rapidan River. Originally named the Rapid Ann after Queen Ann, the name of the river had been shortened over time. The plantation encompassed flat to gently rolling river-bottom land, some of the richest soil in the county. As he gazed across the river, Frank saw the high peak of Clark Mountain to his right and sharply rising hills directly across the river, the boundary line between Culpeper and Orange counties. Slightly over a mile downstream was the mill town of Raccoon Ford, located near Summerduck, the home of his uncle, Reverend Thornton Stringfellow.

Constance strolled out, properly attired in a black riding dress and holding her riding hat and whip. "I'm ready."

When they reached the stables, Abraham had Liz saddled. Her glistening chestnut coat caused Frank to whistle. "Whew, Connie. She's a beauty!"

Constance stroked the horse's nose. "I've named her after a spirited influential woman whom I greatly admire – perhaps the most powerful woman who's ever lived – Queen Elizabeth. I call her Liz."

"She looks like a queen and even has the coloring of Elizabeth. Her markings are unique." Frank admired Liz's long muscular legs. The horse had almost a star between her eyes, white at her hooves, and a marking like a white handprint on her right thigh.

"Let's take them around the track and do a few jumps to warm up," Constance said, swinging into the saddle.

The two of them trotted around the track several times. Liz took every hurdle easily in stride. After about fifteen minutes, Constance called out to Frank on his gray mare, "Are you ready to accept the challenge?"

He nodded yes and said, "We don't want to work them too hard in this heat. Let's go one time around the track and then down and around that large oak tree off in the field. Who ever returns and goes across the first hurdle will win."

"You're on!" Constance stopped beside him. "Are you ready?" He nodded. "Go!"

The two horses ran neck and neck most of the way around the track. Liz took the jumps quicker but then Frank's mare gained a slight lead on the straight-of-way when they sped across the field. Constance urged Liz on and she took the inside curve as they rounded the oak tree. Then when they raced for the last hurdle, hooves thundering, Frank pulled slightly ahead. "Come on, baby!" Constance leaned forward and gave her the whip. Liz glided over the last hurdle a nose ahead of Frank's mare.

"We beat you!" Constance crowed.

"I'm not ready to concede defeat." Frank slowed his horse. "That was a hairline finish."

"Balderdash, Frank Stringfellow! We beat you fair and square and you know it," she exclaimed defiantly. "If I'd been riding astride, we'd have beaten you worse."

"Well, maybe," he acquiesced with a smile. "Let's go down by the river."

When they reached the cool shade encompassing the rapidly flowing river, they led the horses down the gentle bank to drink. "I want to go wading," Constance said. She sat on a log, lifted her skirt, and took her boots off. Suddenly, amidst an abrupt thrashing noise, two creatures scurried out from under the log. "Oh!" She jumped up and dashed towards Frank.

He spied the ringed tails of the rapidly retreating assailants and laughed. "Coons. Now we know how Lafayette felt when the same thing happened to him during the revolution." Lafayette had named the place Raccoon Ford.

"They scared me to death!" Constance gasped. "But I won't be deterred." She sat back down, and took her boots and socks off. Frank did likewise.

He grabbed her elbow to steady her, she lifted her skirt, and they waded into the dark swift current. "I remember what fun we had swimming here when we were children," Frank said.

"I'll never forgive you for that day when you frightened me so badly. You remember." Frank rolled his eyes in an innocent look. "You started swimming under water and you didn't come up for several minutes. I became frantic and screamed for Mandy and Martin. I was sure you'd drowned. None of us could see you, and then we finally heard you laughing around the bend. I still can't believe you swam that far under water."

"It's because I'm so skinny." His lips turned up in a devilish grin. "But you and I were always the youngest and the biggest daredevils. Hide and seek was my favorite game."

"I'll say! We could never find your crafty hiding places.

"I'm only creative." He waded out of the water. "Come sit on the log. I'll protect you."

Constance pointed to the large rock outcropping to her left and followed him. "We used to think that big rock on top looked like a duck." She dropped onto the log. "And the two rocks under it were the nest."

"Oh, yes, I remember how we hid secret messages and treasures between the two rocks." He turned to look her in the eye, and paused a minute. "But seriously, Connie, there's something I want to share with you. I haven't told this to any of my family yet. Will you keep my secret?"

"Absolutely," she answered in earnest. "You know you can trust me. I'd trust you with my life."

He looked down, color creeping up his cheeks. "Connie, I've been smitten. I'm in love with Emma Green, Eliza's younger sister from Alexandria."

"Frank! I had no idea. I'm so happy for you."

"The miracle is, she appears to return my affection. At times I believe I'm dreaming. We've talked of marriage, but her father has let me know that I can't ask for her hand until she's a year older. I must be patient."

"How can you be so certain she's the one?"

31

"It's the way I feel when I'm with her. When it happens, you know. I have no doubt that I want to share my life with her."

"I wonder if I'll ever feel that way?" she mused. "But what of your immediate plans?"

"Next week I'll leave for an extended trip through the South. I intend to visit friends in Richmond, Charleston, Savannah, and New Orleans. Then I'll travel to Mississippi where I have a job teaching Latin and Greek to the little darlings of the plantations. Next summer I hope to return with money in my pocket and ask for Emma's hand."

"I hope you'll write to me." She swatted a dragonfly away. "I've always wanted to spend time in Charleston. Everyone says it's a beautiful city, full of art and culture."

"I'll be your faithful correspondent. But, tell me Connie, what else do you dream of?"

She pulled a piece of bark from the log and tossed it into the middle of the river. They watched it spin in a small whirlpool and then break out into the main current. It sped downstream only to be wedged against a rock. The sun glistened on the water whirling around it. Suddenly it broke loose and was swiftly carried around the bend of the river where they heard the children frolicking in the water.

"I wonder if we have any more control over our destinies than that piece of bark. Life catches us and thrusts us into the currents where we spin helplessly out of control. But," she sighed, "it's still fun to dream. I've inherited Father's love of history and politics. Most related professions are closed to me, but I long to write. Perhaps if I use a pseudonym, I can have some small influence in current affairs. The pen is mightier than the sword. One thing I know for certain; I'm in no hurry to marry. Naturally, I'd love to travel, but eventually I know I'd return to Culpeper. I love the sense of community and kinship here…the rich farmland. This is home."

The two friends spent the remainder of the afternoon sharing their dreams on the bank of the dark, then peaceful, river until a violent thunderstorm forced them to run. The days were numbered until tramping feet and booming cannons would destroy the tranquility of their spot.

2

Don't Tread On Me

December 24, 1860 – April 17, 1861

"Whenever any form of government becomes destructive to these ends, it is the right of the people to abolish it, and to institute a new government."
The Declaration of Independence

"...any people, anywhere, being inclined and having the power, have the right to rise up and shake off the existing government, and form a new one that suits them better."
Abraham Lincoln, 1848

Almost six months later, December 24, 1860: Culpeper Court House

Constance took a deep breath of frigid air, stepped from her front porch to the frozen ground of Coleman Street[i], then hurried towards Davis Street to finish her last-minute Christmas shopping. When she turned the corner by the courthouse, the mountains suddenly loomed so clear she felt she could reach out and touch them. She looked two blocks down Davis Street and saw a large crowd around the depot. Her pulse quickened. She had not heard a train come in, so a message must have come over the telegraph. Now that the worst had happened and Lincoln had been elected, everyone wondered what will transpire next. Would southerners subject themselves to the rule of an abolitionist tyrant, who only got forty percent of the popular vote? More than a million more people voted against him than for him. Of course if anybody considered the opinions of women, that would make it two million. She scurried by the jail and the Baptist Church.

When she reached the boisterous crowd a wealthy planter thrust a flyer into her hand "What's happened?" she asked.

"South Carolina seceded. It's been confirmed. We're calling a meeting at the court-house day after tomorrow."

Constance felt numb. This bold move by the South Carolinians had been frequently threatened, but the reality of it still shocked her. "Calling a meeting so soon," she stammered. "For what purpose?"

---

[i]Now Main Street

"Read the flyer."

She read, *A meeting is called so that we may consult together upon the present condition of the country, and the best means to protect the rights and honor of the South.* So the hour of decision had been thrust upon them.

Walking forward, Constance went over it all again in her mind. The southern states had voted unanimously for Breckenridge, while the three border states of Virginia, Kentucky, and Tennessee went for Bell, the compromise candidate, by the smallest of margins. Lincoln had narrowly carried the northern states, except for New Jersey and Delaware. What would the three border states do if the union shattered? She entered Rudasill and Stark Mercantile, crowded with shoppers. The aroma of spices and coffee welcomed her while she threaded her way to the back counter.

"Merry Christmas, Miss Armstrong." John Stark, Jr. pulled an item off a high shelf. "What may I help you with today?"

"I looked at a pair of riding gloves several days ago for my father." She leaned over the back counter, pointing. "I've decided they would be the perfect surprise for him. They're in the lower drawer."

"Ah, yes. I remember." He lifted the gloves from the drawer. "I'm sure he'll be delighted with these. Will there be anything else?"

"No." She pulled some bills from her purse, then looked up to see Annie Crittenden and her widowed mother, Catherine, laden with bundles.

"Hello, Constance," Annie said. "And greetings to you, Mr. Stark." She batted her eyelashes.

"It's good to see you, Miss Crittenden. You look lovely today." Stark returned her gaze.

"Hello Annie, Mrs. Crittenden," Constance said. "I hate to dampen your spirits, but have you heard? South Carolina's seceded."

"Sakes alive!" Catherine gasped. "So soon? We were all afraid of that."

"I had heard," John Stark said. "There's a meeting at the courthouse on the twenty sixth. I believe we all feel it's time to prepare to defend our homes. I understand that the Culpeper Minute Men of Revolutionary fame will be revived."

"I know my brother Charles will enlist immediately," Annie said. "Mother, we must hurry home to tell him the news." She beamed at John Stark. "Merry Christmas, Mr. Stark."

"The same to you, ladies."

Constance followed the Crittendens out of the store, pulling her scarf around her face in the brisk wind

"Isn't John Stark just the handsomest man?" Annie sighed.

"Indeed, he is. Have a good trip home and a nice Christmas." Constance smiled inwardly. What a flirt Annie was. The two ladies climbed into their carriage and headed to their seven-hundred-acre farm, Cloverdale, at the base of Slaughter's Mountain, on the road to Orange.

Constance darted into the post office and then back out into the street clutching two letters. Almost blinded by the bright sunlight, she squinted to read Frank Stringfellow and Robert Beckam.

She leaned into the wind, rounded the corner by the courthouse, and walked the remaining block home, glancing at the Virginia House Hotel on the corner of Coleman

34

and Cameron streets. Pine garlands draped across the railings of the porches on both stories of the building that covered half the block.[ii] Directly across the street sat the Armstrong home, built in 1750 by Constance's great-grandfather. She looked affectionately at the whitewashed two-story structure formed by two houses joined together. The original portion, recessed on the left, had a porch across the lower level with the front door on the far right, flanked by two windows to the left. Three equally spaced windows sat above the porch and were framed by chimneys on each end. Two wooden signs hung from the porch: "Armstrong and Yager, Attorneys at Law" and "Sisson's Book Store." The right portion of the house, added in 1775, reached all the way to the street on both the Coleman and Cameron Street sides. Two windows on the left and one on the right framed the off-center front door over a simple stone stoop. Above both front doors hung Harriet's beautiful fan shaped arrangements of fruit and magnolia leaves. Simple green wreaths with red berries and bows adorned the front doors. The Armstrongs always spent the winter months in town and enjoyed celebrating Christmas amongst the thousand residents.

She sprinted up the porch steps to get out of the wind, and entered the narrow hall where the aroma of her father's pipe filtered from the two offices in the rear. She took her scarf off, then went left into the bookstore. "Hello, Mr. Sisson."

A short man near thirty peered over his spectacles. "Well, Miss Armstrong, I have good news. The children's Bible you ordered has come in."

"Wonderful! I was afraid it wouldn't get here in time." She flipped through the small book he handed her. "This is perfect. Put it on our account and tell Mrs. Sisson and the children Merry Christmas."

"I will, and the same to all the Armstrongs."

Constance continued down the hall into her father's waiting room. She heard voices behind the closed door of his office, decided not to interrupt, and opened the door to the parlor, located in the new portion of the house. A fire blazed in the fireplace of the huge room where the aroma of cedar and popcorn welcomed her. Amanda and her two boys sat cross-legged on the floor stringing popcorn to decorate the nine-foot-tall cedar tree. "Look," Hudson exclaimed. "We're making the tree pretty."

"That is undoubtedly the most beautiful tree in the world." Constance relaxed on the carved rosewood red velvet sofa. "I've finished my shopping. The children's Bible I ordered for Sadie came in on time, thank goodness." She picked up a gingerbread cookie from the table beside her and munched.

"That's such a thoughtful gift, dear." Harriet was knitting by the window. "I know the Bible will be a source of strength to her as she copes with the loss of Mary and the baby. It's been almost two months. I'm sure she's not over it yet."

"No, she's not." Constance's eyes brimmed with compassion. "But she's progressing with her reading, and I'm confident she'll be able to read this herself."

Amanda spied the envelopes on the sofa. "Who are your letters from? Don't keep secrets, sister."

[ii]This building still stands on Main Street. The porches have been enclosed and the lower level houses a music store, gift shop, and other shops.

Constance resented the intrusion on her privacy. "If you really must know, they're from Frank and Robert Beckam."

"Ah, the handsome Robert Beckam!" Amanda cleaned up popcorn from the floor.

"I'm going to my room to wrap my presents and read my letters," Constance said.

Later, Constance heard the voices of her father and Alex below. She grabbed the wrapped packages and flew downstairs to spy her father warming his hands in front of the blazing fire. After she placed the gifts under the tree, she slid her arm around his waist and he kissed her on the forehead.

"And what wondrous treasures might these be?" He pulled her close.

"Surprises. Father, I heard this afternoon that South Carolina seceded and there's to be a meeting at the courthouse the day after tomorrow."

"I'm afraid it's true." He puffed on his pipe. "James Barbour visited me a few moments ago. He's extremely concerned that Virginia may be caught in the emotion of secession fever. You know how strongly he supports the Union. He believes we should not act hastily but give President Lincoln a chance."

Alex grabbed David, lunging to undecorate the tree. "But if, as I suspect, war is the design of the North, we can't delay arming ourselves," Alex said. "We must make every effort to defend our land. I'll continue drilling with the Little Fork Rangers."

"I received a letter from Robert Beckam today." Constance sat in the maple rocking chair. "He reports that sentiment in Detroit and the northwest states is almost evenly divided between the Lincoln Republicans and the Douglas Democrats. War rhetoric isn't popular. Almost half of the population there is as apprehensive about Lincoln's actions as we are. I mean, after all, he doesn't have the authority to declare war. He's supposed to have the consent of Congress."

"But can we trust him to do that?" Alex asked while wrestling with David. "We'd be foolhardy not to prepare for our defense."

"On the other hand, Frank says Mississippi is a powder keg. He's confident that if South Carolina secedes, the other states in the Deep South will follow immediately."

Charles said, "We mustn't let fanatics determine our course."

"That's enough talk about unpleasant subjects," Harriet interuppted. "It's Christmas Eve, and we're celebrating the birth of the Prince of Peace. After dinner we'll go caroling as usual, and enjoy the wonder of the season."

"My dear, once again, you're absolutely right." Charles kissed her on the cheek.

The stars twinkled brightly in the crystal clear sky while the warmly clad Armstrongs and Yagers marched up Coleman Street. "I'm going to check on the Paynes," Constance said before she rushed onto the porch of the Virginia House.

She entered the empty tavern room and called out, "Who's going caroling?"

"We're coming," a female voice replied. The four daughters, ranging in age from twelve to nineteen, rushed through the door.

"We thought you'd forgotten us," said Millie.

"You know I wouldn't do that," Constance said. "Everyone's meeting in front of the courthouse."

The group of about thirty carolers huddled close together as they paraded south on Coleman Street with Amanda and Alex leading the singing and the way. Their torches and candles flickered to the strains of *Silent Night*. Amanda held Alex's hand tighter than usual, and Constance wiggled between her parents and locked arms with them both. She stared at them intently, striving to imprint the memory of this night on her brain forever. Doors opened and neighbors waved or joined the throng when they passed Bell Tavern.

Amanda's rich, clear voice sang out, "Oh come all ye faithful, joyful and triumphant." Candles in the windows flickered back warm greetings to the crowd. The procession reached Mason Street, then turned left to cross over to East Street, where the newest and most prestigious homes backed up to the recently constructed railroad. They then turned right on East Street.

"We have to go to Dr. Ashby's," Constance said to Alex.

When the carolers arrived at the Ashby house, the last one on East Street, Dr. Charles Ashby flung open the door. "Merry Christmas. Come in!"

"Thanks, but we've all been invited to the Hills' for hot cider and wassail. Join us," the judge said.

"In that case, give us a minute to get our coats." Constance stomped her feet and blew on her fingers to keep warm. Soon the Ashbys and their four daughters joined the throng. Dr. Ashby's booming voice led them in *It Came Upon A Midnight Clear.* Constance and Lucy Ashby snuggled close together while the melodious group swarmed towards the Episcopal rectory. Amanda broke into *Hark the Herald Angels Sing* when smiling Reverend John Cole and his wife came to the door.

"Surely, I have heard the voices of angels," the minister said when they finished. "Merry Christmas and God bless you all."

"Come with us to the Hills'," Amanda replied.

"Thank you, but I'm still working on tonight's sermon. I'll see you in church."

Ambrose Powell Hill stood in front of the floor-to-ceiling pier glass mirror located in the parlor of the East Street mansion of Edward Baptist, his older brother. A dashing figure in his army uniform, he bounced four-month-old Netty in his arms. "See Netty, see Da Da," he whispered. The baby cooed at her image and reached for his auburn moustache. The mirror reflected a 5-foot, 10-inch, one-hundred-sixty-pound soldier of slight frame with sparkling hazel eyes.

Over in the corner, his wife of a year and a half, the former Kitty Morgan McClung of Kentucky, rustled through the sheet music at the piano. Three years ago, the young widow had met Powell while attending the party of a friend in Washington. The gay blade, twice previously engaged, was immediately taken with this vivacious woman nine years his junior. He soon wrote his best friend and former West Point roommate, George McClellan, *"I'm afraid there is no mistake about it this time, old fellow, and please God, and Kentucky blue-grass, my bachelor life is about to end, and I shall swell the number of blessed martyrs who have yielded up freedom to crinoline and blue eyes. I know that you will like her, and when you have come to know her, say that I have done well."* [1]

"Dolly" Hill, nicknamed by her nanny because she looked like a china doll, walked up behind her husband and put her hands around his waist. Leaning around him she made faces at Netty in the mirror. Netty squealed with glee.

"Dolly, I'm convinced that we have the best behaved baby on the face of the earth."

"Absolutely." She laughed and tickled Netty's chin. "I hope Amanda Yager will be here tonight. I enjoyed her company when we visited here after our wedding."

"I'm sure she will be. I'm delighted that you two songbirds have so much in common."

Baptist and his two daughters entered the room carrying plates of cookies. "Now, girls, don't eat these until the carolers get here," Baptist ordered. He peered out the floor-to-ceiling front window.

"I'll go down and see if Mildred and Lucy need any help in the dining room," Dolly said. She walked through the spacious entrance hall and descended the curved stairway. The English basement room radiated the season with cascades of mistletoe and holly hanging from the crystal chandelier and an enormous arrangement of running cedar and fruit in the center of the Chippendale table. Mildred, Baptist's wife, arranged the cups around the bowl of wassail while Lucy, Powell's favorite sister, stirred the hot chocolate.

"How beautiful it looks," Dolly exclaimed. "It's wonderful to spend Christmas here. I must admit it eases my homesickness for Kentucky."

"I'm thankful we can all be together," answered Lucy. "Powell's the happiest he's ever been because of you. We're delighted to have you in our family. "

"And just think, tomorrow Top and his clan and Margaret and Evelyn and their families will all be here," Mildred said. "Baptist is ecstatic. It's the first time since his father died that all of the Hills have been together. This will be a Christmas to remember."

"I hear the carolers. They're coming!" One of the daughters ran across the heart pine floors to the front door.

Momentarily, laughter and Christmas greetings echoed from the twelve-foot ceilings, while the throng rushed inside to the warmth. The children and servants transported coats upstairs, and the guests quickly consumed the hot refreshments, then warmed themselves in front of the marble fireplaces. Constance, flanked by her father and Alex, held her numb fingers close to the flames.

"Merry Christmas, Judge Armstrong." Powell Hill shook his hand.

"Lieutenant Hill, welcome home. You remember my son-in-law, Alex Yager, and my daughter Constance." He nodded towards the two of them.

"Indeed, I do." Hill shook hands with Alex. "My wife has been looking forward to visiting with your Amanda."

"Amanda feels likewise. I'm sure we can persuade them to sing for us tonight," Alex answered.

Powell Hill stepped back and bowed dramatically to Constance. "Can this be the little girl in pigtails who brought me flowers five years ago when I was home recovering from Yellow Fever?" He kissed her hand. "Miss Constance, you've grown into a beautiful young lady. I'll bet you're turning the heads of every eligible man in Culpeper. I almost regret that I'm an old married man of thirty five."

Blushing slightly, Constance replied "I'm flattered, Lieutenant Hill. You have an excellent memory. I'm amazed that you recall my visits. I hope my questions as a twelve year old weren't too boring to you."

"On the contrary. You encouraged me to speak of my adventures in Mexico, Florida, and West Point. And I remember that you customarily brought me several newspapers and asked my opinion of the current political situation. It helped to pass the time during my convalescence. We all love attention when we're sick."

"Since you've just arrived from Washington, Lieutenant Hill, could I again implore you to share your thoughts on the current crises?" Constance asked.

Alex cleared his throat and shifted weight on his feet. "Constance, it's not proper for women to discuss politics in public, and we don't want to spoil the spirit of the evening."

"How do you feel about that, Lieutenant Hill?" Constance's eyes blazed.

"Actually," he replied amicably, "I have a wife who's very outspoken on the subject. I believe it's important for everyone in our country to know what's transpiring. Washington's in a state of panic since the announcement of South Carolina's secession. There's fear of a riot, and I heard before we caught the train this morning that large numbers of troops are being called in. I'm sure there will be a strong military presence in the city to ensure Mr. Lincoln's inauguration." He paused as lines of anxiety creased his face. "Tensions are running high, and those of us who are southerners feel more uncomfortable each day. A minority of our citizens elected Mr. Lincoln, and there are many who don't support him in the North. I'm not sure our nation can survive his presidency."

"What are your feelings about secession?" Charles asked. "You know a meeting has been called at the courthouse on the twenty sixth. Will you be able to attend?"

"No, we have to return to Washington tomorrow night. I believe that any state has the legal right to secede. We entered this union of our own free will and should be able to exit it in the same manner. I do not support slavery and own no slaves. I was enraged when I learned several years ago that a black man was hung in Culpeper for murder and later evidence proved him innocent. Such injustices should not happen." His voice rang with indignation. "The real issue here is states' rights. The constitution explicitly states that all powers not designated to the Federal government go to the states. Slavery is clearly in that category. To free the slaves without financial restitution to their owners would be grossly unfair and the financial ruin of the South. The British gave financial compensation when the slaves of the West Indies were freed. Why won't the North consider it? "

"But this appears to be the goal of Mr. Lincoln," Alex said. "We should prepare to defend our property in case hostilities break out."

"Let's pray that doesn't happen," Hill said. "The eyes of the nation are on Virginia. We remain the strongest state in the nation."

"If most of the southern states secede, do you believe there's a chance the North and Mr. Lincoln will let them go in peace?" Judge Armstrong asked.

"I suppose that's possible. The northern Democrats are certainly sympathetic. I see no reason the two nations couldn't exist side by side in peace. We have no aspirations to conquer them. It all depends on Mr. Lincoln. However, I'm not encouraged by the fact that he's appointed Mr. Seward Secretary of State. Seward's known to be an ambitious man who's most hostile to the South."

"Lieutenant Hill," Constance began, "if war breaks out, you'll have to make an extremely difficult choice. What will you and the other southerners in the army do?"

"That's the question I've been contemplating for months," Hill replied with a pained expression. "Undoubtedly my strongest loyalty is to Virginia. I will defend her with every ounce of my being."

A piercing sob erupted from the back of the room. Netty exercised her lungs while Dolly pushed through the crowd. "I believe Miss Henrietta has had enough excitement for one evening. It's time to tuck her in, but she needs a good night kiss from Daddy."

Powell kissed the baby on the cheek. "Sweet dreams, dearest," he whispered softly. "Dolly, we've had a request for you and Amanda to sing together."

"Yes," Charles said to Amanda, who followed Dolly through the other carolers. "Please do us that honor."

"Of course." Amanda beamed and linked her arm through Alex's. "We've got some time before the church bells call us to worship. I'll get the music."

Rotund Reverend John Cole watched his flock file in for Christmas Eve Eucharist at Saint Stephen's Episcopal Church in the soft candlelight. From his seat in the front of the sanctuary he clearly discerned the expressions of anxiety and fear on their faces when they knelt to pray. He noticed Constance Armstrong look up to the balcony and smile at her two servants, Sadie and Abraham, who responded with looks of affection.

What could he say to lighten the burden on these heavy hearts tonight? Should he preach the normal sermon about peace on earth and good will towards men? Surely he must reaffirm the fact that God is a refuge in times of peril. He would rely on God to put the right words in his mouth when the time came.

All day long, the story that fellow from England, Dickens, had written haunted his mind. Every time he read the section about the Ghost of Christmas Future he got chills. Tonight he kept thinking, perhaps it was a blessing that these people could not see a vision of future Christmases.

Two days later, December 26, 1860: Judge Armstrong's office

The blood vessels pulsed in James Barbour's neck when he slammed his fist on Charles Armstrong's desk. "We cannot allow Culpeper to arouse Virginia into a frenzy of secession fever! How embarrassing for me to be representing the first county to call a meeting to discuss secession. I'll fight disunion at every turn. I want to go to Richmond and recommend that Virginia send a Peace Delegation to Washington to negotiate with the Lincoln administration!"

"Calm down, James." His brother John put a hand on his shoulder. "This is a time for rational thinking, and you're as emotional as the secessionists. I'm afraid that the meeting today will be so dominated by secession fever that the crowd won't listen to reason. Perhaps, unionism will be better served by being quiet until the emotional frenzy passes. It's difficult to reason with a crowd. We can talk with the merchants. They can be convinced that their commerce and trade are tied to the North."

"I agree with John." Charles leaned forward on his walnut desk. "Perhaps the best course is to listen today and see where sentiment lies. You don't want to be shouted down by a mob. Let people cool down. Remember, you're highly respected in this community. Organize your supporters, and perhaps call your own meeting in a few weeks." He puffed on his pipe and looked at James intently. "If you can arrange a meeting in Washington, I'll accompany you and do all in my power to negotiate a peace agreement."

"You know you can count on me, too," John added, gesturing with his hands.

"Thank you." James ran his hand through his brown hair. "I feel in my heart that I must do everything in my power to hold our union together. If we can get Lincoln to agree that slavery as it exists in the southern states is constitutional and will not be tampered with, a great tragedy can be prevented. But," he sighed and leaned back in his chair, "at the moment I feel that my constituents have betrayed me and are endangering my peace efforts."

"Come now, James, you know how fickle public sentiment is. It changes with the wind," John said.

"Many people, my son-in-law included, feel that Lincoln can't be trusted, and that we must arm ourselves immediately to protect our borders," Charles added. "They will most likely be the most vocal today. I propose that we go to this meeting with the intent of listening and absorbing the consensus of the crowd. If the majority opinion is in favor of secession, I feel we must remain silent. We will plead our case at a later date."

James stood and extended his hand. "Charles Armstrong, you're a man of great wisdom and integrity. But you're asking me, a politician, to do the impossible...keep my mouth shut. I'll try."

"I think we'd better be going." John put his coat on. "I'm sure a crowd is already gathering."

Constance pulled the curtains back from the second floor bedroom window and peered at the scene below. Numerous men walked up Coleman Street towards the courthouse, their breath steaming in the cold damp air. Her father emerged from the porch with James and John Barbour. Shortly thereafter she heard the front door of the main house close when Alex departed.

Tingling with excitement, she went across the hall to find Amanda rocking David gently. "Amanda, I must hear what's said at the meeting. This is history in the making! Please come with me."

Amanda stroked David's hair and looked up at her sister, shocked. "Connie, you know Alex would be furious. He insists that a woman's place is in the home. I do want to hear the debate, but it's not possible. Oh, I'm so terribly frightened by it all."

"We could sneak in the back after the meeting starts. Alex will never know you're there. Of course, we can't dare speak, but at least we can listen."

Amanda hesitated. "I can't defy Alex. Our domestic tranquility is more important. I'm sorry."

"I understand. I'll go alone."

Constance raced down the steps and grabbed her cape from the hall tree. Her mother called out from the parlor, "Where are you going, dear?"

"I'm going to the meeting, Mother."

"What?" Her mother stormed into the hall, bristling with indignation. "That would be most improper, young lady. We must trust our men to make political decisions."

"I understand how you feel, Mother," Constance said defiantly. "But what harm is there in listening? This is a momentous occasion."

Harriet glared at her with reproachful eyes. "Your boldness will shock the town. Don't you think you've raised enough eyebrows by riding astride in the hunt?"

Constance lifted her chin, meeting Harriet's icy stare straight on. "I don't have time to argue, Mother. I'm going." She threw back her head and bolted out the door.

When she dashed into the street, Mary Payne, proprietress of the Virginia House Hotel, waved from the porch. She called out, "Are you going to the meeting?"

Constance spun around, surprised. "Yes. Will you come with me?"

The gray-haired, gaunt lady quickly fell in beside her. She had managed the hotel since her husband, twenty years older, had become feeble. "This secession foolishness is the work of the devil," the plain-faced lady said.

"We could enter after the meeting has started and sit in the back," Constance suggested. "Are you willing?"

"Can't see as they can hang us for listening." Mary laughed nervously. "I'm a businesswoman and I've got as much right to know what's happening in this town as anybody else."

When the two women finally slipped into the back of the courtroom, there was standing room only. Mute stares of disapproval met them in the bristling excitement. The speaker completed his call to arms. "Let us join our brothers in South Carolina in creating a new nation and fighting for our constitutional rights if we have to!" The crowd roared its approval. Constance saw Alex stand up and applaud. Several rows behind him she spied her father seated between the Barbours, who sat silently.

"Now it's my pleasure to introduce to you Culpeper's former Congressman, the Honorable Jeremiah Morton."

Jeremiah Morton, wealthy slaveholder and trader, strolled to the front amidst cheers and applause. The tall, white-haired, distinguished gentleman, known for his oratorical eloquence, scanned the faces of his audience. "My friends, eighty-four years ago our fellow Virginian, Thomas Jefferson, penned a document which declared these states to be free and independent. Patrick Henry cried 'Give me liberty or give me death!' Our fathers and grandfathers shed their precious blood to win our liberties. For seven long years they fought a cruel war against a stronger enemy...one of the most powerful empires in the world. Many were the hardships and suffering which they so nobly bore. Food and supplies were scarce. How can we ever forget the fight for survival of our poorly equipped army that harsh winter at Valley Forge? But," he said, strolling across the room, "did they persevere?" His voice rose.

"Yes!" the crowd yelled.

"Yes," he answered in a whisper. "Led by a noble Virginian, George Washington, they held on. And with the help of Almighty God and foreign intervention, they outlasted a stronger foe. By fearless determination, our precious liberties were won. And through the genius of our own James Madison the Constitution was drafted. This document states explicitly that all powers not expressly designated to the Federal Government are left to the states." A cheer rang out. The blood of the crowd was surging now.

"The words that ignited our first Revolution were 'No taxation without representation.' I ask you," he said walking into the aisle. "Is our situation today any different? While it is true, we have representatives in Congress, we are always outvoted on issues of taxation. The South is an agrarian society while the North is industrial. We import most of our manufactured goods. The tariff that they've placed on imports puts the tax burden of the nation on the South while it protects the manufacturing interests of the North. Millions of dollars of tax money have been paid by the South and used by the North to build roads in the Northwest Territories, which give more votes to the North. We have no voice!" he cried emphatically. "Isn't this taxation without consent?" The crowd jumped to its feet cheering. After several minutes he motioned for quiet.

"And then there is the question of preserving our Constitution," he continued

42

moving back to the front of the room. "Be not deceived by this Republican administration. It believes in a higher law than our Constitution and cannot be trusted[2]. Southern security can no longer be guaranteed in this union. Let all the southern states secede, and then hear any propositions the North may make for reconstruction. Surely, Mr. Lincoln will not challenge such a coalition. But," he said shaking his fists, "should he initiate bloodshed, let us fight as nobly to preserve our freedom as our forefathers did to win it!" The crowd went wild. Constance watched Alex wave his fists during the several minutes it took to restore order. Her father looked at James Barbour and shook his head negatively.

Motions were quickly passed to petition the state Legislature to call a Secession Convention and to organize a Southern Rights Association in Culpeper. Constance and Mary Payne slipped out before the majority of the crowd. While she stood in the shadows Constance heard a farmer say, "If Virginia does not secede, I'll go to South Carolina if I have to wade through blood up to my armpits."[3] Although she had been moved by Morton's speech, the rampant talk of bloodshed shocked her.

Two weeks later, January 10, 1861: Armstrongs' back yard

The softness of the gently falling snow muffled the sound of hooves on the street. Constance stared up at the towering magnolia tree, the focal point of the gardens behind her house. She watched the lacy white flakes cling to the large dark leaves briefly, only to slide off the glossy surface. An inch of snow covered the well house and gazebo to her left and the geometrically arranged boxwoods in front of her. Smoke slowly curled skyward from the chimney of the brick kitchen to her right that backed on Cameron Street. Two small servants' cabins stood behind it and the stable and carriage house faced East Street at the back of the yard. White flakes collected on the ridge of the scalloped white picket fence that enclosed the half-block. Her lips turned up in a slight smile as she stuck her tongue out to collect a few snowflakes. The clicking of the printing press across Cameron Street in the office of *The Culpeper Observer* reminded her of the reason for her outdoor excursion. She opened the side gate and walked across the street to talk to her good friend, George McDonald, editor of the local newspaper.

"Top of the mornin' to you, Miss Armstrong," the bald-headed widower said from behind his desk. His son, Ralph, nodded a greeting from beside the clanking printing press.

"Good Morning, Mr. McDonald. I thought I'd drop by to get a preview of tomorrow's paper. My curiosity is greater than usual with all the secession excitement. Perhaps I could be of some assistance to you today." She sat in the straight wooden chair by the desk.

"Now that I'm editor of the newspaper for the county the Richmond papers refer to as 'that Revolutionary County,' I suppose I could use some help." McDonald's eyes twinkled through his spectacles. "Culpeper has shocked Virginia by calling for a Secession Convention. I'm working on my editorial. Would you like to read it?"

"Of course." Constance took the papers from him. *Southern rights must be guaranteed*, she began reading. Her expression became serious as she read on until her eyebrows creased into a frown at the conclusion…*if war must come, surely every*

43

citizen will fly to Virginia's Banner resolved to conquer or die under the stainless color of her honorable cause.[4]

"You don't look happy." The editor leaned towards her. "I want your opinion."

"The wording is a little strong for me. I'd like it better if you ended with some words of caution. After all, it's much easier to get into trouble than to get out of it. When the Secession Convention convenes on February eleventh, we need to pray for wisdom and moderation."

George McDonald tapped his pencil on his desk thoughtfully. "Miss Armstrong, you've made some good points. I especially like the wording of *it's much easier to get into trouble than to get out of it.* With your permission, I'll conclude with a paragraph of caution and use your wording."

"Oh, yes. Absolutely. Father and James Barbour believe secession this soon would be premature. Caution is important. What other news articles are you working on?"

"Well, there are more reports of military buildup in Washington for the inauguration. However, the big story is that the steamer, 'The Star of the West,' attempted to land supplies and reinforcements at Fort Sumter yesterday. A shore battery fired on her and forced her to turn back."

Constance nodded in agreement. "From what I've gathered from the Washington and Richmond papers, the South Carolinians considered Major Anderson's secret move from Fort Moultrie to Fort Sumter an act of aggression. They've sent envoys to Washington to negotiate for federal property, but have been denied access to the president."

"That appears to be the case. President Buchanan's holding a bear by the tail waiting for Lincoln to take office. Since the two are political enemies, they aren't cooperating." He gathered up some papers and newspapers and handed them to her. "Tell you what. Why don't you glance through these papers and telegraph messages and do a rough draft for an article about 'The Star of the West', while I complete my editorial."

"Oh, I'd be delighted," Constance said eagerly. She had been visiting George McDonald for years and appreciated his kindness. He always made her feel important.

The last rays of daylight faded against the snow while Alex stomped his boots on the back porch before entering the hall. "Daddy! Daddy!" Hudson and David ran and hugged him around the legs.

Amanda rushed in smiling. "We've missed you." She kissed him gently. "Your lips are cold!"

"That's because it's a long ride from Rixeyville and Jeffersonton." He handed her the small cedar chest he had brought, and took off his coat and hat.

"What's that?" Hudson demanded.

"In that chest is a valuable Armstrong family heirloom." Amanda carried the chest into the parlor. "How are your parents?"

"Well." Alex bent over to warm his hands in front of the fire. "And the Little Fork Rangers had a good drill. Our ranks are growing each week. Things appeared to be going fine at the farm. Joseph and Selene have everything under control. Isaac said to tell you hello, Hudson."

"I miss him." Hudson watched Amanda set the box on the tea table. "It's an air what?" He looked up at his mother, confused.

"Heirloom," Harriet said from the rocking chair where she was reading. "I think I hear your grandfather coming. He'll tell you the story."

Charles and Constance entered the door from the law office. "Ah!" said Charles, his eyes sparkling with excitement "I see you brought the Culpeper Minute Man Flag. Let's see how it's holding up." He carefully opened the chest.

Hudson leaned forward to peer into the mysterious wooden box and smelled the strong aroma of cedar chips. "Smells funny," he said wide-eyed.

"The fabric of this flag is more than eighty-seven years old and it's quite delicate. You and David mustn't touch it," Charles sternly told him. He gently pushed the cedar chips to the side and pulled out a tattered flag with several large holes. He carefully unfolded it to reveal a faded rattlesnake coiled in the center.

"Ah!" Hudson ducked under the table. "It's a snake! I'm scared of snakes!"

"This one is too old to hurt you." Laughing, Alex pulled him out from under the table and held him up to see the flag. David reached to grab the fragile cloth, but his mother caught his hand in time.

"You see boys, my father, who was your great-grandfather, carried this flag during the American Revolution when we won our freedom from England. The Culpeper Minute Men, ready to fight at a minute's notice, chose the coiled Rattle Snake as their symbol because of its defensive position, coiled, ready to strike quickly if attacked."

Hudson peeked warily through the fingers of his hands, which he had positioned over his eyes. Alex held him tightly and said, "I'm certain that flag sent terror into the hearts of our enemies when they confronted it on the battlefield. The words *LIBERTY OR DEATH* and *DON'T TREAD ON ME* showed the resolve of the soldiers."

"Your great-grandfather fought under this flag until the surrender of Cornwallis to George Washington at Yorktown," Charles continued. "General Washington allowed him to keep the flag even though he wasn't a high-ranking officer. I suppose it was

The famous rattlesnake flag of the Culpeper Minute Men

because he was Washington's godson. At any rate, this flag is the most precious possession of the Armstrong family. Harriet, you must guard it carefully while you and the other ladies make a duplicate."

"My dear," Harriet replied sweetly, "you know that we will use utmost caution." Several wives of the newly formed Minute Men had asked Harriet to help them sew a duplicate of the flag.

"Does this mean, Mother, that you're taking a stand on the secession question?" Constance asked.

"Absolutely not. I'm simply helping to preserve history. I'll not allow politics to invade my private life."

Twenty days later, January 30, 1861: The depot, Culpeper Court House

The cold pelting rain forced the waiting crowd to seek shelter in the depot and around the overhang of the porch. Fannie Barbour and Amanda pushed into a dry corner inside the building. Filled with anxiety, Amanda listened while Fannie told her how James had penned Virginia's official rejection of petitions from the seceded states and worked diligently to arrange this conference in Washington. He was such an intense person, Fannie worried about his health. Amanda put her arm on Fannie's shoulder and told her it was unbelievable how James's meeting at the courthouse had turned the tide away from secession. Fannie agreed his powerful speech defeated the cause of disunion. He had allowed her to hear it since Constance and Mrs. Payne had broken the ice. Amanda revealed that Alex strongly favored immediate secession, and the mounting tension between him and her father was eating away at her.

The crowd stirred with excitement at the sound of the whistle. Coleman Beckam grabbed his daughter's hand, pushed through the spectators to the door, and looked down the tracks at the lights in the distance. Fannie attempted to fix her hair and opened her umbrella amidst the deafening noise of the steam engine. After the train screeched to a halt, a smiling James Barbour disembarked into the driving rain, followed by his brother John and Charles Armstrong. "Over here!" Coleman Beckam called. "Make room for them under the porch."

The three ran to the covered protection and greeted their families. After giving Fannie a quick kiss on the cheek, James raised his hands to motion the crowd for silence. "My friends." All paused to catch his words. "I cannot tell you how gratified I am to see so many of you here on such an awful night. The support of the citizens of Culpeper warms my heart. I bring good news!" The crowd let out a jubilant cheer.

"We have met with Stephen Douglas, Secretary of State James Seward, and several other leaders in Washington. I believe we've reached a plan for the adjustment of our difficulties." He paused until the enthusiastic cheer died down. "Although I am not at liberty to reveal the details of our negotiations at this point in time, I can assure you that the results will be perfectly satisfactory to every Virginian.[5] Former President John Tyler and other members of our Peace Convention remain in Washington to ensure the success of our plan. Thank you for being here tonight. May you sleep well, knowing that peace has been ensured!"

The elated townspeople engulfed the three peace ambassadors with handshakes, pats on the back, and congratulations.

When the Armstrongs arrived home, Abraham pulled a chair up to the roaring fire in the parlor for the judge. "Sadie's makin' hot tea and I'll heat the water for your bath."

"Ah, Abraham, thanks. You always know my heart's desires." Charles collapsed into the brocade chair. "It's so good to be home. I can't wait to crawl into my own bed." He coughed several times.

"We've missed you, dear." Harriet kissed him on the cheek. "It's been a long four days and we've prayed constantly for the success of your mission. I hope you haven't taken a fever."

Constance pulled the rocking chair up next to him and took his hand. "Father, James Barbour's announcement sounds too good to be true. Please, will you fill us in on all the details?"

"Yes. I hope James isn't suffering from false optimism. We spent three days in discussions with many powerful men in the government. They seemed to appreciate the peace efforts of Virginia. In fact several statesmen from Pennsylvania took me aside and assured me that Pennsylvania would never enter hostilities against Virginia. However, we weren't allowed to talk to Mr. Lincoln personally, so our primary negotiations were with Secretary of State Seward. James feels confident that we have preserved slavery in the South. Seward has agreed that the Lincoln administration will support a Constitutional guarantee that slavery where it now exists cannot be eliminated without the approval of the states in question. Kentucky is introducing a bill in Congress called the Crittenden Compromise to make our agreement law."

"But, all you really have to rely on is the word of Seward," Alex commented.

"That's true." Charles frowned as wrinkles lined his forehead. Puffing thoughtfully on his pipe, he added, "I can't quite put my finger on it, but there's something about that man that makes me uneasy. I felt he was telling us what we wanted to hear. On the other hand, he made it clear that he considers James Barbour 'the master spirit of the Union party in Virginia.' Barbour warned him that if Seward falters on the agreement, Virginia will sever its bond with the Union."

"He's only buying time to build up armed forces. I'm convinced they're determined to destroy us," Alex said.

"The massing of forces in Washington is obvious. At this point we must assume it's for the purpose of guaranteeing a peaceful inauguration. Oh, Sadie," Charles said taking a cup of hot tea. "That smells wonderful."

Harriet munched on a piece of spice cake. "I got a letter from my good friend, Maria Daly, today. She and her husband have been in Washington this week and I think you may be interested in some of her observations." Harriet and Maria had lived together for two years in Paris. Now married to an Irish Catholic judge in New York City, she had met the Armstrongs several times at Democratic conventions.

"I'm glad you reminded me, dear," Charles said. "I did receive a note from Judge Daly yesterday commending our efforts. He invited me to join them for dinner but I had to decline. Our schedule was too full."

"At any rate," Harriet continued while she rummaged through some papers on the carved mahogany desk, "they're extremely unhappy with Lincoln's election and find it very upsetting that we might one day be on opposite sides in a war. Of course the Irish consider free Negroes competitors for jobs. Therefore, she has great disdain for the abolitionists. Here it is." She picked up the letter and read,

47

There is much said about the military readiness of Massachusetts and her being first in the field, but I think it is quite proper that she should be. It is preeminently her own quarrel. Her Wendell Phillips, Garrisons, Beechers, and Stowes are the firebrands which have set fire to the smoldering discontent of the South.

Let those who feel so concerned for the slaves of the South and who ask such sacrifices from slave-owners each buy one and then liberate them by degrees. Then I shall believe in the principle – the philanthropy which actuates the abolitionists.[6]

Alex slapped his hand against his knee. "That's the most intelligent thing I've heard a Yankee say on the subject." Harriet smiled as she continued reading:

Lincoln, though a man of little practical ability, seems to be straight forward and honest, but the Judge seems to think that Seward, the Secretary of State, is not the man for the occasion; he is too wrapped up in self. So long as you will listen whilst he preaches, well, but he cannot believe in anyone else nor see any wisdom in those who differ from him. Father Peltz said that in some difficulty about immigrants which occurred whilst he was governor of New York, he showed himself selfish and unprincipled.[7]

"Once again I agree with Mrs. Daly!" Alex said.

When Abraham announced Charles' bath was ready, he stood up stiffly.

"Good night, Father." Constance kissed him on the cheek. "Sleep well. You've done all in your power to ensure peace."

Five weeks later, March 6, 1861: Armstrong dining room

Constance cleaned the last piece of bacon from her plate hurriedly, knowing the Washington papers should be at the depot. "I'll bring a copy of Lincoln's inaugural address as soon as possible," she told her father as he sipped his coffee.

"I'd appreciate that." Her father, deep in thought, looked at the horses passing the front window of the dining room. "I expect James Barbour to arrive shortly. I'm sure he hasn't slept well the last two nights. With the Crittenden Compromise stalled in Congress, a verbal statement from Lincoln favoring its passage is absolutely essential. Otherwise," he sighed sadly, "I'm afraid we've been betrayed."

After Constance delivered the newspapers to her father's office with a grim expression, the two men quickly leafed through the papers until they found complete copies of Lincoln's inaugural address and read it intently.

"It's lame! It's weak! We've been betrayed!" James Barbour cried in disbelief. "Yes, Lincoln promised not to interfere with slavery where it now exists, but he said nothing about the constitutional guarantees as Seward promised. He has not preserved Southern honor." He slammed his fists on the desk. "I can't believe it!"

"I feel a great sadness," Charles replied, his voice quivering. "We're not dealing with honorable men."

"I put my honor and prestige on the line by backing this agreement." Tears filled Barbour's eyes. His face reddened with fury when he stood up and paced the office floor like a caged animal. "Seward's a bastard! I've written him over and over again, reiterating that he must not waver if we are to keep Virginia in the union. I warned him if he failed to support our agreement, Virginia would be out of the union in two weeks. He assured me that Lincoln would speak in favor of the Crittenden Compromise, while he procrastinated to buy time for the North."

"What will you do now?" Charles asked, his voice hoarse with frustration.

Barbour paced frantically, fire burning in his eyes. "I've been dishonored by this treacherous betrayal. I will publicly denounce Seward and the Lincoln administration. We cannot remain in a nation led by such dishonorable men. I will raise as forceful a voice in favor of secession as I did to oppose it!" He shook his fists defiantly.

Speechless, Charles Armstrong could not believe the metamorphosis taking place before him. Virginia's most faithful unionist was becoming an ardent secessionist. The rest of the state would share his shock.

Ten days later, March 16, 1861: Near Brandy Station

Constance enjoyed the first tingle of spring in the air from the porch of Belle Villa, home of Fannie and James Barbour. The two-story brick house with English basement and hip roof had been built in 1857 by Fannie's father as a wedding present to the newlyweds. She admired the plaster urns between the Doric columns of the full front porch where at least forty formally attired dinner guests gathered on the unseasonably warm March evening. Constance surveyed the vast expanse of open farmland visible from Belle Villa's high location, colored by the first rays of sunset.

About a half-mile in front of her lay the small village of Brandy Station, located five miles north of Culpeper Court House. According to legend, the deep well in the center of the village had been a watering place for wagoneers traveling the five important roads that converged there, including the Fredericksburg to Winchester Road and the road from the Blue Ridge to the Potomac River. The tavern, built at the crossroads, was renown for the high quality of its brandy enjoyed by the soldiers of the War of 1812. Thus the village became known as Brandy until the completion of the railroad. Due to the construction of a railroad station, the name lengthened to Brandy Station. Constance watched the smoke from the approaching engine twirl lazily upward.

Her eyes swept north to the long ridge referred to as Fleetwood Hill, and then to the south, where the rich fields of James Beckam's estate, Auburn, spread before her in the distance. James, first cousin of Coleman Beckam, Fannie's father, owned extensive tracts of land.

Constance sipped her punch, then overheard the jubilant conversation of Fannie and Amanda behind her, who realized they both expected babies in the early fall. Apprehensive about meeting the guests of honor, Constance nervously straightened the white mesh gloves that covered her fingers to the knuckles.

"Miss Armstrong." Aged James Beckam strolled towards her with another couple. "Our guests of honor have asked to be introduced to you."

Constance turned towards them forcing a smile. Her throat dry, she finally found her voice. "It's my pleasure indeed."

"This is my younger brother, John, and his wife, Mary. They've stopped to visit me before returning to Warrenton from a business trip to Richmond."

John Beckham bowed politely. "I must admit, Miss Armstrong, you're every bit as lovely as Robert said."

"Yes, dear," his wife said. "He seemed quite impressed with you last summer."

Constance felt her face growing hot. If only she could stop blushing! "I'm flattered Mrs. Beckam. I enjoyed your son's company. He's been a faithful correspondent this winter."

"Oh, yes," Mary Beckam replied, "you can always count on Robert. I believe he's the most dependable of our eight children."

"He's a hard worker and quite serious. At times I think he works too hard," John Beckam added. "Perhaps, Miss Armstrong, you can convince him to spend more time having fun and less time working." Constance's eyes twinkled and her face relaxed into a smile.

"My friends, my good friends," James Barbour called from the lawn below them, "Fannie and I want to welcome you here tonight. It's an honor for us to host this dinner party for Fannie's 'kissin' cousins,' John and Mary Beckam of Warrenton." He waved his hand towards the Beckams standing on the porch and everyone applauded.

"However, before we dine, there's another matter that rests heavy on my heart. Please pardon me for bringing up the great controversy that confronts our nation, but I must enlist your help." He paced in front of the porch. "The citizens of Culpeper elected me to represent them at the state's Secession Convention, expecting me to try to preserve the union. I traveled to Washington and struck a compromise with Secretary of State Seward, which I believed would be acceptable to all Virginians. Unfortunately," he said growing red in the face, "today I must denounce Seward for the double-dealing politician he is. His promises are as chaff on the wind!" The guests applauded enthusiastically.

"Virginians," Barbour continued, his voice rising, "cannot expect the Lincoln government to protect their property, liberty, or rights. The remarkable revolution that began in Culpeper December twenty sixth has swept across the state. Slaveholders and nonslaveholders recognize that secession is the only safeguard for their freedom and prosperity."[8] Alex led the loud applause. "With this in mind, I have called a meeting at the courthouse tomorrow night. I intend to ask for a vote in favor of secession. I hope you will be there." Barbour raised his hands for silence.

"Virginians should not fear the consequences of secession. If Virginia secedes, bestowing its weight and power on the Confederate States, North Carolina, Arkansas, Kentucky, Tennessee, Missouri, and perhaps Maryland will do likewise. The Confederate States of America will be a viable and vital nation. The United States Government has become so decrepit, both morally and financially, that it would not dare," he said shaking his fists, "I reiterate, not *dare* oppose a united South. These lands," he turned towards the horizon and dramatically swept his hands from Fleetwood Hill to the south, "will never be attacked by the Yankees."

Sadly, the lands within his view would be fought over, marched over, and camped upon more times than any other place in America. Fleetwood Hill would witness the largest cavalry battle ever to take place in North America.

Almost a month later, April 12, 1861: Rixeyville

The freedom of being back in the country lifted Constance's spirits. Liz raced across the newly greened meadow towards Rose Dale, the home of Constance's great aunt Martha, the gregarious socialite of Rixeyville. When she rode up to the cheerful yellow farmhouse, Constance spied the round silhouette of Martha Rixey bent over, picking jonquils. Martha looked up, recognized her visitor, and let out a cry of delight. "Yahoo! It's about time you came to see me, Constance! Come here and let me look at you!" the slightly deaf lady called loudly.

Constance dismounted and tied Liz to the hitching post. She turned with a warm smile and her aunt engulfed her in her ample breasts. "It's so good to see you, Aunt Martha." Constance pulled back to look into her aunt's sparkling cobalt eyes.

"You grow more beautiful every day. I think you're finally getting some meat on your body!" Martha laughed.

"Actually, I have gained a little weight this winter." The two of them walked arm in arm towards the front porch. "Sadie says I'm finally developing a figure."

"I'll say you are, a figure that any young lady would envy. Now, tell me truly, Constance, how many young beaus have you got?" Martha motioned for her to sit in one of the rockers while she plopped her fleshy body into the other chair.

"Well, actually, there's not a lot to tell. I'm in no hurry to get tied down. Most of the local fellows seem immature to me. However," she slowly arched her even brows mischievously, "I did meet someone interesting last summer."

"Uh huh, I knew it! Don't you keep anything from me, young lady." Martha leaned forward waiting for Constance to confide.

"His name is Robert Beckam and he's a West Point graduate. His father built the courthouse in Warrenton."

"Oh, yes, I've met the Beckams. They're very well to do, I might add," Martha said with a raspy chuckle. "So what is it about Robert that attracts you?"

"I've only met him once, so it's rather difficult to explain." Constance felt comfortable confiding in her aunt. "He seems to have depth and maturity, not to mention the fact that he's quite handsome."

"That sounds like an unbeatable combination to me."

"What's the news in Rixeyville?"

"I've spent the winter doing the usual...spoiling the grandchildren, visiting, and of course having parties. Everybody's talking war talk. My son-in-law is actively involved with the Black Horse Cavalry in Warrenton. They're all overgrown little boys playing soldier," Martha said with a hearty loud laugh.

Constance smiled tentatively. "I agree. Perhaps it will all pass. The delegates in Richmond voted against secession two to one April second. There seems to be little outcry for war in the North. Horace Greeley of *The New York Tribune* has even urged that the cotton states be allowed to go in peace. Then abolitionist Wendell Phillips agreed, saying 'Now the South will no longer hate the North.' He realizes the two sections can carry on a profitable trade while setting their own tariff rates."

"Top Hill stopped by yesterday." Martha's expression grew serious. "He said Powell has returned to Culpeper with his family after resigning from the army. Powell feels war is Lincoln's intention based on to the heavy military presence in Washington."

"Yes, I know. Father's spoken with him. After his experience with the Peace Convention, Father distrusts Seward and Lincoln. Lincoln's refused to see the three commissioners whom Jefferson Davis sent to Washington, while Seward stalls and placates them with promises to evacuate Fort Sumter." Aunt Martha leaned forward, cocking her head to understand the words over the squeak of the rocking chair. "Meanwhile, vessels laden with troops, munitions, and military supplies have sailed from Northern ports southward. Father suspects Lincoln is trying to provoke the South into firing the first shots in order to rally support for war in the North."

"What treacherous, deceitful minds these politicians have. But enough of this gloomy talk. Don't you worry your pretty head with it. We must plan a party to welcome y'all back to Rixeyville after your winter sojourn in town."

"Oh, what fun! Let's! You give the most divine parties!"

Hudson and Isaac peered over the top of their newly created fort behind Panorama. "Bang! Bang! You're dead!"

"Ah! I'm hit!" Constance staggered up the hill and grabbed her abdomen, trying to suppress her laughter.

"I'm sorry, Connie. They've been shooting Yankees all day," Amanda called from the back porch where she played with David.

The loud clatter of hooves heralded the arrival of Charles and Alex.

"Daddy, I've killed hundreds of Yankees today!" Hudson dashed towards his father after he dismounted.

Constance noticed her father's pale, somber face. "Are you well, Father?" She linked her arm through his.

"I'm afraid I must share some disturbing news with you," he said in a resigned tone. He looked at them with distraught eyes. "Confederate forces in Charleston are bombarding Fort Sumter. The news came over the telegraph late this afternoon."

"Oh, my God!" Amanda moaned, clasping her hand over her mouth. She turned towards Alex, fear in her eyes. "Has it begun?"

"I'm sure it has. Virginia will secede now. We'll be free from tyranny at last!"

"One Ranger can whip twenty Yankees!" Hudson cried.

Five days later, April 17, 1861: The Culpeper Observer

Constance's head throbbed from the clatter of the printing press and the startling news in the paper before her. Abraham Lincoln had as much as declared war on the Confederacy. By calling for 75,000 volunteers to put down the rebellion, he had taken the power to declare war into his own hands. Congress was not even in session. His actions were a flagrant violation of the Constitution. As if that wasn't bad enough, he demanded that Virginia and the border states supply troops, only to have these troops march across Virginia's soil to attack her southern sisters.

"I can't believe the audacity of this man!" McDonald shouted, pacing around his desk furiously. "Virginia will never comply with his unconstitutional demands. He's going to start a war to protect his image."

"There was not a single casualty at Fort Sumter. The people of Charleston merely protected themselves against a union military buildup in their harbor," Constance sputtered. "The Confederacy has no desire to conquer the North. Why can't they let the southern states go in peace?"

"Do you believe Virginia will now secede?" asked Ralph.

"I'm afraid she'll have to in order to protect her honor and her allegiance to the Constitution," Constance answered in a depressed voice.

"The Culpeper Minutemen have orders to be ready to march immediately. We'll go to Harper's Ferry to protect the northern borders and the arsenal."

Charles Armstrong nodded in front of the fire. Constance, delighted to be able to spend a few days alone with him in town, tried to focus on the book in her lap. Her father had been her willing accomplice as she told her mother she needed to shop, knowing her real intent was to stay abreast of the latest political news in town. She walked over to the front window and pulled the curtain back to see people still milling in the street and waiting on the porch of the Virginia House. Everyone expected news from Richmond soon.

The bells of Saint Stephen's rang loudly. Her father bolted up and looked at her in surprise as a series of rifle shots rang out. "There must be news! Let's get to the depot." They rushed to the back door.

Townspeople carrying lanterns surged towards the depot. The large crowd in front of the train station cheered wildly and danced in the street. "Virginia has seceded!" Baptist Hill cried jubilantly. "We are free of despotism. The flames of liberty are burning in our southern hearts!"

"Do you know what the vote was?" Charles yelled above the din.

"Eighty eight to fifty five," Powell Hill answered. "I'm sure most of the dissenting votes were from the western part of the state."

The frenzied crowd celebrated by singing, dancing, hugging, and rejoicing. Once again Virginia would lead a new nation. Exhausted after an hour, the judge insisted they go home. Constance noticed that many onlookers did not seem overjoyed. She spied Mary Payne and others sitting on the porch of the Virginia House Hotel. When her father headed home, she decided to approach the others.

She stepped on the porch and addressed Mary Payne. "Have you heard the news?"

"Hard not to," Mary replied shortly. "I'm opposed to this secession business. It's the work of the hotheads and politicians."

A New England native who had moved to the Brandy Station area three years earlier, sat beside her. Frowning, he said, "This will be a Negro war. Virginia will go too far if she fights against the Union to uphold slavery."

Sensing the tension, Constance said diplomatically, "Let's hope there won't be a war and that the North will let us go in peace."

She entered the house to find her father slouched on the sofa, his head back and his eyes closed. Constance snuggled in beside him. "How are you, Father?" She wrapped her fingers around his.

"Exhausted," he mumbled, his eyes still closed.

"How do you feel about it all?" She caressed his hand.

He lifted his eyelids slowly. "Great sadness that we've dissolved our ties with the Union. But," he sighed, "Abraham Lincoln has made the Confederacy. The power of Virginia has strengthened a weak coalition. North Carolina, Tennessee, and the other border states will follow. Virginia has laid herself down as a shield between Lincoln and her weaker southern sisters. I am afraid a blood bath may take place on our soil."

"Then you believe the North will attack?"

"Lincoln seems determined. However, there's much dissention in the North. One thing is certain…we can't win a long war. They have more than two-and-a-half times more fighting men. The South has no industry or facilities to make weapons. We're more brave and gallant than smart."

"What are the chances of foreign assistance?"

"It's a possibility. England, especially, may be sympathetic. Our greatest hope is that the people of the North don't have the determination for war."

"Will you support Virginia's war effort?"

"As an old man, I'd like to enjoy the luxury of neutrality. Unfortunately, I don't believe that's possible." He paused in thought. "I feel secession is legal. Lincoln's declaration of war is undoubtedly unconstitutional. If we are attacked," he said with resignation, "I'll support our men as they fight to protect our homes."

"It's already obvious to me that everyone will be forced to pick a side. Neighbors will no longer be friends and families will be split." She searched the depths of his eyes.

"My greatest fear," he lamented, his voice breaking as tears formed in his eyes, "is that after today we will never be the same again."

He pulled her tight against him and she felt their hearts throbbing together. Clinging to him desperately, apprehension like she had never known before welled in her throat. Even her father's protective arms could not calm her overwhelming sense of foreboding.

3

Who Will Take Stringfellow?

May 2 – July 24, 1861

*"I came home to invasion-threatened Virginia, fully prepared to die from a
Northern bullet or a Southern cough."*[1]
Frank Stringfellow

Two weeks later, May 2, 1861: Culpeper Court House

Dogwoods and redbuds dotted the green hills along Frank Stringfellow's route from
the Retreat towards Culpeper Court House. The crisp Virginia air felt refreshing to his
lungs as he breathed deeply. A chronic throat ailment and hacking cough had plagued
him during the long wet winter in Mississippi. This mysterious illness, first diagnosed
as tuberculosis, had pulled his weight down to slightly over a hundred pounds. Nevertheless, he possessed strength of spirit and eagerness to fight for his convictions and the
defense of his homeland. Culpeper, because of its strategic location, had been selected
as a site to stock supplies, rendezvous men, and train recruits.

The mountains, bedecked in blue shrouds, beckoned him as he spurred his horse
towards town to observe the military frenzy. Hearing rifle fire and the shouting of
commands, he rode to a hill overlooking the west side of town. He marveled at the
several hundred men drilling and marching below him in the valley surrounding Mountain Run. When he reached crowded Coleman Street, he observed men in every
imaginable type of uniform. Confederate flags hung from many homes, as well as
flapping in the breeze over the Courthouse and Post Office. Turning up Davis Street, he
spied John Stark, Jr., unloading a wagonload of supplies in front of his mercantile.

Stark informed him that there were over 700 recruits in town, with more flooding in
daily. They were temporarily housed in basements, sheds, storage buildings, and churches.
General Philip Saint George Cocke had taken command on the twenty eighth and was
laying out plans to build a camp northwest of town, on land owned by Cumberland
George. It would be named Camp Henry in honor of Patrick Henry, orator of the first
revolution. Stark said he sold his stock before he could get it on the shelves; everything
went: candles, rope, axes, spades, saws, nails, frying pans, coffeepots, sugar, and salt.
He couldn't enlist because he had to keep the business going. Stringfellow announced
his intent to join the cavalry, the most elite group, and rode towards the depot.

When he tied his horse to the hitching post, he saw a group of soldiers nailing a
proclamation on the side of the depot. "Is this where you want it, General Cocke?" an
officer asked of the slight man in his early fifties.

"Yes. The volunteers can't miss it when they get off the trains. We must write General Lee and demand arms for our men. Most have no guns and only a few have sabers."

"Don't you fret none, General," called one of the thirty-odd men gathered around the tracks. "We'll whip them dang Yankees with rocks and our bare fists if we have to." The crowd let forth a lusty cheer.

"Gentlemen, your spirit is commendable. However, if we are to hold the Potomac border between Harper's Ferry and Fredericksburg, we must have arms," Cocke replied with authority. He headed down the street.

"Where you fellas from?" Stringfellow asked the crowd.

"Georgia," one group shouted proudly. "North Carolina," responded the others.

"We're proud to have y'all here to help defend Virginia's borders," Stringfellow said with an easy smile as he walked inside the depot. Peering through the glass windows into the office he spied John Barbour at work with several staff members. Barbour looked up and waved at him through the window.

"Frank!" He hurried out to shake hands. "Welcome home. We've been running this railroad nonstop. I've got every possible engine in use. Our people are united in spirit. But I must admit, I'm exhausted."

"This railroad is the lifeline to our existence," Stringfellow said gesturing with his hands. "Looks like we're located in a dangerous spot

"You may be right. Some have even speculated that the first battle will be fought in Culpeper. Many think the Yanks will fuss and fume but won't really fight much. Let's hope that's the case." Barbour turned to look at a southbound train approaching the station. "Looks like I'd better get back to work. Good luck to you, Frank."

"Thanks. We appreciate your skill in running the railroad."

He sauntered out of the station to see two young men disembarking from the train, satchels in hand. They walked towards him. "We've just arrived from Baltimore and want to enlist in the army."

"From Baltimore?" Stringfellow said surprised. "Now, we've even got volunteers from the North."

"You'd better believe it, and there'll be lots more. We were there when that pro-Confederate mob attacked the Massachusetts Militia that marched through Baltimore towards Washington. We saw how innocent civilians were shot. If you don't agree with Lincoln, they lock you up without a trial. Freedom of speech is dead in Maryland. That Lincoln's become a military dictator," the taller one said as he spat with disgust.

"You mark my words, they've taken military control of Maryland to keep her from seceding. We've left our homes to come here and fight for freedom," the other one added.

"You Maryland boys come on over here and join us," the group from North Carolina called. "We'd be glad to have anybody that fightin' mad."

Stringfellow stood there amazed at what he had heard, then read Cocke's proclamation: *All brave men in this district are hereby summoned to defend Virginia against Northern aggression. The North has not openly, nor according to the usage of civilized nations, declared war on us. We make no war on them; but should Virginia soil be polluted by the tread of a single man in arms from north of the Potomac, it will cause open war.*

After reading the proclamation, Stringfellow remembered the other reason for his trip to town…Constance.

Constance concentrated on setting type when the door opened. She raised her eyes to see those familiar gray-blue eyes twinkling at her. "Frank! You're home!"

He hugged her tightly and kissed her on the cheek. "Connie, you look wonderful," Frank said warmly as he stood back to peruse her.

"But you," she gasped, "you're emaciated. Are you still sick?"

"I think I'm beginning to recover," he said with a cough. "But I can't seem to gain any weight back. You, however, have rounded out beautifully."

"There you go, teasing me already." She took Frank by the hand and introduced him to Mr. McDonald, who told her to take the afternoon off.

"Quite a busy young lady, aren't you?" Frank teased when they walked across Cameron Street. "Sadie told me all about your job. She's fixing tea and cake for us in the gazebo."

They settled into the built-in seats in the white gazebo. Sadie meandered up with a tray of refreshments and encouraged Frank to eat some of her cake to put meat on his bones. Constance nibbled on a piece of cake and looked at Frank thoughtfully. "How are your brothers?"

"Good, but they've both left. Martin's become a sharpshooter in the command of an eccentric colonel named Thomas Jonathan Jackson at Harper's Ferry. The soldiers are all complaining about his uncompromising discipline. He's a former Virginia Military Institute professor and extremely religious. Robert's in camp at Richmond. Eliza was visiting him when Virginia seceded. She told us of the torchlight procession and marching bands down Marshall Street, the fabulous celebration with rockets and Roman candles. She said one speaker predicted the Confederate flag would be waving over the White House within sixty days. That's why I'm so anxious to enlist. I don't want to miss the war."

"Well, you have your choice of units," Constance said. "The Minutemen left the day after Virginia seceded. But there's the Culpeper Riflemen at Brandy Station, the Hazelwood Volunteers at Stevensburg, the Lecher Artillery, Grove's Culpeper Artillery, the Ready Rifles, and the Little Fork Rangers, the only cavalry unit."

"Oh, I'll only enlist in the cavalry. I'm an experienced horseman and good shot. The cavalry will be the elite units. I won't consider anything else. Do you know where and when they're mustering?"

"Yes, Alex is enthusiastically involved. They muster Friday through Sunday at Little Fork Episcopal Church. Obviously, you have to provide your own horse and weapons."

"Excellent. I'll enlist this weekend, then I'll stop by the farm to see you. Will you be there?"

"Yes, I'm working for Mr. McDonald Tuesday through Thursday. He needs help since Ralph left with the Minutemen. We've also been printing Confederate stationery and order forms for General Cocke. I'm donating the little money I make to the Cause."

"Connie, you're an energetic young lady and a true Southern belle. Tell me honestly, now that you're surrounded by hundreds of men, how many hearts have you stolen recently?" he asked with a devilish smile.

"Stop teasing! It's almost scary having so many men around. They've all been gentlemen, but it's obvious they're longing for feminine attention. However," she said, her eyes flickering with merriment, "I will confess I've been corresponding with Robert Beckam since last summer."

"Aha! The handsome soldier who whisked you away at Salubria. I should have been suspicious. Anything serious?"

"Oh, I'm not sure. He'll be returning home soon from Detroit. I suppose time will tell. And how about Emma?"

"The fair Emma still holds my heart. She turns eighteen in two months, and I intend to ask for her hand. I've missed her dreadfully this winter."

"I hope war doesn't interfere with your plans. Life is so indefinite now."

"That's true. We don't know what tomorrow will bring." He squeezed her hand. "Now, sister dearest, I must hurry home to mother. She's a strong woman, but having three sons enlist is difficult for her. I need to spend as much time as possible with her before I leave."

They moved out into the yard. "Mother will invite her to visit soon. I'll see you in a few days at the farm."

He kissed her on the cheek, winked, and departed.

Four days later, May 6, 1861: Little Fork Episcopal Church

Frank Stringfellow bristled with excitement when he rode into the yard surrounding Little Fork Episcopal Church, so named because of its location within the Little Fork, the area between the confluence of the Rappahannock and Hazel rivers. The Great Fork consisted of the area between the Rappahannock and Rapidan rivers. He admired the beauty and simplicity of the rectangular brick church, where he had attended numerous services with the Armstrongs. Built in 1774, the county's oldest church had walls twenty-two inches thick. Three tall windows with semi-circular arches flanked each side of the arched center door. The hipped roof and wooden modillion cornice revealed the church's colonial origin. He watched several men on horseback gather under the trees. Anxious to enlist, he had left home before dawn. The group eyed him warily as he asked, "Who's in charge of this company?"

"That'd be me son. I'm Captain Robert Utterback." A middle aged man moved his horse beside Stringfellow. "What can I do for you?"

"I'm Frank Stringfellow from over on the Rapidan. I've come to enlist."

Captain Utterback sized up the smooth faced scrawny youth in front of him, who didn't look over fifteen. "How old are you, boy?"

"Twenty one, sir, and I can ride and shoot like the best of them."

"Well, I'm sorry son. We can't accept you. I'm afraid you don't fit the image of a Little Fork Ranger. Why don't you try the infantry?" Utterback said firmly but kindly.

Stunned, Stringfellow stammered, "But sir, I've got a good mount and two guns, and I'm determined to be in the cavalry. I can fight as good as any man here."

"Sorry boy, we can't take you and that's final." Utterback turned back towards the other men.

Smarting, Stringfellow sat in stunned silence until a familiar figure rode up. "Don't take it so hard Frank. It's nothing personal. You're just too small," Alex said.

"But Alex, the fact that I'm small or thin doesn't mean I can't fight!"

"Look at it his way, Frank. Suppose you're on picket duty with another fellow. Now he's got the right to expect you to hold up your end if the Yankees come. And what about when we take Washington City? We can't have a bag of bones like you riding with us when we parade through town."[2]

Stringfellow stared at Alex disgusted. "Rally at the foot of the hill, men," Captain Utterbuck ordered. Stringfellow watched the group line up behind the church. He tied his horse to the post and wandered into the open church. The sunlight flooded through the arched windows and illuminated the white walls and colonial teal enclosed pews. He stared up at the raised pulpit directly in front of him and the hexagonal ceiling-hung canopy above it. He had heard many an inspiring sermon from that pulpit. Distracted by the sound of the pounding hooves outside, he ambled towards the altar at the end of the room. Kneeling, he looked up to God for a sense of direction. Surely, God would help him find a way to fight for such an honorable cause. He felt strengthened after a short time, walked out, and decided to find Constance. She always lifted his spirits.

Constance braced her feet firmly, held both arms out straight, and squeezed the trigger of the pistol. When the smoke cleared, she saw a hole in the outside ring of the target. Well, that was an improvement. At least now she could hit the target. She carefully took aim again and squeezed the trigger without moving her arms. Pleased, she spied a hole on the inside circle. She had been practicing for weeks, determined to become an expert shot to defend herself if necessary. She took careful aim and fired again. This time she saw nothing. She walked closer to inspect the target. Had she missed completely? No! She had hit the bull's eye! Unable to control herself she jumped up and down with excitement.

"Those Yanks won't have a prayer against a sharp shooter like you," a male voice said from behind one of the trees in the woods. Startled, she let out a blood-curdling scream. A laughing Frank Stringfellow slunk out from behind a large poplar tree.

"Oh, my God, Frank, you scared me to death! Don't ever do that again. How did you possibly get in those woods without me seeing you?"

"Now calm down, Rebel lady. You know that's a special talent of mine. Are you planning to enlist?"

"I intend to be able to defend myself if necessary." She paused and stared at him intently. "You know, Frank, I've never told anyone this, but at times I fantasize that I'm a man." He raised his eyebrows in shock. "Now, don't laugh. Although I never before wished I was a man...now I feel so keenly my weakness and dependence. I can't do or say anything, for it would be unbecoming to a young lady. How I'd love to fight and even die for my country...what a privilege I'd consider it, but I'm denied because I'm a woman,"[3] she concluded dramatically.

"Constance, I'm in awe of your brave spirit. Perhaps you could disguise yourself as a man," he said with a half smile.

"Actually I've given it serious consideration. But, because of my small size, I don't think I'd get away with it. Some women will fight in disguise, I'm convinced."

"Well, right now you've got a lot better chance of fighting the Yankees than I do," he admitted, his voice heavy with sarcasm.

"What do you mean Frank? I don't understand."

He looked down kicking dirt with his boot, his face growing red. "Damn it, Connie, the Rangers rejected me! At a time when they're taking everybody with a head and a horse, they turned me down."

"Frank," she cried sympathetically, grasping his hand. "I'm so sorry. Why?"

"Said I didn't fit their image…too small," he muttered, his gray eyes moistening.

"Well, maybe Alex can help you."

"Pshaw! His help I don't need. He told me they couldn't ride up to the White House with a bag of bones like me along."

Constance paced furiously. "Alex isn't known for his sensitivity. He considers himself a fierce warrior." She paused, speculated thoughtfully, "Perhaps, Frank, God is sending you a message. You need to regain your health and some weight before you destroy the entire Union army singled handed."

His eyes glimmered again. "You mean I'm going to have to drink cream and eat eggs until I can moo and cackle? Bawk, bawk, bawk," he cackled.

She erupted with infectious laughter, giggling for the sheer joy of it. It felt so good to break the tension. She shook until tears rolled down her face. "Promise me Frank, that no matter what happens, you'll never lose that sense of humor."

He kept cackling like a chicken. "Look at the two of us, Connie," he blurted out. "A five-foot, three-inch girl and a hundred-pound scarecrow. If the Yanks knew they'd have to face such dangerous opposition, they'd be quaking in their boots. There wouldn't be any war." He threw back his head and let out a great peal of laughter.

She wiped the tears from her face, still giggling. "Undoubtedly! We'd put the fear of God into any army. Listen, why don't you stay for dinner. Sadie's cooking will be just what the doctor ordered."

"Well," he paused, trying to regain his composure. "Maybe I could. Mother thinks I'm drilling with the Rangers."

"Of course you can. Amanda's in Jeffersonton with Alex's parents. The women are assembling uniforms for the Rangers, made from wool provided by the Waterloo mill. Of course Alex won't be back. You won't have to see his arrogant face. My parents are dying to see you."

"You've captured me, fair lady," he said as the two of them meandered up the hill towards the house. "And once again you've revived my spirit."

Twelve days later, May 18, 1861: East Street

Constance carried a basket of fruit, bread, paper and pens through her back gate to East Street. She gazed up at the tall steeple of Saint Stephen's while she waited for Lucy and Jane Ashby and their grandmother to catch up with her. She smiled at "Granny," a spry little lady not five feet tall. Mouselike, she scurried around town taking small quick steps, her gray hair piled in a knot on top of her head and her spectacles perched on her pointed Roman nose. She always carried a cane, although she did not need it to walk. Rather, it served as a weapon for use against those who irritated her. Sharp-tongued, she never failed to speak her mind. Pedestrians knew not to cross the eighty-year-old spitfire. No one wanted to arouse the wrath of Granny Ashby, the best known and most feared character in town.

"How are you, ladies?" Constance fell in beside them.

"I'm just as feisty as ever," Granny said. She scurried along in front on the young girls. "I'm surprised your high-falutin' mother will let you work in the hospital." Her two granddaughters shrugged at Constance in apology.

"Actually, she doesn't think it proper for ladies to serve as nurses and be around men in their nakedness," Constance answered. "Who else will take care of the hundreds of sick men, with most of the males already at the front? She only consented to let me go when I told her you'd be along to protect my honor."

"Yes indeed, that's right. If any of those men get out of line, I'll just whop 'em with my cane. But they're so sick with measles, typhoid, diarrhea and dysentery, they won't be a problem." She spun around to look at the three young girls. "Y'all hurry up. We've got a lot of work to do today."

Picking up their pace, they turned right on Piedmont Street. "I'm afraid we're going to lose a third of our army from disease before we ever have a battle," Lucy said.

"It's true. They're living in horrible conditions, all crowded together. Sickness spreads like wildfire. Disease will probably kill more soldiers than bullets,"[i] Constance shifted the weight of the basket. "I heard that Powell Hill's been made Colonel of the Thirteenth Virginia Infantry. The Minute Men and several Culpeper and Orange regiments will be under his command at Winchester."

"Do tell?" Granny squeaked in dismay. "You mean 'Little Powell Hill'? I remember when that scrawny boy used to hang onto his mother's apron strings. Heaven help us if Powell Hill is going to be a colonel in the Confederate Army!"[4]

"Now, Granny, he's a West Point graduate and highly esteemed by his men. We should be proud that a Culpeper man is one of the leaders of our new army," Constance said.

Granny grunted. The foursome headed down the Brandy Road towards Mountain Run. "I'm going to leave early today," Constance informed them. "Robert Beckam telegraphed Father yesterday and requested permission to call on me this evening."

"Constance, how wonderful," Jane exclaimed. "So the handsome Lieutenant Beckam has finally returned from Detroit."

"Yes." Constance's lips curled up in a grin. "He's been trying to secure an appointment as an engineer in the Confederate Army." They headed up the hill towards Camp Henry. "I'm nervous about seeing him. After all, I've only met him once."

"Now don't you worry. If he's got eyes in his head, he'll be charmed by a pretty little thing like you," Granny said.

The plank huts and tents of Camp Henry sprouted on the knoll like mushrooms.[ii] The women saw nearly 600 men marching and practicing all types of military movements with enthusiastic shouts. The north corner of the camp had been designated the "hospital area" where numerous huts and tents housed nearly 300 patients. Doctor Daniel

---

[i] Of the approximately 850,000 men who fought for The Confederacy, 94,000 died from wounds , 166,000 died from disease.
[ii] Mystery still exists over the location of Camp Henry. One theory places it on the Old Dominion Manufacturing site near the current Wal-Mart. This high location was close the railroad and Mountain Run.

Green walked out of a large tent to greet them. "Thank God for you women to watch by the bedside of the sick and suffering. I'm overwhelmed with patients. Please do what you can for these poor men."

"We're glad to serve in our country's struggle," Lucy said. She and Constance walked into the first tent where the stench of body excrements and vomit nearly overwhelmed them. At least forty men lay on cots less than two feet apart. With the tent flaps pulled back, flies buzzed everywhere, but little air circulated. Constance took a deep breath.

"Let's get busy," she said to Lucy with determination.

Exhausted by two o'clock, Constance knew she must go home. Newly arrived patients lay outside on the ground unattended. She spotted Dr. Green in one of the huts and approached him. "Doctor Green, I'm sorry, but I must leave now. I'll be back in the morning."

"Thank you, Miss Armstrong," he answered while examining a soldier. "I'm desperate for places to put these new patients. Do you think you could take some into your home?"

She hesitated a moment, knowing that her mother would object. "Yes, of course," she answered slowly. "I'll send our servant with a wagon for them in the morning. I'll also ask others to open their homes."

"You're a noble servant of the Cause, Miss Armstrong."

While dressing for dinner, Constance stepped into the modesty panel Sadie held. The servant fastened it over her tightly laced corset. "Yes indeed, Miss Constance, your figger is shapin' up mighty fine. I'm lookin' forward to seein' this Lieutenant Beckam I've been hearin' 'bout."

Constance stepped into her hoop. "Oh, Sadie, I'm so nervous. You're all making this such an important event. Alex, Amanda, and the boys are coming from the farm so they can scrutinize him. He's simply a friend coming to visit…that's all."

"Hold your arms up." Sadie lifted the rose dress over Constance's head. "We jist wanna make sure any young gent'man that calls on ya is good enough for ya. You's pretty special 'round here." She buttoned the dress. "Now, don't ya look pretty!"

Constance walked over to the mirror and looked at her image critically. "Thanks, Sadie. Do you think this color is good on me?"

"Of course it is. Ya jist trust Sadie. Now sit down an' let me brush your hair."

Constance settled into the boudoir chair. "I don't know what I'd do without you, Sadie. But promise me you'll always be honest with me. Don't tell me something because you think it's what I want to hear."

Sadie brushed her shiny black hair vigorously. "I's the most honest person in the world. The Good Book says, 'Thou shalt not bear false witness.' Thanks to you, I've read it mahself."

"Sadie, I need for Abraham to take the wagon over to Camp Henry in the morning. They've run out of space for the sick soldiers, and conditions are deplorable. I promised I'd care for three patients here."

Sadie rolled her eyes. "Now, I'm gonna tell ya what I honestly think of that, Miss Constance. Your momma is gonna have a fit! She don't want no dirty soldiers in her house. Not only that, Miss Amanda don't want the boys 'round 'em."

"I'm fully aware of that." Constance held a deep rose ribbon up for Sadie. "Let's try this. Nevertheless, I can't let those men lie outside and die. Mother and Amanda can go back to the farm tomorrow if they object. You'll help me care for them, won't you Sadie?"

"Yes'm, I've always helped anybody who's sick." She pulled Constance's hair back and tied the ribbon in a bow. "Now, what do ya think?"

Walking and twirling, Constance appraised her appearance in the mirror. She held up a pearl-handled mirror to see the back of her hair. "I think this is as good as I'm going to look."

Sadie gave her a big hug. "Ya jist smile yo' pretty smile an' everything will be fine. I've gotta go finish cookin' y'all's supper."

Robert Beckam took a deep breath before he knocked on the Armstrongs' door. Naturally introverted, he had difficulty overcoming his shyness around young ladies. Constance Armstrong's vivaciousness had attracted him, and he had eagerly anticipated her letters for almost a year now. He rapped firmly on the doorknocker and straightened his tie. It felt strange to be in civilian clothes. Abraham opened the door with a big smile. "Good afternoon, sur. Ya must be Mista Beckam. Please come in."

"Thank you." Beckam stepped into the hall when Charles Armstrong entered from the parlor.

"Lieutenant Beckam, it's a pleasure to see you again." He reached his hand out.

"Likewise, Judge Armstrong. I saw an old friend of yours yesterday, who asked to be remembered to you."

"Ah, I suspect that might have been my one time neighbor and political cohort, 'Extra Billy' Smith," Charles said. "Is the old geezer about to win the war single-handed?"

"Indeed he is." Beckam laughed. "At sixty four, he's preparing to go to Manassas where he's obtained a command."

"The energy of that man never ceases to amaze me." Smith had served Virginia as Governor, Legislator, and several times as Congressman. "I have no doubt he'll make an outstanding leader for our army, even though he's had no military training. Please Lieutenant Beckam, come into the parlor."

Alex rose to greet the guest with a smile and extended hand. "Lieutenant Beckam, I'm Alex Yager, Constance's brother-in-law."

"Yes, I remember you from Salubria. Are you involved in the war efforts?"

"Absolutely." Alex poured a glass of wine. "May I offer you some wine or brandy?"

"No, thank you, I don't drink. However, I'd love a cup of tea if you have it. "

"Certainly, Sadie will bring some shortly. In answer to your question, I've enlisted with the Little Fork Rangers, Culpeper's only cavalry unit." Alex sipped his wine.

Charles poured a glass of brandy. "What is your military status? Are we correct in calling you Lieutenant Beckam?"

"Indeed you are. I'm currently assigned as a lieutenant in the Provisional Army of Virginia in the Engineer Corps. While in Detroit I was negotiating by mail to obtain an engineer appointment in the Confederate Army. I waited until the third of May to resign in the hope that I'd receive that position or that this crisis could be averted. One of my West Point friends has written letters on my behalf."

"So at this point you have not received a position in the Confederate Army?" Alex asked.

"No, I'm sure the two armies will merge soon. I've thought about asking other influential men to write letters on my behalf. Perhaps Jeremiah Morton will aid me," Beckam said.

"He's certainly influential," Charles agreed. Morton's plantation along the Rapidan encompassed over 6000 acres and his slave auctions reaped huge profits.

The clatter of feet on the steps and the rustle of skirts in the hall caught their attention. Harriet, looking elegant as always, entered the room first. Robert Beckam bowed formally. "Mrs. Armstrong, you look lovely this evening."

"Thank you, Lieutenant Beckam. It's good to have you in Culpeper," she replied in her usual dignified manner.

Amanda followed her in a lovely empire waist dress that concealed her pregnancy. Bowing again, Beckam said, "Mrs. Yager, it's good to see you."

"Welcome back," Amanda said.

Constance's face colored slightly when she entered the room. She felt the warmth of his stare while his eyes bathed her in admiration. His mouth dropped slightly in surprise; she had filled out, was even more beautiful than he remembered. Pleased, she watched the light twinkle in the depths of his black eyes. He appeared every bit as handsome as she had envisioned him in her dreams throughout the year. Charles cleared his throat.

Jarred back to reality, Beckam bowed while Constance curtsied. "Miss Armstrong, you look radiant this evening."

"Thank you, Lieutenant Beckam. Welcome home to Virginia," she said with a broad smile.

"It's wonderful to be back. I hated the cold weather in Detroit. The city didn't have the gentility of our Southern cities."

Sadie entered with a tray of tea, and Charles invited everyone to sit down to be served. When they were comfortably situated he asked, "What is the pulse of the public in Detroit and the other cities you traveled through?"

For once Constance tuned out the political conversation and used the time to study his face freely, outwardly, unhurriedly, feature by feature. In the distance she heard him say that sentiment was evenly divided with the Democrats, now called Copperheads, not favoring war. People were afraid to speak out against the war because of the tyrannical events in Maryland. Alex protested that Butler's army was holding Maryland captive, sending many of her finest citizens to northern prisons and her legislature to Fort Warren. Lincoln had destroyed the Constitutional rights of Maryland's citizens to keep Maryland from seceding. In addition, Northern armies had moved quickly into Missouri and western Virginia to accomplish the same thing. The Confederacy feared Kentucky would soon suffer the same fate. Lincoln's move to blockade southern ports the day after his call for volunteers clearly proved war had been his intent all along.

Robert agreed that Lincoln's government had employed heavy-handed tactics to remain in control and also had used Fort Sumter to sway sentiment. Robert reported seeing war preparations in every town he passed through. Now that the capital of the Confederacy had been moved to Richmond, attack on Virginia's borders appeared imminent. Time was of the essence. He would be leaving for Winchester day after tomorrow. Constance melted under the intensity of his gaze.

Robert made dinner a pleasant event, keeping them entertained with stories of West

Point, army life, and Detroit. When they left the table Constance decided that she must take the bull by the horns if the two of them were to spend any time alone. "Lieutenant Beckam, would you like to see our gardens?" she asked innocently.

"That would be a pleasure," he replied with a smile that sent her pulse racing. Harriet's jaw dropped at her daughter's boldness. Constance looked at her father who nodded his approval and winked.

They strolled through the yard where she pointed out the Culpeper Observer and explained her work there in great detail. Then she took him to the back fence and showed him Saint Stephen's. Retracing their steps through the boxwoods, she expounded on conditions at Camp Henry, her service to the suffering, and Frank Stringfellow's dilemma. He drank in every word, while devouring her with his eyes. They approached the gazebo. She said, "Come sit down. I have a birthday surprise for you."

He raised his dark eyebrows in surprise, and slid onto the gazebo bench close to her, noticing a small wrapped present on the table. "You seem to have planned this very well. So, you were going to lure me here all the time?"

"Yes." She laughed with her musical voice. "You've been under the scrutiny of my family long enough."

"That's only proper." He reached for the present, shook it, and heard a slight rattle. "Now, what can this be?" He ripped open the package to find a box of Confederate stationery and a gold trimmed pen.

"Now you will have no excuse for failing to correspond," she said softly. "I printed that stationery myself."

"What a wonderful gift." His eyes searched her face. "I find it frustrating that most of our communication has to be by mail, but your letters will be more important than ever to me now." He reached out and laced her fingers with his. "Unfortunately, that's what army life does to you. It sends you places that you don't want to go, and away from those you care for. I don't intend to have a military career. I went to West Point to get the best engineering education possible."

"You are your father's child." She enjoyed the warmth of his fingers.

"Yes. I want to build things, not destroy them. I get great satisfaction out of drawing and designing structures. When I've served my time in the army I'd like to be an architect, marry, raise a family, and live happily ever after in Virginia."

"How sad that the impending war might interfere with your goals." She moved her fingers lightly against his.

"It is, but one thing West Point has instilled in me is discipline. I've learned orders must be obeyed whether you like it or not." The evening shadows had faded into darkness. "Are you chilly?"

"A little." Her blue eyes flashed with azure fire. He slid his arm around her, pulling her close.

"If I cannot get an assignment in the Engineering Corps, then I am requesting Ordnance, and lastly the Dragoons. I don't want to be in the infantry and absolutely not in the artillery. Anyone who survives in the artillery will be deaf." His fingers moved slowly over her arm.

"I hope you get your first choice. Do you have to go soon?" His finger tenderly traced the line of her cheekbone.

"I'm afraid so. I'm spending tonight with Uncle James at Auburn and then returning to Warrenton tomorrow to tell my family good-bye." She leaned against him slightly, tilting her face towards his. "My parents were impressed with you when they met you at the Barbour's. Mother would like to have you come visit. You'd love my nine-year-old sister."

"I'd like that very much. Your father told me that you worked too hard, and I should persuade you to have more fun." Her lips turned up in an inviting smile. He cupped her chin in his hand and his lips slowly descended towards hers, giving her time to stop him, but she did not. She shivered at the sweet tenderness of his kiss.

"I'm all for having more fun, but look who's talking about working too hard, the newspaper lady and nurse." His lips brushed hers again. "I...find that you've become...quite special to me." His arms encircled her, and this time she felt herself returning his kiss. His quiet sincerity touched her deeply, instilling a sense of trust in her.

"Constance," her father called. "Time to come in."

They both sighed. "We can't keep your father waiting...I want to stay on his good side." His lips brushed her forehead. He picked up his gift and they walked arm in arm towards the house.

Nine days later, May 27, 1861: Armstrong back yard

After a long day at Camp Henry, Constance entered the back gate and walked through the garden. She still had three patients in the house to care for. "MOOOO!" she heard from behind a large boxwood. She froze, startled. Then "Cackle, cackle, cackle," caused her to erupt in laughter.

"Come on out, Frank. I know it's you. Let's see if you've drunk enough cream and eaten enough eggs."

A grinning, heavier Frank Stringfellow bounded out from behind the boxwood. Flexing his biceps, he asked, "Do I look like a Dragoon yet?"

She analyzed his appearance. "I believe you do look heavier and yes, definitely healthier."

"I've gorged myself. I think I've gained about fifteen pounds. I've been turned down by the Madison, Goochland, and Prince William Dragoons. I just learned that the Powhatan cavalry has returned from picket duty in Manassas. They're bivouacked in the woods southwest of town. This may be my last chance.".

"Did you know the Federals have occupied Alexandria? We've had our first casualty in Virginia."

"Yes, I know." His mouth thinned with displeasure. "That means I'll have to penetrate enemy lines to see Emma."

Constance's looked at him alarmed. "That would be suicide, Frank. Don't do anything foolish."

"I will see her. I have a strategy that's either going to get me killed or accepted by the cavalry today."

She eyed the pistol stuck in his belt. He had a will of iron. Arguing with him now would be useless. "God be with you, Frank." She suppressed her sense of uneasiness.

He hugged her, kissed her on the cheek, whispered, "Good-by, Connie," and was gone.

* * *

Leaving his horse tethered at the edge of the woods, Stringfellow made his way carefully through the trees. Ahead of him he heard the buzz of many voices, the clink of metal, and the occasional whinny of a horse. He kept the sun at his back, and shortly he saw the first picket, a tall bearded fellow leaning indolently against a tree. He was able to get within three feet of the picket before he was heard. When the sentry turned around, Stringfellow poked his revolver at him and said, "Don't move! Don't make a sound!"

The picket kept working at his tobacco and obeyed orders. With his eyes on the revolver pointing at his middle, he finally screwed up enough courage to ask, "You a Yankee, maybe?"

Stringfellow said, "Could have been, easy enough. Now let your gun down easy. No noise, you hear me?"

The picket did as he was told and awaited Stringfellow's next move. "Call in the pickets on your left and right flanks," Stringfellow told him. "But make it natural-like. No tricks if you don't want to get into trouble."

"Don't know what you've got in mind young fellow, but you ain't going to get away with it. There's seventy men in there and they'll skin you alive."

"I'm doing all right so far. Now call those pickets, and do it nice and easy."

Stringfellow picked up the man's musket and moved back until he was partially covered by a tree. The picket called to his companions and they came, grumbling, pushing heavily through the underbrush.

They entered the little clearing and one of them said, "What's the matter, Jed? See a snake or something?" Then they caught sight of Stringfellow standing with his gun trained on them. They froze.

Stringfellow said, "You won't get hurt if you do as I say. Drop your guns, quick. That's good. Now, head for the camp."

Jed whistled in amazement. "You figure to capture the whole Powhatan Troop?"

Stringfellow answered, "Maybe if I have to. Now, get going."

He herded his prisoners before him into camp and headed for a large tent before which were planted the Confederate flag and a pennant with "CO. E." stamped on it. A sentry before the tent ogled them as they came up.

"Call the commanding officer," Stringfellow told him.

The sentry didn't get a chance to do it. The tent flaps pushed open and a tall bearded officer in a smartly tailored gray uniform stepped out. The sentry saluted; Stringfellow's prisoners looked embarrassed.

"I'm Captain Lay," the officer said brusquely. "What the devil is the meaning of this?"

"Sir," Stringfellow said, "I've been trying to join the cavalry, but I've been turned down numerous times for being too skinny. Now I figure I can do as much riding, shooting, and fighting as the next fellow, so I captured your pickets to prove it."

Captain Lay's face grew red through his beard. "You mean you bushwhacked my pickets? This is wartime young fellow. Don't you know you've committed a serious offense?"

Stringfellow didn't like the tone of the captain's voice, but stood his ground. "Can't see it that way, Captain. I didn't bushwhack them. I *captured* them. And if I can do that to your pickets, I ought to be able to do more to the Yankees."

Captain Lay remained silent for a moment, torn between rage at his pickets for being so careless and growing admiration for the thin, smooth-faced youth who had taken such desperate means to prove that he was "fit" for the cavalry. Finally he turned to his men.

"Get back to your posts, the three of you. And dammit, keep a better lookout. The next time it could be a Yankee knife in your back or a bullet in your belly. All right, get out of here."

When the pickets had left, he turned to Stringfellow. "All right, young fellow, let's have all the facts about yourself. If you're who you say you are, I'll be happy to have you in my command. But tell me, would you have used that revolver if one of my pickets had given the alarm?"

"No, sir," Stringfellow said with a grin. "I couldn't have. It wasn't even loaded."

The next day, May 28, 1861, Frank Stringfellow, who was to become recognized in some northern circles as "one of the most dangerous men in the Confederacy," was sworn in as a private in Company E, Fourth Virginia Cavalry.[5]

Five weeks later, July 4, 1861: Jeffersonton

The sun shone brightly on the nearly 2000 residents of the Little Fork gathered at the village of Jeffersonton to bid farewell to the Rangers. With rumors of fighting in western Virginia, Federal troops in the Shenandoah Valley, and General Irvin McDowell advancing with a large Union army, the Rangers had been ordered to march to confront them at Manassas. Many of the spectators, positioned in front of the Jeffersonton Baptist Church, occupied the highest elevation in the town with a vista of the Blue Ridge Mountains. They overlooked the T intersection of the road from Washington to Georgia, on their right, and the road to Culpeper, in front of them entering from the left. Shops and business establishments lined the Culpeper road; Alex's father, Hans Yager, owned the Rock House mercantile situated on the corner.

Alex, handsomely arrayed in his new gray uniform, walked around his muscular black stallion checking its hooves and shoes, while his family watched from the porch of the store. Hans Yager, a stocky balding man of fifty one, swelled with pride. His wife, Marta, and their three daughters, age fifteen to twenty two, fought back tears. "Rangers eat Yankees for breakfast," exclaimed Hudson, who chased a kitten across the porch. Everyone laughed to break the tension.

Alex stepped up on the porch and embraced each one individually. He picked up Hudson and David, kissing them both, "Now look sons, you've got to take good care of your mother while I'm gone."

"You can count on us Daddy," Hudson replied. "We'll protect her."

Putting the boys down, he embraced Amanda, crushing her against his muscular chest. "I love you my darling," he whispered. "Be strong, and take good care of my baby."

Amanda looked into his brown eyes, her lips quivering and her eyes moist. She had to maintain her composure in front of the boys. Taking a deep breath to swallow the lump in her throat, she murmured, "We'll be praying for you."

He turned, kissed Harriet on the cheek, and said, "Watch over them for me."

"I promise," she answered. "I'm sorry Charles and Constance couldn't be here."

"I understand. The town has become a giant hospital. They're serving well there by caring for the sick." A bugle sounded.

The Rangers formed up in the road, and stood facing the Fishburn house and the Jeffersonton Academy. Miss Emma Latham, an attractive twenty-year-old, walked down from the porch of the house and presented Captain Utterback a hand-stitched flag. "Boys," he asked, "will you follow this banner into the face of the enemy, defending it with the last drop of your blood?"

They responded with a deafening "Yes, yes!"[6]

The crowd applauded the stirring ceremony. Utterback ordered the men to mount. The spectators continued to cheer while they watched the prancing steeds snort and wheel into columns as the new flag unfurled in the brisk wind. The men displayed jubilant spirits even though many of them departed without firearms. The band struck up "The Bonnie Blue Flag" and the men sang lustily, *We are a band of brothers, and native to the soil...*

The homefolks shed tears and waved handkerchiefs and flags proudly until their heroes disappeared from view.[7]

After the boys were asleep, Harriet heard loud sobs coming from Amanda's room. She entered quietly to find Amanda lying face down on the bed, sobbing into her pillow. Rubbing her back gently, she said, "I know how depressed you are, dear."

"Alex is my life." Amanda rolled over to look at her mother. "I'm afraid we'll never finish our own home. Will he live to see this baby?" she blurted.

"Try to be strong, darling." Harriet stroked her hair.

"I don't approve of this war!" Amanda declared vehemently. "What do I care for patriotism? Alex is my country. What is country to me if he's killed? I have no ambition for him to garner fame...or glory; I want him to secure a post as far away from the fighting as possible," she gasped between sobs. "Alex is dearer to me than my country and I can't willingly give him up!"[8]

Harriet pulled her close, trying to calm her erratic breathing. "The men make this seem more like a pageant or parade than a war. As helpless women we can only pray. We must trust in the will of Almighty God."

Seventeen days later, July 21, 1861: Armstrong town home

<u>5:30 a.m.</u> After tossing and turning all night, Constance stared at the ceiling in the first soft rays of dawn. Sporadic fighting and skirmishing had taken place for the last two days in the vicinity of Manassas. McDowell slowly marched west with a large Union army while Beauregard held a defensive position along a creek called Bull Run. John Barbour had told them yesterday that the railroad was running around the clock to transport Johnston's army from Winchester to Manassas. She prayed they arrived in time. She thought she heard the muffled sound of cannon fire in the distance. Were they Robert Beckam's cannons? He had been bitterly disappointed on July eleventh when assigned to Grove's Culpeper Artillery. Command of the unit had fallen on Beckam in Grove's absence. With his strong work ethic, he had thrown himself into training the men for the impending battle. She understood why he had not written in ten days. Restless, she got up quietly so as not to awaken Amanda, and walked over to the table

in front of the window. She picked up the book of poetry Robert had sent her for her nineteenth birthday and removed the letter she had received from Frank late yesterday. She began to read it again in the soft light.

My dear Connie,

I have seen Emma and kissed her sweet lips! Praise God, she loves me still! I'm sure you are curious as to how I managed this feat. I can only give you a brief account. Please do not tell my mother, because I'm sure that news of my foray would only worry her more.

Captain Lay informed us that we had informants in Alexandria who had valuable information for us in reference to McDowell's pending movement. He emphasized that it was a dangerous mission, and asked for two volunteers to go into the occupied city. I immediately stepped forward and told him that I was familiar with the city, and would go. Another brave man, a bugler, agreed to accompany me. Getting through the picket lines required some creativity, but did not stop us. The bugler sounded the alarm and I cried "Charge!" In the dark, the picket thought that he was being attacked. After he ran, I waded across a shoulder height river. Once in the city, a Union soldier requesting to see my papers stopped me. Having none, I smiled and pulled out a letter I had in my pocket. He didn't look at it, thank God, and waved me on. I reached Emma's house only to find it occupied with Union soldiers. I snuck into the pantry and had Emma's maid go upstairs and fetch her, but not tell her the reason. You can imagine her shock, and I must admit...joy, in seeing me! Emma knew the locations of our informants' homes, and insisted that she go receive the documents since I had no pass. She bravely risked all for the Cause, and returned safely with the documents. Obviously, I also got out alive. It was worth all the risk to be able to look into her eyes and re-confirm my love for her.

Our brigade has combined with the Little Fork Rangers under the command of Captain Lay. It is good to be with them, and we are all on the same level now.

July19: Battle is impending and I must write hastily. Today I was detailed to guide Colonel Jackson's troops from Manassas Station to their position behind Mitchell's Ford. After all Martin had written about the Presbyterian Deacon, I half expected to see a man ten feet tall waving a six-foot sword. Instead I saw a rather shabby, seedy fellow of medium height and build. If there was anything unusual about his appearance, it had to be his eyes. They were cold, blue, quick, and hard.[9]

I must make haste to get this letter on the train. The impending battle could determine our independence. Pray for us.

With brotherly affection, Frank

Anxious about news of the battle, many women from outlying farms had come into town yesterday to learn the fate of their loved ones. Anne Stringfellow, her daughters-in-law, Catherine and Annie Crittenden and their neighbor Columbiana Nalle, had all spent the night. Constance listened carefully and thought she heard some of their guests stirring. Amanda sat up in bed, wiped her eyes and stared at Constance.

"Did you sleep?" Constance asked.

"Not much," Amanda said yawning. "I had nightmares most of the night."

70

"Listen." Constance held up her hand. "Did you hear it?"

"Yes," Amanda said frightened. "The sound of cannons in the far distance. I'm sure a great battle will take place today. I believe it will be the longest day of my life."

Women, children, and old men packed the churches that Sunday morning and prayed with a fervor never before witnessed. Following church, the Armstrongs invited all their friends to their house to stand watch together. The women vowed to sew and roll bandages, while Charles promised to remain at the depot to bring any news that came over the telegraph.

Noon: "Listen!" Anne Stringfellow said to the women rolling bandages around the dining room table. "The cannonading is increasing. We who stay behind find it harder than those who go."

"There's nothing left to us but prayer," said Columbiana Nalle. "I have a husband on a blockade runner, but you...heavens..you have three sons on the same battlefield."

"Baptist is serving as head of Commissary for Powell, while Top's son, Frank, is on Powell's staff. We have three family members together, also," Mildred Hill said while picking up a long strip of cloth. "You know, Dolly refused to be separated from her husband and followed him to Winchester,"

"Amanda told me Dolly is expecting again," Harriet said.

"Yes, she's gone to Kentucky to see her family. The situation there is dangerous," Mildred said.

Catherine Crittenden paused from her work. "Charles is overjoyed to be serving under Powell. He writes that he likes him very much. On parade he's very strict...off duty he's a perfect gentleman and soldier."

"I'm delighted to know the men feel that way about him," Mildred said. "We've always felt he was a born leader, but," she sighed and paused, "he must learn to control his temper and sensitivity."

"Because our army is greatly outnumbered, we'll need brave and daring leaders." Harriet placed several rolled bandages in a basket. "I recently received a letter from a dear friend of mine in New York City. You might be interested in her view of our leaders. She's a democrat and opposed Lincoln, but seems to think Fort Sumter has united the North." She walked into the parlor where the younger women were working, and returned with the letter and Granny Ashby. "Let me read you some of it," she said flipping through the pages.

Lee is a good scientific officer, but is only capable of carrying out the orders of others. Jefferson Davis is probably the best of all, with the exception of Bragg, but we have never heard much of any of them.[10]

There is rumor that the war will be over by August, but it seems too good to be true.

Mayor Wood has suggested that New York City secede from the Union along with the departing Southern States. Papers in Newark, New Jersey are strongly pro-southern and Delaware remains a slave state.

That's what we need," said Granny. "We'll surround Washington and run Lincoln out." She paused listening to the sound of a train. "Do you think that train is stopping?"

Several minutes later the back door closed and the judge entered the hall. The ladies from both rooms surrounded him quickly.

"Is there news?" Constance demanded.

Catching his breath, he replied, "All we know at this point is there is a great battle taking place. That train that just steamed through town carries President Davis. He's traveling to the battlefield to observe first hand."

8:30 p.m. "I believe the firing of the cannons is less frequent now," said Fannie Barbour. "I've been knitting socks for almost eight hours, but all I can see is James's face." Barbour served with General Ewell.

Constance rushed to the window. "I see Father coming in the back gate! Perhaps we can learn the outcome of this battle and the fate of our new nation!" The women pushed and shoved to get out the back door. Granny wielded her cane to get to the front of the crowd. The servants, cutting canvas for tents, dropped everything to hear the news. The judge panted under the stately magnolia tree. "Ladies, our men have won a great victory! The news just came over the telegraph. The Union army has been routed and is retreating back towards Washington!"

"Praise be to God!" Granny Ashby raised her hands and cane toward heaven. The women cried, shouted, and embraced each other.

Tears streamed down Amanda's face. She grasped her mother. "Maybe the worst is over now," she cried in sobs of relief.

Reality soon set in after the jubilant celebration. "Now we must wait to learn the fate of our loved ones," Anne Stringfellow said to Mildred Hill.

Next day, July 22, 1861: Armstrong dining room

The faint sound of the train whistle in the distance captured the attention of the Armstrongs, Stringfellows, and Crittendens, finishing a late afternoon lunch. "I believe that came from the direction of Brandy Station," Judge Armstrong observed. "It sounds like a southbound train."

"Then we have to go see if there are details of the battle." Constance jumped up from the table and the others followed in her footsteps. By the time they reached the depot, breathless, several hundred residents had gathered. The crowd watched anxiously while the train, only containing a few cars, ground to a loud halt. A brown-haired distinguished gentleman with a goatee disembarked waving to the spectators. His cheekbones were too high and his jaws too hollow for him to be handsome.

"It's the president!" John Barbour rushed forward to greet him. "President Davis," he exclaimed when they shook hands. "Welcome to Culpeper. What can you tell us about the battle?"

"First Mr. Barbour, I must congratulate you on the excellent job you've done with the railroad. It's our lifeline." The crowd engulfed Jefferson Davis. "I see another familiar face." He reached his hand out to Charles Armstrong. He shook as many hands as possible while he made his way up on the platform, where all could see him.

"Comin' through!" Granny Ashby screeched, swinging her cane. The crowd parted as the Red Sea, while she forced her way to the front.

"Good citizens of Culpeper," the president began in a most eloquent voice. "God has blessed us with a great victory!" After exuberant cheering, he continued, "I arrived at the battlefield late yesterday afternoon, and was escorted by some very fine fellows called the Little Fork Rangers." Over the applause, he said with a smile, "I believe you know them. The scene before me was almost indescribable. The tide of the battle, after a long and bloody struggle, had turned in our favor. The Union army was in full rout, running as fast as possible back to Washington. Many ladies, dignitaries, and Congressmen had packed picnic lunches and parked their carriages on a hill to watch the Rebels get drubbed. They too were overrun by the army in their great haste to escape." The crowd laughed in disbelief. "And I'm happy to report, their army graciously left us enough guns, cannons, knapsacks, and supplies to fully equip our men." That remark evoked more mirth and laughter from the crowd.

"I can give you only a brief account of the battle as it was related to me. The Federals mounted a strong attack on the far left of our line where our men were greatly outnumbered. After fighting courageously our forces were forced to retreat and the tide of battle was going against us. General Bee, trying to rally his troops, pointed to Jackson's men who were holding fast in a pine thicket. 'Look there at Jackson standing like a stone wall!' he cried. 'Rally behind the Virginians!' Jackson held firm until the Yankees were within fifty yards of him. Then his men burst forth with a sheet of flames followed by hand-to-hand combat. The tide of the battle turned in our favor as the enemy began to flee." Spellbound, Anne Stringfellow gripped her daughter-in-law Nellie's hand. They knew Martin was with Jackson.

"At about that time Colonel Stuart mounted a successful charge with his cavalry, who were ably supported by our artillery. Our artillery were fully employed all day, and these gallant men were instrumental in our victory." Constance felt her heart skip a beat. She supposed Robert to be in the thick of the battle, but hearing it now still sent chills through her.

"But regretfully," Davis continued somberly, "our victory has come at a great cost. Many of our noble soldiers, including General Bee, have sacrificed their lives for our independence. The battlefield was strewn with the injured and dying. Our doctors and surgeons worked around the clock last night, but we do not have facilities to house our injured men. That is why I've stopped to address you, the good and compassionate citizens of Culpeper. You have unselfishly cared for the sick at Camp Henry. Unfortunately, we will not be able to house all of the injured there. Shortly trains will begin arriving with the injured. I pray that you will open your hearts and homes to these gallant warriors who have fought for your freedom. When I return to Richmond, I will make every effort to encourage others to travel here and aid you in this mission of mercy. Medical supplies will be forthcoming. The entire Confederacy is grateful to you for your tireless efforts and sacrifice. And now, I must make haste to reach Richmond. We have two cars of less seriously injured to take to the capital."

"President Davis," Annie Crittenden called. "Can you tell us anything about the Thirteenth Virginia?"

Pausing to think a minute, Davis asked, "Were they commanded by Colonel A. P. Hill?"

"Yes," the group shouted.

"You will be relieved to know that they served as the rear guard from Winchester.

Therefore, they did not arrive on the battlefield until the main fighting was over."

President Davis walked towards the train, but Granny Ashby scurried up behind him and tapped him on the shoulder with her cane. He turned around surprised. "Mr. President, now that we've routed them, our men are going to march in and take Washington, aren't they? We could end this fool war right now."

"Madame," Jefferson Davis replied irritated, "we do not want the rest of the world to see us as the aggressors in this war. Our mission is to protect our borders." He boarded the train.

"Damned politicians," she sputtered when she turned around. "Doesn't he know they've got more than twice as many men as we do? We've got to win this war fast. I'm afraid we've got an idiot for a president."

Many of the onlookers agreed with her.

Later in the day, Charles Armstrong wiped the sweat from his brow while Abraham pulled their wagon up next to the railroad tracks to join the throng of townspeople waiting for the train to come to a complete stop. "I'm glad Mother agreed that taking in these soldiers is the Christian thing to do." Constance fanned herself. "I don't see how many of them could have survived the train trip in this heat."

After the train stopped, the men rushed forward to throw open the doors of the boxcars. They were not prepared for the scene before them. Men writhed in the darkness like snakes, moaning, crying out for help. Abraham's foot slipped on the blood-covered floor when he stepped inside. He took Charles's hand and pulled him up. Turning to Constance with a fear-stricken face, he said, "Ya stay out there, Miss Constance."

They bent down to the first man they reached whose abdomen was covered with blood. His fixed eyes stared at the ceiling. Charles touched him and felt for a pulse. "It's too late for him." He pushed him to the side and touched the soldier next to him.

"Help," the soldier moaned, "water."

His eyes adjusting to the darkness, Charles discerned the bloody stump where the soldier's arm had once been. He and Abraham slid their hands under him and lifted him gently. "It's all right son, we're going to take care of you." They lifted him down from the car into the wagon. Stunned at the sight of the filthy, blood soaked victim; Constance gently lifted his head and gave him water.

He choked a little and then drank gratefully. "Thanks ma'am," he mumbled. "We were so thirsty after the battle, we fell down and lapped water from mud puddles like dogs."

"Where're you from?" She wiped his face.

"Alabama," he said weakly. "Our regiment was cut to pieces." He paused to get his breath. "Did you see what they did to my arm?" Tears rolled down his face. Constance wiped his face again, not knowing how to console him.

"You'll be fine." She watched a second man being placed on the wagon. Caked blood covered the location of his missing right ear and the tremendous deep gash in his face. Flies swarmed on the wounds. She turned aside while she gagged and tried to maintain her composure. He moaned, but appeared to be delirious. All along the railroad for a quarter of a mile the sad scene was the same. The Rebels received prompt attention while an occasional Union soldier lay in the merciless sun ignored. So this is war, glorious war, she thought.

"We'll take these two home and come back again," she heard her father say. "All of the churches will be opened too. It's going to be a long night."

Two days later, July 24, 1861: The depot

"Now everyone of you just back off right now!" Mr. Aylor, the postmaster, said to the mob of women rushing him. He took a defiant stance in front of the mailbag. "If you don't, I'm going to sic Granny Ashby on you!"

"That's right," shouted Granny, raising her cane ready to strike. "Just calm down and let him call the names."

The unruly crowd gradually backed away. Every recipient uttered cries of relief and joy when they received letters from their soldiers. After all the mail had been distributed, they celebrated the fact that each of their men had been accounted for. Unbelievably, it appeared all of Culpeper's heroes had survived the great battle.

Constance and Amanda rushed home clutching their treasures. Constance stopped in the gazebo and tore her two letters open, but Amanda ran inside to share the good news with her mother. She grabbed the one from Robert first, her eyes scanning the lines.

Dear Constance,

Please forgive me for not writing since I took command for Grove's Culpeper Artillery and the briefness of this letter. There does not seem to be enough time in the day. As soon as the men in this battery learned that I had been born in Culpeper, they readily accepted my leadership. Knowing that a battle was imminent, we spent an intense ten days in training and preparation. I believe our efforts paid of. I am most proud of the way the men conducted themselves.

We arrived on the battlefield about 11 a. m. Cannon balls began to fall around us, and in order to break the tension; I told the men half-jokingly that 'they must not dodge without permission.' They held fast. Several hours later I received word that my brother, Madison, had been wounded. I was of course, greatly alarmed. Shortly thereafter, I was ordered to report to Colonel Stuart, who ordered me to use two of my guns to support his cavalry charge. We opened fire on the Federal right flank and pushed forward until they were in full retreat. I was most anxious to clear them from the field where I knew Madison to be. The rout of the Federal army was a spectacle to behold, and I am proud that my men played a small part in our victory.

I have seen men wounded in every conceivable way. I will never forget the horror of the battlefield. The night following the battle our men gathered to give thanks for our survival and success. I read to them from the Testament. Thank God, I have received word that Madison's wounds are minor. We have pushed forward to Centerville in pursuit of the Yanks. I am confident that this war will end by fall. Surely, the Yanks must realize the futility of their effort to conquer us. We are anticipating orders to march on Washington.

I think of you daily and eagerly await your letters. Please do not disappoint me!

Affectionately,
Rob

Constance swelled with pride at Robert's modesty. One of the Richmond papers had commended the performance of his battery in support of Colonel Stuart. However, stories of the new savior of the Confederacy, "Stonewall Jackson," dominated the papers. She eagerly opened Frank's letter.

Dear Connie,

Sweet victory is ours! I will endeavor to give you a brief description of my observations and involvement. We were assigned as escorts for the generals and I saw no action until the battle turned in our favor and Beauregard ordered a staff officer to ride to Colonel Stuart and order him to attack.

I was detached to accompany the staff officer. Riding towards the Stone Bridge I was determined to join the action if possible. We approached Colonel Stuart, flashily dressed, and the staff officer gave him the command to attack. Before he could turn back to his men, I saluted and said, "Private Frank Stringfellow of Company E, 4th Virginia Cavalry, sir. I respectfully request permission to join your command in action." Permision was granted and as the staff officer rode off, he turned to me and laughed, "All right, trooper, remember this was your doing and not mine. You will ride with my staff."[11]

We charged in echelon a squadron of scarlet-clad New York Zouaves. A horse went down in front of me, and I had to dodge to miss the rider. We were enveloped in a sea of dust and jabbing sabers. I was in a desperate hand to hand fight, when saved by one of our men. Any man who tells you he is not afraid in battle is a liar! Colonel Stuart ordered us to regroup for a second charge. It was so successful the Zoaves broke and ran. Shortly there after, Jubal Early's brigade arrived as reinforcements. We had them in full rout. We pursued the demoralized Yanks, but were so burdened by prisoners that we were unable to strike.

I worked late into the night guarding prisoners to Manassas. Wild rumors were flying...there was to be a peace conference the next day between Lincoln and Davis Beauregard was on his way to Washington with 35,000 troops...the federal government had fled leaving the city in flames. I gave little credibility to most of them, but was more concerned by a prisoner who said, "We ain't done with you yet, Johnny Reb. We'll be back."

I must return to duty. We are moving again, I hope towards Alexandria. Write!

Your hero,
Frank

Constance smiled. Irrepressible Frank had finally proven himself in battle. She hoped he was satisfied.

4

John Pelham

September 27, 1861 – March 18, 1862

Now the phantom guns creak by, they are Pelham's guns,
That quiet boy with the veteran mouth is Pelham.
He is twenty-two. He is to fight sixty battles, and never lose a gun.

Stephen Vincent Benet, *John Brown's Body*

Two months later, September 27, 1861: Camp Henry

Constance's head throbbed from the loud and ceaseless banging of hammers at Camp Henry. She stood outside one of the newly constructed 250-foot by 35-foot hospital wards and surveyed the frenzy of building in the field below her. Each day new huts and storage buildings sprouted on the horizon. Obviously, supplies for Johnston's army were being stockpiled here. Were the new buildings to house more sick and wounded, or would the troops be moving back here from Manassas, she wondered? Two unfamiliar young ladies joined her and introduced themselves as Hetty and Jenny Cary from Baltimore. They explained that they had been forced to flee for hanging a Confederate flag from their window when Union troops took control of the city. Determined to oppose tyranny, they had smuggled a cache of drugs and uniforms to Richmond before they ran the blockade to escape. Living with relatives, they had come to nurse the brave fighting men of the South.

Constance expressed her sympathy and told them that many women from all over the Confederacy had come to help with the sick. With the building of two new wards and a kitchen, conditions were greatly improved and, the majority of the sick were housed here instead of in private homes. She offered to show them around.

The three of them entered the neatly whitewashed ward to discover a well-ventilated, clean interior, where pine bunks, set two feet apart, lined both sides of the building. Whistles and a few cheers of appreciation greeted the three comely young ladies. "Gentlemen," Constance said, "please be on your best behavior. I want to introduce you to the Misses Cary who have left their home in Baltimore to come south and aid us."

"Well, three cheers for Maryland," said a young man with an amputated leg. "Ma'am, I'd be most grateful if you'd write a letter for me to my mother in Mississippi," he pleaded to Hetty.

Bettie Browning and Annie Crittenden plodded towards Constance from the other end of the room, their arms filled with bloody bandages. "Come with us while we get rid of these, and we'll go to the kitchen and get supper for the men," Annie said weakly. As the three ladies walked out, the Cary sisters serenaded the patients with their own composition, a stirring southern version of "My Maryland."

While they walked through the grass to an open fire pit, Bettie Browning told them that her Daniel Grimsley had written that he believed the most severe fighting was over. After visiting a hospital at Manassas, he was convinced that if sent to one, he'd never come out alive. She threw the bloody bandages in the fire, lamenting their inadequate efforts to help the sick. Constance nodded agreement as she contemplated the hillside cemetery covered with hundreds of wooden grave markers. They climbed up the hill towards the newly constructed kitchen while Annie complained of going home exhausted and drained day after day. How she longed for happier times and the company of healthy, virile men.

They emerged from the stifling kitchen straining to push a cart with two large caldrons of soup and several loaves of bread. Bettie grimly informed them of Culpeper's first battle fatality, twenty-two-year-old Joseph Embrey, killed in a skirmish at Hall's Hill. They paused to catch their breath while Constance revealed some good news: Amanda and Fannie Barbour were both doing well after the births of their children, and the Barbours had changed the name of their home from Belle Villa to Beauregard. They did it at the request of Major Wheat of the Louisiana Tigers, recovering there. He asked them to rename their home in honor of his commanding general and fellow Louisianian. When they reached the first ward, Bettie and Annie said they could feed the men if Constance would find Reverend Slaughter and get the next cart of food.

Constance located kindly, white-haired Reverend Philip Slaughter in one of the older, less ventilated barracks with earthen floors. When she entered, he pulled the sheet over the face of a recently expired patient. "I'm afraid we've lost another one," he sighed sadly. "Typhoid again."

Becoming numb to death, she mumbled, "I'm sorry. We'll have to write his family." She noticed two empty bunks at the end of the room. "What happened to the two Union patients? They appeared almost recovered yesterday."

"They disappeared last night," he answered disgusted. "Or perhaps, escaped is a better word."

"How could that happen?"

Reverend Slaughter's brow creased into a frown while he gave water to another patient. "I think William Soutter helped them escape, since they were about to be sent to prison in Richmond. He's a strong Unionist and refused to serve in the militia. He agreed to serve as a hospital steward only for Union prisoners."

Constance shook her head in disbelief. "It's hard to believe that one of our citizens would do that."

"I wish no one harm, but I'm having trouble tolerating the treachery of some of our citizens. I don't know why we don't arrest them."

"I can't tolerate anyone who won't help our wounded," Constance said irritated. "But we can't do away with freedom of speech. Then we'll be stooping to the same level as Lincoln."

"Yes, I suppose that's true. However, my patience is wearing thin." He looked at his watch. "It's time to feed these men, isn't it?"

"Yes, I came to see if you'd help me bring the food from the kitchen." The two of them walked outside.

"Would you like to ride home in my carriage after we finish? I'm taking Annie," asked Reverend Slaughter, who lived on Slaughter's Mountain near the Crittendens.

"Oh, indeed, I would," Constance replied gratefully. "I don't have the strength to walk home."

When Constance entered the back gate she heard hammering in the carriage house. Abraham and his oldest son, John, must be building more pine coffins to sell to Camp Henry, she thought. What a morbid sign of the times. The aromas drifting from the brick kitchen drew her inside where she found Sadie stirring a big pot of succotash. Constance's eyes lit on cornbread, tomatoes, and squash, piled on the large pine table. "Ya look mighty peaked, Miss Constance." Constance collapsed on the bench. "Hard day at the hospital?"

"Of course. I'm exhausted and I can't seem to shake this melancholy mood. Another man died today. I'm tired of writing sympathy letters." She leaned forward with her chin in her hands.

"Now, ya know what I've done told ya," Sadie lectured shaking her finger. "You's workin' so hard you's gonna git sick. Then, how ya gonna help anybody?"

"I know," she answered nibbling a piece of cornbread. "I'll feel better when we get to the farm for a couple of days and I can ride Liz. Trouble is, I'll have to listen to the squalling of young Alexander Hans Yager all hours of the day and night."

"He's a little thing, comin' so early an' all. He has to eat often. That's jist the way it is."

"Remind me, Sadie, that I'm not ready to get married and have kids. Don't even let me think about it for ten years."

"I 'spect ya might change your mind 'bout that. That reminds me, ya got some mail today. I put it on your bed."

"Thank you," Constance replied, perking up a little.

Constance sprawled on her bed and eagerly opened her letters. She had not heard from either Frank or Robert in almost two weeks. She scanned Robert's letter first:

Dear Constance,

I suffer from the boredom and frustration of camp life. I cannot understand the inactivity of our army and our failure to take the initiative to win this war. Valuable opportunities are slipping away from us. Unfortunately, this war may last for another year. Rumor has it that part of Beauregard's command may be falling back to Culpeper. With that fact in mind, I decided to renew my efforts to obtain an appointment in engineering or ordnance. Meanwhile, General Stuart, who now commands all of the cavalry, approached me and began to relate his desire to form a battery of Horse Artillery to support his cavalry. He proposed using Grove's Culpeper Battery as the nucleus around which he would build his Horse Artillery. I felt it necessary at this point, to inform him of my desire to obtain an appointment in engineering or ordnance. He expressed great disappointment that I did not wish to remain with the artillery, and was complimentary of our performance in the battle. He wished me well and said he would do what he could on my behalf.

About a week later Captain John Pelham was assigned to my battery with orders to begin work forming a battery of Horse Artillery. He was two years behind me at West Point and I remember him as being popular with his peers. Since I outranked him, I told him to proceed with his plans and that I would not interfere with his authority over the men. Yesterday, I received orders to report to General Gustavus W. Smith on October 1 as a staff officer and aide-de-camp. I am elated about this new assignment and look forward to the change.

Your last letter lifted my soul out of the depths of depression. You are an angel of mercy. I know that the vision of your loveliness is healing the sick and injured men in Culpeper. How I wish I could see that same vision. I don't know when I'll be able to obtain a leave. My parents would like to have you come for a visit the next time I'm home. I hope that your parents will grant permission and that I may see you in the not too distant future.

We must trust Almighty God to end this conflict and aid us in our just cause. I eagerly await your letters.

With affection, Rob

With her spirits lifted, she turned to Frank's letter:

My dear Connie,

How my life has changed! About two weeks ago, while on picket duty near Dranesville, I received orders to report to General Stuart's headquarters. You can imagine my apprehension as I rode those five miles through a driving rainstorm. Had I committed some breach of conduct? Did I not conduct myself well in the charge? Did he think me unfit? He seemed to sense my uneasiness when I entered his tent, and a smile came over his bearded face. He laughed as I dropped my hat in a stream of water.

The general began to expound on his ideas about the war. He feared it may last a long time and that Southern valor could not compensate for our deficiency in men and material. Therefore, the South had to wage war as it had never been waged before. Gain local superiority at selected points, strike fast and hard, and then slip away to attack again. Such strategy called for complete knowledge of the enemy's strength and intentions at all times. He said he had heard good things about me. He especially liked the way I had gotten myself into the cavalry. That took imagination and imagination would be a precious commodity as the war went on. He had also heard about my soiree into Alexandria and had observed me in battle. Finally, he told me he wanted me as a personal scout.

He emphasized that I could refuse this dangerous assignment. He said I would be sent often on secret missions, entirely on my own. I would have to depend on myself and survive by my wits, and the quickness of my hands and eyes. It would be my job to flank enemy pickets, penetrate to the heart of their camps, capture stragglers or even officers in their tents, and learn Federal strength, positions, and plans. He concluded soberly, "If you lose your life in the depths of some forest, we'll mourn your passing, but we'll mourn the loss of your information more."[1]

I did not hesitate to accept his offer and said I hoped I would be able to measure up to his confidence. I was transferred to Stuart's escort and given the title of "aide." I joined an illustrious company of about ten other scouts. The three that I feel most at ease with are Redmond Burke, a big, burly older man, John Mosby, a Virginian and graduate of The University, and Will Farley, a South Carolinian who also graduated from the University of Virginia. They have put me through weeks of intensive training. I've learned that a piece of wire looped around a picket's throat can kill quickly and quietly. A weighted knife can kill a man from fifty feet. I've spent endless hours throwing at a target. We've played "patsy" in the woods, where I go out and the others attempt to track me down. No matter how careful I am, I always find a string around my neck or a knife lightly in my back with one of them grinning at me. There have been endless hours of classwork. Only when the "patsy" ends in a tie will I be ready to go out on an assignment. I'm getting close and know that as a scout I can make a difference in this war.

I must conclude by telling you about Will Farley. He comes from a well-known South Carolina family, which has recently moved from Virginia. After his graduation from The University, he took an extended hiking tour over northern Virginia and knows and loves the terrain well. He is a talented writer and admires Shakespeare and the early English writers. He is tall, slender, and genteel. With his dark brown hair, I believe you would agree he is one of the handsomest men in the Confederate army. I admire his bravery and sense of adventure. I consider him my most trusted friend. In short, Connie, I believe he is the perfect match for you. Nothing would give me greater pleasure than playing cupid for my two dearest friends. Do not give your heart away until you have met Will Farley.

Your scout, Frank

Constance chuckled. She could imagine Alex's chagrin when he learned that Frank was a personal scout for General Stuart and a member of his staff. She could not wait to see the expression on his face this weekend when he came home to see his new son. Deep inside, she realized she envied Frank's exciting life. Could she make him understand her frustrations? She sat at her small writing desk and took out a sheet of paper.

Dear Frank,
I must admit I envy the daring and exciting life you will lead as a scout. At times, I'm like a pent-up volcano. I wish I had a more productive field for my energies. I hate this common life of visiting, sewing, rolling bandages, nursing, which seems to devolve on women, and now that there is better work to do, real tragedy and real romance and history weaving every day, I suffer, I suffer, leading the life I do.[2] I read of Belle Boyd delivering messages to Colonel Stuart and shooting a Yankee soldier, and I wonder, what use can I be to our poor stricken country? Are we women worthless in wartime?

She sighed and rubbed her forehead. Folding the paper, she slipped it into her desk drawer. When she had more energy she would enter these feelings into the journal she kept about the war. Her dark mood would pass in a few days, enabling her to write cheerful letters to Frank and Robert.

Six weeks later, November 15, 1861: East Street

Powell Hill raced up the walkway to Baptist's East Street mansion. Striding the steps two at a time, he quickly reached the front door. Throwing the door open, he cried, "Where are my girls?" to the empty hall.

"Powell!" He heard a shout from upstairs. Dolly flew down the steps and threw herself into his arms. He smothered her mouth with demanding intensity, then whirled her around.

"I've thought of nothing but kissing you and hugging you for over five months now," he said. He took her face in his hands and gently kissed her.

"Our separation's been agony for me," she said, seeing the desire in his hazel eyes. "I'll never allow us to be apart so long again." She caressed his beard. "You look rather distinguished with that, but I think you're a little thinner."

"That's what army life does for you." He planted a kiss on the hollow of her throat. "You're more ravishing than ever."

Mildred walked down the stairs carrying a baby and holding Netty's hand. "Welcome home, Powell. Meet your new daughter."

"Thank you, Mildred. Please, let me hold her." He took the three-and-a-half-month-old girl gently into his arms. She opened her blue eyes and looked up. "She's beautiful, Dolly. She has your eyes."

"So you think you'll keep Miss Francis Russell," Dolly teased.

"There's no doubt about it. I'll call her my 'Russie,'" He kissed the baby on the forehead and then glanced over at Netty, shyly clinging to Mildred's skirt. "But now I must have a kiss from my beloved Netty." He gently handed the baby to Dolly and knelt down beside his oldest daughter. Holding his arms out, he said, "Give Daddy a kiss." Netty pulled back and hid her face in Mildred's skirt. Powell's faced became etched with disappointment. "Doesn't she remember me?"

"Remember, darling, it's been over five months since she's seen you, and you didn't have a beard then. You may need to give her some time to get used to you again."

"Netty," he said softly, then reached over and took her hand. "Netty, it's Daddy."

The brown-haired child peeked out slowly from behind Mildred's skirt. "Daddy?" she said quietly, sucking her thumb.

"Yes, sweetheart." He slowly pulled her to him. "Your Daddy has missed you terribly. You've gotten so big." He smiled and kissed her on the cheek. She shyly reached up and touched his beard. Gathering her into his arms, he walked towards Dolly and the baby. "You and the girls will have my undivided attention this week."

Next day, November 16, 1861: The Hill house

As the first soft glow of dawn lit the bedroom, Russie whimpered in her cradle. Her parents' bodies remained intertwined, the way they had finally fallen asleep. Powell stirred and pulled Dolly closer. He slowly cracked his eyes to discover her deep blue eyes staring at him lovingly. "I must be in heaven," he whispered. "For the past five months, I've dreamed that my first vision each day would be your beautiful face."

"Where you are, I will be." Her fingertips ploughed his wavy, chestnut hair. "Like the other refugees, I have no home. My place is with you. After all, this is my war too. I have a husband, six brothers and a brother-in-law fighting for the Confederacy."

"There's nothing I want more," he sighed. "But it's not that easy. I'd never forgive myself if I endangered you and the girls. However, I don't expect another major battle before spring. Perhaps I can find a house for you near camp. The men would love to see you. They're so proud of the flag you made for us from your wedding dress." Russie let out a loud cry.

"Someone's hungry." Dolly climbed down from the four-poster bed. He admired the silhouette of her round, full breasts through her sheer gown while she changed the baby.

"I worried constantly about y'all escaping from Kentucky. Tell me about it."

She picked up the whimpering baby, climbed up into the bed, stretched out, and unbuttoned her gown. Then Russie greedily sucked a red nipple into her mouth and nursed vigorously. "I was still with my mother in Lexington, when it became apparent that the Union was not honoring Kentucky's declaration of neutrality." The baby grasped her little finger. "Union troops began to flood in all over the state. Most southern sympathizers, my brothers included, felt forced to leave their homes and escape south to Tennessee. Around September twentieth, John Hunt and a group of his supporters stole a wagonload of guns from the Union armory and smuggled them south. From then on, he and his cavalrymen began making raids into Kentucky. They travel at night, strike fast and hard, and then retreat to the safety of Tennessee."

"I've seen his raids mentioned in the paper." Powell caressed Russie's head. "He's adapting a type of guerrilla warfare that many think is the best way to fight the Yanks. Did he help you escape?"

"Yes. As soon as I felt Russie was old enough to travel, I got word to him. He arranged for us to stay in several safe houses in Kentucky. One night he and his followers met us and guided us through the enemy lines. Once we got to Tennessee, we took the train to Virginia."

"That was a long, hard trip for you." He climbed out of bed. "Thank God y'all made it safely. I'm going to get Netty. I want all of my girls here together." He pulled his gray pants over his long johns and grabbed a red flannel shirt. "I hope you'll make me more of these shirts. I intend to wear them under my jacket. I'm not much for military garb. I want the men to be able to spot me when we go into battle."

Dolly furrowed her brows, then lifted Russie to her shoulder and patted her back. "It scares me when you say that." He walked towards the door, then pivoted to face her.

"I can't expect my men to do anything I wouldn't do myself. You have to understand that I must lead them into battle," he explained, meeting her eyes. A few minutes later he reappeared with Netty in his arms. They climbed under the covers and the sleepy child snuggled against his chest. "This is contentment. A man can ask for no more."

Dolly lay back down and Russie began to nurse again. She slid her hand on his. "What are you feeling, my love, now that Mac is commanding the Union army?"

He squeezed her hand and looked at her with pain in his eyes. "I can't actually discuss it with my men, but you understand. It doesn't seem possible that it's been only a year and a half since I was groomsman at his wedding. So much has changed. I'm glad I took the time to visit him when I resigned in March. I told him I'd fight to the death to defend the soil of Virginia. He said he understood and in my place, he'd probably do the same. We shook hands and parted friends. We may meet soon on the battlefield, but he'll always be my friend."

She kissed him on the cheek. "What kind of a general do you think he'll be?"

"Mac's smart. He has the ability to be a great general. However, he's a Democrat and definitely not an abolitionist. I question how vigorously he'll prosecute this war. I know that he'll try to achieve his goals with as little bloodshed as possible. That may work to our advantage." Netty opened her eyes.

"And how about Jackson? He's been getting unbelievable coverage in the papers."

His expression grew tight with strain as he recalled his first year at West Point and meeting Jackson, a fellow Virginian. Hill had found him to be a loner, rather dour, and a religious fanatic who studied all the time. They had nothing in common and Hill had

Courtesy Museum of Culpeper History

General Ambrose Powell Hill, C.S.A.

84

much preferred the gregarious company of "Old Burn" and Mac. "If he's the general he's proclaimed to be, he'll have my respect. I admire any man who performs well on a field of battle." Netty reached up and pulled his beard. "You can imagine how frustrating it was for my men to miss the battle at Manassas. I believe them to be the best-trained unit in the army. I don't understand why Davis has us sit by while the North builds strength. Furthermore, he keeps Lee behind a desk in Richmond. It makes no sense."

Netty reached up and grabbed the small ham bone, dangling from a piece of cord around his neck. "You can't have that, young lady." He gently removed her hand. "Your dear grandmother gave me that bone as a good luck charm, and I promised to wear it forever. If you're a good girl today, I'll take you to see the house Daddy lived in when he was a little boy."

"Daddy house," Netty gurgled.

Later that afternoon, Netty held tightly to her father's hand while they shuffled on the brick sidewalk along Davis Street. Crowds of soldiers milled around the street and shops, enjoying the crisp late fall air. Hill stopped to visit with friends along the way and was surprised to learn that Camp Henry was full and there were camps at each end of town. They stopped at the corner of Davis and Coleman Streets and Hill hoisted Netty into his arms. He pointed to the imposing three story brick building across the street. "Look Netty, that was Daddy's house."

"Daddy's house," Netty mimicked, pointing.

Hill smiled and pondered the fond memories he had of his parents and siblings in that house. After his parents died, his family decided they could not part with the house. They had rented it to Joe Gorrell, who ran a thriving drug store in the two front rooms while enjoying comfortable family living quarters in the rest of the house. Hill walked across the street intending to let Netty inspect Mr. Gorrell's inventory of candy.

Almost three weeks later, December 5, 1861: Near Culpeper Court House

John Pelham peered out of the dingy train window at the hills and vales of Culpeper County. "The mountains are so intensely blue, they look like a bank of dark clouds on the horizon," commented the youth from Talladega, Alabama, seated beside him.

Pelham nodded. "Yes, this is beautiful country and we're almost at the end of our long journey." The sandy-haired, smooth-faced young man looked around the car at the forty recruits for his Horse Artillery that he had enlisted from Mobile and New Orleans. Many of them remained asleep after the exhausting trip. This array of men, including several of French and Italian heritage, would join at least twenty-five members of Grove's Culpeper Artillery who had returned home to await his arrival. As the train began to slow down, the men woke up and looked sleepily around them.

"Is theeze the place?" asked Jean, a small dark-haired Frenchman from New Orleans.

"Gentlemen, we are here at last. Welcome to Culpeper Court House, Virginia," Pelham said enthusiastically, then stood to disembark. A strong cold wind chilled them while they walked around the depot.

"Lieutenant Pelham, you didn't warn us it would be this cold up heah," drawled an Alabama youth.

Pelham smiled at him with his laughing gray eyes. "I couldn't. Then you wouldn't have come. I confess I'll use any type of deception to aid our cause." The men scoffed good-naturedly. Looking at the hotel across the tracks, Pelham motioned, "Let's go over there and see if we can get a good hot meal."

A week later, December 12, 1861: Camp Henry

Constance stood mesmerized by the spectacle taking place on the field below her. For the last week she had taken frequent breaks at Camp Henry to observe John Pelham drilling his men in horsemanship. The intensity of purpose and cooperation among so many men amazed her. "Mount!" he ordered and seventy-five men instantly swung onto their horses. "Charge!" he cried and they sped down the hill and over several crudely constructed hurdles. "Dismount!" and they came to an abrupt halt and the men jumped to the ground.

"That was a good effort, men," Pelham said, catching his breath. "Remember we've got to improve our speed and teamwork." He paused for a few minutes while the men rested. "Limber," he ordered. Quickly several men slid the two wheeled carriages under the two guns while the others rapidly hitched a team of horses to each. "Rear! Gallop!" He smiled with approval as they sped across the field pulling the guns. "Halt," he ordered.

His second in command, Jim Breathed, rode up beside him. "Looks like your secret admirer is back, Lieutenant Pelham." John Pelham turned to see a dark haired girl on the hill above. Feeling his stare, Constance fled into the hospital.

"Wish I could figure out some way to meet that young lady."

Eight days later, December 20, 1861: Coleman Street

Charles Armstrong wrapped his scarf around his face, but the howling wind still pelted him with sleet. He leaned into the wind and struggled forward from the court-house towards the Virginia House Hotel, where he had been summoned by Mary Payne. Gasping for breath, he stomped up the steps and attempted to shake the ice from his boots. He opened the door to find the tavern room overflowing with a boisterous crowd of soldiers, enjoying the piano playing of Millie Payne.

An irate Mary Payne stormed up to him. "Judge Armstrong, look at this outrage," she sputtered indignantly, then handed him a written order. The order from Colonel A. S. Taylor, commander of Camp Henry, prohibited the sale of liquor to soldiers in the bar-rooms at the two hotels. Charles Armstrong thought to himself that this was a wise move on the part of Colonel Taylor. The rowdy behavior of the drunken soldiers was a detriment to the army and disturbed the peace of the town. "This is an abomination!" Mary Payne declared defiantly. "It's an attack on my civil liberties. Surely this colonel has no authority over me. Do you feel I'm legally bound to obey his ridiculous order?"

The judge paused thoughtfully. "I, of course, have no jurisdiction over military laws. It's my belief that any officer has the authority to issue orders for the welfare of his troops. However, your best course is to appeal the matter to Governor Lechter."

"Are you saying that if I continue to sell liquor, Colonel Taylor can arrest me?"

"It's my belief that he has the legal right to do so," Judge Armstong responded in an authoritative voice. Mary Payne stomped off indignantly. Charles felt a cold blast of air when John Pelham and eight of his men entered the barroom.

"Excuse me, sir," Pelham said to him politely. "I'm Lieutenant John Pelham from Alabama. Could you tell me who I must see to obtain a room for tonight?"

"Lieutenant Pelham, it's a pleasure to meet you. My daughter, who's a nurse at Camp Henry, has told me about the outstanding training you're doing of your Horse Artillery. I'm Judge Charles Armstrong."

Smiling warmly, John Pelham shook hands with the Judge. "Sir, it's a pleasure to meet you. Tell me, does your daughter by any chance have dark hair?"

"Indeed she does. Have you met her?"

"I'm afraid I haven't had that pleasure yet. However, I believe I've seen her." He looked around the room. "Is that the lady I need to see about a room?" he asked pointing to Mary Payne behind the bar.

"Yes, but I must warn you, she's not in the best of moods."

Pelham walked erectly to Mary Payne and bowed politely, clicking his heels. "I apologize for disturbing you, madam, but I would like to inquire about a room for my men. I have the greatest concern for their health on such a bitter night. You see they've all recently arrived from the Deep South and are not accustomed to this freezing weather. I was hoping to find them a warm place to sleep tonight instead of a drafty tent."

"Sorry, fella, we're full up. Even have men sleeping on the floor in the halls. Don't 'spect you'll find room anywhere tonight."

John Pelham's features fell and he ambled back towards his men. "Lieutenant Pelham," Charles said, "I have three empty bedrooms in my house across the street. I'd be honored to accommodate you and your men."

"Sir, that's a most generous offer." Pelham's face radiated good cheer. "However, I don't wish to impose on your family."

"It's no imposition. We feel we aren't doing enough for the war effort, and would like the opportunity to keep your men warm and healthy tonight." The men smiled broadly and nodded their heads.

"Lieutenant, Pelham, I hope I'm not out of line, sur, but I feel it would be rude to reject the Judge's Southern hospitality," a soldier from Mobile said, causing everyone to chuckle.

"Judge, you're a true Southern gentleman," Pelham said. "Lead the way."

Constance rushed into Amanda's room carrying three dresses. "Mandy, quick, tell me which dress should I wear? I can't believe Father asked John Pelham and some of his men to spend the night!" Her eyes gleamed with excitement while the sleet pounded against the windowpanes.

Smiling at her sister's frenzied state, Amanda said, "I believe I prefer the navy blue one. You're all aflutter about meeting Lieutenant Pelham."

"Here, unbutton me." Constance turned her back. "I've stood in awe as I've watched him train his men in horsemanship. Of course I want to know more about this Horse Artillery he's attempting to build." She stepped out of her dress and quickly pulled on the blue one. "Please, button me up."

"There, you look wonderful." Amanda finished the last button. "I hear the men coming in from the stable. Now, relax, and enjoy the evening. We'll have a merry time on such a frightful night."

* * *

John Pelham held his one-hundred-fifty-pound, six-foot frame erect while he conversed with Harriet and Charles. "Mrs. Armstrong, I must tell you what a pleasure it is for us to smell the cedar and view the beauty of a house decorated for Christmas. It eases our pain of being away from home."

"It's our privilege to provide a home away from home for you brave men," Harriet replied warmly. "Tell me, where are most of your men from?"

"New Orleans, Mobile, and Talladega." Pelham motioned Jean and several of his friends to join them. "I call these Frenchmen my Napoleon detachment. Allow me to introduce Jean. He is a sponger for my guns."

Jean bowed. "Bonjour, Madame. My job is to cool zee Napoleon gun and put out zee sparks after she go boom!"[5]

Harriet laughed at the short man. "I lived in France for several years before I married. Perhaps you'd be more comfortable if we conversed in French."

Jean's face lit up. "Oui, Madame." He introduced Harriet to the others and a lively French conversation ensued.

Charles smiled at Constance and Amanda, entering the room. "Lieutenant Pelham, allow me to introduce my daughters." John Pelham pivoted around to stare into Constance's enormous blue eyes. She appeared even lovelier up close. "This is my older daughter, Amanda Yager. Her husband is with our cavalry near Centerville."

Pelham focused on Amanda and bowed politely. "Mrs. Yager, it's a pleasure. I feel guilty being here tonight with my men while your husband's on the front. We'll be returning to cavalry headquarters in Centerville on the twenty sixth. Since so many of my men are from Culpeper with Grove's Artillery, I decided to bring them here for a month to train. I thought allowing them to spend Christmas with their families would boost morale and membership."

"That was very considerate of you Lieutenant Pelham. I know their families are thankful to have them home. I miss Alex dreadfully during this Christmas season," Amanda responded with a note of sadness in her voice.

"And this is my daughter, Constance, who's been admiring your training tactics at Camp Henry," Charles said with a twinkle in his eye.

John Pelham's clear, gleaming skin glowed when he bowed. "Miss Armstrong, I'm flattered that you would find such military matters of interest."

She perused his perfectly formed, fine features. "I'm an avid horsewoman, myself, Lieutenant Pelham, but I didn't realize to what extent horses would be used in this war. I must admit my ignorance—I don't fully understand the purpose of the Horse Artillery." She studied his boyish face.

"You're not alone in that respect. Use of Horse Artillery has been abandoned in this country since the Mexican War. However, the French have used it since the late fifties. In theory it gives firepower to the cavalry and can hold the enemy at a distance. I believe it's also possible to utilize the artillery during a cavalry charge. According to my West Point professors, the Horse Artillery should be bold, well maneuvered, even venturesome, appearing and disappearing from different points, thereby multiplying its short decisive action. That's why constant drilling and teamwork are necessary for its success."[4]

"Are you saying that horses can pull those guns and still keep pace with the cavalry?" Charles asked skeptically.

"Yes sir, I believe it's possible, even though our guns weigh up to a ton and a half," Pelham replied.

"Whew!" Charles whistled. "That's going to consume a huge number of horses and be unduly expensive. Do you believe it's worth that risk?"

"That's a good point, Judge Armstrong. I have a great concern about our horses and intend to give them the best of care. I agree with General Stuart, who thinks our cavalry superior to the North. Our horses and horsemanship are second to none in the world. He believes we'll win this war by hitting hard and fast and using our cavalry to harass the enemy."

The judge nodded thoughtfully. "In a slug 'em out infantry battle we'll be outnumbered two to one. With that in mind, I can see that the Horse Artillery may be well worth the investment."

"Yes," Pelham continued, animated, "as in the cavalry, each mounted man must provide his own horse. The government will provide those horses serving the guns. That's why I'm working frantically to raise funds and procure horses."

Constance asked, "So how many horses and men do you project you'll need?"

"Each gun will have eleven cannoneers, all of them mounted, two of these holding the horses of the others when they dismount to serve the piece. A six gun battery with its caissons, battery wagon, forge wagon and other equipment will require a hundred and ten horses and a hundred fifty men." The color rose in his cheeks and he became more animated. "I currently have ninety-four horses and about eighty men."

"I can see merit in what you're proposing," Charles agreed. "Let me think about this. Perhaps I can help you."

A gust of frigid air swept through the house as Sadie and Abraham entered the back hall and butlers closet with a tray of ham biscuits and pots of soup and coffee. "That wind an' ice is fierce out there," Abraham said. "We'll serve these refres'ments in the dinin' room."

"Gentlemen, please help yourselves," Harriet said. "I'm sorry we couldn't provide a full meal at this late hour. After we eat, the Napoleon detachment is going to sing the 'Marseillaise' for us, and I'm sure you handsome men can persuade our daughters to play the piano and sing for you."

"After you, Miss Armstrong," Pelham said graciously as they walked towards the dining room. "Your family has been most kind to us. We'd be honored if you'd sing tonight."

Constance's lips turned up in a soft curve when she looked into his laughing blue eyes. "We'll attempt to do so, Lieutenant Pelham. I must confess my sister is the musically talented one."

Next day, December 21, 1861: Armstrong town home

After dawn broke, the wind continued to howl while large flakes fell thickly on the ten-inch drifts. Charles insisted that his guests could not depart in such a storm and they all enjoyed a hearty leisurely breakfast. Following several lively hours of playing charades, they broke into smaller groups to play cards, checkers, and chess. John Pelham challenged Constance to a game of chess. She found herself strangely flattered by his interest.

Major John Pelham, C.S.A.

"I must tell you Miss Armstrong," he said, then made his first move, "you strongly favor my sister. I miss her greatly during this holiday season."

"Where is your home in Alabama?" she asked making a move.

"A tiny village called Alexandria." He studied the board. "I'm truly a country boy." He slid a pawn forward. "Going to West Point was a huge adventure and change for me."

"Did you graduate?" She quickly made her move.

"Afraid not," he answered, leaning forward pondering the board. "I remained as long as I could, but, after Fort Sumter and Lincoln's call to arms, I felt I had to return to defend my native land. I was only a few weeks shy of graduation."

Amanda walked over to watch them with baby Alex in her arms.

"What a handsome baby," Pelham said. "Please may I hold him?"

"Certainly," Amanda answered, flattered.

The baby cooed while Pelham rocked him gently. "How old is he?"

"Three and a half months," Amanda answered as he contemplated the board. "I think it's your move."

"Oh, yes," he said playing with the baby. "I was distracted." He made his move and continued to cuddle baby Alex. Constance stared at him, thinking she had never known a gentler, more unassuming young man. It did not seem conceivable that this boy could lead men into battle and kill.

"How long have you been a volunteer nurse at Camp Henry?" he asked her.

"Practically since the beginning," she said moving her rook. "The death toll from disease is astounding. Over three hundred."

"That many," he said surprised. "That's why I had so much concern about my men sleeping in those drafty tents last night. Many of our battery went home with our Culpeper boys, but I couldn't let the rest endanger their lives. Your family are lifesavers."

"We all wish we could do more to lessen the hardships suffered by our brave men." She paused, contemplated the board and lifted her eyes to meet his. "How much longer do you think this war will last?"

"I believe the North is building a huge army to descend upon us in the spring. With the help of Almighty God, I think we'll hold them off and that will end the issue."

The baby began to fidget. "I'll take him," Amanda said. "Look, I think the snow's stopping."

Several of the men rushed to the windows. "Sounds like the wind is letting up."

"In that case, we may have to drag ourselves away from this Utopia and return to army life. But first, I've got to win this chess game," Pelham boasted in a teasing manner.

About thirty minutes later, the sun broke through the clouds. "Checkmate!" Constance said triumphantly. The room burst into laughter.

"No!" Pelham shouted in surprise, then jumped up. "I can't believe it! Gentlemen, I hope you've witnessed my first and last defeat of this war," he said good-naturedly. "Miss Armstrong, promise me you won't join the Union army."

"You're safe, Lieutenant Pelham," she laughed, merriment twinkling in her eyes.

As the men prepared to depart, Constance slipped beside her father and whispered, "Father, don't you think we should invite these lonely men to spend Christmas Eve with us?"

"Splendid idea. I was thinking the same thing myself."

"Gentlemen," he said loudly. "I want to invite all of you to join us for a festive Christmas Eve Celebration. Consider our house your home away from home this Christmas season."

The men responded with jubilant cheers and thanks. "You've been extremely gracious to us, Judge Armstrong. We gratefully accept your generous invitation." Pelham looked at Constance, his smile matching hers with enthusiasm. "And Miss Armstrong, I demand a rematch."

Three days later, December 24, 1861: The depot

Frank Stringfellow stepped down from the train in Culpeper Court House to see crowds of soldiers and a large stock of supplies around the depot. He took a deep breath of the cool air and stepped over a patch of snow into the milling crowd. A South Carolina soldier angrily debated the performance of a brigade of Georgians at Manassas, fists started swinging, and a free-for-all broke out. Frank ducked a blow, scrambled to safety, and navigated his way up Davis Street to purchase Christmas gifts for his family.

Constance and Sadie busily arranged the dishes for the evening's festivities when they heard a knock on the door. "I hope that's Frank." Constance raced to the door. He had sent a telegram saying he would arrive on the twenty fourth.

She threw open the door to be greeted by Frank's impish grin. "Frank! Welcome home! Come in!"

Setting his packages on the floor, he whirled her around and kissed her on the cheek. "Miss Armstrong, you must be overwhelmed with attention from the thousands of soldiers who surround you."

"What a tease you are! However, I do admit life is more exciting now than it was several months ago. Come sit in the parlor so we can visit." They settled onto the sofa. "Now, tell me all about your exciting adventures as a scout."

Frank's expression grew serious. "The glamour disappeared after my first scouting experience. I realized that death could come quickly and quietly." She registered surprise. "You see," he continued, "McClellan began throwing out scouting parties around Falls Church and General Stuart sent Redmond Burke and me to see what was afoot. For three days we watched the Federal columns and sent couriers back to Stuart with information. In the drizzling rain of early dawn we separated to watch both flanks of any enemy detachment. Burke reminded me to watch out for their pickets. I smelled the wonderful aroma of their coffee and remembered how hungry I was. Not being able to light a fire, we had lived off of hard bread and rancid meat for three days."

"Frank, I don't think I ever understood your hardships." She placed her hand on his.

"Suddenly I heard the whir of a knife cutting through the air, followed by the deadly thump it makes striking home. I whirled around to see a picket standing up with his gun leveled at me. Frozen, I watched him fold gently at the knees and topple to the ground, the knife protruding from beneath his shoulder blades." Constance gasped and squeezed his hand. His eyes grew moist. "I had heard and seen nothing, yet death had stood at my elbow. When I came to my senses, I saw Redmud Burke seated on his horse some forty feet away. He smiled at me as I crept up to him and said 'close.' We've never spoken of the incident again, but remain strongly bound to each other."

"Oh, Frank," she whispered softly. "Thank God you're alive! I fear for you. Why don't you resign from scouting?"

"No," he said resolutely. "I realize each time I go out that I may not return. I'm fully prepared to die for our cause, but I believe I can accomplish more on my own initiative as a scout than in the cavalry. I'm inspired by the brave men who surround me."

"I marvel at such valor," she said in awe.

"Now," he continued, "I must tell you about the intrepid Will Farley. On November twenty seventh, he and two men were scouting beyond Dranesville when they ran into the First Pennsylvania Cavalry consisting of about five hundred men. Farley knew that Johnston's wagons were foraging a few miles to the west relatively unprotected. If the Federals captured them, our army could starve this winter. Without hesitation, Farley decided to attack hoping to throw the column into confusion and delay their advance. And so they charged firing as they rode, three against five hundred."

"I can't believe such audacity."

"The Federals scattered with two men and a horse shot. Then they fanned out and surrounded the three Confederates and captured them. One of our patrols arrived to see our three men being taken to the rear. Upon learning the news, Burke and I prepared to go out on a rescue attempt. Direct orders from Stuart prevented it. He said the area was swarming with Federals and he needed us at headquarters."

"And was Farley taken to prison?"

"I'm afraid so. He's in Old Capitol Prison in Washington. However, even though he was captured, he did his job well. The Federals didn't advance, fearing a large force lurked in front of them, allowing our wagons to complete their foraging. Efforts are being made to get Farley exchanged." He looked at Constance in earnest. "Connie, Will Farley is an extraordinary young man. Don't give your heart away until you've met him. Now tell me, how many men are vying for your affection?"

"Oh," she said coyly, "a few. I must admit I'm impressed with all you've told me about Mr. Farley. Tell me, have you met Lieutenant John Pelham, commander of Stuart's Horse Artillery?"

"No, but I've heard talk of him at headquarters. Why?"

"Father has taken him and some of his Alabama soldiers under his wing. They're here training and we've invited them to a Christmas Eve Party tonight. I'm trying to convince father to roll up the rugs so we can dance."

"That sounds like a merry time."

"Then, the day after tomorrow, I'm going to Warrenton for three days to visit with Robert Beckam and his family." Her eyes sparkled with excitement.

"Well, aren't you the socialite this holiday season!" Frank teased with his eyebrows raised. "Have a wonderful time, but maintain your independence. Hey…that means we'll be able to ride the northbound train together on the twenty sixth. We'll have more time to visit. Now, I must rush home."

"I promise to remain aloof." She walked into the hall with him. "Abraham's expecting you to borrow one of our horses. He'll be in the kitchen or stable. Tell your family Merry Christmas."

"Thanks Connie." He kissed her on the cheek and opened the back door. "Promise me not a single word about my escapades to anyone. I don't want to worry Mother needlessly."

"You can always trust me, Frank."

93

Most families in Culpeper Court House entertained soldiers on Christmas Eve, 1861. With many of their loved ones away on the front, the residents reached out to the lonely soldiers around them and brought them into their families. They realized instinctively that any opportunity for fun and fellowship should not be wasted. Laughter, music, and the strains of familiar Christmas carols filtered through the cold crisp air. The Armstrongs invited Dr. Charles Ashby and the six females of his household to join their celebration along with Pelham's group of soldiers. Dr. Ashby strummed his banjo and Amanda played the piano while the others, young and old alike, danced the Virginia Reel. Granny Ashby demonstrated her spryness as she do-si-do'd with Charles. Harriet and the little Frenchman, Jean, not to be outdone, clapped their hands and skipped between the two rows of dancers. John Pelham's strength surprised Constance when he spun her around with his sinewy body.

After thirty minutes of dancing, Granny admitted to being slightly tired and volunteered to call for the other dancers. Taking a position of authority on a stool, she energetically directed the steps of the others while pointing with her cane. It took the aroma of turkey, yams, ham, fresh rolls, and pumpkin pie to bring the dancers to a halt. After feasting, the jubilant throng gathered around the piano and sang Christmas carols with gusto, with a few renditions offered in French. When the church bells pealed, the Ashbys and five of the soldiers departed for the Baptist church. John Pelham and four of his men strolled with the Armstrongs to Saint Stephen's.

"Lieutenant Pelham," Charles said, "I've been thinking about the merits of your Horse Artillery and I've decided to donate a horse to your cause. However, it's located at our farm in Rixeyville. Can you have someone pick it up?"

"Judge Armstrong, that's very generous and patriotic of you," Pelham replied elated. "Could I send one of my men to pick it up on the twenty sixth?"

"Yes, that will be fine. Have him come here and my servant, Abraham, will ride with him out to the farm."

"Gentlemen, I'm afraid I must warn you of the dilapidated condition of the interior of our church," Harriet said. "You see, it's been used as a hospital and barracks for our men."

"Mrs. Armstrong, we're thankful to have the opportunity to nourish our souls inside any type of church," Pelham responded. "I'm sure the interior of your church surpasses the huts at Camp Henry."

Reverend Cole preached a stirring sermon based on First Jeremiah, an increasingly popular text in the South: *Then the Lord said unto me, out of the North an evil shall break forth upon the inhabitants of the land, and they shall fight against thee, but they shall not prevail against thee; for I am with thee."* Seated beside Pelham, Constance watched him out of the corner of her eye as he knelt to pray, sang fervently, and listened to the sermon intently. She sensed that he was a devoutly religious young man, an inspiring soldier.

The group re-entered the Armstrongs' back gate and the soldiers expressed their appreciation for the evening. "The only good outcome of this war is the fact that we've made so many new friends from across our land," Harriet said philosophically. "I want you all to know that you're welcome to our home at any time."

Pelham moved close to Constance, engaging her with his eyes in the moonlight. "Miss Armstrong, we didn't have an opportunity for a chess rematch tonight. I was

hoping I might have a chance to redeem my honor and self-esteem before I departed."
"I'd like to give you an opportunity to retaliate, Lieutenant Pelham. However, I'm leaving on the twenty sixth to visit a friend in Warrenton for three days," she murmured in a silky voice.

"In that case, I won't have another chance to see you before I leave." His voice had a tone of disappointment. "I hope you'll be kind enough to write a few words of encouragement to this soldier on the front." He bowed, took her hand in his and kissed it softly. "You can count on it." She smiled, enchanted by his laughing gray eyes.

Four days later, December 28, 1861: Near Brandy Station

Constance's mind drifted while she watched the rolling farmland flow by the window of the train chugging south. Conscious of Sadie seated beside her, babbling away about the nice Beckams, she tried to sort through the last three days in her mind. Being around Robert's gracious family, especially his two sisters, had been delightful. She had found him honest, dependable, and of great depth, but more reserved in person than in his letters. Would she ever be able to truly penetrate his thoughts? She admired and respected him, had deep affection for him. But—was she in love with him? She simply wasn't sure—which must mean she wasn't, at least not yet—but maybe in the future. He would make a wonderful husband and in fact had indicated his interest in a more serious relationship. She had tried tactfully to tell him that she was not ready for any type of commitment, especially with the war raging. Church bells had been ringing in a rush of weddings, fifteen since July. Everyone seemed anxious to have someone to write to, pray for, and pine over. That was no reason to get married. She refused to get caught in the frenzy! Besides, with thousands of soldiers around, why not follow Frank's advice and remain independent?

She stared intently out the window while the train passed Camp Henry, and noted sadly that John Pelham's cannons were gone.

Ten weeks later, March 9, 1862: Near Brandy Station

The cold driving rain stung Robert Beckam in the face. General Gustavus Smith's division, the vanguard of Joe Johnston's army, slogged towards Brandy Station. Chilled to the bone in the forty-degree temperature and exhausted from the two-day march through a sea of mud, he escorted a group of reluctant soldiers towards one of his ordnance wagons, stuck in a small creek. He dismounted and examined the wheels mired several inches down in the mud, prohibiting the horses from pulling the wagon up the slight incline. Weak from hunger, he leaned over and felt the depth of the mud around the wheels.

"All right, I want at least six men on a wheel," he ordered. "We've got to get this wagon out and make Culpeper Court House by nightfall." The men took their positions; several of them knee deep in water and mud. Helping on one of the back wheels, he ordered "Push!" The men groaned and strained while the driver whipped the horses. The wagon moved forward slightly. "We've almost got it. Again, push!" Beckam's muscles strained while the wagon slowly moved up the incline. It gained a little speed, splattering mud over the laborers.

The men shouted numerous obscenities, then they wiped mud from their faces. After sweeping a wet sleeve across his face, Beckam mounted his horse and shouted, "Well done, men." He spurred his horse forward into the pelting rain in search of General Smith. He intended to volunteer to ride ahead into town and locate a house to accommodate the general's staff for the night. He felt sure the Armstrongs would willingly open their home, and the prospect of sleeping in a warm dry place, plus seeing Constance, caused his spirits to soar.

At the newspaper office, Constance and George McDonald listened to the ceaseless sound of the trains slowly passing through town for the second day in a row. The shipping of the army's supplies south indicated that Johnston must be retreating, but none of the Confederate army had arrived in town yet.

Her face drawn, she asked, "Do you think we're going to be the front?"

"I'm afraid it's quite probable," he sighed. "The Northern papers are hailing McClellan as their young Napoleon and leader of the most powerful army ever to be seen on the face of the earth. Some say up to 100,000 men. Johnston appears to be retreating, either out of fear or to seek a better defensive position."

Her stomach churned with anxiety while she contemplated all of the recent bad news: Western Virginia was in Union control following Lee's defeat at Cheat Mountain, Fort Donelson had fallen, Nashville was evacuated, most of Kentucky was lost, plus the embargo choked the South. She could not even buy soap, hairpins, woven cloth; prices soared on salt, lamp oil, sugar, and coffee. She failed to understand why the British had not come to their aid and broken the embargo. Surely, they were feeling the shortage in cotton. Britain had sent troops into Canada after the Union unlawfully arrested Confederate ambassadors, Mason and Slidell, on the sea en route to London. The prompt action by England had forced the Union to back down and release the two men. But now, England stood by idly observing. Certainly, they must take action soon.

McDonald tapped his pencil on the desk, "I'm afraid I'll have to put out a smaller paper due to the paper shortage. I have few ads because the merchants have so little stock. I'm not sure how much longer I can remain in business."

"Well, let's hope for the best and get busy," Constance said, attempting cheerfulness. "I think all the rain has sunk our spirits."

When Constance returned home, she discovered her mother and Sadie scurring around frantically. "Your father saw Lieutenant Beckam a little while ago, and he invited General Smith to use our house as his headquarters tonight. They'll be here soon," Harriet said.

"What?" Constance asked stunned. "Are you telling me Robert will be here shortly?" Sadie ran by wide-eyed shaking her head affirmatively. Constance dashed up the steps.

When the general and his staff arrived, they left their muddy boots on the back porch and went up to the three front bedrooms. They attempted to dry their clothes in front of the roaring fires, and Abraham delivered coffee and sandwiches to their rooms. Robert Beckam joined the Armstrong family in the parlor at a late hour. He appeared in a wrinkled but dry shirt with several days' growth of beard. Constance noticed the lines under his eyes and the thinness of his face. "Please excuse my appearance," he said as he coughed. "The last few days have been grueling."

96

West Point Cadet Robert F. Beckam

Charles rose to shake hands with him. "We're glad to have you here, Lieutenant Beckam. Please come in and have a seat." He motioned him towards the sofa beside Constance.

"Thank you." Beckam smiled at the three ladies, his eyes resting on Contance.

"We know you're exhausted," she said sympathetically.

He sat down beside her and her hand reached for his in a gesture of comfort. "It's a pleasure to see all of you. The rest of the staff sends their thanks and hopes that you'll understand that they've decided to retire for the evening."

"I can't imagine an army being ordered to march in such horrid weather," Harriet said.

"We'd hoped not to be forced to relocate until warmer and dryer weather," Beckam said. "And the idea of a relocation or retreat is embarrassing to us. The remainder of the army will be arriving here within the next week. You can imagine my concern for my family who will then be in enemy territory."

"I'm afraid for them." Constance squeezed his hand sympathetically. "Do you think the two great armies could collide here?"

"No one seems to know in what direction McClellan will march. Obviously, Johnston thinks this a good defensive position. Anything could happen." He tried to sound calm. "Sooner or later the two armies will do battle and decide the outcome of the war."

"What do you know of the cavalry?" Amanda asked.

"They, of course, are serving as rear guard for the army, and harassing the enemy. They'll be the last to arrive."

"Speaking of the cavalry, we befriended your replacement, Lieutenant Pelham," Charles said. "He and some of his men stayed with us during the ice storm in December. Quite a likeable young man."

"Oh, you did," Beckam said quite surprised. "Yes, uh...he's very popular with the men." He glanced at Constance but could detect no change in her expression, as she masked her inner turmoil with deceptive calmness. "You must forgive me, but I'm so exhausted. I can't tell you how much being in this warm, dry place and seeing all of you has lifted my spirits." He shot Constance a smile eager with affection, kissed her hand, and pulled himself stiffly to his feet. "But I must bid you good night."

"We understand." Charles stood. "The general is welcome to use Alex's office tomorrow and stay as long as necessary."

"Thank you. Unfortunately, our men are sleeping in this rain without tents tonight. I expect we'll join them in camp within a few days."

"Good night, Robert," Constance said with a radiant smile. "I'll look forward to seeing you in the morning."

A week later, March 16, 1862: Armstrong town home

"Extra Billy Smith! My God, if you aren't a sight for sore eyes!" Charles pulled his old friend inside the hall and the two embraced.

"Charles, I can't tell you how wonderful it is to see you again. I've missed you as my political sounding board since I moved to Warrenton," said tall, aristocratic Extra Billy Smith. "Too bad it took a war to bring us together again. How are your family?"

"Oh, they're fine. I have three grandsons now. Come into the parlor."

"Well of course I've not had military training, and don't really see the need for it," Extra Billy told Harriet, Amanda, and the boys. "Some of the West Point types laugh at me when I drill my men. You see, I just sit on a fence with a cloth umbrella over my head to keep the sun off, and call out the marching commands from a book." They all laughed. "But, you should have seen my men charge alongside Jackson at Manassas. All I had to do was call 'Forward' and they helped capture Rickett's artillery," he said proudly.

"You never cease to amaze me," Harriet said. "How many men do you command?"

"At Manassas I had gathered about two hundred boys from Warren, Amherst, and Prince William counties. Since we were successful in that battle, I was commissioned a Colonel and seven companies from Fauquier, Rappahannock, Nelson, and Prince William were added. We're the Forty-ninth Virginia. At sixty four, I'm the oldest colonel in the army."

"How could anyone who's served five years in the Virginia Senate, one term as governor, and five terms in Congress not be successful?" Charles said.

"Actually, I wasn't too successful managing my finances and politics, too," Extra Billy said, his long face falling. "How I hated having to sell my house here. Fortunately, I was able to go to California and recover financially. But, my heart never left Virginia."

98

"Extra Billy" Smith

That's why I came back when issues heated up. I was thankful to be re-elected to Congress and debate Lincoln."

Constance, returning from the Observer, entered the room. "My heavens," Extra Billy exclaimed, jumping up. "This can't be little Connie that I used to bounce on my knee!" He hugged her and kissed her on the cheek.

"Thank you, Colonel Smith, and welcome home."

They sat back down and he admired her further. "I shouldn't be surprised at how lovely you've grown. I understand there's been some sparking between you and my young friend Robert Beckam. He's a very fine young man."

Constance felt her face glowing. "Yes," she said quietly. "We enjoy each other's company."

"Lieutenant Beckam and General Smith's staff spent two days with us when they arrived in town," Harriet explained. "Unfortunately, Lieutenant Beckam was sick most of the time. They've since moved to their camp south of town."

"I never thought I'd see fifty thousand soldiers in Culpeper County," Extra Billy commented. "I stopped by the depot to see John Barbour before I came here. He's still frantically trying to move supplies south, but the lines have been so clogged travel is slow. He's furious because Johnston is blaming him for having to destroy 750 tons of food and forage at Manassas."

Amanda cried, "What a terrible waste. Our men could have lived on that for a year."

"There's no doubt this retreat has been hasty and wasteful," Extra Billy said, his face drawn. Charles got up to answer a knock at the door.

Excited to see Robert enter, Constance gratefully accepted his invitation to join him for a walk on such a sunny day.

They enjoyed the warmth while they strolled along Coleman Street. The numerous soldiers along the way eyed Constance with appreciation when the couple passed. Proud to be with her, Robert realized that hundreds of young men yearned to take his place.

"We have orders to march tomorrow," he told her somberly.

"No!" she cried. "Do you know where you're going?"

"Only that we're to march south of the Rapidan. Rumors abound, but the most prevalent is that we'll be sent to Richmond. Looks like McClellan is landing his army at Fort Monroe and plans to march up the peninsula to take Richmond."

"That's a surprising change of tactics. Will the entire army go?"

"According to rumor, Ewell with his five thousand men and Stuart's cavalry will be left here to guard the Rappahannock. Does that make you feel safer?"

"A little." She held his arm tightly and stared at his pale face. "Are you feeling better?"

"I'm still weak, but I can keep food down. I believe I must have the most rotten luck in the world," he said with a chuckle.

"What do you mean?"

"I mean that I'm fortunate enough to be a guest in your house for two days, and what happens? I'm sick as a dog. I couldn't even talk intelligently to anyone."

"That was pretty rotten luck."

After walking several blocks, they entered the back gate and strolled through the gardens. "I'd really like to sit in the gazebo," Robert said with a twinkle in his eye. She laughed as he picked a few daffodils and stuck them in her dark curly hair and then led her into the gazebo. He put his arm around her, pulling her close. "Constance," he began seriously. "I don't know when or if I'm going to see you again. It's bad enough knowing we're fighting an army twice as large as ours." She thought she saw fear in his eyes for the first time. "But, it's even worse knowing I'm leaving you here with thousands of dashing cavalrymen and soldiers, all wanting to seek your favor."

"Robert, you're flattering me and overstating the situation."

"No, I'm not. I've seen how they look at you, and I certainly don't blame them. What bothers me most is that I won't be here to compete." She cast her eyes downward.

He placed his finger under her chin and gently lifted her face towards his until their eyes met. "Constance, I want you to remember one thing while I'm gone. I was here before the hordes appeared, and if God is willing, I'll be here after they've left and this war is over."

"Robert," she said softly. "I pray that you will be, but I don't deserve that kind of loyalty."

"I think that you do." His lips pressed against hers, then gently covered her mouth. She enjoyed the strength and warmth of his body as his arms moved around her midriff, pulling her tight against him. Returning his kiss, she slid her arms around his shoulders, caressed his neck. Throbbing with emotion, she found it difficult not to love him.

"Rob," she whispered, "you're so very special. God be with you."

Two days later, March 18, 1862: The Hill house

The rain beating against the windows dulled the noise of the creaking wagons leaving town. Powell Hill pulled on his gray coat over a red flannel shirt and Dolly buckled on his sword. "You make a very handsome Brigadier General." She straightened his collar and brushed her lips against his.

"I hate leaving the Thirteenth Virginia. I believe them to be the best trained unit in the army." He pulled her against him, her soft curves molding to the contours of his lean body. "But I look forward to a new challenge." He detected the glint of fear in her eyes. "Don't be concerned that we're going up against a larger army, Dolly. I'm confident of success. They can never subjugate us. We'll whip the damned Yankee hounds yet—and then God grant that a gulf as deep and wide as Hell may stand between us."[5]

She buried her face against his neck. "I pity your opposition."

"I intend to drive them from our soil!" he swore defiantly. Pausing thoughtfully, he brushed his lips across the top of her head. "I'll send for you and the girls as soon as I believe it to be safe. Promise me that you'll go south if there's any indication that the Federals are moving into Culpeper."

"I promise." She rigidly held her tears in check. "Now let's go get the girls."

Dolly, Mildred, and their children waved handkerchiefs and blew kisses from the front porch while Powell and Baptist rode up the muddy street. Dolly knew she had never seen a more talented horseman than Powell, riding gracefully on his black stallion. Tears slowly found their way down her cheeks when the two men joined the throng of soldiers marching south. Finally, she yielded to the compulsive sobs that shook her.

5

They Came Like Locusts
March 28 – July 21, 1862

"I have come to you from the West, where we have always seen the backs of our enemies..."

General John Pope, U.S.A., to his troops, July 14, 1862

Ten days later, March 28, 1862: North of the Rappahannock River

Confederate scouts John Mosby and Redmond Burke peered cautiously over an embankment at the one cavalry and four infantry brigades advancing southward along the Orange and Alexandria railroad. Both realized it was a big enough group of Lincoln's hirelings to force a crossing of the Rappahannock. Mosby agreed to apprise General Stuart of the situation while Burke warned General Ewell that his outnumbered infantry needed to retreat safely across the river fast as lightning.

General Jeb Stuart rode out to meet Mosby, galloping towards him at full speed. Breathlessly, Mosby explained the situation to him and Stuart responded immediately, "We've got to slow them down so Ewell can withdraw his infantry." He galloped back to his men and had them divide into two groups to slow the advance of the Federal column as dismounted skirmishers. The cavalrymen took their positions in the woods on both sides of the railroad bed, holding fire until the bluecoats were directly in front of them. The Rebels poured a deadly fire into both flanks. Mosby dashed forward with his Sharp's carbine pelting the Yanks. Alex, with the Rangers, took careful aim on the other flank and watched numerous bluebellies fall. The Yanks immediately returned fire, moved forward slowly, and Alex heard bullets whistle by his ear for the first time.

"Fall back and form a new line," Captain Utterback ordered. The outnumbered Confederate cavalrymen, defending their homes, slowly and grudgingly gave ground.

Around three miles north of the Rappahannock, Stuart spotted 300 of Ewell's infantry frantically boarding a southbound train. "Hold them back a few more minutes," he called to his cavalry. After the train sped southward he ordered his men to mount and make a dash for the river.

Hearing the action from the south side of the river, John Pelham moved his guns into position to cover the bridge and retreating cavalry. When they moved into protective range he ordered "Fire!" His guns shot over the Rebels and with deadly accuracy stopped the advance of the Yankees. Ewell's artillery on the other side of the bridge also opened fire. Stuart and his men cut for the fords, then dashed and swam their horses through the cold water to safety. Drenched as he dismounted below the bridge, Alex spun around and fired across the river, his pulse surging from the excitement of battle. No sooner had the last car of the train hurtled across the bridge at Rappahannock Station, than two deafening explosions rose above the din of the artillery. The Rebels had been ready.

The stone pillars supporting the bridge collapsed and the wooden part of the structure burst into flames and portions crashed into the water.[1]

Howard, the Union commander, halted his pursuit and positioned his men and artillery on the bluffs. The level of fire increased with the battle becoming mainly an artillery duel. Crashing shells spewed dirt around Pelham, who coolly repositioned his guns for more accuracy. After about an hour, near dusk, Ewell ordered his infantry to withdraw out of gun range towards Brandy Station. The Yanks pulled back, too, to bivouac for the night. With light casualties, the first attempt by the Federals to cross into Culpeper County had been stymied. "I can't believe those brazen Yanks attempted to cross the river," Pelham said to Breathed as he wiped the soot from his face. "I'm sure the sound of the artillery frightened the civilians." He wondered how the Armstrongs had reacted.

Two days later, March 30, 1862: The depot, Culpeper Court House

Alex enjoyed the task of guarding the fifty Union prisoners he had marched to the depot at Culpeper Court House. He looked forward to spending the night in town with his wife and children. Amanda beamed with pride from the crowd while Hudson and David stared at this strange lot of men—the first Yankees they had ever seen. "Damned Yankees," Hudson muttered. He tossed pebbles at the invaders.

Constance, Lucy, and Granny Ashby heard the commotion when they returned from Camp Henry. "Tell us how you captured them, Alex," Constance asked.

Obviously relishing the role of hero, he answered, "A large force of these impudent bluecoats attempted to cross the river day before yesterday. We of course held them off, but an artillery battle ensued. I can assure you it sounded worse than it was."

Lucy eyed a young captive. "The noise was frightening."

"Yesterday they finally realized the futility of their efforts and began to retreat. General Stuart decided we couldn't let them get off that easy, so the cavalry followed and harassed them, picking up these fifty rascals. Take my word for it, there's nothing to worry about. Our border is safe."

"Serves you fellas right for coming down here and invading our peaceful land," Granny jeered while she poked one with her cane. "What're you here for anyway?"

"We're here for the flag," he replied sullenly.

"Well, you can take your damned old flag and go home. We don't want it!" she taunted, evoking laughter from the crowd.

The spectators found comfort knowing their gallant knights had protected them and punished the intruders, but the sight of the enemy in their town still unnerved them.

Five days later, April 4, 1862: Coleman Street

Charles Armstrong emerged from the barbershop owned by Ira Field, an elderly free black. Walking up Coleman Street, he spied a soldier tying his horse in front of the Armstrongs' home.

"Good afternoon, Judge Armstrong." John Pelham crossed the street to shake hands.

"Ah, Lieutenant Pelham, I'm glad to see you survived the attack at the river."

"Yes, my guns were engaged for a short while, but our involvement was minor," Pelham said modestly. "However, I'm happy to tell you that I've built the Horse Artillery to full strength and the men are ready for action. General Stuart has established his headquarters at the beautiful Barbour estate, Beauregard. He sent me to town to acquire some items for him."

"The Barbours are very dear friends of ours. You couldn't enjoy finer hospitality," Charles said after they crossed the street and stood in front of his house. "So you're on the general's staff now? I hear he's a jovial fellow."

"Indeed he is," Pelham replied with a broad smile. "He's twenty nine and treats me like a kid brother. I couldn't ask for a finer commanding general."

"I've heard nothing but good things about him from our son-in-law." Charles motioned to the porch. "Won't you come in for a visit?"

"Actually, I hoped to challenge Miss Armstrong to a game of chess. Is she home?"

"I hate to disappoint you, but the ladies of my household are visiting with Dolly Hill, General A. P. Hill's wife. You see, we'll be returning to our farm in Rixeyville tomorrow for several weeks to oversee the spring planting, and they wanted to say good-bye to their town friends."

Disappointment registered on Pelham's face. "Perhaps I could arrange another time to call on her?"

"Why don't you bring General Stuart and his staff to a party at our farm in a few days," Charles said. "We'd be honored to entertain the general and provide better food than army rations."

"Judge Armstrong, you're most gracious. General Stuart will bring his banjo player, Sweeney, to add to the festivities."

Charles gave Pelham directions, established the time and date, and Pelham rode off to complete his shopping. Judge Armstrong walked onto the porch and noticed the bookstore sign hanging loose. He unhooked it. Since the Confederacy had passed a conscription act requiring all men age eighteen to thirty five to serve three years, Garland Sisson had been forced to enlist and close his store. Charles regretted the loss of income and remained undecided about what to do with the space. The noise of creaking wagons and livestock coming form the corner of Coleman and Davis Streets disrupted his reverie. He walked out into the street to observe a large assortment of animals and wagons moving southward. Curious, he decided to investigate.

On closer inspection, he discovered about 600 head of cattle and sheep being herded south by close to 60 slaves. Numerous wagons piled with household supplies and furniture followed the throng. Countless refugees had passed through town, but this migration was larger than any other he had seen. Startled, he watched a familiar stately carriage at the end of the procession stop, and Richard Cunningham, one of the county's wealthiest residents, leaned out the window. He revealed that he was fleeing south because he felt his estate on the Rappahannock was too vulnerable after last week's artillery duel. But he had left it in the good hands of General Ewell, who was drinking a bottle of Madeira wine and lounging on the furniture when Cunningham departed. He reported Ewell was fuming and cussing about the stupid ignorant Dutch on the other side of the river and he longed to attack and knock the hell out of Lincoln's thieving hired immigrants. Reportedly, they were robbing, stealing, and wantonly killing all the stock in Fauquier County. Unfortunately, Lee had ordered him to stay in place since he might be needed elsewhere—perhaps Jackson would call him to the valley.

Charles observed that, even though Jackson had been defeated at Kernstown, still his little army in the valley had scared Lincoln enough to keep a large force watching him, and therefore away from Richmond. But if he summoned Ewell, Culpeper would be unprotected.

Cunningham agreed that as long as the river stayed high from the spring rains, the Rappahannock formed a moat protecting Culpeper. But when the water receded in a month or two, and the river became fordable, he believed the despicable foe would descend like an unstoppable swarm of locusts. He had instructed Wiltshire, his mill operator, to torch the house rather than have the Yankees occupy it.

The two friends bid each other an emotional farewell and Charles reflected glumly on the depressing situation.

Four days later, April 8, 1862: Panorama

"Would you get these back buttons for me dear," Harriet said to Charles as they dressed for the party. "I'm looking forward to meeting General Stuart and his staff."

Charles buttoned her emerald brocade dress. "We must make merry while we can." He contemplated the grim situation: General Albert Sidney Johnston had been killed at Shiloh; Yankee hordes approached Richmond and the Shenandoah Valley, and when the Rappahannock receded they may move into Culpeper. "This might be one of our last times for laughter."

"What a dreadful picture you paint," Harriet said with alarm. She turned to look into his sad blue eyes. "Surely it can't be that bad."

"Forgive me dear, for being pessimistic. Let's enjoy tonight." He kissed her on the cheek.

"Actually, I thought you arranged this for Constance's benefit. She seems rather enthralled with John Pelham."

"In reality, I'm anxious to meet Stuart, but I must admit Pelham is an impressive fellow. However, I believe she could do no better than Robert Beckam. He's a steadfast, dependable young man from a fine family. His father's the second largest stock holder in the railroad." Charles put on his well-tailored black coat. "Beckam is my choice for Constance. But, I certainly haven't told her that."

"Perhaps that's wise," Harriet replied while he hooked her pearls around her slender neck. "She's so strong-willed and independent. It's your fault. You've raised her that way."

"If I told her I thought she should marry Robert, she'd probably never see him again," Charles chuckled. "I'm not about to make that decision for her. And perhaps it's my fault that she's so headstrong. But it could be worse. I'd rather she be independent than selfish and self-centered like so many of her contemporaries." He stood back and looked approvingly at Harriet. "You look gorgeous."

Abraham and Joseph waited in front of the house to take care of their guest's horses. After the sun dropped low in the sky, they heard the strumming of a banjo and saw a gray-clad band of men riding up the hill. They gaped open-mouthed at the leader, knowing this man, a spectacle to behold, must be important. General Jeb Stuart wore a brown felt hat with the brim looped up and held by a star in front and crowned by an ebon feather floating above. A heavy brown curled moustache and a huge chest-long beard dominated his face. With a high forehead, prominent nose, and clear penetrating brilliant blue eyes, he had been nicknamed "Beauty" at West Point, because a beauty he was not. All agreed the beard hid his receding chin and improved his looks. He wore a double-breasted jacket buttoned back, gray waistcoat and pantaloons with a bright yellow sash wrapped around his waist and tied so that the tassels fell in full view. His belt buckled over the sash and held his weapons, a light French sabre and a pistol in a black holster. A wreath of jonquils and fruit blossoms hung around his horse's neck.[1]

The broad shouldered, barrel chested, five-foot, nine-inch cavalier conveyed strength when he bounded from his horse. His arms and legs appeared long compared to his relatively short body. "Gin'el Stuart, sur, I'm Joseph Jordan. Judge Armstrong told us to take real good care of your horses." Joseph took the reins of Stuart's horse, patting it on the neck.

"Thank you, Joseph. I can tell you're a good man with horses," Stuart said jovially.

"Oh, yas'r. The judge has some fine horses. I've been takin' care of 'em for years."

"Let's serenade our hosts," Stuart said to his men after they dismounted. "Sweeney, strike up *The Dew is on the Blossom*." His banjo player strummed the notes, and Stuart led the singing in a clear, sonorous voice. The Armstrong family and guests Aunt Martha and Uncle James Rixey, Top Hill, older brother of Powell and Baptist, and his wife Sarah walked out on the front porch and clapped in appreciation. Stuart took off his hat and made a broad, sweeping bow. "James Ewell Brown Stuart at your service, Judge Armstrong and friends."

The gold spurs on Stuart's knee-high patent leather boots jingled while he marched up the steps and shook hands with the judge, who made introductions. Stuart kissed the hands of all the ladies and when he greeted Constance, laughed and said, "Miss Armstrong, it's a pleasure indeed. Lieutenant Pelham has a talent for locating the fairest damsels, no matter where we're camped." He laughed again boisterously. Pelham, standing behind him, shifted uncomfortably on his feet as the color gleamed in his cheeks. Stuart then presented the men who had accompanied him: Captain Dabney Ball, Lieutenant Chiswell Dabney, Captain John Esten Cooke, Lieutenant Redmond Burke, and Lieutenant John Mosby.

"Gentlemen," Charles called out, "you are like chivalrous knights of old to us. We're indebted to you for courageously guarding our border and protecting us. Please accept our appreciation by coming inside and partaking of the feast we've prepared for you."

Charles, Amanda, and Alex escorted General Stuart, Lieutenant Dabney, and Captain Ball into the parlor while the remainder of the men huddled around the dining room table heaping their plates with Sadie's delicacies. "May I offer you gentlemen some wine, brandy, or coffee?" Charles inquired.

"I promised my mother I'd never touch a drop of liquor," Stuart answered, his eyes twinkling. "I'll have coffee."

"The same for me Judge," seventeen-year-old Chiswell Dabney said. "I dropped out of my first year at The University when the war broke out. I'm not old enough for anything stronger than coffee."

"Likewise for me," Dabney Ball said. "I left the Methodist ministry in Baltimore to join up. I'd always strongly opposed secession, but when I observed the unlawful and high-handed tactics used by the Union forces in Baltimore, I knew I had to fight for the Confederacy and against despotism."

"That's why we call him the 'Fighting Parson.'" Stuart slapped Ball on the back. "Poor Maryland, the North has its heel upon her, and how it grinds her!"[5]

"Where are you from, General Stuart?" Alex inquired, then he poured a glass of wine for himself.

"Patrick County, Virginia, and proud of it by God!" Stuart responded loudly and enthusiastically. "There was never any doubt that my loyalties would be to Virginia. I can't understand or tolerate a Virginian betraying our state and fighting for the Union. Traitors, that's what they are!" He paused and sipped his coffee, fire in his eyes. "I still can't believe my father-in-law, a Virginian, is in the Union cavalry." He shook his head.

"How terrible!" Amanda said. "That must difficult for your wife."

"It is. She has a brother, husband, and cousin fighting for the Confederacy while her father remains with the Union. We had named our son after her father. However, I felt we couldn't let him grow up with the dishonorable name of a traitor. Flora finally agreed with me, and we renamed him after me," Stuart said proudly. "We call him Jimmy. I must tell you, I dream of capturing my father-in-law."

"Speaking of captures," Alex said, "everyone's impressed with the captures made by the 'Rebel Raider,' John Hunt Morgan. He's captured horses, Union prisoners, supply wagons, and burned boats and railroad bridges. He's even disguised himself as a Union officer to achieve his means. What do you think of his type of warfare?"

"There's a cry in Richmond for more partisan warfare. I believe the powers that be will soon give us their consent for more raids behind Union lines. We've got to do it in order to gain badly needed supplies and horses," Stuart said.

"The more miserable we make their lives the less likely they are to occupy our territories for long. It's one way to work on them psychologically and shorten this war," Ball commented.

"But," Stuart stated emphatically, "such actions must be approved by the officers in charge. Otherwise, we will have outlaws stealing for their own gain."

John Pelham gravitated towards Constance. They stood beside the dining room table deeply engrossed in a conversation about horses. "Her name is Queen Elizabeth, shortened to Liz, and she's a beautiful chestnut mare." Constance nibbled on a cookie. She noticed John Mosby and Redmond Burke talking quietly in the corner. "If you'll excuse me for a moment, Lieutenant Pelham, I must enquire about my good friend, Frank Stringfellow."

"And who is this Stringfellow?" Pelham said with his eyebrows raised. "I've heard his name around headquarters."

"He's like a brother to me and he's a scout for General Stuart, but I haven't heard from him in months. It'll only take a minute," she said with a dazzling smile. "Help yourself to some more food."

"Gentlemen," Constance said to the scouts. "My friend, Frank Stringfellow, has written me about you. I know he has the highest regards for you."

"Stringfellow's learned fast," Burke said quietly. "He's a good scout."

"He wrote me in early January that he was going on a special mission and that I may not hear from him for several months. However, it's been over three months now, and I cannot help but worry about him. Can you tell me anything?"

"He's on a dangerous mission," Mosby whispered. "As far as we know, he's doing his job well and we believe he's still alive."

Constance sighed with relief. "That's encouraging. Do you have news of Will Farley?"

"Unfortunately, he's still in Old Capitol prison. We hope he'll be exchanged soon," Burke said while enjoying a ham biscuit.

Aunt Martha had watched Constance and John Pelham from across the room. Because of her impaired hearing, she had missed his name when he was introduced. She swayed up to him while Constance talked to Burke and Mosby. "You must be that nice Robert Beckam from Warrenton that Constance has been telling me about," she said gregariously.

Taken back by her remark, Pelham couldn't find his voice for a moment. He wondered, was it Robert Beckam that Constance visited in Warrenton after Christmas? How involved was their relationship? She certainly wasn't wearing an engagement ring. Returning to reality, he replied, "I'm sorry you must be mistaken, madam. I'm Lieutenant John Pelham from Alabama."

"Oh!" said Aunt Martha, realizing she had put her foot in her mouth, "Forgive an old lady, Lieutenant Pelham. I get easily confused these days."

Jeb Stuart strutted into the room and helped himself to a plate of food. "Eat up, men, so we can sing some more. The evening wouldn't be complete without a rousing rendition of *Jine the Cavalry*."

"General Stuart," Aunt Martha said loudly. "Are you headquartered at Beauregard?"

"Today General Ewell pulled rank on me and moved his headquarters into the house. We're now camped on the grounds. However, I can't complain." He wiped his moustache with a napkin.

"I simply must have the honor of entertaining you while you're here," Aunt Martha said vivaciously. "My son-in-law is with the Black Horse Cavalry and compliments you constantly. I want to invite you and everyone here to a party at our home, Rose Dale, on the twelfth."

"I must inform you, General Stuart, that my Aunt Martha throws the most divine parties in Culpeper County," Constance said, joining them.

"In that case, how can I refuse?" Stuart threw back his head in a hearty laugh. "Mrs. Rixey, we accept with pleasure. Now tell me, where do you live?"

Constance leaned close to John Pelham and whispered, "I believe Aunt Martha has met her match in General Stuart."

Ten days later, April 18, 1862: Panorama

After two days of rain the clouds lifted, revealing the mountains, while John Pelham rode towards Panorama. White dogwoods dotted the forests and the emerald fields burst forth with life again. Unfortunately, he mused, armies also come alive again in the spring. He spotted two riders in the field behind the stables and decided to investigate. He rode closer, recognized Constance and her father, and waved his hat. Seeing his blonde hair, they saluted back and rode towards him. "This is a pleasant surprise, Lieutenant Pelham," Charles shouted.

"I'm afraid I've come to say good-bye." His somber face startled them as they stopped beside him.

"Good-bye!" Constance cried, her eyebrows raised in alarm. "What's happened?"

"Jackson summoned Ewell to join him in the valley immediately. He's marching south today. The cavalry has been ordered to Richmond. Only three companies will be left here to picket the Rappahannock. We leave day after tomorrow."

"Is the Fourth Virginia marching?" Charles asked, riding towards the stable.

"Yes, I believe so. General Ewell ordered Camp Henry torn down. He's left a small crew behind to do the work. If you want any of that lumber, you should get a wagon over there tomorrow."

"Does that mean he's afraid the Yankees will come and use those buildings?" Constance asked horrified.

"I'm sure that's the reason, dear," Charles answered. "It would be a terrible waste to see all that wood destroyed. I'll definitely go tomorrow with Abraham and Joseph." They dismounted and Abraham took the reins of the horses. "I need to go tell Amanda. Surely, Alex will spend his last night here tonight."

"Yes, I saw him as I left camp. He said he was going to see his parents first." Pelham stroked Liz's muscular neck while Charles started up the hill to the house. "She's as impressive as you said, Miss Armstrong."

Constance leaned her head against Liz's nose affectionately after giving her reins to Abraham. "She's beautiful."

"I know this proposition might upset you," Pelham said calmly when they walked up the hill. "But due to the circumstances, I'd like to purchase Liz from you for the Horse Artillery."

Constance froze, then stared at him aghast. "You're serious aren't you? No, I can't let her go!"

"I didn't mean to rile you." He took her hand. "But you must be realistic about this. If I don't take her, the odds are good that she'll be captured by the enemy. Do you want her serving the Yankees?"

"Of course not! I'm not about to enlist Liz in either army. I'll protect her. I can shoot a gun."

He looked at her warily, fighting an inner battle not to smile. "Perhaps you can. I wish you luck. However, that's really not my purpose for coming here today. We've enjoyed three parties together, but I still haven't had an opportunity to redeem myself at chess. This may be my last chance for a good while. What do you say?"

With a bemused smile she looked into his laughing blue eyes, enjoying the warmth of his hand. "Lieutenant Pelham, I accept your challenge and I'll show no mercy. Come relax in the study while I change out of these riding clothes." Thankful that today she was properly attired in a riding dress, she scraped the mud off of her boots. "I can't believe Ewell's men are marching in this mud, and on Good Friday, too."

An hour later Pelham sat in the brown leather chair, studying the chessboard intently. Then David toddled into the room and crawled into his lap. "Welcome, young man. Help me beat your aunt."

Constance, perched ladylike on the sofa across from him, said, "No fair teaming up on me. But then you do need all the help you can get."

"That one." The three-year-old pointed to a castle.

"Great minds work alike." Pelham moved the castle.

David looked up at him and asked, "Where's Daddy?"

"I suspect your Daddy will be here shortly." Pelham watched Constance move.

"Bye, Bye." David jumped down and ran out of the room.

"According to the rumors I hear," Pelham said moving carefully. "There's no doubt that McClellan is moving up the peninsula towards Richmond. However, I'm confident we can stop him. He's got greater numbers but we've got spirit, determination, and good generals."

Constance studied every feature of his youthful face. "I'm worried about our dangerous situation here, and yet you show no fear going into battle."

"I'll share with you my one adage of life: 'Fear God and know no other fear.' I don't think a man can be strictly honorable unless he's brave." [5] She saw an inherent strength in his face as his eyes glowed with an inner fire.

"You're inspiring, Lieutenant Pelham. You'll lead your men well." She contemplated the board and moved thoughtfully.

"I hope you'll continue to write to me," he answered, calculating his move. "Letters keep up our morale."

"Yes, of course I will. That is if I'm not too busy fighting off Yankees myself." She moved quickly.

A broad smile lit up his face. "Checkmate," he said triumphantly after he made his final move.

Constance's jaw fell in disbelief. "I can't believe it. You outmaneuvered me!"

He stood up and slapped his hand against his leg. "Yes! My confidence is restored. Bring on the Yankees!" He plopped on the couch beside her, gloating. "Swear to me that you didn't let me win simply to heal my male pride."

"I swear. I'm much too fierce a competitor to do that. As much as I hate to admit it, you won fair and square."

He took her hand in his, lifted it to his lips and kissed her palm gently, his eyes consuming her. "I want you to know how much I've enjoyed your warm friendship."

"And I yours." Every time his gaze met hers, her heart turned over in response. "I believe it's because we laugh together so much."

He leaned over and brushed her cheek with his lips. His nearness overwhelmed her. She wanted more, much more, but realized it would be easier to let him go if she kept it light. "Swear to me that you aren't flattering me so I'll sell you my horse."

"I swear." He squeezed her hand, his eyes sparkling with merriment. "I've got to get back to camp. I slipped away without General Stuart knowing it. I'm sure his dander will be up when he misses me."

When they walked out into the hall, her father came down the steps. They bid him farewell together.

Two weeks later, May 4, 1862: The Courthouse

Judge Armstrong fumbled through the papers on his desk. "Next case." In the dead silence, he looked up to see five blue clad soldiers standing in the back of the courtroom, pistols drawn.

"What's the meaning of this?" he asked, his heart beating rapidly.

The sound of the soldier's boots clomping against the wood floor echoed through the room when two of them swaggered to the judge's bench. The spectators sat frozen with fear, their eyes following the two invaders. "You're under arrest, judge," the tall one said with his gun pointed at the judge. "Come with us."

Charles protested, still seated. "On what charge?"

"By order of Major Porter Stowell, First Maine Cavalry." The shorter one sauntered behind the judge's bench. "Now get moving."

Charles stood up slowly, unfastening his robe. He lifted it over his head, then the Yankee moved behind him and jabbed his gun in his back. "That's good," the soldier said sarcastically. "You got a horse, judge?"

"Yes," Charles replied quietly. "It's at my house about a block away."

"Me and Owens are going to find the judge's horse so he can take a little trip with us," the tall soldier said to the three standing by the back door. "We'll meet you out front in the street."

Charles and his two captors approached Davis Street to see at least fifty Union cavalrymen surrounding seven other town citizens. "Join your friends." Owens motioned Charles towards the group. Charles nodded grimly to the other prisoners: John Barbour, John Stark Jr., John Stark Sr., George McDonald, and three other acquaintances.

The sound of rapidly galloping horses from the direction of the depot captured their attention. The soldiers saluted Major Stowell and his staff in the late afternoon sun. "Major Stowell, sir, we've reconnoitered the town and have seen no evidence of enemy cavalry. We've taken eight civilian prisoners and some rifles," Owens reported.

"Let's take one more ride through the town so the citizens can see these prisoners leaving with us. This should ensure our safety," Stowell replied. The soldiers mounted up and guided their horses down Coleman Street. A sea of blue surrounded the prisoners who had pistols pointed at them from every direction. Townspeople peered helplessly out of their windows burning with fury and indignation.

The current flowed swiftly in the Rappahannock River while the horsemen assessed the situation at Beverly's Ford. It appeared the river had risen six or seven inches since their crossing at 1 a.m. that morning. Major Stowell pulled out his pocket watch. "It's almost six o'clock. We must return to Warrenton tonight. It's going to be a slow crossing, so let's begin. Get half of our men across and then we'll send the prisoners over."

The captives watched the soldiers slowly make their way through the strong current for nearly forty minutes. The horses had to swim in the middle and several stumbled in the perilous crossing.

"You, judge, get going," Owens ordered. Charles slowly edged his horse down the bank. "Easy boy," he whispered, then he felt the shock of the cold water rushing up to his waist as they progressed slowly to the middle of the river. Suddenly, one of the horse's legs slipped and horse and rider tumbled forward into the swift current. Gasping for breath, Charles struggled to hang on to the reins, but the swift current dragged him under.

"Don't risk your lives to save him," Major Stowell ordered his men.

Unable to sit by idly, John Barbour nodded to John Stark, Jr. The two of them spurred their horses into the river in the direction the current carried the judge. "I'll stop him," Stark called. His horse struggled towards the center of the river. He arrived in the knick of time and the limp body came to rest against the front quarter of his horse. Barbour struggled to get his horse close beside them. They reached down and grasped the judge's jacket, but were unable to pull him up. "Hold the reins of my horse. I'm going in." Stark tensely slid into the water. He struggled to get his arm under the judge's chest and lift his head above water. "Try to pull him up on your horse," he gasped to Barbour, who grabbed the judge's arms. The two struggled desperately with the dead weight and after several laborious minutes managed to lay him over Barbour's horse in front of the saddle. Water gushed from the judge's mouth. Barbour slapped him on the back and applied pressure. After a few endless tension-filled seconds, Charles panted for breath and coughed.

"Thank God," Barbour gasped to Stark. Even some of the Yankees cheered.

Five days later, May 9, 1862: Culpeper Court House

Constance rushed home from the post office clasping six letters. Everyone in town vented their rage about the cowardly Yankees' kidnapping civilians to shield their retreat. For the last five days, she had frantically waited and prayed for her father's safe return. Consumed by nightmares and endless days of terror, she moved in a world pervaded by gloom and bad news. She thought of how that horrid General Benjamin Butler harassed the women of New Orleans who called him 'Beast Butler.' Still, they bravely defied him. The Richmond paper at the post office told of a battle near Williamsburg, but Johnston continued to retreat towards Richmond. She had burst with pride when she saw Stuart's Horse Artillery commended for its performance in the battle.

Entering the parlor, she announced to her mother and Amanda, "The mail's finally gotten through. Two from Alex," she said, handing the letters to Amanda, who nursed the baby while Hudson and David looked at a book on the floor.

"And one for you mother, from Mrs. Daly."

Harriet tore the letter open. "Perhaps this will take my mind off your poor dear father for a few minutes."

Constance sat down on the sofa. She had one letter from John Pelham and two from Robert Beckam. Still no word from Frank, she mused. She opened the letter from Pelham first.

"As grim as things are here," Harriet said, "it's encouraging to know that there are problems and discontent in the North. Mrs. Daly and I promised to relate events honestly to each other, and maintain our friendship in spite of this terrible war. Listen to a few of her comments,"

No one seems to feel the danger in which we stand, or to realize that we are a bankrupt, ruined nation should this war continue longer. The corruption of every part of the government is so great that we despair of it. For my part, if the South would consent to yield the border states, the rest of the slave states might go. Mediocrity is king, and money our ultimatum. What can be done with a people who worship these gods?

We visited Mr. William Astor recently, and he shares our low opinion of the administration. We freely commented upon the assurance of the wife of a second-rate Illinois lawyer being obliged to choose her company and select five hundred elite to entertain at the White House. It is too comical, too sad, to see such extravagance and folly in the White House with the country bankrupt and a civil war raging.[5]

They all heard the back door close. "I've returned," called a dirty, wrinkled, exhausted Charles Armstrong.

"Father! Grandpa! My darling Charles," they screamed as they engulfed him with hugs and kisses.

"Oh, my dearest, you look terrible," Harriet moaned in tears. "What have they done to you?"

"I've been through a harrowing experience," he whispered hoarsely. "But God has seen me through it."

"Come, sit on the sofa," Constance said, clasping his hand. "Hudson, run tell Sadie to bring food and drink for your grandfather. Now, Father, can you tell us about it?"

"I'll try," he said weakly. They sat aghast while he related his near drowning in the river. "After I regained my strength, we proceeded to Warrenton, arriving about midnight. They forced us to sleep in a shed with no blankets or hay. The next morning I was so stiff I could barely move. They interrogated us individually, but of course we told them nothing. Their primary purpose, other than protecting their retreat, seemed to be to determine if there were Southern soldiers in the county. I lied and told them that a strong force was stationed north of the Rapidan. We spent another dreadful night in the shed and they released us the next morning, minus our horses of course."

"How did you manage to get home?" Amanda asked, rocking the baby.

"We walked to John Beckam's house. He took us in, fed us, and put us up for a night while he searched for a horse and wagon to transport us to the river. The Union cavalry has confiscated such items and stripped the citizens of crops and forage. The next night he took us under cover of darkness to Beverly's Ford. We had no way to cross the river. We called and called for help, and finally Mr. Wilthsire at Cunningham's came to our rescue. He brought several horses to ferry us across the river. We spent the remainder of the night in Cunningham's deserted mansion. This morning he took us to Beauregard. Fannie Barbour had one of her servants bring us to town in a wagon," he concluded coughing.

"Never would I have dreamed our foe would treat a seventy-two-year-old man so shamefully," Harriet said bitterly. "We must get you a hot bath and put you to bed immediately. You're obviously sick."

Five weeks later, June 15, 1862: Davis Street

Constance walked along Davis Street, listening to Granny brag about how Stonewall Jackson had Lincoln shaking in his boots. Jackson knew how to trick and deceive the enemy and win. Undoubtedly, he'd stunned the world by running all the Yankees out of the valley and saving the Confederacy with his little band of men.

Constance's mind raced as she tried to comprehend it all. First he caught Milroy off guard and defeated him at McDowell. Then he surprised the Federals at Front Royal, and with the information Belle Boyd bravely brought him on the battlefield, easily took that town. Next he liberated Winchester and advanced to Harper's Ferry to threaten Washington. And then, when Lincoln sent two armies to annihilate him, he defeated them both, one at Cross Keys and the other at Port Republic. His name sent fear into the heart of the Yankees.

"Right now they're all wondering, where's Jackson?" Granny said, waving her cane. "When northern children misbehave, their parents tell them if they aren't good, Stonewall Jackson'll get them."

They paused in front of the courthouse to enjoy the warm sunshine. Constance said, "Now that McClellan's been stopped outside of Richmond and Lee's taken command, there appears to be hope. What do you think Granny? Will he be a good general? The papers call him Granny Lee because of his age."

"You'd better believe it! Bob Lee comes from a noble Virginia family and he'll lead us well; with age comes wisdom. After all, he was offered command of the Union Army and turned them down. Besides, the only thing Johnston knew how to do was retreat. Mark my words, Lee will fight!"

"I hope you're right," Constance said soberly. "It all comes at such great cost. The names of casualties have been coming in slowly." She paused and looked down Coleman Street. "We're returning to the farm tomorrow. We've discussed going south, but decided we wouldn't leave our lands to the marauders. Richmond is bursting at the seams with refugees. If the Yankees come, we'll meet them boldly and bear misfortune the best we can."

"That's the spirit," Granny said.

Constance hugged the outspoken little woman affectionately. "Good-bye, Granny." When Constance turned, she looked above the front door of the courthouse at the small second floor balcony filled with slaves waiting to be sent south for safekeeping. Many would work in the Richmond hospitals and munitions factories. She hated to see them locked up like that and wondered about their thoughts on this terrible war. One, who had murdered her mistress, had been sent to Richmond to hang. It made her shudder.

Sixteen days later, June 31, 1862: Panorama

The sweat ran down Abraham's face after he nailed the last board from Camp Henry over the floor joists in the attic, concealing twenty hams and the Armstrong family silver, jewelry, and valuables. He stood up, wiped his brow, shoved boxes of old clothes on top of the newly installed floor, and then walked down the stairs out into the yard to the well house. He enjoyed a cool drink of water in the breeze, and saw the judge strolling up the hill from the stable.

"How's everythin' in town, Mista Armstrong?" he asked taking another drink.

"There's quite a stir of excitement," Charles said reaching for the dipper. "News came over the telegraph of fierce fighting below Richmond for the last six days. Rumor has it that Jackson's joined Lee. It sounds like Lee is attacking McClellan and is pushing him back towards the river."

"I sure hope we win this here war soon," Abraham said wiping his ebony skin. "When do ya think it'll be over?"

114

"I never dreamed it would last this long, Abraham. I can't answer that question. We must accept the possibility that the Yankees may appear here at any time and be ready."

"I put the floor down in the attic like ya told me, an' hid the ham an' valu'bles," Abraham said proudly. "What else kin I do?"

"We need to hide some barrels of flour and cornmeal, and perhaps containers of sugar and coffee."

Abraham scratched his gray head. "I kin bury the sugar an' coffee, but the barrels are tougher. Maybe I kin hide 'em in the hay or take 'em into the woods an' cover 'em with leaves."

"I think that might be best. Abraham, I want you to understand that the Yankees might try to force you to go with them."

"There ain't no way they kin make me leave mah home," the old back man said shaking his head violently. "I'm free an' I'm stayin' right here."

"You and Sadie, Joseph and Selene are part of our family. We always want you here," Charles said looking Abraham in the eye. "But if circumstances change, and you decide to leave, I'll understand. I don't want you to do anything that endangers your life."

"Thank ya, Mista Armstrong, I 'preciate that. No matter what, ya kin count on me."

Charles hugged his grandsons, playing in the yard under Selene's supervision, and entered the house to find the ladies sewing uniforms in the parlor. He related the news about the fighting around Richmond and pulled out a newspaper from his jacket pocket. "I finally got a copy of the Richmond paper that relates the details of Jeb Stuart's bold ride around McClellan's entire army. The astounding feat has revived the sinking spirits of the Confederacy."

"It's encouraging to know that Richmond may be saved," Amanda said, her face pale, "but at such a terrible cost. Thousands of men are laying down their lives for our noble cause. I pray an all-powerful Providence will end this wretched conflict soon. Surely, our enemy must see the futility of their efforts."

"We all pray for peace," Charles said lighting his pipe. "But we must brace ourselves for a longer conflict. Lincoln has called General John Pope from the West to lead a newly formed army. Rumor has it that this army's mission will be to march south and take control of the vital rail connection at Gordonsville, thus cutting off supplies to Lee's Army in Richmond."

All three women leaned forward listening intently. Constance dropped the jacket she was hemming. "They'll have to march through Culpeper to do that! We'll be in the eye of the storm."

"It's certainly possible," Charles said, trying to appear calm. "We decided to remain here on the land where our ancestors are buried, rather than going south. Does anyone want to change their mind?"

Harriet's eyes sparked with determination. "We will not let Lincoln's hirelings push us out of our home. We stay. We could go to my sister's in Fredericksburg, but their location is probably as dangerous as ours."

"I agree," Constance said stubbornly, pacing the room. "The war could follow us wherever we go. We can't let fear paralyze us. We'll continue life as usual."

"I'm greatly concerned for the safety of the children, "Amanda said in a quivering voice. "But we'll stay with you. We must be together and strengthen each other."

"God will give us the strength to deal with our misfortunes," Charles replied with confidence. "But we must be prepared and make efforts to conserve our food supply. Also, understand that we may be cut off without mail. John Barbour left on the last train south yesterday to run the railroad from Gordonsville. He fears the Yankees will capture any trains coming into Culpeper. Who knows when we'll get mail from the army again. Dolly Hill and her girls also left to go to Richmond."

"I don't know how I can exist without knowing if Alex is well," Amanda said with a tear trickling down her face. "It'll be torture."

Constance walked over and took her hands."It may not be for long, Mandy, and remember the telegraph is still operating."

Charles pulled two letters from his inside coat pocket. "I saved the best for last," he said with a grin. "I have two letters that should make my dear daughters happy."

Constance grabbed hers and shrieked, "It's from Frank! He's alive!"

"Thank God," Harriet said. "Poor Anne's been frantic with worry."

Amanda had already ripped her letter open. "Alex was with Stuart on the ride around McClellan," she exclaimed.

Constance began to read Frank's letter:

My dear Connie,

I safely escaped from my secret mission, but cannot give you details in writing. However, in order to flee undetected, I had to spend some anxious minutes submerged in a stream breathing through a straw.

I returned to duty to find General Stuart near Yorktown. I was delighted to be greeted by my dear friend, Will Farley, who had been released recently from prison. Burke and Mosby related their pleasant visit with you in Culpeper.

General Stuart sent Burke and me to watch McDowell's force north of Fredericksburg. They were advancing towards Richmond to join up with McClellan. We sent word that we predicted they would be there by May 30th. Things looked quite bleak for the Confederacy. Richmond could not withstand the assault of both armies. Then suddenly, McDowell began to retreat towards Manassas. We did not understand the reason for this miracle, and watched for a time to be sure we were not being deceived. We later discovered that Jackson's victories in the valley had caused Lincoln to halt McDowell to guard Washington. Jackson saved the Confederacy!!

We reached Richmond to witness the end of the bloody Battle of Seven Pines. Now let me briefly relate my exciting experiences on Stuart's "Ride around McClellan." 1600 cavalrymen and two pieces of artillery under Breathed departed to gain information about the enemy's troop locations. We had ridden some distance behind the enemy lines and determined vulnerable spots, when Stuart ordered Farley and me to scout back to see if we could return by the same route. We reported that the bridge we had crossed at Totopotomoy Creek had been destroyed and a considerable body of troops waited in ambush. Stuart bravely decided to push forward, which meant we would have to circumvent the entire army to return to Richmond. I scouted forward to Tunstall's Station, a Federal supply depot, and reported three companies of infantry. Stuart attacked and the enemy broke and ran. Burke and I burned the bridge over Black Creek while Farley chopped down the telegraph poles. Meanwhile, squads tore up the railroad tracks.

We then rode towards the Chickahominy River, knowing the Federals would be close behind us. When we reached the river, to our dismay it was swollen and the bridge had been washed out. Burke and I were given the challenging job of building a bridge, and quick! Our lives depended on it. We had squads tear down an old warehouse nearby. We found a small skiff that helped us transport the boards to build a shaky bridge. The men were able to cross it, swimming their horses. However, Stuart refused to leave the guns. Our only recourse was to knock the building down with battering rams and carry the heavy uprights to the stream and then push them laboriously in place. No sooner had we gotten everything across and destroyed the bridge than a small group of Federals began to fire from the other side. We quickly escaped back to Richmond, having ridden 100 miles in 48 hours. Stuart's outstanding feat, executed with consummate skill, revived our morale and will go down in history. I have no doubt Lee will aggressively use the information we gathered to plan an attack on McClellan.

Happy belated twentieth birthday. I didn't forget. This war demands every ounce of my energy.   Frank

Twelve days later, July 12, 1862, Monday: Culpeper Court House

Judge Armstrong dismounted and placed his horse in the stable on East Street, sweating in the warm humid air. He had left the farm before dawn to come to town to convene court for the week, but he questioned the wisdom of his decision. Union cavalry raids had been rumored through the county for the last several weeks, but he had seen no bluecoats in the Rixeyville area. On his early morning ride he observed the destruction wrought by these intruders. Burned fences, fields of wheat cut down with sabers, carcasses of farm animals, and burned structures witnessed the wanton destruction. Perhaps he had been wrong to leave the women alone at the farm. They had pledged to continue life as usual, but he felt uneasy about the situation. He pulled out his pocket watch while he walked from the stable into his back yard. 9:10 – he still had time before he convened court at 10:00 to check with George McDonald for a news update.

"Good morning, Judge." McDonald motioned him to a chair beside his desk. "Haven't seen you in a couple of weeks. Is everything well at Rixeyville?"

"So far, but I witnessed considerable destruction en route. We've had little news. What can you tell me?"

"Much has transpired," McDonald said, rummaging through the newspapers on his desk. "We've sent couriers to Orange to pick up newspapers and mail since the trains are no longer running." He pulled out a Richmond paper with pictures of Powell Hill and Robert E. Lee on the front. "Miraculously, our army has hurled McClellan's horde back to the river, and it appears they're retreating to Washington."

"God has blessed us," Charles said in amazement. "To be honest, I wasn't sure it was possible even considering the fighting spirit of our men." He looked at the newspaper pictures. "Tell me about Hill."

"He's made quite a name for himself. His command, which he dubbed 'The Light Division' due to its quickness of movement, has been acclaimed as the hardest fighting machine in the army. They call them men of steel. These men were at the center of the fighting for seven long days of bloodletting. Hill valiantly led his men into the midst of

117

the conflict, day after day. We should be proud of the achievements of our native son."

"I've always had the highest respect and regard for Powell. His success comes as no surprise to me. But, with the intensity of the fighting, casualties must have been high."

"Sadly, yes, we have paid a great price. Almost twenty thousand of our men have died," McDonald answered, his voice breaking. "Casualty lists are filtering in. I anguish over Ralph, but haven't heard anything."

"I pray for his safety." Charles touched his friend's arm.

"No one visualized the magnitude or horror of this war." McDonald shook his head. "And now Lincoln is sending another army, The Army of Virginia, against us under this pompous braggart, John Pope." He picked up a Baltimore paper. "Listen to this announcement to his troops:

I have come to you from the West, where we have always seen the backs of our enemies; from an army whose business it has been to seek the adversary and to beat him where found...I hear constantly of 'taking strong positions and holding them,' of 'lines of retreat...' Let us discard such ideas. The strongest position a soldier should occupy is one from which he can easily advance against the enemy...My headquarters are in the saddle.

"All this he says while he remains behind a desk in Washington. Meanwhile his cavalry ravages our county."

"He won't be known for his modesty," Charles chuckled. "We'll see where his boasting gets him." They both looked up startled at the sound of thundering hooves followed by a gunshot. Momentarily, a small group of Confederate cavalry galloped by the window and a shot pierced the glass. Both men ducked behind the desk while a large brigade of Union cavalry followed in hot pursuit. Charles peered out cautiously, listening to the noise of galloping horses from several directions. He heard shouting from Coleman Street. "I think the fray is taking place on Coleman Street." He stood up carefully and peered out the door. "No soldiers in sight. Shall we make our way to my back door and try to see what's happening out front?" McDonald nodded affirmatively.

The Payne family watched the drama unfold from the window of the Virginia House. Bluecoats galloping in from every direction quickly surrounded the Confederates, who fought fiercely, jabbing with their sabers, attempting to cut their way through the Yankees. A saber slashed across one young Rebel's neck, fatally wounding him. The group finally surrendered after several others were injured. "Senseless slaughter," poor old Mr. Payne kept muttering, staring at the bloody bodies.

By noon, General John Hatch had moved his cavalry corps into the town while a brigade of infantry and battery of artillery set up camp on the edge of town, placing Culpeper under Union control. Soldiers knocked on doors, demanding surrender of any firearms and food to feed their army. They arrested citizens who failed to comply. Charles carefully edged his way up Coleman Street towards the courthouse. He nodded politely to the Union soldiers he passed. "Halt," one commanded. "Do you possess any weapons?"

"I do not." They searched him roughly.

"State your business."

118

"I'm Judge Charles Armstrong and I'm on my way to the courthouse to retrieve my personal papers from my desk."

"General Hatch is establishing his headquarters in the courthouse."

"Very well, I request permission to see the general." Charles stared him in the eye.

"Proceed." He stepped aside.

General Hatch curtly granted the judge permission to remove items from his desk before it was carried into the courtroom for the general's use. Charles entered the clerk's office where Clerk Fayette Mauzy shook his head in disbelief while two Union soldiers removed record books. "What are you doing with those?" Mauzy demanded. "They're irreplaceable record books."

"We need paper to start our campfires," one of the soldiers answered with a cruel snicker.

"By whose authority do you defile our historical records?" Charles inquired angrily, blocking the doorway.

"By permission of General Hatch. Get out of our way Reb." He shoved Charles roughly against the wall and pushed by him.

Fury welled up inside of the judge as he straightened his coat and turned to Mauzy. "We can't allow these scoundrels to destroy our history," he whispered. "They respect nothing."

"I agree," Mauzy answered quietly. "My covered wagon is in the tie-lot behind the office. Will you help me remove the record books under the cover of darkness tonight?"

"Absolutely," Charles said with determination. "Come to my house and we'll make plans."

Next day, July13, 1862: The Courthouse

2 a.m. Charles and Mauzy placed the last record book in the covered wagon in the pitch-black darkness provided by the moonless night. "So far, so good," Mauzy whispered.

"Let me scout ahead, and motion you forward," Charles replied. Mauzy nodded and took his place on the driver's seat. Charles groped his way down the alley to Cameron Street. His eyes adjusting to the darkness, he looked for any movement in both directions. Seeing no signs of life, he went back and motioned Mauzy forward. The wagon moved slowly, but the creaking wheels echoed in the stillness. Charles waved him on when he reached Cameron Street. He saluted the judge when the wagon turned right and then left on East Street.

The creaking of the wagon aroused the sleeping Union picket who sat in the shadows at the corner of Cameron and Coleman Streets. Wiping his eyes, he detected the movement of a figure across Cameron Street. "Halt! Who goes there?" He sprang to his feet.

Startled, Charles dashed forward towards his back yard, hoping to hide in the boxwoods. A bullet whistled by his ear. "Halt, or I'll shoot." The picket ran towards him.

The judge slowly raised his hands. "Don't shoot."

"Who are you, sir, and what is your business at this hour?"

I'm Judge Charles Armstrong. I couldn't sleep in this stifling heat, so I decided to take a walk," Charles said calmly.

"That's a likely story," the picket replied sarcastically. He poked the gun barrel into the judge's back. "Move forward. You're under arrest for being a spy."

Three days later, July 16, 1862, Friday: Panorama

Constance watched Joseph plowing down by the creek as she rode Liz along the tree line. Her eyes swept towards the stable and house, detecting a cloud of dust approaching the stable. It must be Father, returning from town, she thought. But when the cloud came closer, she distinguished three riders. Squinting, she inhaled in horror at the sight of blue uniforms. Yankees! She guided Liz into the woods and tied her to a tree to conceal her. She stumbled back to the edge of the woods to observe the three Yankees dismount and swagger towards the stable.

Abraham stood squarely in the door to the stable, his legs spread and his arms crossed."Get outta the way, nigger," the tallest soldier snarled.

"Y'all ain't got no bin'ess here." Abraham stood his ground firmly. "Go 'way an' leave us alone."

"We'll go after we get those horses," a Yankee replied maliciously, motioning to the stable. "What's it matter to an old slave? Why're ya protecting white man's property?"

"I'm no slave, I'm free. Without horses we can't raise our crops or git to town. Ya got no right to steal. Jist go on 'way from here!" Abraham's face hardened as he stuck out his chin defiantly.

The tall soldier nodded at the other three. He struck a hard blow to the old darkie's stomach with his fist, doubling him over. Another soldier crammed his rifle against the back of the old man's head and he reeled forward. Thud! Thud! Fists struck his face causing blood to spurt everywhere. A fierce blow under the chin sent Abraham reeling out of control. When he tumbled backwards with great force, his head crashed against the corner of a plow behind him. The three Yankees heard a cracking noise when his skull struck the plow and blood flowed freely. They stepped over him and took the reins of the four horses. When they led them outside, Sadie rushed down the hill after hearing the commotion. She screamed hysterically at the sight of Abraham sprawled on the hay, his head in a pool of blood.

The three Yankees rode up the hill and tied the horses behind the house. They kicked open the back door and marched in boldly. Harriet confronted them in the hall, her heart hammering. "Sir, what is the meaning of this?"

"Stay out of our way, Rebel lady, and you won't get hurt," the tall one snorted, then they stalked into the dining room. One of them grabbed a pair of brass candlesticks and thrust them in his pouch. They rummaged through the drawers of the hunt board. "No silver," one hissed in disgust. He took his saber and slashed the portrait of the two girls, painted by Harriet.

Harriet recoiled in horror against the wall. "Please, don't," she pleaded bursting into tears. "Those pictures can't be replaced." The soldiers laughed while ruthlessly smashing china. They then stormed into the parlor and study to continue their pilfering.

Constance crept silently up on the back porch. She slipped in the back door and ascended the stairs undetected while the soldiers ransacked the parlor. Intending to change out of her riding clothes so they would not search for Liz, she found Amanda and the boys huddled in a bedroom.

"I'm so frightened," Amanda whispered. "What should we do?"

"Stay put," Constance said firmly. "They may not come up here."

After changing clothes, she closed the door to her room and listened intently in the hall.

"Ready to go, Jack?" one soldier asked.

"No, I want to check upstairs first."

"We'll ride over to that yellow farm house and then come back by here for you," the other said. "And we expect to be fed when we get back, lady." The two of them swaggered out the back door and rode off.

Jack marched up the stairs to discover Constance in the hall. "Well, well, ain't you the pretty one." His eyes raked her body from head to toe. "Now I see what all them secess boys are fighting for," he snickered crudely.

Constance's eyes blazed defiantly. "You Yankees seem to steal better than you fight."

"Don't push you luck, lady." He entered her parents bedroom. She followed him in, and watched him search her father's dresser. He pulled out her grandfather's watch and shoved it in his sack. Then he found some old pictures.

"Those have no value for you, but are priceless to us," Constance said curtly. "Don't take them."

"I can take anything I want," he sneered, dropping the pictures in his pouch. He rumbled through her mother's clothes and then decided to get down on his hands and knees and look under the bed. "Aha!" He pulled out the small cedar chest. "What have we here?"

Constance took a quick sharp breath as her body stiffened in shock. The Minuteman Flag! How could they have forgotten to hide it? She couldn't let him steal it. He placed the chest on the bed and opened it. Slowly, he pulled out the tattered flag. "Sir, that was given to my grandfather after the Revolution. It's a family heirloom. I beg you not to take it," she pleaded.

"Looks like a secess flag to me." He folded it up. "This'll bring a big price in New York."

Constance shook with rage. Desperate and furious, her eyes swept the room for a weapon. Adrenaline surged through her arteries. She gripped the fireplace poker with both hands and mustering all of her strength, struck the Yankee on the head. He tumbled to the floor. Overcome with hatred, she smashed his head again, and again, and again. Thud! Thud! Thud! Blood spurted profusely from his skull and eye sockets.

Amanda and Hudson raced into the room. "Oh my God, Connie, have you killed him?" Amanda screamed.

"I think I may have." Her voice shook. "He was stealing the Minuteman flag and I... I lost control."

"Grandma, Aunt Connie killed the Yankee!" Hudson flew down the steps.

"If they find him when they come back, we'll all be hanged," Amanda wailed.

"We've got to drag him to the cellar," Constance said, clipping her words. "But there's so much blood." She pondered, glanced around the room. "We'll have to wrap his head first." She grabbed a small throw rug and wrapped it around the Yankee's mangled head and secured it with one of her father's belts. "Now, take one of his arms and let's drag him," she ordered Amanda with ragged breath.

The two sisters struggled with the dead weight. They got him to the head of the stairs

121

and stopped. "Mandy we have to do this. Our lives depend on it! Going down the steps will be easier." When they pulled the soldier down the steps his spurs cut small gouges in the wooden treads. They reached the bottom, then Harriet and Hudson helped them drag him through the hall to the cellar steps.

Joseph rushed in the back door. "Daddy's been bad hurt by the soldiers," he blurted out. Then he stopped, wide-eyed, trying to understand the scene before him.

"We killed a Yankee!" Hudson yelled.

"Joseph, hide his horse in the woods immediately," Constance ordered, her voice rising hysterically. "His companions could return at any time. Take the horse. and go!"

"Yas'm," Joseph said with his eyes bulging. He ran out the back door, mounted the horse, and galloped towards the woods.

Amanda and Constance dragged the victim down the cellar steps. Constance panted to her mother, "Go get a blanket to cover him."

Constance rushed towards the kitchen to get food for the Yankees when they returned. Joseph met her coming up the hill. "I tied the horse, like ya said, Miss Constance."

"Good. The Yankees are coming back for food. After they leave we'll bury the dead one in the woods." She spewed out the words. Joseph followed her into the kitchen and related what they had done to Abraham.

"We have dinner prepared for you, gentlemen," Constance said politely to the two Yankees entering the back door. They followed her into the dining room where Amanda served their plates.

"If we'd known there were such lovely ladies here, we'd of behaved ourselves better." The tall sat down to eat. "Where's Jack?"

"He left shortly after you did," Constance answered innocently. "Said he was riding to meet you."

"We ain't seen him." The other one stuffed food into his mouth.

"Perhaps he decided to go elsewhere," Amanda said with a forced smile.

The soldiers seemed to be eyeing them suspiciously while they devoured the food. Suddenly, there heard a loud noise from the cellar. Constance's heart skipped a beat. Wasn't the Yankee dead? "We have some cats in the cellar. They're always knocking something over," she explained, her heart pounding.

"Would you like some more bread," Amanda asked, trying to keep their attention. Another thud pierced the air. The two women's eyes met in frozen fear.

"Sounds like some pretty lively cats," the tall one mused, eyeing them.

"Please have some of our delicious apple butter for your bread," Constance said with a flirtatious smile, her eyelashes fluttering like humming bird wings. It was time to turn on the feminine charm.

"Well, thank you, young lady. I believe I will." He smiled back, assessing her figure.

They engaged in polite conversation and the Yankees left smiling and thanking them for dinner. The women told them they hoped they would find their friend, Jack. Constance collapsed against the door with weak knees after the soldiers rode away. When she went to the cellar she did, indeed, find two cats atop a turned over crock.

* * *

Three days later, July 19, 1862: Rixeyville

Captain Aaron Adams Ames of Portland, Maine, marveled at the mountain vistas that unfolded before him near the Hazel River. Suffering intensely from the sweltering Virginia heat and humidity, he rejoiced when the soldiers were allowed to rest and swim in the river. While the cool refreshing water flowed over his muscular six-foot-two body, he noticed the pickets on each side of the river keeping a watchful eye. Snipers and guerilla bands had been a nuisance, picking off soldiers and firing from the woods when least expected. Day before yesterday two cavalrymen had reported the mysterious disappearance of one of their comrades in this vicinity. The civilians appeared secessionist to the core. Nevertheless, Ames could not condone the harsh policies of that braggart, Pope

Just this morning he had been appalled as he read Pope's General Orders Nos. 5, 6, and 7, his latest directives to subdue the civilian population. *The army was authorized to confiscate from local citizens whatever food, forage, animals, and other supplies they might require; to exile beyond Federal lines all male citizens who refuse to swear allegiance to the United States; to execute all persons who fire upon Federal troops; to destroy the property of all such persons; to force local residents to repair any railroads, wagon roads, or telegraphs destroyed in their neighborhoods; and to deny guards for the homes of citizens who seek protection.*[6] Ames considered these orders unprecedented in civilized warfare and feared that depredations and pillage would take place against helpless women and children. He was fighting to preserve the Union, Ames thought, not to force starvation on helpless civilians. This matter should be decided among men on the field of honor. A May graduate of Harvard, he had just completed his training when elected Captain due to his education and popularity with the men. He had yet to participate in his first battle.

The Armstrong women watched the Union soldiers down by the river from an upstairs bedroom window. "Look how many there are," Harriet moaned wringing her hands. "If only Charles were here."

"He's four days overdue from town now." Constance pulled back the curtains. "We must accept that he's been arrested, or perhaps worse. Let's deal with this situation ourselves."

"Look," Amanda cried in alarm. "Some of them are marching towards our house."

Constance stared at the two soldiers on horseback and about thirty infantrymen, obviously heading in their direction. "We can't stay here and quake with fear in front of them. We must put them on the defensive. I'm going out to meet them."

"Oh, no! Please don't, Constance. It's much too dangerous," her mother begged.

"I'm going, Mother." She pulled away and flew down the steps. "Even the Yankees can't be low enough to shoot a defenseless woman."

Aaron Ames squinted at the figure rapidly marching towards them from the large white frame house on the hill. It appeared to be a small woman whose dark hair was like shining glass in the sunlight. "What do you make of it, Williamson?" he asked the corporal riding alongside him.

"Either she's a Union sympathizer coming to welcome us, or we're being attacked," he replied with a grin.

Constance stormed towards them rapidly, head held high and blue eyes flashing. She planted her feet firmly on the ground and positioned her hands on her hips defiantly. "Who commands this group of men?" she demanded testily.

Aaron Ames gaped in stunned silence at the smooth white skin, delicate features, silky sable hair, and comely figure of this brazen young lady confronting him. Did she actually think she could stop them? "I do, ma'am. I'm Captain Ames, Tenth Maine Infantry."

"I'm here to complain about the brutal conduct of your cavalry," she said, spitting out the words with contempt as she edged closer, shaking her finger. "Several days ago three Yankees descended upon us and severely beat an elderly free Negro servant who attempted to save our horses. He died last night from the injuries they so cruelly inflicted. They stole our horses and ransacked the house, destroying family portraits and taking irreplaceable pictures and heirlooms. Only the basest cowards would steal from helpless women and children and murder servants. What kind of barbarians are you?" she demanded, irate sparks shooting from her eyes.

Ames dismounted and looked down her into her scorching eyes. "I can assure you, Miss...uh..."

"Armstrong," she shot back.

"Miss Armstrong, we are not barbarians. Unfortunately I can't speak for the men who aren't under my command," he continued in a calm voice with a New England twang. "We've been ordered to camp here for the night, and have no provisions. General Pope authorized us to seek provisions from the civilians."

"Don't you have any food in the North?" she protested. "It's despicable that you steal from us and force us into starvation because Lincoln won't provide rations for you."

"Miss Armstrong, unfortunately, I do not decide policy. I'm faced with the task of providing sustenance for my men in enemy territory. I pledge to you that we will not ask for more than we need to sustain us while we're camped here," his smooth, deep voice said sincerely. "It would be a more agreeable situation if you'd provide food for us rather than forcing us to steal it."

She stared up into his hazel eyes, determining him to be a man of integrity. "Very well, Captain Ames. You may take what vegetables you need from our garden. You will find corn, beans, peas, squash, and potatoes. We'll provide you with milk and eggs. However, I ask that you refrain from slaughtering our livestock or chickens."

He admired her courage and felt enough compassion to compromise with her. "I accept your generosity, Miss Armstrong. You have my word that we will not touch your livestock."

"Please camp a respectful distance away from our house," she concluded, tossing her head in defiance. "Good evening."

"Good evening." Ames watched her march proudly back up the hill.

"She's about as feisty as she is beautiful," Williamson said with a teasing grin.

"I have to admire her courage... her spirit. She's not the image of a sedate southern lady that I had imagined," Ames said thoughtfully, then mounted his horse. They headed towards a grove of trees to pitch tents. He intended to make it perfectly clear to his men what food they could and could not procure.

* * *

124

Next day, July 20, 1862: Panorama

Aaron Ames watched from a respectful distance while the funeral procession moved from the house to the fenced family cemetery about a half-mile down the hill. He listened to the singing, Amanda's beautiful voice rising above the others: S*wing low, sweet chariot, comin' for to carry me home...*

At the cemetery, the lone Negro man pushed the pine coffin off the wagon into the grave. The dark-haired Miss Armstrong read from the Bible and led the prayers. Amazed, he saw the three white women and two children embrace the two black women, one black man, and three children. This show of affection contradicted all he had been taught—that blacks hated whites. The lovely Miss Armstrong walked back linking arms with the tall Negro lady in black, obviously the widow.

"Sadie, I remember how Abraham used to bounce me on his knee. He was a devoted and kind man. We'll all be lost without him," she said, her voice breaking.

"I know he be in paradise with the Good Lawd." Tears streamed down Sadie's face. "But I can't forgive them Yankees for killin' him an' robbin' us. People like that don't deserve to be on the face of this earth. We was happy people 'til them horrible soldiers came along."

"Sadie, no matter what, I want you to know you've always got me." Constance looked up into the sad bloodshot eyes.

"Yas'm Miss Constance, I know that. I'll never leave ya." They clasped each other's hands tightly. "Ya know ya can't trust them Yankees out there. I heard them thieves in mah chickens last night. Look't the feathers," she said pointing.

Constance stared at the chicken feathers sprinkled in the grass beside Sadie's cabin. "Those sorry liars," she muttered.

The sun dropped behind the deep blue mountains as Aaron Ames knocked on the Armstrongs' front door. Constance cracked the door a few minutes later and peered out. "Captain Ames." She stepped out on the porch.

"I felt that I should inform you, Miss Armstrong, that we've been ordered to march to Culpeper Court House at dawn tomorrow. You should know that we're the vanguard of a larger army. Within a week, thousands of soldiers will be marching by here." He paused and watched her face fall. "I fear for the...um... personal safety of young ladies alone in the country," he said, trying not to show emotion. "I could escort you safely to town tomorrow if you choose to leave."

She stared intently at the handsome Yankee with honey-brown, wavy hair, moustache, and a well-formed, rugged face. "I appreciate your concern, Captain Ames. We have a house in town and would like to go there. My father's a judge. He didn't return from town four days ago as scheduled. We're gravely concerned about him and fear he may have been arrested."

"I hope he's safe," Ames said politely.

Constance's eyebrows furrowed as she contemplated her problem. "There is one complication. We only have one horse left to pull our carriage. The weight would be too great over that distance. Could I possibly impose on you to loan us a horse?"

Ames brushed his fingers over his horseshoe moustache and pondered the situation. It would be highly irregular, but he understood her plight. If he was reprimanded, so be it. "I'll let you use my horse, and I'll drive the carriage." His lips turned up in a smile.

"That's most generous of you, Captain Ames." She returned his smile. "It's encouraging to find a gentleman in the Union Army. However, I must tell you that someone from your company killed several of our chickens last night."

"I find that difficult to believe," he said shocked. "I gave them strict orders. However, perhaps I need to refresh their memories. Now if you'll excuse me, I must make preparations to march. Please be ready at daybreak."

"Thank you, Captain. We'll be prepared." She watched his broad shoulders disappear down the hill.

Next day, July 21,1862: Panorama

Constance woke up abruptly in the pitch-black darkness to a ruckus coming from the back yard. "Help!" a male voice screamed. "Let me loose!" She jumped out of bed, lit a candle, and hastily threw on a robe. After running downstairs and lighting a lantern, she raced into the back yard. Shocked, she discovered a Union soldier writhing in pain on the ground near the cabins, one foot caught in a metal trap. Sadie stood beside him, her arms crossed, with a look of smug satisfaction on her face.

"That is our chicken thief!" Sadie said triumphantly.

Joseph rushed up and spied the suspect. "We caught him Momma!" He laughed. "I knew that bear trap would come in good of somethin'."

Constance burst out laughing. "You two are a fearful team."

"Please, let me out," the soldier moaned.

"Joseph, go down to the camp and tell Captain Ames you have something up here to show him"

Aaron Ames surveyed the scene. Irritated about being awakened, he still had difficulty suppressing a smile. "Private Smith, I believe you've disobeyed my orders," he said with his eyes twinkling.

"Please, Captain, get this damned thing off my leg. I'll fight Rebels on the battlefield any day rather than these people."

Captain Ames and Joseph removed the trap. "I believe justice has been done," Ames said while the prisoner crawled to his feet.

They all watched him slowly limp down the hill muttering, "Damned niggers."

"I hope your soldier isn't seriously injured," Constance said with a malicious grin.

"He got what he deserved," Ames conceded with a smile. "I see the first light of dawn in the sky. We must prepare for our journey."

Joseph harnessed Liz and Captain Ames's horse to the carriage. "Joseph," Constance said, "you need to understand that many more Yankees will be coming. We're leaving you and Selene here to watch over things, but don't risk your lives. You've got a mule and the captured horse, so if it's safe, please bring a load of vegetables and food to town. We'll have very little to get by on."

"Yas'm, Miss Constance, I understan'. We'll do the best we kin." He loaded the trunks on the carriage.

After Amanda, the three children, and Harriet got settled in the carriage with their extra trunks and food, it became obvious that there was only room for one more person. Sadie held her ground defiantly with her arms crossed. "I won't ride beside no murderin' theivin' Yankee, Miss Constance. I ain't never disobeyed ya, but I ain't gonna sit beside that damn Yankee!" she declared, her eyes flashing.

The scene irritated Aaron Ames. He believed that slavery was morally wrong and should be eradicated, plus he was risking his life for these people. Yet this Negress refused to sit beside him. He couldn't explain the paradox. "We have to go ladies," he ordered crisply from the driver's seat.

Constance knew Sadie's stubborn streak. "Captain Ames, there isn't enough room for all of us inside the carriage. Would you allow me to ride beside you?" she inquired politely.

"Certainly Miss Armstrong." She accepted his proffered hand and dropped her sapphire eyes discreetly.

They proceeded towards town, Corporal Williamson riding beside them and the soldiers marching behind the carriage. Other companies of soldiers camped nearby fell in behind them. Neither spoke for a good while, but the closer they got to town the more destruction they observed. Constance vented her feelings about the vandalism. Ames admitted that he was embarrassed by the conduct of the Union Army and feared much worse was yet to come. Constance then related the story of her father's efforts in the peace movement and his later arrest and near drowning. When they entered town they saw soldiers everywhere, but few town residents could be seen. Questioning stares followed the unusual entourage. Captain Ames praised the beauty of the town and commented on the imposing house with twenty-foot columns and a curved stairway, occupying the entire block between Edmondson and Spencer Streets.[i]

"That house was built by former governor and congressman, Extra Billy Smith." Constance adjusted the brim of her hat to keep the intense sun off her face. "He's a close friend and political ally of my father and now serves as a colonel in our army. Have you heard of him?"

Ames thought for a moment. "Yes, I believe I read some of his speeches while he was in Congress. He's an eloquent orator. But tell me, how did he get the nickname 'Extra Billy?'"

"As a young man he obtained the mail contract from Washington to Culpeper. He continually opened up new territory for his stage lines and extended the route to Georgia. Consequently he frequently demanded extra payments from the postal service, and was soon referred to in Congress as 'Extra Billy.' If you'll turn left on Spencer Street," she said pointing, "we can go to the carriage house and stable."

Anxious for news of her father, Constance rushed to the Culpeper Observer building. "Mr. McDonald, where's father?"

"I'm surprised to see you. How did you get to town?"

"I'll tell you all about it later," she said frustrated. "Please, do you know about Father?"

"Yes. He was arrested late Monday night for being a spy. He and the clerk had rescued the courthouse record books from the hands of the destructive Yankees, when

---

[i] The County Office Building (former post office) on Main Street occupies the site of the Smith mansion.

127

a picket discovered him walking home about 2 a.m. He's imprisoned on the second floor of the courthouse. These demonic Yankees even dragged Reverend Cole from Saint Stephen's last Sunday, because he dared pray 'for the welfare of the Southern Confederacy and the success of its arms,'" McDonald concluded in disgust.

"I can't believe the tyranny. There's no freedom of speech," Constance sputtered furiously. "Is Father all right?"

"Yes, but he's suffering from the heat and poor food. No one as noble as your father should be treated so cruelly. But," he added with gleam in his eye, "there's hope. Rumor has it that Jackson's in Gordonsville and we'll soon be liberated."

"I hope he'll drive these devils away. I must go see Father." She ran out the door.

"Father," Constance cried from below the second floor balcony of the courthouse. "Father, it's Connie!"

Her pale, disheveled, sweat-soaked father appeared on the balcony. "Oh Connie, darling," he said weakly. "How did you get here?"

"I'm so glad you're alive!" she cried, tears in her eyes. "We've been frantic over you! Abraham was killed trying to protect our horses from the Yankee soldiers. I managed to hide Liz, and with the help of a gentleman Yankee we all came in the carriage to town."

"I'm sick about Abraham. I begged him not to risk his life. Is everyone else safe?"

"Yes, but how are you faring?"

"It's stifling up here during the day and cool at night. The hard floors are all we have to sleep on and little food. I'm overjoyed to see you, darling," he concluded in a breaking voice .

"Be strong Father. Jackson's coming...he'll save us. You must hang on. I'll get food to you and see what I can do about your release."

"I pray that we're liberated soon. But, please be careful. They arrest citizens for practically no reason."

"I understand. I must go tell Mother and Amanda where you are. I love you." She blew him a kiss.

Aaron Ames's athletic body leaned against the brick building that housed Gorrell's Drug Store, while his men rested on Davis Street before proceeding to the south side of town to make camp. He witnessed the touching scene between father and daughter. Spotting him, Constance crossed Coleman Street to speak to him. "I apologize for rushing off without thanking you properly for your assistance, Captain Ames. I was frantic about my father. As you can see, he's imprisoned in deplorable conditions. He was arrested after rescuing the record books in the courthouse from certain destruction by your army.[ii] He's falsely accused of being a spy."

"I'm glad he's alive, Miss Armstrong, but regret the circumstances."

"Jackson will free us soon. Have you heard of General A. P. Hill?"

"Yes, I'm well aware of his success on the peninsula."

"You're leaning against his boyhood home. I'm sure he realizes that your army has

---

[ii] Fayette Mauzy took the record books to the home of Henry Hitt, a tanner, and they remained safely hidden under the tanbark until the end of the war.

destroyed our county like a swarm of locusts. I suspect he'll accompany Jackson and fight with a bitter vengeance to liberate his home. I pity you, Captain Ames, if you confront the wrath of A. P. Hill on the battlefield. Good day."

The iciness of her stare sent chills down his spine. He, too, realized that a brutal battle would soon take place.

6

The Inferno of Cedar Mountain

August 1 – August 11, 1862

"Rally, brave men, and press forward. Your general will lead you. Jackson will lead you!"

Stonewall Jackson at Cedar Mountain

Eleven days later, August 1, 1862: On the train to Gordonsville

Netty Hill slept in her father's lap while the train rattled westward from Richmond to Gordonsville. Dolly cuddled Russie in one arm. Proud to be sitting by the youngest Major General in the Confederate army, Dolly realized she needed to soothe and calm him. A bit hotheaded at times, Hill had challenged Longstreet to a duel in a fit of anger. The conflict occurred when a Richmond reporter printed exaggerated compliments about Powell's men during the Seven Days Battle. Maxey Sorrel of Longstreet's staff wrote a scathing rebuttal on Longstreet's behalf, which Hill felt insulted the honor of the Light Division. Lee's intervention and Dolly's convincing her high-strung and sensitive husband to vent his wrath against the Yankees averted the confrontation. Lee decided to defuse the tension by sending Hill to reinforce Jackson in Gordonsville.

Hill glanced up from the Richmond newspaper. "It's not hard for me to hate that bombastic miscreant, Pope. Listen to what the paper says: '*If pompous and pretentious proclamations could make a soldier, Julius Caesar would be a baby in the hands of General Pope. The man is simply a compound of vulgar self-conceit, impudence and brutality.*'[1] I'm appalled at the way he's ravaging Culpeper. I can't wait to drive him from my home."

"I pray that Mildred and the children are surviving. She doesn't even know that Baptist is sick in Richmond. When you join Jackson with your twelve thousand men, you'll be successful against Pope." Dolly stroked Russie's hair. "Are you resentful to be under Jackson's command after he failed to support you so many times on the peninsula?"

Hill repositioned Netty, then glanced around the car at his staff and the other soldiers. He leaned close to Dolly and whispered, "My men outshone his at every engagement. For a man who was known for speed of movement in the valley, his slowness around Richmond is incomprehensible. Time after time he failed to appear promptly or to support my men. We were cut to shreds and bore the brunt of the most brutal fighting because of it. I believe his tardiness kept us from annihilating McClellan's army. How can I help but feel resentment?"

"Your feelings are understandable darling, but don't let them interfere with your duty." Dolly placed her hand on his arm. "You and Jackson have to cooperate in order to destroy Pope before Mac reinforces him."

"You're right, as usual," Hill whispered. "Mac's problem is he's too slow. Let's hope that continues while he moves his men by boat. Nobody wants to destroy Pope more than I do. I'll work with Jackson. I only wish he wasn't so danged secretive about everything."

Netty sat up and wiped her eyes. "Are we there yet?"

"Almost, sweetheart." He pulled her nose.

Dolly looked across the aisle at her brother, Richard, Assistant Adjutant General on Powell's staff. "Let me hold her for a while," Richard said. Dolly carefully handed his sleeping niece to him.

"Thanks Richard. It's so good having you here in Virginia." Dolly's thoughts turned to their mother, a widow in Federal occupied Lexington, Kentucky. She had not heard from her in weeks and worried constantly. Besieged in her own home, Union troops camped on her lawn while five of her sons fought for the Confederacy. John Hunt had become the folk hero of the South, referred to as "the Marion of the West" after the Revolutionary War hero. His successful raids had done untold damage to the Yankees occupying Kentucky. She feared the closer he came to Lexington, the more her mother became the focus of bitter wartime hatred. Hostile eyes watched her house to the point that she was afraid to venture outside. The slowing of the train near Gordonsville brought Dolly out of her reverie.

Stonewall Jackson had enjoyed the hour-long religious discussion with the visiting Presbyterian minister in his tent headquarters. "General Jackson," the clergyman said, "I know that you've read the unprecedented orders of General Pope including the atrocities with which he has threatened our citizens. Surely, Pope's a candidate for your immediate attention."

The deeply devout general replied, "Yes, and by God's blessing he shall receive my attention. I'm confident that I can defeat any general who doesn't know his headquarters from his hindquarters."

The cleric laughed and stood up. "I'll pray for your success, general. Now, I must return to the Lord's work."

"Good day, sir. Please come back again when you have time to visit." Jackson, shabbily dressed, stood up to shake hands. He sat down and picked up the letter impeccably courteous Robert E. Lee had sent him, subtly suggesting that he keep Hill and his generals informed of his intentions. Jackson opened the letter, and read: *A. P. Hill you will find I think a good officer with whom you can consult and by advising with your division commanders as to your movements much trouble will be saved you in arranging details as they can act more intelligently.*[2]

Jackson understood Lee's message, but he had learned the necessity of total secrecy at the battle of Kernstown. He would strike Pope when the time was right and the element of surprise would be essential. This operation would be a one-man show in the same manner as the valley campaign. He ignored the obvious difference: he now commanded over 24,000 men, half of Lee's army. With a firm, iron mouth and determination in his eyes, he folded the letter and set it aside.

131

Jackson walked outside in the heat, observing the lush pasturage of the Green Springs area of Louisa County, several miles south of Gordonsville. He had relocated his camp there to take advantage of the forage. He addressed his medical officer, Hunter Holmes McGuire, eating a raw Bermuda onion. "Dr. McGuire, how can you eat anything with so pungent a taste and odor?"

"It dispels the heat and thirst, sir, and helps prevent scurvy. I highly recommend it."

"I'll stick with lemons. By the way, I'm expecting General Hill to arrive later today with his men. Please have him make camp and locate me if I'm not here." General Beverly Robertson, commander of the cavalry, rode up. Jackson strongly disliked Robertson and lacked confidence in his ability. "Where are the enemy?" Jackson asked.

"I really don't know," Robertson responded calmly with a smile.

A scowl came over Jackson's face. He turned away abruptly and mounted his horse. He decided to telegraph Lee and insist on the services of Jeb Stuart. As he rode through the lush green fields, Jackson noticed an enlisted man up in a nearby tree picking peaches. A stickler for discipline, he rode up to him and inquired, "Who is you commanding officer?"

"Sir, I do not know," the small man replied, not recognizing Jackson.

"What is the meaning of this?" Jackson insisted.

"Sir, I was told that old 'Jack' ordered us not to tell anybody anything. I don't know my name, where I'm going, or where I've been. Those are old 'Jack's orders. Don't tell nobody nothing."

Stonewall chuckled and rode off. "Carry on," he called.

Two days later, August 3, 1862: Near the Rappahannock

Frank Stringfellow rode quietly in the darkness along the south side of the Rappahannock River. With no moon, he almost rode over the enemy picket snoring heavily as he leaned against a tree. Dismounting soundlessly, Stringfellow cautiously crept up on the soldier and pressed his gun to the man's temple. It took several pokes of his revolver to nudge the Yank awake. The startled soldier reached for his rifle, forcing Stringfellow to club him over the head.

The picket regained consciousness, rubbed his head, and moaned, "Why'd you have to go and hit me? I wasn't going to do nothing. You just startled me, that's all."[5]

"Just cooperate and you won't get hurt." Stringfellow held his gun to the old soldier's head. "What do you know of General Pope's intentions?"

"The small man said, "I tell you, young fella, I'm too old for this war. I only joined the army to get away from my wife. She's enough to run a man crazy. I'm only a private so General Pope hasn't called me in for a conference lately."

Stringfellow smiled. "You hear rumors. What's going around camp?"

"From what I hear you Johnny Rebs are really in for it. We'll be crossing the Rappahannock in a few days, and there'll be a great battle. Ol' Marse Lee is going to catch it."

"Where's the rest of Pope's army?" Stringfellow pushed the gun tighter against his prisoner's head.

"Don't push that thing so hard. I'm tellin' you all I know. Rumor has it that General Banks is at Little Washington and General Siegel's at Sperryville. That's all I know."

Stringfellow stared at the little man, debating his fate. He couldn't let him go enabling him to sound the alarm and likely trap him and Burke who was upriver. He hated to kill this likable old fellow. The only alternative left was to take him with him and hope they would not cross any Federal cavalry. He tied his prisoner's hands securely and hoisted him up on the back of his horse. Stringfellow climbed into his saddle and the Yank held onto his belt. He rode silently towards his pre-arranged rendezvous spot with Burke near Brandy Station.

Not finding Burke when they arrived, he made the Federal dismount while they waited. Stringfellow pondered the situation. It had been more than two weeks since Stuart had sent him along with Burke and Mosby on independent duty to watch Pope. They had hidden by day and traveled by night. He and Burke had left Mosby near Beaver Dam Station, and he wondered why Mosby had not caught up with them. Stringfellow was unaware that Mosby had been captured and spent the last two weeks in prison. However, several days ago while on a prisoner exchange boat near Fort Monroe, he observed Burnside's troops being shipped from North Carolina to reinforce Pope. At this very moment, Mosby was relaying that information to Lee who would telegraph Jackson and prompt him to act quickly before Burnside's men joined Pope. Stringfellow and Burke had made contact with outlying Confederate pickets, and knew that Hill had joined Jackson, giving him 24,000 men to oppose Pope's dispersed 47,000. The sound of firing from upriver interrupted Stringfellow's thoughts.

A few minutes later, Burke galloped up, clenching his left wrist.

"Hit?" Stringfellow asked alarmed.

"Yep," said Burke, grimacing in pain. "Rode up on a picket before I saw him. Damned good shot, too."

"Ought to catch 'em sleeping like I did mine." Stringfellow nodded towards his prisoner. "Let me see that arm." The wound was a clean one; Stringfellow bound it as well as he could. The two scouts decided that Burke would take the prisoner and report to Jackson. Stringfellow would stay on the Rappahannock to observe any movement of enemy troops.

"Take care of yourself, pal," Burke said before he rode off. "They're comin' over the river soon, sure as shootin'."[4]

Three days later, August 6, 1862: Armstrong town home

Hudson stared at the small bowl of beans before him with a long face while his stomach roared from starvation. With most of the food they brought from the farm gone, the family had to ration the little they had left. They realized grimly that unless Joseph could smuggle food past the Yankees soon, they would starve.

"How can these heartless soldiers take food out of the mouths of women and children?" Harriet asked indignantly. "The world has never known such barbarity."

"There are several sources of hope," Constance replied. "Jackson will liberate us soon, and hopefully food can be brought in from the South. Rumor has it that the Yankees have almost rebuilt the railroad bridge over the Rappahannock. They'll soon be able to ship in supplies. Perhaps then they'll quit stealing from us."

"Humph!" Amanda said. "They'll only dole out food to us if we take the despicable oath of loyalty. What southern woman would sell her birthright for a mess of pottage?"[5]

"Not I," vowed Constance defiantly. "I'd rather starve!"

"We must quit worrying about ourselves while your poor father suffers imprisonment in that hot, crowded hellhole," Harriet said despondently. "Pope's latest edict states that all Rebels suspected of being spies shall be executed and their property confiscated. His life and the possession of our home hang by a thread."

"We must pray that Jackson gets here before that happens." Constance's eyes glimmered with determination. "It's a race against time."

General A. P. Hill's men had been marching northward since early morning. The intense sun beat down on the soldiers unmercifully and dust permeated the air distorting their vision. Some men put leaves under their hats to help keep cool. Many stragglers collapsed along the route, while all rationed the precious water in their canteens. Hill rode at the head of his column when Captain Charles Blackford, an old friend, galloped up beside him. "Where are you going?" Blackford asked.

Suffering from the broiling heat, Hill answered sarcastically, "I suppose we'll go to the hill in front of us. That's all I know."[6]

The secretive Jackson had not told him that he was marching towards Culpeper to destroy a portion of Pope's army before it could be reinforced. The tired men would march until 9 o'clock that night.

Frank Stringfellow watched Rickett's Union infantry division cross the Rappahannock from his well-concealed hideout in the woods. Sick at heart, he knew they were advancing south and his home lay in the path. He didn't know where the two armies would collide, but he realized those fields that he loved so well might soon become a battlefield. He wanted to go to his mother and to warn his friends. But with Burke disabled, the responsibility of keeping the Confederates posted on the advance rested squarely on his shoulders. When it became dark, he must move safely through the Union lines to report to the nearest Confederate pickets.

Two days later, August 8, 1862: Orange Court House

Dawn: Powell Hill stood anxiously at the head of his lead brigade looking down the street for Ewell's Corps. The irritated general and his men had been waiting for almost an hour to begin their march northward from Orange. The preceding day they had endured a grueling march through plantations and by-roads, fighting the dust and heat until almost midnight. The exhausted, hungry soldiers fell along the road to sleep.

During the night, Hill had received orders for today's advance: Ewell would lead, followed by Hill, with Jackson's division under General Charles Winder bringing up the rear. As the sun rose, Hill grew more frustrated that there was no sign of Ewell. He complained to a chaplain, "I tell you, I do not know whether we march north, south, east, or west, or whether we will march at all. General Jackson simply ordered me to have the division ready to move at dawn. I have been ready ever since, and have no further indication of his plans. That is almost all I ever know of his designs."[6]

Shortly thereafter, a Confederate brigade passed down the street in front of him. When a second brigade marched past, Hill noticed the battle flag, which he thought belonged to Winder, not Ewell. Perplexed, he rode forward and questioned the officer in charge. "Yes," the officer replied. "We're with General Winder. We were informed this morning that General Ewell had been sent by an alternate route to the west, and to proceed marching." Furious, Hill wondered why he had not been informed of the change of plans. He rode back to his men and determined that it would be improper to break into Winder's columns. To his surprise, Winder's supply wagons followed his men. Should he barge in and separate Winder's wagons from his infantry? No, he decided, it would be best to let them pass.

Jackson rode up, his face dark with anger. "General Hill, you were ordered to march at dawn. Why do you stand here idle?" he asked abruptly.

Seething, Hill spit out his words. "I was ordered to follow Ewell. My men and I were ready to march an hour before dawn and waited here where we believed Ewell would pass. No one informed me that Ewell would take an alternate route."

Jackson rode off brusquely. He knew from his scouts that Pope's troops remained scattered along the turnpike from Sperryville to Culpeper. He intended to strike today before they could be united. Otherwise, he would lose the element of surprise. The march had not progressed as he hoped. He would take out his wrath on Powell Hill.

Mid-morning: Aaron Ames, accompanied by several of his men, knocked on the door of Mildred Hill. She cautiously cracked the door, and addressed the Yankees, "Yes, what do you want?"

"Madam, we've been ordered to prepare your house for use as a hospital," Ames said while the first train from the north steamed into the depot. "Since a battle is imminent, we need to remove the furniture to make room for the wounded."

Mildred Hill stood speechless. Her beautiful home would be ruined if overrun by wounded men, but it appeared she had no choice. She slowly opened the door, and the soldiers entered and began piling the furniture on the front porch. She had hidden the family silver in a compartment behind the large mirror in the parlor. Fearing it might be discovered, she tiptoed into the parlor after the soldiers had removed the furniture. Since they appeared occupied in the other room, she slid the mirror aside, and removed the bag of silver. Startled by footsteps in the doorway, she spun around and dropped the bag of silver on the floor. Captain Ames stared at her after she quickly moved to cover the bag with her hoop skirt. He suspected the bag contained valuables but would not violate her modesty. Bowing politely, he left. She smiled knowing she was not the first Confederate woman to employ the hoop skirt to conceal or smuggle prized items.

Constance tied her bonnet before she walked out the front door into the oppressive heat. Determined to go see her father even though her mother and Amanda were too afraid to leave the house, she entered the street packed with soldiers. Obviously more had arrived last night. She negotiated her way through the blue uniforms across to the porch of the Virginia House Hotel. The Payne sisters had openly mocked the soldiers and she felt they would be brave enough to accompany her. She noticed a reporter sitting in a rocking chair, making notes. "Sir, I hope you're telling your readers the truth about Pope's treatment of civilians. We're being starved to death."

He looked up at her and smiled. "I have written that even the very dogs are skinny and savage from want of sustenance. The war in Culpeper is being waged in a way that casts mankind two centuries back towards barbarism."[7]

She nodded her approval. "You seem to have grasped the situation."

* * *

The soldiers stepped aside as the three young ladies threaded their way up the street, heads held high. "We're almost completely out of food. I'm sorry I don't have anything to give to Father today. He's crammed up there with barely room to sleep on the floor." The group stepped out in the street to avoid walking under the American flag.

"Our situation's almost as bad," replied Millie Payne. "We have little to offer our guests. I'm sick of listening to those Union soldiers brag about what they're going to do in this upcoming battle. Jackson'll whip them soundly!"

Near the courthouse, they saw a large group of soldiers standing in Davis Street, apparently surrounding many prisoners, escorting them towards the depot. Constance pushed forward for a better view, her heart pumping spastically. She glimpsed two rows of prisoners, their hands tied behind their backs and tied together in a line. She froze rigid with terror at the sight of her father, Reverend Cole, and numerous other civilians and soldiers. They even had Miss Ella Slaughter, a lovely young lady from a fine family, who had drawn a pistol on a soldier who entered her house and grossly insulted her. Gulping air furiously, Constance shoved forward to get closer. "Father!" she shrieked.

Her father turned a hollowed drawn face towards her. "Constance," he answered weakly. His filthy clothes were drenched with sweat, while dark shadows outlined his eyes.

She shuffled alongside the group, frantically trying to reach through the guards to touch him. One of the guards pushed her back rudely. "No!" she screamed in a voice shrill with horror. "You can't do this to him. He's a judge and innocent of all charges!" When the group neared the depot, her mind spun in a frantic frenzy. She could not allow them to put him on that train. "Please," she pleaded. "Tell me who's in charge?"

She rushed towards an officer standing by the freight car, checking off names. "Sir," she begged, tears streaking her face. "My father is seventy-two years old. He's innocent of all charges. I beg you, don't send him away."

"I'm sorry, madam. My orders are to send these prisoners to Washington. We have to make room for the prisoners who'll be taken in battle soon," he said coldly.

Constance shook, then erupted in uncontrollable sobs. When they marched the prisoners to the waiting car, she ran forward again, trying to touch him. "Please," she let out in a strangled cry, "at least let me kiss him good-bye."

"Connie, I love you," her father stammered with tears rolling down his cheeks. "Be strong."

She lunged forward one more time with all her strength, reaching out to touch him before he entered the car. "Father, I love you…I love you!" The guard shoved her back with so much force she almost lost her balance. The two Payne girls rushed forward to steady her, and the door to the boxcar slammed shut. She sobbed violently while the person she loved most in the world disappeared from her view. "I don't think…I'll ever see him again!" She collapsed in the arms of her two friends.

Aaron Ames observed the heart-wrenching scene from the sutler's wagon where he had just purchased cigars. Overcome with compassion, he longed to go to her, to try to comfort her, but he knew she would only see him as the hated enemy.

Noon: The martial music played loudly while Crawford's division marched through the streets of Culpeper Court House with thousands of bayonets glistening in the sun.

The men cheered and raised a loud "Huzzah! Huzzah!" Aaron Ames tingled with excitement but had difficulty cheering. The soldiers marched south to reinforce the cavalry along Cedar Run about six miles south of town near Slaughter's Mountain.

Early afternoon: Dark-haired John Pope, forty, puffed on a cigar and talked confidently to those around him at his headquarters at Douglas Wallach's house. "I believe the reports yesterday of Confederates approaching either Culpeper or Madison may simply be a feint or reconnaissance in force. Since we aren't sure of their destination, I've ordered Crawford's brigade forward from Culpeper, and Rickett's is to move to Colvin's Tavern to watch the road from Madison.[i] I also ordered a signal station be established on top of Thoroughfare Mountain so that we can watch them closely." An attractive man, Pope impressed his listeners with his never-ceasing rhetoric. Wallach, editor of *The Washington Evening Star* and a Union sympathizer, had advised Pope in Washington for the last several weeks on the terrain of Culpeper. He was happy to offer his house as headquarters. David Strother, another renegade Virginia Unionist, had also given advice on topography.

The pounding of hooves suddenly startled the group. The First New Jersey Cavalry came riding pell-mell up to the house and the large-framed general and his staff rushed out to meet them. "Sir, a large Rebel force including an immense number of cannons and artillery have crossed the Rapidan at Barnett's Ford," the commanding officer blurted breathlessly.

Pope's face registered concern. He must rapidly unite his forces in Culpeper. "Send orders to General Banks, about eight miles out on the turnpike from Sperryville, to march here immediately. Then ride on to Sperryville and order General Siegel to do the same," he ordered a staff officer. To another officer, he snapped, "Telegraph General King at Aquia Harbor to march to Culpeper at once."

Early evening: The day's march had been the sorriest performance in Stonewall Jackson's career. He had failed to reach Culpeper in time to give battle and only a small portion of his troops had crossed into the county. With the element of surprise lost, he finally called a halt to the fiasco and ordered his troops to bivouac where they were. Men lay along the route prostrate or dead from heat stroke.

A major bottleneck had occurred when Ewell's troops merged back into the main road to Culpeper at the same time that Winder reached that point. Wagons, artillery, and troops clogged the road, encumbering forward motion. Hill sweltered in Orange most of the day unable to move forward but a few miles. He had ridden forward and seen the bottleneck caused by more that 1200 wagons. Wasn't Jackson known for traveling light? He sent word to Jackson that the trains were delaying the march. Did he really want the trains mixed into the columns? Hill received no reply.

After dark his men settled into camp and Hill rode forward to seek Jackson. He found the general at the head of the column near Crooked Run Church, where he prepared to sleep on a porch. Jackson ignored Hill when he rode up. Determined, Hill dismounted and saluted him. "General Jackson, it will be impossible for my men and artillery to

---

[i]Colvin's Tavern was located in the wooded area across from the T intersection where The White Shop Road joins The Old Orange Road behind Fairview Acres Subdivision.

137

advance tomorrow if the wagon trains still occupy the roads. I'm a native of this area and know the roads and fords well. May I suggest that I take an alternate route by a lesser ford? I will be able to rejoin you wherever and whenever you designate."

Jackson stared at him with icy blue eyes. "General, the wagons have been ordered off the road tomorrow. You will advance as ordered. Good night, sir."

Hill rode back seething. He had endured one of the most frustrating days of his life. The riff between Hill and Jackson would fester until Jackson's death.

Next day, August 9, 1862: Orange Court House

2 a.m. Powell Hill prepared his men to march under the bright full moon. Determined to catch up with the troops ahead of him, he would not be criticized for being late today. The troops north of him had gotten little sleep. Twice during the night gunshots and a threatened Union cavalry raid aroused them.

7 a.m. The temperature had already risen to 84 degrees when Aaron Ames stared at Cedar Mountain (Slaughter's Mountain) from his camp along Cedar Run, four miles north of Jackson at Crooked Run Church. Well concealed in a ravine, he perused the morbid row of ambulances behind the camp. From the firing of the cavalry during the night, he assumed a battle would take place today. The cavalry had bragged last night about destroying a small church at the base of the mountain and ransacking the house of Reverend Slaughter, visible on the side of the mountain. They had even strewn the books from his classical library across the lawn. "We will be punished for our sins," Ames wrote in his journal. A staunch Episcopalian, he read his Bible for the next half-hour. He was not afraid to die but wondered how he would perform in this, his first battle, the supreme test of manhood.

9 a.m. Harriet sat in an upstairs front window, her eyes turned upward, and her arms stretched towards heaven. The blue regiments pouring into Coleman Street glanced up at her with a sense of foreboding while she implored heaven to rain fire and brimstone upon them. A member of Banks's Corps, which had arrived during the night, looked up at her and muttered, "That Rebel lady gives me chills." Scores of bands played simultaneously while officers shouted commands above the din. The Germans, Celts, and Saxons roared their native ballads: *St. Patrick's Day*, *Bonnie Dundee*, *The Star Spangled Banner*, and choruses of German sword-songs. As far as the eye could see, thousands of bayonets glistened like waves in the sun. Suddenly, as if by rehearsal, all hats went up in unison followed by deafening cheers.[8]

Constance, Amanda, and the children stared solemnly out of an adjacent window. Dark circles outlined Constance's eyes. "I spent a fretful night last night. I kept seeing father locked in a cold, clammy prison cell."

"I understand," Amanda said, her face contorted in agony. "Plus the wagons creaked all night long. Did you see the destruction of the garden the Yankees caused when drawing water from our well?"

"Yes, I'm afraid so. They trampled the boxwoods and practically drained the well. We have no food left and Jackson's one day too late to save father," Constance sighed.

Amanda bounced the fussy baby in her arms. "Listen," said Hudson. They all heard the strains of *Dixie* coming from the piano at the Virginia House.

A Slow March to Battle

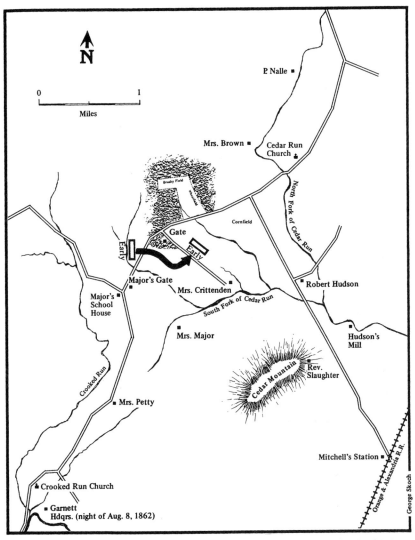

From STONEWALL JACKSON AT CEDAR MOUNTAIN by Robert K. Krick. Copyright 1990 by the University of North Carolina Press. Used by permission of the author and publisher.

The Battlefield and Its Approaches

Amanda smiled slightly. "We must keep the faith. God will deliver us today." Column by column, the blue soldiers marched in front of the courthouse heading towards Cedar Run. Several of the remaining Confederate prisoners jeered from the upstairs balcony. "Just wait until Ol' Jack gets hold of you. You'll be marching back on the double-quick, if you come back at all. That general with the movable headquarters better commence moving!"

Pope sat on the porch of the Wallach house, optimistic and refreshed. "Banks will have his men in position by noon," he said confidently to David Strother and several of his aides around him. "He understands that he's to take a defensive position until Siegel arrives."

"Siegel's ignorance is inexcusable," sneered Strother, a topographer. "I can't believe he wrote you last evening and asked which road to take to Culpeper. There's only one road from Sperryville to Culpeper."

"Damn fool." Pope puffed on his cigar. "I ordered him to march all night to make up for lost time. He doesn't seem to understand the urgency of the situation, but I expect him to arrive shortly."

Jackson's army crawled northward slowly on this sweltering morning. Several cavalrymen rode up and informed Jackson that General Banks, whom Jackson had soundly defeated in the valley, commanded the Union troops in front of him.

Riding forward, Jackson overtook his trusted physician, Hunter McGuire. "Do you expect a battle today?" McGuire inquired.

"Banks is in our front and he is generally willing to fight," Jackson said, drawing his thin lips into a smile, "and he generally gets whipped."[9] Jackson's troops referred to their old adversary affectionately as "Commissary Banks." Once defeated, he could always be depended on to feed them when they were hungriest and to clothe their ragged backs. Jackson nodded back to the elated civilians who waved and cheered the army that would liberate them from Pope's reign of terror.

Noon: Catherine Crittenden stared apprehensively out of her front door at the Union cavalry moving across the rolling fields of corn.[ii] Off in the distance towards town, she saw the great clouds of dust signaling the movement of Bank's troops into position near Cedar Run. "I don't think there's any doubt. A battle will soon take place," she lamented to Annie, standing behind her.

"We've got to try to escape behind the lines." Annie waved to the Union cavalry. Shortly, Chaplain Frederic Denison of Rhode Island approached them.

"Sir," Catherine implored. "I beg you to escort me and my children behind your lines so that we may escape out of harm's way to Culpeper."

"I'm sorry, Madam," he replied pleasantly. "We're too occupied with the Rebel cavalry to assist you. You will fare as well as we do."

They watched him ride off and Annie scowled. "So much for northern chivalry."

[ii]The Crittenden house no longer stands. It was located near the silo, seen at the base of Cedar Mountain, across from the intersection of The Orange Road (Route 15) and General Winder Road (Route 657)

Bald-headed General Dick Ewell coaxed several small children out on the porch at the Petty house and talked "baby talk" to them. A small blonde girl toddled over to him and giggled. Elijah White and his independent cavalry company, the Comanches, loafed under the large shade trees in the yard. Stonewall Jackson rode into the tranquil scene, stirring up a cloud of dust. He nodded to Ewell and spread maps on the porch floor. His blue eyes twinkled as he reached for the little girl, then bounced her on his knee. Children were his weakness, and he longed for one of his own. He pulled a button off his coat and handed it to the child before her mother smiled and took her away. The two generals scrutinized the maps, quickly agreeing on the battle plan. Ewell's troops would lead the way and take position on the edge of Slaughter's Mountain and along the Crittenden lane. Winder would follow and place his men to the left of Ewell to the Crittenden gate and into the adjoining woods. "I suggest we take a brief nap," Jackson said. "It's going to be a long day."

Columbiana Nalle paced nervously in the grand hall of her stately brick mansion, Val Verde. She had seen and heard the Union troops marching out to Cedar Run when they passed along the east side of her plantation. "Children," she said. "I want every one of you to stay close to the house." They listened to the sound of skirmishing off in the distance. "Anything could happen today. I'm afraid a great battle may take place."

William Nalle, thirteen, slipped out the back door and found his servant, Fayette, lounging under a locust tree. "I'm not afraid to go watch the battle," he bragged. "Are you a chicken, Fayette?"

"No, Marse William. Ya know I ain't scared of nothin'. I'm kinda curious to see how these white folk make war."

His sense of adventure overwhelming his common sense, Will said, "Let's go!"

1 p.m. Brigadier General Jubal Early of Franklin County, Virginia halted his troops at the Major Schoolhouse near the Y intersection of the Culpeper and Madison Roads. A West Point graduate, the irascible lawyer had strongly opposed secession until the very end. However, when the decision was made, he cast his lot with Virginia and was now only partially recovered from a wound received at Williamsburg. A rising star, he would fight his men valiantly today. He wiped the sweat and intolerable dust from his face as Sandie Pendleton of Jackson's staff rode up. "General Jackson sends his compliments to General Early, and says that he must advance on the enemy, and he will be supported by General Winder."[10] Pendleton stated.

In deep earnestness, Early drawled, "Tell him I will do it."

Glancing at the column of dust behind him signaling Winder's approach, Early rode forward with General Robertson of the cavalry to scout the area of the impending battle. He observed the enemy cavalry in a skirmish formation in the fields of Mrs. Crittenden's farm. Fortunately, he discovered a route enabling him to move his men to the right, concealed by woods, and burst out onto the Crittenden lane to attack the exposed flank of the Federal cavalry.

After returning to the schoolhouse, Early immediately put his troops into motion. Without hesitation, he designated the stalwart Thirteenth Virginia to lead the assault. This original regiment trained by A. P. Hill and containing the Culpeper Minutemen and many local soldiers never failed. "Colonel Walker," he called to their commander.

"Your unit is to lead the way as skirmishers. I feel secure with you in the lead." A rousing cheer went up from the men.

"General Early, my men consider this our personal battle. We would be honored to lead the attack against that scoundrel Pope!" Walker replied excitedly. With a broad grin on his face, he motioned his men forward.

3 p.m. Catherine and Annie Crittenden huddled together in a corner while the house shook from the artillery fire. The younger children and several slaves had taken refuge in the cellar. Pictures crashed to the floor and china shattered. "We're trapped in the middle," Catherine moaned.

Annie rose up enough to peek out of a side window.

"Our troops have moved up along the lane and are putting cannons in place under the cedars," she reported nervously. The house shook when enemy artillery plowed into the yard around them. The two women clung together tightly. "We've got to stay here to tend the wounded," Annie said quietly.

"Oh, my God, we're doomed," Catherine cried in agony. "How can we survive?"

"Trust in God, Mother. We will survive. I wonder if Charles is out there?"

Captain Charles Crittenden dove behind the rise of ground along his lane. No sooner had the Thirteenth Virginia fired on the Federal cavalry and come out into the open, than the enemy artillery opened fire on them. He heard the whiz and shriek of shells passing overhead. A projectile plowed up the ground in front of him, while several hundred yards to his right, he contemplated his home. He prayed that his mother and Annie had escaped. He heard the Rebel artillery in front of him returning fire and shortly thereafter Confederate guns fired north of the cedars and on the other side of him at the gate. The first two hours of this battle would be an artillery duel.

The remainder of Ewell's Corps pushed upward along the shoulder of Slaughter's Mountain, hidden in the woods. Ewell had ridden forward to the open farm of Reverend Slaughter and recognized it to be the ideal location for artillery. He sent Trimble's infantry ahead to secure the position and remain hidden in the woods. Riding up to Elijah White's independent cavalry, he said, "Gentlemen, we must drag the artillery up the mountain to a commanding position. There are no roads for horse teams."

White stared back at him in the sweltering 98-degree temperature. "Sir, are you telling us to dismount and bodily drag those guns up that mountain in this heat?"

"Yes and we must do it promptly. We'll be able to rake the whole enemy line with those guns. I'll have the Georgia Infantry help you," Ewell ordered abruptly.

Shaking his head, White dismounted and walked towards the guns. "You heard him boys. Let's get ropes around these guns and start dragging." With immense effort and unbelievable strain the determined Rebels slowly dragged the guns up the mountain. Several Georgians passed out from sunstroke along the way. Captain Joseph White Latimer, commander of the guns, hastily rode ahead to start calculating distances and cutting fuses. Latimer, eighteen and a brilliant artillerist, gazed at the vista before him. He observed a cannoneer's dream and perhaps the best position occupied during the war. Before him lay the entire valley battlefield, with the Union line to his right and the

Confederates to his left. Because of the commanding height, he should be able to do heavy damage to the enemy on any part of the field.

Under Ewell's personal supervision the exhausted draymen moved the guns onto Slaughter's front lawn. In doing so they crunched over at least a thousand books thrown there by Yankee vandals. One Georgia officer shook his head in disgust. "Damn northern iconoclasts. Whenever the barbarians see a library they systematically destroy it."

"Let's send some of these shells we captured from General Banks back to him," the smooth-faced Latimer said with a grin. When Latimer's guns belched smoke and threw shells from the side of the mountain, the Federals far below looked up shocked by their enemy's superior position.

4 p.m. Powell Hill pushed forward through the suffocating red dust and heat towards the cannonading several miles in front of him. He couldn't believe it. It sounded like Jackson had commenced the battle with only half of his men on the field. Stragglers and those suffering from heat prostration lined the road. Hill had no idea of the battle plan, but he moved his men forward as quickly as possible.

Aaron Ames hugged the ground while a shell whizzed overhead. From his position in a ravine with the Tenth Maine, he felt relatively protected. His tongue stuck to the roof of his mouth in the heat. He debated and finally took a drop of precious water from his canteen. He observed smoke belching from the side of the mountain. Why had his generals allowed the Rebs to get their artillery in such a dangerous position? The Yankees had been there all day and could have taken the high ground. From his position on the far right of the Union line with Crawford's Division, all he saw in front of him was woods. Men pinned their names on their coats and several brigades formed up for a charge.

William Nalle and Fayette had watched the battle from a position on the edge of the woods between the two lines, slightly forward of the Tenth Maine. Suddenly, they spied Union soldiers advancing in the woods. Latimer focused his cannons in that direction and a shell fell near the two boys, spewing dirt over them. "C'mon Fayette, let's get outta here!" William yelled, then dashed away. Fayette attempted to follow but tripped on a tree root and fell. Another shell struck only inches away covering him with dirt. The frantic black boy felt his legs to see if they were still there, then jumped up and ran.

William flew out of the woods into an open field on the other side. He paused and looked back to see Fayette dashing after him, eyes big as saucers. "Marse William," he gasped, "Ya almost lost yo'self a good nigger that time! I done seen enuff of this war." The two boys broke all speed records as they fled home safely.

General Charles Winder of Maryland had left his sickbed against the advice of his physician to take command in this fierce battle. He directed his artillery near the Crittenden gate. Shells screeched overhead, knocking down trees. The enemy heavily bombarded this bottleneck where the Culpeper road came out of the woods. He worked to position his troops on the left of the gate in the woods and to the right along the lane to connect with the Thirteenth Virginia.

General Pope puffed on his cigar on the porch of the Wallach house, directing the battle through dispatches. He looked at the immense wagon trains surrounding him. That idiot Siegel had finally begun to arrive, but his troops had no rations. They would have to be fed before he could order them into battle. He paused to listen to cannonading, growing hotter and heavier. "Sounds like something may be going wrong," he said to General McDowell and David Strother. Deciding to finally put his "headquarters in the saddle" he stood and said, "Mount up. Let's go assess the situation. McDowell, move your reserves forward to reinforce Banks."

4:30 p.m. Winder, still directing his artillery, leaned forward to shout a command to one of his gunners. A shrieking Federal shell struck between his left side and arm, mangling him severely. His horrified men watched him fall straight backwards on the ground where he lay quivering, a bloody gaping gash in his chest. Several of his men gently laid him on a stretcher and carried him back to the schoolhouse, knowing the wound was fatal. William B. Taliaferro assumed command, although he remained totally ignorant of Jackson's plan of battle.

5:30 p.m. General Nathaniel Banks, a Massachusetts politician with no military training, wanted desperately to retaliate against Jackson. He decided now was the time to attack. At the moment of decision, he had 9000 men on the field opposed by Jackson's 12,000. He did not know how many men would arrive with A. P. Hill, but intended to assault Jackson's left in the woods across the wheat field with a charge by Crawford's division. Crawford's men moved through the woods to get into position. At the same time he would have Auger's men advance across the cornfield towards the Crittenden lane.

Jubal Early thought he detected bayonets glistening in the woods across the wheatfield. He sent a message to Winder to prepare for an assault on his left, unaware that Winder had just been killed.

5:45 p.m. Ewell and Latimer saw them coming from their vantage point on the mountain. A wave of blue rushed forward through the cornfield in front of the Crittenden Lane. Latimer directed his fire towards them, causing severe damage but not stopping the charge. The brave Federals ran forward rapidly, concealed in the corn, suffering from the merciless heat in this hottest battle of the war. Smoke covered the Confederate line when Early's and Taliaferro's men fired at the advancing blue troops in the cornfield. The intense cracking of the muskets drowned out the sound of artillery fire. In just the nick of time, Thomas's Brigade under A. P. Hill's command arrived on the field and secured Early's right. Jackson approached the Georgians, hat in hand, so they would recognize him. A loud cheer went up and he personally guided them into position. The Yankees emerged from the corn and friend and foe confronted each other in an open field. The musketry raged with terrifying fury, followed by the sickening thuds of bullets hitting flesh.

6:00 p.m. The cornfield boiled, then Latimer saw the blue coats rush forward from the woods into the wheat field on the Confederate far left. He turned his projectiles in that direction, hoping to slow the 1500 enemy soldiers. Many fell, but the assault

Confused Preparations in the Woods

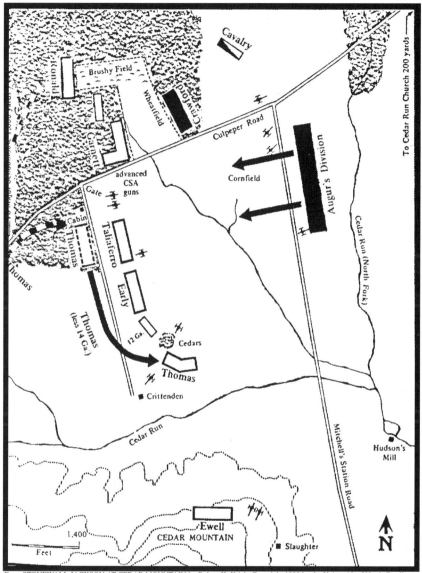

Thomas Arrives, Augur Begins to Move, 5:30-5:45

proceeded forward furiously across the field until the stubbornly brave Federals entered the opposite woods and began a fierce hand-to-hand fight with the Rebels. In the thick forest, men jabbed with bayonets and clubbed with gun butts with intensity never seen before. The Rebels gave way, then many broke and fled to the rear.

Banks watched through his binoculars. A wave of blue rushed from the woods and attacked Taliaferro's men at the Crittenden gate. The Rebel line reeled back from the vicious assault. Elated, Banks smelled victory. Finally, he had the mighty Stonewall where he wanted him!

6:15 p.m. Powell Hill, in his sweat-soaked red battle shirt, stood in the Culpeper road several hundred yards behind the gate. He had deployed Branch's men to assist Early and now frantically tried to move his men into battle while they marched up the road. In an effort to halt the flow of retreating infantry from the woods, the fiery redhead drew his sword and stormed into the retreating stampede. "Soldiers, I order you to hold your ground. Regroup and return to the front. Reinforcements are here!"

He took his wrath out on a lieutenant he spotted heading the wrong way. "Who are you, sir, and where are you going?"

The shaken lieutenant replied, "I'm going back with my wounded friend."

His blood boiling, Hill ripped the insignia from his collar. "You are a pretty fellow to hold a commission—deserting your colors in the presence of the enemy, and going to the rear with a man who is scarcely badly enough wounded to go himself. I reduce you to the rank, sir, and if you do not go to the front and do your duty, I'll have you shot as soon as I can spare a file of men for the purpose."[11]

Jackson, who for once held the numerical superiority in battle, flirted with disaster. His left shattered, the Yanks rolled up his line towards the center. He dashed up to Hill. "General, you're behind time. Deploy your men to the front immediately."

Hill, who had been doing just that, controlled his temper and replied in a civil tone, "Yes sir, at once." He ran back to the servant holding his horse, vaulted into the saddle, and sped towards the men further down the road. He would send these men, marching since 2 a.m., on the double-quick through the woods to the wheat field.

Jackson rode over to Branch, who was giving his men a rousing speech before moving forward, and stared him coldly in the eye. "Push forward, general, push forward," he ordered. Branch moved his men forward at once, ignoring the fact that they were not fully formed into line.

Jackson galloped back to the critical area of melee around the gate,[III] determined to turn the tide of the battle. Tree branches and bark fell thickly from the pounding enemy artillery when he dashed into the thickest fire he had ever faced personally. His adrenaline pumping, Jackson attempted to draw his sword, only to discover the darned thing was rusted in its scabbard. Unperturbed, he unsnapped it and waved scabbard and all over his head to attract the attention of his panic-stricken, fleeing troops.[IV] He dropped his reins and grabbed a Confederate battle flag with the other hand. Waving both, he yelled to his men above the din and smoke, "Rally, brave men, and press forward. Your general will lead you, Jackson will lead you!"[12]

[III]The Crittenden gate was located where the fenced monument now stands on Gen. Winder Road, Route 657
[IV]The Battle of Cedar Mountain is the only time Stonewall Jackson drew his sword.

Retreating men stopped and stared. Could this dynamic warrior be the usually slouching, dour Jackson? They called him "Old Blue Light" because of the fierce light flashing from his eyes in battle. Jackson's eyes never blazed more fiercely than at Cedar Mountain. His face lit with inspiration, Jackson called, "Remember Winder! Forward men, forward. Follow Jackson!"

In the swirling chaos, men cheered, loaded their guns and formed a line. Who could defy the mighty Stonewall? A Union prisoner being carried to the rear became caught up in the excitement and drama of the moment. When he discovered that the magnetic general was Jackson, he waved his broken sword over his head and cried, "Hurrah for General Jackson! Follow your general, boys!"[13]

Seeing that order was restored, Taliaferro rode up to Jackson, and shouted, "General, I insist that you retire. This is no place for the commander of the army."

Somewhat surprised, Jackson seemed to think his argument logical, and replied "Good, good," as he rode to the rear. Relieved, Taliaferro felt Jackson's escape from death was nothing short of miraculous. Jackson's heroic performance had changed the emotional tide of battle, but A. P. Hill's reinforcements would carry the day.

6:30 p.m. James Walker's stalwart Thirteenth Virginia held it's ground with grim determination. The combined assault of Crawford's men coming out of the woods and Auger's men advancing across the corn field shattered the lines to the left, and some men on the right began falling back. The Thirteenth now became caught in the crossfire from three directions. "Hold firm, Virginians!" Walker shouted to his men. Charles Crittenden heard the sickening plunk, plunk, of bullets felling his comrades around him. This small band of men, clearly outnumbered, held its ground against all odds. The one piece of artillery that they protected poured deadly fire into the advancing Federals. Their heroic stand saved the Confederate right from total collapse and possible destruction. These hometown boys, fighting on their own soil, became unquestionably the heroes of the day.

Aaron Ames felt relief at being out of range of the Confederate artillery. The Tenth Maine moved through the woods to the edge of the wheat field. They had been left behind to guard Union artillery while the rest of Crawford's brigade surged across the field. In that open position, artillery fire had reined upon them with a vengeance. Now, after delay and confusion in orders, they prepared to advance alone. Disgusted with the delay, Ames shouted, "We will go forward if anybody will lead us!"

Major Louis Pelouze of Bank's staff, responded, "I will lead you forward!" They emerged from the woods to hear their comrades fighting in the Confederate woods, but saw nothing. They moved quickly down a gentle slope and then up to the rise in the middle of the field. There had been little opposition, but after they moved down from the rise to the stream below, Ames spotted remnants of their brigade retreating towards the woods. Their charge must be too late, Ames decided. "Give them three down-east cheers!" a soldier shouted. After the nasal New England yells rang out, their retreating comrades called back; "There's too many Rebels in the woods to handle." Looking ahead Ames spied numerous gray soldiers inside the tree line; Branch's reinforcements were in place.

Colonel Beal used common sense and ordered his men to "about face" and return to the friendly woods. When they crested the midfield ridge, Pelouze approached and ordered them to halt. Beal and Pelouze engaged in a violent argument with much gesticulation of fists. Beal grudgingly and unwillingly ordered his regiment into line to fire on the Confederates in the woods.

Ames cursed the insanity of the order but loaded his rifle. He watched the Rebels crouching behind the fence at the edge of the woods, while his regiment remained exposed and unprotected in the middle of the field. The Tenth Maine loosened a mighty volley and smoke covered the line. The enemy returned fire with deadly accuracy. He heard bullets whistle by while comrades tumbled in the line. The setting sun blinded the New Englanders as shadows lengthened along the woods. Ames dropped to his knees and fired again. All bedlam broke loose. Fire soon opened on them from the north end of the wheat field as well, and Latimer got the blue line in his sights. Bullets knocked men over with a sudden shudder or jerk. Ames watched some throw up their arms and fall backwards while others reeled around and around. He attempted to reload when he heard the thud and felt a sharp pain in his left arm. Flinching, he raised his gun and fired towards the woods. Suddenly, a shell exploded behind him, and he lurched forward with a violent pain in his buttocks. When he tumbled to the ground with great force, his right arm became entangled with his rifle. He felt it snap with the impact of the hard earth as the adjacent soldier collapsed on top of him simultaneously. Riddled with pain, he felt several more comrades fall into the mound of wounded above him. Lying on his stomach, he managed to move his head and observe the activity on each side of him. He heard bullets plunking into the bodies above him and realized his smitten comrades saved him from certain death in the crossfire. He soon heard Beal order the remnants of his brigade to fall back. Their useless stand had cost forty percent casualties.[V]

6:45 p.m. Ames heard the thundering hooves of the First Pennsylvania Cavalry courageously making a last-ditch charge to save the retreat of Union artillery. He saw them ride in from his left, circle in front of him, and retreat from his right. Vicious fire from every direction picked them off. By this time the Thirteenth and Thirty-first Virginia and Fourteenth Georgia had advanced to the south end of the wheat field surrounding the cavalry. Horses and men fell in droves.

7 p.m. The tide of the battle turned as A. P. Hill's well-trained massive reinforcements sprang into action. Seizing the moment, Hill ordered his troops to advance. Ames saw thousands of Rebels pour out of the woods and surge across the field. He heard musket fire coming from the woods behind him as Confederates tumbled. His brigade must be making a defensive stand in the woods. Although more bodies littered the bloody wheat field, the determined Rebels surged forward again after a brief pause. He watched a general in a black slouch hat and red shirt wave his sword. "Forward, men!" the Reb shouted. "Revenge to Pope!" The Rebels let out their piercing yell and Ames knew the day was lost. Who was that general, he wondered? It didn't look like Jackson. Was it Hill?

[V] A monument to the gallant stand of the 10th Maine is visible from Route 15.

Pope watched the retreating and wounded Federals stream by him. He escorted Rickett's division from Colvin's Tavern to reinforce Banks, obviously too late. Darkness set in and the rout continued in full force. A soldier running by called, "Give 'em hell boys, we got 'em started."

Frank Stringfellow had been observing the battle from a concealed position in the woods behind Union lines. Exhausted and weak from hunger, he had lived off of berries and forage for the last several days. He saw the Federal troops retreating towards him at an alarmingly rapid rate. Lord, they were coming fast! Jumping to his feet, he realized from the approaching noise that they would overrun his position in a few moments. Gasping for breath, he knocked away twigs and tree limbs in a dash for his horse. He bounded onto his mount and sped away praying the dusky shadows would camouflage him.

8:00 p.m., Armstrong back yard: Gnawing hunger and a throbbing head motivated Constance to walk outside towards the kitchen. Surely, there must be some food that Sadie had overlooked. Startled, she spied a Union soldier standing by the well. He informed her that he had been ordered to secure the water for wounded Union soldiers. Livid, she said nothing but wondered what they were supposed to do. She listened to the rapid exchange of musket fire and stumbled forward, worrying about Frank, John, Robert, and Alex. Were they alive? Were they out there famished for food and water, fighting for her deliverance? She boiled with bitter hatred at this army that had taken her precious father away from her.

"How hard-hearted these despicable creatures are!" she erupted to Sadie when she entered the kitchen.

"I agree with ya," Sadie said with fire in her eyes, looking up from her loom. "They've taken the two people we love most 'way from us."

Constance looked at Sadie forlornly, her eyes moist. "How tragic that we have that in common. I believe Father's too weak and old to survive long in prison. Poor Abraham never had a chance." The two women sat quietly for a minute, seeking comfort from the other's presence. So close, they could often read each other's minds; each felt the other's pain. Constance walked over to the cook stove and lit a candle. "Are you sure there's nothing else here to eat? I'm famished."

"I can't find nothin', but ya take a look," Sadie said, walking towards the recessed pantry area near the back door. Constance held the candle up to the empty shelves. Then she got down on her hands and knees and peered under the lowest shelf. Empty handed, she stood up and shook her head dejected. "If that Stonewall Jackson don't git here soon, we's all gonna be starved to death," Sadie said.

The two spun around when the door opened. "Joseph!" Sadie ran over and kissed her son.

"Are ya all right, Momma?" he asked hugging and kissing her.

"We's practically starved to death. Did ya bring us some food?"

"I sure did. I knew you'd need it. I heard all that shootin' goin' on an' thought they might be fightin' on the other side of town. I waited 'til dark to sneak into town so the Yankees wouldn't steal what I brung ya," Joseph said proudly.

"Thank God, Joseph!" Constance cried. "You're the answer to our prayers. There's a

Union soldier guarding the well. I suppose we'll have to unload everything in the stable, and then figure out where to hide it. Maybe I can sneak some food in under my hoop skirt."

"That sounds like a good idea. I wanna git back to the farm 'fore all those soldiers show up," Joseph said. "I've got lots to tell y'all." He sat down at the table and pulled two plums from his pocket. Sadie and Constance greedily consumed the fruit. "Several days ago, thousands of those blue soldiers came through the farm. They slaughtered mosta the livestock an' then left half of it out in the fields to rot. A few of the chickens got away so I brung some eggs. They destroyed the garden an' cut the crops down with their sabers. I ain't seen nothin' like it. And then, jist for meanness, they threw some of the dinin' room chairs outside an' broke 'em to pieces for their campfires."

Constance slammed her fist on the table. "Those were antiques! Mother will be heart-broken!"

Joseph continued, "I went up in the attic after they left, an' got out five hams to bring ya'll. I also loaded half of the flour an' cornmeal, hidden in the woods, plus some potatoes, onions, beans, an' sugar. I hid it all under the hay in the wagon an' used the mule to git heah. That dead Yankee's horse is still tied in our woods. I was 'fraid to bring any more, in case the Yankees captured me."

"Joseph, you're a life saver. We appreciate your loyalty, but don't risk your life," Constance said. "Now, let's unload the wagon so you can return to the farm."

8:30 p.m. The rising full moon cast an eerie light over the chaotic battlefield. The Rebels had rolled the Union line back over a mile, but the assault sputtered in the darkness and confusion. It was difficult to tell friend from foe and even generals became disoriented. Jubal Early cursed thunderbolts. He couldn't locate the gallant Thirteenth Virginia and suspected they had retreated to the rear. Spotting Colonel Walker in the moonlight, he galloped up and rudely inquired, "Where in the hell is the Thirteenth?"

Exhausted, Walker spun around, astounded at the question and obvious insinuation of Early's anger. This was too much for a sane man to handle, after the heroic performance of his men. "General Early, damn it! If you want to find the Thirteenth, go closer to the enemy. It's a mile in front, holding on for you to come up. The Thirteenth don't stay with the wagontrain!"[14]

Jackson and Hill sat on horseback at the intersection of the Culpeper and Mitchell's Roads. "General Hill, I want to use our advantage and push on to Culpeper Court House," Jackson said. "Owing to the darkness of the night it will be necessary to move cautiously."

"I suggest that we seek Captain Charles Crittenden of the Thirteenth Virginia to guide us. We have fought on his land," Hill replied. "Should I order forward my unused troops under Field and Stafford?"

"Yes, to both questions." Jackson chewed on a wild onion. "Move your artillery across Cedar Run and commence shelling the woods in front of us. The cavalry are coming up soon; I'll order them forward for reconnaissance."

Frank Stringfellow observed thousands of bayonets gleaming in the moonlight while reinforcements filed in behind the enemy's line. It looked like at least a corps from his

150

hiding place, but he had to confirm his suspicions. He crouched behind a bush and waited until a straggler approached him. Quietly, he crept forward, hooked his left arm under the soldier's neck and held a pistol to his temple. "Be quiet, Yank, and you won't get hurt." The frightened soldier complied as Stringfellow dragged him behind the bush. "Whose corps are you with?"

"Siegel's," the boy answered. This confirmed Stringfellow's suspicion. Pope had finally united his army and now outnumbered Jackson.

"I'm sorry to have to do this, young fella," Stringfellow said, then knocked him unconscious with his revolver. He crept silently through the woods to his horse and rode carefully through the Federal camps. When challenged to identify his command, he replied "Pennsylvania Bucktails," and rode on as if he belonged, expecting a bullet to hit him in the back at any time. It took self-control not to spur his horse and make a dash for it. Keeping a cool head, the scout soon reported his vital information to a fellow scout named Farrow.[15]

9:00 p.m. General Pope and his staff lounged on the grass watching new troops file by. Discovering the general, they let out a loud cheer, attracting the attention of the Rebels. A shell screamed over their heads and burst just beyond the high command. The shelling increased and Pope unceremoniously scampered to a safer location. The generals sat on the ground, holding their horse's bridles while the fiery missiles screeched overhead. After about thirty minutes the shelling ceased. "I think they've had their fun for the night," Pope said cheerfully.

Suddenly, Confederate cavalry burst from the woods and spurred towards them. The horsemen came on yelling and pouring a continuous carbine and pistol volley into the Federals. Without dignity, the officers scrambled onto their horses. Bullets hissed through trees and sent sparks flying from rocks. Banks fell in the chaos, struck by the hoof of the horse of a wounded orderly. His hip badly hurt, he finally managed to mount his horse. Pope immediately stuck his head down and, striking spur, led off at full speed, showing no hesitation in "turning his back to the enemy." The balls struck around David Strother so rapidly that he feared it was impossible for anyone to escape. A staff officer beside him fell. Apparently the Confederates were shooting too high. "Grumble" Jones and his Seventh Virginia cavalry did not realize their quarry was the infamous Pope. They would never have let such a prized prisoner escape.

When the northern staff officers sped away a friendly regiment mistakenly opened fire on them, killing several horses. They escaped severe damage because they fled through a hollow. Strother swerved to the left to avoid the U.S. troops while several others plowed into a split rail fence five rails high. Thinking horses and men killed, Strother rode over to discover a cursing knot of men and horses attempting to right themselves. The only loss was a broken sword.

The group rode forward for two hundred yards to get out of fire range and stopped to count noses. "General Pope and Major Meline are missing," said Banks.

"Meline is afoot and may have been captured," Strother said. "I'm uneasy about the general." A shell burst nearby, causing the officers to flee further to the rear. Strother thought for a while that Pope was killed or captured and the game was up. However, after a couple of hours he located Pope, Banks, McDowell, and Siegel sitting on a pile of fence rails under a tree.[16]

* * *

151

11 p.m. Prisoners captured by Jones's cavalry confirmed the information Jackson had received from Stringfellow. Siegel had indeed arrived, giving Pope numerical superiority. Deciding it would be imprudent to press the attack, Jackson ordered his men to bivouac where they were. This day in hell, which would go down in history as the Battle of Cedar Mountain, finally drew to a close.[VI]

The exhausted survivors fell into Cedar Run and its tributaries and lapped the life-sustaining water. The fact that the stream ran red with blood did not deter them. Either they didn't care or couldn't see the color in the moonlight. Most quickly dropped to the ground and fell asleep. Utterly exhausted, Jackson rode up to his headquarters where one of his officers offered him food. "No, I want rest, nothing but rest!"[17] The officer spread a cloth on the ground under a tree. Without ceremony, Jackson rolled up in it and fell instantly asleep.

Powell Hill marched his men from the front several miles back to the bloody battle-field to bivouac. Sleep did not come as quickly for Hill. He looked up at the stars and reflected with pride on the performance of his men. His cheering brigades had mounted a fierce charge, dealing the Federals a knock-out blow in short order. The scrappy Light Division not only enhanced its reputation, but was well on its way to becoming the best fighting machine in the Confederate Army. Yet, despite near disaster and poor communication, Jackson would get the glory. Hill rolled over and closed his eyes knowing, he had done his best and that his men had clinched the battle. In reality, the hometown boy had saved the day.

Aaron Ames moaned from excruciating pain and the weight of the dead bodies pushing down on him. He listened to the groans and imploring cries for water of the other 2500 wounded and maimed on the battlefield. Almost every inch of the wheat field was covered with human flesh. The various liquids draining down from those lying above him…blood, excrement, sweat, and vomit, drenched him.[VI] He heard a few Confederates succoring their friends. Others scavenged through the bodies taking money, clothes, boots, food and anything useful. "Water," he begged. His parched throat made swallowing painful. He felt himself weakening from loss of blood; life seemed to be draining from him. He had to hang on. He thought of his parents, his five older brothers and one sister, and longed to see them again. Visions of the many lovely ladies he had courted while at Harvard passed before him. They all seemed the same, so compliant, eager to please. He felt himself slowly slipping away. Through the haze he glimpsed the vision of a beautiful dark-haired young lady sobbing at the train station. He wanted to reach out to her, to comfort her. He concentrated, trying to focus on her face. He could see her enormous blue eyes, long dark lashes, delicate mouth, lily-white skin. Suddenly the realization became clear to him; he wanted to live to see that face again. If he could just focus on that face, perhaps he could hang on.

Next day, August 10, 1862: The Crittendens'

Dawn: As the first gray rays of dawn radiated across the sky, Catherine Crittenden

---

[VI] Total losses of dead, wounded, and missing were: 1418 Confederate, 2403 Union picked her way through the wounded soldiers moaning on the floors of her house. She stared at the walls, riddled with bullet holes. An unexploded shell lay in the parlor while another that had crashed through the roof, lodged in her poster bed upstairs. A soldier screamed out in agony while several others held him down. The sound of Dr. McGuire's saw grinding through his arm bone sickened her. Sweat rolled off the forehead of the doctor, who had worked frantically all night. She stared at the pallid exhausted face of Annie, gallant Annie, assisting him. She was the only one who had bravely ventured out of the cellar during the battle to aid the wounded soldiers who flooded into the house. Catherine's foot slipped on the slick blood-soaked floor. Regaining her balance, she pushed forward to get outside for fresh air. Somehow, she must escape this ghastly night of horrors.

After she stepped off the front step, the freshly dug grave of a Confederate Lieutenant confronted her. The pale dawn light revealed furrows, fresh dirt; her yard had been completely plowed by shells. The corn in the field lay flat on the ground, cut to shreds by the muskets. The scene before her, the most macabre ever witnessed in Culpeper County, exposed bodies, living and dead, littering the ground in every direction. The stench of death penetrated her nostrils as she surveyed the pile of dead horses and men blocking her lane. Scalding tears streamed down her face. She could never blot this horrendous vision from her mind. How could she continue to live here? A crack of gunfire made her jump. "Oh, God no!" she prayed. "Don't let it all start again!"

A soldier walked towards her in the mist. Something about him looked familiar, but she could not see the features of his dust-crusted face. "Momma? Are you all right?" he asked softly, then reached his arms out to her.

"Charles! Oh, my God, you're alive!" She collapsed in his arms. "By a great miracle of Almighty God, we have all survived!"

"It's over now." He stroked her hair. "I fought right out here in the lane most of the day. Surely, you and Annie didn't stay in the house?"

"Yes," she sobbed while he rocked her gently. "We were here through every…single… hellacious… minute."

Mid-morning: The shelling and skirmishing came to an end. Neither side had the energy to attack as the merciless sun rose in the sky. Instead, they licked their wounds. Columbiana Nalle fought fatigue and tore bandages. Her house of refinement had been turned into a butcher's block. The rich carpets lay bundled in the corners while bloody blankets and sheets covered the floors. The furniture not removed was spattered with blood. She watched the Union surgeon work at the amputating table next to the piano, his tools strewn on the mantle. "The air's becoming so close in here I believe it would be best if we moved outside," he said to his assistants.

Shortly, the soldiers set up the amputation table in the shade of the large locust trees in the front yard. The wounded lay on blood-soaked stretchers, flies swarming over them and on their festering wounds. William Nalle and his young friends watched the horrid scene from an upstairs window. The pile of amputated limbs eventually reached to the top of the table. The glamour of war had disappeared for the children, who now gaped at brutal reality. John Pope, who made Val Verde his headquarters, sat on a crate under an apple tree with McDowell and Strother. "It's blood, carnage, and death among the sweet shrubbery and roses," Strother observed.

They watched a squad of soldiers carry a dead man on a litter, others following with picks and spades. "Well, there seems to be devilish little that is attractive about the life of a private soldier," Pope remarked without feeling.

"You might say, General, very little that is attractive in any grade of a soldier's life," McDowell answered.[18]

The majority of the Federal wounded lay unattended on the Confederate controlled battlefield. Aaron Ames felt the merciless sun blistering his face and heard a distant voice say, "Look at this beauty of a gray stallion I found for you, General Hill." He slowly focused his eyes to see the man in the red shirt stroking the nose of a horse.

Struggling to make sound come from his parched throat, Ames softly moaned, "Water, please, water." Hill looked for the source of the voice and realized that the man on the bottom of the pile was alive. He removed the canteen of one of the dead Yankees and knelt beside Ames, tilting the wounded man's head and putting the canteen in his mouth. Ames gulped greedily. "Slow down, Yank. Take a little at a time. Lieutenant Morgan, remove these bodies and get this man in the shade with a supply of water," Hill ordered. Looking at the horse he said, "I think I'll name that beauty Prince."

Ames wrenched with pain as the ragged Rebels laid him in the woods and built a canopy of Poplar leaves over him for shade. "Sorry, Yank, but I'm going to relieve you of these boots and your pistol," one said. "You'll be comfortable here until one of your doctors can get to you. We've got to take care of our own first." He placed two canteens beside Ames.

"Arms hurt," Ames whispered. The Rebel realized one arm was broken and the other wounded. Thoughtfully, he rolled Ames on his side and leaned the canteens against him, placing his wounded left arm against them. "See if you can drink." Ames struggled with his left arm and finally got the canteen to his mouth. He nodded and whispered, "Thanks." He slipped in and out of consciousness during the afternoon. When coherent, he watched Rebels burying their dead, placing many Union soldiers in a shallow ravine, and covering them with a thin layer of soil. Grotesquely, hands and feet protruded. He tried to blot it all from his mind and focus on the face, the beautiful face. He had to hang on.

Willis Madden and his son Jack sat on the porch of Madden's Tavern. "Sounds like that pow'ful big battle's finally over. What ya make of it all, Daddy?" Jack asked, whittling on a stick.

Willis Madden shook his head and puffed on his pipe thoughtfully. "All I know is mah bin'ness has practic'ly died since this fool war started. There ain't much traffic 'long this road now. These Yankees are supposed to free the slaves, an' that's good. But then what?" he pondered tapping his pipe on the floor. "I wish no harm to mah white friends an' bin'ness partners."

Hearing noise from behind the house, Jack walked around the corner for a look. He saw thousands of blue soldiers marching towards him. "Looks like we got comp'ny Daddy, an' a lot of it!"

The dusty men of King's regiment, marching from Aquia Harbor to reinforce Pope, made a beeline for the well. The parched soldiers pushed and shoved for the precious water, yelling in some guttural language unfamiliar to Madden. Perhaps it was German or Dutch, he thought. He quickly diverted his attention to the soldiers who rushed into the barn and emerged with two horses and a cart. Running to an officer nearby, he

154

pleaded, "Please, sir, don't steal mah prop'ty. I can't run mah farm without horses. You people are supposed to be here to help us Negroes!"

The irate officer shoved him away saying, "Old man, that isn't your property. It belongs to some white person and you're taking care of it. I don't believe any colored man in Virginia owns so much property."[19]

"But I do," Madden yelled. "All of this is mine, the tavern, barn, an' all the land ya see. I have the deed to prove it."

"Stay out of the way, old man, and you won't get hurt." The officer watched his men haul away everything they could carry. Helpless, the Maddens sadly observed the destruction. Realizing the precious water could no longer be brought up with a bucket, a resourceful Yankee went down into the well on a rope and brought the liquid up by the cupful. When Willis Madden's Yankee "friends" finally departed, they left his well bone dry and stole two horses, a cart, 40 fowls, 40 bushels of corn, 200 pounds of bacon, and 8000 pounds of wheat.[20]

Next day, August 11, 1862: The battlefield

Morning: The steamy weather continued after Jackson granted permission for Union soldiers to tend their dead and wounded under a flag of truce. The sickening stench of the already putrefying bodies almost overwhelmed the soldiers attempting to identify the bloated, hideously blackened corpses. Groups of men silently, grimly, buried their own while the officers overseeing the truce chatted congenially, sitting on a log. Jeb Stuart, who had arrived the morning before, and Jubal Early represented the Confederates, while Generals Roberts and Hartsuff stood in for the Union. Stuart and Hartsuff, who had been contemporaries at West Point, greeted each other warmly while the sullen Early sat silently on his horse. A surgeon uncorked a bottle of whiskey and toasted an early peace. Generals Bayard and Crawford arrived with a basket of food which added to the cheerfulness of the party. "I can assure you," Stuart stated boldly, "that Jackson's thrashing of Pope will be reported as a Union success in your lying Yankee papers."

"You're mistaken, Jeb," Crawford argued, "not even the *New York Herald* would have the audacity to publish such a whopper." The two men wagered a hat on the debate; Crawford paid off several days later when the press proved him wrong.[21]

Jubal Early rode through the battlefield and became irate when he discovered some of Siegel's men violating the truce by attempting to haul away captured weapons. He angrily halted the offenders and sent the six loads of rifles to the Confederate rear. Early heard one of the Federals say, "It's hard to see our nice rifles going that way," to which an open-minded friend answered, "Yes, but they are theirs, they won them fairly."[22]

Aaron Ames was unconscious when they finally loaded him on the ambulance.

Early afternoon, Armstrong town home: Harriet's eyes blazed at Constance. "No! I will not have any wounded Yankee soldiers in my house! They've cruelly arrested your father and killed Abraham. I have no sympathy for them now. They came of their own free will to our soil to destroy and kill."

Realizing the futility of continuing the argument, Constance hurried out the front door to assist the wounded at the Virginia House. She hated the Yankees as bitterly as her mother, but her Christian compassion compelled her to go to the aid of these mangled human beings. Alfred Townsend, the reporter, greeted her. "Miss Armstrong, I have visited both hotels, the courthouse, several churches, and the depot. All are overflowing with wounded. Several boxcars full were just shipped north from the depot. About half the homes are flying hospital flags. The doctors are performing amputations in the courthouse and outside. Pleading eyes stared at me from every sidewalk. I've never seen anything like it. This shady little town has become a sort of Golgotha."

"It's a grotesque scene. Will you be renting a room from us tonight.?"

"Yes, I'm appreciative. I'll pay you in U.S. money as you stipulated." Yankee soldiers' distribution of counterfeit Confederate money had rendered Confederate currency practically worthless. They threaded their way through the wounded littering the porch of the Virginia House.

"They stop at nothing," she replied before they entered the furniture-bare tavern room where bloody soldiers covered the floors. Old Mr. Payne tottered through with a tear in his eye mumbling, "My good Lord! Who is responsible for this?" [22]

"Northern fanaticism, tyranny, and injustice are responsible for this," Constance shot back, then picked up a pail of water to serve the men.

She and Townsend went upstairs where he interviewed some of the survivors. "I hear Siegel took the field and Jackson's dead," one man said.

"Oh! Get out! That's all blow. We're lathered; that's the long and shawl of it," an Irishman exclaimed. [24]

Townsend took notes while several black boys fanned the wounded with cedar boughs to keep the swarms of buzzing flies away. Constance worked tirelessly with the patients, breathing the putrid odor of gangrene for several hours, before she stepped outside for a break. She rubbed the small of her back as she stood on the hotel steps, her whole body engulfed by waves of weariness and despair.

The doctor conversed with an ambulance driver in the sweltering sun. "There's simply no room here," the physician lamented. "Every inch of the floor and porch are covered. Our only hope is that some merciful citizens will take these suffering men into their homes."

"These poor fellows have been lying on the battlefield unattended for almost two days. They're suffering from dehydration and exposure. I can't leave them out in this sun," the driver argued desperately.

Constance ambled over and looked at the three men in the ambulance. She noticed something familiar about the tall one with curly brown hair, causing her to move closer and scrutinize his blistered, grimy face. "Oh, no!" she gasped. "It's Captain Ames!" A sense of compassion overwhelmed her. Recalling his kindness to her, she knew she could not allow this man to die in the broiling sun.

"You know this soldier, Miss Armstrong?"

"Yes." She stared at Ames's swollen lips and bloody arm. "Carry these men to my house across the street. I'll take care of them if you'll give me medical supplies."

The doctor smiled with relief. "I will indeed. I appreciate the compassion of the citizens, who have been so badly abused by this army."

7

Jeb Stuart Trades A Hat for A Coat

August 11 – August 24, 1862

"You have my hat and plume; I have your blue coat. I propose a cartel for a fair exchange of the prisoners."
General J.E.B. Stuart, C.S.A. to General John Pope, U.S.A., August, 1862

(continued) August 11, 1862: Armstrong town home

Constance ignored her mother's cries of protest as she stubbornly led the soldiers carrying Aaron Ames up the steps and into the front corner bedroom. She threw back the covers on the bed and they lifted him over from the stretcher. "You can put the other two in the next bedroom," she said pointing. "They'll have to share a bed."

She unbuttoned his filthy clothes, drenched with blood and sweat. Grabbing the bottoms of his trousers, she struggled to pull them off, but couldn't do it alone. Sadie stomped into the room carrying a basin of water with a disapproving scowl on her face. "Ya done stirred up a hornet's nest this time, Miss Constance, bringin' them Yankees in here."

"Captain Ames treated us kindly, Sadie. I couldn't leave him out there in the broiling sun to die. We must be good Samaritans. Please, help me get his jacket off."

Sadie set the basin by the bed and grudgingly helped pull one bloody arm out of the sleeve causing Ames to groan. "I know that story 'bout the Sama'tin, but I don't think it applies to Yankees. Ya see, there warn't no Yankees when the Lawd Jesus told that story."

Constance whirled around to confront Sadie. "Sadie please don't be stubborn! I need you to help me take care of these men. I can't do it alone."

Sadie stood firm with her arms crossed. After a few moments, her expression softened. "All right, Miss Constance, I'll do it 'cause ya asked me, but not 'cause I wanna."

"Thank you, Sadie. Now get on the other side of the bed and help me get all of his clothes off so we can wash him and determine the extent of his injuries."

Constance found herself admiring Ames's muscular physique while she bathed him. This man was wonderfully made, tall, broad shouldered, and narrow waisted with a taut, firm abdomen. Totally masculine, he reminded her of the statues of Greek gods she had perused in her history books. She felt the color creeping up her face. Proper southern ladies should not have such thoughts, but he was the most virile male she had ever seen—and of late she had seen many. She glanced at Sadie, hoping she couldn't read her mind. Forcing herself to concentrate on being a nurse, she examined his bloody left arm. It appeared the bullet had passed through the bulging biceps. If it had not shattered the bone, the wound should heal unless infection set in. She felt confident the arm could be saved. She tried to move his swollen right arm. He cried out in pain, causing her to suspect it was broken.

"Help me roll him over Sadie." The two women struggled with his weight to get him on his stomach. The large gaping gash in his right buttocks, oozing blood and pus, shocked them both.

"Umph," Sadie exclaimed shaking her head, "that's one nasty lookin' wound!"

"I'll say! It's ragged and deep—must be from artillery shrapnel. We've got to completely clean it and get all of the metal out. If we don't, the infection will kill him." Constance's stomach churned with anxiety. "Go down and bring me a knife and a needle and thread. This isn't going to be easy." She washed and probed the deep wound while she waited for Sadie. Having watched the doctors do this before, she knew now it was up to her to do it right.

When Sadie returned, Constance probed the festering wound with the knife, bringing out several pieces of metal as Ames tossed and cried out frequently in pain. She clenched her teeth to control the waves of nausea, and continued probing deeply until she was satisfied the wound was clean. Constance pushed a wisp of hair out of her face, wiped the beads of sweat from her forehead, took several deep breaths, and stared at the ceiling to ward off dizziness. This was the toughest thing she had ever had to do. "I need you to push the flesh together while I try to sew it up."

"Yas'm, but are ya sure ya know what you's doing?" Sadie held the bloody edges of the gash together.

"No, but I've got to try to do the best I can." Constance slowly pushed the needle through flesh and closed the wound. "We'll have to clean this every couple of hours. Too bad we don't have any mustard to make a poultice. Let's put a pad under him and roll him back over." When they had him on his back, she put several pillows under his head. "We've got to get water into him. Go tell that soldier guarding the well we need water for our Yankee patients. Bring me a soupspoon and some bacon grease. Since we have no balm, it's all we have to put on his blistered lips and face."

When Sadie fetched the requested items, Constance placed her arm behind Ames's head, tilting him forward. She raised the cup to his lips and slowly let the water drip into his mouth. He sputtered and choked at first and then began to swallow. Thank God, she thought. She spooned several cups of water slowly into his mouth and he swallowed them spoonful by spoonful, then he tossed and muttered. "What did he say?" She rubbed the grease on his scorched lips and face.

"Sounded somethin' like 'face' to me. Don't make no sense."

"He's weak and he's lost a lot of blood. I hope he's strong enough to fight off this infection." Constance stood up, and heaved a long, exhausted sigh. "Now, let's tend to our other patients."

Next day, August 12, 1862: Armstrong parlor

Harriet joined her two daughters in the parlor and said in a revolted tone, "My German is rather rusty, but from what I can gather, the one with the abdominal wound is from Amsterdam. The Yankees hired him to come here and fight. They promise these immigrants that they can have everything they steal from us. It's deplorable. The noble sons of the South are being pitted against the trash of Europe."

158

"Half the Union army doesn't speak English,"[i] Amanda agreed. "Our genteel culture is being destroyed by coarse uneducated immigrants. Lincoln sends them down because not enough northern men will volunteer to fight in his war of aggression."

"So many of them are dying, and for what purpose?" Constance mused. "That poor little man upstairs won't last much longer. There's nothing we can do to treat his wounds. The other one has a head wound and seems to be coming around. Captain Ames hangs on by a thread in burning delirium."

Alfred Townsend entered the front door and joined them. "Good evening, ladies. I trust I'm not disturbing you."

"No, please sit down, Mr. Townsend," Constance said to the gawky young reporter. "What can you tell us of today's events?"

"I visited Pope's headquarters at that lovely mansion, Val Verde. Unfortunately, it is still overflowing with bloody soldiers. When Pope awoke this morning he discovered that the Rebels had disappeared, apparently having recrossed the Rapidan and retreated."

"Surely Jackson hasn't deserted us. He won the victory!" Harriet said.

"You should have heard Pope gloating over *his* victory. Why else, he asked, would Jackson retreat? He must have been defeated," Townsend said with a laugh. "I can assure you ladies, from what I observed, Pope was soundly whipped."

"I'm sure Jackson has a reason for his action. Haven't more troops arrived to reinforce Pope?" Constance asked.

"It appears so. I'm not good at estimating numbers, but I know King has arrived. Don't be too concerned about the wisdom of Jackson's decision. I suspect he's trying to lure Pope into a trap. He may be successful. Pope is making preparations to move south."

"I pray you're right, Mr. Townsend, because we cannot hold out much longer for want of food." Amanda said, her face grave.

"Here's how I've described it for my readers," Townsend said, looking at his notes. "Vegetables, fruit, corn and everything that could be used are swept as clean as if a swarm of Pharaoh's locusts had been here."

Townsend told them that he had decided to depart for New York in the morning and then travel to England where he intended to capitalize on his observations by writing a book about the American war. The ladies begged him to encourage the English to come to the Confederacy's aid and break the blockade. He agreed to take a letter to Harriet's friend in New York.

The Wallach House: Douglas Wallach paced furiously and turned to wife. "Pope must be reined in! His harsh treatment of civilians has alienated those loyal to the Union. He's done us far more harm than good."

"Just look at the losses we've incurred," his wife agreed. "We were kind enough to let him use our house for his headquarters, and yet we've suffered destruction. If he treats prominent Unionists this way, how cruelly he must be treating others."

Wallach sat down at his desk and began writing. "I'm going to deliver this letter to Halleck when I go to Washington tomorrow. Help me list our losses...let's see, sixteen

---

[i] 500,000 Union soldiers were foreign born.

cattle, three horses, hundreds of sheep butchered in the field and half left unused, bushels of corn, wheat, and timothy."

"Don't forget the handfuls of silver snatched from the breakfast table," his wife said. "We've received no payment or vouchers for anything. Officers permit their men to plunder with no restraint whatsoever."

Two days later, August 14, 1862: Coleman Street

Constance reveled in the twenty-degree-cooler air when she walked out the front door to enjoy the relief from the stifling heat. However, she worried about the effect of last night's chill on her father in prison and the sick who still remained outside. She walked across Coleman Street and noticed a plain square-faced woman about forty, leaning over one of the many soldiers on the porch of the Virginia House. She carried a case of scarce items: dressings, salves, and clean cloths. "Excuse me, Miss, I'm Constance Armstrong. I'm caring for three Union soldiers in my house across the street and wondered if I might trouble you for assistance."

"Yes, Miss Armstrong," the brown-haired woman said as she stood up. "I'm Clara Barton. I arrived yesterday and brought supplies to aid our wounded. I'm shocked at the deplorable conditions. You see, this is my first visit to the front. Men are dying from neglect."

"That's my thought exactly, Miss Barton. I've been trying unsuccessfully for two days to get a doctor to look at my patients. Now, one has died and I have no way to remove the body. Another is delirious with fever and needs to have a broken arm set. I'm running out of supplies and food," Constance explained with a sense of urgency.

"I brought a doctor with me. He's working inside but I'll see that he helps you soon. Take what supplies you need from my box. We have a crew removing bodies. I'll send them over. I'm sorry I can't help you with food, yet," the Yankee nurse said with a smile.

"Thank you, Miss Barton. May I ask where you're from?"

"I was born in Massachussetts and have worked in Washington in the patent office for many years. I felt compelled to come to the front to help the suffering. It's far worse than I ever imagined."

Ames thrashed in the bed, burning with fever and soaked with sweat. Constance wiped his body with a cool cloth. "Hot," he mumbled in his delirium. "On fire." She held a piece of piece of precious ice to his face, and then brushed it across his lips allowing it to gradually melt into his mouth. Having already given him water and cleaned his wounds every couple of hours, she didn't know what else to do except pray.

She heard the doctor climbing the stairs, and rushed to the door. "Please, doctor, see what you can do for him. I'm sure one arm is broken."

The elderly gentleman examined both wounds and Ames's arm. He whistled when he saw his hindquarters. "That's a nasty one. It's inflamed, but I've seen worse. Did you sew him up?"

"Yes," she replied, chewing her lip nervously. "I didn't know what else to do. Do you think he'll live?"

"He's fighting the infection now, but he looks like a sturdy fellow to me. You've done an admirable job. I brought you some salve. Just keep putting this on. That's all you can do. Now, let's see that swollen arm again." He felt it and tried to move it. "Yes, it's broken, just above the elbow." He manipulated the bone and finally got it in place as Ames cried out. "I'm going to wrap it and put it in a sling. He's not going to be able to use this for about six weeks. Get as much water as you can into him and change his dressings frequently. The next day or two will tell the story. His chances of survival are much greater here than in one of our hospitals."

Constance rubbed her fatigued eyes later that night while she sat with Ames and gave him more water. Her mother entered the dimly lit room. "Constance, I want to tell you that you were right to bring Captain Ames here. Compared to the way most of our acquaintances have been treated, we were fortunate to have his assistance." She stood close to her daughter and placed her hand on her shoulder. "I'm sorry I acted so rudely. I'm just so upset about your father," she whispered in a trembling voice. "I miss him terribly."

Constance stood and wrapped her arms around her mother, her eyes growing moist. "I understand Mother; I don't know how we'll get along much longer without him. I write him every day to tell him how deeply I love him, but I wonder if he ever gets my letters."

Harriet sniffled and stroked her daughter's hair. "I admire your courage and strength, and the way you've helped these soldiers. Why don't you go to bed now? It's nearly midnight. I'll stay with Captain Ames."

"Are you sure, Mother?" Harriet nodded and wiped her eyes. Constance felt relief that the tension between them had vanished. "I'm glad you aren't mad at me any more." She kissed her on the cheek. "Be sure to give him plenty of water."

Two days later, August 16, 1862: Armstrong town home

The little Union soldier stared blankly at Constance. His only wound had been a gash in the skull, but he seemed to know nothing since regaining consciousness. "What's your name?" She was not sure if he had permanent brain damage, loss of memory, or did not speak English. Getting a piece of paper, she began to write and then gave him the pen to see if he could do likewise. He pushed it away. Discouraged, she went to check on Ames.

Ames saw the beautiful face through the haze. He had been swirling for days in the hot fog, seeing the face, always the face. "Captain Ames, can you hear me?" He tried to focus on the face until he saw her clearly, looking down at him. Was he in heaven? Where was he? "Captain Ames, it's Miss Armstrong. Can you hear me?"

"Yes," he whispered weakly, focusing on the luminous blue eyes.

"Thank God!" Her eyes sparkled with joy. "Here, let me prop you up." She pulled him forward, put several pillows behind him, wiped his face, and lifted a cup of water to his mouth. "Try to drink."

He drank the water appreciatively and stared at his surroundings, trying to comprehend the situation. "Am I...alive?"

"Yes, I'm delighted to report that you are." She pulled the sheet back and looked at his wounded arm. "You've been delirious with fever for almost a week. You feel much cooler today. Do you remember the battle?"

He cringed as visions of the smoke and firing muskets flashed before his eyes. "Afraid...so." She applied some salve to his left arm and rewrapped it. "Where... am.... I?" he asked slowly.

"You're in our house in town. They brought you in on an ambulance two days after the battle." She wiped his arms and chest with a damp cloth as he enjoyed the sensation of her closeness. "Do you feel like you can eat anything?"

"Too...tired," he whispered with a slight smile before he drifted to sleep. This might be better than heaven.

Champing at the bit, Stonewall Jackson led Robert E. Lee and James Longstreet to the top of Clark Mountain,[ii] the highest foothill south of the Rapidan River in Orange County. When the three generals emerged from the tree line to the open orchard and fields on the summit, Lee admired the extensive vista. "Magnificent." He dismounted and studied the landscape. "God's creation is beyond description."

Longstreet, a South Carolinian in his early forties, pointed to the vast rolling forest to the right. "That's the direction to Fredericksburg, past the wilderness area."

"In front of you are the fertile plains of Culpeper," added Jackson. "And farther to the north you can barely see the Bull Run Mountains and the Manassas Plateau. That green-crested peak directly ahead is Slaughter's Mountain, site of my recent encounter with Pope. To the left is Thoroughfare Mountain, all framed by the Blue Ridge range. To your left you can see almost to Charlottesville."

"You were wise to establish a signal station here General Jackson. You say you've had Hotchkiss make maps of this entire area?" Lee asked, reaching for his binoculars.

"Indeed, sir. I've been observing Pope for the last week, anxiously awaiting your arrival so we can destroy him," Jackson said, his eyes gleaming.

Lee and Longstreet studied the camps of the unsuspecting Union Army some twelve miles away. Only a few pickets were visible; the cavalry appeared idle. White dots of tents spread randomly over a large area while gray smoke curled lazily from the camps. The sun glistened on guns stacked around the camps. "They're like sitting ducks," Longstreet commented.

"Exactly!" exclaimed Jackson, his face flushed with excitement. "We've got them trapped between the two rivers, and I believe we outnumber them. They don't know your army is hidden behind this mountain. We can move in behind them and cut off their retreat to Washington. We must strike at once before more reinforcements arrive!" he said slamming his fist into his hand. "Now is the time!"

Lee lowered his glasses and stared Jackson in the eye. "All of our cavalry have not yet arrived. I would prefer to have them destroy the bridge at Rappahannock Station first, to hamper Pope's retreat across the river."

Jackson paced frantically shaking his head. "We don't need the cavalry to annihilate that army. We can't let this golden opportunity slip away! If one of their scouts discovers your army behind this mountain, Pope's going to disappear before we can destroy him."

"Our supply wagons haven't arrived either," Longstreet argued. "We'll have no provisions for our men if we go into battle immediately."

"We can live off the land for a day or two," Jackson exclaimed, his frustration mounting.

[ii] Clark Mountain is now also known as Moormont Mountain.

"Green corn and green apples are readily available. In addition, my scouts have informed me there's a large cache of food at Brandy Station. We can capture that initially. We must not hesitate!"

Lee rubbed his hand over his gray beard and walked thoughtfully, staring at the enemy camps. "I believe that it is to our advantage to have the full use of our cavalry. I will order General Stuart to burn the bridge at Rappahannock Station. We will commence our attack before dawn on the eighteenth, day after tomorrow."

Jackson, a stickler for military discipline, would never defy Lee. Trying to control his disappointment, he walked several feet away and let out a moan.

"Sir," Longstreet whispered to Lee with a slight smile, "I believe General Jackson is ill. He moaned."

"I heard," the normally courteous Lee snapped back. Regaining his composure, Lee mounted Traveller and said, "Your reconnaissance has been outstanding General Jackson. Come, we must return to camp."

Next day, August 17, 1862: Armstrong town home

"Good morning, Captain Ames," Constance said cheerfully as she pulled the curtains back. "It's time to wake up. You need to eat today."

Ames tried to focus through the haze. He seemed to be drifting, drifting...there was the face again. He hadn't been dreaming. "Good morning," he whispered.

"How do you feel?" She set a tray beside the bed.

"Weak, tired...drifting," he answered, trying to keep his eyes focused. She put her arms behind his back, struggling to prop him up.

"Ugh, you're heavy," she gasped, then shoved two pillows behind his head.

"Sorry, not much help...too weak."

"That's understandable. You've lost a lot of blood and haven't eaten for a week. Here, try some of this." She raised a spoonful of yellow grits to his mouth.

He swallowed and grimaced. "What's that?"

"Grits. It's ground cornmeal cooked with a little ham. I'm sorry we can't offer you something better, but we have little food." She wiped the leftovers from his beard and gave him some water to wash it down. "Here." She poked another spoonful in his mouth. "You've got to eat this entire bowl."

He obeyed, never taking his eyes off her face. Sadie came in with a basin of water and they proceeded to wash him. Ames realized for the first time that he was naked under the sheet. "We've got to roll you over to clean your other wound," Constance said. He felt the throbbing pain in his hindquarters when they rolled him over. "It looks a lot better, today...not as much drainage. You're beginning to heal. I think we can pull the thread out tomorrow."

"What an...embarrassing place...to be wounded," he mumbled.

"You jist be thankful that's where you was hit," Sadie said brusquely. "Been that deep anywhere else, you'd be dead. Miss Constance saved your life by gettin' that metal out an' sewin' ya up." They rolled him back over.

"I'm most...grateful," he whispered to Constance before he drifted off.

Late evening: Thick darkness set in as Jeb Stuart, Heros Von Borcke, John Mosby and Samuel Gibson rode towards the tiny village of Verdiersville, about ten miles south-east of Raccoon Ford and the Rapidan River. Expecting to intercept the cavalry under General Fitz Lee, nephew of Robert E. Lee, at the village, Stuart had orders to move across the Rapidan and destroy the bridge at Rappahannock Station (now Remington) the next day. Von Borcke, a Prussian soldier who had run the blockade to join the Confederate cause, leaned forward towards Stuart. "How much farther, General?" the six-foot-four, 240-pound Prussian asked.

"I believe it's just around the bend, Von," Stuart responded. "Not tired are you?"

"Me? Never!" Von Borcke boasted. "I'm ready to take on the whole Yankee army."

Stuart let out a boisterous laugh. "I know Mosby's well rested after his vacation in prison."

"I'm never going to hear the end of it," Mosby quipped with a smile. "I can assure you it won't happen again."

When the cavalrymen rounded the curve and entered the village, they located Norman Fitzhugh and Chiswell Dabney of Stuart's staff, who had been sent ahead to make contact with Fitz Lee. "General Stuart, sir, our men have not yet arrived," reported Fitzhugh.

"Are you sure major?" Stuart questioned, completely surprised. "Perhaps you missed them and they've moved towards the river?"

"No, sir. I've questioned all of the villagers. No cavalry have passed through here today."

"It makes no sense. They should have been here before now." Irritated, Stuart dismounted and contemplated the situation. He was ten miles outside of his lines in an exposed position until his men arrived, but surely they would appear soon. He decided to wait.

"Major Fitzhugh, I want you to ride about a mile down that road to the intersection of the Richmond and Antioch Church Roads. General Fitz has to pass that way. Await his arrival and urge him to move here quickly. Meanwhile, we'll make ourselves comfort-able on the porch of that house," Stuart said, nodding towards the small farmhouse on the right.

"At once." Fitzhugh spurred his horse down the road.

The others walked through the narrow gate into the yard of a farmhouse surrounded by a picket fence. Stuart tied his horse to the fence, took the bridle out of its mouth and allowed it to feed. "Best leave the saddles on in case we have to mount in haste," he said to the others. "We may as well get some shut-eye while we wait." He spread his gray riding cape on the porch, took off his hat, and stretched out to sleep.

Dabney removed his belt and laid it aside, along with his pistol and saber. He then curled up in the grass, noticing that Von Borcke still retained his weapons. "Why do you make yourself uncomfortable by leaving your weapons on?" he asked the Prussian.

"I believe it is a wise decision considering our location," Von Borcke responded as he rolled over. "I feel safer this way."

Next day, August 18, 1862: Verdiersville

4 a.m. Major Fitzhugh had reached the designated intersection and waited several hours for General Fitz Lee. When no soldiers appeared, he finally tied his handsome sorrel and went inside a deserted house for a brief nap. The noise of hooves on the road outside aroused him, and he rose to meet his comrades. Instead, he saw a swarm of blue-coated cavalrymen surrounding the house, one of them gleefully capturing his shiny sorrel. A group of soldiers burst through the door and pushed pistols at his breast. "Surrender!" they commanded. Furious at his dilemma, he reached for his pistol and cocked it. A Yankee attempted to wrench it from him, but he twisted his hand back firing two shots to no avail. The group threw him to the floor, wrestled his gun from him, tied his hands behind his back, and then took him to the commanding officer.

"Well, my Rebel prisoner, can you tell me where this road leads?" the officer asked.

Fitzhugh shook his head and refused to answer any questions. The officer, returning from a raid to Louisa, was obviously lost. Fitzhugh feared for Stuart, who could be surprised and captured, if the column went in that direction. His heart pounded as the Yankees forced him to ride towards Verdiersville. How could he warn Stuart of his peril? Stuart would undoubtedly mistake the column for Fitz Lee. He prayed for a solution but felt his situation could not have been more hopeless. He saw no earthly means of giving an alarm and knew he might have to witness the capture of his beloved general.

The sound of the approaching horses and wagons stirred Stuart from his sleep. He arose from the porch and walked to the gate, assuming it to be Fitz Lee. Unable to see the horsemen in the early morning mist, he decided to be cautious. "Captain Mosby, Lieutenant Gibson, ride forward and determine whose command is approaching."

As the two Confederates rode towards the column in the mist, the Federals fired when they became visible. "Halt! Surrender!" the Yankees commanded. The firing continued while the two Rebels rapidly retreated. The bluecoats thundered down upon the house, where Stuart stood observing at the fence. Acting promptly, Stuart and Dabney instantly bridled and mounted their horses. Stuart dug his spurs into the sides of his mount, who cleared the fence and galloped into the open field amidst hot fire. Dabney followed close behind.

Von Borcke ran about fifteen steps to reach his horse. He hastily unfastened the bridle but had no time to throw the reins over the horse's head. He managed to hold on as the excited animal reared. Von Borcke forced him through the gate into the face of the enemy, who demanded his surrender. Slapping his horse on the head, and digging his spurs into its flanks, the Prussian dashed forward. A shower of carbine and pistol bullets flew past him, and the Yankees followed in hot pursuit. Fitzhugh, witnessing it all, closed his eyes. He didn't want to watch his friend killed. The speed of Von Borcke's black charger saved the day. He gradually outdistanced his adversaries, who soon gave up the chase.[1]

Stuart watched mortified from the woods while the Yankees gleefully rushed to the porch and captured his hat, cape, and haversack containing important maps and documents. They triumphantly raised his treasured brown hat, looped up with a gold star and decorated with a black feather, on the point of a saber with great mirth and laughter. "I'm going to make them pay for this insult," he vowed to his companions, who had rallied and joined him.

Von Borcke rode up breathlessly and eyed Dabney. "Are you quite comfortable now, without your arms?" he asked maliciously. Dabney glared at him.

Major Fitzhugh, seated beside the Federal colonel, burst into laughter as he witnessed the escape of his general.

"Major, what is the humor in this situation? Who was that party that escaped?"

Unable to contain his triumph, he exclaimed, "Do you really wish to know who that was, Colonel?"

"Indeed, I do."

"Well, sir, that was General Jeb Stuart and his staff!"

"General Stuart!" shouted the shocked officer. "A squadron over here! Pursue that party at once! Fire on them! It's General Stuart!" The Federals charged forward but Fitzhugh knew from experience that they did not like the woods, fearing surprise attack. The squadron soon returned without any captives. Fitzhugh was their only prisoner, but unfortunately he carried a detailed copy of Lee's planned attack on Pope.

No one enjoyed a joke more or was a more devilish prankster than Jeb Stuart. The sun began to rise in the sky as he led the mortified Rebels towards their lines. Stuart took out his handkerchief, tied the corners in knots, and covered his bare head. The entire group erupted into boisterous laughter at the undignified appearance of their fearless leader. "General Stuart, sir, I believe this time the joke is on you," Mosby said with a smug smile.

"I can't deny it," the jovial Stuart laughed heartily. "I need to have a good laugh. Soon I'll have the unpleasant task of informing 'Marse Robert' that Pope will expediently have a copy of his plan of attack and Fitz Lee is heaven knows where. His plans for today have been foiled."

Late afternoon, the Armstrongs': From the window beside his bed, Aaron Ames had a clear view of Coleman Street in front of the house and up to the corner of Davis Street. He watched the wounded from the Virginia House being loaded onto ambulances and quickly spirited away. Supply wagons had been rumbling up Davis Street for several hours now and he had heard numerous trains depart. The wild flurry of activity could only indicate one thing—Pope was retreating. He pondered his situation. Too weak to feed himself, he couldn't use either arm and knew he remained vulnerable to exposure and disease. His life still hung by a thread. Could he survive the intense daytime heat and cool nights if he joined his evacuating army?

Constance entered with a triumphant smile on her face. "Well, Captain Ames, it appears that the bombastic Pope is turning his back to the enemy." She slid the tray onto his bedside table.

Ames leaned forward as she put the pillows behind his back. "I can't disagree." She poked a spoonful of grits into his mouth. "Um, grits again."

"If your army hadn't stolen all of our food, you would have a more varied and delectable menu," she answered sarcastically. "Should you desire to be evacuated with your army, I'll make the arrangements for you. I believe it's reasonable to assume that our army is approaching. If you decide to remain here you must understand that you'll be sent to prison as soon as you're strong enough to travel."

He gulped down another mouthful of grits and stared at her intently. She fascinated him as no woman ever had in the past. He wasn't ready to leave her yet, regardless of the consequences. "Neither alternative holds much attraction, Miss Armstrong. But, I believe my chances of survival are greater if I remain here…that is if you will be merciful enough to allow me to stay."

She wiped his face. "Certainly, you may stay. I believe that's a wise decision. I'd hate to have you die en route and my masterful stitching job be all for naught."

166

They both smiled. She walked to the window and held the curtains back allowing them to watch Clara Barton directing the evacuation. "Besides," Ames quipped, "the nurses are prettier here."

Constance stared at him coolly. She was not about to let this Yankee charm her. "Even though Miss Barton's plain, she's a tireless and inspiring worker." She pulled a letter from her pocket. "I've written a letter to your parents telling them that you're alive and on the road to recovery. I need their address; is there anything else you want to tell them?"

"Yes, tell them I'm blessed to have a compassionate caretaker."

Next day, August 19, 1862: Behind Union lines

Early morning: Redmond Burke located Frank Stringfellow in his wooded hideaway, where he watched the rapidly retreating Union army. "How's the wrist?" Stringfellow asked in greeting.

"It's a little stiff, but I can't complain," Burke responded. "There's been big goings on at headquarters." He related the story of Stuart's narrow escape and lost hat, as well as the botched invasion. "The whole army's laughing about it. Everywhere Stuart goes, he's greeted with 'Whar's your hat, Jeb, or some other taunt. I'm not sure he appreciates the humor in the situation."

Stringfellow laughed. "That hat was his pride and joy." He paused to look at the dust caused by the retreating army. "But, now Pope has skedaddled across the Rappahannock. Too bad. We could have destroyed him here."

"I think General Jeb is planning to retaliate against Pope. He wants you to scout in the direction of Warrenton to find out if troops could be passed over the river near there, and to fix exactly the extreme right of Pope's army."

Stringfellow's eyes glowed with excitement. "That's the kind of challenge I thrive on. I'll be off at once." He stood and shook Burke's hand.

Late morning: Constance paraded the soldier with the head wound before Ames. "Do you recognize him?"

"No," Ames said scrutinizing the little man. "He wasn't in my company. I've never seen him before."

"I'll take him to Miss Barton shortly." She motioned for the little man to sit in the chair. "This wound looks less inflamed." She examined his arm carefully. "See if you can move it." Ames managed to raise his left hand a few inches. "A little," he sighed. "It's still painful," he said above the loud marching feet of the retreating soldiers.

Sadie flew through the door. "Miss Constance! Ya ain't never gonna guess who's out in the kitchen to see ya! It's Mista Frank!"

"What!" Constance exclaimed spinning around. "Frank, here now? In the midst of the Union Army? Oh, my God. You finish here, Sadie." She dashed out the door.

Ames tried to comprehend the situation. "Who's Frank?"

"Frank Stringfellow. He's a good friend of Miss Constance, like a brother to her. He's a scout for Gin'el Stuart. But, that ain't none of your binness, anyhow. Why don't you damn Yankees go away and leave us alone!" she said, her dark eyes smoldering.

"Why do you hate me so?" he asked bewildered.

"Because you is a murderin', thievin', damn Yankee! Now roll over and let me look at your behind." She pushed him over none too gently. He groaned.

"The only reason you's alive is 'cause Miss Constance is a good Chris'ian woman. Her momma, her sister, and I forbid her to bring any damn wounded Yankee soldiers in this house after the way your army done treated us. But she done it anyway!"

"Frank!" Constance cried as he swept her into his arms and spun her around. "Thank God, you're alive, but it's so dangerous for you to be here!"

"The Yanks are too busy retreating to notice me," he said as he put her down. "Besides I had a Federal officer's jacket over my uniform. If I'm caught in my uniform, I'm a scout and sent to prison. If I'm not in uniform, I'm considered a spy and will swing from a rope. So, Lord willing, I hope this combination saves me from the rope. Anyway, I need a safe place to sleep for a few hours and get a meal before I go on an assignment."

"Of course, sit down and I'll slice you some ham and bread. We have little else."

"The conduct of Pope's army is deplorable. We'll retaliate." He sat at the table. "But Connie, there's so much I want to tell you, and I only have a little time. For three months I lived in Alexandria gathering information for General Stuart."

"So that's where you were." She placed the food on the table and sat down.

"I assumed the identity of a dental apprentice during the day. Learned a lot about teeth." He devoured the food. "The dentist was supposedly a southern sympathizer. At night I condensed the information in the newspapers and dropped it to be picked up by a courier, who delivered it to our army. After several months, who should walk into our office but my beautiful Emma! When she saw me she gasped, and cried 'Frank!' I told her she had mistaken me for someone else. She immediately understood the situation. Several days later the dentist's wife warned me that my identity was known and that her husband would betray me. I fled in great haste only to discover that the man who had smuggled me into the city had been killed. Then I went swimming and finally arrived safely behind our lines."

"What a narrow escape! What next?"

"Then I joined Stuart on the peninsula. Farley performed incredibly daring acts there. At Tunstall's Station he rode along a train and shot the engineer. You must meet him, but at the moment he's watching McClellan's army land near Alexandria." He told her about Stuart losing his hat and his current assignment. She related her father's imprisonment, the help they had received from Aaron Ames, and his injuries.

"Be careful Connie, we don't want any Yankees falling in love with you," he teased.

"Don't worry!" Her eyes bristled with anger. "I hate that army and everyone in it because of their brutal treatment of Father." He nodded his approval and yawned. "You can sleep safely in Sadie's cabin. I'll wake you up in three hours. God go with you, Frank." He kissed her on the cheek and walked out the door

Noon: Robert E. Lee stood again on the summit of Clark Mountain, staring at the terrain he would know so well over the next two and a half years. Vexed, he watched the dust raised by the retreating Yankee army as they escaped across the Rappahannock, thus slipping from his grasp. Jackson had been right; they had missed the golden opportunity. It had been a comedy of errors. First his orders had been captured with Fitzhugh, next Fitz Lee had arrived a day late because he was foraging for food, then Toombs had failed to guard the ford of the Rapidan, allowing the Yankee cavalry with Fitzhugh to slip through. Now he was two days behind schedule and facing an entirely different situation. Time was of the essence. McClellan's troops were arriving at Aquia Harbor and marching to join Pope. Every day Pope grew stronger, but Lee knew he had no hope of reinforcements. The Confederates would move in the morning. He must make haste to destroy Pope.

Late afternoon, Panorama: Selene glared defiantly at Joseph, paced in the cabin, then pulled down her blouse to reveal her scarred back. "Look at those marks," she yelled. "That's where Mista Kelly whipped me. I fought back, and bit his arm. Served him right that he got blood poisonin' an' had to have his arm amputated. Justice was done! I ain't never gonna be a slave again an' I don't want mah kids to be slaves." She shook her fists angrily. "These Yankees say we'll be free if we go with them, and I'm goin'."

"Selene, you're wrong!" Joseph protested. "I begged Mista Armstrong to buy ya to get ya away from mean ol' Mista Kelly. He said he didn't want to own no more slaves, but he finally did it to make me happy. I'm paying him back. You's gonna be free soon. These Yankees killed mah Daddy and they ain't never gonna treat ya as good as ya been treated here."

Selene stalked around the cabin floor, holding the children's gaping stares. "Mista Armstrong is an old man an' he's in prison. If he dies, mah kids kin be sold away from me. Ya know it kin happen. Besides there's not much food left. The crops are destroyed. These soldiers'll feed us."

Joseph shook his head. "This is our home and these are our people. I don't trust those Yankees."

"Momma, I don't wanna leave Hudson. He's mah friend," Isaac begged.

They heard the sound of horses outside. "You niggers come on out of there, or we'll drag you out," a Yankee soldier called. Joseph walked outside. "Come and work for us and you'll be free. You can take anything out of your master's house you want. It's yours."

"No, sur, we ain't going," Joseph said defiantly.

"Guess we're going to have to burn that house, boys," the officer called to a group of soldiers near Panorama. They lit a torch and rode towards the house.

"No," Joseph cried, "please don't burn the house."

"Come with us and we'll spare the house," the Yankee said.

Joseph had tears in his eyes when his family followed the Union army north. Selene strutted proudly, dressed in one of Miss Constance's finest outfits.

Stringfellow rode northwest to Waterloo Bridge. He cautiously crept through the woods, saw only a few Union pickets on the north side of the river, and decided the Confederates could cross without much difficulty. He then rode a mile upstream to Hart's Ford to discover the river was rough and rapid at that point. There were no pickets, and he determined the river could be forded.

Nightfall: Stringfellow crossed the Rappahannock and rode through the pickets with no difficulty. Wearing his Federal officer's coat, he rode into Warrenton and stopped at the Warren Green Hotel. Across the street he noticed a Negro woman ironing clothes in the window of a house. He crossed the street and standing on the sidewalk outside the window, said, "Excuse me, ma'am, I wonder if you could assist me? Could you tell me where our wagon train is?"[2]

Seeing his blue coat, she replied rudely, "I haven't the slightest idea. Why don't ya ask one'a your own folks over there on the hotel porch."

Looking up at the porch filled with Federals, Stringfellow had an uneasy feeling in his stomach. Knowing the risk, he approached them cautiously. "Can I help you soldier?" one asked.

"You sure can," the scout replied, "if you can tell me where our wagon train is. I've got some orders for the quartermaster."

The soldier shrugged in disgust. "That's the trouble with this damned army. Nobody knows where anything is. The wagon train's at Catlett's Station. Where else would it be?"[5]

"Thanks, I'm much obliged." Stringfellow hastily mounted and rode down the street. He began to relax when he was out of sight. Feeling more confident, he decided to visit some long-time family friends, who informed him that Pope had ridden through town the day before. Shortly, a man named Marshall, the father of Colonel Charles Marshall of General Lee's staff, dropped by and said that this morning a large wagon train had passed through headed to Pope's headquarters at Catlett's Station.

Later that night Stringfellow rode towards Catlett's Station to corroborate the information he had received. He observed only a few pickets about, and they didn't appear very alert. This would be easy pickings for Stuart who would get revenge for the loss of his hat, Stringfellow thought with a grin.

Next day, August 20, 1862: Raccoon Ford

4 a.m. The Confederate liberation of Culpeper began as John Pelham's Horse Artillery splashed through the waters of the Rapidan at Raccoon's Ford while Fitz Lee's cavalry led Longstreet's advance into Culpeper. Simultaneously, Robertson's cavalry, accompanied by Stuart, led Jackson across at Somerville's Ford. Anxious to clear the hated enemy out of Culpeper, Pelham worried about the welfare of the Armstrongs. No sooner had he forded the river than he spotted squadrons of Federal cavalry ahead under Buford, disputing the progress of the Rebels. The gray cavalrymen charged and began to push them back. Alex and the Little Fork Rangers dashed into the center of the action, fighting to liberate their homes. In his element, Pelham executed the type of maneuvers that were making him famous. His quick eye instantly selected the most advantageous position. As he sent his batteries dashing up a hill, his voice rang out alive with excitement. "Give it to'em men! That's the stuff, boys!"[4] His infectious enthusiasm instilled courage in his men. The running fight continued as the Federals fell back towards the northeast in the direction of Kelly's Ford.

Noon: Willis Madden heard the gunfire coming closer. Soon he spotted the Federal cavalry heading in his direction and the smoke of Pelham's guns. Perhaps the safest place to hide would be under the bed. Pelham's cannons surged forward to occupy another hill. "Let'em have it, boys! Revenge to Pope!" he cried eagerly. A brisk encounter took place on Madden's farm before the Yanks fell back towards the river. Alex heard a bullet whistle by as he galloped forward in hot pursuit.

Early afternoon: The Federals decided to make a stand at Kelly's Ford. "We've got to push them across the river," Fitz Lee ordered. His men lined up for a charge. Both sides fought hot and heavy for a short period of time until the enemy finally withdrew across the river, leaving their dead and wounded behind.

John Pelham wiped his brow in the intense heat and walked among his command. "Good work, men. We must have driven them back a good eight miles."

Robert Beckam stopped at the Doggett farm outside of Stevensburg for a drink of water with sweat pouring off him. He had heard the cavalry fight at Kelly's Ford and knew they had cleared the way for the infantry. For days he had looked forward to marching into Culpeper Court House. He'd escorted numerous attractive ladies around Richmond but had been unable to erase Constance from his mind. He heard a commotion up ahead where a group of soldiers stood under a large tree. "What's going on?" he asked old Mr. Doggett, standing near by.

"You missed all the excitement," the old farmer said with a smile. "A little while ago General Longstreet and his staff were sitting under that cherry tree when a courier rode up and ordered him to fall back at once. 'By whose order?' Longstreet asked. The courier had obviously mistaken him for a division commander. 'By General Longstreet's,' the poor guy answered. Realizing something was awry, the general's staff pulled their guns and arrested the fool. When they searched him they found papers that General Longstreet had sent by one of his couriers several hours earlier. One bullet was missing from the suspect's revolver. He was obviously a Federal spy who had killed Longstreet's courier and assumed his identity."

Beckam stared at the body swinging from a rope in the tree, eyeballs bulging. "It appears his punishment was swift."

"Oh, they held a real quick trial and convicted him of spying and murder. And you see the price he paid for being a spy."

Mid-afternoon: Fannie Barbour stared out the window of Beauregard at the large open plain between her home and Brandy Station. This plain, so conducive to cavalry engagements, was about to witness its first battle. Before her stretched 3500 Union cavalry, with arms glittering in the sun and battle-flags waving. Jeb Stuart, who with Robertson's cavalry, had pushed the enemy back from Stevensburg, arrived on the scene. He rapidly deployed the one regiment with him as sharpshooters and ordered Von Borcke to ride back and bring the rest of his men into battle with great haste. Realizing their numerical superiority, the Federals mounted an attack. The small regiment of Confederates fought bravely but were relieved to hear the wild Virginia yell of their comrades charging to their rescue.

Within a few moments the Virginians charged into the midst of the Yankees, sabers crashing in fierce hand to hand combat. A Union soldier aimed to fire on Von Borcke, who slashed his saber at his antagonist's neck, nearly severing his head. The Yankees fell back and reformed to charge several times. Again and again they were beaten back by the fierce advance of the Rebels. Finally, they retreated, leaving behind 50 wounded, 15 killed, and 64 prisoners.

Elated by the victory, Von Borcke wiped the blood from his saber on his horse's mane, and rode to look for Redmond Burke, whom he had seen fall while charging gallantly at his side. He soon found Burke, sitting up placing a tourniquet on his leg. "Where are you hit?" Von Borcke asked as he dismounted.

"Took a bullet in the calf muscle," Burke replied, obviously in pain. "Can't seem to dodge these bullets lately."

Von Borcke promised to get him to a house immediately. Stuart galloped up and surveyed the scene. Relieved to know Burke's wound was not serious, Stuart informed Von Borcke that a prisoner claimed the enemy had gone for reinforcements around the Hazel River and planned to return and attack again. Stuart had dispatched a messenger to Fitz Lee to send his men and guns to reinforce them.

Late afternoon, Culpeper Court House: "Praise God, here come our liberators!" screeched Granny Ashby, waving her cane to the strains of *Dixie* in the distance. The euphoric townspeople gathered along the sidewalks while Confederate flags waved from windows. For the first time in weeks they could walk freely and converse with each other. Each had a fearsome story to tell of how they had survived Pope's occupation. The cruel treatment of his army had only strengthened their unity and resolve to resist tyranny. Their spirit had not been broken.

Deafening cheers arose as the ragged gray columns marched down Coleman Street. Constance, Amanda, Harriet, and the boys waved handkerchiefs in front of Gorrell's Drug Store, where Gorrell had set up a large tub of iced lemonade for the dusty heroes. Amazingly, he had been able to hide these delicacies from the Yankees.

"Oh, my country how I bleed for thee," sang a shoeless soldier with his shoes tied together and strung over his shoulder. He greedily dipped into the cold lemonade. "Best lemonade I ever drank," he cried in appreciation.

"Why don't you wear your shoes?" Hudson asked.

"'Cause they don't fit so good, and I'm savin 'em for cold weather. But don't worry kid. I don't need shoes to kill Yankees!"

Granny Ashby and several older men and women fell on their knees in thanks. Harriet rushed out to kiss a battle flag. The band stopped in front of the Virginia House to play while the columns of soldiers marched down Davis Street and out the Brandy Road. Chants of "Lee, Lee, Lee!" rose from the crowd. Constance strained to see the distinguished gray-haired gentleman riding towards them, hat in hand. Appearing a master of the situation, he dismounted and partook of the lemonade. "Just think of it! Ice cold lemonade, with plenty of lemon in to make it taste sour, and plenty of sugar to make it taste sweet, and ice to make it cold. You, sir, have provided a cherished delicacy for these weary, dirty, dusty soldiers. I thank you," he said to Gorrell.

Gorrell beamed. "General Lee, sir, you have led our army to victory and liberated us from the persecution of Pope. We thank you."

Constance pushed through the crowd determined to address Lee. "General Lee, sir, I beg a moment of your time," she said. "I'm Constance Armstrong, and my seventy-two-year-old father, Judge Charles Armstrong, has been taken prisoner by the Yankees on false charges of being a spy. His health is frail, and I fear he cannot survive long in prison. I beg of you," she said with tears in her eyes, "will you seek his release?"

"Is this the Charles Armstrong who served in our legislature?" Lee stared at her with honest eyes.

She felt this man searching her heart and brain. "Yes," she answered. "He also went to Washington to seek a peace agreement with Seward."

"Your father is a man of integrity, Miss Armstrong, and I deplore Pope's unprecedented treatment of innocent civilians. President Davis has written Lincoln a letter of protest and notified him that for every civilian he executes, we will execute a Union officer prisoner. I don't think you need fear his execution," Lee said compassionately. "However, I understand your concern for his survival. I will have one of my staff write a letter urging his immediate release."

"I am most grateful, General Lee." She was pushed aside when townspeople crowded around him.

"Good people of Culpeper, I must make haste to punish Pope." He pushed through the crowd to mount his horse.

"I can't believe you talked to General Lee," Amanda exclaimed while they watched him ride off.

"We are blessed to have such a Christian gentleman lead our army," Constance replied in awe.

The columns of soldiers filed by, flirting with the ladies. A tall soldier on horseback dismounted, tethered his horse, and maneuvered his way through the crowd towards them.

"Connie," he called. "Over here!"

She focused on the dirty soldier with a beard but had difficulty identifying him. He pushed closer until she saw his dark eyes smiling at her. "Robert!" She reached for his hand. He pulled her towards him and enfolded her in his arms.

"Please," he said, holding her tightly. "Let a filthy soldier hold you for a few minutes."

She clung to him. "We're two of a kind. I haven't had enough water to bathe in a week."

Laughing, he looked into her eyes and kissed her tenderly. "You're a sight for sore eyes. How I've missed you."

"Lieutenant Beckam, we're so happy to see you alive and well," Harriet said. She and Amanda rushed to greet him. "Were you in the battle at Slaughter's Mountain?"

"No, we were still in Richmond watching McClellan retreat. We arrived several days ago and are now in hot pursuit of Pope. I've been so worried about all of you. I'm sickened by the destruction."

"We've almost starved to death," Amanda complained. "The farm was raided and would you believe Connie beat a Union soldier to death?"

"No!" He stared at the two of them to see if they were teasing him. "Are you telling me the truth?"

"Do you have time to visit?" Constance inquired with a twinkle in her eye. "I'll tell you all about it."

Beckam looked at the soldiers marching forward. He shook his head sadly. "Unfortunately, I must stay with our regiment. We're moving towards the Rappahannock to encounter Pope. A major battle will take place soon." His eyes blazed eagerly down into hers as the band played. "Walk down the block and dance with me before I go."

Smiling, she took his hand. "My pleasure. Lead the way."

He held her snugly as they whirled among the other revelers celebrating the return of the Confederates. She told him about her father's dilemma and briefly related the demise of the enemy soldier.

"That was brave of you, but dangerous, very dangerous." They stood in front of the Virginia House.

"Compared to the risk you've been exposed to, my encounter was mild."

He encircled her with his arms. "I can't tell you the slaughter I've seen," he said somberly. "But we pushed an army much larger than ours back to the river. Lee's an amazing leader. If we can push Pope out of Virginia, hopefully the war will end. Our fighting spirit is unstoppable. I don't know what will happen in the next few days, or when we'll give battle. I hope to be able to come back and see you again."

"I'll pray for your victory and return," she said softly while looking into his depthless black eyes. He brushed his lips against hers.

"I must go now, before it becomes more difficult." He turned and walked towards his horse.

Aaron Ames had observed the whole scene from the bedroom window. The wild celebration and joy the citizens expressed at the sight of their liberating army touched him. Suddenly, he was a captive at the mercy of the enemy. The tables had turned. He watched attentively and helplessly as the dark handsome soldier whirled Constance around and kissed her good-bye. Who was he? It was none of his business…but it bothered him.

Sunset: John Pelham watched the sun slowly set from his position at the right of Stuart's line of battle on the beautiful grassy level field just past Brandy Station. What a splendid picture the 3000 riders made with their drawn sabers reflecting the last russet rays of light. Pelham held his guns in limber, ready to dash forward wherever needed if the enemy attacked. He had careened across five miles of rough terrain with two regiments of Fitz Lee's cavalry to reinforce Stuart. Overcome with exhaustion, they stood ready to face an enemy charge if necessary, but it appeared no charge would come. The ranks dispersed along the Rappahannock to make camp and Pelham collapsed in the high grass to sleep. He thought of Constance and wanted to see her, but not tonight. He was tired…too tired.

Late evening: Constance and Amanda had just gone to bed when they heard the rapping on the back door. Constance lit a candle, and the two of them threw on their robes and dashed down the steps to the continued rapping

"Amanda, it's Alex!"

"Alex, oh thank God!" Amanda hastily unlatched the door.

He grabbed her into his arms, devouring her with kisses. "My darling, my love, how I've missed you," he whispered. Finally seeing Constance, he reached out and pulled her to him also. "Thank God you've survived Pope."

"You're alive…thank goodness!" Amanda moved her lips over his bronze face. "My love…your baby's walking

"That's great. I've been fighting Yankees since 4 a.m. and would give anything to crawl into a bed. I must go back tomorrow, but we can talk in the morning."

Constance pulled away. "I'll sleep in the front room. Alex, what do you know of John Pelham?"

"I just left him at Brandy Station. He's becoming quite famous." He and Amanda climbed the steps arm in arm.

Next day, August 21, 1862: Armstrong town home

Ames looked at Constance with eager anticipation when she placed a dish in front of him. "Applesauce? To what do I owe this delightful change?"

"To the fact that your army finally withdrew and I was able to barter with some of my neighbors for different items. It's wonderful to be able to walk freely now and visit friends again." She lifted a spoonful to his blistered lips.

He ate the applesauce greedily. "Delicious! Now, let me try to do it myself." He took the spoon in his left hand. She watched with an amused smile as he manipulated the spoon into the dish awkwardly. With great concentration he slowly raised it to his mouth, managing to eat about half and spilling the rest down his front.

"Almost!" She snickered and wiped the mess off his beard and hairy chest. "You're making a lot of progress."

"I refuse to give up. But, now I know why I'm not left-handed. That hand is completely uncoordinated." He worked to procure another spoonful of applesauce, managing to get more in his mouth. "There. Aren't you proud of me, nurse?"

"Indeed I am. You're the best patient I have at the moment." She turned to see Alex walk into the room. "Captain Ames, I'd like you to meet my brother-in-law, Alex Yager. I'll leave you two to get acquainted."

"I trust you're receiving good care," Alex said after he sat down.

"The best, and I'm most grateful. I owe my life to your sister-in-law," Ames said sincerely, looking at Alex's uniform. "Are you in the cavalry?"

"Yes, Fourth Virginia. I understand you're from Maine. My wife tells me you were kind to them and assisted in their flight from the farm to town. I want to thank you for that. My family is everything to me. You appear to be a man of integrity." He paused, his eyes assessing the patient. "Tell me, why are you here, invading our peaceful land?"

Ames looked out the window for a minute, at a loss for words. "Let me first say that I detest the cruel policies of Pope and his brutal treatment of civilians. He's an embarrassment to the North, and the actions of his army are inexcusable. I'm ashamed to say that I fought with his army, but we don't get to pick our generals." He stared at the ragged Rebel, grasping for words. "When I graduated from Harvard in May, I decided to seek some excitement, and my family felt one of us should support the war effort. Since I'm the youngest son and unmarried, I was the obvious choice. I believe in the preservation of the Union and the eradication of slavery. However, I must confess that after my first battle, I admire the fighting spirit of your men. I've always assumed southern men fought so fiercely because they frequently employed violence to control their slaves."

Alex shook his head, his eyes smoldering in disbelief. "Let me explain why your assumption is totally false. I own no slaves and neither do ninety per cent of the men in our army. In 1860 only six per cent of southern whites owned slaves. This war is not about slavery. Look at the leaders of our army who aren't slave holders: Robert E. Lee,

Joseph Johnston, A. P. Hill, Fitzhugh Lee, Jeb Stuart, Jubal Early, just to name a few. Our ragged barefoot army fights courageously because we've been attacked. We're fighting to protect our homes and loved ones." His voice rose as his face reddened. "We're determined to preserve the sacred right of self-government. We want to be a free and separate people from you and to live by the Constitution as our forefathers originally designed it. We'll no longer make the coffers of your government rich by paying unfair tariffs. You don't want to let us go because you'll lose those revenues. It's all about greed!"

"I understand your feelings and thank you for being honest with me," Ames said quietly, hoping to calm Alex down. "I've truly experienced southern hospitality and am thankful to be in the hands of merciful Christians. It's obvious that I have much to learn from you."

Alex stood up and gave him a look of conciliation. "Captain Ames, you sound like a rational man and I wish you a speedy recovery. I hope to be able to continue our debate again, but at the moment I must return to the battlefield to subdue Pope. Good day, sir."

"Ames seems like an honorable man," Alex said to Constance while he prepared to depart.

"Yes, he's quite pleasant." Her face clouded with uneasiness. "Alex, the Yankees stole Liz the night they retreated. I'd tried to keep her hidden in the stable. I hate the thought of her serving the enemy." Her eyes glazed with tears. "Please be on the lookout for her. Her markings make her distinctive. Perhaps you can get her back."

"That's a tough assignment, Constance. However, if the opportunity arises, I'll do my best." He kissed her on the cheek. "Now, I must go and tell my family good-bye."

Unflappable, Robert E. Lee listened to the artillery duel warming up between Longstreet and Pope who confronted each other across the Rappahannock River between Kelly's Ford and Rappahannock Station. He turned to Jackson, who after arriving with his wing of the army from Stevensburg, had just breakfasted at Beauregard. "General Jackson, you're to position your men along the river from Rappahannock Station all the way to Jeffersonton. This will stretch our line thin but will force Pope to do the same thing. We have to determine his weakest spot in order to mount an attack. Time is of the essence."

Jackson pulled his dirty VMI cap down over his eyes. "We will move at once, sir."

"General Stuart," Lee continued, "have your men probe every practicable ford. This will keep Pope guessing as to where we'll cross. We must locate the most advantageous crossing for our infantry."

"We'll pursue our activities vigorously today sir," Stuart replied, saluting. "I hope to have word from our scouts that will give us a better idea of Pope's distribution of troops."

"I desperately need that information. Contact me immediately with any vital dispatches."

By late afternoon the artillery duel had reached a fierce intensity. Broken tree limbs, bark, rock fragments, screeching of projectiles, and exploding shells showered the Confederates in the woods. Because the Federals possessed the higher riverbank, they appeared to have the advantage. Stonewall Jackson remained stoic through it all. He sat on a stump, writing a dispatch to Lee. Oblivious to the shells kicking up dirt around him, he continued to write as a wounded infantryman fell almost at his feet. When another shell covered him and his dispatch with bushels of dirt, he nonchalantly stood up, walked around the stump and sat back down to finish his writing.[5] Staff officers observing the behavior of their leader questioned his sanity.

Ames awoke abruptly from a brief catnap with the feeling that he was being watched. He looked around the room and listened to the thundering cannons. Then his eyes fell to the foot of the poster bed where he spied Hudson and David staring at him intently. Their eyes only were visible because they crouched below the mattress. "Hello," he said to the two pairs of eyes.

"Are you well yet?" Hudson asked, remaining partially concealed.

"Not completely, but I appreciate your concern. Why don't you stand up so I can see you?"

Hudson slowly raised up to reveal his face. "We want you to hurry up and get well so we can shoot you. Mother says we can't kill you while you're sick. It wouldn't be proper."

"Ah!" Ames said shocked. "Perhaps we could negotiate my sentence, General... um...what's your name?"

"Hudson. You're our prisoner now and we can do anything we want to you."

"Well, yes, General Hudson, that's true. My only recourse is to beg for your mercy," Ames said, trying not to smile.

"You talk funny," David said, still hidden below the bed.

"Why do you talk so fast through your nose?" Hudson moved closer to his prisoner.

Constance entered the room carrying a tray and said sternly, "Now, boys, you know you're not supposed to be in here bothering Captain Ames." The two assailants fled from the scene while she set a bowl of soup on the table.

"We were having a fascinating conversation," he chuckled and reached his left hand towards the soup bowl.

"Oh, no you don't!" She pulled the bowl away from him. "I'm not about to let you attempt to feed yourself this soup, because I don't want to clean up the mess!"

He scowled at her, knowing he was beaten. "Are you always this bossy?"

"Only with my Yankee prisoners." She sat close to him and lifted a spoonful of soup to his mouth, admiring the swath of tawny hair that fell across his high forehead. He swallowed several spoonfuls of soup, drinking her in with his eyes, smelling the sweet aroma of the rose sachet bag that hung around her waist. A loud burst of cannon fire shook the house. When she jumped involuntarily, he saw fear, stark and vivid, glitter in her eyes. "It sounds as if these two mighty armies are about to fight to the death at any moment," she said. "Then we'll again be overrun with wounded and maimed men." Her body grew rigid as she gave him more soup. "I don't think I can bear it."

"Your life has been hell," he said softly. "You never know when this volcano called war will erupt around you, or what devastation it will spew forth. I admire your strength." Constance saw compassion in his green-edged hazel eyes. She felt this man had penetrated her innermost being—unlocked her soul. "I want you to know that I witnessed the incident at the depot when your father was sent to prison. It broke my heart and I longed to comfort you."

She gulped hard, hot tears gathering in her eyes and spilling down her cheeks. He had suddenly released the grief bottled up inside her. She looked down, then he awkwardly manipulated his left hand to wipe a tear away. "Do you want to talk about it?" he asked gently.

Tears blinded her eyes and choked her voice. She looked into his eyes and shook her head no. "Can't…yet," she gasped and fled from the room.

Next day, August 22, 1862: On the Rappahannock

Dawn: Jeb Stuart looked up from the desk in his tent headquarters when Stringfellow entered in the soft morning light. "Stringfellow!" He sprang up. "I've been anxious to hear from you. What have you learned?"

"Plenty," Stringfellow said with a grin. "I've had an exhausting ride. May I sit down general?"

"Of course, of course." Stuart motioned to a stool. "Now, proceed."

"Pope's headquarters are at Catlett's Station. It's sparsely guarded. We can take it easily. The safest route is by Waterloo Bridge through Warrenton."

Stuart's blue eyes gleamed while he paced the floor and questioned Stringfellow closely about the bridge, the ford, and the approach to Catlett's Station. Satisfied with his answers he let out a hearty laugh. "Old Headquarters-in-the saddle, eh? Well, we'll put a torch to his hindquarters!"[6]

He quickly scribbled a report to Lee requesting permission to raid Catlett's Station, guaranteeing that he had a scout who could lead him within twenty feet of Pope's headquarters. "Stretch out and take a nap, Stringfellow, until I get a reply from General Lee. We're going to have a tiring day."

John Pelham positioned four of his guns advantageously at Freeman's Ford and began inflicting heavy damage on the enemy across the river. Chew's Batteries were likewise employed at Welford's Ford. "Aim higher." Shells whistled and crashed around them. The duel raged for several hours with heavy casualties on both sides.

10 a.m. Jeb Stuart received a one-word reply from Lee—"Go." He hurriedly gathered together 2000 cavalrymen under Robertson and Fitz Lee, including the Little Fork Rangers. John Pelham stared at his orders, disappointed. *Detach two of Chew's guns for a mission with General Stuart.* Was he being left behind again as in the famous *Ride around McClellan*? He sent orders to Chew and rode to seek out Stuart.

Pelham rode up to the gathering forces. "General Stuart, sir, I request permission to accompany you."

"I know you don't want to miss the fun, Major Pelham, but I can't spare you from the artillery duel here on the river. You're too valuable." Stuart tried to soothe the feelings of this young man he admired so greatly. "I'm going after my hat," he added with a devilish grin. Pelham ruefully watched the expedition move out in the rain, with Stringfellow leading the way.

Mid-afternoon: The Confederates had little trouble driving in the enemy pickets at Waterloo Bridge and fording the Rappahannock in two columns at Hart's Mill and Waterloo. With a single charge they were able to capture the few Federals who occupied Warrenton. Stringfellow eyed the prisoners, recognizing the Yankee who had given him directions to Catlett's Station several days earlier. The duped Yankee looked at Stringfellow and spat on the ground. "Damned spy," he muttered.

The townspeople lined the sidewalks and cheered Stuart's men as deliverers. Confederate flags, hidden for several months, now hung from every house and store. Stuart, enjoying the limelight, stopped and questioned the citizens about enemy troops between Warrenton and Catlett's. A young lady learning of his intended raid burst out laughing. "General Stuart, I hope you'll capture Major Charles Goulding. If so I'll happily lose a bet I made with the officer."

Intrigued, Stuart asked, "Why madam are you joyous about losing a bet and who is this man?"

"You see General," she giggled, "he's the Federal quartermaster who boarded at our home while the Yankees occupied Warrenton. We had many heated discussions about the war, and he bet me a bottle of wine that he would be in Richmond within thirty days. I of course accepted his wager. If you were to capture this man, he would win, though not in the way he assumed."[7]

Stuart let out a hearty laugh. "Yes, he would enter Richmond as a prisoner of war instead of a member of a victorious army. Blackford, write the man's name down in the unlikely event that we encounter him. What a marvelous joke!"

The cavalry rode out of town in the steadily heavier rain. Stringfellow rode forward to inspect Cedar Run, a stream they would have to cross. Reporting back to Stuart, he said, "The stream ahead is now wide and deep, and the water's rising fast."

Evening: "Move forward quickly," Stuart called to his men. When they reached the stream, some of the smaller horses had to swim through the deep water. "We'll have to double-team the guns to get across," Stuart ordered. Stringfellow watched with concern as the columns struggled to the other side. If they had to retreat back through this strong current under fire, they would be sitting ducks. They approached Catlett's Station in the gathering darkness. Stuart sent Tom Rosser's regiment forward to capture the Federal picket.

When Stuart and his staff rode forward they encountered a Negro walking on the road outside of Pope's camp. Joseph looked up surprised at the Confederates surrounding him. Stringfellow thought, what a stroke of luck, as he recognized the darkie. "Joseph, it's Frank Stringfellow."

"Mista Frank! I's so glad to see ya. Please, ya gotta tell the Armstrongs that the Yankees made me come with 'em. They threatened to burn the house!"

"I'll tell them, Joseph. General Stuart needs your help," Stringfellow replied.

Joseph turned to Stuart with wide eyes. "Ya know I'll help ya, Gin'l Stuart."

"Joseph, can you tell us the location of Pope's tent and the layout of the camp?"

Joseph smiled broadly. "I sure kin, Gin'l Stuart. I'll be delighted to take ya right to his tent and show y'all where all the supplies are stored." The sky opened up and suddenly the rain fell in torrents. Lightning flashed and crackled while Stuart questioned Joseph and the captured pickets further, then sent a scout to verify their information. Satisfied with the correctness of his information, he divided his men into three groups whose objectives were Pope's tent, destroying the railroad-bridge over the stream, and seizing and destroying supplies at the depot.

179

"When the bugle sounds, charge forward with a yell. They'll never know what hit them in this darkness," Stuart ordered.

The thunderstorm covered the noise of the invading Confederates while the unsuspecting Federals relaxed securely in their tents at the end of a long day. Several officers listened to the rain on the tent roof while they played cards next to Pope's tent. "Now this is something like comfort," one said after sipping his toddy.

"Yep," another agreed with a laugh. "I hope that scoundrel Jeb Stuart won't disturb us tonight."[8] Suddenly, a bugle sounded and they heard wild yells followed by the sound of thousands of horses charging through the camp. The officer banged his fist on the table. "There he is, by God!"[9]

The Rebels dashed everywhere using the element of surprise to their advantage. It was difficult to tell friend from foe in the darkness. Guns blazed; several men fell injured by friendly arms. The Rebels chased the stunned Yankees through camp corralling them at the station and taking 300 prisoners. Joseph, as good as his word, unerringly led Fitz Lee's men to Pope's tent. When they charged in, they discovered to their disappointment that Pope was not present. "Damn it!" Fitz Lee shouted. "He's not here. Take everything." He grabbed Pope's personal papers and dispatch book, and opened two chests containing $500,000 in greenbacks and $20,000 in gold. He whistled. "Look at this! It must be a payroll."

"I've got his uniform," an officer bragged. "General Stuart will love this."

The rain pelted Alex who approached the railroad bridge. He and several of the Rangers struggled to ignite the wooden supports, but the driving rain foiled their attempts to set it aflame. "It's not going to burn," an officer shouted. "We'll have to try to chop it down!"

In a flash of lightning, Stringfellow spotted the telegraph line. "Give me a boost up that pole so I can cut the line," he called to Von Borcke. Standing on his comrade's shoulders, the wiry scout scaled the pole but lightning revealed him to the enemy. A shot sent splinters of wood onto his face. In the darkness again he reached the line and quickly severed it with his knife. Lightning flashed a second time and several shots whizzed by him. He maneuvered to the backside of the pole and rapidly descended. "That was close!"

At the supply depot, Rebels absconded with as much booty as they could carry back— guns, canteens, field glasses, watches, and clothes. They set fire to the flammable items and took axes to destroy everything else. When a train pulled out, Blackford charged after it pulling up close to the engine and firing on the engineer. He swore he shot him, but that could not be confirmed. One crew tore up sections of railroad track.

Jeb Stuart questioned some of the prisoners about Pope's whereabouts. "He rode towards the Rappahannock to inspect fortifications," one volunteered.

"Wouldn't you know it!" Stuart muttered. "Lucky scoundrel!"

An ecstatic Tom Rosser rode up. "General, I've been giving them hell!"

"Keep it up!" Stuart shouted.

Alex chopped at the wooden bridge support with all of his strength. The Federals opened fire from the other side of the creek. Undaunted, the Confederates worked frantically with bullets whizzing around them. Alex saw one of his men fall into the stream while a bullet struck the wood by his foot. He continued to swing the ax, but their task appeared unachievable. "General Stuart says mount up," an officer soon called.

"We're going to pull out." Greatly relieved, Alex threw himself into his saddle and fled as bullets hit the ground around him.

Stuart watched his raiders safely recross Cedar Run with their valuable booty, prisoners, and several hundred captured horses and mules. "Well done," he said to Stringfellow, halted beside him. "I want you to stay here and watch for a Federal pursuit force. If they follow, ride forward and let me know the size of their unit."

"Yes sir," the tired, wet, miserable scout responded dutifully. Stringfellow waited over an hour to be sure Stuart was not being closely pursued. He then rode to the home of an old man he knew and requested shelter in order to get a few hours of desperately needed sleep. The old man promised to keep watch for Yankees. Stringfellow entered the upstairs bedroom, threw off his wet coat, unbuckled his guns, laid them on a table, then fell into the bed and fell asleep instantly.

Shortly, he awoke abruptly to cries of "Yankees in the yard! Frank, wake up!" He leapt to his feet, buckled on his guns, and looked out the window the to see numerous Yankees with his horse. Leaving his coat behind, he dashed down the steps, out the back door, quickly jumped a fence and sprinted for his life. He heard the cavalry company closing in behind him and bullets whizzed by, much too close. The chances of his survival looked grim.

By the grace of God, the several ditches and fences in his path slowed down the cavalry. Panting, he managed to stay ahead of them and reached Cedar Run. Without hesitation he dashed into the swollen stream and swam across. He climbed up the steep bank and took shelter behind a large tree, drawing his guns. He vowed to shoot as many Yanks as possible if they crossed the stream. The Yankees stood their horses on the other side and discussed the situation. After several minutes they laughed and rode away. Stringfellow stretched out on the ground gasping for breath. Fury welled up in him at the loss of his coat, dispatch book, and a highly prized watch. Vowing to make the Yanks pay for the insult, he contemplated his dangerous situation; he was ten miles from his comrades without a horse.

After recrossing the stream, he remembered having seen several closely guarded horses in a meadow nearby. Not about to walk back, he advanced to the meadow and spotted a deep ditch that led out to the horses. He slithered through the ditch until he was in the middle of the horses. Nearby, he spotted a handsome gray with a bridle. He took a halter off another horse, vaulted on to the gray, and quietly rode to the edge of the meadow before a guard called out, "Hey, who are you? Where're you going with that horse?" Stringfellow mumbled something but kept riding towards the trees. The confused Federal hesitated and then called "Halt!" Stringfellow politely waved his hand but kept riding. The irritated Federal fired with his carbine. Stringfellow kicked his horse in the sides and took off at a gallop. Realizing the situation, the Federal cavalry pursued him hotly again. This time Stringfellow had a lead and a fresh mount. He rapidly outdistanced them.[10]

Next day, August 23, 1862: Warrenton

Morning: In his element, Jeb Stuart led one of his prisoners, Major Charles Goulding, into a familiar house in Warrenton. "We southerners keep our word, major. You've won your bet fair and square."

"Major Goulding, with great pleasure, I present you with this bottle of wine," the young lady of the house said triumphantly. "You will indeed be in Richmond within thirty days." Boisterous cheers went up from the Confederate spectators. Goulding, realizing his only recourse was to enjoy the situation, accepted the wine with a laugh.

"May I drink this now?" he asked Stuart. "I don't believe they serve wine in Libby Prison."

"By all means, Major. Sit down and enjoy your wine. It may be your last for a good while."

Next day, August 24, 1862: On the Rappahannock

Morning: In a grim mood, Stonewall Jackson had spent several hours standing hip-deep in the Rappahannock River supervising the construction of a bridge. Two days ago Early's men had advanced across the river to feel out the enemy position. The heavy rainfall during the night caused the river to rise, leaving Early trapped in a dangerous situation. If his men were discovered, the overwhelming Federal forces could annihilate or capture the Confederates. The bridge, which would accommodate the retreating artillery, neared completion. A large body of the enemy appeared to be massing near Warrenton Sulphur Springs, once a resort for the wealthy. Jackson did not consider a direct assault across the river advantageous to the Rebels. Instead, he contemplated more daring tactics.

Jackson reclined on a rail fence when Stuart and his cavalry galloped up. An exultant Stuart dismounted and held up Pope's coat before Jackson, displayed scarecrow style on two poles. "We had a rewarding visit to Pope's headquarters."

Jackson smiled and examined the fine blue broadcloth coat, glittering with brass buttons bearing its label: John Pope, Major General. "I take it you did not encounter the boastful general personally?"

"No, the lucky scoundrel wasn't there. Nevertheless, we got his papers, personal belongings, money, three hundred prisoners and horses. I've retaliated for the humiliating loss of my hat and have written Pope a proposition." Stuart handed Jackson a piece of paper.

Jackson unfolded the paper and read aloud, *"General, You have my hat and plume. I have your blue coat. I have the honor to propose a cartel for a fair exchange of the prisoners."*[11] The dour Jackson threw back his head in a hearty laugh, that Stuart alone seemed able to invoke. "Very good, very good," he chuckled. "I'm sure General Lee is anxiously awaiting you. His headquarters are in Jeffersonton."

Stringfellow rode confidently towards the outskirts of Warrenton, where he believed Stuart would be found. He heard a horse close behind him and someone asked, "What regiment, trooper?"

Without looking around, he answered, "Fourth Virginia." He realized he had made a careless mistake the moment he spoke. Spinning around he discovered a squad of Federal cavalry charging towards him. He wheeled his horse and dashed across the Warrenton and Alexandria Pike. Galloping into the yard of a farmhouse, the scout found the rear gate open and tore through. He then kicked it shut, causing the pursuing horsemen to pile up against the gate. Gaining a few precious moments, he spurred his horse forward.

However, since he steadily lost ground he realized his mount was worn from the previous chase. He saw only one alternative; he would leave the road and head for the mountain about a mile away. Pulling to the left, Stringfellow kicked his horse and tried to make him jump a stone fence. The weary animal crashed into the barricade, sending the scout sailing over his head. He hit the ground hard; but gasping for breath, he pulled his aching body back to the fence. Meanwhile, the pursuing Yanks, unable to stop their horses, sailed over Stringfellow's head. Before they could halt, the clever scout had clambered back over the fence, managed to get his horse to its feet, mounted the stunned animal, and galloped away down the road. Glancing over his shoulder, he saw the Federals standing still, apparently too frustrated to pursue him further.[12]

When he finally found himself outside enemy lines for the first time in a week he chuckled to himself, "Just another exciting day in the life of a scout."

Captain B. Frank Stringfellow, C.S.A.

8

Punishing Pope

August 24 – September 10, 1862

A Yankee horde, a mighty band, came down to invade our peaceful land,
A place beneath the ground, a cold, cold, spot, is all that this Goddamn Yankee got!
Inscription on a wooden grave marker

August 24, 1862 (continued): On the Rappahannock

Midday: John Pelham admired Pope's uniform with a smile. "I've been dodging shells for the last two days while you've made the headlines with your daring raid," he said to Stuart. "Casualties have been high among our artillerymen. Jackson's men had to make coffins from the pews in Saint James church near Brandy."

"I'm sorry you had to miss the excitement," Stuart replied. "With the information I brought from Pope's headquarters, Lee will figure a way to end this standoff."

"I'm ready for aggressive action. What will you do with the coat?"

"I plan to send it to Richmond where it can be displayed to all. This should show the Yanks what happens to boastful generals."

"I believe the good people of Culpeper Court House should see it first. After all, they've suffered the most at Pope's hands. I propose that we take the coat to town and pay a visit to our good friends, the Armstrongs," Pelham said, his eyes sparkling.

Stuart let out a guffaw. "I see through you, Romeo. You want to visit the lovely Miss Armstrong. It sounds like a rollicking good time to me. First, I have to meet with General Lee to discuss his plans. I'll let you know later if time will permit us to make the foray."

Late afternoon, Jeffersonton: Alex stood with his parents and sisters on the porch of their store at Jeffersonton and watched the curious scene before them. The soldiers carried a table from the Davisson's house, where Lee had his headquarters, and placed it in the center of the field before them. They observed the four generals approach the table, checking to be sure no one else was in earshot. "That's Lee sitting at the table and spreading the map," Alex whispered. "The tall man sitting to his right is Longstreet. The one on his left, with the curled mustache is Stuart. Jackson's standing and pacing in front of them."

"All of the commanding generals are before us," his father said. "Surely we're fortunate to be watching them. This has to be history in the making."

"I believe you're right," Alex said. "With the information we brought back from our raid, Lee should know the strength and position of Pope's army. He's got to act immediately before Pope receives more reinforcements from McClellan."

"It's all been so terrifying," his mother said. "With cannons booming all around us and thousands of soldiers from both sides swarming through our village, we've lost almost everything. I pray Lee's cunning will defeat Pope and end this terrible war."

They watched silently for a few minutes, until the generals stood up. Lee and Jackson walked forward into the road. Jackson appeared excited. He moved the toe of his boot through the sand, then gesticulated earnestly about the apparent map he had outlined. Lee listened and nodded his head. He knew that within the next two days, Pope's strength would grow to nearly 75,000 men, while the most he could muster was 52,000. He had to act now and he was willing to gamble. Defying conventional military wisdom, he decided to split his smaller force before Pope's larger army. Jackson would soon leave on a flanking march to Pope's rear at Manassas, while Longstreet kept Pope distracted on the Rappahannock.

Shortly, Stuart commanded his cavalry to be ready to march within twenty-four hours. Learning the news, Alex got permission from Captain Utterback to spend this last night with his family.

Early evening, Armstrong town home: "Yahoo!" Alex entered the front door. "We've been to raid Pope's headquarters!" Everyone rushed to meet him. He lifted the baby up over his head and kissed him. "Your Daddy has had the adventure of his life!"

"Daddy, what did you do?" Hudson shouted in the excitement.

"Jeb Stuart has done it again! We rode to the rear of Pope's army and captured his uniform, dispatches, three hundred prisoners, and several hundred horses. It was exhilarating. Frank Stringfellow was the scout who made the discovery and led the way!"

"Anne will be so proud," Harriet said.

"Constance, come outside. There's someone to see you," Alex announced.

"Do tell?" Constance walked out the front door. "Who can it be?" Seeing no one, she looked around and finally spotted Liz tied to the hitching post. "Liz!" She dashed up to the horse and put her head against her nose, caressing her.

"She was among the horses we captured. I asked permission to make her my own, as my horse is growing lame."

Constance scratched Liz's chin while the horse nuzzled her. "I hate to have her in the war, but I know it can't be helped. At least she's on the right side this time."

"As I was leaving camp, John Pelham told me he and Stuart would soon be following me to town to show all of you Pope's coat."

"What!" Constance took a quick breath of utter astonishment. "They're coming here now? I look a sight! I have to go change clothes." She charged up the steps.

"Captain Ames, I want to invite you to a celebration," Alex said. "You must get dressed and come downstairs to join the festivities."

Surprised, Ames replied, "That would be very difficult. With both arms injured, I cannot use a crutch nor can I put weight on my right leg yet. I don't believe I'm up to it. But thank you for the invitation. What's all the excitement about?"

"We raided Pope's headquarters and made away with tremendous treasures, including the good general's coat. Jeb Stuart will be here soon to show it off. You can't pass up the opportunity to meet the famous General Stuart."

Uncomfortable with the thought of being the only Yankee at a Rebel party, Ames demurred. "I'm honored, but I don't feel well enough for a party."

"I won't take no for an answer. Surely there's a way for us to get you downstairs." Alex's eyes searched the room. "I've got it. We'll put a pillow in that straight-back chair to pad your wound, and then carry you down in the chair. Can you sit in a chair?"

"I don't know," Ames said reluctantly. "I haven't tried yet." He realized protesting further would be pointless. Alex pulled back the sheet and helped him into his pants and a shirt. The fabric felt abrasive and uncomfortable against his wounds. Then Alex slid the chair next to the bed and put a pillow in the seat. With difficulty, he helped Ames balance on his left leg and lower himself into the chair. Ames grimaced at the discomfort in his buttocks.

"Now, you wait here until the others arrive and we can carry you down."

"I don't have any choice."

The strumming of Sweeney's banjo attracted a crowd while Stuart paraded Pope's coat through town. The spectators laughed gaily at the scene and rejoiced that Pope had gotten his due. In the last rays of light, Stuart gave a brief account of the raid to the townspeople gathered in front of the Virginia House. Alex invited him inside, and following a sweeping bow, Stuart kissed Harriet and Amanda. He then introduced Von Borcke and Blackford, who were followed in by Pelham, Dabney and Sweeney. When Alex explained that he had a wounded Yankee prisoner upstairs, Stuart dispatched Von Borcke to help transport the Yank down to see his general's coat.

Stuart inquired about his old friend the judge and listened spellbound to the story of his arrest. "What!" he exploded. "That's the most dastardly thing I've ever heard! It only strengthens my resolve to destroy Pope." He watched the prisoner's arrival. Ames' clenched mouth evidenced his pain until the chair was lowered to the parlor floor.

"Well, welcome to our Yankee guest," the gay cavalier exclaimed.

Pelham edged beside the chair, then introduced himself to the prisoner. Ames replied, "I'm Aaron Ames from Portland, Maine. I believe you may know two cousins of mine from West Point—Adelbert Ames and Armstrong Custer."

"Of course." Pelham squatted beside the Yankee, meeting his eyes. "I knew Del well and considered him one of my most treasured friends. Delightful fellow. We even lived together for a while. Custer was in my company. What a character! He sent me a telegram when I was promoted, saying, *We rejoice, dear Pelham, at your success.*"

"Del's spoken warmly of you on several occasions," Ames told the smooth-faced officer. "I barely know Custer myself, since he's from Michigan."

Stuart spied Constance, radiantly beautiful in a flattering aquamarine dress, swaying through the door. "I get the first kiss." He shoved Pelham aside and kissed Constance. "Now it's your turn, Romeo," he quipped to his starry-eyed major.

Blushing slightly, Pelham kissed Constance warmly on the cheek. "You see the type of derision I'm subjected to by being on General Stuart's staff."

"I'm thankful you have survived the torture." His burning eyes held her still.

Von Borcke decided to turn the tables on Stuart. "By jove, you should have seen the good general fleeing for his life when he lost his hat at Verdiersville."

"Now, Von, that's enough of that. I've retaliated for the insult and here's the coat to prove it. I must tell you that my raid would not have been such a success without the assistance of two friends of the Armstrongs." Stuart strutted across the room displaying Pope's coat.

"We know about Frank Stringfellow. Who else?" Constance inquired while Pelham led her forward by the arm.

"Your servant Joseph kindly directed us to Pope's tent."

The mouths of the family dropped at the news about Joseph. "You mean Joseph left the farm and is with Pope's army?" Alex asked.

"Yes, he asked us to tell you that he was coerced. They threatened to burn your house if he didn't agree to come with them and serve their army," Stuart said disgusted.

"Oh, my God," Harriet sighed. "Now both Abraham and Joseph are gone. We have no one to tend the farm. How will we manage?"

Hudson, furious at the thought of losing his friend Isaac, shouted, "We killed a Yankee! Aunt Connie beat him to death."

Constance felt the color creeping up her face when all eyes focused on her. "Is this true?" Pelham asked in disbelief.

"Well, I…um…yes, but you see I didn't intend to," she stuttered. "He went into my parents bedroom and stole photos and family mementos. Then he found the Culpeper Minuteman flag that my grandfather carried in the Revolution." Her voice rose an octave. "You see, I couldn't let him steal that. It's a priceless family heirloom. Before I knew what was happening, I hit him on the head with the fireplace poker."

The men, especially Ames, stared at her thunderstruck. Stuart took her hand away from Pelham. "Miss Armstrong, I'm in awe of your courage. You're a brave servant of our cause. Soon, you will be as famous as one of Major Pelham's other lady friends, Belle Boyd."

Now it was Pelham's turn to blush. "You know Belle Boyd?" she inquired.

"Actually…well, yes…I met her near Martinsburg. She's a good friend," Pelham said evasively.

Realizing he had tormented Pelham enough, Stuart turned his attention to Ames. "Tell me, Captain Ames, why are you sitting on a pillow?"

"I have a wound on my…um…hindquarters." Ames was irritated at the embarrassment.

Stuart and the other Rebels let out a boisterous laugh. "Why am I not surprised that a member of Pope's army would be wounded in the hindquarters?" Stuart taunted.

Ames seethed with anger and humiliation. He would not be the subject of their derision. "General Stuart." His deep voice bristled with indignation. "I was with the Tenth Maine when they made a gallant stand in the middle of a wheat field, completely exposed to the enemy. Nearly half of my friends were lost. I was facing the enemy when a shell exploded behind me. I may be a Yankee, sir, but I am not a coward." A hushed silence fell over the room. Her patient's rebuff of Stuart impressed Constance.

Stuart swaggered over to Ames and put his hand on his shoulder. "I admire your courage, Yank. Let's enjoy the party. You need to have some fun before your sojourn in Richmond. Sweeney, strike up a song!"

Amanda played the piano and the soldiers sang a rousing version of *If you want to have fun, jine the cavalry,* as well as numerous other patriotic songs. Stuart led the singing with his sonorous voice. All of the soldiers treated Ames cordially and were delighted to learn that he had rowed on the crew team with Rooney Lee, Robert E. Lee's middle son, while at Harvard. Ames found himself envious of their irrepressible spirit and sense of unity to their cause. He watched intently and observed that Constance's eyes followed Pelham's every move. Concluding that she was infatuated with him, he was disturbed when they slipped away to the front porch.

Constance and Pelham stood in the moonlight stroking the horse's neck. "You were right about Liz," she said. "The Yankees stole her and Alex recaptured her in the raid. I should have sold her to you."

"I understand your reasons. As brave as you are, you could have protected her. You did a crazy thing, but I admire your courage." He slid his hands around her slender waist and pulled her gently against him.

His laughing gray eyes glistened in the pale light of the moon, captivating her. "Major Pelham, congratulations. You're the one who's becoming famous for courage. The newspapers call you the gallant Pelham."

"I'm only doing my duty like every other soldier. Tomorrow we're marching, I know not where. One thing is certain: a battle with Pope will follow. I pray God will grant us another victory that will end this war." He paused while his hands caressed the hollows of her back. "I want you to know that your letters have been a source of strength for me. No matter how terrible the situation, I think of you and I feel better."

"You are constantly on my mind also." Her pulse raced in anticipation.

"You've become much more than a friend to me." His stare bore through her while he grasped for words. "I want to…kiss you…if you deem it proper."

She inhaled sharply. "During war, we don't have time for…proprieties. I deem it proper." Parting her lips she raised herself to meet his kiss. The touch of his lips was a delicious sensation. He held her close against his taut, lean body. Shocked at her own eager response, she caressed his neck and ran her fingers through his blonde hair.

The sound of boots on the front porch heralded Stuart's departure. "Pelham my boy, I know you're out here," called Stuart loudly. "Enough romance for one night. Duty calls."

"You see what I have to put up with." Pelham released her reluctantly. "He never lets me out of his sight. I have no privacy."

"I suspect you enjoy every minute of it."

He squeezed her hand and mounted his horse. "Good night, fair damsel!" Sweeney strummed his banjo and the band of Rebels rode into the night.

Next day, August 25, 1862: On the Rappahannock

Dawn: Powell Hill followed Ewell when Jackson's Corps marched before daybreak. Once again none of the generals had any idea of their destination. The men filed by the gruesome sight of an open grave containing the bodies of three deserters whom Jackson had executed the day before. The message was clear: desertion would not be tolerated. As the columns entered Amissville and turned west towards the mountains, a cheer went up because the men assumed they were returning to the valley. However, they promptly turned northward on a back road and crossed the Rappahannock undetected at Hinson's Mill. Were they headed towards Manassas? No one knew. Jackson gave directions at every intersection. The barefoot men left a bloody trail along the rough twenty-five miles they covered before stopping at Salem for the night.

Morning: The Armstrongs' "Good morning, Captain Ames. I hope you weren't too badly abused last night," Constance said over the cannons booming again in the distance.

"Good morning," he said sleepily. "I'm still sore from sitting in that chair. I don't think those muscles are healed enough to be stretched yet. What smells so good?"

"Scrambled eggs and bacon. Several farmers have brought food from the valley to sell. However, prices are outrageous. Without Father's salary, our financial situation is grim."

"Delicious!" Ames awkwardly fed himself. "I'll repay you one of these days."

"Thank you for offering. For now we'll take one day at a time." She straightened his covers and folded his clothes over a chair. "So tell me, what did you think of General Stuart?"

"If you want an honest answer, I found him obnoxious and arrogant. However, I must admit I admire his daring bravery." He munched on a piece of bacon. "I realized last night how little I know about your family history. Would you be kind enough to share it with me, especially the part about the flag?"

A thoughtful smile curved her mouth. "Yes, I'll do that if you'll do likewise. In fact, I'll come back after I've finished some chores and show you the flag."

"Wonderful!" He devoured every morsel of the eggs. "I'll look forward to that."

Afternoon: Hudson and David sprawled one on each side of Ames, while he read to them from *Moby Dick*. "I've seen lots of whales off the coast of Maine where I live. They're beautiful when they jump out of the ocean and spray a fountain of water up from their backs. Sometimes they slap their tail fins against the waves."

"How big are they?" David asked.

"Huge! As big as this house," Ames replied.

Constance walked in with a small cedar chest. "It seems you already have visitors."

"He's telling us about whales," David said wide-eyed. "They're this big." He spread his arms to the limit.

"I tell you what boys, if you'll let me visit with your aunt now, I promise I'll finish reading the book later." Ames handed the book to Hudson.

The two boys reluctantly climbed down from the bed. "Remember, you promised," Hudson said as they left the room.

"Looks like you've made some new friends." Constance sat in the chair beside the bed.

"Actually I'm doing it in self-defense. They threatened to shoot me a few days ago." Ames chuckled.

"Do tell?" She laughed. "I must apologize. Are you ready for the Armstrong family history?"

"I'm all ears, teacher. Begin the lesson."

"My great-grandfather, Charles Hudson Armstrong, arrived here in 1749 at age twenty four with his new bride. A graduate of William and Mary, he decided to venture to the frontier to practice law. Fortunately, he came well financed: his father was a wealthy

189

tobacco merchant in Williamsburg. He built a house, which is the left wing of our current house, where the law offices are located. The courthouse was constructed in 1750. A seventeen-year-old surveyor, pursuing his first job, arrived about the same time and worked for three years laying out the town and surveying the surrounding area. He and great-grandfather became hard and fast friends, and the surveyor boarded with them while he worked in town. When my grandfather was born in 1752, the surveyor became his godfather." She tilted her head and grinned mischievously. "The surveyor's name was George Washington."

Ames's eyebrows shot up, then he eyed her skeptically. "Am I to assume we are speaking of *the* George Washington?"

"None other," she said with a smug look. "Grandfather was twenty four when our first Revolution began. Then, as now, the flame of independence and defiance burned brightly in the hearts of Culpeper's young men. They formed the Culpeper Minute Men, one of the first units to react when Patrick Henry called for men to march to Williamsburg in response to Governor Dunmore's removal of powder and military supplies from the magazine." Her voice became animated. "You can imagine what a stir the backwoodsmen caused when they marched into Williamsburg wearing green home-spun jerkins lettered with their motto 'Liberty or Death,' arrayed with toma-hawks, scalping knives, and buck-tailed hats." She opened the cedar chest on the table and pulled the tattered flag out. "And this was their battle flag."

Ames whistled. "Very impressive. How did you come into possession of the flag?"

"My grandfather became close friends with another Minuteman from Warrenton by the name of John Marshall."

Ames rolled his eyes. "You're connected with all the F.F.V.s,[i] aren't you?"

She smiled and nodded. "They fought with General Washington until the surrender of Cornwallis at Yorktown. The good general presented the flag to his godson at the conclusion of the war. You can understand why I couldn't allow the Yankee to steal it."

"You were courageous to defend that flag. I, too, would have killed under the same circumstances."

"I brought the flag to town when you provided us safe passage. The Culpeper Minutemen have been revived and are fighting in this our second War of Independence as part of the Thirteenth Virginia Infantry. The women made them a new flag, an exact replica of this one." She carefully folded the flag and put it back in the chest.

The music of her voice and her slow sultry southern drawl hypnotized him. "Please, continue. Tell me what happened to your grandfather."

"Following the Revolution he returned here to practice law with great-grandfather. He married Katherine Rixey, whose wealthy family owned large tracts of land in the area where our farm is located. Her parents gave the newlyweds five hundred acres and fifteen slaves. They prospered and built our farmhouse and added on to this house, making a portion of it law offices. My grandfather lived to the ripe old age of eighty eight. He had never really approved of slavery and freed his slaves in his will. How-ever, that left my father the difficult job of deciding what to do with them."

---

[i] First Families of Virginia

"I'm not sure why that was difficult," Ames said bewildered. "Elaborate for me."

"First of all, none of them wanted to leave. All cried and begged to stay. Sadie and her husband and children were part of our family. Father wanted them to remain here, but he had to petition the legislature for permission and guarantee that they would be cared for and not become indigent. Free blacks are not welcome anywhere and many northern states have laws preventing them from entering the state.[ii] Another farmer, J. Pembroke Thom, confronted the same situation when he attempted to free his eighteen slaves. After he bought a suitable tract of land for their settlement in Pennsylvania, his slaves refused to go. It was as if his whole plantation was in mourning. Determined to complete his good work, he had them hauled there against their will. Within a year, practically all had returned to Culpeper."[1]

"This is an aspect of emancipation I never considered," Ames said thoughtfully. "It sounds as if it's not as simple in practice as it sounds in theory."

"No, it's an extremely complex problem. At any rate, when Sadie's children grew up, Father hired Joseph to stay as his overseer. One son was killed working on the railroad, one works as a cook at the hotel, and another went to New York and was never heard from again. We suspect he was kidnapped by some Yankee and sold into slavery in South America, as so frequently happens to freemen in New York."

"I believe such occurrences are rare. But tell me more about your family. Do have just one sister?"

"Yes." She leaned back in the chair and folded her hands. "My father lost his first wife and child in childbirth. Broken hearted, he threw his energy into politics and served in the legislature. He met Mother when he was forty four. The daughter of a wealthy shipping tycoon in Fredericksburg, she had lived in Europe many years studying art. When they married Father knew he would have to give up politics in order to earn enough money to support his family. He re-entered the practice of law and left the farming operation to Joseph. He always kept abreast of the political situation from the sidelines. Since he didn't have a son, he allowed me to share all of those activities with him. He's taught me all I know about law, government, history, and politics."

"I'm impressed with your knowledge and intellect," he said sincerely. "It's obvious that you're very close to your father."

"Yes, he's everything to me." She swallowed the lump in her throat. "But I've talked enough. It's your turn. I want to know about the Ames family."

"My great-grandfather, Adelbert Aaron Ames, came from a seafaring family in Liverpool, England. At age twenty eight, in 1740, he immigrated with his wife and two children to Salem, Massachussetts. He brought with him enough capital to open a small shipbuilding business. He worked diligently and his business prospered. His wife…"

"Excuse me, Captain Ames, but may I ask what kind of ships your great grandfather built?"

"He built many types of vessels, but of course he had to cater to his clients' needs."

"I would assume that since Salem and Liverpool were leading ports for slave ships, that a good portion of his income was derived from building slave vessels. In the 1760s

[ii] New Jersey, Indiana, Illinois, and Oregon had laws prohibiting free blacks from immigrating into their states. Massachusetts had them publicly whipped if they remained too long.

when the crown attempted to levy a tax on molasses, Massachussetts objected saying 700 slave ships, 60 distilleries, and 5000 men would be out of work."

"You have an excellent memory!"

She shrugged matter-of-factly. "Father and I have studied the slavery issue carefully."

"I can't deny that a portion of his business was from slave ships, but I don't know the percentages. His wife died shortly after his arrival and he later married a woman who was the daughter of a wealthy distillery owner. They had five children, the first of which was my grandfather."

"You can't deny that the source of her wealth was brewing rum for the slave trade," she asked innocently.

"I will concede that it was a partial source of profit." His voice had a tone of irritation. "My grandfather went to Harvard and continued to work in the family business. He was also interested in politics and participated in the Boston Tea Party. He married the daughter of a prominent lawyer near the beginning of the Revolution. He immediately enlisted and rose to the rank of major before he was killed at Saratoga. My father was born five months later."

"He paid the supreme price for our freedom. You must be proud. Who raised your father?" She leaned closer to the bed, her eyes sparkling with interest.

"Of course he remained with his mother, but unfortunately she died a year later. Then he went to live with his uncle, grandfather's brother, who was running the family shipping business. He became an accepted member of that family and actually had a very happy childhood, along with his six cousins. While at Harvard, he fell in love and married a Boston lady. She died at the birth of their second son. Several years later he returned to Boston and was smitten with my mother, twelve years his junior and the grand niece of John Adams."

"Aha!" An easy smile played at the corners of her mouth. "Of course we are speaking of *the* John Adams."

"Absolutely!" He laughed. "I won't let you outdo me. But she refused to marry him unless he sold out of the Salem shipping business, which at that point was, I must admit, heavily into slave ships. You see my mother's a very religious woman, and she refused to live in Salem around that environment." He glanced at Constance who gave him a mute "I told you so" smile. "So father sold his share of the business to our relatives for a sizable sum, and they married and moved to Portland. There he established a thriving shipbuilding business and fishing fleet. I have five older brothers and one sister, two years older. I'm the baby."

"You're blessed to have such a large family. Are your brothers involved in shipping?"

"Yes, they each have several boats and concentrate on cod fishing and whaling. My sister is married; I adore her. My parents have been blessed with longevity; he's eighty two, she's seventy."

"Do you intend to join the family business?" She stood and walked to the window, listening to the cannons.

"No. After two years at Harvard, my parents suspected I had succumbed to the sins of the city and was neglecting my studies. They insisted I come home to work with the fleet and rethink my priorities." His full mouth parted in a devilish grin, displaying dazzling straight, white teeth against his tanned face. She wondered, did he think he could disarm her with that irresistibly devastating smile? How many women had he seduced with that smile and his sensuous physique? No sane woman would ever trust a man with such magnetic sexual appeal. His deep voice caught her attention again. "I grew bored after over a year and knew it wasn't the life for me, so I decided to finish college and take my studies a bit more...um... seriously. I love writing and literature. I've thought about working for a newspaper and I also have an interest in medicine. After the war, I'll pursue a career in one of those fields."

"We share a common interest in writing." She examined his arm. "Your wound is healing. The provost-marshal is coming to check on your progress tomorrow."

Her words struck him like a bolt of lightning. "Oh, of course...I understand...it's inevitable. I can't impose on you much longer."

"Captain Ames, don't you see the hypocrisy in your situation?" she asked sharply. "Your family's wealth, as that of most New Englanders, was built on the slave trade. And now, you, who have made fortunes by selling men into slavery, are here destroying our land to supposedly free those same slaves. Not only that, you're punishing the ninety-four percent of us who are not slave owners."

He stared at her face, hot and pinched with anger, and did not know how to answer. "I...uh...well...I've never thought of it that way. You're forcing me to look at my preconceived ideas differently."

"There's much you don't understand about slavery. My father and I have done extensive research on the subject. It's such an emotional issue, but I'd like to share some facts and statistics with you that tell the true story."

"I would greatly appreciate that Miss Armstrong. I feel our debates are beneficial to both of us." He eagerly anticipated the opportunity to spend more time with her.

"Very well. Prepare yourself for a lecture tomorrow." She left the room carrying the treasured cedar chest.

Next day, August 26, 1862: Armstrong town home

Ames cringed when Sadie stalked into the room to bathe him. She had assumed that task because she believed it improper for Constance to be exposed to a naked man, especially a naked Yankee. It was never a pleasant occasion. He laid aside the volume of Shakespeare Constance had loaned him and attempted to smile. "Sadie, there's something I've wanted to ask you." She threw the sheet back.

"What's that?" she replied sullenly while wiping him off.

"What's your last name and how did you get it?"

"Mah last name is Jordan. I picked it mahsef 'cause of the River Jordan in the Good Book. When we was set free, Mista Armstrong said we had to have our own name. I named all mah chil'en after folks in the Bible."

"Why did you choose to stay with the Armstrongs when you were freed?"

"'Cause we is their people. They care 'bout us. Where else we gonna go? How we gonna make money? Who'd take care of us? Don't ya see, this is mah home. Mah great-grandmother was born here. I've raised those two girls. We was happy people 'til you damn Yankees came along!"

"If you had the opportunity to return to Africa with the other freed slaves, would you go?"

She rolled him over roughly. "Africa! They got wild animals an' snakes in the jungles over there! Lan' sakes no, I wouldn't go. I'm a Christian. Ain't no Christians over there. Besides, I'm a *Vah-gin-yan*. I 'spect mah family has been here as long as yours has been in Maine. How'd ya like it if somebody told ya to leave your home an' go 'cross the ocean to wherever ya came from?"

"I never thought of it that way, but no, I suppose I wouldn't want to leave. But, your son has gone with Pope's army."

"That's 'cause they forced him to! They threatened to burn the house. Now they'll make 'em work for 'em, an' he won't have a roof over his head. He'll never fight 'gainst his people. They'll be back; this is their home. When you Yankees quit fightin' an' killin', they'll be back!" she shrieked.

"I wish I could make you understand that we're here to help you."

"Help us! I don't 'member askin' for your help. If stealin' our food an' killin' anybody who gets in your way is help, we don't need it." She scrubbed him roughly. "Look's like your behind is 'bout healed. Seems like it's time for ya to go 'way from here. We don't need another mouth to feed. That other Yankee with the head wound, that we thought we was rid of, he showed up on our doorstep again." She rolled him back over, her black eyes shooting sparks.

"I'll be going to prison soon."

"Well, good riddance!" She stomped out of the room causing the furniture and pictures to rattle in her wake.

Constance rummaged through her father's desk for the information she wanted to show Captain Ames. She pulled out the census statistics on Negroes in the South. Yes, that was important. She kept searching until she found the two newspaper editorials Mrs. Daly had sent them that proved greed was the North's motivation for war. Finding them she read them again:

The first was from the March 30, *New York Times:*
If a manufacturer in England can send his goods into the Western States through New Orleans at a less cost than through New York, he is a fool not availing himself to his advantage. If the importations of the country are made through Southern ports, its exports will go through the same channel. The produce of the West, instead of coming to our own ports by millions of tons, to be transported abroad by the same ships through which we received our importations, will seek other routes and other outlets. Once at New Orleans, goods may be distributed over the whole country duty free… The process is perfectly simple…The commercial bearing of the question has acted upon the North….We now see clearly…what policy we must adopt. With us it is no longer an abstract question…one of Constitutional construction…or of delegated power of the State or Federal Government, but of material existence and moral position both home and abroad…We were divided and confused until our pocketbooks were touched.

And from the *New York Evening Post*, March 12:
That either revenue from duties must be collected in the ports of the rebel states, or the ports must be closed to importations from abroad…If neither of these things be done, our revenue laws are substantially repealed; the sources which supply our treasury will be dried up.[2]

194

Captain Ames was obviously an intelligent man. She would put these articles in front of him and let him draw his own conclusions.

David and Hudson were curled up beside Ames, totally entranced while he read to them. Constance observed the touching scene. "Please don't make us go, Aunt Connie," Hudson begged. She raised her eyebrows and gave her patient a questioning look.

"Boys, I promise I'll finish reading you this book before I leave, but I'd like to spend some time with your aunt now." He closed the book; they frowned but obediently slipped away. "I'm glad to see you. I need some intellectual conversation. I hope we can have this debate and remain friends. Otherwise, we should skip it." He searched her face for some sign of emotion.

"We're on opposite sides in a brutal war, but you're right. We must respect the other's point of view. Let's promise each other we'll end the debate as friends, no matter what." She pulled the chair to his bedside and placed her books and notes in her lap.

"I'll agree to that," he responded with an engaging smile. "Now, proceed to indoctrinate my Yankee brain."

"I have a considerable amount of information to share with you, so forgive me if I sound like an old school marm giving a lecture."

"At least you don't look like an old school marm."

Ignoring his compliment, she began, "Slavery has existed since recorded time. We southerners didn't invent it, but we've never known a world without it. I, too, would like to see the practice ended, just as I dream of women being granted the right to vote. I also believe that working children fourteen hours a day, six days a week in deplorable conditions, as in your New England mills, is morally wrong. In 1832 one third of your factory work force was under the age of ten. Our slave children don't work those hours at such an early age." She paused. "But, I'm digressing; where we strongly disagree is how to abolish slavery without bankrupting the South."

Ames nodded. "I'm with you so far."

She opened her notes. "Contrary to what you may have learned at Harvard, the first permanent English colony was established at Jamestown in 1607." He chuckled and nodded his agreement. "An English ship brought the first twenty Negroes here in 1619. Virginians did not seek Negro labor. It was dropped on our doorstep. These first arrivals were treated as indentured servants and were able to earn their freedom."

She glanced at her notes. "The first colony to pass a law legalizing slavery in 1641 was the home of your ancestors, Massachusetts. In 1646 the good New Englanders passed a law by which Indians could be seized and sold into slavery in the Caribbean. They turned a healthy little profit selling thousands of them to Bermuda, Barbados, and the other islands. Meanwhile, Virginia passed a law protecting its Native Americans. The intolerant Puritans also shipped off Quakers and those of other faiths to bondage. The first slave ship equipped in America was the *Desire*, which was built in Salem and sailed in 1637. For the next two hundred years massive fortunes were made in New England as the African slave trade became the cornerstone of Yankee commerce." She looked up from her notes to see him frowning at her.

"I can't dispute any of your facts, but I believe you've exaggerated."

"I'll be glad to let you see my sources when I'm finished," she said crisply. "But now let's look at the three steps of the slave trade. First, slavery began in Africa where blacks enslaved blacks. Warring chieftains soon learned they could capture weaker tribes, march them to the coast, and make a hefty profit selling their native brothers to the slave ships anchored off shore. No white men ever went into Africa and captured slaves. They would have died from disease and the chieftains would not have tolerated the competition. So, if you want to end slavery, why not go to the source? Conquer the African chieftains and make them free their slaves."

"I get your point," he said begrudgingly. "But we have no right to invade Africa."

"Neither do you have any right to invade the South," she snapped. "But let us continue and look at the middle passage. The human cargo was crammed into a space three and a half feet high for a voyage of two months. The shackled slaves had to sit or lie in excrement and filth. Is it no wonder eight to ten per cent died? Think of the cramped quarters, the seasickness, and try to begin to grasp the torture. New Englanders built and owned those ships. When the slaves were sold in the Caribbean, molasses was loaded to take back to New England to make rum. Your great-grandparents greatly profited from the slave trade."

"That may be partially true, but that was in the past," he said defensively.

"So your family is guiltless because they profited, and never saw the slaves? Your family fortune was built on profits from the slave trade, but that was in the past, so you're now sinless? I suspect the Ames family has gained far more from slavery than the Armstrongs, and yet you're invading our land!"

"I can't change the past," he protested. "I can only hope to change the future."

She took a deep breath, trying to keep from erupting. "I think you're being evasive, but I'll continue." She stood up and held a piece of paper in front of him. "This column is the number of slaves brought out of Africa and where they were taken. The second column is the current Negro population of each country. Only five percent of all the slaves taken out of Africa were brought to this country. The others were sold in South America and the Caribbean. That's where the Yankee shippers made and are still making massive profits.[iii]"

Ames studied the figures carefully. "Do you mean that the 450,000 slaves brought here had increased to 3,953,760 by 1860. A number almost…what…nine times larger?"

"Yes, and at the same time the nine and a half million taken elsewhere have decreased to almost half the original number. Their death rate is appalling." Ames whistled as he studied the figures. "Is there any doubt that the slaves brought here were the lucky ones? They've thrived and multiplied because they've been well fed and cared for. We aren't the cruel ogres described by the abolitionists."

"Those figures are food for thought," he acquiesced. "I admit I've always visualized a plantation owner sipping on mint juleps and beating his slaves. I was surprised to see the affection between your family and your servants."

"I can't deny that there are cruel masters. We have a few here, but they're social outcasts and definitely the minority." She sat back down. "I suggest that the only reasonable solution to the slavery problem is a gradual economic one. Financial compensation should be made to the slaveholders as the British did in the West Indies in 1833."

[iii]According to black historian W.E.B. DuBois, during the Civil War more than 1200 slaves were brought to the Western Hemisphere by ships flying the U.S. flag.

"But the North did away with slavery. Why can't the South?" he asked innocently.

Her body became rigid and her eyes smoldered. "Let's take a closer look at that so-called magnanimous gesture by the North. You're industrial, we're agricultural. When you could hire white immigrants to do the necessary work, keeping slaves was no longer financially advantageous. So you sold the young physically able ones to southerners, thereby recouping your investment. The elderly were set free to live in poverty and squalor. We're legally obligated to care for our elderly slaves. The North lost no money by freeing its slaves." She shot him a withering glare of blue ice. "Southerners have freed far more slaves at their own expense, the way my grandfather did in his will. Our two main money crops, tobacco and cotton, are grown throughout the world with slave labor. If we went to free labor, we couldn't compete. And where, may I ask you, would all of our slaves go if they were suddenly freed? Abolitionists may hate slavery, but they don't love the slaves."

"I had always thought colonization back to Africa was the logical solution. However, when I mentioned it to Sadie today she let me know in no uncertain terms that she was a *Vah-gin-yan* and she was not about to go over there with all the snakes and wild animals."

She managed a small smile. "You can't suddenly transplant people against their will for the second time. If Culpeper's seven thousand Negroes suddenly appeared on the doorsteps of the good people of Portland, would they take them in? Would they find jobs for them?"

He pondered for a moment and shook his head. "I doubt it. People like my mother would, but the vast majority would not welcome them."

"How many Negroes have you known well, Captain Ames?"

"To be honest, none. There're only a handful in Portland; they work on the docks and live in poverty."

"And when your army arrived here, did the blacks rush out to welcome you as great deliverers?"

He shrugged his shoulders in resignation. "I was surprised. They seemed very wary of us. Sadie is the only black I've really ever talked to. She told me today that *mah* behind was better and it was time for me to go away from *he-ah*."

Her soft laughter rippled through the air. "I couldn't have said it more eloquently myself."

His mouth twitched with amusement and then he broke into a deep, rich laugh. "May I suggest, Miss Armstrong, that we cease hostilities and declare a truce?"

"I will consider that in a minute, but as Jeb Stuart would say, I have one last charge to make."

"Proceed. I'll hunker down in a defensive position." He sank down into the bed and pulled the sheet up until only his eyes were visible. He enjoyed watching her and found her beautiful even when angry. Her quick mind and fiery spirit excited him. Although they had completely opposite perspectives, he found everything she said logical. She challenged him at every turn.

She glanced down at her notes. "When the states of the deep South first seceded, there was little outcry in the North. Horace Greeley and several other abolitionists came forward and said, let them go in peace…we can be peaceful trading partners. However, when the Confederacy adopted its own Constitution and adopted a lower ten percent tariff on imports, powerful people in the North soon realized how much revenue would be lost. The Federal coffers have been filled for years by the grossly unfair tariff southerners have paid on imports. Abraham Lincoln was even quoted as saying, *Let the South go! Let the South go! Where will we get our revenues?*[5] Here are two editorials from northern papers proving my point. I hope you'll consider them."

She handed him the newspaper clippings, which he scanned with attentive eyes. "This war is not about slavery, Captain Ames. That's the emotional issue that has been used to incite hatred. We no longer want to be your economic colony and are fighting for independence. You do not want to let us go because your pocketbooks will suffer. Plainly and simply, this war is about Yankee greed and imperialism!" She defiantly slammed her notebook shut.

He sat up, allowing the sheet to slide down his well-developed chest to his waist and stared at her in deep thought. "I'll read these clippings. I don't know the motives of our leaders or others involved in this war. There certainly may be some truth to your argument. I can only tell you one thing. Look at me, Miss Armstrong." His compelling eyes riveted her to the spot. "I did not risk my life in the middle of that wheat field because of greed. *That is not why...I...am...here!*" he said slowly, deliberately.

As she looked into his hazel eyes, she became convinced of his honesty. "I believe you," she said softly. "Perhaps you've been duped."

"If I've been duped, then so have the Rebels who're fighting to preserve slavery for the wealthy planters." The rigid muscles in his square jaw gradually relaxed until a half-smile crossed his face. "The provost marshal is coming for me day after tomorrow. I'd like to enjoy the pleasure of your company again before I leave. Perhaps we could indulge in a more friendly confrontation. Do you play chess or checkers?" he asked, his eyes twinkling.

"Yes, both, but I prefer chess," she replied with a challenge in her voice.

"Ah!" His thick eyebrows shot up. "You may want to reconsider. I must warn you, Rebel lady, that I was champion of the Harvard Chess Team."

Typical Yankee arrogance, she thought. She might have to bring this Harvard man down a few notches. "And I must warn you Yank, you will be defeated."

Next day, August 27, 1862: Manassas

The flags fluttered gaily in the dawn sky as Jeb Stuart's cavalry lines advanced on the irregular town of storehouses, barracks and tents at Manassas Junction. "Open up on them, men," John Pelham ordered. His horse artillery shelled the redoubts protecting the town. Dense clouds of white smoke covered the area while masses of blue troops frantically fled to the woods. Taken totally by surprise, the Federals put up little resistance. Delighted with his success, Stuart captured twelve pieces of artillery in the redoubts with little fighting. The cavalry quickly claimed a gaudily painted sutler's wagon drawn by four excellent horses, which Stuart claimed for his horse artillery.

"What wonderful gifts you've brought me," Pelham exclaimed to Von Borcke when he arrived with the steeds. The cannoneers gathered around the captured wagon to distribute the booty while the Prussian slashed the boxes open with his sword. "Look, shirts!" Pelham passed them to the men. "Oh, thank God, fresh fruit!" He tossed oranges and lemons to starving comrades. The Rebels grabbed and fought over wine, hats, handkerchiefs, and cigars.

Jackson rode over to the scene, astounded at the captured stores. He immediately put a warehouse full of whisky under guard and ordered Fitz Lee to picket the roads east and destroy lines of communication to Washington. Sheds brimming with food and clothing lined the streets of the town. Round shot stood in rows and shells were piled in high pyramids. Barrels of flour, pork, biscuits, and cases of tinned meats covered acres of the surrounding fields.[4] "I believe our men deserve a brief holiday," he said to Stuart when he rode up. "But have the heads knocked out of the barrels of whiskey and wine."

Stuart laughed heartily. "We can't have our army inebriated. When we captured the supply post at White House, my men had already gotten into some of the liquor before I could stop them. I had Stringfellow and Farley spread a rumor that the Yanks had shipped their embalming fluid in whiskey bottles. You should have seen the troops suddenly become deathly ill and grasp their stomachs." Jackson threw his head back and laughed.

The ragged, ravenous footsoldiers charged the storehouses of incredible wealth. Powell Hill sat on a barrel enjoying lobster and caviar, while he watched the Rebels fall on their faces to guzzle the liquor trickling through the ditches. Men tumbled over one another and scrambled in a frenzy of greed for the coveted luxuries. Stringfellow stood on a barrel auctioning off some goods. The swapping continued at a frantic pace while they bartered underwear for blankets, coffee for tallow candles, toothbrushes for sugar, sardines for caramel candy. The delighted soldiers gorged themselves and pillaged until late afternoon. All that could not be consumed or carried away was destroyed.

John Pope arrived at Bristoe Station at twilight to discover supply trains derailed by Confederate marauders. Startled, he looked east towards Manassas and saw a volcano of flames shoot high into the air. Shells exploded and sudden jets of flame rose and receded in the sky, sounding like a great battle. A courier galloped up to him at full speed. "General Pope, sir, I report that the Rebels at Manassas are more than a cavalry raid. It's Jackson's whole corps of thirty thousand!"

"Jackson!" Pope exclaimed. "So it's Jackson! Now we have the mighty Stonewall where we can destroy him!" Pope believed he could at last back up his boasting by defeating the most elusive prize of the war. Jackson! Even the northern papers thought Stonewall a hero. Pope smiled. He would bolster his sagging reputation by finally destroying the deceptive Jackson. He forgot that Longstreet was behind him.

"Issue orders for my army to move forward from Gainesville," he barked to his aides. "We shall bag the whole crowd, if my men are prompt and expeditious."[5]

The Armstrongs': When Constance entered the bedroom carrying the chess game, Ames greeted her with a warm smile. "I thought you had stood me up."

"I've had a busy day." She placed the board on the bed beside him and sat down on the edge of the bed. "I've been helping Mr. McDonald prepare an edition of the paper. He hasn't published one since Pope's occupation."

"So you're already in the newspaper business?" He helped her position the pieces on the board. "Ladies first. Your move."

"Yes, I've been helping him since his son went off to war." She moved and stared at the volume of Shakespeare beside him. "What's your favorite work?"

"*Romeo and Juliet* without a doubt. I'm deeply touched by the tragedy of the star-crossed lovers." He pushed a pawn forward. "It's especially relevant in light of our current conflict." He stared at her intently but she would not let her eyes meet his.

She carefully made her move. "But so are the plays about military ambition such as *MacBeth,* and Hamlet's soliloquies are classic debates about morality during wartime."

He took a handkerchief and wiped the sweat from his face. "The heat and humidity have been oppressive today. I don't know how you tolerate it." He moved again.

"We grow used to it. But I'm sure it's difficult for you to adjust to. Tell me about Maine." She looked up at him with an interested smile. In his element, Ames went into a long, detailed dissertation about the beauty of his home state, elaborating on the jagged coastline, towering evergreens, rolling mountains, rushing rivers, and serene lakes. Then he expounded on the delicacies pleasing to the palate: lobster, fish of every kind, and blueberries.

She enjoyed his rambling travelogue while the game progressed. "Listen." She held her hand up. "Did you hear that muffled sound in the distance? It sounds like the cannons at the battle of Manassas."

"Yes, I hear it. The bombarding has quieted here today. What do you make of it?"

"I believe Lee and Jackson have shifted the scene of battle northward. Perhaps they're trying to cut Pope off from Washington. I'm thankful this conflict will not take place on our soil." She pushed her knight forward.

"And would you care to predict the outcome?"

"Pope will be defeated. I'm positive of that. Lee and Jackson are the two greatest generals alive and our men are angrily seeking revenge for Pope's deplorable treatment of civilians. Would you like to wager on the outcome?"

Ames contemplated the chessboard and her question. "No. I'm not fool enough to bet on Pope. In fact, I believe I'm fortunate to be here tonight and not on the battlefield. I fear his men will be like lambs led to the slaughter."

She took his castle. "If Pope's defeated, Lee will have accomplished the impossible. He will have pushed two armies twice his size from our soil and Virginia will be free of Yankees at last. Then I believe England will recognize us and break the blockade. If we can get supplies, you will never defeat us."

Ames studied the board, realizing he was in trouble. He took her knight. "You may win this battle, but you will not win the war. Our numbers and resources are too great."

"Checkmate!" She tossed her head and eyed him with cold triumph.

An unwelcome blush crept into his cheeks. He became overwhelmed with a deflated feeling of humiliation. "I'm impressed," he stuttered. "I never lose at chess. If all Rebels are as crafty as you, Miss Armstrong, perhaps we are doomed. Where did you learn to play like that?"

"My father and I played frequently." She coolly packed up the chess set, pulled a letter out of her pocket, and handed it to him. "I will not be here in the morning when they come for you. I'll be helping print the paper. I've written a letter on your behalf explaining your kind treatment of us, and requesting that you be treated well in prison and exchanged promptly." For reasons she could not explain, she did not want to see them take him away.

"That was thoughtful of you." He studied her face, feature by feature, striving to permanently imprint it in his memory. "I pray that your father will be safely returned home soon. I would be honored if I could be exchanged for him." He reached his large square left hand forward and took her hand. "You saved my life. I hope to repay you for your mercy, although I do not know where or when." He lifted her hand to his lips and kissed it gently. "Thank you, Miss Armstrong."

She could not miss the invitation in the smoldering depths of his eyes. Withdrawing her hand, she cast her eyes downward. She had no intention of succumbing to the charms of this Yankee Apollo. "I wish you well, Captain Ames. I hope no harm comes to you." She slowly stood by the bed and picked up the chess set. "We southerners who've fed your army and cared for your sick and wounded ask only one thing of you."

"And what is that?" he asked skeptically.

"Simply, that you go away and leave us alone. Leave us in peace." Her words were as cool and clear as ice water. "Good-bye," she said with a tone of finality. Then she turned and rushed towards the door.

"Good-bye," he replied in a husky whisper. For the first time in his life he felt the searing pain of total and complete rejection. He must be crazy to want this sassy southern spitfire. And yet he knew in his heart, he wanted her more than he had ever wanted anything or anybody.

Eight days later, September 4, 1862: Davis Street

Constance clutched her four precious letters tightly and hurried towards the courthouse. Thank God, they all had survived this second battle at Manassas: Frank, Alex, Robert, and John. The whole town had celebrated the defeat of the braggart Pope. She pushed through the crowd and her eyes scanned the recently posted list of dead and wounded. She gasped. Ralph McDonald, Mr. McDonald's only child, had been killed. She must go to him. In addition, Generals Ewell and Taliaferro were seriously wounded. Jackson's men had suffered heavy losses. Thank God Powell Hill escaped injury. Dolly had been frantic with worry. She walked home with the eager anticipation that her father might be released soon.

Sadie pouted with her hands on her hips while the family stared at the little Yankee soldier with the head wound from Cedar Mountain, seated on the back steps. She had gotten rid of Ames but mysteriously, this man had returned to them. "I try to shoo 'em away an' he jist keeps comin' back."

Constance shook her head sadly. "Poor man doesn't seem to know or remember anything. We can't let him starve, but we certainly don't need another mouth to feed. I wonder if the Yankees left him behind when they retreated, or if he came back here on his own?"

"Nobody wants him. Even our provost marshal refused to take him prisoner. Looks like we're stuck with him," Amanda said. Hudson leaned over and made faces at the soldier.

"Let's call him Billy," Hudson said, "Billy Magnum."

"I suppose that's as good a name as any," his mother replied. "If he's going to stay here he'll have to work. Maybe we could show him how to chop wood and clip the bushes."

"Let him sleep in the other cabin until we figure out what to do with him," Constance said to Sadie. "We'll have to feed him."

Sadie stood with her hands on her hips, her eyes shooting sparks. "The last thin' in the world I need is a damn Yankee hangin' 'round here! Ain't we got enuff problems already?" The Armstrongs went into the house and left her alone with the unwelcome vagrant.

Two days later, September 6, 1862: Armstrong town home

Constance opened the front door to see a thinner Reverend John Cole standing before her.

"Reverend Cole!" She gulped air furiously. Her eyes darted maniacally, searching beside him, behind him. Her breath caught in her throat and her heart pounded wildly. She whispered, "Where's Father?"

He stared at her, unable to speak, while a tear slowly trickled down his melancholy face.

"Oh, no!" Her voice was shrill with horror. She stepped backwards and braced herself against the wall. "Please, God, no!"

"Miss Armstrong," a glazed look of despair spread over his face, "I'm so sorry to have to be the one to tell you." He stepped forward and grasped her in his arms. "Your father died of pneumonia a week ago."

A flash of wild grief ripped through her. She let out a strangled cry. "They killed him!"

Hearing the commotion, Harriet, Amanda, Sadie and the boys rushed into the hall wild-eyed. "Father's dead!" Constance sobbed hysterically. Sadie caught Harriet when she reeled backwards.

"Let's get her on the divan," Amanda cried in numbed horror. She helped carry her mother into the parlor. Reverend Cole held Constance in his arms until he finally calmed her enough to lead her to the other room.

After about fifteen minutes of uncontrolled sobs of anguish, the family members began to regain a slight degree of control. "He had been sick for several weeks. The changes from hot to cold in the prison were difficult to adjust to. The food of course was terrible and barely enough to sustain life. I had so hoped he could survive until Pope was defeated, and they finally decided to release us. I was with him until the end." The cleric wiped his face with a handkerchief.

"Where is his body?" Amanda asked, rocking David in her arms.

"They buried him in the prison cemetery. I asked that his grave be marked so that we may move him after the war."

"I can't believe... my dear and honorable husband... buried in a prison cemetery like a common criminal," Harriet wailed from the divan. "That's the supreme insult...not to be able to place him in the Armstrong family cemetery."

Constance's sorrow festered like a huge, painful knot inside her, while she seethed. "The Yankees have no mercy."

"His last thoughts and words were of all of you. I brought two letters, one that he wrote and one that he dictated to me towards the end." The pastor pulled the letters from his pocket and handed them to Constance. "Judge Armstrong was one of the most highly esteemed men in our community. We must hold a memorial service in his honor. It will take several days to pass the word amongst the community. Would four days from now be agreeable with you?"

"Yes, that'll be most appropriate. It'll give us an opportunity to share our grief with our friends," Harriet sniffled.

Constance's misery was so acute that it was a physical pain when she lay in bed that night. She caressed her father's letters tenderly, and read them again and again.

My darlings,

I have received numerous letters from you, which have sustained me during this torturous time. I do not know if you have received my letters, as everything is censored and I believe rarely sent.

Reverend Cole and I are in the same cell and we are forbidden to communicate with the other prisoners. However, notes are passed and a very sufficient line of communication exists. We sustain each other. I understand that Major Fitzhugh of General Stuart's staff has recently arrived. He confirmed Jackson's victory near Slaughter's Mountain. I pray that all of you have survived that terrible ordeal and have had enough food to sustain you.

The famous Belle Boyd is also incarcerated here and I have caught several glimpses of her. Constance, she is about your age and a most attractive young lady. Her insuppressible spirit and devotion to our cause have inspired us all. I cannot comprehend a foe that would treat a lady so cruelly. She serenades us frequently with 'Maryland, My Maryland.'

My food is barely palatable and I find that I am growing weaker. The dampness of the cell has had an adverse effect on my cough and I have been ill for several days. I pray that we may be released in the near future. My deepest love and affection to each of you.

My dearest loved ones,

I have to dictate this letter, as I am too weak to write. I do not believe I will survive much longer. Rest assured that I do not fear death because of my deep faith in Jesus Christ. I believe that my death, as that of our gallant soldiers, will be for a just and righteous cause.

There are countless civilian prisoners who have been incarcerated here without writ of habeas corpus or due process of law. I even met an old man, Mr. Mahoney, who is editor of an Iowa paper. Because he stated firmly that our Constitution should not be altered, he was arrested and his paper shut down. I believe that our soldiers are the last representatives of free government or the rights of States and peoples to govern themselves. If they fail, despotism more galling than any tyranny of Europe will be forced upon the land by a party of brutal men, uneducated, unprincipled, and inhuman.[6] With my last breath, I urge you to resist such tyranny with all your strength.

I feel the deepest guilt that I may not be there to protect you or sustain you through the perils which you will face. I love each one of you with all of my heart. You have been my life. May Almighty God sustain you and protect you.

Father

Constance snuffed out her candle and attempted to cry herself to sleep. She tossed and turned all night, trapped in a web of nightmares while visions of her father flashed before her: he was lying in a damp cold cell, calling to her for help, telling her to resist tyranny. She watched his lifeless body being carried away and she could not get to him, could not touch him. The restless, fitful night seemed endless, and when morning came she felt too weak to get out of bed.

Next day, September 7, 1862: Constance's bedroom

"Miss Constance, I came to check on ya. Don't ya' know it's time to git up?" Sadie pulled the curtains back to let the sunlight flood the room.

"I'm too exhausted," Constance moaned weakly. "I just want to lie here forever. I have nothing to get up for."

"Now ya jist listen to me, young lady." Sadie sat down on the bed. "Ya ain't the only one that's lost somebody ya love. You can't jist lay there an' feel sorry for yourself." She took Constance's hands and pulled her up until she could rock her in her arms.

"Oh, Sadie, how did you keep going after Abraham died?"

"The Good Lawd, He give ya the strength. Ya jist have to ask Him." She rocked her dearest child gently. "Ain't nobody loved her Daddy more than you, but your Daddy didn't raise no quitter. He taught ya how to think for yourself an' now ya gonna have to do it. Who else's smart enough to take charge 'round here?" Sadie pushed Constance's rumpled hair out of her face. "We gonna make them damn Yankees pay for this."

"Sadie, how are we going to survive?" she asked in a childish whimper.

Sadie wiped the tears from her face. "Ya jist use that brain of yours an' you'll figger it all out. We will survive, and we'll do it together!"

Next day, September 8, 1862: Armstrong town home

Constance's sense of loss was beyond tears. Yet Sadie had forced her to face reality; she must take charge if they were to survive. She studied her mother's proud anguished face across the dining room table. Her world of aristocracy had been swept away. How would she ever adapt to their grim financial situation? Amanda was weak, compliant, but perhaps she would have the stamina to be helpful. Now that the boys were asleep, she must make them face reality.

"I know this is difficult," Constance began. "But we must discuss our financial situation and plans for survival."

"But we're helpless women," her mother sighed despondently.

"Mother, the fact that we're women does not mean we're helpless. We have brains and now we must use them. I went to the bank today and we only have five hundred dollars in savings."

"Oh, I'm sure you're mistaken. I had a huge dowry. We must have a great deal more money that," Harriet said arrogantly.

"Father could never deny any of us anything. He spent more than he made and then invested heavily in Confederate bonds. We only have five hundred dollars in cash," Constance insisted firmly.

"That won't last long with the high price of food," Amanda said, her brows furrowing. "Alex's salary from the army is small and paid erratically. We must have a source of income or sell property."

"I agree," Constance said. "I believe it would be foolhardy to sell real estate at this

204

time. Confederate currency may end up being worthless and then we'll have lost the value of our property. We must keep both houses for the boys."

"So, what are our alternatives?" Amanda wondered, her voice a sinking tone.

"I've been contemplating that," Constance continued. "There are two fairly simple possibilities. First, we can rent out the three front bedrooms whenever the opportunity presents itself."

Her mother stiffened, shock covering her aristocratic face. "You mean become a boarding house? Who will do all the work?"

"We all will," Constance replied in a voice of authority, boldly meeting her eyes. "Second, I propose that we reopen the bookstore. Reading is our salvation, our escape during this turbulent time. There's also a demand for more newspapers and a lending file of newspapers."

"I agree, there's a demand, but could we make any money?" Amanda asked, her voice heavy with apprehension.

"I believe we can," Constance said. "The work would be fun. I propose that we take two hundred dollars to stock a bookstore. That's a relatively small amount of money to experiment with."

"Southern ladies don't work," her mother protested. "What will people think of us?"

"Mother, we all have to survive. Most of our friends are in desperate straits, too. Times have changed," Constance said.

"I believe we should try it," Amanda agreed. "We'll take turns running the store."

"We must be frugal with our money. That means we can't afford any additional hired help. The workload is too great for Sadie. We must all pitch in and help with the cleaning, washing, ironing, cooking, everything."

"My arthritis is so bad in my hands and ankles, I don't know what I can do," her mother whined, on the verge of tears.

"You can care for the children, help them with their lessons," Amanda said sympathetically. "The important thing is that we all pitch in and work together. There's a lot the boys can do, too."

"This is all so sudden for me," Harriet moaned.

Three days later, September 11, 1862: Saint Stephen's

Constance clasped her mother's hand on her right and Sadie's hand on her left, and stared at the beautiful stained glass windows of Saint Stephen's. The church was packed and about fifty mourners stood reverently outside in the drizzling rain. Deeply touched by this display of respect for her father, she gazed up to the balcony. She saw Willis Madden with several members of his family, Sadie's son John and his wife and four children, the barber, Ira Field, and several other Negroes she did not know. She had insisted that Sadie sit downstairs with her today against her mother's arguments and social protocol. Her presence strengthened her. She knew this memorial service would help her accept the finality of her father's death, but she still had the sensation of drifting in a bad dream.

Reverend Cole rose to the pulpit. "Dearly beloved, we are gathered here today to celebrate the life of Charles Hudson Armstrong III. He was many things to us: friend, legislator, judge, father, grandfather and Christian. Above all else, he was a man of honor and integrity who loved his Savior. Devoted to his family, he put them above everything and everyone else. That such an honorable man of peace should die a cruel death at the hands of our oppressive foe is incomprehensible to us. I was with him when he died and his last words were *we must fight tyranny.*" Constance wiped the tears from her eyes and listened to the remainder of the service in a daze. John Barbour and Coleman Beckam gave stirring eulogies, followed by scripture readings and her father's favorite hymns. The Armstrongs invited the mourners back to their house following the service.

Although all had suffered severely from Pope's occupation, food brought by friends covered the dining room table. The overwhelming outpouring of love and sympathy from their neighbors lifted the family members temporarily out of their depression. For the first time in months, neither army occupied the county, allowing the residents to come together and share their sorrow and stories of survival.

Fannie Barbour and Dolly Hill embraced Amanda. Fannie lamented that James could not be there. Recently recovered from illness, he had returned to Ewell's staff while Ewell recovered from a leg amputation. She told of the deafening noise from the cannonading along the river. Several wounded soldiers remained at Beauregard, and the Yankees had burned Richard Cunningham's beautiful mansion when they retreated. A group of Yankees had been captured in her icehouse, none of them able to speak English.

Dolly Hill reported that Powell had written her that more than 4000 lay dead in front of his line at this second battle at Manassas. His men held on until the end, when they were almost out of ammunition and had to use stones. Two horses had been shot from under him, and she rejoiced that he was unhurt. At least they had the satisfaction of knowing Pope had been pushed back to Washington and relieved of command. Powell reported Lee was moving north, to take the war to the Yankees.

"It's time for the Yankees to smell southern gun powder and suffer depredations on their land. I hope they suffer enough to be heartily sick of their wretched war of aggression," Amanda said.

Granny Ashby pushed her way through the crowd to the dining room table. She helped herself to a piece of apple pie and cackled to the Starks and Gorrells about how she had saved the meat in her smoke house. When she knew the Yankees were approaching, she threw it all out in the garden. When they rode up, she yelled, 'there it is, take it all!' This surprised them greatly and they assumed the meat was poisoned. They left it all alone. Of course, they got even by beheading her geese with their sabers.

Joe Gorell bragged that he had built some secret compartments in the house and managed to hide salt and coffee. With the shortage of salt becoming acute, they would be unable to cure meat. John Starke assured him that the governor promised him Culpeper would receive an allotment of salt soon from the salt mine in southwest Virginia.

Constance stood encircled by a group of her friends in one corner of the parlor. Annie Crittenden, no longer the carefree flirt, told them soberly of staying in the house during the Battle of Cedar Mountain and the indescribable horrors she had witnessed. She warned them not to go to see the battlefield because they would be plagued by nightmares.

Constance mumbled that she had cared for the sick and wounded until she was emotionally and physically drained. Becoming numb, she feared her heart had turned to stone. Bettie Browning pleaded that they must not allow the war to harden them so much that that they could not love. Her dearest Daniel Grimsley was optimistic England would recognize the Confederacy any day now.

Lucy Ashby commented that John Pelham and the Horse Artillery were making quite a name for themselves. Surely the war would end soon. Constance must be proud. Constance, blushing slightly, admitted to being quite proud. They all expressed shock at the stories of the women who had been ravaged by the Yankee soldiers. Of course their identities must be kept secret, but the slave women had been assaulted most.

Aunt Martha waddled up and embraced her great-niece with words of deepest sympathy. Sadly, she reported that about half of her servants left with the retreating Yankees along with Joseph and his family. She had seen Selene strutting in Constance's beautiful pink dress. Stunned, Constance could not believe Selene would steal from them after all her father had done for her. How desperately they needed that $1500 he had paid for her now! Aunt Martha continued that she had opened their house to travelers seeking to run the blockade north to Baltimore for supplies. The most interesting people passed through. They had a gay time every night.

Harriet thanked John Barbour for the beautiful eulogy and told him it was good to have him back operating the railroad. He explained that he had a crew rebuilding the bridge at Rappahannock Station to reopen the line north, and hoped to be better able to transport the wounded south, plus get supplies to the army.

Anne Stringfellow, Catherine Crittenden, and Columbiana Nalle showered Harriet with affection and condolences for the tragedy. Harriet told them that she needed them more than ever, begging them to spend a few days with her. With a stricken face, Anne agreed to stay until her wounded son, Martin, arrived. Then she would take him home and try to nurse him back to health from a serious stomach wound. Columbiana said she must return to the children and attempt to put her bloodstained house back in order. She knew the hideous memories would never fade.

"It was too ghastly to explain," Catherine commented somberly. "My house is riddled with bullet holes and everything is bloodstained. I do not know if I can continue to live there with all the memories that haunt me. I may stay here for a few days, but I cannot impose on you forever. I've written to Governor Lechter protesting the conscription of my overseer. Without him I can't make any attempt to operate the farm. Only about a third of our Negroes remained."

"Many of the poor darkies believe the Yankees are their friends. They will be sorely disappointed," Harriet said.

"It's so sad," Columbiana said. "They've gone to homeless poverty, an unfriendly climate, and hard work. Many of them will die without sympathy. They have deserted their houses, beds, and many comforts, the homes of their birth, and the masters and mistresses who regarded them not so much as property, but as humble friends and members of their families."[7]

"Poor, deluded creatures," Anne exclaimed. "I grieve not so much on account of the loss of their services, though that is excessively inconvenient, but for their grievous disappointment.[8] Most of our older servants remained loyal, and of course Uncle George and Aunt Felicia would never desert us."

Harriet turned around and took a letter from her mahogany desk. "I want to share portions of this letter I received yesterday with all of you. It's from a friend of mine in New York. The northern people are disheartened by the defeat of their massive armies by our smaller ones. Most wish Lincoln was out of the White House. However, their lives go on as usual. I don't believe they comprehend our suffering. Listen to this:"

Can our countrymen be so blind, so stupid, as to again place such a clod, though an honest one in the presidential chair? What may the country be, and whose may it be before that time? Would that God would raise up a deliverer![9]

There seems to be a panic in the North at Jackson's success. As far as I am concerned, I would as willingly be ruled by Jefferson Davis as by poor Lincoln, and I suppose many feel the same.[10]

The wretched heads of departments know nothing of their duties and the <u>honest</u> fool at their head is content playing president. God forgive the authors of these horrors and enlighten the mind of the poor creature who dared to take upon himself the high office of President in such a time with no ability to fill the office! Better a dishonest but clever man! Honesty, unfortunately, is often an attribute to imbecility.

I am sure I would not willingly sit at the table of Lincoln or his wife, much less receive them at mine. In the *World* this morning there was a very bold article against the administration. I hope it is a sign of public opinion. I wish the army would take Washington and defend it for the nation, and drive Lincoln and his host of locusts, like those which infested Egypt of old, into the sea![11]

"<u>She</u> wishes Lincoln and his horde of locusts would be driven into the sea!" Catherine exclaimed. "My farm is a desecrated bloody battlefield, and <u>she</u> wants them driven away! Don't they understand what Lincoln has done to our land? Why don't they rise up, join us, and drive him out of office?"

"We must hope that popular opinion in the North will end this terrible war," Harriet said. "But unfortunately, the tyrant continues to imprison those who oppose him and closes newspapers that criticize him.[v] The people in the North have lost their precious freedoms."

---

[v] According to estimates 30,000 to 40,000 *northern* civilians were imprisoned for speaking out against the war. 200 to 300 newspapers and publications were closed or censored for the same reason.

9

From Sharpsburg to Fredericksburg

September 24 – December 15, 1862

"With a Pelham on each flank, I believe I could whip the world."
Stonewall Jackson at Sharpsburg

Thirteen days later, September 24, 1862: Panorama

Hudson's sandy hair glistened in the fall sunshine as he climbed to a higher limb and reached upward for the few apples remaining on the tree. He grunted, plucked one, and dropped it into the basket his mother held below. Slowly he worked his way forward, and within a short time had cleaned the tree.

Amanda, in her newly made homespun dress, carried the last basket of fruit to the large table beside the kitchen where Constance and Sadie rapidly peeled apples. The warm glow of autumn lifted Constance's spirits. She drank in the beauty of the indigo blue mountains and the red glow of the sumac and dogwoods in the woods around her. Deciding to start the fire for the apple butter, she headed for the stack of wood Billy piled up. The little man looked at her quizzically when she pointed to the big copper pot and indicated they must light the wood. Understanding, he went into the kitchen and brought out several scoops of hot coals that soon ignited the wood. Hudson blew on the flames and supervised.

Constance realized they would need all the apple butter they could put up to get through the winter. After the bloodletting at Sharpsburg, she feared this war would not end any time soon. Thank God the four soldiers dear to them had survived the slaughter. Both sides claimed victory when 30,000 Rebels held off 90,000 Yankees for most of the day. It had been an amazing display of valor, with Powell Hill's regiment arriving from Harper's Ferry just in time to save their army. But she suspected it was just a matter of time before McClellan moved his horde back into Virginia. They must brace for the worst.

Constance pulled back the skirt of her homespun dress and sat down beside the others. When her hand brushed the rough butternut fabric, she thought of the many hours of labor it had taken to spin the cloth. Since the Yankees burned the mill at Waterloo, home production was the only source of cloth. The plain dress gathered at the waist was comfortable to work in, and that was the type of clothing she needed now. No longer could she afford to indulge in skirts consuming fifteen yards of fabric. With great joy, she had tossed the hated hoop aside while her mother ranted about not being able to distinguish upper-class ladies from lower-class ones. But that's the way it was now; they all faced the same challenge—survival.

She sliced her knife into the apple and contemplated Lincoln's proclamation freeing the slaves in the Confederacy. She considered it a crafty political move. In the area where he had no power or authority he freed the slaves; in the states he governed, such as Maryland, Delaware, Kentucky, and West Virginia, he left slavery intact. Obviously, he hoped the slaves would rise up, kill their masters, and fight for him. He could ill afford to alienate the citizens of the border states by freeing their slaves because he desperately needed their votes.

Amanda sliced the apples and dropped them into the pot while Sadie grumbled about not having any spices. "We have to be thankful for anything edible we have and not concern ourselves with the flavor," Constance said after she stood up. "I'm going to find a crowbar and get Billy to help me remove the boards in the attic floor so we can retrieve the silver and remaining hams. Then we'll try to locate the barrels of flour and cornmeal hidden in the woods." Amanda took Hudson to the garden to search for cabbages, turnips, and potatoes.

The forlorn appearance of Panorama depressed Constance. Weeds filled the borders amongst the broken and trampled bushes, and the porch railing had been torn off; she saw only the skeletal remains of Amanda and Alex's house. Once inside the back hall, she discovered the interior of the house in shambles; mud and smashed china covered the floors and rugs. The antique dining room chairs were gone, but most of the other furniture remained. Upstairs, all of the bedrooms had been ransacked and anything of value stolen. Most of her clothes were gone, thanks to Selene, she assumed. Climbing to the attic, she discovered the floorboards in place. Thank God, their treasures had not been discovered. She grasped the crowbar and attempted the hard and strenuous work of prying up the boards. Billy soon understood the task and assisted her, and after much toil they unearthed the precious silver and hams.

Upon safely removing the cache to the dining room, Constance motioned to Billy to follow her back outside into the autumn sunlight. They walked through the tall grass and Queen Anne's lace to the Gorrell's generously loaned horse and wagon. Constance climbed up to the driver's seat, grasped the reins and motioned to Billy to join her. The two of them rode through the meadow, down the hill to the woods, enjoying the splendid vista of the mountains. The beauty of nature's splendor always renewed her spirit. She had to think positively. The house was still standing. With some effort it could be made habitable again, and there was food. They would survive.

When they reached the edge of the woods, she picked up the crowbar, climbed down, and motioned to Billy to follow her. She knew Abraham had covered the barrels with leaves in a ravine. Twigs crunched and leaves rustled under their feet as they hiked towards the closest ravine. Constance poked through the leaves with her crow bar, finding nothing. Billy stared at her baffled. Poor creature, she thought. What does he really know or understand? She continued walking and probing in the warm sunlight with no success. Becoming most discouraged after thirty minutes, she leaned her head against her hands on the bar and rested a minute, wiping her brow. The barrels had to be here somewhere. She must not give up. Following several minutes of rest, she moved forward, probing again. Suddenly, she heard the plunk, plunk of metal against wood. "Yes," she cried. "We've found them!" Still mystified, Billy watched her slide down into the ravine and toss the leaves aside with her hands. He finally spotted the wooden barrels underneath and came forward to help her. They struggled to roll one of the barrels out of the ravine. When they got it on level ground, she opened the top to see flour. "It's almost half full!" she said. The bugs in the flour did not deter her.

They labored to roll the two barrels back to the wagon. When they rode up to the kitchen, Constance triumphantly displayed her treasures. Amanda pointed to her prizes: a dozen cabbages, a basket of turnips, and a few potatoes. They decided to make sauerkraut with the cabbage in order to prevent scurvy during the winter.

"It's cookin.'" Sadie stirred the mixture of apples in the large copper pot. "'Gonna take a long time."

Constance glanced at the rays of peach highlighting the clouds. They'd have to take turns stirring the apple butter during the night and return to town in the morning. It seemed prudent to transport their valuables while there were no Yankees in the vicinity. That situation could change at any moment.

Next day, September 25, 1862: The Hills' house on East Street

"Dolly." Powell Hill kissed his sleeping wife. "It's time to get up. We must get an early start today. It's a long way from Culpeper to Martinsburg."

She snuggled into his arms and looked at his sunken cheeks. "Darling, I've been thinking about your conflict with Jackson. If he's willing to drop the charges against you after your stellar performance at Sharpsburg, why not let it go?"

"Because my pride and reputation are at stake," he said sharply. "Justice must be done. Without a court inquiry I cannot clear myself of his false charges of neglect of duty. I'm smoldering inside." His eyes blazed. "I'll never get over the humiliation of being removed from command in Maryland and then being forced to walk at the rear of my division. I'm like an old porcupine—all bristles. That's why I had to come get you and the girls. Otherwise I couldn't endure vegetating under that old Presbyterian fool all winter."[1]

"You are two irreconcilable personalities. He's dour, quiet, reclusive, and from a middle class background. You're jovial, outgoing, fun loving, and a cavalier. The two of you are exact opposites. You'll never see eye to eye."

"The Almighty will get tired of helping Jackson after awhile, and then he'll get the damndest thrashing. And who will get blamed? I will, for the people will never blame Stonewall for any disaster."[2]

"Calm down, dearest," she whispered. "I can see I'm going to have a full time job soothing your soul. But how happy I am to be going with you. I think it's time for another baby."

His hazel eyes flickered with passion. "That's a challenge I enthusiastically accept." Netty came into the room bleary-eyed and crawled into bed with them, coughing loudly. "Come here, sweetheart." He cuddled her in his arms. "I worry about her Dolly. She's always sick."

Three days later, September 28, 1862: Armstrong town home

Constance dusted off the shelves in the bookstore before unloading the boxes of books from Richmond when she heard a knock at the front door. She rushed to open it. A ragged Confederate soldier greeted her and she spied an ambulance and a Negro out front. "Miss Armstrong?" he asked.

"Yes, I'm Constance Armstrong. May I help you?"

"Yes, I hope so. I'm Captain Robert Funkhouser of the Forty-ninth Virginia and this is George Hunter." He nodded towards the servant. "We're transporting Colonel Smith, who was badly wounded at Sharpsburg, to Orange to recover. He suggested you might allow us to spend the night here."

"Do you mean Extra Billy Smith?" she asked alarmed. The soldier nodded affirmatively. She rushed out to the street. "By all means, bring him in!" She looked down at the pale handsome face of the old man. "Colonel Smith." She took his hand. "I'm so sorry you've been wounded."

He opened his eyes and smiled weakly. "Constance, we held them off. You've never seen such valor."

"Your bravery is legend. How are you feeling?"

"My arm and shoulder are mangled," he moaned. "But don't look so worried. I'll recover. Lincoln calls me that old gamecock, Extra Billy Smith. I hope my good friend, the judge is here."

While she explained the circumstances of her father's death in a choked voice, a tear rolled down the old gentleman's face and his eyes flashed with outrage. "I will fight again. I will avenge the death of my honorable friend."

After they had the patient settled in bed, Captain Funkhouser joined the family for dinner and told them about the battle. "We were outnumbered two or three to one. The first fierce assault came on the left, controlled by Jackson. As his line wavered, we reinforced with Early. We repulsed wave after wave. Colonel Smith, wounded three times, refused to leave his command. His bravery was conspicuous as he dripped blood and fought on."

"That's astounding!" Harriet said in awe.

"They may claim victory, but we know better," Funkhouser continued. "Colonel Smith is loved by his men. He has no idea of military tactics, but a braver commander never faced an enemy. When we were advancing through deadly fire and thick undergrowth on the peninsula, he told us to 'move forward Forty-ninth, fire, and flush the game.' We followed that old man into a place where I didn't think a mosquito could live."

"We've known he was amazing for years," Amanda said. "But why is he traveling to Orange?"

"He's going to Selma, owned by the Grymes family, relatives of his wife. He's afraid he might be captured if he goes home to Warrenton."

Almost three weeks later, October 17, 1862: Armstrong town home

Amanda carefully cut open the seams of an old cotton dress while her mother darned socks. Yes, she thought, there is enough fabric in this skirt to make Hudson a shirt. He might not like the color, but he desperately needed play clothes. Constance entered the bedroom with a crestfallen face and handed Amanda the only letter.

"Wonderful!" Amanda tore into her mail. She read for a few moments with a smile on her face. "Jeb Stuart has done it again. He made a successful raid behind McClellan's army to Chambersburg, Pennsylvania. They brought back hundreds of horses, prisoners, and other booty. Alex is elated. They've returned to cavalry headquarters at The Bower, a lovely plantation near Charlestown."

"That's good news," Constance said soberly. "Does he mention John Pelham? I haven't heard from him in several weeks."

"Yes, he does." Amanda scanned the letter. "He says that Pelham's artillery saved them when they recrossed the Potomac back into Virginia. His reputation shines brighter every day." She read on and paused, as her face grew pensive. "He also relates that John Pelham spends most of his time with Sallie Dandridge, daughter of the proprietor of The Bower. The dancing and singing never cease. Alex says according to rumor, they will soon become engaged."

Constance's blood pounded. Her face grew scarlet from humiliation. "I don't believe that! If Alex wasn't so busy drinking and strutting in front of the ladies, he wouldn't hear such rumors."

"How dare you insult my husband!" Amanda snapped.

"Now girls, remember that you're sisters," Harriet said firmly, attempting to establish peace. Constance, tears brimming in her eyes, fled from the room.

"What on earth is the matter with her?" Amanda asked incredulously.

"I'm not sure. She never confides in me and I've always thought she loved Sadie more," Harriet answered in a strained tone. "I suspect she, like half the young women in the Confederacy, is totally infatuated with John Pelham."

"Perhaps I shouldn't have told her the truth," Amanda mused. "But Alex felt she should be aware of the situation. He's quite fond of Robert Beckam and hates to see her jeopardize her relationship with him."

"I understand dear. You did the right thing. She'll get over it."

Two days later, October 19, 1862: The bookstore

Constance hurried up the front steps with her letter from Frank, and made herself comfortable behind her desk in the bookstore. She ripped open the envelope and devoured the letter:

My dear Connie,

At last I have time to write you a more detailed letter. In my opinion, Sharpsburg was the fiercest, bloodiest,[i] and most indecisive battle of the war. Our relentless foes seem to have an unquenchable appetite for blood, blood, and more blood. Our gallant men held off an enemy more than twice our strength. We now know that McClellan had a copy of Lee's orders, which were found wrapped around three cigars. We must never let our security be so lax! It almost caused our army to be destroyed, as the Yanks attacked before Lee could reunite his entire army. I served as a courier throughout the battle. Initially, a fierce assault was hurled against the left of our line commanded by Jackson. Miraculously, our brave men held due to the support of the artillery, which was all under the command of your friend, John Pelham.

[i] Sharpsburg or Antietam was the deadliest day in American history, with nearly 25,000 casualties.

Following the battle, I overheard General Jackson's comments to General Stuart. He spoke warmly of Pelham, saying, "He is a very remarkable young man. This morning he commanded nearly all of the artillery on the left wing of the army, and I have never seen more skillful handling of guns. It is really extraordinary to find such nerve and genius in a mere boy. With a Pelham on each flank, I believe I could whip the world."[5]

During the afternoon, McClellan shifted the brunt of his attack against the center of our line, but General Longstreet's sturdy troops held steadfastly, refusing to budge from their excellent defensive position on a hill. By late afternoon, Burnside finally got his blue coats across the bridge on Antietam Creek and was moving forward in an attempt to crush the right of our line. If successful, our line of retreat back to the Potomac would have been cut off, thus endangering our entire army. I rode back into the town of Sharpsburg where General Lee was watching the battle from a high vantage point. With a worried face, he scanned the horizon behind us, searching for a sign of A. P. Hill's men coming up from Harper's Ferry. Our survival depended on their arrival. We all cheered when we spotted the column of dust approaching. As Hill appeared on the horizon in his red battle shirt, General Lee rode out to meet him. I watched with tears in my eyes, as he dismounted and embraced Hill. By pushing his men forward at a relentless pace on that momentous afternoon, Hill saved the day. Culpeper should be overflowing with pride at the achievement of its native son. He expertly moved his five brigades into action at the critical points and kept our line from crumbling. General Lee boldly and resolutely held the field the next day, staring McClellan down. The love and respect the men feel for him is indescribable.

After our withdrawal across the Potomac, we made our headquarters at the Bower, near Charlestown. Following several weeks of rest and recuperation, General Stuart decided to make a bold raid north, behind McClellan's lines. Farley and I scouted ahead with two others and found a safe crossing fifteen miles above Williamsport. We moved north to Chambersburg, where we burned vast supplies for the Union army and captured hundreds of horses plus several prominent citizens for exchange purposes. John Pelham's guns protected our return across the river. In two days we traveled 125 miles, the last 80 without a halt.

Pelham has the love and respect of the whole cavalry. I have gotten to to know him around camp and understand his popularity. He remains modest despite his fame. The Horse Artillery is considered the most elite and respected unit in the army. However, as your friend I must also inform you that he is referred to as "the grandest flirt in the Confederate army." You have much competition for his affection. At the moment he is enjoying the attention of one of the Dandridge daughters. However, she's not as pretty as you are! I still believe Will Farley is the perfect match for my dearest sister.

Her face twisted in pain, Constance folded the letter thoughtfully and placed it back in the envelope. Amanda came in the door carrying several newspapers. "I'll file those, Mandy." She stood up and took the papers. "I want to apologize for speaking unkindly about Alex. I realize you weren't trying to hurt me, but rather striving to inform me of the situation."

Amanda scanned her sister's eyes with concern. "That's true. Alex is quite fond of Robert and doesn't want you to jeopardize your relationship with him. Would you like to talk about it?"

Constance looked at her pensively. "I was deeply hurt when you told me John may be engaged. That's why I lashed out at Alex. I still don't believe that he's engaged, but I'm sure many young ladies are infatuated with him. But, that doesn't make me care for him any less…if anything it makes him more attractive. At the same time I continue to have the greatest affection and respect for Robert. Do I sound like a silly, moonstruck school-girl?"

"No." Amanda smiled and hugged her sister. "You're surrounded with handsome, dashing, gallant soldiers. It's perfectly acceptable to care for more than one of them. Just don't wear your heart on your sleeve."

"Thanks, Mandy." Constance's faint smile held a touch of sadness. "I'll be a lady of great mystery as I enjoy the company of several enticing young gentlemen."

Two weeks later, November 2, 1862: Coleman Street

Constance stood on her front porch with Granny and Lucy Ashby, pulling her cape tighter to ward off the brisk wind. "Look at their red hands and bare feet," Lucy said. Column after column of ragged Confederate soldiers marched through the muck of Coleman Street.

"No army has borne greater hardships with such good spirits as this one." Constance wrapped her wool scarf around her chin. "But we must help make clothes to keep our poor thin soldiers warm. I think I'll donate one of our rugs as a blanket."

"I've got a little wool yarn. I'm going to knit some more socks," Granny said. "There's no way we can feed that army. The county has been stripped. I hope food will come over the railroad."

They cheered and waved handkerchiefs when the band struck up *Dixie*. "We're in a most precarious situation," Lucy said gravely.

"We mustn't be so glum," Constance said. "After all we're suddenly surrounded by thousands of men who need to hear an encouraging word from a female."

"That's right! You young'uns do some sparking while you can!" Granny cackled.

A sudden deafening cheer rose up from the men. "Look!" shouted Granny. "There's General Lee! He's the handsomest man I've ever seen. Not only is he the greatest general in the world, he's the best looking too. He even makes my old heart flutter." The distinguished gray-haired gentleman tipped his hat to the ladies with a smile.

That evening, Constance placed the dinner plates on the table. "With half of the army here, our business is booming. I believe we should telegraph Richmond tomorrow for another shipment of books."

"I concur," Amanda answered, placing the knives and forks. "We need to increase the number of newspapers, too."

Constance heard a knock at the door and rushed anxiously to the hall to answer. She opened the door to look into the dark eyes of Robert Beckam. "Robert!"

He gathered her into his arms. "Oh, how wonderful it feels to touch a woman, especially one as pretty as you." His kiss was as tender as a summer breeze.

"You are a welcome sight, although a bedraggled one." Her free hand closed the door.

"Yes, I'm one of many dressed in rags, but at least I have shoes. We have thousands of men without shoes in the frigid weather. Lee's working frantically to get more shoes."

He looked much older with the moustache and thinner face. "Come into the dining room. You must join us for dinner." Beckam greeted Harriet and Amanda warmly. Staring at the three women dressed in black, he said, "Allow me to extend my deepest sympathy. The judge's cruel death was another tragedy of this terrible war."

"Thank you," Constance responded. "We're attempting to move forward with our lives and provide some income. We've reopened the bookstore."

"You'll be overrun with soldiers looking for reading materials to pass these long nights. May I have a tour later?" His eyes probed Constance, who nodded in agreement. Over a dinner of ham, rolls, and baked apples, he related numerous events at Sharpsburg and several stories making the rounds in the army.

"When a courier rode up to General Jackson at Harper's Ferry to inform him that McClellan's army was rapidly advancing towards Sharpsburg, the normally dour Jackson inquired, 'Do they come well-provisioned?' The courier responded, yes, that they had a whole herd of cattle. Jackson smiled, and said, 'My men can whip any army that's well-provisioned. We will proceed to General Lee's aid posthaste.'" The women and two boys chuckled.

"Robert, how has the army reacted to Lincoln's proclamation of emancipation?" Constance asked.

Beckam paused thoughtfully stroking his mustache. "It proves Lincoln is a stooge of the abolitionists, but we already knew that. I fear that by making slavery appear to be the issue in this war, he may have stopped England from recognizing us. If so, it was a crafty political move."

"The outcry in the North over his usurping of power is encouraging," Amanda said. "The war grows more unpopular by the day. I believe the elections will go against him."

"That's true," Robert agreed. "Desertions in their army have increased dramatically. Vallandingham is openly speaking out against Lincoln's administration and calling for peace at any cost. But," he sighed, "it's all speculation. I for one welcome the brief pause in hostilities and am delighted to be in Culpeper. When do I get a tour of the bookstore?"

"There's no time like the present," Constance said. He stood and pulled her chair back.

They walked arm in arm while he read the titles of the many books on the shelves. "You've got a good variety. I assume you have the Richmond papers."

"That's correct. I'm trying to get some from Charleston and Atlanta. I'm keeping one copy on file and checking them out for a penny a day. At least it will help people keep informed. We've sold quite a few books, and hope to rent out three bedrooms. Our financial situation is not too bright."

He stared down at her, his eyes radiating tender concern. "I'm sorry to hear that. I thought your father would have left you well off."

"No, we have little savings. He invested in Confederate bonds, and I refuse to sell real estate now for Confederate currency. It's too risky. We must earn enough income to buy food."

"I admire your strength and ingenuity." He clasped one of her hands in both of his.

"We have to do what we have to do," she answered quietly. "Look at you dressed in rags, sleeping out in the cold. That's far more heroic than our sacrifice."

He wrapped his arms around her midriff. "I never dreamed it would last this long, that we would come to this. McClellan's army of nearly 90,000 is close behind us. The cavalry did an outstanding job of screening our movement from Winchester. We weren't harassed, but we heard them fighting daily. Though greatly outnumbered, they fought valiantly."

"Wasn't it dangerous for Lee to divide the army again?" She enjoyed the strength and warmth of his body. "Can't McClellan fall on you and destroy you here?"

"It's certainly possible." He admired the faint rose color of her mouth. "But Lee seems to understand that McClellan is slow and pensive. I have great faith in Robert E. Lee. It's my hope that hostilities will not resume until spring and I can spend the winter near you."

"That sounds like a dream, but we must enjoy every moment available. Opportunities for pleasure are few and far between." Her eyes crinkled.

He moved his lips over hers, devouring their softness. Slowly, his lips left hers to nibble on her earlobe. "Fair Connie, how many men are vying for your affection?" he whispered into her hair.

"I'll never tell," she replied with a giggle.

"At least tell me that I'm still in the running." He squeezed her tight against him.

She pulled back and looked him in the eye. "Of course you are, Robert."

"Well, that's good news, but unfortunately I must return to duty. I have to replenish our supply of ammunition as supplies arrive from Richmond, so we can be ready to fight at any moment. I'll be very busy for the next week, but will strive to see you as time permits. Now, come with me to tell your mother and sister goodbye."

Three days later, November 5, 1862: Waterloo bridge

Darkness had fallen when Jeb Stuart's cavalry clattered across the bridge at Waterloo to the safety of Culpeper County. Stuart watched Pelham's exhausted men position their guns to protect the bridge with a nod of approval. "Your performance today was outstanding as usual." He slapped the youthful artillerist on the back. "Bivouac your men here."

After being in constant engagement with the Yankees and incurring staggering losses of horses and men since dawn, Alex and the Rangers cooked the few squirrels they had killed and fell asleep on the cold ground. For the last week the cavalry had fought gallantly each day and then fallen back towards Culpeper, screening the movement of Longstreet's troops. Alex stared up at the stars, thankful to be close to his family once again.

Stuart and his staff rode back about a mile and established headquarters at the house of a friend. After roasting and eating several turkeys, they soon fell asleep. Von Borcke read a few dispatches by candlelight until a courier arrived from Culpeper Court House with a telegram for General Stuart. Following his instructions from Stuart, he opened the telegram and read it with a pained face. It announced the death of Stuart's beloved five-year-old daughter, little Flora. Von Borcke hung his head in grief. The child had been dangerously ill in Lynchburg, but Stuart felt unable to leave his command at such a critical time. He had written his wife, "My duty to the country must be performed before I give way to the feelings of the father."[4]

217

Von Borcke gently awoke Stuart who looked at him bleary-eyed. Seeing his grave expression, Stuart asked, "What is it, Major? Are the Yankees advancing?" Unable to speak, Von Borcke handed him the telegram. Stuart read the painful message and was no longer a fierce warrior, but a tender, loving, father. Tears streamed down his face. "My dearest child…I wasn't there…I'll never get over it." When Von Borcke reached out to comfort his general, Stuart threw himself against him and wept bitterly.

Next day, November 6, 1862: Waterloo Bridge

The morning passed quietly at Waterloo Bridge with no enemy in sight. "Hold your fire," two men called from the north side of the river. "It's Stringfellow and Farley." The two scouts, who had been probing for the enemy, galloped across the bridge with a captured Yankee wagon. "We brought you a present," Stringfellow said with a boyish grin as he dismounted in front of Stuart and pulled the cover off the wagon. Inside they discovered an enormous shipment of Havana cigars and a large number of fine bowie knives.

Delighted, Stuart stuffed several cigars in his pocket. "It's been a long time since I've had a Havana cigar. And we can always use these knives."

Farley stuck a knife in his belt. He prided himself on being fully equipped due to the generosity of the Yankees. "I'm not sure how good this will be for killing Yankees," he quipped, "but it will come in handy for cutting the tough meat the army provides us."

Stuart smiled. "What did you see of our adversaries?"

"Only a few scouting parties," Stringfellow said. "The main body has not arrived yet."

Stuart became restless by midday and decided to lead a squadron across the river on reconnaissance. They soon confronted an advancing column of the enemy who attacked vigorously. The Yankees drove the Confederates back towards the bridge in a disgraceful stampede, much to the mortification of Stuart. Hearing the action, Pelham had his guns poised to fire when his comrades raced to safety across the bridge. "Open up on 'em, boys!" His guns punished the enemy with deadly accuracy. Alex joined the sharpshooters firing along the river amidst whizzing bullets. The battle raged furiously until dusk. The enemy artillery opened up on Pelham, who held his ground despite losses in his ranks.

When the light faded from the sky, Stuart decided to retreat. "Ignite the bridge and fall back to Jeffersonton," he ordered. Already prepared with combustibles, the bridge burned quickly while the retreating Rebels watched the fiery timbers crash into the water.

Hans and Marta Yager heard the galloping horses from their residence above the store. Hans cautiously peered out the window. "A large body of cavalry is approaching. Let's hope they're ours. Looks like they're coming to the door." They immediately heard a loud rapping. "Stay up here," he ordered his wife and daughters.

He slowly cracked the door and the frigid air flowed inside. "Dad, it's Alex."

Hans threw opened the door and embraced his son warmly. "Thank God, son. We've been so worried about you."

"I'm thankful to be home. It's beginning to snow. May I bring my men inside?"

"Of course! They can sleep on the floor in the store and upstairs." Alex went outside and searched for General Stuart but was informed he had already settled in an abandoned house. About fifty cavalrymen rushed inside to sleep in the warmth.

Next day, November 7, 1862: Jeffersonton

Stuart and his staff shivered around a campfire while a fine rain mixed with snow pelted them. They complained of the miserable night they had spent in the dilapidated building. Between the howling wind and the smoke from the broken down chimneys nearly suffocating them, they had not slept a wink.

"You'll all warm up when our uninvited guests arrive and attack. The roads are slippery and horrible in the extreme, but we must draw up in lines to receive the attack," Stuart said, striving to revive the spirit of his hungry, cold, bedraggled men. The Yankees arrived and a hot fight continued until after ten o'clock.

Stuart, fearing the Hazel River would rise behind him, ordered a retreat around noon. The exhausted artillery horses could scarcely pull the guns through the mucky roads. Late in the evening, the Confederates safely forded the river and took a position on the heights near Rixeyville. John Pelham stared at the forlorn sight of "Company Q" slowly struggling up the hill. The continuous marching and fighting had taken its toll on both horses and men. Nearly 500 non-combatants consisting of sick, disabled, and dismounted men plus broken-down and lame horses comprised "Company Q." The starving men plucked persimmons from the trees and ate voraciously. Pelham gazed towards Panorama recalling the pleasant times he had enjoyed there. He hoped to visit Constance soon.

No Yankees appeared on the opposite side of the river. At nightfall, the rain changed back to a heavy snowfall. The main body of troops pulled back a couple of miles and bivouacked in a dense forest of oak and pine. A blazing fire warmed the blanket-wrapped men. After a dinner of baked potatoes, a courier arrived from Culpeper Court House with mail, which greatly lifted the spirits of the men. Von Borcke was deeply absorbed in reading the first mail he had received from home when his blanket caught fire in the embers. "Von," Stuart called, "what are you doing there? Are you going to burn yourself like an Indian widow?"[5] The whole camp laughed boisterously.

Two days later, November 9, 1862: Culpeper Court House

The sun glistened on the snow as Amanda and Hudson picked up the two bundles of newspapers at the depot. They wandered towards the post office maneuvering through the swarming soldiers and their visiting loved ones, collected one letter for Constance, and plodded up Coleman Street.

Hudson kicked the powdery snow. "When's Daddy coming home?"

"Soon, I hope," his worried mother replied. "The cavalry are protecting the front." They stomped the snow off their shoes before entering the hall.

"I've got the papers," Amanda called to Constance, who unloaded a box of books while several soldiers browsed in the bookstore. "And you have a letter from Maine."

"What?" Constance abruptly pulled herself up. "Captain Ames must have been exchanged." She grabbed the letter and sat down at her desk while Amanda sent Hudson into the parlor to stay with Harriet. When she unfolded the letter a check fluttered onto the desk. Surprised, she picked it up to see that it was made out to her. "Oh!" she gasped. Two hundred dollars in Federal money would come in very handy. She read quickly:

Dear Miss Armstrong,

Fortunately, I stayed in Libby Prison only two weeks before I was exchanged. I believe your kind letter worked in my favor, and once again I am indebted to you. I rejoiced the day I left, and let me suffice by saying I pray I never return.

I was sent home to Portland to recover from my injuries. I arrived to learn the sad news that my father had died of a heart attack and was buried two days before my arrival. The shock devastated me. I continue to mourn his loss as I realize how much I valued his advice and wisdom. He left a void in my life which no one else can fill. I pray that you and your father have been joyfully reunited.

While in prison and since returning home, I have had much time to contemplate this cruel war and our debates. You have forced me to look at the situation with a more open mind. I believe that neither side is completely right or completely wrong. This tragic war never should have happened. If cool heads had prevailed we could have resolved our differences without violence. But sadly, we are suffering for the shortcomings of our politicians. In a war there must be a winner and a loser. I believe that we will eventually prevail and the sooner this terrible conflict ends, the better. You must understand that I am as loyal to my state and the righteousness of our cause as you are to yours. We need to respect our opinions and differences.

I enlisted for two years. After much soul searching, I have decided to fulfill my obligation rather than hiring someone to take my place. That would not be honorable. However, Jeb Stuart has convinced me that the men in the cavalry have all the fun. I am now making arrangements to "jine the cavalry." I believe a man on horseback is more difficult to hit than one standing in the middle of a field. Since I hope to survive this conflict, I will take my chances as a cavalryman. It is also apparent to me that we must improve our tactics to beat Jeb Stuart at his own game. Perhaps, I can play a small role. You will be pleased to know that my derriere has healed to the point that riding a horse is comfortable. Thank you for a superb stitching job. I am striving to improve my equestrian skills and am lifting weights to strengthen my arms. Regaining use of my right arm has been slow since the sling came off. If all goes well, I should return to the front within a month.

Lincoln, with the help of God, has taken a bold step by freeing the slaves. I would have preferred that his proclamation applied to all the states. I'm sure you see his actions as hypocritical. I believe the tide of this war has turned in our favor since our victory at Antietam. Let it end soon!

I think of you often and pray that you are surviving this terrible ordeal. I have enclosed a small check from my back pay and hope that it will be helpful to you. It is my most ardent prayer that we may soon meet again under more pleasant circumstances, and renew our warm friendship.

Your humble servant,
Aaron Ames

The soldier cleared his throat to get her attention. "I'd like this book," he said with an admiring smile. Glancing at the headline on the stack of papers, he added, "And give me one of those papers, too. I've got to read about Burnside replacing McClellan."

"Oh, yes of course," she said distracted. "Let me cut the twine. That's big news." She made change for him while he read the paper. "Thank you, and come back."

She unbundled the papers and reread her letter, aware that someone else had entered the store. "General Lee, sir," a soldier said as he saluted. Constance looked up at the distinguished gentleman with her mouth open.

"Where are you from, soldier?" Lee inquired politely.

"Louisiana, sir."

"I trust you are surviving our cold Virginia weather," Lee replied kindly.

"It's tough on us Louisiana boys, but I can stand it, sir. Shucks, sir, I'd invade hell with a bucket of water if you'd lead us!"

Lee leaned back and laughed. He glanced at Constance and said, "How can we not win the war with men like this in our army?"

"We are blessed to have you lead our army, General Lee," she said. "May I help you find something?"

He studied her intently. "You look familiar to me. Have we met?"

Amazed that he recognized her, she answered, "I'm Constance Armstrong. I implored you to write a letter on behalf of my father last time you passed through Culpeper."

"Oh, yes." He nodded thoughtfully. "Your father is Charles Armstrong. I hope he has returned home safely."

"No," she answered, feeling her throat tighten. "He died of pneumonia in Old Capitol Prison."

"I'm so sorry. I've written Lincoln many letters deploring the treatment of civilians."

"Thank you for your concern," Constance said. The soldier nodded cordially to Lee and departed. Constance handed Lee a newspaper and he scanned the headline. "It seems Lincoln did not consider McClellan a match for you, sir."

"I must tell you, Miss Armstrong, that I hate to part with McClellan," Lee said with a slight twinkle in his eyes. "For we have always understood each other so well. I fear they may continue to make these changes until they find some one I don't understand."[6]

"I pray that doesn't happen. You have the total confidence of your army."

"Nothing can surpass the valor and endurance of our troops. I have been blessed to lead the bravest army the world has ever known." He browsed her bookshelves. "I need something inspirational to read."

"We have a whole section over here." She led him across the room where he perused several books before selecting a collection of sermons.

"This one should be helpful. I'm concerned my men may become too distracted by the gambling and drinking. Several ministers are in camp leading a religious revival."

"That's most important." He paid her for the book and paper. "We must feed their souls."

"Yes, we certainly aren't doing a very good job of feeding their bodies. Good day, Miss Armstrong."

"Good day, General Lee, and God bless you." She, too, had utmost confidence in the leadership of this calm, Christian gentleman.

About an hour later, Robert poked his head in the door as she and Amanda stocked the shelves. "I've come to take you away from your labors," he said to Constance. "There's an outstanding minister preaching a revival service on the edge of town. Come with me?"

Constance glanced at Amanda. "Well, um, I don't know."

"Oh, go ahead. I can handle things here," Amanda insisted.

"In that case, I'd love to," she said to Robert with a smile.

He beamed. "Better dress warmly."

Next day, November 10, 1862: North of the Rappahannock

Heros Von Borcke galloped to the top of a high hill and took in the magnificent view around him. He had been sent ahead by Stuart to reconnoiter the area. The Prussian observed several miles towards the town of Warrenton, where many encampments revealed the presence of the entire Union army. The Rebels had fought through Union lines to discover this vital information. Immediately in front of him, he saw three brigades of infantry and several batteries of artillery reinforcing the force opposing the Confederates. The blue coats advanced on the double quick. He spurred his horse and galloped back to warn Stuart of the perilous situation.

Von Borcke galloped up to his comrades and realized they were already retreating. Reaching Stuart, he exclaimed, "The whole Union army is at Warrenton! Heavy reinforcements are advancing towards us."

"That's what we wanted to know. I already perceived the additional strength," Stuart shouted as the enemy artillery opened on his troops. Irritated, he gathered about thirty infantry riflemen. "Follow me." He led them to the corner of a wood. "Don't fire until they are within two hundred yards. We're going to punish those impudent Yankees."

When he rode out of the woods into the field, Stuart greatly exposed himself to the enemy. Concerned, Von Borcke rode up and dismounted beside his general. "Sir, it is my duty to tell you, that in my opinion, you are not in your proper place. In a few moments the whole fire of the enemy will be concentrated on you."

In a very bad humor, the usually jovial Stuart replied curtly, "If this place seems too hot for you Major, you are at liberty to leave."

Von Borcke cautiously positioned himself behind a large tree and said, "My duty attaches me to your side, sir. No place could be too hot for me where you choose to go."[7] Instantly, bullets whizzed by and plunked into the opposite side of the tree. He saw Stuart pass his hand quickly across his face. Even in this perilous moment, Von Borcke could not control his laughter when he realized one of the whizzing missiles had cut off half of Stuart's beloved mustache. "I believe our Yankee friends have saved you a trip to the barber, sir!" Stuart, too, was forced to laugh. He motioned to Von Borcke to fall back.

When the returning cavalry entered camp with their thirty prisoners, Pelham and those who had not been on the expedition rushed forward to learn the results. After giving a condensed version, Stuart said to Von Borcke, "Major, I want you to ride with haste to Culpeper to inform General Lee of what has been done."

"General Stuart, sir, I request permission to accompany the major as his bodyguard," Pelham said with a straight face.

Stuart arched his eyebrows and eyed the two of them suspiciously. "Von, do you feel you need a bodyguard?"

"Absolutely, sir. I'd feel much more secure," the giant Prussian answered, his eyes twinkling.

Pelham looked at Stuart innocently. Stuart loved this gallant cannoneer as a brother. He could deny him nothing. "Very well," he said with a smile. "I suspect this is a ruse to visit a certain young lady, but the two of you had better be back here tonight."

Constance lit several candles and dropped into her desk chair exhausted. It had been a busy day with all the hustle and bustle of activity generated by visitors to the army. Several customers browsed in the bookstore. All eyes turned to stare at the tall fashionably dressed young lady who entered. With curled brown hair piled on her head, she carried herself like a lady. Possessing a long face and nose, Constance considered her attractive, but not beautiful. "May I help you?" She admired the jewelry of her visitor.

"Yes, I hope that you can. I need a room tonight for my servants and myself. We're traveling to Charlottesville."

"We have a room available. Are you visiting a friend in the army?"

"Oh, they're all my friends. I've been forced to leave my home in Martinsburg, which is now occupied by our enemy. I could not risk arrest again."

Constance grew more curious. "Why were you arrested?"

"Because I love the Confederacy and have served it with all of my energy. They accuse me of being a spy. I'm Belle Boyd."

"Oh! It's an honor to have you here Miss Boyd. My dear father was imprisoned in Old Capitol Prison while you were there. He wrote that your spirit inspired the prisoners."

"What is his name? Has he been released, Miss...uh?"

"Armstrong, Constance Armstrong. My father was Judge Charles Armstrong, but sadly, he died in prison."

"Please accept my deepest sympathy, Miss Armstrong. They treated us cruelly, but they can never conquer our spirit." She paused and held out her arm. "See this watch? It was a gift to me from my fellow inmates at Old Capitol, which I received after arriving in Richmond. I was deeply touched." Constance admired the handsomely enameled gold band with diamonds. "These clothes were a gift from one of the wardens. I charmed him into believing that I would soon be married, and he presented me with a beautiful trousseau. All is fair in love and war, Miss Armstrong. We women must use our feminine wiles to serve our cause."

"I'd never really thought of it that way. At times I feel useless. By the way, I believe we have a mutual friend."

"Who is that?" Belle inquired with her eyebrows raised.

"John Pelham," Constance answered, watching her eyes light up.

"Ah, the gallant, irresistible John Pelham. Yes, I met him at the beginning of the war near Martinsburg. I even introduced him to Jeb Stuart. Then, when I worked in the hospitals after First Manassas, we renewed our friendship." She smiled wistfully. "I confess that I was quite infatuated with him. Unfortunately, there were many young women vying for his affection, and I fear I did not win. We are close friends. I suspect, Miss Armstrong, that you are also charmed by his innocent grin."

A woman dressed in black entered with her son pulling on her hand. "Mommy, let go!" The boy, about three, broke loose and raced around the store.

"Jimmy, that's enough. Calm down!" the ordinary, sturdy looking woman in her late twenties ordered. "I must apologize," she said to Constance. "He's been on a train all day from Lynchburg, and has too much energy to burn off. I was hoping you could rent me a room for the night. All the hotels are full."

Constance felt sympathy for the tired, melancholy woman. "Of course, we'll be glad to have you, Mrs. Um...."

"Stuart, Flora Stuart. I'm General Stuart's wife." She caught the hand of her son as he ran by.

"Mrs. Stuart, it's an honor. We all hold the general in the highest esteem. I'm Constance Armstrong, and this is the celebrated Belle Boyd."

"Miss Boyd, it's a pleasure to meet you. My husband has written me about your deeds." Lines of sadness creased her face. "Unfortunately, I've come to be with him while we mourn the recent death of our five-year-old daughter." Flora's voice broke.

"Oh, no!" both women exclaimed

"I'm so sorry to hear of your loss." Constance walked towards the door. "Please follow me and I'll show you to your rooms. We'll have dinner in about an hour."

Following dinner, all the women and children had gathered around the fire in the parlor when they heard the knock at the door. "I'll get it." Hudson raced through the hall. Delighted, he saw a somewhat bedraggled John Pelham standing outside. "Come in, Major Pelham," he cried excited. Pelham shook his hand. "Where's my Dad?"

"I haven't seen him in several days, but I suspect he's at camp. You see I had to sneak away," Pelham whispered, then hung his hat and cape on the hall tree.

"Aunt Connie, its Major Pelham!" Hudson raced back into the parlor. Startled, Constance jumped up and swayed gracefully out into the hall.

"Major Pelham, I'm delighted to see you alive and well. I haven't heard from you in so long, I feared for your safety," she said coolly.

He took her hand and kissed her on the cheek. "Forgive me. I've had little time. It's wonderful to see you."

"Please come into the parlor. We have two friends of yours staying with us tonight."

"Really?" He appeared quite taken aback at the sight of Belle Boyd. "Miss Boyd, I heard you had returned safely from prison. Welcome back." He bowed politely and kissed her hand.

"I'm overjoyed to be free again, even though I've been forced to leave my home," she said with a radiant smile. "You, Major Pelham, have become renown. It's a great pleasure to see you again," she continued, batting her eyelashes.

Pelham bowed to Mrs. Stuart. "Mrs. Stuart, the whole camp is mourning the tragic death of your daughter. Please accept my sympathy. The general looks forward to your arrival tomorrow."

"Thank you, Major Pelham. He's sending a wagon for me in the morning. I hope to have a good night's sleep tonight. My husband's every letter sings your praises. You're to be greatly commended for your valiant efforts at Sharpsburg."

"All of our men were valiant at Sharpsburg." Color slowly crept into his smooth cheeks. "Mrs. Stuart, I slightly...um...deceived your husband to get permission to come to town tonight." He smiled mischievously. "I hope you won't mention to him that you saw me here."

Flora Stuart laughed. "If you've put one over on my husband, more power to you. He's usually the one playing the tricks. I will not betray you."

Pelham turned to Harriet and Amanda and bowed. "Please allow me to express my deepest sympathy on the death of the judge. The story of the tragic civilian deaths of this war will never be fully revealed."

"Thank you. We're attempting to go on with our lives and have re-opened the bookstore," Amanda replied.

With all the seats occupied, Harriet said, "Please, Major Pelham, bring in a chair from the dining room and make yourself comfortable."

"Actually, it's time for me to get Jimmy in bed." Flora looked at her yawning son and stood up. "It's been a pleasure visiting with all of you. Sit down, Major, and I look forward to seeing you at camp." She picked up her drowsy son.

"Good night, Mrs. Stuart," they all said.

Pelham sat down and leaned forward. "I didn't wish to alarm Mrs. Stuart," Pelham whispered while she climbed the stairs, "but I must tell you what happened to the good general today." They all laughed when he related the tragic loss of half of Stuart's cherished mustache.

"That curled mustache was his pride and joy," Constance chuckled.

"Tell us some of your adventures, Miss Boyd," Harriet said while she knitted.

Belle Boyd dramatically related how she ran between the bullets on the battlefield at Front Royal to give vital information to General Jackson, penetrated Union lines to flirt with soldiers while gathering classified orders, shot a Yankee to protect her mother, suffered untold hardships and psychological abuse while in prison for several months, was welcomed as a celebrity when returned to Richmond, visited with many generals and dignitaries, and was given a commission as Captain and honorary Aide-de-camp by her dear friend, Stonewall Jackson. Pelham caught Constance's eye during the long dissertation and winked. "There are times when I feel I have the weight of the Confederacy on my shoulders," she continued.

Before she could catch her breath, Pelham interjected, "Major Von Borcke will be returning soon and I must ride back to camp with him. I'd like to have a good book to read. Would you allow me to select one from your bookstore, Miss Armstrong?"

"Of course." Constance stood up. "I'm sure you'll find something to your liking."

Belle looked miffed as they departed. "Whew," Pelham whispered when they entered the bookstore. "I thought she would never stop."

Constance set the candle on the desk. "I assumed you would be delighted to see her. I understand you enjoyed a warm, close friendship."

His eyes studied her with curious intensity while he tried to penetrate her thoughts. "I admit we were involved for a short time. I soon realized what a notorious flirt she is and how she loves to be in the limelight. That ended the romance for me."

Constance chuckled. "That's an interesting comment from the young man who's known as the grandest flirt in the Confederate army."

"Where did you hear that gossip?" he asked with a wounded look.

"I have my sources."

"Well, don't believe everything you hear. I tricked General Stuart and rode an hour and a half in the cold rain for one reason." His earnest eyes sought hers. "To see you and only you."

Her resistance softened as his gray eyes became pools of appeal. "Then I'm honored and flattered, Major Pelham."

He took both of her hands in his. "I didn't want to alarm the others, but we learned today that the whole Union army is camped at Warrenton. The situation is precarious. Anything could happen at any time. Burnside's an unknown to us. At least we could predict McClellan. We've been involved in the bloodiest of conflicts almost continuously since April. Let's not waste the few precious moments we have together picking at each other over trivialities."

"You're right." The pulses in their fingers throbbed together. "What type of book would you like?"

"Something romantic." He heard footsteps on the front porch. "Oh, no, there's Von!"

He pulled her into the shadows and in one forward motion; she was in his arms. Her mind told her to resist, but her body refused. The urgency of his kiss was more persuasive than she cared to admit. Her calm was shattered by the tingle of body contact; she responded to his caresses. He held her tightly while they listened to the knocking on the door. "I'll be back, but I don't know when," he whispered. "Now give me a book."

She grabbed the candle and pulled a book of love sonnets off the shelf. "You should enjoy this."

"Coming, Von," he called.

Two days later, November 12, 1862: The bookstore

Business in the bookstore had been brisk all morning. The frenzied activity distracted Constance from the shadow cast on her heart by her father's death. She and Amanda greeted a distinguished man in his sixties and two women from Florida inquiring about a room for the night.

"We'll be happy to accommodate you." Constance appraised the two well-dressed ladies. "Are you visiting someone in the service, Mr. Um?"

"Bailey. Actually our story is unique. We were told our son was killed at the Battle of Cedar Mountain. Several days ago we received a telegram from two Confederate soldiers who reported that they had found him alive, hidden in a hut in the woods with his old Negro servant."

Amanda joined the group. "I can imagine your shock and joy at receiving that news."

His wife continued, "You see Uncle Reuben was terrified of the Yankees. He hid our son to protect him. Unfortunately, he was also afraid of the other Confederate soldiers and didn't seek help. We can only imagine the misery they've endured over the last three months."

"I pray we've arrived in time to save my husband," the attractive young lady said. "We have no idea the extent of his injuries. We know they've suffered since the weather has turned so cold. It was the smoke from a fire that finally attracted the attention of the soldiers who discovered them. Uncle Reuben refused to leave but insisted they telegraph 'Old Massa,' who would know what to do."

"So are you now going to search for them in the woods?" Constance asked.

"Yes, we visited General Lee at his headquarters nestled in a pine thicket. When he heard our dilemma he offered to loan us a horse and wagon plus several soldiers to aid in the search," Mr. Bailey said. "Our general is the kindest gentleman."

"Indeed he is, Mr. Bailey. May I ask, are you related to the governor of Florida who bears that name?" Constance inquired.

The gentleman looked down blushing slightly. "I _am_ the governor of Florida. I'm honored you Virginians know my name."

Amanda's chin dropped. "It's our honor to have you here, Governor Bailey. We hope you'll find your son alive this afternoon. We'll have two warm rooms waiting for you when you return." After the three Floridians exited, Constance and Amanda stared at each other in disbelief. "I believe that is the most touching and incredible story I've heard during this war," Amanda said.

"The loyalty of their servant defies all reason. Unfortunately, by being so protective of his soldier, he may have impeded his recovery," Constance mused.

The Bailey's finally returned after dark. The Armstrongs watched in melancholy silence, while two soldiers carried the son in on a stretcher. A ghastly sight, all skin and bones, he was a skeleton hanging by a thread to life. "I knew Ol' Massa would come. I took good care of Massa Hugh," the poor old emaciated Negro kept saying. "I wouldn't let no soldiers git 'im." Sadie took the old servant out to the kitchen to feed him. The two women followed Hugh Bailey upstairs while Governor Bailey collapsed into a chair in the parlor and sobbed.

"If only we could have gotten to him sooner," he lamented. "They were in a drafty old hut infested with bats and owls. Poor old Uncle Reuben foraged for food at night with little success." He paused to wipe his face with a handkerchief. "The old servant thought he was protecting Hugh, but in reality he caused him to starve to death."

"It's a heartbreaking tragedy," Harriet said sympathetically. "Please, let us get you some dinner."

"No, I can't eat," the governor replied between sobs. "We'll take him to Richmond tomorrow and attempt to nurse him back to health, but I'm afraid we're too late. We were so hopeful when we received the telegram. I'm horrified at the thought of losing him now." [ii]

Five days later, November 17, 1862: The bookstore

"Alex!" Amanda screamed when her ragged, muddy, husband marched into the bookstore. "Thank God!" She threw her arms around him, showering him with kisses.

"At last I get to see you, my darling!" He crushed her against him. "You look beautiful."

"And you're a sight." She examined the patches on his tattered uniform.

"Take me to my children." The entire family gathered around him while he romped on the floor with the boys in the parlor.

Amanda watched her family contentedly. "Why has it taken you so long to get home, darling?"

"The situation has been too tense to allow anyone to take leave. We've fought and

[ii] Hugh Bailey died several days later in Richmond.

skirmished non-stop. John Mosby returned from a week's scout and reported that he suspects the Yanks are moving towards Fredericksburg. The general gave us the night off since we may be marching in the next day or two." He bounced baby Alex on his stomach.

"Does that mean we'll have only one night together?" Amanda asked.

"I'm afraid so, so let's make the most of it. I invited General Stuart and his staff to join us tonight. The general and Mrs. Stuart prefer to spend some time alone, but Pelham, Von Borcke, Dabney, Stringfellow, and Farley will be coming with Sweeney. We're going to have a party!"

"Oh, you mean they're all coming here!" Constance asked wide-eyed. "We'll have to invite the Ashby girls to join the festivities."

"I don't think it's appropriate for us to have a party so soon after your father's death," Harriet said. "It wouldn't be proper."

"Mother, I understand your feelings, but they'll all be leaving soon. Who knows when this opportunity will arise again?" Amanda walked over and hugged her mother. "Father would want us to seize the moment,"

"Well, dear, I suppose you're right," Harriet agreed reluctantly. "If Charles is watching, I know he'll understand." The boys giggled, pulled their father's hair, and crawled over him.

"Alex, I want you to tell me the truth," Constance said seriously. "What do you know about John Pelham's romance with Miss Dandridge?"

"Well, Connie," he gasped as Hudson got him in a neck clinch, "he's the most loved man in the cavalry, next to Stuart. Those of us who've seen him in action realize he's a military genius and a truly deserving hero. Women flock to him like bees to honey. He and Sallie Dandridge were inseparable while we were at the Bower. It's a beautiful estate encompassing 1000 acres with 100 slaves. Rumor had it that they would become engaged, but to my knowledge there was no formal announcement. You've simply got to understand that you've got stiff competition. She's wealthier than you, but no prettier. I must confess he appeared quite anxious to see you when I spoke to him today."

"I appreciate your candor, Alex. When will they be here?" Constance stood up.

"In about an hour or two, I suspect." He rolled over and winked at Amanda.

Sadie entered Constance's bedroom, her eyebrows arched above her bulging eyes. "Sadie, what on earth has you all aflutter?" Constance asked from her dressing table. Sadie walked behind her and took the brush to continue grooming her.

"Miss Constance, ya ain't gonna believe who's down there with Mista Alex." She peered over Constance's shoulder into the mirror.

"Who? Have our guests arrived?" Constance pinched her cheeks for color.

Sadie rolled her eyes. "It's Major Beckam, an' Mista Alex jist invited him to stay for the party."

"Oh!" Constance gasped and grabbed Sadie's hand, her pulse racing. "How am I going to handle this? I mean it was complicated enough knowing John Pelham and Will Farley would be here together, but now with Robert. Oh, my!"

"Now, ya jist listen to Sadie. You's gonna be cool as a cucumber. Let them fight for your attention. Look at yourself in that mirror." She turned Constance's head towards the mirror. "Those gen'men are all gonna wanta be with ya."

"Oh, Sadie! I'm so nervous. See, my face is already turning red. I go months without an interesting man in sight, and suddenly three of them show up at once. Why?"

"'Cause when it rains, it pours. That's the way life is. Now stand up an' let me see ya."

Constance stood up and whirled around. "Ya look beau'ful, Miss Constance. Jist remember, cool as a cucumber."

Constance put both her hands on Sadie's shoulders and stared into her dark eyes. "But Sadie, you don't understand. When John Pelham looks at me with those laughing gray eyes...he captures me with his eyes... I...I...melt, I lose control...I can't help it!"

Constance strolled into the parlor in her royal blue dress. "Good evening, Robert." Beckam rose from the divan where he had been chatting with Alex, and walked over to greet her with a kiss.

"You look lovely. Alex informs me that this is going to be a festive evening."

"It's an opportunity for gaiety in these bleak times," she responded with a smile, masking her inner turmoil with deceptive calmness. "I hope you'll join us."

"Thank you. I'll be delighted to stay for a while, but I can't be too late returning to camp, since we'll be marching tomorrow." Sorrow filled his voice. "I had hoped we would spend the winter here, but it appears we're going to Fredericksburg,"

She recognized the sincerity in his eyes. "I had no idea you'd be leaving so soon. Is the whole army moving?" Mixed feelings surged through her.

"No, only our brigade. I suppose General Lee is waiting to confirm Burnside's intent."

The two of them sat on the divan next to the chair where Alex relaxed in his civilian clothes while Amanda washed and mended his uniform. Shortly, Hudson raced into the hall to answer the door. "It's Frank! It's Frank!"

"Ah! We must greet the famous scout!" Alex stood, followed by Constance and Robert.

Skinny, ragged Frank bounded into the room, grabbed Constance and spun her around. "We are here at last, dearest sister!" Constance tried to focus on his companion as she whirled around. Of medium height and build, he possessed dark brown hair and a moustache. His bushy dark eyebrows and lashes shaded his gray eyes, making them appear black. Frank kissed her on the cheek and released her. "Allow me to introduce my friend and comrade, Captain William Downs Farley."

Will Farley bowed gracefully, took her hand and kissed it. "Miss Armstrong, it is a pleasure to meet you at last. Your reputation precedes you," he said in a low voice.

"The honor is mine, Captain Farley," she answered with a radiant smile. "We have all heard of your daring and heroic service to our country." She then turned to introduce him to Robert and Alex, while Harriet and Amanda entered and embraced Frank.

"Frank it's wonderful to see you." Harriet linked her arm through his. "Anne is always frantic with worry. What dangerous escapades have you been up to lately?"

"We're ceaselessly scouting behind enemy lines to see what information and booty we can secure. Farley captured a colonel and his adjutant several days ago with two excellent horses. Their regiment was marching only a hundred yards away. Can you imagine their surprise when their commander mysteriously disappeared?"

Everyone laughed. "That's quite an achievement, Captain Farley. How do you feel the Yankees are reacting to the outcome of the elections and Burnside's appointment?" Constance said, watching him speculatively.

"McClellan was most popular with his men. The election shows the tide of public opinion is turning against Lincoln. We perceive that their desertions are high, and many Yanks have entered our lines to surrender or fight with us because of his proclamation freeing the slaves."

"I must share with you the insight of one of my good friends in New York who's a Democrat," Harriet said, then walked towards her desk. "Listen to a few of her remarks."

Our friend, Mr. Barney, reported that Lincoln spoke of raising Negro brigades, which my husband disapproved. He said that if that were done that he would wash his hands of the whole matter; that recruiting was difficult enough because of the everlasting Negro question.[8]

Judge Pierrepont tells us that the president told him that the Emancipation Act was his own doing. The Cabinet was not consulted. What supreme impertinence in the rail-splitter of Illinois! 'It is my last trump card, Judge,' said Lincoln. 'If that don't do it, we must give up.' Father O'Reilly says we are under a worse despotism than France or Russia. There is no law but the despotic law of Abe Lincoln. Yet he only stands between us and internal revolution. It is terrible. God help our unhappy country![9]

We see so much invasion of our rights that the abolitionists might establish a reign of terror with little trouble. Raasloff says that some opposition must be shown to avoid this. What is most disastrous is the enormous debt and depreciated currency. Raasloff thinks peace on any terms would be better than this ever-lasting frightful debt.[10]

The election is over and Seymour, an opponent of emancipation and the war, was elected governor of New York by a large margin! Democrats gained strength in New Jersey, Pennsylvania, Ohio, and Lincoln's own Illinois. There has never been so great a revolution of public feeling!

"Those are encouraging words," Farley said. "Many believe McClellan will lead an uprising amongst the Democrats and remove Lincoln from power."

"Oh, pray God that it will happen soon," Harriet said. They heard the rustle of skirts in the hall. "I believe the Ashby ladies have arrived." No sooner had the four attractive young ladies been introduced than they heard the strumming of a banjo and Pelham, Von Borcke, Dabney, and Sweeney swept into the room.

"I might have known the two scouts were out in front of us as usual," Pelham said with a boyish grin when he spotted Stringfellow and Farley. "These two intrepid gentlemen are the bravest in the army. We only follow where they dare to lead."

"Amen," Von Borcke said.

Pelham walked over to Constance and kissed her on the cheek. "I promised you that I would return, and I have the good fortune of bringing Sweeney with me." He did not see Beckam, standing behind Alex.

Constance, her mind swirling in mixed emotions, replied, "I'm delighted we have this opportunity for merriment. You remember Major Beckam, don't you?" She motioned towards Robert.

Pelham's cheeks colored while he shook hands with Robert. "It's a pleasure to see you again, Major Beckam. How do you like your position on General Smith's staff."

"It's quite agreeable," Robert responded cordially. "You're to be commended for the outstanding achievements of the Horse Artillery."

"Well, you had them so well trained when I took over, there was little for me to do." Beckam smiled. "Balderdash! You've built that unit into the finest unit in the army and the credit is entirely yours."

"I need some help rolling up the rug so the dancing can begin," Alex said. All of the soldiers pitched in and had the rug out of the way in short order. "There are some meager refreshments on the dining room table. Please help yourselves. Now, we want everyone to dance. Sweeney, strike up the music."

When the fiddling began, Robert reached his hand out to Constance. Amanda and Alex joined them, followed by Farley and Lucy Ashby, Von Borcke and Harriet, and Frank, Pelham, and Dabney with the other three Ashby girls. "At times like these, I'm glad we have a huge parlor," Constance said with a smile as he held her firmly.

"Yes, this is great fun. I haven't danced in a good while. It feels good." Beckam searched her eyes. He sensed that she was distracted. She carried on a pleasant conversation, but her eyes wandered. She seemed to watch Pelham's every move.

Will Farley graciously asked for the next dance. "Where is your home in South Carolina, Captain Farley?"

Obviously a gentleman of the highest order, he danced gracefully. "Laurenville, but I'm part Virginian. My father came from Charlotte County. At age seventeen I made an extended walking tour of northern Virginia. The knowledge that I gained concerning terrain and roads has helped me significantly as a scout. After graduating from the University of Virginia, I returned home to assist my ailing father and practice law. I like to claim that I was the first South Carolinian to come to Virginia's aid when she seceded."

"From what Frank tells me, we're fortunate to have you here." With his dark eyes and olive complexion, she found him as handsome as Frank had told her. "I understand you have a passion for literature."

"Yes, my greatest pleasure is to wander into the woods, stretch out under a tree and reflect on Shakespeare and the elder poets. I never ride without a volume of the bard in my bag. I must confess," he said with a twinkle in his eye, "that from an early age my ardent love has been poetry. It's my favorite medium of expression."

"Then you write as well as read?" she asked. He rolled his eyes and nodded affirmatively. "I also have written some verse, but I've never shown it to anyone." She cast her eyes in the direction of Pelham.

"You shouldn't hide your talent." He twirled her effortlessly. "I'd like to read some of your work."

"Perhaps, someday. I've opened a bookstore since my father died, since we desperately need a source of income. However, it's been a Godsend for me. I love the intellectual challenge. I've read everything that's graced our shelves."

"You're to be commended for your incentive." He admired her delicate features and high forehead but felt frustrated that he did not hold her undivided attention. At the conclusion of the song, Pelham appeared immediately at their side, requesting the next dance.

He held her tightly and smiled contentedly into her cobalt eyes. "I know I've mentioned this before, but you remind me so much of my sister, Betty."

"Please tell me about her." Constance returned the intensity of his gaze.

"She has beautiful dark hair and blue eyes, like you, and is about the same size. She'll be twenty one in December. Growing up with six brothers made her quite a tomboy. I'm afraid my brothers and I were known as 'those wild Pelham boys.' We were always into mischief and even hid all the school furniture in a barn once, to torment our schoolmaster." Constance laughed musically. "As long as I can remember, I was riding, fishing, and swimming, and good old Betty always hung in there with all of us. We had to walk five miles to school, and occasionally we would even stop in an adjacent field and ride a bull."

"Your sister and I do have much in common. I admit I grew up riding, swimming, and fishing with Frank. He was the brother I never had, and we were together continuously since our mothers were best friends. I can't tell you how much I've missed not being able to jump on Liz and fly across the fields these last few months. I hate not having a horse," she continued with sadness in her eyes. "I was shocked at her thinness, but Alex said she's in better shape than most of the horses."

"The condition of our horses is deplorable." Pelham whirled her around gracefully. "We've lost so many, and most of the others are in poor condition. When we were fighting the Yankees every day, we eventually didn't have enough horses to pull all the guns. I've never lost a gun to the enemy and never intend to," he said with fire in his eyes. "The men stayed up all night and dug a hole big enough to bury the two guns we could no longer carry with us. We were determined to keep them from the Yanks."

She raised her eyebrows in amazement. "I don't believe I would have thought of that solution."

"You know I always felt like I could talk to Betty about anything. I feel the same way about you. I enjoy your directness and the fact that you usually have something worthwhile to say." Constance felt her cheeks glowing. "Betty has grown into a beautiful young lady. I idolize her." It became obvious to everyone watching them dance, that they never took their eyes off each other.

When there was a break in the music, Lucy Ashby scurried by Constance and whispered, "I think Captain Farley is the most divine man I've ever met." Constance smiled in agreement.

Stringfellow took Farley aside and asked, "What do you think?"

"Constance is everything you said, but I believe she's infatuated with Pelham. How can I compete with him? Not only that, Beckam is next in line."

"I'm surprised Pelham is so attentive, considering his involvement with Miss Dandridge," Stringfellow replied frustrated. "Don't give up."

"I believe for the time being I'll enjoy the company of Miss Ashby, whom I find most attractive and attentive." Farley walked towards Lucy to ask her to dance.

Robert Beckam had come to the same painful conclusion as Farley. Constance was infatuated with Pelham, and he felt helpless. How could he compete with the most popular man in the cavalry? Deeply hurt, he didn't want to stay any longer. If Pelham chose her, his cause was lost. He walked towards the two of them. "Constance, I have to leave now. We march at dawn tomorrow."

Surprised, she saw the unspoken pain glowing in his eyes. Deeply disturbed, she probed, "Must you go so soon, Robert?" He nodded affirmatively. "Then I'll walk you to the door."

"No." He took her hand and kissed it. "That won't be necessary. Enjoy the music."

Confused, trying to maintain her fragile control, she said, "Good night, Robert. God go with you." Sweeney strummed his banjo and John took her into his arms. The revelers danced in front of the flickering light of the fire for the next half-hour while singing drifted though the air from the Virginia House. Pelham never left her side and Farley enjoyed Lucy's company. Young Chiswell Dabney appeared fascinated with the youngest Ashby daughter, Blanche. Later, Amanda played the piano and the group sang lustily. Around eleven, Farley, Stringfellow, and Dabney escorted the four Ashby girls home.

When Von Borcke and Sweeney bid their hosts good night, Pelham said, "You two ride ahead. I'll catch up with you shortly." Von Borcke gave him a knowing smile. Pelham then turned to Constance, "I realize I haven't paid you for the book I took last time and I'd like to get another one."

"Of course." She picked up a candle and led him into the bookstore. After she set the candle down, he traced his fingers tenderly over her arms. "Miss Armstrong, I don't know exactly how to say this, but I hope my being here tonight didn't interfere with your relationship with Major Beckam. I realize that you are close and that you spent several days with his family last year after Christmas."

She inhaled sharply with surprise. "How did you know that?"

"I have my sources," he answered with a knowing smile. "I assumed that since you were not engaged, that it would be proper for me to call on you."

"I have a great deal of affection for Robert, but we're not engaged. I'm not ready to make that commitment. It's quite proper for you to call on me, and I'm glad you were here tonight," she said softly, anxiety spurting through her. "But I have a similar question for you. Rumor has it that you are engaged to Miss Dandridge."

Even in the soft light his blush was visible. "And I must give you the same answer. I'm quite fond of her, but I wasn't ready to commit to an engagement. Her family seemed anxious, and I suspect that's how the rumor started. It appears we're both in the same boat." He contemplated her, his eyes betraying his ardor. "I enjoy your company immensely and feel that I can talk to you about anything. I believe we should nurture the compelling attraction that exists between us, and see where it leads us." He slid his arms around her waist and pulled her against his lean body.

Her pulse pounding in her ears, she moved her arms around his shoulders. "That's what I'd call living dangerously. But why not live dangerously during these perilous times? Opportunities wasted can never be regained."

"Amen." His finger slowly traced the outline of her lips. "You have a beautiful mouth and the softest lips." He kissed her on the forehead, the end of the nose, and then softly on the mouth. She did not pull away. Her body tingled. She wanted more. She felt his moist breath on her cheek and his hands locked against her spine. His lips touched hers like a whisper. She inhaled sharply and his lips recaptured her, more demanding this time. Her hands moved over the strong tendons of his neck as they melted together. "Um," he sighed breathlessly. His hands moved persuasively over the small of her back. "After a kiss like that, I believe I can whip the world. Those Yankees at Fredericksburg aren't going to know what's hit them."

* * *

Eighteen days later, December 5, 1862: The Hill mansion on East Street

Amanda and Dolly Hill watched baby Alex, David, Netty, and Russie pile the wooden blocks in the floor at the Hills' East Street mansion. "You've certainly got the handsome sons for my daughters to marry," Dolly quipped. Netty coughed loudly. "The trip back over the mountains was difficult in the extreme cold and snow. I'm afraid Netty's coming down with something."

"We're glad to have you back, but I know you miss Powell. Do you know where he is?"

"Not exactly. You should have seen the bloody footprints in the snow after our devoted men marched south in the valley. This army has an utter disregard for hardships, which I believe no modern army has been called upon to bear. Powell never knows his destination. Jackson is so secretive. The two of them are still feuding. I assume they're marching to reinforce Lee at Fredericksburg, but by a southern route." Netty coughed again and laid her head in her mother's lap. Dolly felt her forehead. "My goodness, she's burning up. I'm sorry, Amanda but I need to get her in bed."

Six days later, December 11, 1862: Armstrong town home

Harriet wrung her hands, nervously paced the bedroom floor, and listened to the dull thud of cannons coming from the direction of Fredericksburg. "Those cannons are the death knell for many a brave young soul," she lamented to Amanda, putting cool cloths on baby Alex's forehead. "I'm afraid the beautiful town and my home place are in rubbles.[iii] I pray Sissie and her family have fled."

"He's still burning up." Amanda stroked the baby's sweat-soaked auburn hair. "I feel so helpless. I don't know what else to do."

Constance entered the room, her face drawn. "Is something wrong, dear?" Harriet asked.

"I'm afraid so," Constance answered solemnly, then walked towards Amanda. "Mandy, I'm sorry to have to tell you this, but I just saw Mildred Hill." She placed her hand on Amanda's shoulder. "Little Netty died of diphtheria yesterday."

The color drained from Amanda's face. "Oh, my God," she muttered. "Poor Dolly!" She looked at the baby, fear in her eyes. "Netty and the baby played together several days ago."

Harriet wrapped her arms around her daughter. "Don't jump to conclusions, darling. Your boy is as strong as an ox."

"We're here with you," Constance reiterated. "How I hurt for Powell. They telegraphed him yesterday, and now he's attempting to lead his men into battle. He adored that child."

Four days later, December 15, 1862: The depot

"Fredericksburg was Lee's most overwhelming victory yet!" Granny chirped to Lucy

---

[iii]The Federals shelled Fredericksburg at a rate of 100 rounds per minute.

and Constance, waiting at the depot. "Those damn Yankees should have had enough by now."

"I can't wait to see the Richmond papers. We know so few details," Constance answered. They watched the train steam in.

"Constance, I got a letter from Captain Farley," Lucy said elated. "I'm smitten."

"That's wonderful," Constance said. The train stopped and a bundle of papers was tossed towards them. She ran to the papers, cut the twine off, grabbed the top paper and examined it. She gasped when she saw John Pelham's picture on the front page. Her heart stopped. Had he been killed? The caption under the picture read,

The Gallant Major John Pelham of Stuart's Horse Artillery. The whole army watched in awe as Major John Pelham, with only one gun positioned on a plateau, held off the advance of the Union Army for almost two hours. Spotting their assailant, the enemy turned a barrage of artillery on Pelham. By moving his gun, and using the screening of a hedge and cedars, Pelham held out against overwhelming odds and did heavy damage to the enemy. When encouraged to withdraw, he remained bravely on the field until his ammunition was expended. While observing the action from a high vantage point, General Robert E. Lee commented, "It is glorious to see such courage in one so young." Later in the battle Pelham was given command of half a dozen batteries of Jackson's Corps. He fought them ably and bravely, inflicting severe punishment on the enemy. The day following the battle Jackson is quoted as saying to General Stuart, "General, if you have another Pelham, I wish you would give him to me." The handsome Alabamian earned a place in history at Fredericksburg.

Constance exploded with joy. Granny had been reading the paper along with her. "Sounds like your Pelham is a knight in shining armor."

Constance wiped a tear from her face. "I must run and show this to Mother and Amanda!"

"Miss Armstrong, I just received a telegram for your sister," a depot clerk called. He rushed forward and handed her a slip of paper. Breathlessly, she read:

Mrs. Yager, Your husband has suffered a shoulder wound and broken leg. Is being brought home to recover. Capt. Utterback.

Well, at least Alex was alive and the injury didn't sound too serious, she mused as she hurried home.

Constance raced into the bedroom, but was shocked to find Amanda sitting in a rocking chair holding her still, lifeless baby while tears streamed down her ashen face. Harriet, perched on a near-by cedar chest, sobbed in grief. Amanda muttered in a trance, "My darling is with the Savior now."

"Oh no, Mandy!" Constance wailed. "We all loved him." She rushed forward to embrace her sister knowing she couldn't show her the telegram yet.

10

The Battle of Kelly's Ford

December 31, 1862 - March 23, 1863

Somebody's watching and waiting for him, yearning to hold him again to her breast,
Yet there he lies with his blue eyes so dim, and purple, childlike lips half apart,
Somebody's darling, so young and brave, soon to be hid in the dust of the grave.
Somebody's Darling, a popular song

Sixteen days later, December 31, 1862: On the Rappahannock

The icy water of the Rappahannock numbed Pelham's legs while his horse swam across at Freeman's Ford to the safety of Culpeper County. His men double-teamed two guns across the river, horses and men slowly struggling against the rapid current to the south side. In the last rays of daylight he joined Stuart, watching his 1800 cavalrymen escort 200 prisoners, 200 captured horses, and 20 wagons southward.

"Our Christmas visit behind enemy lines has netted great gifts for the Confederacy," Pelham quipped. "You're to be congratulated on your most brilliant raid yet. It's been an exciting six days."

Stuart's blue eyes twinkled. The Rebels' circuitous raid had left Fredericksburg, crossed the river at Kelly's Ford and proceeded to Dumfries, Burke's Station, Fairfax, Centreville, Middleburg, and Warrenton, leaving the Yankees confused and embarrassed. "I'm satisfied. We should be able to find shelter at Culpeper Court House for the night."

The Armstrongs': Constance and Harriet worked diligently patching the sheet spread out before them in front of the crackling fire. All the washing and ironing had taken its toll on their bed linens. However, they had earned enough money from the boarders and the bookstore while the army was here to last them several months. Constance worked carefully, pulling the needle through the fabric. This was not the most exciting way to spend New Year's Eve. She found life painfully dull with the army still at Fredericksburg.

"I'm glad 1862 is finally over. There are empty chairs beside every hearth. It's been such a tragic year for us," Harriet said in a shaking voice. "The loss of your father, Abraham, the baby—will 1863 be as dreadful? I hate to think. I'm tired of this tedious life."

"Mother, you mustn't let depression and gloom consume you. You're very important to us. Without your help with the boys, Amanda and I couldn't have run the bookstore. We must try to see the bright side of each dilemma. Alex being wounded has been almost a blessing for Amanda. The two of them have been able to share their grief over the baby. They desperately needed this time together."

"You're right, dear. I have difficulty seeing anything positive in such trying times. I suppose having Billy here is a blessing of sorts, too. Without him, we'd have no man to chop and haul wood and help with the heavier chores. Poor soul..." They both looked up startled as they heard thundering hooves in the street and the piercing Rebel yell.

"It sounds like a large body of cavalry!" Constance said. She heard pounding on the door, rushed to the hall, and threw open the door to see Jeb Stuart, John Pelham, and hundreds of cavalrymen milling in the street.

"Best wishes for the New Year, fair damsel." Stuart took off his hat and made a sweeping bow. "Would you give shelter on this freezing evening to some wandering knights?"

"Of course," she laughed. "Come in, as many of you as possible."

The jubilant Stuart motioned to those behind him to follow, then rushed into the hall and kissed Constance. "Thank you for your hospitality. We've returned from a six day visit with our adversaries across the river."

Pelham hurried forward and swept her into his arms. "What I have to go through to get to see you." The touch of his lips sent a warming shiver through her.

"It appears this New Year's Eve isn't going to be as boring as I thought." Joy bubbled in her laugh and shone in her eyes. "You're freezing and wet. Come in by the fire." She pulled him forward through the crowd to the fireplace in the parlor. Amanda and the boys rushed downstairs to see the cause of the excitement.

Stuart greeted Amanda and Harriet warmly, his spirit buoyant. "We've had great fun deluding our enemy. We struck along Burnside's line of communication from Fredericksburg to Washington. We picked up prisoners and supplies in dozens of skirmishes, keeping the Yanks confused and uncertain of our next move. Of course the incomparable Pelham was ever up with his guns, choosing the most advantageous positions. On the twenty seventh, two of his guns ran out of ammunition and had to be sent back. He always does the very best that can be done!"

Embarrassed by the compliments, Pelham answered with rosy cheeks, "General Stuart was clever enough to take along his own telegrapher, who could intercept their messages and send his own to add to their confusion."

"Yes," Stuart snickered. "I must admit I did have a little fun with that. You see, I wasn't happy with the mules we had captured to haul our seized booty away. I sent several messages to General Meigs, Quartermaster-General U. S. Army, and informed him that I was unhappy with the bad quality of the mules he had lately furnished, and found them unsatisfactory for my needs. I expressed my hope that he would provide me with better quality mules in the future. Then we cut the telegraph lines."

Everyone laughed boisterously. Channing Price, a new member of Stuart's staff, stepped forward and said, "General Stuart, this raid was the longest, most dangerous, and most brilliant expedition undertaken by your cavalry to date.[1] You've given your admiring public something else to cheer about!" The soldiers let out several hearty cheers, flustering the unflappable Stuart.

"General Stuart, my husband's upstairs recovering from a wound he received at Fredericksburg," Amanda said shyly. "I know he'd be honored if you'd go up and tell him about your raid."

"Corporal Yager wounded? Of course, I'll visit him. We can't allow him to lie around here too long. He's needed in the field!" Stuart and several others ascended the stairs.

After warming themselves by the fire a good while, the exhausted soldiers began to sit or lie on the floor wherever they could find space. "We have three empty bedrooms upstairs. Why don't some of you go there to sleep?" Harriet said. A large group eagerly climbed the stairs.

Pelham and Constance picked their way through the sprawled bodies to the privacy of the dark hallway leading to the bookstore. A cold draft inspired them to seek warmth from each other. She wound her arms inside his jacket and around his trim waist while his hands caressed the planes of her back. "Congratulations, gallant Pelham. Your fame has spread across the nation since Fredericksburg." She looked into his eager eyes.

"I'm completely embarrassed by all the publicity," he replied in an apologetic tone. "I don't deserve or want it. There's something you must understand. When I positioned my guns that day, I selected the best defensive position. It never occurred to me that my actions would be observed so clearly by both armies. I'm afraid that people think I did it so I could be seen, to get the glory. I don't care what the world thinks, but your opinion is important to me. You must understand that I was not seeking glory."

"No, I don't think you were," she teased in a casual, jesting way. "I credited it all to the inspiration of our parting kiss."

He threw back his head and let out a peal of laughter. "You're correct. Your touch inspires me." He enjoyed feeling the soft curvatures of her body against him. His lips brushed her hair. "I've told you before, I believe our scouts are the true heroes of this war, but they get little publicity. Did you know that Redmond Burke was killed?"

"No!" She pulled back and looked at him. "How?"

"He went to his home in Shepherdstown. Someone informed on him and the enemy sent a raiding party. He and one of his sons were killed. We suspect that they were not allowed to surrender. General Stuart plans to erect a monument on his grave."

"I'm so sorry. I know Frank's depressed. Where is he?" He tenderly moved his hands over her shoulders.

"He's scouting near Fredericksburg. Farley was with us on the raid. He and Dabney found shelter at the Ashby's tonight. He seems quite taken with your friend."

"She's captivated. Her father has returned home seriously ill after serving as a doctor at Fredericksburg. I'm sure Captain Farley's attention will cheer her." She laid her head against his chest. "I certainly didn't expect to usher in the New Year with you. I'm so apprehensive about what's to come."

He trailed his knuckle across her cheek in a gentle caress. "The Yankees' morale is low after the slaughter at Fredericksburg, plus Vallandingham and others in the North are crying for peace at any cost. I think it will end soon. I hope I can spend more time with you in the coming year."

She looked up into a smile that sent her pulse racing. "That sounds like a dream." Her lips found their way instinctively to his. His lips feather-touched hers with tantalizing persuasion, the intensity quickened, and she relaxed into his cushioning embrace.

All too soon, Jeb Stuart called from the parlor, "Happy New Year! It's midnight! This is the year we'll whip the Yankees!" A few drowsy men cheered. "Let's get some shut eye. We'll start before dawn tomorrow. Pelham, where are you? Quit hiding. Enough sparking for one night."

The two lovers laughed and separated reluctantly. "Happy New Year. I'll try to see you again soon," he breathed in her ear. "You know how difficult it is for me to get away from General Stuart."

Sixteen days later, January 16, 1863: The bookstore

Constance and Amanda were in the bookstore when General Wade Hampton of South Carolina sauntered in. Tall and distinguished, with a receding hairline, he was one of the wealthiest men in the South and had armed and outfitted his cavalry brigade at his own expense, even importing brass cannons from Europe. "Good afternoon, General Hampton," Constance said. "Are you still camped at Brandy?"

"I'm afraid so," he sneered in an angry tone. "I feel cut off from the world. My men and horses are starving while we picket the west section of the Rappahannock. Meanwhile, the Virginia Brigades remain comfortable at Fredericksburg. Any newspapers?"

Surprised at his hostility, Constance replied, "We got papers yesterday, but you know they only come about twice a week now from Richmond. It's the best I can do. I'm sorry your men are suffering such hardships."

"Thank you, Miss Armstrong." He picked up a paper. "I apologize for my rudeness. It isn't your fault that General Stuart shows such partiality to his fellow Virginians. Everyone knows of his close friendship with General Lee while he served as superintendent of West Point. It's no surprise that Fitz Lee and Rooney Lee command two brigades of his cavalry while my South Carolinians have been assigned the most arduous duty and are being broken down by the harsh conditions."

"If it's any consolation, we appreciate your efforts," Amanda said. "Good day, General." He nodded and exited while Fannie Barbour entered the store and embraced Amanda.

"I have the most distressing news," Fannie said, a look of annoyance on her face. "Those terrible Unionists, the Botts, have finally moved into Auburn. Now they're my neighbors. Our family's so upset by it all. We think Botts swindled poor old Uncle James by paying in Confederate money. I don't think we should tolerate Unionists in the county. They weaken our cause and should be arrested."

"Wasn't John Minor Botts in the secession convention?" Constance asked. "I believe he voted against secession until the end."

"Yes, that's correct. James detests the man. He's a big bag of wind. I don't know why he had to move here from Manassas."

"Fannie, I'm sorry this has upset you. Please stay and visit awhile. I know Alex would love to talk with you." Amanda waved her hand towards the door.

"Yes, of course Amanda. I hope he's doing well." Fannie followed her friend.

Constance worked at her desk a good while until she looked up to see Annie Crittenden breeze in. "Annie, it's so good to see you at last!"

"It's difficult for us to get to town in this terrible winter weather. Reverend Slaughter gave me a ride in today. Constance, there's something I must tell you." Her face beamed with joy.

Constance walked around the desk to her friend. "You look elated. I surmise this news has something to do with a man."

Annie rolled her eyes and took off her gloves with a knowing smile. "You are correct!"

"Tell me. The suspense is killing me!"

Annie grasped both of her friend's hands. "I'm engaged to be married in May! His name is Major James Richard Smoot of Alexandria. He's one of the soldiers I nursed after Cedar Mountain."

"Annie, I'm overjoyed for you!" Constance hugged her. She knew Annie had been depressed when John Starke, Jr. married someone else. "You're sure he's the one?"

"Absolutely! Love blossoms when you care for someone intimately day after day. Many a soldier has fallen in love with his nurse, and vice-versa."

A month later, February 17, 1863: Near Madden's Tavern

The howling wind whipped the snow against John Pelham's face while he prodded his horse forward through the thickly wooded wilderness towards Culpeper Court House. The intensity of the storm had increased dropping almost a foot of snow since he, Von Borcke, and Price had departed from Fredericksburg. Men and horses neared exhaustion and the thickly falling snow obliterated the track of the road in the gathering darkness. Still more than ten miles from their destination, Pelham realized they would have to seek shelter if they were to survive. In the distance ahead he thought he saw a faint glimmer of light at Madden's Tavern. Having traveled this road following Cedar Mountain, he hoped his memory served him correctly. "I believe there's a tavern ahead," he called to his comrades above the howling wind.

Von Borcke rode close beside him, his head held down into the wind. "Our horses cannot go on, and we will surely become lost in this vast wilderness." The horses trudged slowly towards the salvation of the light. The three almost-frozen soldiers eagerly dismounted and rapped on the door with numb knuckles.

Willis Madden cracked the door enough to reveal a blazing fire, a beacon like heaven to the three vagabonds. At the sight of the soldiers he muttered, "I don't want nothin' to do with no stragglers," and slammed the door in their faces.

"Oh, I can't believe it," Channing Price said in stunned disappointment. The desperate Rebels stood in shocked silence for several minutes.

Finally, Pelham declared, "This won't do at all; we can't possibly go on. To remain outside in this terrible weather means certain destruction. We're obligated to preserve our lives for the sake of our cause and our country."[2]

"We're armed. We could shoot our way in," Von Borcke suggested.

"No, I hate to do that to the poor old nigger," Pelham replied. "Let me think a minute. Perhaps I can come up with a better plan."

Willis Madden paced the floor. He wanted to maintain his neutrality in this fool war, but every time soldiers appeared on his doorstep from either army, he suffered pillage. Still it was a frightful night, and these men looked like officers. Perhaps he should reconsider his harsh decision. He didn't want to antagonize either side.

Pelham blew on his numb fingers. "I'm going to fool this ignorant old man, and play a trick on him which I believe is pardonable under the circumstances." He knocked loudly on the door repeatedly until Madden cracked it again and peered out warily. "Mr. Madden, I'm a friend of yours and you don't know what you're doing when you treat us this way. That gentleman there," he said, pointing to 6-foot, 4-inch Von Borcke, "is General Lee himself; the other one is the French ambassador," he continued, indicating Price, "and I'm a staff-officer of the general's. He's quite mad at being kept waiting outside so long after riding all this way to see you."[3]

General Lee, indeed, Madden thought to himself while he stared at the dark-haired, twenty-nine-year-old giant. Everyone knew General Lee had white hair, was older and of medium height. He had friends who had seen him in town. He smiled inwardly and decided to play along with their game. Perhaps it was to his advantage if they believed him an idiot.

"In fact, if you let the general stay any longer here in the cold, he'll shell your house as soon as his artillery comes up,"[4] Pelham said in a perfectly serious countenance.

"Gin'nel Lee, sur, please come in," Madden said. "I'm sorry I didn't realize it was somebody as important as you." He opened the door and the three surged into the warm paradise. "You can put your horses in mah stable and there's corn to feed 'em. Now, ya'll dry yourselves in front of the fire, and I'll fix a dinner worthy of such important guests." He walked towards the kitchen with a big grin.

After Price had taken care of the horses, the three toasted themselves in front of the fire and inhaled the savory odors emerging from the kitchen. "I'm proud of my diplomatic ruse," Pelham said with a laugh.

"It appears he's preparing a dinner worthy of his distinguished guests, " Von Borcke chuckled. "By jove, I've never felt so important before."

"We'll pay him well in the morning and reveal our hoax," Pelham said. "He deserves that." However, Madden refused to be undeceived the next day, and continued to play the role of an important innkeeper, honored with a visit from most distinguished guests.

Next day, February 18, 1863: The Virginia House Hotel

Constance and Pelham laughed at the antics of the minstrel show being conducted by Fitz Lee's men, with the assistance of Sweeney. Looking around the packed audience at the Virginia House, Constance contemplated Fitz Lee. Sporting a dark beard and hair, the attractive bachelor nephew of Robert E. Lee had relieved Wade Hampton of picket duty on the Rappahannock. Hampton, there with his staff, appeared in a more cordial mood because he was leaving for South Carolina to recruit horses and men for his unit. The ever-jovial Stuart laughed loudly. He had joined Pelham in an inspection of both Lee's and Hampton's brigades. In rapture, she stared at the handsome, boyish face of Pelham who laughed heartily at the show. When the show concluded, Pelham took the stage and acted out the scenario that had transpired between him and Willis Madden, much to the delight of his audience.

"What did you think?" he inquired after he sat down beside her.

"Your impromptu skit was quite comical, but I don't believe for one minute that you deceived Willis Madden. Von Borcke doesn't look a thing like Lee."

"Of course I fooled the dumb old man," Pelham said surprised at her observation. "We couldn't even convince him otherwise when we left."

"Willis Madden is a respected businessman in this community. He's far from dumb. Might I suggest that he played along with your little ruse, and the joke's actually on you."

His pride was wounded. "You believe that don't you? If you're correct, then I made a total fool of myself."

"Don't take it so hard," she teased. "I'm delighted you were clever enough to survive the blizzard and arrive here safely. How long do you think you'll stay?"

His eyes lit up. "You don't know how much finagling I had to do to get here in the first place. General Stuart's going to Richmond for a few days and I've appealed to him to let me stay here. He hasn't given me a reply."

"That would be wonderful!" They exchanged conspiratorial glances. "Do you think I could use my feminine wiles on General Stuart?"

"They always work on me," he said in his sweet Alabama drawl. "Why not give it a try?"

She glided up to Jeb Stuart, who greeted her warmly with a kiss. "General Stuart, I have a problem I was hoping you would assist me with," she began in a silky voice.

"Certainly, Miss Armstrong. How can I help you?"

"Since my father's death and the loss of our servants, we have had difficulty getting and chopping fire wood. Our supply will only last a few more days. I thought perhaps you might allow Majors Pelham and Von Borcke to stay and chop wood for the next few days. I understand that you're going to Richmond. Surely you don't need Major Pelham there, and he would be of great assistance to us if he stays here," she concluded, batting her long lush lashes.

Stuart threw back his head in a robust laugh. "You should be a lawyer, Miss Armstrong. That Pelham will stop at nothing! I'll give your request serious consideration."

Next day, February 19, 1863: Armstrong town home

Amanda and Constance giggled at the scene they watched from the parlor window. "What's all of that fuss about out in the street?" Harriet asked when she walked in.

"The street's a sea of red muck since the snow melted so rapidly," Amanda answered. "It's impossible to cross it without sinking a foot deep in the mud. It appears the gallant Pelham and Von Borcke are building a bridge across from the Virginia House."

The three women stared at the spectacle before them. His blonde hair glistening in the midday sun, Pelham balanced precariously on a plank and dropped two large stones in the mud in front of him. He then carefully placed the plank Von Borcke handed him on the two stones. Laughing heartily, the two friends in like manner completed the bridge across the street and stomped triumphantly on the porch. "They did it!" Constance raced to the front door.

"Fair ladies, we have bridged the muddy gorge which separates us, and can now call on you morning, noon, or night without tracking mud into your lovely home!" Pelham said with a bow and then swept Constance into his arms.

"How inventive you are!" she laughed. Von Borcke greeted Harriet and Amanda.

"We're free! Stuart has gone to Richmond and left us here to enjoy ourselves in this paradise," Pelham boasted.

"By jove, we're going to have a jolly good time!" Von Borcke added. "What shall we do first? Anyone interested in a game of charades?"

"I am," Alex said. He hobbled down the steps, followed by the boys.

"You're much improved since our last visit," Pelham observed as they shook hands. He picked up David and gave him a hug.

"Yes, my leg's still stiff," Alex replied, "but I'm regaining use of it rapidly, and my shoulder is healed. The fall from my horse was worse than the wound. I'm delighted you're here. Let the games begin!"

And so the days of gaiety and laughter began. Channing Price, the couriers and other of Fitz Lee's men who visited the Virginia House frequently joined them. The Ashby girls often added their beauty and charm to the gatherings. Even though mourning the recent death of their father, the young ladies refused to miss out on the gay fellowship. The group played games, sang, talked, laughed, debated, and danced. On many occasions Constance and Pelham would steal away from the others and talk of West Point, his childhood, her love of riding, music, books, and current events. They read aloud to each other from the classics, poetry, and the Bible, and spent long moments looking deep into each other's eyes. When Constance studied his gentle, boyish face, she had difficulty believing he was the one who aimed his guns to kill, kill, and kill. Surely it was someone else. There were no lines of harshness in his face. He drank in her beauty, the silkiness of her hair, and the dancing depths of her eyes. They constantly engaged in an evenly matched battle of wits to see who could outsmart or defeat the other. Private moments for stolen embraces were few and far between and exceedingly cherished. Pelham went to church with them, and townspeople eager to meet him and shake his hand surrounded the hero. The women openly flirted with him. Brimming with pride, Constance floated on a cloud of euphoria.

Nine days later, February 28, 1863: Constance's bedroom

Singing to herself, Constance whirled around when Sadie entered her bedroom.
"Well, now, ain't ya the happy one this morning." Sadie laid some clean clothes on the bed.
Constance danced in a circle around her, singing and humming. "Sadie, I'm exploding with joy!" She gave the tall black woman an energetic hug. "These last ten days have been the happiest in my life!"
"Miss Constance, you's something else," Sadie laughed. "But ya gotta keep control of yourself."
"No I don't and you can't make me." She twirled around to look out the window into the back yard.
"What's all the ruckus about?" Harriet walked in and joined Constance at the window. They watched Pelham, Von Borcke, and Billy split the load of wood they had cut the preceding day, while David supervised. David suddenly tripped over a log and skinned his knee. Pelham picked up the crying child, brushed off the snow, and comforted him. "Never have I known a gentler young man with a sweeter disposition," Harriet said. "I don't believe he could ever get mad. He's such a splendid boy. He doesn't look a day over sixteen."
"I think he's divine," Constance sighed.
"That's obvious!" her mother replied with her eyebrows raised. "It's scandalous the way the two of you keep disappearing. What will people think?"
"Oh, Mother, don't be such a prude! We rarely get any time together. He's a perfect southern gentleman and you know there's nothing improper about it."
"Nevertheless, as innocent as he looks, he has a reputation for being quite a lady's man."
"I'm fully aware of that. However, I intend to enjoy every second that I have him to myself. Please don't destroy my few days of happiness." Constance pranced out of the room.
Harriet shook her head. "Sadie, I'm afraid she's going to be badly hurt."

"Yes'm. But there ain't nothing ya kin do about it. She's powerful bull-headed."

John Pelham placed two pieces of wood on the pile, then a snowball slammed into his face and another smashed against his chest. "Ow!" he yelled stunned. Wiping the snow from his face, he looked towards the back fence and stable, the direction from which the missiles had come. He thought he saw someone dart around the corner of the stable. "Did you see anybody, Von?"

"Not a soul," Von Borcke said mystified.

"Somebody's going to pay," Pelham vowed before he raced towards the stable. He slowly opened the door, seeing no one. Constance, plastered against the wall behind the door, saw his moist breath. "I believe the guilty party should come forth and beg for mercy," he challenged as he closed the door. Turning, he spied Constance, who gave him an innocent smile. "Now, Miss Armstrong, is that any way to treat your humble servant?"

"Major Pelham, whatever are you talking about?" she drawled seductively.

He leaned over her, placing his left hand against the wall. Amusement flickered in his eyes for a few minutes while he debated her fate. Then, without warning, he pulled his right hand from behind his back and smeared a fist full of snow in her face. "Ah!" she cried, spitting out snow. "It appears that chivalry is dead!"

"I'll forgive you," he said with a satisfied grin, "if you confess that this was a ruse to lure me in here so we could be alone."

"Ah, typical male conceit," she sputtered. He wiped some snow from her face and then proceeded to kiss the rest away. His mouth found hers and they melted together in a long embrace.

"You're driving me crazy," he whispered against her neck. "It's wonderful to be able to see you day after day, but not to be able to touch you is torture."

"I know. Let's enjoy these few minutes before they send out a search party." She slid her arms around his neck and they kissed again…and again…and again…until Liz's whinnying finally brought them back to earth.

"Come look at her," Constance said. They walked to the horse with their arms around each other. "I've been paying the exorbitant price for grain to try to fatten her up." She stroked the animal's nose. "How I long to fly through the fields on her before Alex reports back to duty and takes her. Mother thinks it improper for me to ride outside of town with so many soldiers about."

"Then I'll go with you, if the roads dry up enough." He reached over her shoulder to touch the chestnut horse.

"That would be wonderful! We could ride out to the farm and see Aunt Martha. But we'd have to have a chaperone for Mother to approve. She's given me a lecture today on proprieties and our scandalous behavior."

"I'm sure Von will go with us. I believe I'll have to use some of my Alabama charm on your mother. We'd better get back before we're missed." His body felt heavy and warm against her. His lips moved over her neck.

Von Borcke addressed the group seated around the hearth in the parlor that evening, "Let me tell you about Major Pelham's twenty-fourth birthday party. It was September the seventh, while we were enjoying the beautiful countryside of Maryland. We had strict orders against any pillaging because the citizens of Maryland are sympathetic to our cause. Febry, one of our gunners, cooked us a delicious meal of barbecue pork to celebrate the gala event. When questioned about the source of his meal, Febry said, yes, he knew about the order against any despoiling of the Maryland farmers. But this enormous pig had the audacity to viciously attack him. He had no choice but to slay it in self-defense!" The ladies all laughed.

"I of course saw the joke," interjected Pelham, "but was flattered by the banquet on my behalf and naturally joined in the feast. However, the next day General Stuart soberly issued new orders directing that even vicious pigs should be spared."

"There is no one quite like General Stuart," Alex said. "One minute he frolics and laughs like a child, and the next minute he leads us in and out of the jaws of death."

"There's not a one of us who would not unquestionably follow where he leads," Pelham agreed. "He's requested my promotion which has not yet been granted. I believe my youthful appearance and inability to grow anything but peach fuzz are the problems. There was a rumor that I would be promoted to take command of Longstreet's artillery. I would never accept any promotion that would take me away from General Stuart. I love him like a brother."

"Even when he torments you?" Constance teased.

"It's his buoyant sense of humor that keeps up our spirits," Pelham admitted with a grin.

"His ceaseless energy is an inspiration," said Von Borcke.

"But I must say, his flirtations and kissing of all the ladies has raised many eyebrows," Harriet said, "not to mention his dapper attire."

"He obviously enjoys the attention of the ladies, but I can assure you he's devoted to his wife. He has never done anything improper. Since I'm almost always with him, I would know," Pelham said.

"She's been with him at Fredericksburg, and rumor has it that she is with child, as is Mrs. A. P. Hill, and Jackson is ecstatic finally to be a new father. He still hasn't seen his daughter," Von Borcke added.

"Jackson has a reputation for being so stern, I can't imagine him as a father," mused Lucy Ashby.

"Oh, but he really has a heart of gold, you have to penetrate his outer shell," said Pelham. "He talks of his baby constantly." They heard cheering and horses outside. Pelham jumped up and walked to the window. "It's Fitz Lee returning from a raid. I'm going to invite them in."

"Allow me to introduce my good friend and West Point roommate, Colonel Tom Rosser," Pelham said to Constance and Harriet, standing in front of the fire.

"Miss Armstrong, Mrs. Armstrong, it is a pleasure," the sturdy 6-foot, 2-inch soldier said, then he bowed politely.

"Tell me Colonel Rosser, what was it like living with Major Pelham for almost five years?" Constance inquired, watching Pelham's expression.

"He managed to put up with me and never lost his temper," handsome, dark-haired Rosser replied. "I'm the hot-tempered one. It was a full-time job for him to keep me out of trouble. He liked athletics better than academics."

"I'm afraid I must plead guilty," Pelham admitted. "Now tell her how shy I was around young ladies. She'll never believe me."

"Ah, that's true. John would watch the women with a telescope from the window of our room. That's as close as he ever got. I'm delighted to report that he has finally come out of his shell."

Constance rolled her eyes looking from one to the other. "This I find difficult to believe. I suspect the two of you are conspiring to deceive me."

"It's the truth," Pelham said innocently.

A jubilant Fitz Lee and Will Farley joined them with Lucy and Jane Ashby in tow. "I brought you a bag of coffee from our successful raid." Fitz Lee handed Harriet the small bag.

"Coffee! We haven't had that luxury in months. We'll brew some up right now." Harriet took the bag and walked towards the hall.

"Good hunting?" Pelham asked.

"The best! We caught them off guard near Hartwood Church, drove in their pickets, and routed the camp. Brought back a hundred and fifty prisoners, their horses, arms and equipment. Averell is an old West Point pal of mine. I left him a note saying, 'Go away, and if you won't go away, bring me some coffee,'" Fitz Lee chuckled.

"And what information have you picked up, Captain Farley?" Lucy looked at him in adoration.

Farley paused thoughtfully for a minute, and then said in his low voice, "The man they call 'Fighting Joe Hooker' has replaced Burnside and is making plans to take Richmond soon. He's an attractive guy who talks big."

"Have you seen him?" Lucy asked surprised.

"Oh, yes, I've infiltrated his camp several times," Farley said modestly. "Their army's in high spirits. You see, he's the first general who's allowed ladies of ill repute to follow the army in great numbers. He's made the term 'hooker' more appropriate than ever."

"That's scandalous!" Lucy exclaimed. "The Yankees have no sense of morality."

"Amen," Constace chuckled. "I understand Frank is on a secret mission. I suspect it will take him to Alexandria and the fair Emma."

"It's true, he's on a dangerous mission," Farley confirmed. "I can't divulge the details. And Mosby has been given an independent command and will harass behind enemy lines using guerilla warfare of the style of John Hunt Morgan."

"Explain that," Lucy said. "I don't really understand."

"He will use fast hit-and-run tactics to raid their supply lines, probably in Fauquier and Loudoun counties. He and his men will hide in secret quarters or stay with families. It's going to be impossible for the Yankees to find them. All the youngbloods are anxious to sign up with him for the excitement. If I know Mosby, he's going to do serious damage to the enemy and they'll never catch him."

"Well, hats off to Mosby! Let's sing to celebrate your successful raid," said Pelham.

When they gathered around the piano, Lucy whispered in Constance's ear, "I love these rowdy cavalrymen, all boots and spurs. Their very look, scent, and bearing is erotic."[5] Constance blushed slightly and nodded in agreement.

Two days later, March 2, 1863: Panorama

The cold, crisp air exhilarated Constance as Liz galloped up the hill towards Panorama. Her eyes drank in the magnificent blue snow-capped mountains. "The ride was fantastic!" Pelham helped her dismount from her sidesaddle, admiring the way the sun glistened on her dark hair.

"Von, we need to get some water for the horses. I expect the well is frozen. Would you take them down to the creek while we check the house?"

"Be my pleasure."

Pelham handed him the reins of the horses and whispered, "And take your time." Von Borcke smiled knowingly with a nod.

The sun streamed through the crystals of ice covering the windows. "It's like a beautiful ice palace," Constance said when they walked inside. She moved close to one of the windows to examine the crystals. Pelham slipped his arms around her waist and kissed her on the back of the neck. "Alone at last," he said softly.

"It's like a dream." She tingled at the sweetness of his kisses.

He took his right hand and etched a small J.P. into the ice and glass with the diamond in the ring he always wore. "That's so you won't forget me."

When she spun around to look into his eyes, she saw sad resignation for the first time. "I will never forget you. Don't speak of it!"

"Every day of life is a gift. Spring is coming and hostilities will begin soon."

She put her arms around his waist and laid her face against his chest. "Hold me tight."

He kissed her gently on the forehead. "Come let's sit on the sofa. There's something I need to tell you."

He dusted the debris off the sofa, pulled her down beside him, encircled her in his arms, and rubbed her red hands. "Your hands are like ice. May I call you Constance?"

"Of course, John. I'd like that, but don't do it in front of Mother. She'd accuse us of being too familiar."

"Constance, there are some things I want to explain to you. What Rosser told you about me at West Point was the truth. As a backwoods boy from Alabama, I was intimidated by young ladies, and had little social involvement. When the war began, women constantly flirted with us soldiers and I grew more confident. My involvement with Belle Boyd was brief, because I met Sallie Dandridge. I was quite taken with her. She's beautiful and comes from a very prominent family. I wrote my family glowing letters about her and confessed that I hoped to marry her." He paused thoughtfully and kissed her red fingers as her heart pounded in confusion. "But, then I met you and I found myself intrigued. Everything about you reflects intelligence, education, and breeding. It's the ease with which we converse that attracts me to you. Your beauty is an extra-added bonus. I wasn't sure of the extent of your involvement with Beckam or if you would ever think of me as more than a friend. That first time that I kissed you, out in the street after Cedar Mountain, you kissed me back. That gave me hope. So even though I spent four wonderful weeks with Sallie at The Bower, I couldn't commit to an engagement. You haunted me. Constance, I had to find out about you." His voice echoed her inner longings.

Searching his face, she swam through a haze of feelings and desires. "And what have you found out?"

"That _you_ have become increasingly important to me. That I want to tell _you_ my innermost thoughts. It's _your_ blue eyes that I see when I close my eyes at night. I believe the eyes are the windows to the soul. I'm not sure where it all will lead us..." He paused, groping for words.

"John." She laced her fingers with his. "Because of you these last two weeks have been the happiest of my life. Your laughing eyes haunt me also. We both entered this relationship with no strings attached. It's been wonderful so far…let's keep it that way." She caressed his face softly with her hand.

"And you're willing to give me your affection under those circumstances?" he asked amazed.

"Absolutely. If we make no promises then we'll tell no lies." She moved her lips slowly over his face.

He kissed the pulsing hollow at the base of her throat. "Connie, dear Connie, I hunger for your touch." His mouth engulfed hers and he slid his hand under her cape to caress her.

A short while later, they were too engrossed to hear the first knock at the door. Von Borcke cleared his throat loudly and then knocked again more forcefully. "John," she finally said. "Von's at the door."

"Make him go away." He squeezed her tighter. "And then make the war go away."

"How I wish I could." She slowly pulled away, stood up, and prodded him up from the sofa.

Aunt Martha, now twenty pounds lighter, ushered the three into her large parlor. "Our house is a rendezvous spot for blockade runners north to Baltimore. We have a steady stream of adventurers here every night and we enjoy a gay time around the fire. It's all so exciting that at times I actually enjoy this war. Mrs. Grey, Mrs. Smith," she said to the two ladies seated by the roaring fire, "allow me to introduce my niece, Constance Armstrong, the gallant Major Pelham, and Major Von Borcke."

The two soldiers bowed politely. "Major Pelham, it's an honor to meet such a celebrity," the younger lady said. "My husband, Dan, is in the cavalry and he writes of your brave feats."

Pelham blushed slightly and the four of them took seats. "Thank you, Mrs. Grey. What has prompted you to run the blockade? That sounds rather dangerous, especially for two women."

"We hope to attach ourselves to a larger group so that we won't be traveling alone. Of course there's danger involved, but many do it successfully every day. We want to visit our mother in Baltimore. I stayed with Mrs. Rixey in November when Dan was here and watched blockade-runners pass through each day. They said that by traveling west and crossing the Potomac above Shepherdstown, they could sneak through the enemy pickets. Then it's only a matter of going southeast to Baltimore. That prompted me to go to Petersburg and fetch some gold and my sister Milicent. My husband's uniform is in shreds. I'm determined to bring back gray wool to make him a new one."

Constance said, "Because of the blockade we desperately need so many items. My bookstore is our livelihood, but I may not be able to get many more books from Richmond. Ladies, I wonder if I might beg you to locate me a source of books and periodicals in Baltimore?"

"You mean find a supplier who will sell to you?" Milicent asked.

"Exactly. You see I have a two hundred dollar check in U.S. money that I could endorse to a supplier for my first purchase. Surely there's a way to get the books here through Union lines."

"And where did you get such a check?" Pelham asked with his eyebrows raised.

"Captain Ames sent it to me. He was generous enough to compensate us for taking care of him," she replied, avoiding his eyes.

"Ah, yes, the soldier from Maine. He seemed like a nice chap." Pelham scrutinized her face.

"Miss Armstrong, we understand your situation. I'll certainly try to locate a supplier for you," Marta Grey said. "I've seen your bookstore on Coleman Street. If I'm successful, I'll visit you on our return."

When Pelham and Von Borcke returned to the Virginia House late that afternoon, a telegram from Stuart awaited them, summoning the two back to Fredericksburg. Thus, the days of gaiety and laughter came to an abrupt end. Alex returned to duty with Fitz Lee, and Amanda and Constance resumed the daily drudgery of trying to survive.

Eight days later, March 10, 1863: The bookstore

Granny Ashby scurried into the bookstore moving at a pace even faster than normal. She handed Constance a note, with a gleam in her eye. Startled, Constance said, "What is it?"

"Read it for yourself," Granny said excited. Constance read the scribbled note: *If you want some excitement, come to the depot at once. John*

"John! Is he here?"

"I've been sworn to secrecy," Granny squeaked. "You'll have to come see for yourself."

Without a second's hesitation, Constance threw on her cape and ran to the depot, leaving Granny in the dust. Arriving breathlessly, she saw numerous Union soldiers guarded by a few Confederates. Pelham, Stuart, and Mosby waved to her. "John!" When she ran up, he grabbed her and kissed her. "What's happening?"

"I tagged along with General Stuart to pick up these prisoners that Mosby captured at Fairfax Court House night before last. You know I wouldn't miss a chance to come to Culpeper," he said with his arm around her.

"Miss Armstrong, surely you have a kiss for the benevolent general who allowed Major Pelham to vacation here." Stuart kissed her on the cheek. "I trust he chopped enough wood for you."

"Oh, yes, it was a great help to us. Thank you, General Stuart." The soldiers began loading the prisoners on the train.

Mosby nodded to her. "We had a successful raid," the 5-foot, 9-inch wiry partisan said with a grin. "In the dark of the night twenty nine of my men entered Fairfax. My scouts discovered the location of General Stoughton's headquarters. We took his orderly at the door, and I mounted the steps to his bedchamber. Finding him serenely asleep, I ordered, 'Get up, General, and come with me!' The groggy general suddenly sat erect, indignant at my lack of ceremony. 'Do you know who I am, sir?' he asked rudely. 'Do you know Mosby, General?' I retorted. 'Yes,' he said with eager excitement. 'Have you got the damned rascal?' 'No,' I answered, 'but he's got you!'"

Everybody laughed, including Granny who had arrived on the scene. "Hooray for Mosby!" she shouted. "I bet old Lincoln is shaking in his boots after hearing about this! He's probably moved the gold out of Washington!"

"Mosby, I couldn't be more elated," Stuart said, slapping him on the back. "You've brought me a general, two captains, thirty prisoners, and fifty-eight horses. Without the loss of a single man, it's an unparalleled feat! Keep up the good work, my man." Mosby nodded with satisfaction.

"I've missed you," Pelham said to Constance while attention was focused on Mosby.

249

"It seems like an eternity since you left."

After the last prisoners climbed on the train, Stuart said, "Sorry Pelham, but we have to head back." Pelham kissed her quickly and the two soldiers climbed aboard. He blew her a kiss while the train pulled away. She stood there several minutes waving. Granny put her arm around her.

One week later, March 16, 1863: North of the Rappahannock

Dawn: Stringfellow turned to see one of his scouts galloping up to him and the small band of men he commanded. "There's a large number of Federal cavalry gathering at Morrisville, about six miles east of Kelly's Ford," the scout reported breathlessly.

Stringfellow pondered the information. He was traveling south after establishing a line of communication from Washington to Richmond, which would provide vital information to the Confederacy until the end of the war. His small command had recently had several brushes with the active Federal cavalry moving west. "I suspect they're going to force their way across the river and threaten the railroad at Culpeper or Orange," he said thoughtfully. "They'll probably cross at Kelly's Ford. I need three couriers to leave fifteen minutes apart to take this vital information to Fitz Lee in Culpeper." After sending his three volunteers on their way, he decided to take his men on a circuitous route around the enemy, with the hope of arriving in Culpeper in time to join the impending battle.

Later that afternoon the sun streamed through the windows of the bookstore. Constance straightened the books on the shelf. Amanda, seated at the desk, saw John Pelham enter soundlessly and motion her to keep silent. He stealthily crept up behind Constance, threw his arms around her waist and kissed her on the neck.

"Oh!" she cried. She spun around to look into his laughing gray eyes. "John!" She threw her arms around his neck. "What are you doing here?"

"I'm here to see you. Why else?" He kissed her.

"Major Pelham," Amanda inquired, "I heard that General Stuart was at the court-house today to testify in a court-marshal case. Are you involved in that?"

"No, actually I was so bored with camp life, that I got permission to visit Orange to inspect Moorman's Battery. I was at the train station several hours ago when the train from Culpeper came in to get extra ammunition for Fitz Lee. Seems our scouts have reported Federal cavalry massing on the other side of the river. It appears that a battle is imminent, so I decided to return with the train to join Stuart in Culpeper. I want be available to assist."

Both women's faces registered great alarm at the news. "Oh, no, it's going to start all over again," Amanda said.

"John, this will not be your battle. Your artillery isn't here," Constance said.

"But I have to protect the fair damsels of Culpeper. If we don't stop the Yanks, they'll be in town in no time. But let's not fret about that now. General Stuart, Harry Gilmor from the valley, and several other officers have invited me to join them for dinner at the Virginia House. With your permission, I thought perhaps I could entice them over here later in the evening to enjoy some singing around the piano."

"Of course, we'd like that," Amanda said.

"Come into the parlor and tell me how you've been occupying yourself for the past two weeks." Constance led him forward by the hand.

They settled onto the sofa and he slid his arm around her. "Our tent has been reasonably comfortable. John Esten Cooke and I have built a wood floor and chimney that make it almost cozy. He's a rather droll fellow, a first cousin of Mrs. Stuart. He writes all the time…says he'll make me immortal," he chuckled.

"You deserve that." She slipped her hand in his.

"I had the opportunity to visit with my younger brother Sam and hear about home. Mother's holding up fairly well, considering she has six sons in the war."

"I don't envy her. John, I'm dying from the boredom here. I've missed you terribly."

"I'm afraid you've spoiled me." He twirled a ringlet of her hair in his fingers. "After two weeks with you I can't readjust to the drudgery of camp." He leaned towards her, slowly moving his lips towards hers. "Give me a few precious moments of rapture."

Just before the battle, Mother, I was drinking mountain dew,
When I saw the Rebels marching, to the rear I flew.

Pelham, Stuart, Gilmor, Rosser, Puller, and several other officers sang lustily, enjoying their version of a northern song. "Can't you just see Lincoln shaking in his boots. Since Mosby's raid, he has the boards removed every night from the bridge across the Potomac," Stuart chuckled. Glancing at his pocket watch, he continued, "Gentlemen, the hour is growing late. We'll need our rest if all three thousand Yanks over there decide to cross the river tomorrow. Ladies, thank you for your hospitality."

When the soldiers began to file out, Harriet caught the arm of Harry Gilmor. "Captain Gilmor, please tell me a little about yourself."

"Certainly, Mrs. Armstrong," the youthful cavalryman replied. "I'm from Baltimore. When Beast Butler unlawfully took control of the city, I attempted to flee south to join the Confederacy. Because of my secessionist leanings I was arrested for two weeks. When I finally obtained my freedom, I joined Turner Ashby in the valley. After Sharpsburg I attempted to visit my family, only to be captured and spend five months in prison. I'm here to see General Stuart on business and hope to assist him in action tomorrow, should the situation arise."

"My, that's quite a story," Harriet said. "You're welcome here any time. Good night, gentlemen." Pelham lingered in the hall with Constance. Eyeing the two of them closely, Harriet said, "Constance, come upstairs in a few minutes. I want to talk to you."

"I'll be up shortly Mother." Harriet and Amanda climbed the stairs and closed the doors to their rooms.

"I don't think she trusts me," Pelham said, pulling her close. "She just gave me the evil eye."

Constance laughed and slid her arms around his neck. "She doesn't think you're as innocent as you look." He kissed her gently at first, and then so passionately, she finally had to gasp for air.

"Oh," she sighed, trying to breathe. "Perhaps there's some truth in Mother's accusation."

He smiled at her with that innocent grin. "I have to leave now, so you have nothing to fear, fair lady. John Pendleton invited me to spend the night at Redwood.[i] He's such a distinguished gentleman, I couldn't refuse. Sweeney's loaned me his horse."

"He'll be honored to have you." She took his face in her hands and looked deep into his engaging eyes. "John, I'm so frightened about tomorrow. How many men does Fitz Lee have to meet the enemy?"

"Men aren't the problem. It's lack of horses that hampers us. I doubt if he has more than eight or nine hundred mounted." He saw the stark fear in her eyes. "Don't look so forlorn. We've been greatly outnumbered before and won. This time tomorrow night, I'll be back in your arms. I promise."

She pulled his face towards hers and kissed him. "Forgive me for wanting to cling to you," she whispered. "I know you have to leave."

"Watch for me in the morning. The sight of your face will inspire me." He kissed her on the forehead and was gone.

"I'll be here, John. You can count on me," she whispered softly as she watched him cross the street.

Next day, March 17, 1863: Kelly's Ford

Dawn: Aaron Ames swung the ax over his head, chopping into the abatis of fallen trees that the Rebels had placed on the north side of Kelly's Ford to impede their passage. Rebel sharpshooters in the rifle pits across the river sent welcoming missiles in his direction. When the last log fell away, passage was cleared for a first attempt to cross the river. He watched several men fall from their saddles when a detachment forded the river. They whacked at the barrier on the south bank but were turned back by the accurate rifle fire from the Rebel pits. Several more detachments crossed before the way was finally cleared. In the soft light of dawn, he cheered Simeon Brown and the First Rhode Island Cavalry who dashed across the river and captured all but three of the Rebels.

The Yankees positioned a gun to cover the crossing of the remaining cavalry. "Mount up, men, and take a nose bag of artillery ammunition," his commander called. Ames held the ammunition above his head when his horse waded into the chilly water. His legs and lower body became numb from the cold before he reached the other side. He had mixed emotions about his arrival in Culpeper. He had returned to duty in time to witness the sickening slaughter at Fredericksburg. Having participated in several small actions and skirmishes, he felt comfortable and confident in his new role of cavalryman. This, however, was his first major battle. He wondered, who would he face…obviously Fitz Lee, but what about Stuart, Pelham, Rooney Lee, and Alex Yager? He did not have any problem killing Rebels to bring a quick end to this rebellion, but killing an acquaintance would be emotionally troublesome. Ordered to rout and destroy Fitz Lee's men and then take control of the railroad at Culpeper, he felt their superior numbers and excellent horses should achieve that goal. Anxious to be in Culpeper Court House, he glanced at the 900 men left behind to guard the ford. Then

---

[i]John Pendleton, former Congressman and minister to Chile, Argentina, Paraguay, and Uruguay built Redwood in 1830. The house is located one mile west of town off Route 522.

his eyes swept up the hill on his left to Kellysville, domain of John Kelly. With 500 inhabitants, it encompassed a woolen mill, post office, dye factory, stagecoach factory, shoe factory, and grain mill. Where would the battle take place?

8 a.m. Constance paced in front of the windows of the bookstore. John had just ridden up and rushed inside the Virginia House, tying Sweeney's horse in front. She put on her cape. "I think they'll be leaving soon. I'm going out on the porch," she said to Amanda. Shortly, Pelham, his cheeks rosy, came out the front door and saw her waving a handkerchief. He mounted up and admired her from a distance. "God be with you, John," she called when Stuart and Gilmor rounded the corner of Cameron Street. She threw him a kiss.

He lifted his hat and called to her, "Save that kiss for tonight," then rode towards the two officers. Constance leaned over the railing and continued to wave her handkerchief until they turned the corner by the courthouse. When he rounded the corner, he looked back for one last glimpse of her silhouette against the morning sun.

"Mandy, I have a terrible sense of foreboding," she exclaimed after she rushed back into the bookstore.

Amanda put her arms around her sister. "We must watch and pray together. I know that Alex will be in the thick of it. The odds are against them, and if they fail, will our town again be in enemy hands?"

"God help us all," Constance moaned.

Midday: "The roads are wretched," Stuart said as the three approached the impending battle. "Thank God General Fitz has been able to use the railroad to move his men forward and get the dismounted men and lame horses to the rear."

"Breathed is struggling to move his guns through the mud. It's going to take him a while to get them up," Pelham replied.

Fitz Lee rode up to them. "The enemy has taken a defensive position ahead in Jamison's Woods on the Wheatley farm," he explained to Stuart who scanned the area with his field glasses. The Yankees had moved forward only a half-mile from the ford, obviously seeking an attack before tiring their horses. "I think there are only a few platoons in the woods. Hadn't we better 'take the bulge' on them at once?"[6] he asked Stuart.

"Yes, proceed."

Fitz Lee formed the Third to charge and sent Captain Bailey forward with a squadron of sharpshooters. As the charge surged forward, sabers glistening, bullets flew from the tall stone wall in front of the Rebels. Bailey's horse collapsed beneath him. The Rebels charged the stone wall and the Yankee sharpshooters, including Ames, poured deadly fire into them. Federal artillery, hidden in the woods, opened fire. The Yankees held a strong position. The charge ground to a halt, then disorder occurred when the men retreated. At that moment, Stuart dashed in amongst them, waving his hat. "If you run men, you'll leave me by myself," he cried. Gilmor stared at him apprehensively, fully expecting to hear the dull thud of a bullet and see him fall. "Confound it men, come back!" Stuart ordered. Inspired by their general, the Rebels reformed.

"Give it to them, men!" Pelham shouted. While the men reformed, a shell exploded, killing three. Gilmor was sent to order the Third to charge the woods, and Pelham, still cheering, rode towards the back to check on the artillery. When he reached Breathed on the muddy road, Breathed began putting his guns into action at long range. Consulting with him, Pelham concluded, "Captain, don't let your fire cease. Drive them from their positions."[7]

The second charge of the Third had been costly and unsuccessful. Gilmor was sent to Colonel Rosser of the Fifth to order him to charge on the extreme left and cut the enemy off from the ford. The fighting became general all over the field while different parts of the valiant, out-numbered Confederate line charged and counter charged. The fighting was hand to hand, saber to saber, as horses lunged and thrashed. Alex, in the middle of the melee, thrust his saber into a Yank, only to swing around and see another charging from the rear. He felt the pain when the saber cut his left arm but continued to fight vigorously.

Mid-afternoon: Gilmor and Pelham rejoined Fitz Lee, forming his men into line for another charge while severe artillery fire burst among them. "Keep cool, boys; these little things make a deal of fuss but don't hurt anyone,"[8] Lee cried. The whole regiment gave him three hearty cheers and moved towards a gap in the stone wall with Gilmor and Pelham joining them.

Pelham stood up in his stirrups, waved his hat overhead, and shouted, "Give it to 'em boys! There they are! Give it to 'em!"[9]

The explosion of a shell behind him deafened Gilmor. He did not look back until he heard Bailey shout, "My God, they've killed Pelham!" Turning quickly in his saddle, Gilmor saw Pelham's horse, without his rider, moving slowly off, and Pelham lying on his back in the mud, his eyes wide open, and looking very natural, but obviously critically hurt. At that moment a line of Federal cavalry appeared directly in their front and uncomfortably near.

"My God, we can't let them get Pelham's body!" Gilmor yelled. With the help of Bailey and a Lieutenant, they laid him in front of Gilmor's saddle. Pelham was bleeding profusely from the back of the head. After traveling to safety, Gilmor placed Pelham over the saddle of his own horse, which had followed. Seeing two dismounted men, Gilmor approached them and said, "This is Major Pelham. Get him to the nearest ambulance and call a surgeon at once."

Galloping off, he sought Stuart to tell him the sad tidings. Seeing the blood on Gilmor's uniform, Stuart exclaimed, "My God, Captain. Are you wounded?"

"No, General, the blood you see is that of poor Pelham. I regret to inform you that he was wounded, mortally I fear, and taken from the field a few minutes ago," Gilmor reported with tears in his eyes. Stuart's face registered distress and horror. The battle raged around them, almost cutting the two men off from their own troops. They made their way rapidly through dense woods towards their line, then Stuart halted and demanded, "Tell me everything that happened, Captain."

After Gilmor recounted the details of the disaster, Stuart, who had lost hundreds of men in battle, threw himself against his horse's neck and wept. "Our loss is irreparable!"[10] After several minutes, he managed to regain his composure. "I need for you to go to Culpeper and send a telegram to General Lee."

The Federal cavalry gradually pushed the Confederates about two miles back towards Brandy Station. Breathed positioned his artillery strategically and with fierce determination the gallant Rebels made a brave stand.

Late afternoon: Gilmor overtook the two soldiers he had placed in charge of Pelham's body en route to Culpeper. To his horror, the gallant boy's body was still draped across his saddle, with his head and hands dangling on one side and legs on the other like a sack of potatoes. His face, hair, and hands were caked and clotted with mud and blood. "What is the meaning of this? Didn't I order you to find an ambulance and doctor?"

"We couldn't find one, and besides he's already dead," one of them said lamely.

Incensed, Gilmor dismounted and examined Pelham closely. Yes, he detected a faint pulse! "This man is alive! Help me lay him out on the grass."

Irate, Gilmor believed that Pelham's life could have been saved if doctors had given him prompt attention. "You idiots!" The two men hung their heads in shame. Trying to subdue his temper, he continued, "I want one of you to go find an ambulance and doctor immediately. The other will stay here with Pelham. Do not move him until the doctor arrives. Then I want you to take him to the Armstrong house, directly across from the Virginia House Hotel. Do you understand?"

"Yes, sir," one replied. "We're sorry. We didn't mean no harm, sir."

After Gilmor had completed his task at the telegraph office, he went to the Armstrongs' to inform the ladies of the grim task before them. When they heard the knock on the door, Constance and Amanda answered it together, hand in hand. Shocked by his forlorn face and bloodstained uniform, Constance stammered, "Captain Gilmor, are you wounded?"

"No, Miss," he answered, his voice breaking. "I regret that I must inform you that Major Pelham has been gravely wounded and will soon be brought here with the doctors."

"Oh, no!" Constance gasped, panting in terror as her legs melted away below her. Amanda supported her sister. "But he's alive?" she cried, tears blinding her eyes and choking her voice.

"Yes, but his situation is critical. A fragment of shell struck him at the base of his skull," Gilmor replied fighting back tears.

Amanda put her arms around her sister and held her tightly as Constance yielded to the compulsive sobs that shook her. "Be strong, Connie," she whispered. "He's still alive."

7 p.m. Ames stared at the wounded and dead who would be left behind, while he prepared to recross the river. He wondered, why in the name of God were they retreating? They outnumbered the Rebels more than two to one. He went over the battle in his mind. They had fought the enemy bravely and pushed them back towards Brandy. Disappointed that they had not advanced to Culpeper, he felt nothing had been accomplished. He kept seeing the vision of a young blonde Rebel waving his hat in a charge and then falling. From the glimpse he got from the wall, he could have sworn that it was Pelham. It must be his imagination. Pelham would be with the artillery, not in a charge. Spying a sack with a note on it perched on a rock, he decided to investigate. He dismounted and read the note: *Dear Fitz, Here's your coffee. Here's your visit. How do you like it? Averell.* Ames chuckled, replaced the sack, and forded the river.

* * *

Sadie set the basin of hot water, soap, and towels, on the bureau and turned back the covers of the bed in the front bedroom. She hugged Constance, leaning against the wall and shaking with convulsions of grief. "It's all right baby, Sadie's here, Sadie's here. They bringing him up. Why don't ya leave and let Sadie wash him?"

"No," Constance said, her voice breaking miserably, "I'll take care of him."

"This ain't gonna be easy, honey." Sadie pulled Constance's face against her bosom while they laid him on the bed.

"The doctors will be here shortly," one of the soldiers said before they left.

Constance pulled her head away slowly to gaze at his pale face and uniform covered in caked mud and blood. "Oh!" she moaned, as a suffocating sensation tightened her throat. The room began to spin wildly.

Sadie held her arm. "Take deep breaths," she ordered. Constance closed her eyes and took several deep breaths, struggling to regain her fragile control. "I'm ready." Sadie pulled his boots off and unfastened his pants. Constance's shaking hands gently wiped his face with a clean cloth. "John, it's Connie. I'm here," she whispered softly, over and over. Sadie pulled off his pants, jacket, and shirt. After they tenderly washed his front, they gently rolled him over. Sadie began to dab at the blood caked at the base of his neck, where his hair curled.

"There's jist a little cut right there," Sadie said. Constance stared at the small wound and could not believe that was the source of his injury. After they had finished washing him, they pulled up the covers and called the doctors.

When three doctors, Gilmor, and Amanda entered, Sadie took Pelham's uniform to wash and hang before the fire. "Miss, you may want to leave," one of the doctors said to Constance.

"No, please let me stay." Amanda took her hand and pulled her against the wall. They poured a little brandy in his mouth and then attempted to relieve the compression on his brain. They probed and removed a piece of shell no larger than the end of a little finger.

"The shell entered at the curl of hair and raked through the skull without piercing the brain," one doctor commented.

"Yes, and then came out two inches below. The skull was badly shattered in between," another agreed.

They looked and probed further and the third doctor sighed. "If we could have gotten to him earlier, we might have been able to save him. I'm afraid the rough handling and swelling make the situation hopeless."

Delirious with grief Constance let out a low, tortured sob. Amanda rocked her back and forth while she wept aloud. "I'm so sorry," the doctor said. "There's nothing else we can do. One of us will check on him in a few hours."

Gilmor picked up the small piece of shell from the table. He wanted a memento of one of the most gallant and highly esteemed officers of the Confederate army. "I'll stay with him," he said.

Amanda gently tried to pull Constance towards the door. "No!" She tore herself away with a choking cry. "I will not leave him!" She pulled a chair up to the bed, took his hand and laid it against her tear stained face. Amanda placed a chair beside her and sat down, while Gilmor sat on the floor in front of the fire.

1 a.m. Pelham opened his eyes and turned towards Constance with an unconscious gaze. "John! It's Connie!" He drew a long breath and went limp.

Amanda felt his pulse and passed her hand under his nose. "I'm…afraid…he's gone," she said in a broken voice. Gilmor touched him and came to the same conclusion. Spasms of nausea overwhelmed Constance who wept hysterically. Amanda put her arms on her sister's shoulder and lifted her out of the chair. "You're coming with me while Sadie dresses him in his uniform."

Constance re-entered the room, supported by Amanda and her mother. "He looks so handsome," she whimpered. "There's a slight smile on his face."

"He's at peace," Harriet said. She stroked Constance's arm softly.

The door slowly opened and Stuart entered, having just returned from the battle. Great tears rolled down his cheeks while he silently gazed upon the lifeless form of this boy he cherished so dearly. He took Constance's hand, squeezed it, and retired, too overwhelmed to speak.

"Please," she begged those still in the room. "I'd like some time alone with him." They granted her request.

When she leaned over to kiss him softly on the lips, one of her tears dropped on his cheek. "Oh, John, I've loved you with all my heart. We could have been so happy together, if you had chosen me." She gently caressed his face, wiping away the tear. She ran her fingers through his hair, took a pair of scissors from the table and cut a lock of hair, and placed it on the table. She sat down and traced her fingers over the ring on his hand. Another tear fell as she remembered the way he had etched his initials in the window. "I will never, ever, forget you," she whispered, kissing his hand. Pondering the fine features of his face, she thought he was almost as beautiful as a girl. In a society that equated facial hair with masculinity and valor, this smooth-faced boy had captured the hearts and respect of all who knew him, male and female. Gilmor returned and stretched out on the floor. She refused to leave.

Dawn: The soft light of dawn fell on his face, making it glisten like marble. "Connie." Amanda put her hands on her sister's shoulders. "You have to leave now. They're here with the embalming fluid and coffin." Constance stood up and gazed at his handsome face for the last time, while the pain squeezing her heart became a sick, fiery gnawing.

"He represented all that is good about the South." Amanda guided her out. "He was our noble, gallant knight."[ii]

Jeb Stuart had spent a sleepless night. While he dressed, he wondered if his sobs had been audible through the walls of the Virginia House. He had to pull himself together and do everything in his power to honor Pelham's memory. He walked downstairs and

---

[2] Communities in Alabama, Georgia, North Carolina, and Tennessee were named after Pelham.

shared breakfast biscuits with the few other officers. "They'll be bringing the coffin out soon. I'd appreciate it if all of you would march to the depot with me."

"Certainly," one replied. "Here they come now." They walked out the front door to see the pine coffin, draped in a Virginia flag, being loaded on the wagon. The ladies, grasping Constance, watched mournfully from the porch while the somber procession, led by Stuart, marched to the depot. Townspeople followed along and gathered beside the tracks to show their respect. Stuart went inside and telegraphed Von Borcke the sad news, ordering him to meet the train at Hanover and escort the remains to lie in state at the capitol. He then sent the following message to Representative Curry of Alabama, *The noble, the chivalric, the gallant Pelham is no more. He was killed in action yesterday. His remains will be sent to you today. How much he was beloved, appreciated, and admired, let the tears of agony we have shed, and the gloom of mourning throughout my command bear witness. His loss is irreparable."*[11]

Mid-morning: "Daddy," Hudson cried in alarm when Alex walked in the back door, his arm strapped and bloodstained. "You're hurt!"

"Just a little cut." Alex rumpled his son's blonde hair.

"Darling!" Amanda raced down the steps. "Thank God, you're here! Oh, heavens... you're hurt!"

He put his other arm around her and kissed her warmly. "Just a little saber cut."

"Come upstairs and let me look at it," Amanda ordered, guiding him up the steps. "You need to rest."

"It was the hardest fought battle yet," he said while she unwrapped his arm, "and our greatest achievement. There was charge after charge with the saber. Eight hundred held off over two thousand. But our losses were heavy: Puller, Pelham."

"They just took him away in a box," Hudson said with moist eyes.

"I know." Alex took the boy's hand. "I saw them at the depot. It's a terrible loss to the cavalry. How's Connie taking it?"

"She's shattered." Amanda cleaned his arm. "She sat with him all night."

Alex shook his head in sad resignation. "Rosser was seriously wounded. And, we lost so many horses. Their cavalry grows stronger while ours grows weaker. But Liz survived like a trooper."

"Now, you lay down and sleep. You've lost a lot of blood." Amanda pulled the covers up and kissed him.

Next day, March 19, 1863: The Virginia House

Jeb Stuart paced the floor of his room at the Virginia House. He would have the entire cavalry wear black armbands for a month in honor of Pelham. But he had to eulogize him in writing by creating a document that would proclaim forever the achievements and honor of his lost companion. He sat at the table and began writing thoughtfully. After several minutes he balled up the paper and threw it in the fire. It was not good enough! He worked diligently for over an hour, scratching out lines, rewriting, and wiping an occasional tear from his face. Finally, satisfied with his creation, he opened the door and called down the hall. "Sweeney, come here a minute."

"Sir?" Sweeney entered the door.

"Take this document to that newspaper editor, MacDonald. Have him print sixty copies of this for me to take back to Fredericksburg tomorrow. When they're completed, drop one copy off to Miss Armstrong with my condolences."

When Sweeney departed, Stuart paced the floor again restlessly in a moment of introspection, while he faced the possibility of his own death. There were some issues he needed to address with Flora. He walked thoughtfully, stroking his beard. He wanted her to know he hoped Jimmy would grow up to be just like Pelham. But there was more. He had to gently inform her that it was extremely improbable that he would outlive her. He must beg her to promise that no matter what happened, she would never desert the South. She must raise their children on southern soil. He pounded his fist on the table, sat down and scratched rapidly with his pen.

"Miss Constance, ya gotta git outta that bed." Sadie pulled the covers back.

"No," Constance groaned, pulling the pillow over her head. "I can't. Go away."

Sadie removed the pillow, took her hands, and pulled her to a sitting position. She stared into her red-rimmed eyes, encircled with dark shadows. "Come on, baby." She dragged Constance to her feet and held her. "I know you's hurting, honey, but ya can't hide in here forever. Ya gotta face it. Ya got friends an' family who wanna help ya through your grief. Don't ya turn your back on them."

"I'm so tired." Constance sniffled and leaned against Sadie, trying to absorb her strength.

"Miss Amanda has got her hands full with Mista Alex hurt and her so sick in the mornings. She needs ya to run that bookstore. I 'spect she's in the family way again. Ya can't let her down."

Constance sighed and mustered all of her strength to stand on her own. "No, I can't," she said with steel determination as she pushed the tangled mass from her face.

"That's more like it. That's mah girl! What dress ya wanna put on?"

Constance looked at Sadie, her face a study of desolation. "The black one of course."

In the late afternoon, Sweeney entered the bookstore to find Constance behind the desk. "Miss Armstrong, General Stuart sends this to you this with his condolences." He handed her the paper.

"Thank you," she answered in a lifeless monotone as he departed. She pondered the paper.

The Major-General commanding approaches with reluctance the painful duty of announcing to the Division its irreparable loss in the death of Major John Pelham, commanding the Horse Artillery.

He fell mortally wounded in the battle of Kellysville, March 17th, with the battle cry on his lips, and the light of victory beaming from his eye.

To you, his comrades, it is needless to dwell upon what you have so often witnessed…his prowess in action, already proverbial. You well know how, though young in years, a mere stripling in appearance, remarkable for his modesty of deportment, he yet disclosed on the battlefield the conduct of a veteran, and displayed in his handsome person the most imperturbable coolness in danger.

His eye had glanced over every battlefield of this army, from first Manassas to the moment of his death, and he was, with a single exception, a brilliant actor in all.

The memory of "THE GALLANT PELHAM," his many virtues, his noble nature and purity of character, is enshrined as a sacred legacy in the hearts of all who knew him.
His record has been bright and spotless; his career brilliant and successful.
He fell…the noblest of sacrifices…on the altar of his country, to whose glorious services he had dedicated his life from the beginning of the war.[12]

"That's beautiful," she sniffled, then wiped her face with her handkerchief, trying to swallow the lump that lingered in her throat.

Five days later, March 23, 1863: Armstrong parlor

Constance stared into the hypnotic flames of the fire while the dull, empty ache gnawed at her soul. "John's on his way home now."

"Yes." Alex looked at her over the top of the Richmond paper. "According to the paper he lay in state in the capital until 4 p.m. on the twentieth."

"I can just see his casket on a pedestal at the feet of Washington's statue in the great hall, with a sentinel pacing before it," Amanda added pensively. "The paper says they put a glass panel over his face so the hundreds of women and old men filing past could see him. The woven covering of evergreens with the many flowers brought by the mourners must have been lovely."

"It says Sallie Dandridge, accompanied by her father, made her way from Martinsburg through enemy lines to kneel by his casket just before they took him away," Alex continued.

Constance remained mesmerized by the fire, showing little emotion. "It's good that she got to tell him good-bye," she said softly.

"The procession formed at the Capitol's south front," Alex read. "The colors and honor guard preceded the casket, followed by Major Peter Pelham, then delegations of officers, congressmen and other friends. A military band played appropriate dirges while church bells tolled, and guns cracked in the air. It wound its way to the Richmond and Danville Railroad station. Large crowds are expected to greet the train along the way and Major Pelham will lie in state in Atlanta and Montgomery, before being interred in his hometown of Jacksonville, Alabama."

"It's a fitting tribute to a beloved hero." Harriet looked up from her mending to contemplate the circles under Constance's eyes. "You know dear, your friends have been extremely attentive and compassionate, especially the Ashbys."

As if in a trance, Constance muttered, "Yes, I've been blessed." She paused for a moment. "I needed to reach out to his family, so I wrote a letter of sympathy to his sister, Betty."

"Now the question is, who will Stuart select as his successor?" Alex mused. "Breathed and Chew are in line, but neither are West Point men. Pelham's shoes will be hard to fill.

Constance looked towards him with pain in her eyes. "No one can replace John. I pity the poor soldier who's given that impossible task."

"Nevertheless, we must move forward and prepare for the spring invasion," Alex said. "When the river recedes, they will come. I'm going to report back tomorrow."

"No!" Amanda protested to no avail. "You're not ready!"

Six days later, March 29, 1863: The bookstore

"News from camp," Alex announced when he entered the bookstore. "Stuart has named Pelham's replacement."

Constance, holding an armful of books, continued to place one on the shelf. "Oh," she said nonchalantly with her back to him. "What poor soul has been given that awesome task?"

"Robert!" he answered enthusiastically.

She spun around so quickly that the five books in her arms went flying across the floor, clattering in different directions. "Robert?" she gasped. "Robert Beckam?" Alex nodded affirmatively and watched her with a smile. "Are you sure?"

"Absolutely! General Stuart has made an extremely wise decision," he said proudly. "Robert will gain the respect of the men in short order."

11

Beckam Takes Command

March 30, 1863 - June 4, 1863

"Young man, I congratulate you."
Stonewall Jackson to Robert Beckam at Chancellorsville

Next day, March 30, 1863: Armstrong town home

Harriet greeted Stringfellow at the door. "Frank! It's so wonderful to see you here safe! Come in, come in!"

"It's good to be back, Mrs. Armstrong. How's Connie handling Pelham's death?" He stepped inside and hugged her.

"Not well," Harriet sighed. "He spent two weeks here prior to his death, and she fell head over heels for him. But, maybe you can cheer her up. You always make her laugh."

Stringfellow thought for a moment and rolled his eyes. "Give me an hour alone with her in the parlor, and I guarantee I'll have her laughing. But don't tell her who it is."

"Now, just sit on the sofa and wait a minute." Harriet closed the door to the hall and Constance sat down baffled. What on earth was her mother up to?

Frank bounded through the doorway from the bookstore. "Welcome, fair lady to a one man show, *Frank Stringfellow in Washington*. Sit back, relax and let me entertain you," he said with a theatrical gesture.

"Frank!" She looked at him with amused wonder. "Oh, golly, what next?"

"It all began in mid-February when Jeb himself said to me, 'Stringfellow, you can have all the men and money you need to set up a reliable communications system with Washington,'" Stringfellow related pacing the floor, imitating Stuart's voice. 'If a member of Lincoln's cabinet catches cold, I want to hear about it before his doctor!" he said shaking his finger.

"So I began devising my plans." He rubbed his hands together craftily. "And was not averse to the challenge because I knew it would take me to," he raised his eyebrows up and down, "the fair Emma!" Constance chuckled in spite of herself. "I requested the services of a cavalry company under Captain Farrow, plus the services of two scouts from Fairfax County. We searched desperately for a place to safely ford the Occoquan River." He paced the room with his hand over his eyes, searching. "Finally, we discovered the spot and waded across the shallow, icy stream." He continued the pantomime by pulling up his pants legs and imitating wading, wincing at the cold. "I crept up the hill and peered over," he knelt behind the chair and peeked over the top, "and waited for the pickets to pass. We then made our way safely to the home of one of my scouts," he said, crossing the room, "where I obtained a horse and wagon and fake pass. I then rode into Alexandria." He sat on the piano bench and pretended to grab reins and bounce along, "And praise God, passed safely into the city," he said wiping his brow with relief. "The worst was over."

"I left the cart at an appointed place and walked to the store of James Sturrett, a man I'd known for years." He walked across the room. "When I told him of my mission, he suggested that I work for him. It would give me an opportunity to move around freely and I could go to Washington to pick up supplies. I thanked him, but he seemed to notice my distraction. He told me to wait there while he went for Emma."

Frank's eyes lit up and he moved his eyebrows up and down. Constance giggled. "She came into the store, puzzled. When she saw me her eyes went wide, and she grabbed the counter to keep her balance," he imitated as he dramatically grabbed the edge of the table. "She ran to me laughing and crying. Mr. Sturrett kindly left and locked the door." He raced across the room, picked up a throw pillow, hugged it and then kissed it several times. "The audience will have to use its imagination in this scene. It's censored," he said with an infectious laugh. Constance's laughter matched his in enthusiasm.

Putting the pillow down, he continued, "I took two trips into Washington where I made connections with four Southern sympathizers whose names had been given to me. These clerks in the War Department had information as soon as Halleck himself. With each passing day, I knew it became more dangerous for me to remain in Alexandria, but I could not tear myself away from Emma. One day I was walking down the street after work, when I ran smack into a Federal officer at a corner." He turned, crashed into the door, fell back, and looked at the door. "We started to make apologies and then stopped and stared at each other. I recognized him as one of Pope's officers that we had captured in our raid on Catlett's Station. Unfortunately, he also recognized me. 'Stringfellow, by God!' he exclaimed." Frank jumped back from the door and threw his hands up in shock. Constance smiled with delight.

"I fled down the street," he related, then raced around the room. "I heard him shouting and soon there were several soldiers in close pursuit. As much as I dodged around corners and doubled back, I couldn't shake them. When I felt I could run no further," he said panting for effect, "I ran into the open door of a house, slammed it and locked it," he said slamming the door to the hall. "I ran upstairs and saw an old lady working on a table cloth. She looked vaguely familiar to me, and I was too breathless to explain my dilemma. She said, 'Get under here, Frank,' and lifted her hoop skirt."

"Oh, I can't believe it," Constance chuckled.

Frank took an afghan, spread in over a round table, and then crawled under it. "I reached safety none too soon, as the soldiers climbed the steps and questioned her about a Rebel spy," he said from his place under the afghan, dropping his voice. "Calmly the old lady replied, 'I heard someone run through the house a moment ago. Must have gone out the back way. Did you search the alley?' The soldiers apologized and finally left. When I came out of my hiding place." He emerged from the afghan. "I discovered that the old lady was a friend of my mother's. Her hands remained completely steady while I trembled all over," he related, trembling. "I knew I had to get out of Alexandria. Emma insisted that she and a friend ride on the wagon with me. I regret endangering her, but it worked. They flirted with the guard and diverted attention from me.[1] And so, fair Rebel lady, you may rest assured that, thanks to the work of your humble servant, Jefferson Davis knows what happens in Washington almost as soon as Lincoln. The end," he said, making a sweeping bow.

Constance clapped and laughed. "That's an unbelievable story, but knowing you, I'm sure it's true." He sat down on the sofa and kissed her on the cheek.

Looking at the circles under her eyes he said, "You know I'd never lie to you. It's good to see you." He paused searching for words. "I realize how deeply you're mourning Pelham. He will be greatly missed by us all."

Her eyes clouded and her chin trembled. "We had become extremely close. I...loved him."

"I'm sure you did. He was a very fortunate fellow," he said softly, taking her hand. "But realize, Connie, that many women admired him. You're not the only one wearing black. In fact, just before he was killed, he went to Orange to see Miss Nannie from Dundee in Hanover and Miss Brill. They had sent him some candy through General Stuart."

This painful revelation caused tears to well in her eyes. "I...know that he was not exclusively mine. I never attempted to...possess him," she said fighting to maintain her composure. "I don't begrudge him one minute of pleasure he enjoyed in his short twenty-four years, but it doesn't lessen my affection."

Frank squeezed her hand, sensing her pain. "I'm your big brother, Connie. I'm just trying to look out for you. You're too wonderful to waste away. You impressed Farley, but he realized you only had eyes for Pelham."

She raised her dark eyebrows in surprise. "Was it that obvious?"

"Yes," he said softly. "Farley's going to South Carolina for a much deserved furlough. That's means I'll have to be doubly alert watching the enemy. Their cavalry is massing across the river and something big will happen soon. I'm sure they'll come through Culpeper."

"Why are you so sure?" she asked in a small frightened voice.

"Hooker is determined to take Richmond. The easiest place to ford the rivers is Culpeper. Once the Rapphannock and Rapidan flow together, it's too deep. Pontoon bridges are risky, as Burnside learned. I've begged Mother to flee south. She's a determined old girl and refuses to leave her home. I expect you're the same way."

"Where would we go? Our only income is through the bookstore. We'd starve without that income."

"Well, let's look on the bright side." Stringfellow tried to sound optimistic. "The Copperheads in Ohio, Indiana, and Illinois are organizing and growing in strength. My sources say they may rise up at any time and attempt to overthrow Lincoln. There's talk of a raid by John Hunt Morgan to lead them."

"What a Godsend that would be!"

"Nevertheless, I've got to get back to work now." He pulled himself to his feet. She took his hand and walked him to the door.

"Thanks, Frank, for always making me laugh. It felt good. Good hunting." He kissed her on the cheek.

* * *

Several cavalrymen rode by Constance amidst the bustling activity caused by Stuart re-establishing his headquarters in town. She looked past the Waverly Hotel at the newly greened rolling fields that heralded the return of spring. Noticing the shadow of a tall soldier behind her, she spun around to confront the sad eyes of Von Borcke. All the memories of her two weeks with John flooded her mind. "Von," she stammered while her throat seemed to close up. "Oh, Von."

Sharing her grief, he hugged her gently. "Miss Armstrong, I have thought of you often and have several matters to relate to you."

She pulled back to look at him and said in a choked voice, "Not a day goes by that I don't long for his gay laughter."

"And I too. I was given the melancholy task of meeting his body and accompanying it to Richmond. We reached Richmond in the dead of night, and the wagon I had requested did not meet us. I was forced to find a rude wagon and convey him to the capitol in the rough pine box. The next day I procured a more suitable metal casket and helped transfer his cold remains. It was the saddest thing I've ever had to do." His voice dropped to a broken whisper. She took his hand. "I had a window put in the casket over his fair face so the mourners could see him. They came in multitudes. I remained until they put him on the train."

"He's not home yet?"

"No, not yet. I must tell you, that he spoke to me of his deepening affection for you, and his internal debate about how to handle the situation. I never saw him happier than the two weeks he was here."

Her heart sang with joy. She squeezed his hand in the shared moment. "Von, thank you so much for telling me that!"

The train puffed into the station and several bundles were tossed towards them. Constance picked up the bundle of papers while Von Borcke looked for one marked for Stuart. He gathered it up and said, "You know General Stuart has named our camp Camp Pelham. It's a beautiful site overlooking Mountain Run with a view of the Blue Ridge Mountains. The men have enjoyed fishing in the stream."[i]

"Why have you moved here from Fredericksburg?"

"The enemy cavalry are massing across the river. Unfortunately they greatly out-number us, as we only have Fitz and Rooney Lee's brigades. We must be vigilant guarding the fords. Major Beckam has arrived, and he's impressed everyone with the tireless energy he has employed in his new challenge."

Constance nodded in agreement with a slight smile. "He's very diligent. He'll do a good job."

At dinner that night Alex told the family that by using Liz as a plow horse and with Billy's help planting potatoes, he had gotten a good garden in at the farm. Even though they would not be there to care for the garden, hopefully they would get a good yield

---

[i] Camp Pelham was located on the high ridge now traversed by Blue Ridge Avenue and down the hill to Mountain Run between Scanlon and Asher Streets.

from it. With the soaring prices of food, they desperately needed to grow as much as possible. Amanda complained that because of her pregnancy she had no appetite for the bland food they had been forced to eat all winter.

"We have to keep our spirits up," Alex said. He cast his eyes towards Constance. "It's good to have General Stuart back. I suspect he'll drop by tonight with his staff."

That evening Constance sat on the edge of her bed in her nightgown brushing her hair. Her mother tiptoed in and sat down beside her, looking at the framed newspaper picture of Pelham beside her bed and the lock of golden hair tied with a ribbon in a velvet box. "It was good to see General Stuart and his staff," Harriet said. "I'm sorry Robert didn't come."

"He's extremely busy right now."

"Darling," Harriet took her daughter's hand, "there are some things I want to tell you."

"Of course, Mother."

"You know I've really enjoyed taking care of the boys these last several months. It's made me realize that I didn't fully appreciate you when you were small. I was busy with my painting and of course Sadie took care of you. Your father always wanted your undivided attention, so I spent most of my time with Amanda. I regret that now. I've always felt that…you loved Sadie more than me."

Constance was taken back by her statement. "Of course, I love Sadie dearly. She was always there for me. She picked me up when I cried and kissed me good night. But that doesn't mean that I don't also love you, Mother, just as much." She squeezed her hand.

Harriet's eyes grew misty. "I hope we can grow closer. At any rate, I feel compelled to tell you something I've never told anyone else. In fact, I never told your father." Constance looked at her intently, her eyebrows raised. "When I was seventeen, I fell completely in love with a wonderful and handsome young man of twenty. I knew that he was the only one who would ever hold the keys to my heart. But then the war of 1812 broke out, and he was killed a short time later."

"Oh, no!" Constance's breath caught in her lungs and she tightened her grip on her mother's hand.

"Life didn't seem worth living. I fled to Europe and spent the next fifteen years absorbed in art, refusing to allow myself to care for anyone." Her gaze rested on her daughter's questioning eyes. "It was the biggest mistake of my life. I gave up so many years of happiness for a dream…a dream I could never have. Just think if I had come back and met your father sooner, how many more wonderful years I could have enjoyed with him. I loved him with all of my heart, much deeper than that soldier of twenty. I made a mistake, which I can never change. It is possible to love again and love deeply."

"I know what you're trying to tell me," Constance said slowly, searching for words. "But right now I'm empty inside. After losing Father and John so close together, I'm afraid to care for anyone again. I don't think I can. With this terrible war raging on, I'm scared…to love." A hot tear slowly rolled down her pale cheek.

"I understand completely, darling." Harriet wiped her tear away tenderly. "But time will heal that. You're young and beautiful, and have everything to live for. I pray this cruel war ends soon so you may find happiness and security."

"You know how independent I am. I can be happy by myself."

"Perhaps, but now I must tell you something your father said." Constance looked at her curiously. "When we were dressing for that first party we had with Stuart's staff, I asked him if he planned it because you appeared enthralled with John. He replied no, he thought you could do no better than Robert Beckam."

Shocked, Constance eyed her mother suspiciously. "Did he really say that, Mother?"

"Indeed, he did. He said Robert was a wonderful young man from a fine family. However, he would never tell you he hoped you'd marry Robert, because you're so headstrong you'd probably never see him again."

"Of course I will make my own decisions."

"That is your privilege, which no one will deny you," Harriet said diplomatically. "I saw the hurt in Robert's eyes that last time he was here, when you were dancing with John. He's extremely fond of you."

"I never meant to hurt him." A look of tired sadness passed over her features. "I suppose I didn't hide my infatuation very well. I think very highly of Robert."

"He's undertaking an enormously difficult task. He needs your support."

"I understand that." Constance stared into space thoughtfully. "He does deserve my support. I owe him that, and my friendship."

"I want to encourage you to reach out to him. Perhaps you could write him a note of congratulations and invite him to dinner." Harriet caressed her daughter's hand.

"I'll think about it. Just give me a little more time." Harriet hugged her and kissed her cheek. "I'm glad we had this talk, Mother."

"Good night, dear." Harriet limped out the door while Constance cringed at the thought of her mother slowly becoming crippled by arthritis.

Nine days later, April 20, 1863: Armstrong town home

"Now, Miss Constance, which dress is ya wearin' for dinner tonight?" Sadie demanded. "It's been over a month, an' ya ain't wearin' that black one with Major Beckam comin'."

"You're so bossy." Constance frowned and placed her hands on her hips.

"That's 'cause sometimes ya don't think straight. How 'bout this rose one?"

"Yes, that will be fine, but don't be so pushy!"

Robert Beckam took a deep breath before he knocked on the Armstrongs' door. He must not let her know how hurt he had been. If he ever hoped to win her, he needed to appear aloof. It would take time, but she had reached out to him. That was encouraging.

"Robert," Constance said with an easy smile when she opened the door. "Come in. It's good to see you."

He bowed politely, entered, waited for her to shut the door, and then kissed her hand. "Connie, thank you for your kind invitation." He noticed the shadows under her eyes. "I've been quite busy, but I'm glad to have this opportunity to see you."

His dark hair was a little longer, but he looked handsome with his neat goatee and mustache. "Congratulations on your new position. It's a tremendous honor."

"Yes, but I regret the circumstances. Major Pelham's death was a great loss to our army," he said softly.

Her eyes fell. "Yes."

"Robert, welcome," Harriet said as she entered from the dining room. "Please join us. Dinner is almost ready."

During dinner Robert told them that he had 500 men he must get to know immediately, and 24 guns. The Yankees had forced crossings at the fords several times, but so far his guns had driven them back. With the river still high from the snow and rain, he felt relatively secure. However, when the water receded he feared the outnumbered Rebels would face the onslaught of the Union cavalry. They seemed intent on taking Culpeper, but who knew in which direction Hooker's infantry would move. Amanda voiced great concern for Alex and their own plight if fighting should occur soon in the county. Following more pleasant conversation in the parlor, Amanda and Harriet rose to go to bed.

"Well, goodnight, Robert," Harriet said. "Please come back soon." They walked towards the door, leaving the two of them alone.

"Thank you, I hope to," he answered as he stood.

"Robert," Constance said, when he sat by her on the sofa. "I know you never wanted to be in the artillery. Your sense of duty is admirable."

"You're right, but it's an honor and a duty I couldn't refuse. I have a lot to learn about the Horse Artillery since my experience has been in ordnance. I must confess that I'm troubled with doubts about my lack of experience. The eyes of the entire army are focused on me." She detected the apprehension in his eyes. "I know that I can never replace Pelham. I can only hope to do a competent job."

She understood the double meaning of his statement and was overcome with a sense of compassion for him. Despite his closed expression, she sensed his vulnerability. She laced her fingers with his. "Robert, be yourself and you'll be successful. You're honorable, diligent, and dependable. Your men will follow and respect you."

"Thank you, Connie. I needed those words of encouragement, especially from you." His dark, earnest eyes sparkled while he squeezed her hand. "But, now I must return to camp."

She walked him to the door. "Thanks for dinner and a pleasant evening," he said after he brushed his lips against her cheek.

"I know you're busy, but please come back when the opportunity presents itself." Her lips curved up in a sincere smile.

Nine days later, April 29, 1863: Brandy Station

Dawn: "Rest your guns here until we can determine the direction of the enemy," Beckam said to his two battery commanders. "Be in readiness for action at any moment." He rode forward nervously to inspect his batteries in the faint light of dawn. A dense fog covered the plains at Brandy Station making visibility possible for only a few feet. Stuart had placed his small cavalry force in line of battle at Brandy, on the knowledge that a large force of enemy cavalry, infantry, and artillery had crossed at Kelly's Ford using boats and a pontoon bridge. He hoped to give battle to the cavalry on the plains of Brandy, impeding their movement towards the railroad.

Fredericksburg: The loud knocking on the door abruptly awakened Anna and

Stonewall Jackson. Julia whimpered and then let out a loud cry from her crib. Following a brief conversation with a courier, Jackson returned to the bedroom and picked up his beloved daughter. "Now, don't you fret little Miss Jackson," he cooed, holding the daughter he had spent nine blissful days getting to know. "Anna, it appears the enemy is crossing the river. You must take Julia and go to the train station immediately. I cannot endanger the two of you."

"No! Oh, I hate to leave you so soon." Anna spread her protective arms around him and the baby.

"I must go to headquarters at once. If my duties permit, I'll return to see you to the train." He cuddled the baby and kissed her tenderly. "She's such a little gem." Jackson hastily kissed his wife and placed the baby in her arms. "Pray Almighty God will grant us victory." He kissed his daughter on the forehead for the last time.

Lieutenant Smith of Jackson's staff entered the dimly lit tent causing General Lee to stir in his sleep. "General Lee, sir, I have a message from General Jackson."

Lee opened his eyes and sat up slowly. He reached for his glasses and slipped them over his ears while putting one foot on the floor.

"General Jackson wishes to inform you that he has heard firing and cannonading. It appears the enemy is crossing the river before us on pontoon bridges."

Lee smiled and replied, "Well, I thought I heard firing, and was beginning to think it was time some of you young fellows were coming to tell me what it was about. Tell your good general that I am sure he knows what to do. I will meet him at the front very soon."[2]

"Yes, sir." Smith saluted and exited. Unperturbed, Lee rubbed his eyes, regretting that Longstreet and 20,000 men were off on a meaningless expedition to Suffolk. At that point in time, Hooker with 130,000 men and 428 guns faced Lee with 60,000 men and 170 guns. To anyone else the predicament would have looked hopeless. Lee calmly pulled on his coat. He would consult with Jackson and they would determine a way to handle the situation.

Midday, Brandy Station: Hour after hour of uncertainty had passed before the fog slowly lifted at Brandy Station. Skirmishing had been heard from the direction of Kelly's Ford. Stuart scanned the horizon with his field glasses. "It appears to be only a small force of cavalry to keep our attention. I fear our foe has deceived us," he said irritated. "We must move towards Madden's with great haste. Their army must be marching in the direction of Lee at Fredericksburg."

Within minutes Beckam had his guns bouncing and careening over the rough narrow road. They had to move rapidly to do any damage to the enemy before they crossed the Rapidan in their movement east.

Mid-afternoon: Willis and Jack Madden stared out of the windows of the tavern. "It's a sea of blue," Willis said. "They jist keep comin'."

"They've trampled our fields and crops. We ain't got a fence left. I 'spect there's been 50,000 of 'em."

"Oh, no!" Madden shouted. "Here come the gray boys. All hell is gonna break loose. Let's git in the cellar!"

Beckam caught sight of the marching column of the Yankee rear guard, not more that 300 yards away, when he reached the intersection of the roads at Madden's. "Unlimber," he ordered. "As soon as our sharpshooters advance through the undergrowth, we'll open fire simultaneously with them. Take advantage of those openings in the forest." The sharpshooters soon opened up. "Fire!" The shower of shell and canister mutilated the enemy's closely gathered ranks. The Yanks stampeded forward in confusion and panic at the unexpected attack. Beckam poured deadly fire into them again and again until they disappeared from sight. The wounded and dead littered the road. Sixty Yanks were taken prisoner and soon revealed that there were three corps, the Fifth, Eleventh, and Twelfth, and their destination was Chancellorsville.

Stuart wrote a brief telegraph message to be sent to Lee, warning him that at least 60,000 Yanks were moving towards his flank. "I want a party of sharpshooters left here to annoy their trains as much as possible, and then follow us to Raccoon Ford," he said to his staff. "We'll move forward and snipe at Hooker's flank to impede them."

Beckam soon had his guns bouncing over the rough road. When the firing finally ended, the Maddens slowly eased outside from the tavern to help the wounded men lying in the yard and road. "Oh mah God," moaned Jack. He lifted the head of a bloody soldier. "How's we supposed to deal with all this?"

Nightfall: The bitter wind blew sleet in the face of Aaron Ames who sat in line of battle with Averell's cavalry at Brandy Station. The few remaining Confederates did not seem anxious to fight with darkness setting in. "Fall back to the edge on that wood, men, and prepare to bed down for the night," an officer called out. Ames unsaddled his horse and attempted to sleep without shelter on the cold, wet ground. He had not eaten in twenty-four hours. It appeared they would be moving south in the morning, while the bulk of the army advanced on Lee. He prayed for Hooker's success. This wretched war could not end soon enough.

Midnight: The frigid water of the Rapidan numbed Beckam's legs while he directed the movement of his last piece of artillery up the bank at Raccoon's Ford. With the sleet stinging his face, he stretched out beneath a tree, exhausted. He nibbled on a piece of rank bacon, the only food he had eaten all day. His mind drifted as he dozed restlessly. A huge battle would soon take place, and he would be thrust into the middle of it. God help him to be ready….

Next day, April 30, 1863: Near Brandy Station

Aaron Ames, mounted on his horse, watched General Averell knock at the door of the stately white house, Auburn. The Confederate cavalry had melted away during the night offering no resistance. A heavy-set older man with bushy dark hair and eyebrows greeted Averell warmly. The general wished to pay his respects to one of the few Union sympathizers in the county, John Minor Botts. Ames admired Botts for going against his neighbors and sticking with the Union, but he could only imagine how unpopular he must be in Culpeper.

Dead horses presented the only evidence of the Confederate cavalry along their war-torn route. Most houses looked deserted, and Ames saw few white folks. By mid-morning they rode up Coleman Street, followed only by a few Negroes. Constance peered out of the window. "It's Yankee cavalry. God help us. We're at their mercy."

Ames gazed longingly at the Armstrong house, his heart pounding. He did not think his general would approve a social visit at this point in time. "Proceed to the depot and cut the telegraph lines," his commander called out. At the depot they discovered sixty barrels of flour and large amounts of pork and bacon. He figured the Rebels must have been in a hurry if they left food behind. The starving soldiers dug into the food and took as much as they could carry.

Averell, in a show of generosity, decided what remained should be distributed to the poor people of the place. The soldiers watched the Negroes, including Sadie, rush in to claim their prize. Surprised to see her, Ames was eager to inquire about Constance, but did not wish to incite Sadie's hostility in front of the other soldiers.

The column left town and rode hard and fast over the Cedar Mountain battlefield, shocked to see all parts of the human skeleton strewn on the ground with hogs gnawing on the skeletal remains. Visions of his personal hell flashed before Ames's eyes. "Those could be the bones of my comrades from Maine," he called to a friend. They continued moving rapidly south and Ames suspected their mission was to cut off Lee's communications to Richmond and impede his retreat. They had Lee trapped this time with no way out. It would end soon.

Afternoon: A courier from Stuart galloped up to Jackson's headquarters. "General Jackson, sir," he said after he saluted old Stonewall, "General Stuart wishes to report that three corps of the enemy, at least 60,000 men are moving through the wilderness towards Chancellorsville." Jackson nodded thoughtfully, showing no emotion. Hooker had split his army and was attempting to turn Lee's left. "Thank you. Tell General Stuart to keep me posted."

"Look's like we may have to fight on the defensive," one of Jackson's staff remarked.

Jackson whirled around, his blue eyes flashing, "Who said that? No, sir, we shall not fall back; we shall attack them!"[3]

Nightfall: "Fighting Joe" Hooker climbed confidently up the steps of the tavern at the crossroads of Chancellorsville. "Bring me my toddy," he said to one of his aides. He went inside to write an announcement of congratulations to his army—the finest army on the planet. Two more corps would join him during the night bringing his strength to 72,000. Sedgwick, with 65,000, had crossed the river and confronted Lee at Fredericksburg. Lee would be forced to retreat and he would crush him in the process. With each of his wings larger than Lee's entire army, he had a telegraph connecting him to Sedgwick, plus three hot air balloons to monitor Lee's movements. The possibility of fog or cut telegraph lines never occurred to him. He did have a minor concern that his cavalry rode towards Richmond while Stuart observed his every move. He had expected Stuart to pursue his cavalry, but it was not a matter to lose sleep over.

Next day, May 1, 1863: Near Chancellorsville

When the first rays of dawn lit the sky, Stringfellow and a squad of men rode out to scout. With Farley still away, he felt as if he had the weight of the Confederacy on his shoulders. He must find vulnerability in Hooker's lines. They rode silently, ever vigilant, through the thick woods towards the rear of Hooker's army. When they neared a small ridge, Stringfellow whispered, "Dismount." The Rebels slithered forward to the edge and peered over cautiously. Spread out below them were the camps of the Federal infantry, with arms stacked at random and no fortifications visible. Stringfellow whistled softly. The unsuspecting Federals cooked breakfast while a few played ball. To one side, butchers slaughtered beeves. "Find Fitz Lee and bring him here immediately," Stringfellow whispered to two of his men excitedly. He had found the opportunity of their dreams.

Early afternoon: Robert E. Lee watched the soldiers push the last piece of artillery in place on Marye's Heights to strengthen the strong Confederate fortifications at Fredericksburg. "General Early, you are to hold this line at all costs. You must prevent Sedgwick from breaking through."

"We will do it, sir," Early drawled. "I will keep my men constantly moving and visible at different locations to give the impression of a larger force." Lee rode off satisfied that Early's 10,000 men could hold Fredericksburg. Jackson had moved his other 45,000 men during the night and under cloud cover this morning to confront Hooker at Chancellorsville. Sedgwick appeared unaware that only a small force occupied the heights above Fredericksburg. Lee listened to sporadic firing and skirmishing from Chancellorsville where Jackson probed and attacked Hooker.

Late afternoon: "Major Beckam, bring four of your guns forward to support Wright's infantry. Follow my staff and that of General Jackson," Stuart ordered.

Beckam immediately put his guns in motion. They progressed slowly, dragging the guns down a wretched narrow muddy road. The infantry had been creeping forward towards Chancellorsville most of the day. Restless, Jackson rode and probed for a way to do serious damage to the enemy. Beckam's stomach churned with apprehension at being under the watchful eye of both generals. The dense woods and undergrowth made it impossible to see what lay ahead. He heard the enemy artillery pelting their lines and realized it would be his job to destroy those guns.

When they reached a knoll where Stuart and Jackson watched the action, Beckam's men struggled to get a gun in position through the thick undergrowth. After moving one gun into place, Beckam ordered, "Cut the undergrowth with your sabers so we can move another gun up." While his artillerymen worked fiercely to get the second gun in position, Beckam sized up the situation. He carefully calculated the distance to the line of enemy infantry until the remaining men brought up the last two guns. "Fire!" Two guns simultaneously belched forth deadly missiles on the lines below. Blue soldiers fell and gaps opened in their line. "Keep it up, give it to them," Beckam called as the enemy fell back.

Suddenly, hidden enemy artillery pelted the Confederates from close range, wounding one of Beckam's gunners. Beckam spotted the location of the enemy guns, then redirected his fire to fight back. Six Parrott rifles and four Napoleons pounded the knoll with converging fire. Shells fell into the horses, killing several and causing the others to rear and whinny. "Steady men," Beckam called out while he attempted to fire his guns again. A caisson exploded behind him, sending a gunner into the sky. The men tumbled to the ground from the shock of the explosion. Sprawled flat on his back, Beckam struggled to get his breath after the impact of his fall. Through the spewing earth and surging flames, he saw the generals withdrawing. Gasping, he pushed himself up, staggered to his feet and rallied his men to fire again. With several of his gunners injured, he manned one of the guns himself. Shells exploded around him but he struggled to fire until the way was clear on the narrow road to withdraw. "Limber," he yelled to the remaining men. They labored to get one of the guns back to the road, and then chased down the frenzied horses to pull it. A shell exploded behind Beckam as he examined the broken axle of one gun. He lunged from the impact and decided to leave it behind among the pile of bodies.

"We've never been under hotter fire!" Lieutenant Burwell called to him in the chaos. "Every one of my men is wounded."

"We've got to get the guns out!" Beckam worked frantically, sweat pouring off of him. "We'll come back for the men." When the exhausted survivors finally reached safety with three guns, they were relieved to learn that Jackson and Stuart had miraculously escaped injury.

Nightfall: Lee and Jackson sat opposite each other on two discarded hardtack boxes discussing the military situation. Both realized a frontal attack on Hooker would be disastrous. The flickering light of a campfire threw eerie shadows into the pine thicket while a handful of soldiers watched the conference. Jeb Stuart rode up pell-mell and leaped off his horse in a jubilant mood. "Fitz Lee and his scouts report that the Federal right is definitely 'in the air,'" he announced, his blue eyes sparkling. "It does not extend to the Rapidan or rest on any strong point. The enemy is expecting attack only from the south and there are no cavalry in strength along the route."

Jackson smiled at his revelation. It sounded too good to be true. Were there roads that would enable him to move his men in that direction without being detected? He would have to ascertain that possibility during the night.

Next day, May 2, 1863: Near Chancellorsville

1 p.m. "Push on men, push on," Jackson kept repeating to the long column of Rebels marching on a narrow dirt lane towards Hooker's right flank. Robert Beckam pushed his horses to keep the guns moving fast enough. Wiping his brow, he felt the warmth and fatigue because they had been marching since dawn. Powell Hill urged his men, the last in line, forward. Of course he did not know the final destination, but assumed they were flanking Hooker. His feud with Jackson continued, but he would not let that alter his duty today. He knew the performance of his men would be critical.

Fitz Lee galloped up to Jackson. "General, ride with me." The two rode to an observation point of the Federal camp. Jackson's eyes burned with a brilliant glow when he observed the groups of soldiers laughing, chatting, smoking, and feeling safe. Behind them parties drove in and slaughtered beeves. Jackson took it all in, his thin mute lips moving; his face flushed with excitement. Fitz Lee watched him gallop away, his arms flapping as he leaned forward over the head of his horse.[4]

* * *

5:15 p.m. Robert Beckam's adrenaline surged through his veins. The Rebels silently moved into line of battle behind a ridge shielding them from the unsuspecting Yankees. Skirmishers moved out in front followed by three lines: Rodes, Colston, and Hill. Beckam examined the position of his guns, which held the far right while Stuart's cavalry secured the left. Two pieces under Breathed would take the lead and fire simultaneously. Two pieces directly behind would relieve Breathed, while Moorman's battery remained in the far rear. Realizing his guns would be the only artillery in the charge, Beckam eyed the narrow road and heavy woods he would have to penetrate.

5:30 p.m. A bugle sounded in the stillness and the gray lines surged forward screeching the bone-chilling Rebel yell. Startled Union soldiers looked up from their dinners to see deer, rabbits, and quail fleeing through their camp in front of the Rebel hordes. Panic-stricken, they dashed for their guns as gray-clad demons appeared from every direction. "Fire!" Beckam ordered. Two guns simultaneously hurled canister into the stunned enemy. The infantry rushed forward and the two guns ceased firing while the rear section dashed forward in front of the infantry and opened up. "Keep moving, men," Beckam called, watching the gray lines bowl over the Union Eleventh Corps. He realized that the fast movement was causing excessive strain on his men. "Ride to the rear, and bring up volunteers from Moorman's battery," he told a courier. His fast-moving guns continued pouring death and destruction on the enemy as the lines advanced unmercifully. When one of his gunners fell out from exhaustion, Beckam took his place and helped maneuver the gun through several trees. "Fire, men," he shouted in the mayhem. "We've got them in a rout!" Gunners from Moorman soon arrived to give relief.

General Hooker sat on the porch of the Chancellor house enjoying a toddy while writing orders for tomorrow's pursuit of Lee, whom he believed to be retreating towards Richmond. When the guns sounded, one of his staff members picked up his binoculars and gazed towards the field in the west. "My God, here they come!" he shouted.

Within an hour Jackson had crushed Hooker's flank. When there was a slight lull in the battle, Beckam paused, panting, and wiped the sweat and grime from his face. An officer rode up to him, leaned forward, and extended his hand. He looked up into the flashing blue eyes of Old Jack. "Young man, I congratulate you," Jackson said warmly, his face flushed.

"Thank you, sir," Beckam stammered as they shook hands. Knowing Jackson was stingy with compliments, he swelled with pride for his men. It was Robert Beckam's finest hour.

Eleven days later, May 13, 1863: Armstrongs' parlor

"Jackson's dead!" Granny wailed. She took off her glasses to wipe her eyes. "How could the God who has blessed us with so many victories take this heroic Christian away from us?" The women, who had rushed to the Armstrongs' parlor to read the first papers to reach Culpeper in two weeks, sat in stunned silence. With the telegraph lines cut by the Yankee cavalry, they had listened to the muffled guns to the east rumble for four days, wondering the outcome of the fierce battle. Rumors had drifted in that Lee had won a great victory and that Jackson had been wounded. Now that they finally had the facts, the shadow of Jackson's death overshadowed everything else.

Harriet sobbed, "We've lost a gifted general who can never be replaced."

"He was the best Yankee killer we had," Granny continued while she paced the floor. "I buried my own son in February, and now I grieve for Jackson as if he were also my son." She paused to wipe her eyes. "How can we win this war without him?"

Constance looked up from the paper, her face filled with grief. "What a tragedy." She continued reading, "He was mistakenly shot by his own men while riding ahead of his lines to plan a night assault. Powell Hill came to his aid but was wounded by artillery fire when Jackson was carried away."

"Oh, no!" Mildred Hill cried. "Is it serious?"

Constance continued to read. "No, only a slight leg wound, but he turned the command over to General Stuart, who led the assault the next day. Jackson's left arm was amputated, and he appeared to be recovering when pneumonia set in."

"Well, thank God Powell will recover," Amanda said. "I know Dolly is relieved."

Lucy frantically read another paper. "It says Jackson made a brilliant flank attack on Hooker's unprotected right, which turned the battle in our favor. Lee was outnumbered more than two to one. The only artillery supporting Jackson's lightning attack was the Stuart Horse Artillery under Major Robert Beckam, which performed admirably."

Constance smiled with a sigh of relief. "Thank God. Robert was under intense pressure, having to go into such a great battle after being in command only three weeks."

Lucy continued to read. "Huge crowds at every station met the train bearing Jackson's body. A procession led by Davis, Longstreet, and Ewell bore his body to the capitol, where more than twenty thousand mourners streamed past to pay their respects."

"Lee will have to pick his replacement soon. Our army must have leadership," Harriet said wiping her eyes. "Who will it be?"

"Powell Hill is definitely in line, and Ewell has returned to duty with a wooden leg," Constance mused. "Perhaps General Stuart may be under consideration. However, I can't imagine him leading anything but cavalry."

"Powell is most deserving," Mildred Hill said proudly. "But we're all greatly concerned about his health. He suffers from a strange disease that causes flare-ups of his kidneys."

"Humph!" Granny snorted. "There's no mystery about his disease. He contracted it in the brothels of New York his first year at West Point."

"Well, I never!" Mildred sprang to her feet. "I will not listen to these insults! Constance, may I take this paper home?" she asked red-faced.

"Of course," Constance replied. Mildred stormed out the front door.

"Granny, that was unnecessary!" Jane Ashby reprimanded.

"It's the truth!" Granny snapped back. "I don't know why everybody avoids the truth."

"It's a rumor that you cannot substantiate and you had no business saying it," Lucy said firmly. "I expect you to apologize to Mildred." Granny turned her head, refusing to respond.

"Jackson's body will be taken by train to Gordonsville and Lynchburg today, and then by barge to Lexington for burial," Constance read, trying to smooth things over.

Granny spun around. "I'm going to catch the return train to Gordonsville. It should be leaving in about a half-hour. If I don't get to see the casket there, I'll go all the way to Lexington if I have to. I must kneel by the casket of my beloved general!"

"Granny, you can't go alone," Jane said. Seeing the determination on her grandmother's face, she relented. "I'll go with you. Come on, let's go pack."

After everyone else had left the parlor, Constance and Lucy continued to glean information from the papers. "Oh, no!" Constance moaned. "It says that Channing Price and Heros Von Borcke were killed!"

"They were both charming. How we all enjoyed Von when he was here with John." Lucy's voice broke. "I'm sick of this terrible war!"

"You know, Lucy, every time I think I'm too empty inside to shed any more tears, I find myself crying again."

"You've suffered so much, Constance," Lucy said touching her hand. "I know how deeply you're grieving for John." She paused thoughtfully for several minutes as her thoughts turned to Will Farley. "I'm thankful that Captain Farley wasn't at Chancellorsville. At least I believe he's still alive and en route from South Carolina. He's the most exciting man I've ever met."

Constance wiped her eyes and contemplated her friend. With her nutmeg hair and brown eyes, Lucy attracted much attention. Of medium height, she carried herself gracefully. Her Roman nose was perhaps a little large, but she had an ingratiating smile. Although she could not be called beautiful, she certainly caught the eyes of many young men. "Would you marry him if he asked you?"

"In a heartbeat! But I do not believe he's that serious yet. At twenty one, I'm approaching spinsterhood. With so many of our men dying, I'm afraid we're all doomed to be old maids."

A week later, May 20, 1863: Davis Street

Constance carried her precious purchases, a bag of flour and a pound of cornmeal, towards Coleman Street, enjoying the balmy air. She noticed cavalrymen at the far end of Davis Street, close to their old camping ground on the west side of town. Was Stuart returning, she wondered? She turned the corner by the courthouse, looking into the late afternoon sun. "Connie," she heard from two cavalrymen who rode along side her. The sun blinded her, preventing her from seeing their faces. One dismounted and handed his reins to the other. "You take my horse, Alex," Robert said, then rushed over to hug her.

"Robert! Thank God you're back safe and sound!" He picked her up and held her with her feet dangling for a minute. He slowly let her down with an expression of new confidence and satisfaction in his dark eyes.

"You're a sight for sore eyes," he said. His lips brushed hers.

"You're to be congratulated!" She took his arm and they walked towards her house. "I'm proud of you and I've got a surprise for you."

"What?" She shrugged her shoulders and smiled innocently. "Connie, there's so much I want to tell you. The morale of the cavalry has never been better. General Stuart ordered us all new uniforms from Richmond, and recruits are streaming in. Our horses are being replenished. I do not believe we've ever been stronger!"

"That's wonderful news!" They climbed the porch steps. "Come into the bookstore."

They entered to find Amanda and Alex entwined in a long embrace. "Excuse us," Constance said while she walked towards the desk. She took a package out and turned towards Robert. "Welcome home, Alex." The husband and wife stopped long enough to acknowledge them.

After she led Robert into the parlor and they sat down on the sofa, she handed him the package wrapped in brown paper and ribbon. "Happy twenty-sixth birthday. I'm sorry I didn't have any better wrapping paper."

"I'm surprised you remembered." Deeply touched, he unwrapped the book. "*Les Miserables,* I've been wanting to read it, but it's almost impossible to get."

"I know. It's our last copy and I saved it for you. It's a story of the struggles of the poor people of France. I know you'll like it. Books are all that I have access to, but I didn't want to forget your birthday."

"Thank you, Connie. Your thoughtfulness means a great deal to me." Feeling pleased with himself, he took her hand. "Do you want to hear about the battle?"

"Of course, especially your part in it." He talked easily and candidly, attempting to describe for her everything that had transpired over the last three weeks. She listened eagerly, asking questions from time to time.

"There's one other thing." His voice vibrated with new life. "I didn't even include this in my report, but I want to share it with you. After our rapid assault on Hooker's right flank, General Jackson rode over to me and extended his hand. 'Young man, I congratulate you,' he said as we shook hands. I'm thankful that I got to shake the great general's hand before he was shot."

"Robert, that's a story to tell your grandchildren. You should be extremely proud." She paused and looked at him thoughtfully. "But why is the cavalry here? What's next?"

"We're refurbishing and building our strength. I believe Lee will take the offensive. At any rate, General Stuart is planning a review of his cavalry at Brandy Station day after tomorrow. Will you come?"

"Of course, if I can get there."

"Don't worry, we'll be certain to get the fair ladies to the review field," he chuckled.

Next day, May 21, 1863: Along the railroad tracks behind East Street

Stuart, Farley, and Dabney rode along the railroad tracks behind the large back yards along East Street and spied a tall cherry tree. "I do believe those cherries are about ripe for plucking," Stuart said.

Recognizing the familiar area, both Farley and Dabney grinned. "Are you ordering us to harvest the tempting fruit?" Farley asked before he dismounted.

Stuart's eyes twinkled. "Use your own discretion, gentlemen."

With some effort, Farley and Dabney climbed the tree and tossed the ripe cherries to Stuart who caught them in his hat. Stuart devoured several. "Delicious!" A few minutes later, the two men in the tree settled back on a comfortable limb and enjoyed their plunder.

A little old lady charged around the corner of the house at the top of the hill, and descended upon them with the speed of lightning. Wielding a long pole with considerable dexterity, she assaulted the men in the tree. "Sorry, thieves!" she screeched. She walloped Farley with such force that he lost his balance and tumbled to the ground.

Stuart burst into laughter at the sight of Farley sprawled on the ground, his breath knocked out. Catching his breath between bursts of laughter, Stuart called out, "Biggs blow the retreat! Retreat to safety, men!" The woman fell on Farley, continuing to apply her weapon with a vengeance. Dabney climbed down laughing, and mounted his horse.

"Granny, Granny! Stop it!" Lucy screamed while she ran down the hill, followed by her youngest sister, Blanche. Granny delivered one more blow to her victim, before her granddaughter caught her arm. "This is General Stuart and his staff!" She knelt on the ground beside Will Farley, badly bruised and bleeding on the ear. "Captain Farley, I hope you're not severely hurt. My Grandmother is hard to control at times," she whispered looking into his dark gray eyes.

"I don't care who they are, they got no right to steal our cherries," Granny yelled defiantly.

Farley sat up slowly, wiping the blood from his ear. "I fear I have just suffered my first defeat," he said weakly.

"When did you return?" Lucy asked. "I had hoped to give you a nicer reception than this." She took his arm and helped him up. Blanche administered to Dabney's wounds, and Stuart chuckled.

"Yesterday," an embarrassed Farley said after he stood.

"Come up to the house, and let me take care of your wounds. We'll give you some cherry jam and rolls," Lucy said with a flirtatious smile.

"General, my nurse wishes to take care of my wounds." Farley's mouth turned up in a roguish grin. Stuart let out an uproarious laugh and they all headed towards the Ashby house.

Next day, May 22, 1863: Auburn

Constance stood in awe of the nearly 4000 horsemen parading in front of her. Never had she seen so many well-clad cavalrymen in one location. She applauded along with the other townspeople gathered to witness the spectacle on the farm of John Minor Botts. "Surely this group of southern gentlemen can never be defeated," Lucy said. "It's the most amazing display of horseflesh and manliness that I've ever witnessed."

Constance cheered when General Stuart and his staff rode by, flags waving in the warm breeze. She turned her head towards a dark-haired young lady who called her name. It took her a moment to recognize Myrta Grey, recently returned from running the blockade to Baltimore. She reported having many narrow escapes before reaching Baltimore and spending several pleasant weeks with her relatives. She had contacted a Mr. Browning, owner of a large bookstore. When told of Constance's plight, he sympathetically agreed to sell her books. However, he stressed that getting a wagonload through the blockade had risks. He could not guarantee delivery but felt books would be less suspicious than other items. Myrta gave Constance his address and told her he had agreed to accept the check, if she endorsed it over to him. Constance thanked her appreciatively and told her she would take the risk, since few books would be forthcoming from Richmond.

When asked about acquiring wool for her husband's uniform, Myrta announced proudly that she had smuggled it back under her hoop skirt. Now her Dan had a beautiful new uniform. She was staying with the Bradfords at Afton to spend some time with her husband while the cavalry remained here.

After the review came to an end, General Stuart and his staff rode into the crowd and dismounted. Constance grabbed Amanda's arm, stunned at the man she spotted in the crowd. "My God, that looks like Von," she sputtered. "The paper said he was dead."

Sure enough, a very much alive Prussian with a handlebar moustache approached her smiling. "Miss Armstrong, how did you like our little review?" He kissed her hand.

"Von, I thought you were dead!" She grasped his hand. "The paper said so."

The tears welling in her blue eyes touched him. "Many have taken me for a ghost of late. I don't know how that rumor got started. I appreciate your concern. Following Chancellorsville, we rode to pursue Stoneman's cavalry, raiding towards Richmond. The enemy even stooped so low as to capture a train of our wounded en route to the hospital. When Governor Lechtor read of my death in the paper, he telegraphed General Lee requesting my body so he could bury me as an honorable Virginian. General Lee telegraphed back in reference to my body, *Can't spare it: it's in pursuit of Stoneman.*"[5]

"Oh!" she laughed in relief. "General Lee does have a sense of humor. I'm so glad you're safe. What about Channing Price?"

"Sadly, I must report that he was wounded in the leg. Feeling no bone broken he continued to fight. However, an artery had been severed and he bled to death."

"Miss Armstrong," Will Farley said, then bowed and kissed her hand. "You look radiant today. It's a pleasure to see you." The warmth of his smile echoed in his voice.

"I trust that you had a good trip home, Captain Farley," she said, feeling the intensity of his stare.

"I did indeed, but I may be moving a little stiffly today. You see yesterday I suffered my first defeat from an enemy far more fierce than the Yankees." An easy smile played at the corners of his mouth and his eyes twinkled.

She raised her eyebrows in surprise. "And who was your adversary?"

"Her name is Granny Ashby and her wrath knows no limits," he said solemnly.

Constance couldn't control her burst of laughter. Lucy pushed her way through the crowd to get beside Farley. "Captain Farley, are you feeling better?" A radiant smile lit her face.

Farley bowed and kissed her hand. "Thanks to your excellent care, Miss Ashby, I believe that I will survive my wounds."

Robert maneuvered his way towards them. Jane Ashby, batting her long eyelashes coquettishly, called out to him, "Major Beckam, congratulations on your new position. We're all proud to have a Culpeper man in such an important job."

"Thank you, Miss Ashby." He reached Constance's side and kissed her on the cheek. "What did you think?"

"That a more handsome group of men does not exist anywhere on earth."

Not willing to give up her attention, Farley asked, "Miss Armstrong, we discussed some of my poetry, and I was wondering if you would be so kind as to read it and give me your opinion."

Surprised at his insistence, she answered, "I would be honored Captain Farley."

The crowd applauded General Stuart who pushed his way through. "Today was such a great success that I've been inspired," he announced enthusiastically. "When the rest of my troops arrive I will have nearly ten thousand men. We must plan a Grand Review for General Lee and invite all our friends from Richmond and Charlottesville." The group cheered. "Will you all help me plan it?"

"Yes! Yes!"

"Miss Armstrong, Mrs. Yager, may we meet at your house in a few days to make plans?"

"It would be our honor, General Stuart," Constance replied.

Five days later, May 27, 1863: Armstrongs' parlor

Stuart raised his hands to silence the large crowd gathered in the Armstrong parlor. "This review on June fifth will be the grandest pageantry ever staged in the Confederacy! We need a large, open area of several miles. I can think of none more suitable than the lands of John Minor Botts. We will be able to bring our guests out on the train and provide flat cars for them to sit on." Stuart paced restlessly. "I must admit I take great delight in using the farm of a Unionist!" He heard considerable snickering. "Mind you, I do not wish to torment him, but to protect him." Stuart flashed a wicked grin. "If you have any names to add to our invitation list, give them to Major McClellan."

"Who will attend the ball on the fourth?" Rooney Lee, middle son of Robert E. Lee, inquired.

"Staff, officers, and of course our lady friends. Von, you're in charge of decorating the Town Hall and making arrangements. We'll need all the hotel rooms and possible accommodations in local houses for our out of town guests. It may also be necessary to accommodate some of the ladies in tents."

"You know that we have three extra rooms," Harriet offered.

"We have two rooms," Lucy added.

"We'll have several special trains coming in on the fourth, and we'll need every available wagon and ambulance to shuttle our guests to their accommodations," Stuart continued. "Colonel Hampton, will you take charge of that?"

Frank Hampton, the recently married handsome younger brother of Wade Hampton, smiled broadly. "Sir, it will be my pleasure to greet the ladies."

"It's going to be a gala event!" Stuart said.

"If your plans are complete now, sir, may I request that you sing for us?" Amanda said. "We ladies are all dying to hear your version of *Joe Hooker, Wouldn't You Come Out of the Wilderness.*" Stuart chuckled and nodded in agreement.

"Yes! It's the theme song of Chancellorsville," Fitz Lee said while they all gathered at that end of the room.

"Connie," Robert moved alongside her towards the piano, "may I have the honor of escorting you to the gala ball?"

"It would be my pleasure, Robert." During the singing, she felt the eyes of Will Farley boring through her. He had visited her at the bookstore and dropped off several pages of poetry for her to read. Jane Ashby tossed her strawberry blonde curls and stood on the other side of Robert. She smiled radiantly in admiration every time she caught Robert's eye.

Constance contemplated 6-foot, 4-inch Rooney Lee. An impressive figure with his dark hair and beard, he definitely had his father's penetrating eyes. When the singing concluded, she caught his attention. "General Lee, it's an honor to have you here. A soldier from Maine recuperated with us following the Battle of Cedar Mountain, and mentioned that he rowed with you on the crew team at Harvard."

Rooney Lee's eyes lit up. "You must mean Aaron Ames!"

"Why yes," she replied surprised. "He spoke highly of you."

"Ames was the strongest oarsman on our team. Because of him, we won. He was quite popular on campus and extremely bright." He rolled his eyes with a smile. "The ladies adored him. Tell me, has he recovered?"

"Yes, and he's returned to fight in the cavalry."

Lee's face fell. "I hope I don't meet him on the battlefield. That's the terrible tragedy of this war. Friends fighting friends. If you hear from him again, please give him by best regards, Miss Armstrong."

"I will." Will Farley joined her, and Rooney Lee engaged Harriet in conversation.

"Miss Armstrong, I enjoyed the critique of Shakespeare you sold me," Farley said. "I was wondering if you would give me the distinct pleasure of escorting you to the ball?"

She felt his eyes assessing her approvingly. "Oh, I'm flattered that you asked, but I have already promised Major Beckam."

"I was afraid that I might be too late, but I hope you'll save me several dances." He stood so close she felt the heat from his body.

"Of course. I enjoyed your poetry. I found your description of the mountains and our landscape captivating."

Lucy wiggled her way to Farley's side. "Connie, did you know that Captain Farley is a true volunteer? He doesn't accept pay or supplies from our army."

"Is this true, Captain Farley?" Constance asked. Her eyes scanned his attire: a plain suit of gray with a belt tightly drawn around his slender waist holding his pistol, a black cavalry feather adorning his hat, and boots of the handsome pattern worn by Federal officers with patent-leather tops and ornamental threadwork.[6]

"None of my equipment has cost our government a cent. I've captured everything from sutlers or the Federal larder. I appreciate how well the enemy provides for me. My purpose is to roam freely, gathering information and doing as much damage as possible to the enemy."

"That's quite impressive," Constance said. "If you'll excuse me, I want to meet Major McClellan." She walked through the crowd, noticing Jane and Robert still engrossed in conversation. She greeted the newly appointed assistant adjutant on General Stuart's staff. "Major McClellan, I'm Constance Armstrong. I didn't have the opportunity to greet you when you arrived. I must admit I'm curious. Are you related to General George McClellan?"

The fair skinned young man with delicate features bowed. "Everyone asks me that question. I'm his first cousin. I was born in Philadelphia and graduated from Williams College at age seventeen. I wasn't ready to pursue a profession, so I came to Cumberland, Virginia, to teach Latin. I lived here for two years before the war broke out."

"And you decided to fight for the Confederacy? That must have been an extremely difficult decision."

"I love the South and it's people. Secession is completely legal. When this war of aggression erupted, I enlisted in the Confederate army immediately. I've never looked back."

"But your family must have been upset? Do you still hear from them?"

"They bombarded me with letters to return home and threatened disinheritance," he said sadly, "but that didn't deter me. I have several brothers fighting for the Union. Yes, we do still communicate."

Stuart joined them and put his hand on the shoulder of his new adjutant. "The ball and review will be the most exciting social events ever to take place in Culpeper."

Eight days later, June 4, 1863: Culpeper Court House

Culpeper bustled with excitement. Wagonload after wagonload of guests were ferried from the depot to their accommodations. Smiling ladies, hatboxes, trunks, and hoop skirts crowded the streets of this tiny rural town.

Constance saw the throng of guests unloading their trunks at the Virginia House from the crowded bookstore. With Amanda sick again, Longstreet's Corps camped at Pony Mountain and Ewell's on the north side of town; the last few days had been frantic. On top of all that, they had to prepare rooms for the out-of-town guests. She watched a wagon stop in front of her house and several beautifully attired young ladies and their servants disembarked. "Excuse me," she said to one of her customers. Walking to the hall, she called her mother to help escort their guests to their rooms, then opened the front door and greeted the guests warmly, directing them to their rooms upstairs. Embarrassed to be seen in the plain homespun dress she normally wore while working, she stared at the guests dressed in the latest fashion, with their hair piled on their heads in flowing curls. Two young ladies about her age, a petite redhead and a stately brunette, were especially beautiful.

Constance wiped the sweat from her brow and finally locked the door to the bookstore. Too busy to join the others for dinner, she had hastily eaten at her desk. While she climbed the stairs, she heard chattering female voices. Walking down the hall, she overheard, "I believe Robert Beckam is the most desirable man in the cavalry." Stopping frozen, she noticed one of the bedroom doors ajar. "As the head of Stuart's Horse Artillery, he holds a most prestigious position. I will endeavor to gain his attention tonight." She recognized the voice as that of the redhead.

"He was a prominent figure on the Richmond social scene this winter," the brunette said. "We saw him at practically every dance, but he never seemed to pick a favorite lady. I agree, he's handsome indeed."

"He's certainly different from John Pelham," the redhead continued. "How we all loved him! But he was such a notorious flirt. Robert Beckam possesses a quiet sincerity that melts my heart. How I long to gaze into his dark eyes."

"Personally, I don't think there's anyone more dashing than Farley, the scout," the brunette giggled. "His stunning good looks and impeccable manners excite me."

Constance tiptoed to her room. "Sadie, are the curling irons hot?" She prepared for her bath. "You'll have to work a miracle on me. I've got to compete with those stylish ladies from Richmond. How I wish I had a new dress."

"Now, don't ya fret. I put some gold trim on your rose dress, an' it looks beau'ful. When I gits through with ya Miss Constance, you's gonna be the mos' gorgeous lady at that ball!"

* * *

Robert was chatting with Harriet in the hall when the two beauties from Richmond descended the stairs. "Major Beckam," the redhead said surprised. "How wonderful to see you." She thought that perhaps he had come to escort her to the ball. "How did you know I was here?"

Beckam bowed politely. "Miss Hudson, Miss Spencer, welcome to Culpeper. I'm delighted to see you, but actually I didn't know you were staying here."

"Oh," the redhead said, batting her eyelashes. "Then why are you here?"

"I've come to escort Miss Armstrong to the ball."

"Miss Armstrong?" she asked confused. "Oh, you mean the proprietress of this establishment?" she questioned haughtily.

His eyes riveted on Constance who walked gracefully down the stairs, her head held high. Her abundance of silky hair curled in long ringlets crowned her head. "Connie, you look beautiful." He kissed her hand.

"That's because I have such a handsome escort." She shot him an enchanting smile and took his arm. "Your new uniform is magnificent."

"Would you like to join us ladies?" he asked.

"Yes, please walk to the Town Hall with us," Constance insisted. "It's only a block."

"We'd be delighted," the brunette replied. They could only walk two abreast on the sidewalk because of the hoop skirts. Constance and Robert followed the two Richmond socialites.

Stuart's battleflag and those of his brigades adorned the walls and ceiling of the packed Town Hall. All the furniture except for a few chairs around the walls had been moved out. Tallow candles placed in the windows provided the only light. "My eyes will have to adjust to the darkness," Constance said as they moved through the crowd. Will Farley and Lucy Ashby joined them.

"Constance, can you believe that these lavishly clad cavalrymen are the same ragged, dirty soldiers we've known in the past?" Lucy giggled.

"Their change in appearance and attitude is amazing," Constance replied.

"Our morale has never been better," Robert said.

"Alas, should tragedy befall me, I beg you all to wrap me in my splendid new coat and send me home to my mother," Farley said dramatically.

"Oh please, don't speak such things," Lucy begged. "I'm surprised you treasure your coat so highly, since you didn't acquire it from the Yankees."

"They don't provide Confederate coats, but I do treasure every item I procure from a dead Yankee."

Constance studied the glint of excitement in Farley's eyes. She believed he actually enjoyed the killing.

"Welcome friends!" Jeb Stuart called from the center of the room. "It boosts our morale to have you here. We'll open the festivities with a Virginia Reel"

"Shall we?" Robert said. Constance felt her spirits soar in the excitement and glamour of the event. After the fourth song, Frank and Jane Ashby joined them.

"Can you believe this exciting event is happening in Culpeper?" Frank quipped, causing them all to laugh. "Major Beckam, I must have the privilege of dancing with my dearest sister," he said breathlessly.

283

"But of course." Robert stepped aside and Jane's face glowed at the opportunity to dance with him.

Constance worried about Frank's frail condition. He floated like a feather compared to Robert. "You're as thin as ever."

"Thinness is nothing new for me. I've always been in vogue. In fact, I've never felt better. I'm full of optimism about the upcoming campaign."

"It appears that the whole army is converging on Culpeper. What do you think will happen?"

"Lee's not here yet. I don't think he'll see the review tomorrow, but it will be exciting anyway. I suspect he's planning to take the offensive – perhaps invade the North. It makes sense. This area is war torn and the farmers need to get crops in. It would be a bold and dangerous move, but a decisive victory in the North would end the war. Their morale has never been lower."

"Attempting such a campaign without Jackson scares me," she said studying his face. "We're all so proud that Powell Hill is a corps commander, but neither he nor Ewell has had experience leading such a large body of men."

"That's certainly a good point. Hill remains at Fredericksburg to fool the Yankees. The less they know about the location of our army the better. I believe dividing our army into three corps was a wise decision." He smiled at her. "I've enjoyed spending some time with Mother. She's coming to the review tomorrow. Then, I must get back to work. We aren't being vigilant enough."

"It's nice to make the war disappear for a few days," she said philosophically. "Tonight is an event to remember and enjoy to the fullest."

"Dearest sister, you're the most beautiful lady here. The lovelies from Richmond do not compare."

"Oh, Frank!" She laughed. Stringfellow spotted Farley approaching after the music stopped. He winked at Farley and gave him her hand.

Farley bowed. "Miss Armstrong, may I claim the dance you promised?"

"It's my pleasure, Captain Farley." He held her firmly while their bodies moved together with the music.

Lucy and Jane Ashby glared at the two of them from the edge of the dance floor. "Sometimes I'm so jealous of Constance, that I hate her," Lucy said.

"It's not fair," Jane whispered. "First she gets John Pelham, and now Robert and Will are hovering around her. I think Robert is divine; I would treasure his affection."

"She doesn't openly flirt with them or even appear interested, and yet they flock around her," Lucy commented. "Perhaps we shouldn't be so obvious. Maybe that's the secret. I'm going to make Will Farley seek me out."

Constance glanced over Farley's shoulder to see Robert dancing with the red-hot redhead from Richmond. "You look ravishing tonight," Farley said. His dark eyes moved over her intently.

"Thank you." His strong arms held her so close that she found his nearness strangely disturbing.

"There are some matters which I feel compelled to discuss with you tonight. I'm sure my timing is poor, and this is not the correct place, but the opportunity may not arise again," he began, searching deep into her eyes. "We're embarking on a dangerous campaign, and I feel I must speak from my heart. If I make a fool of myself, so be it."

He paused in thought. "I find myself strongly attracted to you. It's not just your beauty, but your wit and intellect. Frank had told me so much about you, that I believe I was enamored with you before I met you."

"You know how Frank exaggerates."

"In this case, I believe he spoke the truth. I hope that I might have a chance of winning your affection."

She stared into his inviting eyes. "Lucy is one of my best friends, and she's smitten with you."

"And I'm quite fond of her. I enjoy her company. But," he emphasized, "I am not in love with her." He paused while she pondered his statement. "And I don't believe that you're in love with Major Beckam."

She looked away and grasped for words. Her mind swam in a sea of conflicting emotions. She was not blind to the magnetism that made this uncommonly attractive man so self-confident. Finally she answered, "My affection for him grows deeper each day." The music stopped.

"Friends, friends," Stuart called to the crowd. "Since it appears that the ladies are in the majority tonight, a fact that we gentlemen are enjoying, it seems appropriate to let them do the asking for one dance. So by request, this next waltz will be a lady's choice. Prepare for the charge men!"

Constance's pulse raced. She realized that the moment of decision had been thrust upon her. "Excuse me, Captain Farley," she said hastily, then rushed towards Robert, standing across the room. Jane, the redhead, and several other ladies rapidly swished towards him.

Robert was amazed at his popularity. "Ladies, I'm honored and regret that I cannot dance with all of you," he said slowly, allowing Constance to reach him. "I hope to dance with each of you tonight, but can only pick one for the moment." He reached his hand over the shoulders of two of the other ladies to take her hand. "Connie, it's my pleasure," he said smiling confidently.

"You've become quite popular and famous," she said when she put her hand on his shoulder and they moved onto the dance floor.

"I'd trade it all in an instant for peace. I detest the killing. I want to get on with my life and start building instead of destroying."

She felt certain that she had made the right choice. His goodness, sincerity, and steadfast loyalty were rare attributes—attributes to be cherished and never again taken for granted. She was comfortable with him and he seemed content with her. Realizing that she had hurt him, she determined to make it up to him.

"Robert, you deserve every bit of attention you've gotten tonight. The people of Culpeper are proud to claim you and Powell Hill as our own local heroes. We support you."

"I do greatly appreciate the support and encouragement I've gotten from the local citizens." He looked down at her with a tender gaze. "But your support, Connie, means the world to me."

"I'm happy and proud to be with you tonight," she whispered, laying her head against his shoulder.

His lips brushed her hair. "I'm always happy when I'm with you."

She noticed that the brunette from Richmond had claimed Will Farley while Lucy sought another. Constance watched Farley bow after the song ended, and then move to Lucy's side. She hoped his pride had not been severely damaged and that he would return Lucy's affection. The two of them remained together for the rest of the enchanted evening, as did Constance and Robert.

12

The Battle of Brandy Station

June 5 – June 24, 1863

"Hurrah! We're going to have a fight!"
Captain William D. Farley, C.S.A. at the opening of The Battle of Brandy Station

---

Next day, June 5, 1863: Auburn

What a perfect day for military pomp and pageantry, Constance thought. The sun warmed the multitude of spectators assembled on the farm of John Minor Botts. She adjusted the brim of her new palmetto-leaf bonnet and opened her parasol before she surveyed the impressive scene. Thanks to Robert's rank and influence, her family enjoyed a spot on General Stuart's review knoll. They sat comfortably on stools atop the two allotted ambulances. She opened her fan and glanced at her companions: Granny Ashby and her four granddaughters sat on her right, and Amanda and the two excited boys were on her left. Her mother, Anne Stringfellow, her daughters-in-law, and Fannie Barbour and children were seated on the other ambulance beside them. Across the review field, hundreds of spectators gathered on the flat cars parked on the railroad track. A mile and a half of immaculately clad cavalrymen awaited the arrival of their general, with Robert's twenty guns lined up on the right. Everyone was there except the guest of honor, Robert E. Lee.

All heads turned towards the sound of bugles. "It's General Stuart and his staff," Lucy said. A deafening cheer arose from the cavalry when Stuart and his entourage galloped past. Plumes waved, sabers clanked, brass glittered, and spurs jingled while the women tossed flowers in their path.

"There's Robert," Constance said, watching him gallop away from the others to take command of his artillery.

Lucy gripped Constance's arm. "How dashing Captain Farley looks."

"I see Frank!" Anne said to Harriet. "Never could a mother be more proud."

Stuart, clad in a short gray jacket, wide-brim white hat with a long black plume, gold sash and black patent boots, galloped up to the review area and bowed low in his saddle to the ladies. A wreath of flowers encircled his magnificent horse's neck. Amid cheers and squeals of delight, the ladies bombarded him with flowers. Constance and Lucy stood cheering and tossing the daisies and roses they had brought. Many of the young ladies swooned at the sight of such an assemblage of masculinity and prowess. Suddenly Robert's guns belched forth a deafening salute to their general. David and Hudson jumped and covered their ears.

"Oh," Constance cried out, "how do they tolerate the noise?"

"What a waste of powder and ammunition," Granny grumbled.

Stuart spurred his shiny mount, then rode forth down the line to inspect each regiment one at a time. Brigade officers fell in behind their commander, and accompanied him back to the knoll to review the troops.

"We must remember every second of this spectacle," Lucy said, "so we can tell our grandchildren."

Bugles sounded commands. "What grandeur," Constance replied. She watched the Horse Artillery positioning itself to march in front of the review knoll. One of three bands struck up a martial tune while the Horse Artillery and guns paraded in front of them, flags and guidons waving in the soft breeze. Constance, her heart swelling with pride, stood, cheered, and tossed flowers towards Robert.

Jane Ashby cried out, "Hooray for Robert Beckam!"

The sight of that many horses and guns instilled a sense of confidence in the crowd. These Rebels were a formidable, undefeatable group. After parading in front of their general, the Horse Artillery unlimbered on the hill behind the crowd.

"What next?" Lucy asked.

"It looks like each regiment will parade by us." Constance watched the first group move into position. The soldiers walked forward, quickened their pace to a trot and, when within a hundred yards of the review knoll, galloped past, lifting their sabers with a spirited yell. The ground vibrated and shook beneath the pounding of countless hooves. As the artillery fired a round in salute, the crowd cheered and applauded exuberantly.

Constance fanned rapidly, trying to remove the dust swirling around her. "It's going to be a long afternoon," she said, then opened her picnic basket. "I believe we may as well eat."

"I'm getting hungry, too," Lucy said. "I feel for the men in all of this heat and dust. It's exhausting on the horses."

"Humph!" Granny sneered. "It's a ridiculous waste of horse flesh, if you ask me."

John Minor Botts paced the front porch of Auburn, incensed by the ridiculous pageant taking place on his farm. "Stuart is basking in the attention of the ladies. It's all a show to feed his pompous conceit," he said to his three daughters.

"Don't take it so personally, Father," Mary, his youngest, replied. "You act as if he planned the whole thing to punish you."

Botts moved his bushy eyebrows together in a frown. "Knowing the cunning of Stuart, he probably did. My new corn has all been trampled. He's not going to get away with it. I'm writing to the Richmond newspapers."

The formal review ended by mid-afternoon. Beckam limbered his guns and moved them to random locations around the field. "What are they doing?" Constance asked Lucy.

"I'm not sure. It seems like they would be exhausted by now."

The spellbound spectators watched the cavalry regiments divide up and charge different guns, simulating a cavalry battle. The guns roared with blank ammunition.

"Look at them! Why aren't they hurt?" David asked.

"It's a pretend battle," Amanda explained. "They aren't using real ammunition."

The men applauded and the ladies squealed at the antics of the mock battle.

"I hope this is the closest I ever get to a battle," Constance told Lucy.

Granny's tolerance had run out. "General Stuart's behavior has been perfectly ridiculous. I'm going to write and tell President Davis how he spends all his time entertaining female companions," she complained. "What other major general would dare stage repeated reviews for the benefit of his lady friends?"

"But it builds morale in the men, Granny," Lucy said. "It's terribly exciting."

"He's a fop! Aren't we supposed to be fighting a war? It's a waste of energy and ammunition. He rides up and down the lines of ladies, all decorated with flowers. In my opinion it's a monkey show, and he's the monkey!"[1]

That evening, Constance and Robert watched the shimmering moonlight on Mountain Run as the music and laughter of the revelers at the impromptu ball drifted through the warm air. "Are you tired?" she asked him, watching the dancing shadows cast by the bonfires.

"It's been an exhausting day. I must admit that at first I considered it a useless expenditure of powder and horses. But the grandeur of it all made me swell with pride. I think my hair stood on end," he chuckled.

The soothing serenade of frogs and whippoorwills pierced the night. "It was a grand spectacle, and tonight is perfect, almost idyllic." The gentle breeze caressed her skin.

He put his hand on her shoulder in a possessive gesture, thinking their headquarters along the stream a perfect location for the festivities. "I'm glad we have the opportunity to dance under a full moon. Fatigue won't prevent me from enjoying this evening or you. Shall we dance?"

Frank Stringfellow lingered in the shadows, watching Will Farley and Lucy Ashby dance around the bonfire. Overcome with depression, he realized that the grim realities of war had been thrust upon him even in this joyous setting. Stuart had ordered him to scout north for a safe place to cross the Potomac. Something big was about to happen. Farley spotted him when the music stopped, came over and slapped him on the back.

"What? Not dancing, Frank?" he asked, his eyes bright with excitement. "It's a perfect evening."

"Yes, it is. But, I'm leaving to scout north. I believe a major battle is imminent."

Farley suddenly became serious, older. "I guess we'll all be leaving soon. I wonder how many of us will dance again. Tonight reminds me of Lord Byron's poem *The Night Before Waterloo*. Do you suppose we're about to meet our Waterloo?" He paused for a minute and tried to shake off the dark mood. "Well, I can't stand here and moan. I've got a young lady waiting."[2] He glanced at Lucy. "Miss Armstrong gave me a lesson in humility, but nevertheless, I'm greatly enjoying Miss Ashby."

Stringfellow smiled. "You should. She's a delightful young lady. Have a good time."

"Good luck, trooper." The two friends shook hands for the last time. "Remember everything I've taught you."

Robert's fatigue disappeared while he danced song after song with Constance. Touching her energized him, and he relished her undivided attention. Aware that Farley had tried to woo her, he assumed she had rejected him. Of course, she had not fully recovered from Pelham's death yet. That would take time, but he had patience.

"Major Beckam." Jeb Stuart tapped him on the shoulder. "May I have the pleasure of dancing with Miss Armstrong?" Beckam could not refuse his general.

Stuart was at the pinnacle of success. Nothing could upset him on this day. "You seem to have a preference for cannoneers, Miss Armstrong."

She resented the tone of his voice and looked up at him with hurt in her eyes. "I grieve for John every day, but all of my mourning won't bring him back."

"I grieve too," Stuart said softly. "He would have loved today. The child Flora carries will bear the name of Pelham."

"What a touching tribute." She paused in thought. "You must understand that Robert and I have been close friends since before the war. You've thrust him into a challenging situation. He deserves my support and friendship."

"That's true, he does. He's fortunate to have it. He's doing extremely well so far. His commitment to duty and his work ethic have won the respect of the men. I've recommended him for a promotion. I hope it's granted. Poor Pelham didn't receive his greatly deserved promotion until after his death,"

"That's a shame. I hope Robert is promoted."

"Yes, yes," Stuart said cheerfully. "Did you enjoy the review?"

"It was the most spectacular event I've ever witnessed. Your men are at the height of performance and enthusiasm."

"I think so, too!" Stuart whirled her around. "Do you know this John Minor Botts?"

"Only by reputation. Why?"

"He came after me today following the review, ranting and snorting. Seems he didn't like having his corn trampled. I wasn't going to let anything ruin the day. I laughed it off. He's a Unionist. What does the big bag of wind expect? That we should ignore the fact that he's a traitor?"

Constance smiled, her eyes twinkling with merriment. "Now you must admit, General Stuart, that you do enjoy tormenting him. It's a great delight for you."

Stuart laughed heartily. "Perhaps," he admitted as the song ended and Robert approached. "Major Beckam, thank you for sharing this delightful young lady with me."

Two days later, June 7, 1863: The bookstore

Amanda pondered the newspapers spread on her desk in the busy bookstore. Many northerners seemed incensed by the treatment of Vallandigham, the former Congressman from Ohio. Because of his outspoken opposition to the war, Union soldiers had smashed in his door, dragged him from his house, and imprisoned him in the middle of the night. In protest the citizens of Dayton had rioted, burning public buildings, stores, and houses. Demonstrations had taken place all over the state with crowds cheering for Jeff Davis, John Hunt Morgan, and Vallandigham. Lincoln then had him moved to prison in Boston. Surely the North must be realizing that their president was a dictator, she thought.

Constance entered the bookstore rubbing the back of her neck. "I'm so tired. I've been helping Mr. McDonald finish printing the general orders, provost-marshal passports, and other military forms for General Lee."

"It's been hectic here." Amanda collected money from a customer. "You missed Extra Billy Smith. He's a general now and fully recovered from his wounds. I believe he's looking forward to the campaign. He said to tell you hello."

"I'm sorry I missed him. He always inspires me."

Amanda wiped her forehead. "I haven't felt well all day. Let's close up soon."

"I'll take over now. Why don't you go and lie down?"

Amanda stood up to see Fannie Barbour sweep into the store. "Amanda!" She embraced her friend. "It's so good to see you. How do you feel?"

"I'm rather exhausted now, Fannie, but I'm glad you're here. What brings you to town?"

"I came to see James off. He spent last night at home but had to rejoin General Ewell today. They're preparing to march in two days. I hate to see him go." The three ladies turned when Robert Beckam entered the shop. "Cousin Robert." Fannie hugged him. "I finally get to congratulate you."

"Thanks, Cousin Fannie, I appreciate that. I've come to invite all of you to another review tomorrow. General Lee has arrived and requested to see the cavalry."

"I can't believe you're going to do it all again," Constance said.

"You should hear the men bellyaching and complaining. But this review won't be as exhausting. General Lee has forbidden firing the guns or tiring the horses. We've orders to march day after tomorrow, and we'll be camped near Fleetwood Hill tomorrow night."

"Robert, you can't leave without having dinner with me," Fannie insisted. "Please come to dinner at Beauregard tomorrow night. In fact, why don't you all come? Amanda you and Constance can spend the night and ease my loneliness for James."

"I'd certainly enjoy that." Robert turned his eyes to Constance. "It would give us some extra time together."

"Yes, it sounds like great fun. I'd love to come Fannie," Constance said.

"If I feel well enough tomorrow, I'll be there," Amanda added.

"Wonderful!" Fannie said. "It's all set!"

"I'll send a wagon to take you to the review tomorrow morning." Robert leaned forward and kissed Constance on the cheek. "Now I have to return and prepare my men."

Next day, June 8, 1863: Auburn

Lucy leaned towards Constance and whispered, "Captain Farley has spent every available minute with me. I'm in heaven. I can't bear the thought of them all leaving tomorrow."

"Neither can I. We've been spoiled these past few days."

Constance fanned herself in the mid-afternoon sun. Not too many civilians had turned out for this review, but General Hood's 10,000 men had marched out to enjoy the show. Constance contemplated Robert E. Lee. No general had ever been more loved or admired than this man. His astounding victories proved he was the greatest general who had ever lived. Yet, he was human and bore the weight of the Confederacy on his shoulders. Perhaps the people should spend more time worshiping God, and quit expecting Lee to be a God, she mused. Today, she had to agree that the review was a useless waste of energy that should be expended winning their independence. The enemy must be lurking on the other side of the river.

When the review came to an end, Robert sought Constance out in the crowd and Alex managed to locate Amanda. When Amanda told Alex she was spending the night with Fannie and sending the boys home with Harriet, Alex agreed to seek permission to spend his last night with her, even if he had to rise before dawn to join his command.

Robert told Constance he would join her at Beauregard after he moved his guns north of Fleetwood Hill.

After a good dinner in Beauregard's stately dining room, Alex savored his cherry cobbler. "We're marching to fight the battle that will win our independence. A decisive victory in the North will break their will to subjugate us."

"The Copperheads' anti-war movement is definitely gaining strength," Robert agreed. "I do believe the Yankees' defeat at Chancellorsville has brought their morale to an all-time low. But enough talk of war. Fannie, thank you for a delicious dinner. For the first time in two years, I ate so much I need to walk it off. Constance, would you like to go for a stroll?"

"Yes, that's a lovely idea."

They walked arm in arm on the front lawn. "What a sight," he said "Look at all the campfires twinkling. Our men are spread out from Oak Shade to Stevensburg."

The lightning bugs twinkled in the warm breeze. "That must be almost ten miles. Is that to help you cross the river quickly in the morning?"

He studied the shimmer the moon cast on her periwinkle eyes. "Yes, then we'll reunite as we march north. Ewell's Corps is marching west to cross the mountains and then head north down the valley. We're to screen them."

"Do you know your destination?"

"I can only tell you that we're marching north." He stopped and pulled a small package from his pocket. "It appears that I will not be here for your twenty-first birthday. I wondered what to give you, with so little available in the stores. I know that only books, flowers and candy are appropriate gifts, but you have access to books, flowers don't last, and there's no candy available. Mother helped me solve the dilemma."

She took the small, beautifully wrapped package from him. "Oh, Rob, it's too beautiful to open!"

"My mother wrapped it." He slipped his arm around her tiny waist. She untied the bow and lifted the lid off the box, holding it up in the moonlight.

"Oh, it looks like a necklace." Delighted, she held up the dainty chain with a pearl on it. "It's beautiful, but I...shouldn't accept such a gift."

"It was my mother's, but she wanted you to have it. We thought you'd accept a gift from her."

She wavered. Should she accept this expensive gift from him? She looked up into adoring eyes full of hope. "My, that's so thoughtful of her. I'll write her a letter of thanks. Will you hook it for me?"

"Of course." He took the necklace and turned her around. She pulled back her long hair and his fingertips tingled when he touched the soft skin of her bare shoulders.

"Thank you," she said softly after he hooked the necklace. He leaned forward and planted a moist kiss on her shoulder. She turned towards him, then he pulled her body firmly against his. Slowly their lips moved together. She did not feel passion, but she felt warmth, affection, and great respect for him. She knew that these feelings were the seeds from which long and enduring love could grow.

Several hours later, Alex admired Amanda's alabaster skin in the shimmering light streaming through the bedroom window. "You're tantalizing in the moonlight." He leaned on his elbow and twirled a ringlet of her blonde hair. "I'm going to remember you just like this while we're marching."

"Alex, I'm so afraid. This pregnancy is not going well. I fear I may lose the baby and you at the same time."

"Don't even speak of it, darling." He nuzzled her neck. "When I return we'll have won the war and you'll present me with a daughter. That's how it's going to be."

"Do you promise?"

He pulled her over on top of him. "I promise." His last words were smothered by her lips.

Next day, June 9, 1863: North of Fleetwood Hill

4:30 a.m. "Damn! Where did they come from?" exclaimed a groggy Confederate picket at Beverly's Ford. He listened to shouts and the pounding of hundreds of horses as the Union cavalry under John Buford splashed across the ford and up the bank.

"We didn't have a hint of a force that big," said another. "Not a noise, not a flickering fire, nothing!"

Captain Bruce Gibson hastily sent a message of the attack to Major C. E. Flournoy, Sixth Virginia cavalry, camped nearby. "Fire your carbines into those shadows," he ordered his men. "We know they're out there." The crack and whiz of carbine fire broke the morning stillness. The greatly outnumbered pickets were soon forced to retreat.

Robert Beckam sat up suddenly in his tent, listening to the firing from the direction of the river, less than two miles away. Quickly pulling on his clothes, he dashed outside into the morning fog. "Wake up, men! It sounds like an enemy attack! We've got to move the guns to protection." He hastily pulled on his boots. All bedlam broke loose in the camp. Frantic half-dressed soldiers raced through the fog grabbing boots, weapons, horses, and saddles.

Major Flournoy reacted quickly. "Whoever's ready, follow me!" he ordered. "We've got to charge the enemy to slow them down while the guns are moved to safety!" No more than 150 men galloped off with him down the Beverly's Ford Road, some riding bareback.

"Limber up men," Beckam yelled. "Hart's battery will stay here to protect our retreat. Everybody else ride at once towards Saint James Church!" Beckam's men frantically harnessed the horses and moved the wagon trains and caissons. He heard Flournoy confronting the advancing Yankees, slowing them up, buying some time. General "Grumble" Jones rode by with a portion of the half-dressed Seventh Virginia Cavalry, rushing to support Flournoy.

"Wheel your two guns around," Beckam ordered Hart, "and pour canister into them." Beckam rushed his other fourteen guns and wagons towards Saint James Church where they could take up a strong defensive line. In the hurried flight, Beckam's camp desk jostled off the wagon and later was confiscated by the Federals.

Hart's guns opened up and blasted canister into the enemy, slowing their advance. The guns continued firing until they became exposed to the Yankees. The gallant artillerymen fought off their assailants and rained canister into the enemy until they had reached the safety of their other artillery at Saint James Church.

Jeb Stuart was camped on the south end of Fleetwood Hill about a mile and a half from Saint James Church. Stuart, aroused by the carbine firing, wondered what mischief the enemy was up to. The boom of Beckam's cannons quickly stirred everyone at

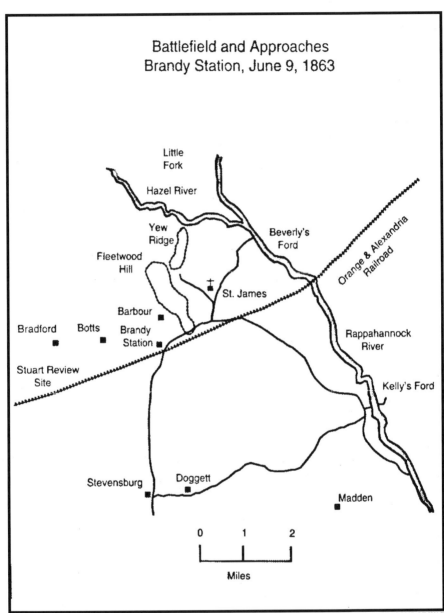

Battlefield and Approaches
Brandy Station, June 9, 1863

Little Fork

Hazel River

Yew Ridge

Fleetwood Hill

Beverly's Ford

Orange & Alexandria Railroad

St. James

Barbour

Bradford

Botts

Brandy Station

Rappahannock River

Stuart Review Site

Kelly's Ford

Stevensburg

Doggett

Madden

0   1   2

Miles

headquarters. Will Farley crawled out of his tent, walked outside and tossed his hat up into the air. "Hurrah! We're going to have a fight!"[3] Stuart smiled and strained his eyes, peering into the dense early morning fog.

The men at headquarters hastily dressed and prepared for action. A courier from Jones arrived and gave a few sketchy details of the large force moving towards them from Beverly's Ford. "Brazen Yankees," Stuart muttered. To McClellan he said, "Send a courier to Robertson at Auburn ordering him to march down the Kelly's Ford Road to confront any Federals who might be coming from that direction. Have Rooney Lee cross the Hazel and take up a position on Yew Ridge. Order Hampton to join me from Stevensburg." Then he turned to Von Borcke. "Von, ride forward and reconnoiter around Saint James Church. The rest of us will saddle up and find the fight."

Alex lifted the saddle onto Liz at Beauregard, then he heard the carbine fire coming from the direction of Beverly's Ford. He debated the situation. The Little Fork Rangers were camped on the other side of Stevensburg. It would take him a good while to reach them. If there was going to be a fight here, he felt he should volunteer his services. He rode towards Stuart's headquarters on Fleetwood, hearing Beckam's guns open up. Yes, the enemy must be attacking. He rode in the direction of the firing to join the fray.

Constance tossed in her sleep, dreaming she heard the roar of cannons. Opening her eyes, she heard it again. That was cannon fire from the other side of Fleetwood Hill. Those were Robert's guns! She jumped out of bed, threw on her robe, raced downstairs and found Amanda and Fannie looking out the front windows. "What do you make of it?" she asked.

"We can't see anything because of the fog," Amanda said wringing her hands. "Alex just left and I fear he rode towards the impending battle."

"Can the enemy be attacking here?" Fannie asked in disbelief. "Surely it's just a skirmish. Let's be calm and have some breakfast."

6 a.m. Aaron Ames sat restlessly on his horse at Kelly's Ford waiting to cross with the left wing of the Federal attack under General David Gregg. They waited for the Second Division commanded by Colonel Alfred Duffie, who had apparently lost his way. Ames heard the cannon fire in the direction of Brandy Station, indicating Buford was hotly engaged with the Rebels. Their assumption that Stuart was located at Culpeper Court House might have been incorrect. At any rate, their orders were to merge with Buford at Brandy Station. Anxious to get into the battle, Ames felt that this time they would show Stuart a thing or two. His cousin, Adelbert, led one of the infantry units under Buford, while his other cousin, Armstrong Custer, rode with the cavalry. This battle would be a family affair. Although proud to be fighting with the First Maine, The Puritans, Ames was not happy to be under the command of Judson Kilpatrick. Brash and ambitious, he had earned the sobriquet "Kil-cavalry" because of his callous disregard for the best interest of his men. Ames felt uncomfortable having his fate in the hands of such an unscrupulous man.

7 a.m. Beckam surveyed the arrangement of his guns on a slight eminence near Saint James Church. He would be able to sweep the open fields before him when the enemy attacked. He did not have to wait long. Buford's cavalry soon charged across the fields on both sides of the road. "Open up on them men!" His fire raked the lines of the enemy. Hard desperate fighting continued most of the morning while the enemy attempted to overrun their position. At one point some of the Federals managed to cut their way through to the batteries. The artillerymen fought them off hand to hand until they were forced to retreat. Beckam noticed that one of his guns, a Blakely, had only some defective rounds and solid shot left. "Take that gun up to headquarters on Fleetwood Hill," he commanded his crew. That decision would prove critical later in the battle.

8 a.m. Frustrated that his charges against the Rebels had not succeeded, Buford surveyed the situation from a high knoll. He decided to attack Rooney Lee's position on his far right on Yew Ridge, a steep slope that joins the north end of Fleetwood. Lee's men, dismounted and dispersed behind a sturdy stone wall, held a strong position. Buford watched the sharp fire of the Confederates force his charges back. Not only that, they had placed two pieces of artillery in a ravine, invisible to him, but firing high into the air and pelting his position in a clever use of indirect fire.

9 a.m. Finally the last of Gregg's cavalry splashed across Kelly's Ford hours behind schedule. Ames rode with the almost 2200 men commanded by Gregg, taking the most direct route to Brandy Station. Duffie, with 1900 men, was ordered to advance towards Culpeper Court House by way of Stevensburg, a much longer route.

Beauregard: Constance and Fannie ascended the steps from the attic to the cupola on top of Beauregard, an observation point slightly higher than Fleetwood Hill. "What a view!" Constance exclaimed. The fog burned off and the day turned bright and clear. "Look at the smoke from the cannons," she said pointing towards the hidden side of Fleetwood.

Fannie observed the smoke and a few cavalrymen in the far distance, but most of the battle remained hidden from them. "I wonder if it's safe for us to stay here," she asked in a trembling voice. "I'm afraid for the children."

"At this point, I believe we're perfectly safe. You've got a deep cellar that will protect us if necessary." Constance took in the 360-degree view. "I'll stay up here and keep an eye out. If anything new develops, I'll let you and Amanda know. She's too upset to watch this with Alex out there."

"I know. I'll try to keep her calm. She's feeling so poorly." Fannie shook her head in dismay. "James never dreamed this would happen, or that the Yankees would fight this way. Most of them don't want this war any more than we do. We never thought Lincoln would become a military dictator."

"No, it doesn't seem possible." Constance raised a window. "It's going to be stifling in here without some air." A cool breeze rumpled her hair. "We must pray for our men. I feel so useless and want to do more. Let me see those old field glasses that James left behind."

Fannie handed the glasses to Constance who scanned the horizon. "I suppose I should begin preparing for the wounded. I feel we'll be overrun." Fannie descended the stairs. Constance adjusted the glasses, bringing them into focus. In spite of the slight crack in one lens, she could see a great distance with them.

Mid-morning: "They're slowing down, men," Beckam yelled. He surveyed the mounds of dead and wounded strewn in front of his guns. "We need to preserve our ammunition." He wiped the sweat and soot from his face, attempting to catch his breath.

Alex sat on Liz, reloading his gun. He had joined Jones's troops and participated in several charges. Jeb Stuart, directing the action at Saint James Church, looked up to see a courier racing towards him.

"General Stuart, sir, about fifty-five hundred Yankees, including one brigade of infantry, have crossed at Kelly's Ford. They've split their forces and half are marching directly towards Brandy, and the others appear headed towards Stevensburg."

Stuart, already aware of the threat, realized he could be caught in a pincer action between the two wings of Federals. He had dispatched Robertson to block the Kelly's Ford Road. "Farley," he called to his most trusted scout. Farley, who had earlier been in the thick of the action, rode beside him. "At least two thousand Yankees are moving towards Stevensburg. Only the Second South Carolina and Fourth Virginia are in that area. They're greatly outnumbered but must delay the advance of the enemy. I want you to ride to Colonels Butler and Wickam and command them to do everything in their power to delay the enemy. They can't reach Brandy. It's imperative. I suggest they take a defensive position on Hansbrough's Ridge or along Mountain Run. Use your discretion to see that this order is carried out."

Farley nodded with a broad smile. "I will do it, sir. You can count on the brave men from South Carolina."

Annoyed at being unable to move his men forward to Brandy Station, Buford never expected to find the Rebels in such strength here. He had believed the main body of Stuart's troops to be in the town of Culpeper. Nevertheless, he must push forward to join up with Gregg. Unable to dislodge Rooney Lee's men from behind that stone wall, he summoned a Wisconsin infantry officer. "Captain Stevenson, we've got to drive those people out from behind that wall."

Stevenson sighed deeply. That was a tough assignment because he was outnumbered two to one. He contemplated the situation. "Perhaps I can sneak some marksmen through that wheat field on the left and create a diversion. Then the rest of the infantry might be able to carry the wall."

Buford nodded thoughtfully. "I don't order you; but if you think you can do it, go in."[4] Stevenson's gallant men succeeded, forcing Rooney Lee to pull his men back to the northwestern end of Fleetwood Hill.

Late morning: Will Farley and a few hundred South Carolinians crouched in a long sparse line hidden in the woods on Hansbrough's Ridge. Below them, they watched the lines of Union cavalry moving towards them on the open road to Culpeper. "Don't shoot until they're in close range," Farley said as he moved among the men. When they finally opened up on the surprised Yankees, the enemy moved forward slowly, assuming a much larger force to be in the woods. When they reached the point where the ridge leveled off and the road went around the end of it, a sharp battle occurred. Determined to stop the advance of the enemy, Colonel Frank Hampton led a bold charge, expecting to be supported by the Fourth Virginia. In fierce hand to hand combat, Hampton slashed at a Union soldier, knocking him off his horse. Suddenly two enemy soldiers were upon him, fighting fiercely. Trying to ward off the blow of one, he turned his head, and the other slashed him across the face and neck as a bullet struck him. He tumbled to the ground mortally wounded. The Fourth Virginia joined in the charge, but seeing the overwhelming number of the enemy, broke and fled. These were the hometown boys, including the Little Fork Rangers, but they did not earn honor on June 9th. Duffie's Yankees pushed forward towards Stevensburg.

John Barbour and his wife heard the nearby firing from their home, Clover Hill, then watched the ambulance coming up their lane. "Looks like they're bringing a wounded soldier here," he said. "I wonder who it is?" He walked out to meet the Rebels.

"It's Colonel Frank Hampton," a soldier said. "He's badly wounded and we don't expect him to live."

"Bring him into the parlor. We'll do what we can for him."[i] Barbour cringed at the disfigured face of Hampton. Soon other wounded Confederates arrived.

Noon, Beauregard: Constance took a sip of water and wiped her face with a handkerchief. The intense heat did not budge her from her position in the cupola. Somehow, she felt her presence gave moral support to Robert and Alex on Liz. What more could she do? She picked up the field glasses and scanned the horizon again. Suddenly, her eyes riveted on the road from Kelly's Ford to Brandy Station. She detected movement through the trees. Yes, there it was again. A large column of Union cavalry was approaching Brandy Station! She saw them clearly in front of her. Did General Stuart know they were coming? If the enemy took control of Fleetwood Hill, they would soon gain control of the battle by possessing the high ground. She wanted to run towards the hill to warn him. No, that was foolhardy. She couldn't get there in time on foot. "The Yankees are at Brandy," she yelled down the steps to Amanda and Fannie.

Captain Daniel Grimsley, of Jones's staff, spotted the approaching enemy and dispatched a courier to Stuart. The courier's message irritated Stuart. He had already sent Robertson to handle that situation. "Tell General Jones," he said curtly, "to attend to the Yankees in his front, and I'll watch the flanks." He held no affection for Jones. Stuart did not realize that Robertson had let the Yankee cavalry advance unmolested while watching their infantry.

When "Grumble" Jones got the message, he was livid. "So he thinks they ain't coming, does he? Well, let him alone; he'll damn soon see for himself."[5]

H. B. McClellan and only a few staff officers remained at Stuart's headquarters on Fleetwood Hill. He spied the columns of Yankees and sent two couriers in succession to warn Stuart. He realized that if the enemy took control of the hill, the victory was theirs. Somehow, he had to slow them down to give Stuart time to shift his cavalry to the critical area. Looking around, he focused on the one gun Beckam had sent back with faulty ammunition. "Get that gun into position to fire towards Brandy." Maybe if he fired it slowly, his ammunition would hold out long enough to slow down the Federals. It was his only hope.

Jeb Stuart read McClellan's message incredulously. Suddenly he heard cannon fire from the direction of his headquarters. It must be true! The Yankees were approaching from Brandy. "Order everyone to advance to Fleetwood at full speed!" he shouted. Robert Beckam instantly realized he must get his guns into position on the crest of the

---

[i] Frank Hampton died later that night at Clover Hill. His body was taken to Richmond where he lay in state.

hill one-and-a-half miles behind him. His efficiency would determine the outcome of the battle. "Limber, men! We must move the guns at once!" Jumping in, he helped harness the horses to the guns. The race was on for possession of Fleetwood Hill.

McClellan's gun halted the forward movement of the enemy while Gregg wondered how strong a force occupied the hill. He wasted valuable time pondering the situation, thus allowing McClellan's ploy to work. Gregg moved artillery into place to shell the hill. "Colonel Wyndam," he ordered. "You're to charge that hill and take it." A shout went up from the men. Aaron Ames sat restless with his reserve brigade. He had been here before and knew that the hill was the key to the battle. He watched the grand sight of his comrades charging forward over the open ground towards Fleetwood with flags waving.

Beauregard: "Oh, my God! Look at them coming," Constance exclaimed. She and Fannie saw the Yankees advancing about a half-mile in front of them. The Union artillery, which had advanced to a knoll a short distance below the crest of the hill, opened up.

"The battle is moving towards us," Fannie gasped. "We could be hit by artillery. I think we'd better go to the cellar."

"You go ahead. I'm going to stay here a while longer. I think it's safe."

The Twelfth Virginia Cavalry, winded and disorganized from their mile and a half gallop from Saint James, crested Fleetwood Hill just before the Yankees reached the top. They charged into Wyndam's men in savage hand-to-hand combat, which would be the order for the rest of the day.

Early afternoon: Will Farley had been busy gathering portions of the dispersed Fourth Virginia to come to the aid of Colonel Calbraith Butler, who had moved his men from Hansbrough's Ridge to a defensive position along Mountain Run. They intended to take a stand there to prevent Duffie's Federals from progressing along the road from Stevensburg to Brandy Station. The Yankees unlimbered their artillery on a high hill behind Stevensburg Baptist Church, which looked down on the Rebels along Mountain Run. Farley rode up to Butler to discuss their position. While they sat side by side with their horses' heads facing opposite directions, the Federal artillery got them in their sights. The first solid shot struck the ground near them, ricocheted, cut off Butler's right leg above the ankle, passed through his horse, through Farley's horse, and carried away Farley's leg at the knee.

Amongst cries of anguish, the men close by rushed to the aid of their officers. Lieutenant Rhett and Captain Chestnut wrapped Colonel Butler in a blanket. Realizing that he was not as seriously injured as Farley, Butler said, "Now that you've placed me in the hands of my men, go and take charge of Farley."

They knelt by Farley, who was in intense pain and bleeding profusely. "Colonel Butler has sent us," Rhett said. Farley controlled his anguish and attempted to smile pleasantly. Some soldiers arrived with a flat trough and gently lifted Farley onto it.

When they raised the trough, Farley said to Rhett, "Bring my leg to me." Surprised, Rhett picked up the bloody severed leg, lying close by, and handed it to Farley. The injured man hugged it to his bosom as one would a child and said, "It is an old friend, gentlemen, and I do not wish to part from it."[6]

Stunned, the two men shook hands with him. "Good-bye, Captain Farley. I hope that we will soon have the pleasure of seeing you again," Chestnut said soberly.

Suppressing his pain, Farley answered, "Good-bye, gentlemen, and forever. I know my condition…and we will not meet again. I thank you for your kindness. It's a pleasure to me that I've fallen into the hands of good Carolinians…at my last moment."[7] Smiling, he nodded his head and the men bore him away.

"Where shall we take you, sir?" one of the bearers asked.

"To Doctor Ashby's house on East Street," Farley answered with a grimace.

Watching him being born away, Rhett said in awe, "I've never seen a man whose demeanor, in the face of certain, painful, and quick death, was so superb. I've never seen anything so brave from first to last."

Butler's stand discouraged Duffie from progressing directly towards Brandy Station. Instead, he backtracked and took a more circuitous route, thus not arriving until the battle was over. Had his nearly two thousand men been employed earlier, the outcome of the battle could have been significantly different. The small band of South Carolinians had performed gallantly, but in doing so they had sacrificed two of their noblest and handsomest sons, Will Farley and Frank Hampton, to the cause they both so deeply believed in.

Mid-afternoon: Charge and counter-charge had been the order of the afternoon on Fleetwood. First one side and then the other took control of the hill. Amidst the dust, rearing horses, firing guns and clanking sabers, Beckam managed to move some of his guns into position on the crest of the hill. Constance had watched the mayhem spellbound. She could see a small group of Union cavalry near Beauregard who had been pushed down from the hill and separated from their regiment. Lieutenant Colonel Virgil Brodrick and a fragment of the First New Jersey debated their dilemma. "We've got to fight our way back through the Rebs to our division," Brodrick said.

"Sir, that means we will have cut our way through those guns unlimbering up there," a subordinate observed.

"Those who are with me, charge!" Brodrick shouted as he exploded forward. All of his men thundered down on McGregor's and Hart's unsupported batteries.

Seeing the impending charge, Beckam fired his pistol. When the Yankees roared into them, the artillerists wielded sponge staffs and pistols in a fight to the death over the guns. The artillerymen fired several times and Brodrick fell mortally wounded. "Hold them off men!" Beckam yelled. One of his gunners collapsed from a saber slash, but the attack quickly failed with only a few New Jersians making it back to their command. "Good work, men. Let's get the guns roaring," Beckam cried above the din of battle.

Late afternoon, Beauregard: Robert E. Lee and Dick Ewell dismounted, and several staff members tethered their horses to the hitching post behind Beauregard. Lee, headquartered in Culpeper, had learned of the battle early in the morning from the signal station on Pony Mountain and dispatches from Stuart. He believed it to be a reconnaissance in force but felt concern that it had raged so long. He hoped it would not be necessary to deploy Ewell's infantry posted in the woods near Auburn. He addressed Ewell. "I don't want those people over there to learn that our infantry is here."

"Absolutely, sir." Ewell limped to the back door on his artificial leg. "They will be used only as a last resort. Let's hope General Stuart can continue to hold them back."

Constance spun around in surprise when the two generals joined her in the cupola. "General Lee!"

"Miss Armstrong, I understand you've been keeping a vigilant watch up here," Lee said pleasantly. "Do you know General Ewell?"

"No, it's a pleasure General Ewell," she stammered. The bald-headed man nodded to her. "I'm shocked by the magnitude of what I've witnessed."

Lee scanned Fleetwood with his field glasses. "Give us a brief summary, Miss Armstrong."

Her voice rose an octave in excitement while she explained to Lee all that she had witnessed, concluding, "The fighting has been a furious jumble of man to man combat, and charge and countercharge. Those guns were taken by us, and then lost again. I believe most of their artillerymen have been killed."

"I'm impressed with the valor on both sides," Lee said, watching the action.

"Sir, our location here may be dangerous," Ewell warned. "The enemy could easily charge this house and take us prisoner."

"But, they don't know we're here," Lee replied calmly.

With the Rebels temporarily in control of Fleetwood Hill, Judson Kilpatrick moved his brigade north from Brandy in order to assault Fleetwood from the opposite side used by Wyndham. If he could take the heights he would reap popular acclaim and fame. His regiments, the Second and Tenth New York and First Maine, formed en echelon facing west towards Fleetwood. Ames was glad they were finally moving towards the fray.

"Drive the Rebels from the hill and hold it!" Kilpatrick commanded the Tenth New York. With a cheer they surged due west toward the southern end of Fleetwood.

"See that house up there?" Kilpatrick said to Colonel Davies of the Second New York. They both looked at the two-story house called Fleetwood where Stuart had his headquarters. "I want you to charge and take it!"

Ames and the First Maine watched the two regiments quickly run into a line of Georgians and South Carolinians charging down the hill to meet them, firing in splendid order. Instantly, the lines became mixed up and confused in the mayhem. Repulsed, the Tenth New York only skirted the base of Fleetwood and then turned sharply to the left to scurry back towards the railroad tracks and safety. The Second New York did not last much longer before fleeing. "Cowards!" Kilpatrick shouted furiously, shaking his fists. "They floated away like feathers in the wind!"

Kilpatrick's visions of glory began to dim. He turned to his last resort, the First Maine, and trotted towards them. "Colonel Douty, what can you do with your regiment?"

"I can drive the Rebels to Hell, sir!" was his confident reply.

Kilpatrick addressed the men, "Men of Maine, you must save the day!" A rousing cheer went up. Ames surveyed the retreating Federals and screaming Rebels before him. Artillery missiles whistled over head while riderless horses reared and galloped frantically. Ames drew his saber and leaned forward in his saddle and the First Maine exploded forward.

They quickly traversed the open ground and shot up the hill to the shock of the Rebels. Alex saw them coming and joined the disarrayed Sixth Virginia who tried to halt the brunt of the attack. The Federals opened fire, forcing the Virginians to fall back.

Ames galloped up to the Fleetwood house and veered to the right with half of his comrades. A bullet whizzed by Alex, who fled for his life. The First Maine had control of Stuart's headquarters, but lunged forward in the excitement of their success. Ames dashed towards a battery, striking at an artillerist who wielded his sponge staff at him. He heard a bullet thud into the man behind him. Douty became separated from his men during hand-to-hand combat at the battery. In the confusion and dust, the men from Maine continued forward, now racing down the opposite side of Fleetwood towards Beauregard.

Beauregard: "They're charging towards us!" Ewell cried. "I believe we should hasten downstairs and be prepared to shoot our way out if necessary."

Lee also recognized the danger. "Perhaps that would be prudent." He walked towards the steps. "Miss Armstrong, are you coming?"

"Let me stay and keep watch for you, sir." She dropped to her knees so as not to be visible. "I'll call to you if they're close to the house."

"I appreciate you valor, but don't risk your life," Lee called back up the steps.

Constance breathlessly watched the Rebels pursue the line of blue coats in fierce hand to hand combat, constantly moving closer to the house. She froze the binoculars on a chestnut horse and gray rider lunging forward. Was it Liz? Yes! She spotted the unusual white markings on her right flank, then the artillery boomed away into the writhing mass. Suddenly, Liz tumbled down, throwing Alex to the ground. "Oh, no! Liz!" Tears welled in her eyes.

Stunned, Alex tried to get his breath. Slowly, he pulled himself up on his knees and searched for his hat. Suddenly, he heard a horse thundering towards him from behind. Aaron Ames leaned forward on his black stallion with his saber raised high in his right hand. If that dismounted Reb did not throw up his hands in surrender, he'd have to kill him. Alex reached for his pistol and spun around to face his assailant. He fired only to discover that the gun was empty. Ames leaned forward, swinging his saber towards his victim. In that split second that their eyes met, there was recognition. Ames abruptly pulled his saber up to avoid striking Alex, who ducked. Alex watched Ames ride away, unable to believe his good fortune. His hands shaking, he looked around him for a way out. He spotted a riderless horse about twenty yards away and made a dash for it. Dirt spewed around him but he grasped the horse's reins, and threw himself into the saddle.

Constance gripped the wall in fear, having witnessed the whole drama. "Thank God, Alex escaped!" she mumbled to herself. It looked like that Yankee on the black stallion had deliberately spared him. Why? She watched the Yankees pull back and begin to disperse. A group of about fifty of them rode towards the house. When they came closer, she scrutinized the tall soldier on the black stallion. She tried to focus on his face, but could not see it under his hat. Then he took off his hat to wipe his brow. She recognized the familiar curly brown hair and ruggedly handsome face. Yes! It was Aaron Ames! Her heart raced at the sight of him. The artillery opened up on the Yankees, and shells plowed into the front yard. She heard one crash into the porch and decided to dash to the cellar.

Ames addressed the others. "I think we'll have to circle around by Auburn to get out of range of their artillery. Let's stay close together so our prisoners can't escape." Little did he know that the most coveted prisoners of all, Lee and Ewell, were in the house in front of them for the taking.

"That's right, we've got to get back with this stand of colors," another soldier bragged, waving a captured flag.

"What do you want to bet that Kilpatrick's going to try to appropriate that flag?" Ames asked, then a shell hit near them.

Galloping forward, the soldier answered, "If Kilpatrick wants one bad enough, he'd better go out and get it himself." They soon raced to safety.

Constance dashed down the three flights of steps to the cellar and saw the Union soldiers galloping away. She flinched when a window shattered. Then it sounded like a shell crashed into the house.[ii] Lee and Ewell had escaped capture, but they were all in danger from their own artillery.

Beckam galloped up to the guns firing towards Beauregard. "Hold your fire! There are civilians in that house!" He had been at the other end of the line, and was frantic with worry about Constance and Fannie when he saw where the shells were crashing.

"Enemy soldiers were there, sir," a gunner replied.

"They're out of range now," Beckam answered shortly. His head pounded from the noise of the guns. He had eaten no food and had drunk little water in more than twelve hours. Many of his men had passed out from exhaustion, and he found it difficult to function. He struggled to remain alert. With the guns finally positioned to control all approaches to the hill, the Rebels had firm possession of it now. He hoped the battle would soon wind down because all he wanted to do was collapse and sleep.

5:30 p.m. Ames saw the sunlight reflecting off of bayonets in the woods when they passed near Auburn. The Rebels must have infantry in those woods. He hurried back to Brandy to report that information. Ames knew they would probably withdraw now. They had not been able to hold the hill, but had for the first time fought the Confederate cavalry as equals. This huge battle had instilled confidence. Both sides would probably claim victory, but the Rebs would never be able to replace their losses while the Union would.

Beauregard: Lee, back in the cupola, scanned the north end of Fleetwood Hill, where he saw smoke. "Sounds like we're mounting a charge."

"Our artillery has secured this end of the hill," Ewell responded. "Now it appears Stuart's trying to force them back on the north end." Indeed, Rooney Lee was mounting a gallant charge against Buford, which would inspire the Federals to retreat across the Rappahannock. In that fighting, Rooney would be seriously wounded in the thigh.

Turning to Ewell, Lee continued, "It appears Stuart has this situation under control. You may march your men back to camp and prepare to move towards Winchester in the morning."

After the two generals departed and the battle ceased, Constance, Amanda, and Fannie stared out the front windows at the field strewn with dead and wounded soldiers and horses. "I think it's safe to go out there now," Constance said. "I've got to get to poor Liz...and Robert."

"That hideous scene is too terrible for you to see. Please don't go," Amanda begged.

[ii] When Beauregard was remodeled in 1950, an unexploded mortar shell was found in its walls.

"But I have to," Constance insisted with staunch determination. "Liz needs me and so do those poor men. At least I can get water to them."

"You're braver than I am. They'll bring the wounded here soon," Fannie said.

Constance dashed down the front steps and raced down the hill towards the small stream. She held her handkerchief to her nose to ward of the stench and swarming flies. Trying not to look at the maimed soldiers around her, she wanted to get to Liz first. She lifted her skirt to cross the small stream where horses and men lapped up the water. The men stared at her in disbelief and several called out. Sweating and breathing heavily, she climbed up the edge of Fleetwood stepping over bodies and horses.

"Liz!" she cried when she spotted her beloved horse. Skirting around a dead soldier, she knelt beside the horse's head. Liz looked up at her with big brown eyes. "Oh, my baby, my poor baby," she moaned as tears rolled down her cheeks. She laid her head against the horse's nose and stroked her softly. Liz pawed the ground with her front hoof and whinnied weakly. "I know you recognize me, baby." Constance stroked her neck softly. "You know I love you. I never wanted this to happen to you, baby." She reluctantly looked at the bloody stump of what had been the horse's hind leg. Liz could never recover and had to be suffering. "I won't let you suffer any more," she whispered in the horse's ear. She kissed her on the nose, and, after weeping for a few minutes, regained her strength. Constance pushed herself to her feet and wiped her tear stained face. She staggered over to a dead soldier, removed his pistol, and with a trembling hand, pointed the gun at Liz's head. "I'm sorry, Liz, but I can't let you suffer." She pulled the trigger twice. Liz lay still and at peace. Shaking all over, Constance lowered the gun to her side.

"Please, lady, shoot me," a wounded soldier moaned behind her. She pivoted around to see a Union soldier whose ruptured intestines were spread on the ground beside him. She flung her hand to her mouth to keep from gagging. "Please," he begged. "Put me out of my misery." Overwhelmed with pity for him, she did not think she could do it. But, surely he deserved the same compassion as Liz. She took a deep breath, edged towards him and pointed the gun at his head. Praying for strength, she pulled the trigger.

"Oh, God!" Her trembling hand dropped the gun. "Forgive me." Shaking all over, she dissolved into hysterical sobs. Through her blinding tears, she glanced at the crest of the hill towards the artillery. She had to find Robert. In a trance, she walked upwards. Men called out to her, but she did not hear. When she reached the guns, she saw most of the men sprawled out on the ground. Were they all dead? Was Robert dead or wounded? She threaded her way slowly down the line of guns in the fading light, examining the blackened faces of the men. Then she saw him, lying on his back, his eyes closed, and his arms stretched out above his head. She scrambled over to him, and knelt beside him as panic welled in her throat. His clothes were filthy and soaked with sweat, but no blood was visible. Had he been hit in the back of the head like John?

"Robert," she said softly. There was no response. She laid her head on his chest and wept aloud. "Please God, no," she whimpered, her voice trembling. Robert slowly awakened from his stupor of exhaustion, his head spinning. He tried to focus on her. Was he dreaming or was that Constance?

"Connie?" he said, reaching his hand towards her.

She raised her bloodshot eyes towards him, and the lines of pain on her face relaxed in relief. "Oh, Robert! I thought you were dead!" She threw her arms around his neck, collapsing on top of him. "I had to find you!"

His head still pounding, he slid his arms around her. "How did you get here?"

She raised her head up, then turned wide concerned eyes towards him. "I wanted to help you." She lowered her lips gently against his.

"Um," he sighed. "This is the way to end a battle. Here help an exhausted soldier sit up." She pulled him forward until he sat facing her. Flies buzzed around them and the stench of already decaying carcasses came with the breeze. "I'm filthy, and I hate to touch you. This is no place for a lady."

"I don't mind that you're dirty. Please, hold me," she begged with tears in her eyes.

He pulled her against him and rocked her like a child. "Oh, Connie. You never cease to amaze me." He kissed her on the cheek while his hands caressed her hair. "Now tell me, did you walk here from Beauregard?"

"I watched the whole battle from the cupola," she answered clinging to him. "I saw Liz get shot. Alex was dismounted but grabbed another horse. I had to get to Liz. When I found her, one of her hind legs was gone. I shot her to put her out of her misery." She trembled. "Then…then a Union soldier who was disemboweled begged me to shoot him." She could not go on.

He pulled her tighter against him. "And did you?" She nodded yes.

He lifted her face towards him and kissed her gently. "You're strong."

"Oh no, no I'm not! I'm so weak! I never comprehended…how horrendous battle really was…until today. I can't fathom what you've endured since dawn. It's you who's strong and brave—you have my greatest admiration."

He absorbed the sincerity of her voice. "You've witnessed the greatest cavalry battle of this war.[iii] I've never seen anything like it. It was almost all fought on horseback as in days of old." He looked up at several horsemen riding towards them. "Oh, no, here comes General Stuart!" He sprung to his feet and pulled her up.

Stuart, still full of energy, looked shocked to see her. "Miss Armstrong, what in God's name are you doing here?"

"I…um…I came to help the wounded."

"Are you wounded, Major Beckam?" Stuart asked concerned.

"No, sir," Beckam replied, his face glowing underneath the soot.

"Well, thank God for that." Stuart leaned forward and extended his right hand. "I want to commend you on the excellent way you deployed your guns today."

"Thank you, sir." Beckam smiled and shook hands.

"I attempted to re-establish my headquarters at the Fleetwood House. Unfortunately, the ground is so bloodstained and covered with dead men and horses that it is uninhabitable. The bluebottle flies are swarming in multitudes and the stench is overwhelming. I'm moving my headquarters to the yard at Afton. See to your wounded tonight and report to me there in the morning."

"Yes, sir."

[iii] The Battle of Brandy Station was the largest cavalry battle ever fought in North America. Of the 20,000 troops engaged, 17,000 were cavalrymen - 11,000 Union, 9,000 Confederate. Casualties: 868 Union, 515 Confederate.

Stuart jerked the reins of his horse and started away. "I appreciate your courage, Miss Armstrong, but I don't believe this place is fit for a lady."

"Do you want me to take you back to Beauregard?" Robert asked.

"No, I'm under control now. You have too much to do. I'm going back and get water to those poor men out on the hillside."

He smiled in admiration and kissed her. "Thanks for coming to check on me. I'll see you as soon as possible."

11:30 P.M. Wounded soldiers covered the porch and yard of Beauregard. Constance imagined that the scene must be the same at every house in the area. A surgeon performed amputations in the yard; the bloodcurdling scream of a victim sent her head spinning wildly. Feeling faint, she dashed over to the bushes and threw up. She heaved over and over, then gasped to regain her poise. If these men could endure such suffering, the least she could do was help them. She staggered back to the porch, grabbed a jug of water, rinsed out her mouth, spit into the bushes, and knelt to give a soldier water.

"Thank you, kind lady," he mumbled. A gentle breeze cooled the night, but on it came the stench of death and swarming, relentless flies. She turned to see a familiar soldier dismount and walk up the front steps.

"Alex! Thank God you've survived."

He rushed towards the familiar voice and her open arms gave him a quick welcoming hug. "Connie, it was the hardest fight of the war. I'm sorry, but I lost Liz."

"I know," she answered, her voice fading. "I watched the whole thing from the cupola. Tell me, was that Aaron Ames who spared your life?"

"Yes! He seemed to recognize me at the last instant. It's because of your compassion for him that I'm still alive. Thank you," he responded with unusual humility.

"God blesses us in strange ways. Amanda is upstairs in bed. She's feeling poorly and the strain of today was too much for her. You need to go to her."

"How I regret that she had to be exposed to all of this mayhem. I'm exhausted and have to get some sleep. I'll take her home in the morning, when I report back to the Rangers."

Three days later, June 12, 1863: Beauregard

Constance and Fannie watched the last wounded soldiers being loaded on the ambulances to be taken to the field hospital or to the railroad for transportation to Lynchburg. The last four days had been a blur for the two of them. Day and night they had tended the wounded, swatted flies, and watched the buzzards circle overhead and devour the hundreds of horse carcasses around Fleetwood. Burying parties had worked continuously digging graves and covering the dead Union soldiers where they fell; eventually the horse carcasses were burned. Most of the Confederate dead had been taken to the local cemetery and buried in a mass grave. Fannie stared at her bloodstained porch and the gaping holes in the roof. Her servants had attempted to cover the broken and cracked windows with boards and blankets. Despite the damage, the house remained basically sound.

"I feel like I could sleep for days." Constance rubbed the small of her back. "Will the air ever smell good again?"

"I hope it will and that this nightmare will end," Fannie answered. "I hate that my children have had to live through this. I don't think they'll ever stop having nightmares."

Constance turned towards the wagon rattling towards them. "Here comes Robert. Can't I convince you to come to town with me? You really need to get away for a few days."

"I must attempt to get things back to normal here first. Then perhaps I'll come spend several days with you and at Clover Hill." She turned and hugged Constance. "Thank you for staying with me and helping with the wounded. Your stamina gave me strength."

Robert embraced both of them. "I've come to take you away from all this. Both of you have served nobly."

"I'm ready to depart." Constance hurried down the steps. "Fannie refuses to go."

Robert kissed Fannie good-bye and helped Constance onto the wagon, loading her bag. "You look exhausted." The wagon creaked forward. "Personally, I'm delighted to finally get a few hours away from camp."

"I can't wait to sleep in my own bed again and to smell clean air." She leaned against him. "Now that it's all over, what's your assessment of this monstrous battle?"

Robert looked at her thoughtfully. He admitted that they were taken completely by surprise. Stuart had his men positioned to march, not fight. Now he had the awesome job of seeking replacements for the horses lost to the artillery and wondered if that was possible with so few horses left in the South. In addition, his desk had fallen off a wagon when they rushed in flight. After the battle he went back and combed the area to no avail. It upset him greatly as his marching orders were in it and now the enemy knew Lee's intentions. He had reported the matter to Stuart.

Constance looped her arm through his and told him he could not berate himself for an accident. Nobody fought harder in that battle than he did. He smiled at her appreciatively and then broke some other bad news—Rooney Lee had been seriously wounded and Will Farley was dead. She listened intently as he related the details of Farley's death. The story had circulated among the entire cavalry.

"Farley died as bravely as he lived. His spirit will abide with us," Robert concluded.

"You say they took him to the Ashbys'? I can only imagine what Lucy's been through. I'll visit her in the morning."

Next day, June 13, 1863: East Street

Constance threaded her way through the crowds of soldiers on East Street in the hot humid morning sun. From a distance, she saw General Lee dismount and stride up the brick sidewalk to the Hills' house. Recognizing her, he tipped his hat. She could see the lines in his face when she waved back. He was a concerned father visiting his wounded son, who had been brought there. For a few minutes the responsibilities of his upcoming campaign would have to be pushed aside.

She fanned herself, then knocked on the Ashby's door. Granny opened the door and squinted up at her. "Oh, Constance, I'm glad you're here at last. Poor Lucy needs you. She's suffering terribly."

"I know." Constance entered the dark hall. "I've been at Beauregard since the battle, helping with the wounded."

"Old Jeb Stuart got caught napping," Granny sneered. "Serves him right for spending his time prancing in front of the ladies. But the South and his poor soldiers had to pay the price. That Will Farley was a brave one."

"There's no doubt about that. Where's Lucy?"

"Upstairs in her room, staring at the walls. See if you can get her outside."

"Lucy, it's Constance." She knocked on the door. When the door creaked open, she stared into the bloodshot melancholy brown eyes of her friend. "Oh, Lucy." She put her arms around her and held her tight. "My heart breaks for you."

"He's gone, Constance. I loved him with all my heart and soul, and now he…he's gone." Lucy wept softly.

"If there's anyone who understands your loss, it's me." Constance stroked Lucy's hair as her eyes grew moist. "You feel empty inside, a hollow shell." Lucy nodded and sniffled. "Come, sit on the bed and tell me about it. It'll help you."

The two of them climbed onto her high poster bed, then Lucy took her handkerchief and wiped her nose. "A soldier came to the door and told us Will was outside in the ambulance, and that his leg had been shot off. I became hysterical, but Jane and Blanche had sense enough to drag a mattress downstairs and place it in front of the fireplace for him. When they brought him in, he was clutching his severed leg to his chest." Her voice broke. "I sat on the floor and cradled his head in my lap." Constance took Lucy's hand and squeezed it. "He looked at the two soldiers and said clearly, 'To your post, men! To your post!' Obviously in intense pain and weak from loss of blood, he told me he was proud to die for the independence of the South, and not to cry for him. He reiterated his desire to be buried at home. He only remained lucid for a few minutes. I caressed his head, wiped his face, and told him how much I loved him. He had slipped into unconsciousness and did not speak again. I could feel his life seeping away and there was nothing," she sobbed, "nothing I could do."

Constance put her comforting arm around her. "Believe me, I know what a helpless feeling it is. How long did he linger?"

Lucy tried to regain her aplomb. "Less than an hour. He was gone by sunset. We had no way to notify General Stuart, and it sounded as if the battle was still raging. Jane and Blanche walked to General Lee's headquarters, but he was not there."

"Yes, I know," Constance said rubbing her back. "He was at Beauregard with me. So what did you do?"

"They could only find a staff officer, who said it would be impossible to get Will to South Carolina. Jane begged him to notify General Stuart to no avail. He did agree to provide a coffin in the morning and send some soldiers to bury him."

"It's wrong that they couldn't give him the honor of being buried at home, as bravely as he has served our army," Constance said indignantly. "Did you bury him?"

"Yes. I sat with him all night. When they brought the pine box, we laid him in it and placed his leg beside him. I wrapped him in his new coat as he had requested. We took him to the cemetery. I was determined that he would not be lost amongst the others in a mass grave, so we buried him beside father in our family plot."

"I'm glad that you did that. I want to go to his grave. Will you walk out there with me? We can take some flowers."

"I'd like that." Lucy stood and blew her nose. "I've been there every day."

The two young women knelt by the fresh mound of dirt and Lucy laid a bunch of roses on the grave by the wooden marker. "Granny read the scriptures. I'm determined to put a permanent headstone here as soon as possible.[iv] He must not be forgotten."

"Can you afford that since your father's death?"

"Father was wise enough to convert our money to gold. We will be able to support ourselves for a year or two. I'll put the tombstone up even if I have to starve."

"I hope that one day I'll be able to put up a monument in honor of John," Constance said longingly. "He died in Culpeper, and I'm determined to honor him. But heaven knows if I'll ever be able to afford it." She contemplated the clumps of red dirt, as visions of the hideous bloodstained battlefield flashed before her eyes. "After watching that battle, I'm convinced of the insanity of this cruel war. It is totally unjustifiable. The money spent to wage it could have bought the freedom of every slave. This useless bloodbath never should have happened."

Three days later, June 15, 1863: Near Gourdvine Baptist Church

Longstreet's Corps wound its way in the stifling heat along the narrow dirt road towards Winchester. Old men, women, and children lined the road waving and cheering their army. With these soldiers went the hopes and dreams of their new nation. Robert E. Lee doffed his hat to the spectators at Gourdvine Baptist Church.

These good people expected so much from him, but he knew his weaknesses. His army was in high spirits despite the fact that many of the soldiers marched barefoot. No army had fought more fiercely for their homes and their independence. He was beginning to believe they were invincible.

Ewell had taken Winchester yesterday, and Hill would be following close behind Longstreet from Fredericksburg. Lee realized his resources were diminishing and thus he decided to make this bold move to subdue the North's fervor for war. The Yankees were a divided people and a victory in the North would weaken their resolve to keep fighting. Unfortunately, he went without his right arm—Jackson. The two of them had planned and discussed a northern invasion throughout the winter. Ewell and Hill, both capable generals, had never had to make strategic decisions before. Jackson's secretiveness had taken that responsibility away from them. Lee prayed they would perform well, but knew there would never be another Jackson. God's will be done.

Next day, June 16, 1863: Afton

Myrta Grey ran to the fence at Afton when she saw the Confederate cavalry departing. Climbing up on the fence, she waved to General Stuart, who stopped to shake her hand. She unclasped the dainty chain holding a Catholic medal from around her neck. Her eyes brimming with tears, she placed it in his gloved hand. "It's been blessed by my confessor. It will bring you back safe. Take care of my Dan."

Touched by her gesture, Stuart said with merriment in his eyes, "We're off to whip the Yankees!"

Still smarting from the scathing criticism of him dominating the southern papers,

---

[iv] Will Farley's grave is easily seen at Fairview Cemetery on Sperryville Pike. It is located at gate 4, a short distance in on the left side of the drive.

Stuart needed that boost. He had been surprised at Brandy Station, they claimed. Some even went so far as to insinuate that he had been defeated. What poppycock! They suggested that the ladies had turned his head and he had grown careless. And who could believe the ridiculous ruckus raised about John Minor Botts' corn? Weren't his men allowed to have any diversion or fun? Yes, it was true that the unfortunate battle had delayed his march over a week and given indications of Lee's plans. But he was on the march now to screen Lee's infantry, moving north on the west side of the mountains.

Shaken by the loss of Farley, his best scout, Stuart knew Farley's talents would be sorely missed. But Stringfellow was to meet him at Salem (now Marshall) with a plan to cross the Potomac. Mosby also scouted for a safe route. His cavalry would be the eyes and ears for Lee's army as it moved into enemy territory. Stuart remained ignorant of how thickly the Union cavalry swarmed north of him. For the first time, he would fail his assignment. His scouting arm was weaker than he realized.

Eight days later, June 24, 1863: Near New Baltimore

Bonetired, Frank Stringfellow pushed his horse forward towards New Baltimore. He had missed Stuart at Salem, because Stuart had left the day before he arrived. Stringfellow had run into unbelievable difficulties, forcing his tardy arrival. Federals thronged throughout the area. First he had almost been captured at the home of some friends, but the loyalty of their Negro servant saved his hide. She had instructed him to lie on a beam in the attic. When the Yankees came up to search, she craftily stood in front of the candle casting a shadow on his hiding place. But the damn Yanks had taken his horse. Not to be deterred, he set off on foot and soon bushwhacked a lone Yankee in the road. The soldier had begged for mercy when the scout left him tied up in the night. Stringfellow called back that he had shown as much mercy as the Yank had shown to the two confiscated southern chickens cackling in his saddlebag. It served the chicken thief right!

For days Stringfellow had probed the fords along the Potomac to find all well fortified. Finally, after talking to local sympathizers, he heard of a little used ford known as Rowser's Ford. Upon inspection, he determined it to be the safest place for Stuart to cross his cavalry. He had ridden hard for thirty miles to get this vital information to Stuart. Stringfellow gazed into the early morning mist, wondering why Stuart had gone south and east from Salem. Was he giving up his intention to cross the Potomac? Unaware of the great battle that had transpired at Brandy Station, Stringfellow reasoned that Stuart was attempting to outmaneuver the enemy and would then make a dash for the river. Even though he had gone without sleep for twenty-four hours, he had to find Stuart immediately to tell him about Rowser's Ford.

An enemy cavalry patrol dashed around the bend of the road in front of Stringfellow. He spun around in his saddle to see another detachment behind him fan out to cut off his escape. He must find a way to escape. Stuart depended on him. The woods in the distance offered his only chance. He whirled his horse around and dug his spurs deep into its side. The horse sprang forward and cleared the ditch alongside the road. The scout raced towards the safety of the woods when a carbine volley cracked behind him. His mount stumbled to its knees and Stringfellow sailed helplessly over his horse's head. He struck the ground with a heavy thud. The early morning sky disintegrated in a sudden, red-tinted flash.[8]

13

The Beginning of the End

July 2, 1863 - September 10, 1863

Three cheers for the homespun dress the Southern ladies wear,
Now Northern goods are out of date, and since old Abe's blockade,
We Southern girls can be content with goods that's Southern made.
The Homespun Dress, a popular song

Eight days later, July 2, 1863: Coleman Street

When the driver removed the canvas cover from the wagon, Constance stared with delight at the shipment of books. "Oh, this is wonderful. Did you have difficulty getting through the lines?"

"It was a little tricky, but most of the army has gone north chasing Lee. That made things a lot easier for me. I brought you fifty copies of *Les Miserables* as you requested, many Baltimore papers, stationery, books, and two bolts of cloth, one black and one natural."

Constance walked around the wagon picking up books and looking at titles, wondering if she was dreaming. She thanked the driver, explaining that these would help keep food on the table. Sympathetic to her plight, he said he was shocked at the destruction he had witnessed. The people of Baltimore longed to be free again. She pointed to the door of the bookstore showing him where to unload.

Constance felt the sweat trickle between her breasts while Hudson and Billy placed stacks of books on the cluttered wooden floor. An attractive, dark-haired young lady entered the store, surprised at the mess. "Sorry, we've just received a shipment of books. I'm Constance Armstrong. May I help you?"

"Yes, I'm Mary Minor Botts. I understand you have the best selection of books in town, and I'm desperate for something new to read. When I read I can forget the ever-present war. Do you mind if I look around?"

"No, please help yourself." Constance was unsure how to react to this Unionist. Mary Minor Botts browsed and asked many probing questions about the books. She and Constance soon engaged in an intellectual conversation and discovered they had much in common. Constance found herself liking the petite young woman, despite her father's political leanings.

Mary placed three books on her desk. "I'll take these. I want to tell you how much I've enjoyed our visit. Few people will have much to do with us, because we're Unionist."

"We all have a right to our opinions, Miss Botts."

"I grow terribly lonely at times. My father isn't against Virginians, but he doesn't approve of the government in Richmond. He feels this is a rich man's war being waged by the poor."

311

Constance looked at her thoughtfully while she took her money. "It's unfortunate that we must choose sides. I hope you'll return soon. Books are our refuge now."

Shortly, Dolly Hill rushed into the bookstore and Constance embraced her. "Dolly, it's wonderful to have you back. We're all exploding with pride over Powell's achievements. I saw him briefly when his corps passed through town."

"Thank you, Constance. He's been overwhelmed with an awesome task. I saw little of him those last few weeks before he left. I just heard that a message came in over the telegraph announcing fighting near a little town called Gettysburg, in Pennsylvania!" Her voice held a rasp of excitement.

"Then it's begun!" Constance's eyes widened. "Do you know any details?"

"No, only that there was fighting yesterday and today. It appears that neither side has prevailed."

"We should gather for prayer tonight."

"I agree." Dolly's voice rose. "I arrived yesterday and Mildred told me of Amanda's miscarriage. How is she?"

Constance shook her head. "She's weak and extremely depressed. She can't seem to get her strength back. She's so fond of you. Perhaps you can cheer her up, but don't tell her about the fighting yet. I'm afraid that will set her back."

Dolly climbed the steps, tapped softly on the bedroom door, and then entered the darkened room. "Amanda." She leaned over the bed. "It's Dolly."

Amanda rolled over to look at her friend with eyes haunted by an inner pain and a face devoid of color. "Dolly," she whispered hoarsely. "Thank you for coming."

Dolly kissed her on the cheek and took her hand, caressing it. "My heart grieves for you. We both lost beloved children, but you've also lost another baby and your father. I know how heavy your burden is."

Amanda gripped her hand. "It's overwhelming me. I feel as if I'm spiraling downward... downward...and nothing can save me. The gloomy fog will not lift from my soul...I have no energy, no desire to eat."

Dolly perched on the edge of the bed beside her. "I understand. Your depression is natural, but you have to pull yourself out of it. Your boys need you."

"I'm drained from the stress and strain. Each morning I awaken in fear that Alex has been killed or maimed. I can...bear it no longer," Amanda sighed in a broken whisper as tears welled in her eyes.

Dolly caressed Amanda's back. "Every wife in the Confederacy lives with that fear. You're not alone. Together we must find the strength to endure."

"You're right, Dolly. I've got to stop feeling sorry for myself." Amanda wiped a tear with her sleeve. "I'm so proud of Powell. Please, tell me all about your winter in Fredericksburg."

"Oh, there's much to tell. I joined Powell after the battle of Fredericksburg. He was distracted during the battle at the shock of Netty's death and didn't perform as well as usual. I found a small house near his headquarters, and we were able to be together, to mourn together. Russie cheered us up. She grows more vivacious each day. We've been so fortunate to be able to be together. That's the privilege of rank."

"Yes, you're blessed, but with rank comes responsibility."

"We know that too well. During the battle of Chancellorsville, Russie and I stayed at Powell's uncle Henry Hill's plantation in Chesterfield. When I returned I found Powell wounded in the leg, but fortunately he healed quickly." Dolly paused thoughtfully. "Powell continued to feud with Jackson, yet when Jackson was wounded he went to his aid and cradled his head in his lap. It was when he attempted to carry Jackson from the field that he was wounded. It's strange, but just before Jackson died, he called for Powell to bring his troops up, and then he said, 'Let us cross over the river, and sit in the shade of the trees.'"

"Powell's been given a big responsibility with little time to prepare before this northern campaign. I hope they treat the civilians as cruelly as their army has treated us. They need to have the war in their backyards for a change." Amanda's voice betrayed her bitterness. "Now tell me of your famous brother, the Rebel Raider."

Dolly stood up and paced before the window. "He's off on another daring raid, but this time he's gone into Ohio. There's much Copperhead support there, and I believe he hopes they'll rise up and join him. It's a dangerous mission, and four of my brothers are with him. Poor Tom was killed in August. I don't know how Mother stands the strain."

"We admire his intrepid service." Amanda looked at her friend's rounding silhouette. "When's your baby due?"

"Late October." Dolly smiled, then took Amanda's hand again. "You must hurry and get better. We need to sing again together."

"I'll try. You've lifted my spirits," Amanda said with a forced smile.

Eight days later, July 10, 1863: Armstrongs' parlor

"*Deo Vindice—defended by God* is the motto of our new nation, and yet Lee is retreating from Pennsylvania and Vicksburg has fallen. How can that be?" Mildred Hill asked the stunned ladies assembled in the Armstrongs' parlor. "Are not God and justice on our side?"

"This is the punishment God has sent upon us for our boastfulness," Granny muttered with tears in her eyes. "He took Jackson away from us and without him we cannot win."

Dolly Hill paced the floor restlessly. "This is a terrible setback, but we must not be so pessimistic. It would be an unusual war if we had only successes. I'm far from being discouraged."

"The Lord loveth whom he chasteneth," commented Harriet. "My faith is strong. I feel that we must and will succeed finally with the help of God."[1]

"We will separate ourselves from the corruptions of the North and their worship of Mammon," said Mildred Hill. "Never for one moment since the struggle commenced, has my mind wavered as to the final result."[2]

"But, we must be realistic," Constance added. "Lee has lost almost a third of his army. Those men can't be replaced and we don't know yet who's survived. Will the army return here?"

"I can't accept the possibility that Lee was defeated," Lucy said. "However, he didn't win a decisive victory. This is his favorite camping ground. I suspect he'll return here."

"His army has been greatly weakened. Meade will be close behind him. We must brace ourselves for the worst," Constance said with her face drawn. "Culpeper could be occupied by the Yankees again."

"Oh, heaven forbid!" said Harriet. "I don't want to think about it."

"You'd be foolish to ignore it!" Granny squeaked. "Better hide all your valuables and be ready to run to the cellar of the rectory if those damn Yankees shell the town."

"Please don't speak of such things," begged Harriet. "You're getting carried away."

"But we must be prepared, Mother," Constance retorted, clipping her words. Her mind consumed with uneasiness, she worried about the Yankees stealing the bell from Saint Stephen's to melt it down for bullets. Somehow she must make these women face reality and prepare for the worst. "I suggest that we meet frequently to strengthen each other. We can read aloud while we spin and make cloth. Escaping into the adventures of books will help us cope."

"That's a wonderful idea!" Lucy said. "It'll encourage us all."

"I agree," Mildred said. "But now we must brace ourselves for the list of killed and missing."

"For the first time our men will be returning as the vanquished rather that the victors," Dolly said, her jaw set in determination. "We must do everything in our power to restore their spirits."

Next day, July 11, 1863: The cellar, Armstrong town home

Hudson sat on the dirt floor of the shallow root cellar and chiseled away at the soft mortar around two big stones with Billy watching mystified. "I've almost got them loose, Aunt Connie," he called to Constance, waiting outside the small door.

"If you can work them loose, get Billy to help you pull them out," she yelled back.

Shortly, he called, "We got them out!" The proud boy emerged from the door and Constance handed him a basket and small trowel.

"Fill this with dirt and I'll dump it for you. You need to dig a big enough hole for the cedar chest with the flag in it."

"Don't worry, we can do it. Those damn Yankees aren't going to get that flag!"

Constance surveyed the pitiful condition of the house and yard. Weeds had overwhelmed the trampled boxwoods, and the house looked like an old beggar in need of new outer clothing. The gazebo was naked without latticework, and gaps marred the fence like missing teeth. Rotten boards on the front and back porches squeaked their need of replacement. Shortly, she carried a basket of dirt and dumped it in Sadie's little garden outside the kitchen. It had provided them with squash, pole beans, tomatoes, peppers, and herbs. She desperately needed to find a way to get to the farm and dig the potatoes Alex had planted in the spring. Since being forced to use most of her cash to pay taxes, she had little reserve for food, while prices soared. She peered inside the kitchen to see Sadie grinding eggshells with a mortar and pestle. "What are you doing?"

"I'm grindin' these eggshells to put in the meal when I make cornbread."

"They must have some nutritional value…we can't waste anything. I wish we could come up with something better than that wretched Confederate coffee."

"I know, but I ain't got nothin' but parched corn to make it from."

Constance carried the basket back to Hudson and then went in the house for the cedar chest and silver. Fortunately, she could fit all the silver in the chest. She thought it would be safe buried behind the foundation of the house, where no fresh dirt would be visible.

* * *

"Hudson, are you ready for another adventure?" Constance asked after they finished a meager lunch of bread and watery soup.

"Of course!" His blue eyes lit up with excitement. "What are we going to do now?"

"We're going to save the bell at Saint Stephen's," she said with a grin.

John Cole and Constance stood in the balcony and looked up the tower towards the bell. He said, "I'm not sure he can get up there. It's going to take a long ladder."

"I know," she replied confidently. "John, Sadie's son who works at the hotel, is bringing the ladder they use to paint windows. I think that will work. If you know the dimension of the opening, we can go ahead and cut the cloth."

"Yes." He unrolled the plans for the church. "Here they are."

Getting the dimensions, she said to Hudson, "Let's lay the cloth out downstairs and cut the first piece."

After John's arrival, Hudson scampered up the ladder with a hammer, nails, and piece of black cloth over his shoulder. He struggled to reach the top of the bell tower. "I can't quite reach the top," he called down.

"Ya jist let me go up there. I can reach it," said six-foot-tall John.

Disappointed, Hudson scampered down and handed everything to John. John climbed up, cut the bell pull, and nailed the black cloth to one side of the belfry wall. He descended the ladder and repositioned it on the other side, enabling him to climb back up and secure the cloth across the opening.

"We've saved the bell," Hudson said astonished. "When you look up the bell tower looks empty."

"I can't believe it. It looks like there's no bell," said Reverend Cole.

"You's pretty smart, Miss Constance," John said.

"That bolt of black cloth is being put to good use," Constance said with a satisfied smile.[ii]

Two weeks later, July 25, 1863: Davis Street

Constance walked from Stark's mercantile towards home in the oppressive heat, weaving between the sun-baked, ragged soldiers clogging the street. The returned army appeared markedly reduced in size and vigor from the optimistic group that had marched north six weeks ago. "I ain't had nothin' but hardtack, berries, and green apples for days," she heard a soldier complain.

When she rounded the corner by the courthouse, a group of soldiers raked their eyes over her appreciatively. "Pardon me, Miss, but I have to tell you how good it is to see a lovely Virginia lady again," one said politely.

"Those Pennsylvania women are the ugliest set of mortals on earth!" another chimed in. "Long-faced, barefooted, big-nosed and everything else that it takes to constitute an ugly woman."

"I'm flattered, gentlemen," Constance said with a smile and continued to walk. "Welcome back."

[ii] The bell of St. Stephen's survived the war by being concealed by black cloth.

"We was repulsed, but we ain't defeated. There's a lot of fight left in us yet!" one called out when she mounted the steps to her house.

Amanda looked up when Constance entered the store. "Any sign of the cavalry yet?"

"No." Constance took off her bonnet. "But don't be upset. You know they're always last to arrive. How do you feel?"

Amanda slowly stood up and walked to the window. "I'm so weak and despondent. I know if I could see Alex, I'd feel much better."

The family was finishing their dinner of squash, green beans, and bread when they heard footsteps on the back porch. Hudson and David jumped up and scampered noisily down the hall. "Daddy! Daddy!" they screamed with joy.

"Oh, thank God!" A look of relief flooded Amanda's face. Alex, filthy and soaked with sweat, entered the dining room with the boys in tow. Amanda threw herself into his arms unable to control her sobs. "Alex, thank God you're safe. I...I...I lost the baby," she blurted out.

"Oh, Mandy, no!" He took her face in his hands and saw the flickering pain in her eyes. "I'm so sorry, darling." His eyes filled with tears. He kissed her, held her close, trying to comfort her.

"We love you, Mommy." David clung to her legs.

"I know you do," Amanda sniffled, then picked him up. "Right now I'm a very lucky lady. Forgive me for feeling sorry for myself. Alex, you must be starved."

"That and bone-tired." Constance and Harriet rushed to hug him. "I haven't had any cooked food in over a week,"

"Now ya jist take what's left, Mista Alex," Sadie said with a grin, "an' I'll go cook ya some more."

"Alex, what about Robert?" Constance grabbed his arm tensely.

"He's fine." Alex consumed a piece of bread. "I'm sure he'll show up soon."

The dusky rose rays of sunset highlighted the sky when Constance walked to the outdoor kitchen and poked her head in the door. "Sadie, cook up everything you've got. I'm hoping Robert will be here soon."

"Yas'm, Miss Constance." Sadie fried bacon and squash. "But I ain't got nothin' else comin' in mah little garden."

"I know, but we have to feed these poor starving men. I'll trade some silver tomorrow to get more food." Constance walked outside and eagerly searched the street. She knew Robert would be downcast and exhausted. Somehow, she had to radiate cheerfulness in order to lift his spirits. No army had fought harder than these gallant men. She scrutinized a horseman riding through the foot soldiers on East Street.

"Connie!" he called from the back gate.

"Robert!" She raced through the tall grass towards him. Throwing open the gate, she flung herself into his arms. "Thank God you're back!"

He enveloped her in his arms, kissing her with an ardor and passion she had not felt before. It was a kiss his tired soul could melt into. After his lips moved over her ear and neck, he sighed, "I've dreamed of that kiss ever since I left. It's what kept me going."

"I've felt so useless. I'm glad I helped you in some small way." She pulled back to look at his filthy matted hair and unshaven grimy face. "My, you're a sight!"

"I know. But I couldn't wait to see you. Forgive me."

She took his arm and led him towards the house. "You know I'm only teasing. You look wonderful to me. I can only imagine what you've endured. You must be starved."

"I'm famished." The aroma from the kitchen reached his nostrils. "I hope she's cooking that for me."

After Robert devoured every bit of available food, Alex leaned back in his chair. Constance studied them both and said, "The newspapers have not been kind to General Stuart. Many are placing the blame for Gettysburg on his shoulders because the cavalry didn't keep General Lee informed."

"That's unfair," Alex snarled. "It's easy to sit behind a desk in Richmond and criticize. They have no idea of the problems we encountered. The massive Union cavalry forced fierce engagements around Middleburg and Aldie. Mosby found a way for us to cross the Potomac, but it was blocked when we tried to cross, so we had to go east, which delayed us. I'm sorry to report that Frank didn't meet us at Salem as we expected."

"What do you mean?" Constance asked leaning forward on the table. "Where is he?"

"We don't know," Alex replied. "He's missing. He's either killed or captured."

"Heavens!" Harriet gasped. "Does Anne know?"

"I doubt it," Alex said shaking his head.

"Not Frank!" Constance slumped in her chair, her eyes brimming with tears.

Robert reached under the table and took her other hand in his. "Don't give up hope. He may be in prison. There's a good chance he'll be exchanged."

Constance sniffled. "I can't bear to lose Frank." Robert moved his fingers tenderly over hers.

"There's more bad news," Alex continued. "Von Borcke was wounded in the throat. We didn't think he would live. However, last report says he's in Richmond and he's hanging on."

"We're all so fond of him," Harriet lamented. "I hope we'll see him again."

"Stuart has named our camp after him. It's Camp Von Borcke." Robert pushed his plate away. "It's true that we didn't arrive at Gettysburg until the second day of the battle. Horses and men were completely exhausted. We had captured numerous Union supply wagons, which slowed us down. The Yankees got between us and Lee, and we lost contact. In retrospect, I believe it was a serious error. Our first duty was to keep Lee informed."

"Hindsight is a wonderful thing," Alex argued. "At the time those supply wagons were extremely tempting. From what I've gathered from the infantry, Ewell failed to seize the high ground on the first day. His timidity lost the battle. Jackson wouldn't have hesitated."

"What's done is done," Amanda said quietly. "It was God's will and we can't change it. Our cause is just and we will triumph eventually. We must have faith."

"God certainly allowed our army to escape safely. I served under George Meade at the Great Lakes and have great respect for him," Robert said. "But he moves slowly and cautiously. Our army could have been destroyed at Williamsport while we crossed the Potomac. Tomorrow has been set aside as a day of prayer and revival at Brandy. Will you come with me?" he asked Constance.

"Yes, of course."

"We aren't the only ones with problems," Amanda said. "Lincoln has his own. The North is revolting against his draft law. Nobody wants to fight in his war of aggression. The fact that the wealthy can buy their way out for three hundred dollars has incensed the working class. Because of the riots, the draft lottery has been suspended in Buffalo, Philadelphia, and Easton. Denver and Iowa say they can't enforce it."

"Oh, but the riots in New York have been by far the worst!" Harriet slowly stood and grabbed her cane. "Let me get a letter from my friend in New York and read it to you."

"Do you want me to get it, Mother?" Constance asked while Harriet hobbled across the room.

"No, dear. I need to make myself move around."

Alex frowned and whispered to Amanda, "She's really given back since we left."

"I know. Her joints are giving her a fit."

"We've been on the march and know little about these draft riots," Robert said to Constance. "Have people been killed?"

"Oh, yes. The Irish killed nearly a hundred Negroes in New York!"

"What?" Sadie exclaimed as she cleared the dishes. "I sure hope mah Joseph didn't go there! Is that what happens to free slaves?"

"It has happened," Constance replied.

Harriet slowly hobbled back to the table. "Now," Harriet said, then sat down and spread the letter in front of her. "Here's what she writes."

The draft began on Saturday, the twelfth, very foolishly ordered by the government, who supposed that Union victories would make the people willing to submit. It gave them Sunday to think it over. By Monday morning there were large crowds assembled to resist the draft. All day there were dreadful scenes enacted in the city. The police were successfully opposed; many were killed, many houses were gutted and burned: the colored Orphan Asylum was burned and all the furniture was carried off by women. Negroes were hung in the street!

"That's jist terrible!" Sadie protested after she set the tray on the table. "They burned the orphanage." Harriet nodded and continued:

All last night the fire-bells rang, but at last by God's mercy, the rain came down in torrents and dispersed the crowds. Fearful that they might attack a Negro tenement house some blocks below us, as they had attacked others, I ordered the doors to be shut and no gas to be lighted in front of the house.[3] The principal cause of discontent was the provision that by paying $300 any man could avoid serving if drafted, thus obliging all who could not beg, borrow, or steal this sum to go to war. This is exceedingly unjust.[4]

We had four days of rioting. Fighting went on constantly in the streets between the military and police and the mob, which was partially armed. The greatest atrocities have been perpetrated. Three or four Negroes were hung and burned. Colonel O'Brian was murdered by the mob in such a brutal manner that nothing in the French Revolution exceeded it. We feared for our own house on account of the Negro tenements below McDougal Street where the Negroes were on the roof, singing psalms and having firearms.[5]

Gaunt-looking savage men, women, and children were armed with brickbats, stones, pokers, shovels, and coal scuttles. This mob seemed to have a curious sense of justice. It destroyed many disreputable houses and did not always spare secessionists. The Superintendent of Police said the draft could not be enforced.[6]

The Catholic priests have done their duty by denouncing these riotous proceedings. One of them debated with a woman in the crowd who wanted to cut off the ears of a Negro who was hung. The priest told her that Negroes had souls. "Sure, your reverence," she said, "I thought they only had gizzards."[7]

"That's the most hateful thing I ever heard!" Sadie said angrily.

"It's an outrage," Constance agreed. "All caused by Lincoln's war policy."

"They're having to use troops to control their own people," Robert said amazed. "That's fewer that we'll have to face."

"Since they can't get their own men to fight, they're trying to arm the slaves who've fled. They'll put them on the front lines where they'll be mown down," Alex said.

"I know mah Joseph ain't never gonna' fight 'gainst his people," Sadie said.

"Sadie, thank you for the best food I ever ate," Robert said.

"Yas'r Major Beckam," she answered as she left the room.

Alex leaned back in his chair and yawned. "I'm ready for one night's sleep in a bed."

"Robert, why don't you stay for the night in our extra bedroom?" Harriet asked.

"Oh, thank you Mrs. Armstrong, but I must get back to my men." He shot Constance a questioning glance.

"You're crazy to pass up the chance to sleep in a bed." Alex stood up. "Who knows where they'll send us tomorrow."

"Why don't you stay, Robert?" Constance's smile was inviting. "Then I can go to the revival with you in the morning."

"I surrender. You've talked me into it." He stood and helped Constance up.

"Then it's settled," Harriet said cheerfully. "Constance, you can sleep with me."

"Yes, Mother. I'll be up in few minutes." She led Robert into the hall. "Alex, we need to dig those potatoes at the farm. Our food situation is critical."

"I'll do it tomorrow," he called down the steps.

Constance took Robert by the hand and they entered the parlor. He put his arm around her after they settled onto the sofa. Her eyes searched his. "Do you want to talk about it?" she asked softly.

He looked down at the floor with a faraway expression. "Maybe I need to." His eyes grew moist. "These last nineteen days of retreating through mud and muck have been pure hell. Our cavalry is in terrible shape. The horses are worn down and too many men are without mounts. Somehow, I've got to find more horses."

"That sounds like an impossible task."

"I know." He penetrated the depths of her azure eyes. "Our ambulances stretched for five miles. Connie, it was the most pitiful sight I've ever seen. We could hear them screaming and moaning for miles." Tears flooded his eyes. "I was sure this battle would end the war. We've never been whipped before. I would give...everything I ever hope to possess if it would end the war. How many more will die?" Tears rolled down his cheeks. "I don't know if we can win now," he whispered in a broken voice. Overcome with emotion, she gently wiped the tears from his face. "You must think I'm weak," he said with a quiet sob.

"Oh, no, Rob. You're one of the strongest people I know." She turned his face to make him look into her eyes. "But you're human and you're exhausted. You have every reason to cry after the sadness you've witnessed. I'm thankful that you've finally shared your innermost feelings with me. I never thought you'd do that."

"I admit I'm shy, perhaps distant, but that doesn't mean I don't feel and feel deeply," he continued, regaining his control. "I feel deeply about you. Thinking of you was the only thing that got me through this ordeal." He cupped her face in his warm hand, "Connie, I _need_ you."

"And I'm here for you, Rob. I feel so much closer to you right now than I ever have before." He pulled her face towards him and felt the softness of her lips against his. She returned his kisses with a new enthusiasm.

Four days later, July 29, 1863: East Street

Constance teased Robert while they walked towards the Hills' house. "I can't believe you haven't met General Lee. I'm sure he'll be there tonight. I'll introduce you."

"You're such a socialite. It's a big army. We've all seen him, but the majority of us haven't met him."

Amanda, walking in front of them, said, "I feel uncomfortable going without Alex. I don't understand why the Rangers were assigned picket duty near Fredericksburg when they could have stayed here close to their families."

"The army never makes sense," Robert answered. They joined the crowd gathered on the Hills' wide lawn.

"I only came because Dolly asked me to sing with her. Then I'm going to leave," Amanda said. Then Dolly walked forward to greet her with a hug.

Powell Hill bowed politely to Constance. Shocked at how thin he was, she said, "General Hill, we're so very proud of your accomplishments. Allow me to introduce Major Robert Beckam."

"It's an honor sir." Robert shook Hill's hand. "I'm sure you're glad to be home."

"Yes, but I'm distraught at how run down and devastated the town looks. You're to be commended for the excellent job you're doing with the Horse Artillery."

"Thank you, sir. We captured many horses in Pennsylvania, but our shortage remains acute."

"Yes, my artillery suffers the same shortage."

"Dolly, the South mourns the capture of your gallant brother," Constance said.

"Thank you, Constance," Dolly answered with a forlorn face. "I still can't believe that all five of my brothers are locked in a penitentiary." Their daring raid into Ohio and Indiana had not caused the Copperheads to rise up and join them as they expected, Dolly thought. She believed the Copperheads to be sympathetic to the southern cause but hesitant to risk their lives.

"He represented the spirit of the South...it's a major setback," Robert said.

"At least they're all alive," Powell said. "I don't believe the North will hang them, because they know we'll retaliate against their prisoners. But, let's try to enjoy tonight. Please meet my staff members who are here."

"Thank you," Constance said, then they walked towards the porch. She pulled out her fan. "The heat's still stifling. I don't believe Powell's position has puffed him up. He remains his congenial self."

"Yes, he's quite pleasant." Robert spied Extra Billy Smith on the front porch. "I believe I see an old friend."

The dignified old gentleman greeted them warmly. "Constance and Robert, two of my favorite young people. How delightful to see you." He hugged Constance.

"General Smith, you look wonderful compared to the last time I saw you. Your recovery is a blessing."

Robert shook Smith's hand vigorously. "I understand you were an ambassador of good will in Pennsylvania, General."

Extra Billy chuckled. "Yes, I endeavored to show our best side to the northern people. They need to know how wonderful we are. Our army behaved like gentlemen, Constance. You would have been proud of us."

"Indeed, I'm always proud. But tell me, how did you interact with the civilians?"

"When we entered Pennsylvania, the farm women made signs at us." He crossed his index fingers. "We learned that they were hex signs. I decided they needed to know us better." Small crinkles appeared around his merry eyes. "Our brigade was in the lead when we entered the beautiful little town of York. I asked my son Fred, who is my aide, to go back and look up those tooting fellows and to tell them to come to the front and march into town tooting 'Yankee Doodle' in their very best style."

"That was a magnanimous gesture," Constance commented.

"Yes," he continued, "I rode ahead bareheaded, and began bowing and saluting the civilians, especially the pretty girls," he related with a hearty smile.

By this time a group of guests had gathered on the porch to hear his oratory. "I'm sure they were captivated," Constance said

"The Yorkers seemed at first astounded, then pleased, and finally by the time we reached the public square they broke into cheers. They crowded around, forcing me to call a halt. I had my men stack their arms and they visited with the good people of York. It was a rare scene, the vanguard of an invading army and the invaded and hostile population hobnobbing on the public green."

"Too bad Pope didn't take lessons from you," Robert said.

"True. I decided to deliver a rather humorous speech that went something like this," he said pacing the porch. "My friends, how do you like this way of coming back into the Union? I hope you like it; I have been in favor of it for a good while. But don't misunderstand us. We are not here with hostile intent. You can see for yourselves, we are not conducting ourselves like enemies today. We are not burning your houses or butchering you children. On the contrary, we are behaving ourselves like Christian gentlemen, as we are."

"Amen," Robert and several soldiers said.

"You see," he gestured with his hands, "it was getting a little warm down our way. We needed a summer outing and thought we would take it at the North, instead of patronizing the Virginia springs, as we generally do." Constance and the guests laughed merrily. "We are sorry and apologize that we are not in better guise for a visit of courtesy, but we regret to say our trunks haven't gotten up yet; we were in such a hurry to see you that we couldn't wait for them. You must really excuse us." Robert laughed heartily.

Smith continued, "What we all need, on both sides, is to mingle more with each other, so that we shall learn to know and appreciate each other. Now here's my brigade—I wish you knew them as I do. They are a hospitable, fascinating lot of gentlemen. Why just think, this part of Pennsylvania is ours today; we've got it, we hold it, we can destroy it, or do what we please with it. Yet we sincerely and heartily invite you to stay. Aren't we a fine set of fellows?"[8]

Everyone on the porch applauded enthusiastically and the old gentleman took a deep bow. "General Smith, I want to congratulate you." Robert E. Lee made his way through the guests. He shook Smith's hand. "Friends," he said addressing the crowd, "I proudly introduce you to the newly promoted Major General Smith, the oldest general in the army! He makes me feel young." The onlookers cheered. "After hearing him tonight, I've decided to send him on a speaking tour where he can enlist his patriotic eloquence in behalf of my new amnesty and furlough laws. Hopefully, these moves will strengthen our army. General Smith, may I count on your services until you take office as our newly elected governor in January?"

"By all means, General Lee. But remember, when I'm governor you may have to listen to me, perhaps even take a few orders."

Lee laughed. "Sir, I look forward to that."

"If I may have your attention for a moment," Baptist Hill announced loudly, "we have two very talented ladies who are going to sing for those of you who would like to come inside."

Constance caught General Lee's eye. "Good evening, Miss Armstrong," he said. "How have you been since our encounter at Brandy Station?"

"Fine, thank you sir. Allow me to introduce Major Robert Beckam."

Lee looked up at Robert who saluted. "Major Beckam, General Stuart has only the highest praise for you. I appreciate your devotion to duty. Keep up the good work."

"Thank you, sir. May I inquire as to the condition of your son?"

Constance looked at the lines on Lee's face and the sadness in his eyes. He seemed so much older than she remembered him. According to rumor, his health was deteriorating and he had written President Davis a letter of resignation after the disaster at Gettysburg. No one could lead the army like him. His men adored him. She prayed he would continue in command.

"Rooney's wife took him to her home east of Richmond to recuperate. Unfortunately, the Yankees sent a raiding party from Fort Monroe to capture him. My oldest son, Custis, was there when they came. He begged them to take him in Rooney's place. It did no good. They carried Rooney away on a mattress. We hope to arrange an exchange, but Lincoln seems unwilling."

Indignant, Robert muttered, "That's the most despicable thing I've ever heard. Taking a wounded man to prison."

"I shudder at the brutal level to which this war has deteriorated," Lee said. "Now, excuse me. I'm going to hear some beautiful singing. Music soothes the soul."

Constance took Robert's arm. "There's a breeze in the yard. Let's take a stroll."

Fireflies twinkled while they walked in the large front yard amongst the soldiers and guests. Robert slipped his arm around her waist.

"You seem in better spirits tonight," she said.

"Yes, it's amazing what rest and a few visits with a lovely lady will do for one's spirits. I've almost forgotten that the Yankees are across the river harassing my family."

"Let's not talk of the wretched Yankees any more. I want to do something exciting tomorrow." She turned and faced him, taking both of his hands in hers. "Borrow a horse for me and take me for a ride in the country. I'm sick of being cooped up in town."

"There's nothing I'd rather do, Connie, but I can't do it tomorrow." Sadness flickered in his eyes. "I'm leaving in the morning to inspect my batteries at Fredericksburg and then to go to Richmond to talk to some government officials about acquiring horses. I didn't want to spoil tonight by telling you."

"I can't believe you're going away so soon. How long will you be gone?"

"At least a week, I imagine." He studied the delicate features of her face, the enticing curves of her body. "I want to be alone with you. Let's go to your gazebo."

Three days later August 1, 1863: Warrenton Junction

Dawn: Aaron Ames sipped his coffee by the campfire and contemplated his cousin, Brigadier General George Armstrong Custer. At twenty three, the "Boy General" was the youngest in the army. His star had risen in a spectacular burst during the Gettysburg campaign. Knowing no fear, he had led his brigade from one success to another, having seven horses shot from under him in the campaign. Ames admired Custer's aggressive style of fighting. That's what it would take to win this war quickly. Strangers to each other, Ames had sought Custer out and expressed his desire to fight beside him. A hard and fast friendship developed between the two cousins who realized they had much in common. After observing Ames in action, Custer requested that he be transferred to his staff as an aide. Ecstatic, Ames said farewell to his comrades from Maine and enthusiastically joined Custer's Michigan Wolverines, the most admired brigade in the cavalry.

Reddish-gold hair fell in curls almost to Custer's shoulders. The fair skin on his face appeared flushed due to sun exposure, and a bushy mustache draped over his coffee mug, which concealed his dimpled, receding chin. With high cheekbones, an aquiline nose, and piercing blue eyes, he was a dashing figure in his bizarre costume. He intended to be as conspicuous as possible both in and out of battle. In appearance he had no peer in the Union army. The broad collar of a blue sailor's shirt fell over a black velveteen jacket ornamented with two rows of brass buttons and gold braid from cuff to elbow. The spurs on his boots jangled when he crossed his legs and brushed a twig from his velveteen trousers with twin gold stripes. He straightened his scarlet necktie and adjusted the brim of his hat with silver stars on each side.[9] "I want to look my best if we're called into combat today," he quipped to Ames.

"Do you think that's likely? Will we get to Culpeper?"

"We're being held in reserve. Buford and Gregg will lead the reconnaissance." Custer adjusted the straight sword hanging from his belt. "Are you disappointed, cuz?"

Early risers, the two of them frequently enjoyed intimate conversation before the rest of the men arose. Ames lit a cigar. "I suppose I am a little. The sooner we move forward, the sooner this war will end."

Custer chuckled, his blue eyes twinkling. "You can't fool me. I know you're anxious to see that southern belle who's gotten under your skin. What's her name?"

"Constance Armstrong." Ames stood up and paced. "I know it sounds crazy, when there are many northern ladies who find me attractive. In fact a wealthy girl in Boston

General George Armstrong Custer, U.S.A.

practically proposed to me when I was home. Maybe it's because winning them is too easy and I want a challenge. But there's something about her spirit that attracts me like no woman has before. Try as I may, I can't seem to get her out of my mind."

"You're an attractive man of the world. If she's the one you want, go after her. You'll never be satisfied with second best. That's the way I feel about Libbie. I'm not going to give up until she's mine. Look at the obstacles I've attempted to overcome. Her father wouldn't let me call on her, so I walked in front of her house where she had to see me, and sat near her every Sunday in church. I've told her *I love you* a thousand times with my eyes. Tenacity is the name of the game. I will win her."

"Don't tell me you're ready to relinquish your wild bachelor days?"

"Maybe," Custer conceded. "You know how it is when these women win our hearts. Suddenly, they want us to give up all our vices. No more smoking, drinking, cussing, gambling. And then, on top of that, we'll have to get religion! If we're such gallant, fierce warriors, why do we let petite little women wrap us around their fingers?"

"That's the question of the ages." Ames blew smoke rings. "Let me know when you find the answer." He straightened his red tie, a duplicate of Custer's. At Warrenton Junction, eight miles north of the Rappahannock, he felt physically near Constance, and yet they remained worlds apart.

3:30 p.m. John Minor Botts and his family looked out the dining room window at the lines of gray soldiers moving towards them. "They're falling back towards us. How much do you want to bet they'll end up fighting in my beautiful field of corn," he grumbled. They had listened to the gunfire since 10 a.m. when John Buford's Calvary pushed forward from the Rappahannock on a reconnaissance in force. Buford's mission was to determine the Confederate strength and location of infantry. Young's Confederates had been pushed back by a force four times larger. Young now took a new line of defense knowing that A. P. Hill's men, camped close by, would come to his aid.

"Do you think we should go to the cellar?" his wife asked nervously.

"Yes, that might be wise." Botts watched the action less than a half-mile away. "This is the thanks I get for allowing the Rebels to fill their canteens with milk from my herd and pay me in useless Confederate money."

"Father, don't assume they're fighting here to torment you," Mary said. "Our farm is a wide-open, level area conducive to cavalry battles. We simply have to live with it."

The other family members went downstairs, while Mary and her father listened to the thundering hooves of soldiers arriving from the west. Suddenly gray horsemen surrounded the house and raced to join Young. Botts saw the plume floating above the general's hat. "Oh, no, there's Stuart. I can kiss my corn good-bye. They're unlimbering the artillery. Come, Mary, let's go downstairs."

4 p.m. Constance nervously paced the floor of the bookstore. "The intensity of the fight has increased. It sounds like they're close to town. Do you think we should go to the Coles' cellar? It's the deepest one in town."

"I don't know what to do," Amanda said, almost crying. "I'm sick of living in the middle of a war."

"Now, keep control, Amanda." Constance peered out the bookstore window. "There are soldiers milling around who seem perfectly calm. It's probably just a cavalry battle.

After all, A. P. Hill's men are camped out there. They'll defend us. At least we know Robert and Alex aren't there."

"Yes, that's a small consolation. But it's all going to start again." Amanda thought about Culpeper's losses in the recent campaign: the Seventh and Thirteenth were in Pickett's disastrous charge. Colonel Tazwell Patton of the Minutemen was dead, and the list went on and on. The worst tragedy was the company from Stevensburg. Two years ago they had a 102 men. Now there was only one officer and six men left. The Brown family had lost five of seven brothers.

Constance paced nervously. "I believe we'll be safe here unless they get closer to town. We don't want to panic and scare the boys."

Confusion reigned in the melee at John Minor Botts' cornfield. Both sides mounted charges and countercharges in the 100-degree heat. The saber became the order of the day. Buford was having a difficult enough time when Anderson's Division of A. P. Hill's Corps joined the battle. Moving on the double quick in the intense heat, the infantrymen opened up on Buford. The Yankees fell back, but the men on foot pursued them for almost five miles to the river. Men and horses fainted from fatigue and sunstroke. Buford accomplished his mission by learning of the infantry's presence in Culpeper. Once again severe fighting made Brandy Station memorable. Stuart could ill-afford the heavy losses incurred by Hampton's Brigade, which saw 500 men killed, wounded, or put on foot by the loss of their horses.

6 p.m. Sickened at the scene confronting him, John Minor Botts saw dead and bloody men covering every inch of his immense, ruined cornfield. Every stalk of corn had been cut down by carbine, rifle, pistol, and cannon fire or mashed flat by the hooves of 6000 horses and the boots of Rebel infantrymen. [10]

Two days later, August 3, 1863: Davis Street

Amanda struggled to force her way across Davis Street amongst the crowd of soldiers and supply wagons, slowly moving south. She put a handkerchief over her mouth to ward off the dust permeating the town while A. P. Hill's men marched in the intense heat. When a slight gap appeared between wagons, she dashed across the street. The town was in turmoil. Her mouth choked with dust until she finally reached the back door. She grabbed a pitcher of water sitting on the dry sink and drank greedily.

Constance rushed into the hall. "What did you find out?"

Amanda gulped down her water. "I talked to Dolly." The two sisters returned to the parlor. "She's preparing to leave with the army. She knows only that they're going south. Powell seems to think that Lee is taking a stronger defensive position in the hills overlooking the Rapidan. However, they could be going to Fredericksburg or trying to outmaneuver Meade."

"Are we being deserted? Is the whole army going?" Constance wondered.

"Yes, all of the infantry. General Stuart and the cavalry are staying here."

"Well, at least that's something," Harriet said. "We'll have some protection."

"We have to make a decision," Constance said nervously. "Do we go or stay?"

"Life holds little meaning for me," Harriet replied slowly. "I'm ready to join your father. I don't want to leave my home. This is where I've lived my life and it is where I want to die."

"You've got to think about life, Mother, not death." Amanda took her hand. "I understand your reluctance to leave. I hate the thought of becoming a refugee."

Hudson looked up from his book. "I'm not afraid of the Yankees. I want to stay and protect our home."

"Me, too!" David chimed in.

"The little cash we have won't last long if we leave," Constance said. "We have a good stock of books and a source of income if we stay. I feel safe with the cavalry here. Robert should be returning any day now, and perhaps he can give us some insight."

"Then it's decided. We stay and trust in Almighty God," Harriet said forcefully.

Nine days later, August 12, 1863: Camp Von Borcke

Jeb Stuart played on the floor of his tent headquarters with his two mongrel puppies, Nip and Tuck. "Come on Nip, get it boy." The puppy grabbed the end of a piece of rope while Stuart pulled on the other end. The puppy growled and shook his head attempting to pull the rope away from Stuart, who laughed merrily. "Can't get it, can you?" Tuck ran and yapped at the excitement. Stuart needed a little fun to break the tension. With a few thousand men, he protected the buffer zone of Culpeper County between Meade and Lee. In addition, he was attempting to reorganize his badly depleted cavalry while suffering from the criticism following Gettysburg. On top of that, Flora, eight months pregnant, was sick in Lynchburg and he could not get away to see her.

Engrossed in the tug of war, he noticed the shadow when a soldier entered his large tent. Still on his hands and knees he looked up at the familiar thin youth. "Stringfellow! By God!" He jumped up and embraced him. "First we heard you'd been killed and then that maybe you'd been captured. Thank God you're back!"

"I'm thrilled to be back," Stringfellow said with a boyish grin. "My sojourn in Old Capitol Prison was too long for me, and I'm still smarting about being captured."

"Come, sit down." Stuart motioned to a stool.

Stringfellow made himself comfortable and then related his difficulties prior to his capture.

Stuart shook his head in remorse. "Lee could have used your information. We didn't know about Hooker until three days later, and I was delayed in finding a way across the river. But, we can't change that now. How did they treat you in prison?"

"They interrogated me without ceasing, convinced I was a spy. I never gave in. Since I was dressed in my uniform, they could prove nothing. Conditions are deplorable. I can't believe how many civilians are there. When new prisoners arrived, confirming Lee's retreat from Gettysburg, we all wept," Stringfellow said with tears in his eyes.

"Yes, I understand. You were lucky to be exchanged. Rumor has it that the North is going to stop prisoner exchange, because they know our men will come back and fight again with vengeance. But, there's nothing we can do about that. I need you here. You know this country better than anybody else. You're the best I've got."

Stringfellow looked at him surprised. "You're flattering me, sir. Where's Farley?"

Stuart's face fell. "I'm sorry. I guess you don't know." He related the details of Farley's death.

Choked up, Stringfellow could barely speak. "I'm going…to make them pay for Farley."

"Yes, I agree," Stuart said. "I've got just the job for you. I've learned that General Bartlett is living in high style in his headquarters near New Baltimore. Security measures are lax, and I believe you may be able to capture him. They've captured several of our generals, including Rooney Lee, and we need one of theirs to exchange."

"I'd take great delight in making that capture," Stringfellow said with vengeance. "Give me a day to rest and make my plans, and I'll do it."

"That's the spirit," Stuart said.

Stringfellow saluted and walked outside. Standing in the bright sunlight, he finally let the tears flow down his cheeks and vowed to make a personal war on the Yankees. He must make them pay for Farley. No opportunity would be passed up to do the enemy harm. They would see how much damage one man could inflict.

"It's so quiet in town with so few of us left," Lucy said to Constance while they walked along Davis Street in the late afternoon sun. "Are you seeing Robert often?"

Constance smiled, then shifted the basket of food to her other arm. "Yes, he comes every few evenings. It's nice having him so close by. Let's hope Meade will remain content to stay north of the Rappahannock."

"You're quite fortunate to have his undivided attention." A lone horseman rode up behind them.

"Connie!" he called.

Constance whirled around and tossed her basket down when she heard the familiar voice. "Frank!" She dashed towards him. "Is it really you?"

"None other!" He jumped down and she threw her arms around him.

"Thank God, Frank!" He picked her up and she kissed him on the cheek. "We were afraid you were dead!"

"God spared me again. But I spent some extremely unpleasant time in prison." He paused to look at her and towards Lucy. Reaching his hand towards Lucy, he pulled her towards them. With his arms around both of them, he said in a breaking voice, "I just heard about Farley. I'm shattered."

Lucy's eyes filled with tears. "He died so bravely, Frank. He thought the world of you."

"I'm going to make the Yankees pay," he vowed, his eyes smoldering. "Tomorrow I'll attempt to capture one of their generals. I'm not going to let them have a moment of peace."

"Frank, don't do anything foolish. You're just one man," Constance begged. "You can't bring him back."

"Do you want to visit his grave?" Lucy asked. "I'd like to go. I haven't been for a few days."

"Yes, of course," Frank said. "Let's go right now. Connie, come with us."

"No, you two go ahead. I'm expecting Robert shortly."

Stringfellow detected the sparkle in her eyes. "I hope he's making you happy. Perhaps we'll stop by to see both of you later."

"Oh, please do. That would be nice."

* * *

Next day, August 13, 1863: Camp Von Borcke

Stringfellow awoke refreshed and invigorated. After he drank his Confederate coffee in front of the fire, he began to carefully formulate his plans. He would take only eleven men. They would have to be completely reliable and experienced in the type of fighting they would likely encounter. He would choose carefully. Next he would scrutinize the horses. He only wanted those that were rested, strong, and well shod. He would have each man take a carbine, a revolver, a knife, cold provisions, and forage for his horse. They could not risk carrying cooking equipment or anything that would rattle at the wrong time. As a final precaution, he would order the men to oil down their saddles thoroughly. He was well aware that creaking leather had cost men their lives.

11 p.m. Stringfellow halted his men in the driving rain about 200 yards from Bartlett's headquarters. They had successfully swung to the far left around the Union pickets and crossed the Rappahannock without difficulty. "Listen carefully, men," he whispered. "I want Bartlett taken alive if possible. According to my information, he should be sleeping in a tent just inside of the farmyard fence. Do not fire unless we're fired upon. We may be lucky enough to get the general out before we're detected. Any questions?" The men shook their heads negatively.

He led them silently forward along a narrow mountain road until a picket cried out, "Who goes there?"

Aware that the Third Pennsylvania was in the area, Stringfellow risked answering, "The Third."

"Pass forward," the picket answered. Relieved, they moved to within twenty yards of the headquarters area. The scout saw a house and some tents in front of him. He picked out the general's tent and motioned towards it with his revolver.

Immediately, a sentry spotted them and ordered: "Halt! Advance one and give the countersign!" Stringfellow trotted forward and pointed his gun in the sentry's face.

"Make no noise or you'll die on the spot!" The brazen Yank failed to take him at his word. He fell back in surprise and let out a yell that raised the hackles on the back of Stringfellow's neck. Then the guard fired practically into his face. The bullet burned so close to Stringfellow's eyes that he felt the heat. The picket dashed through the camp screaming and firing to arouse everyone. Livid, Stringfellow knew they could not take the general by surprise, but would be forced to kill him.

His men poured fire into the third tent, which Stringfellow realized housed a regimental brass band. He heard the bullets pinging when they struck and ricocheted from the equipment in the tent. Apparently his men had not seen him gesture toward the general's tent.

"Quit wasting your bullets," he ordered. "It's this one over here." Three of the men spurred forward and blasted away. Their aim was good, because the scout later learned they had riddled the cot with bullets. Unbeknownst to them, the general was sleeping in the house.

Stringfellow saw a man run out on the porch of the house and bang away at them. Since he was in his undergarments, the scout did not recognize his quarry – the general. Stringfellow exchanged shots with him, but the general soon realized what a perfect target he made in his white garments. He dashed to the rear of the house.

Stringfellow gathered his men and led them out of the headquarters area. On the way he had them drive some horses tethered nearby through the camp. Under cover of the commotion and confusion thus created, the Confederates safely escaped.[11]

Though the expedition failed in it's objective of capturing General Bartlett, there is evidence that Stuart was pleased. In his report to Lee he said: *It so far succeeded as to get possession of his headquarters, the General having saved himself by precipitate flight in his nether garments. The headquarters flag was brought away. No prisoners were attempted to be taken, the party shooting down everyone in reach. Not a man of the selected 12 was touched, though fired on repeatedly. I consider this affair, though only partially successful, as highly creditable to the daring and enterprise of Frank Stringfellow and his band. I send you the flag by Daingerfield Lewis."*[12]

A month later, September 10, 1863: Along Mountain Run

Constance and Robert rode south of town along Mountain Run. "It's exhilarating to get outside on such a beautiful day," she said. "I just regret that we couldn't go out to the farm."

"I'm afraid it's too risky. Stuart's fallen back to the Hazel River. There are constant skirmishes."

"I hate that the Yankees are harassing the poor people of Jeffersonton. I know Alex's parents must be suffering. We'll certainly miss our apple butter this winter."

"Mosby's doing so much damage to the enemy's supply lines that they're punishing the civilians," Robert said irritated. "They know our people are sheltering his men. But I suspect the soldiers have probably devoured all the apples on your trees."

"Well, it's too beautiful a day to talk about unpleasant subjects. Let's just enjoy it."

They picked up the pace, taking the horses to a trot. Constance loved feeling the breeze against her skin. The red berries on the dogwoods decorated the tree line while the bright sumac added its vivid color. She drank in the beauty of the mountains, then a covey of quail whirled up in front of them. Queen Anne's lace danced in the wind. "This is heaven," she shouted. After several minutes they slowed the horses down to a walk.

"Let's stop and let them drink," Robert said. He dismounted, lifted her down from the sidesaddle and enjoyed feeling her body slide down his to the ground. "Have I told you recently how beautiful you are?"

A warm glow flowed through her at the sight of his carefree expression. She always tried to distract him from the realities of war. "Why, Major Beckam, for someone who professes to be such a shy lad, you certainly have become aggressive," she teased with open amusement in her eyes.

"You bring me out," he laughed richly. Putting his arms around her waist, he squeezed her affectionately. "These last five weeks have been heaven. I want to make time stand still."

"I wish you could do that," she whispered. "And make Meade stay on the other side of the river forever." When their lips moved together, he felt like he could devour her. Delighted with the way their relationship was progressing, he would marry her in a minute but realized she was not ready yet. Not about to risk rejection, he resolved to be patient.

"Um," she sighed after a lingering kiss. "Come, let's walk beside the stream."

They strolled silently for a few minutes, his arm around her shoulder and hers around his waist. The birds chirped loudly in the trees while a wood duck glided into the stream. Robert had a deep concern about the military circumstances but decided not to burden her with his suspicions. With the situation deteriorating in Tennessee, he had heard talk that Lee might be forced to send some of his men there. If that happened, Robert feared Meade would attack Lee's weakened army. "Connie, I hate telling you this, but I'm leaving tomorrow to go back to Fredricksburg and Richmond."

She turned to face him, shocked. "No, not again! You got some horses last time."

"I know." He stroked her hair. "But half of my artillery is there. I have to inspect the batteries. We still need more horses. Meade could attack at any time."

"I think you simply enjoy the social life in Richmond," she said with a little pout.

"Do I detect a note of jealousy?"

"Perhaps. You're one of the handsomest men in the cavalry."

"Now seriously, Connie." He took her face in his hands. "You know the last thing I want to do is be away from you. This war is like a raging tornado. It swoops us up, spins us around and around, and then spits us out wherever and whenever it pleases. I have absolutely no control over my life and I hate it!"

She understood the intensity in his eyes. "You know I was only teasing. I don't want you to go, but I understand your sense of duty."

He moved his lips over her mouth…her face…her neck. "I'm going to worry about you," he breathed into her ear. "Anything could happen while I'm gone, and I won't be here to protect you."

14

The Battle of Culpeper Court House

September 13 – September 28, 1863

Man is loved mainly because of two virtues: courage first, loyalty second.

Lucius

Three days later, Sunday, September 13, 1863: Stuart's headquarters

1 a.m. "General Stuart, sir, there's urgent news!" H. B. McClellan tried to arouse Stuart from a deep sleep. Bleary-eyed, Stuart sat up on his cot and looked at the two men before him.

"What's happened?"

"Dr. Hudgins, formerly one of your staff surgeons, has arrived from his home in Jeffersonton," McClellan explained.

Stuart looked up at the familiar doctor. "How did you get through their lines?"

"It was treacherous, sir. I was spending some time at home since my wife recently died. I believe she was frightened to death by Kilpatrick's men. I've witnessed a huge massing of Federal cavalry. I'm positive they intend to attack in force at dawn. I had to get here to warn you."

"I appreciate your bravery." Stuart stood and pulled on his coat. "How many men would you say you've seen?"

"I believe a division is in the area, sir. A friend overheard a Yank say the whole cavalry was moving at dawn."

"Get this man some food," Stuart said to McClellan. "Then order all wagons and disabled horses to begin moving towards the Rapidan." McClellan nodded and the two men left. Stuart sat at his desk and pondered the situation. The Federal cavalry must have close to 11,000 men, and the most he could muster in Culpeper was less than 5000. Fitz Lee picketed from Germanna Ford to Fredericksburg and could not get here in time to help. Moreover, he could not leave that section of the river unguarded. Wade Hampton was still recuperating from a Gettysburg wound and Young commanded his brigade. With "Grumble" Jones under arrest pending court-martial charges, Lunsford Lomax commanded his division. Colonel R.L. Beale commanded Rooney Lee's men. Stuart would have to make do with what he had. If he could not hold the enemy back, he must delay them long enough to move supplies south by wagon and train and to warn Robert E. Lee of the impending invasion.

6:30 a.m. Aaron Ames's heart pounded with excitement while his horse splashed across the river in a heavy downpour at familiar Kelly's Ford. He heard Davies's brigade, who had crossed before them, skirmishing with the Confederates. He knew they outnumbered Stuart two to one and was glad Meade had finally ordered them to push the Rebels out of Culpeper and to occupy the county. Meade had gotten wind of Longstreet's departure to Tennessee and decided to take advantage of Lee's weakness.

8:00 a.m. Lomax, who had fallen back to Brandy Station, now realized his small band of men confronted the three united divisions of Union cavalry under Buford, Gregg, and Kilpatrick. He ordered the three guns of Chew's Horse Artillery to open up. By firing rapidly and accurately, they delayed the advance of the Federals. His dismounted men opened heavy fire from the woods. The overwhelming blue tide finally forced him back to the Botts farm, where he again delayed the Yankees.

11:30 a.m. The stalwart worshipers at Saint Stephen's listened attentively to Reverend Cole's sermon over the gunfire in the background. Constance jumped at the sound of cannonading. She had seen the wagons moving south this morning and feared Stuart might be deserting them. From past experience, the townspeople realized that the battle noises they heard originated from the Brandy Station, Inlet area. Would the battle move to town? "My dear friends," Reverend Cole said after he concluded his lengthy prayer for their survival and the Confederacy, "it appears that our enemy has no respect for the Sabbath and refuses to allow us to keep this day holy. I feel it would be prudent for us to adjourn at this time. I invite all of you to the safety of the cellar at the rectory. It's the deepest in town. We welcome you if you choose to come at this time or later in the day."

Hudson and David whined about being hungry while the family stood in the church-yard. The Armstrong women decided it would be safe to go home for a while, agreeing to go to the rectory if the battle moved closer to town.

2 p.m. Having pushed Lomax back to the east side of Culpeper, Kilpatrick's division formed in a line of battle along a low ridge by the Wallach and George houses, three quarters of a mile east of Culpeper. Lomax had moved his artillery to a small knoll east of the railroad tracks and near the depot. A train steamed into the depot from Orange and Confederate soldiers frantically loaded it with supplies. Jeb Stuart closed up his headquarters and sent word to Lomax to hold the enemy until the train could be loaded. Thus a battle became inevitable.

Pleasonton and Kilpatrick observed the Rebels filling the train through their binoculars from the ridge at the Wallach house. "Capture that train!" Pleasonton said to Kilpatrick.

"Yes sir." Kilpatrick rode towards his two batteries of horse artillery. "Unlimber your guns. I want the fire aimed at the depot, the Rebel artillery, and the town where there might be snipers."

Aaron Ames watched apprehensively while the artillerymen moved the twelve guns into position on the ridge. "Son of a bitch!" he exploded. "The bastard's going to shell the town. Doesn't he know it's full of women and children?"

"He's after the train," a companion replied. Livid, Ames rode forward to seek his cousin.

"General Custer, I volunteer to take a few men forward to sight for the artillery." The lines of his brow and tenseness of his voice evidenced his anxiety.

Four Phases of Battle

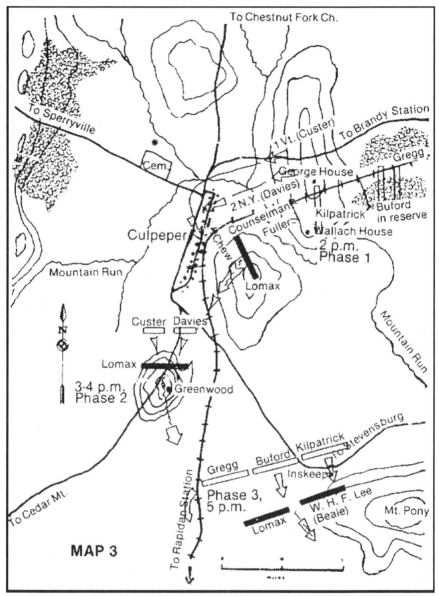

The Battle of Culpeper Court House
September 13, 1863

Staring at him, Custer understood his concern. "Lieutenant Ames, that's a dangerous assignment. Are you sure you want to undertake it?"

"Absolutely, sir."

"Permission granted," Custer said reluctantly. Ames gathered three other volunteers and they rode cautiously down the hill to the edge of the tree line. Then they dismounted and crawled through the tall grass to take a position behind a slight knoll adjacent to the Waverly Hotel. Ames used his binoculars to scan the area. He could see Lomax and his artillery a short distance to his left and the depot directly in front of him. He scanned the town and spotted a few civilians on the streets, with Davis Street to the courthouse being visible. The artillery opened up on Lomax's position.

Everything in the Armstrong house shook from the noise. "That was too close!" Amanda screamed. A vase crashed to the floor. She seized the hands of the two boys. "Quick! We've got to go to the parsonage."

"Come, Mother!" Constance grabbed her mother's arm and helped her out of the chair. "We must hurry! Amanda, you go now with the boys. I'll stay with Mother."

"Are you sure?" Amanda asked terrified as she opened the back door.

"Yes! Now go!" Harriet took her cane and hobbled out the back door. The back porch vibrated from the continued fire of the artillery.

"Constance, you go ahead. Don't worry about me. I'm a old woman."

"Don't be ridiculous, Mother. I'm not going to leave you." They shuffled slowly through the back yard to the gate. Constance saw Sadie racing down the street behind Amanda and the boys. Her heart hammered in her chest while she held her mother's left arm and helped her walk along East Street. A shell shrieked overhead. "Damn Yankees!" she muttered.

Lomax returned artillery fire. The rest of the Federal guns opened up shelling the depot and town. Ames froze and focused on the civilians dashing across Davis Street. It looked like Amanda, the boys, and Sadie. No sooner had they cleared the intersection than a shell exploded near the corner. "They're overshooting by at least a hundred yards," he yelled to one of his companions. "Ride back with that message." The soldier dashed back to the woods and mounted his horse. Ames watched breathlessly while Constance and her mother slowly edged across Davis Street. "Oh, my God," he whispered.

Suddenly, the earth trembled, then a series of shells exploded and kicked up dirt around the fleeing women. Both tumbled to the ground. "No! Dear God, no!" Ames cried in anguish. Constance, overwhelmed by the sharp pain in her leg, attempted to lift herself up on her elbow, noticing blood on the neck of her unconscious mother. Ames saw Constance move and realized she was alive. He yelled to his companions, "I've got to rescue those women." Too shocked to speak, they watched the crazy lieutenant depart.

He dashed through the grass and vaulted on his horse. It would be necessary to ride past the Rebels to get to her. There was no other way. He fiercely jabbed his spurs into the horse's side. They flew across the field and were nearly past the shocked Rebels before they opened fire. Ames put his head down while the bullets whizzed past him. His horse sailed over the railroad tracks at the depot, where one or two Rebels turned and fired at him, but most were too busy loading the train. A shell crashed into the ground in front of him, causing his horse to rear and whinny. "Easy boy," he yelled, managing to hang on and get control of the animal. Shells smashed into the buildings

335

around him, sending debris flying through the air. A piece of wood slammed into the horse's flank and he lunged forward. Galloping through the chaos, Ames soon reached the women. He jumped down to see Constance struggling to pull herself forward on her elbows, tears streaming down her face.

"Miss Armstrong, it's Aaron Ames," he yelled above the crashing shells. He knelt beside her. "I've got to move you to safety!"

Writhing in pain, she gazed up at the familiar face in shock. "What? Captain Ames!"

He instantly slid his arms under her legs and shoulders. "Put your arms around my neck," he ordered as he scooped her up. She could not believe his strength. Knowing another round of shells would be coming in; he dashed left on East Street. They were not more that twenty-five yards away when two shells exploded almost exactly where she had been lying.

"Mother!" she screamed hysterically. "Oh, my God! No! Mother!"

Ames raced into the alley behind the large brick mercantile on the corner of East and Davis. Finding an open grassy area behind two buildings, he laid her down in the grass, observing her blood-soaked skirt.

"Where are you hit?" His heart ached when he looked at the tears streaming down her anguished face.

"My right leg," she moaned. The ground shook from the artillery.

"You seem to be bleeding heavily. May I examine your wound?" he asked urgently.

"Yes," she whispered weakly.

He pulled up her skirt to see her pantalettes red with blood. Tearing away the fabric, he cringed at the large gaping wound about six inches above her knee on the back of her leg. From the amount of blood, he feared an artery had been severed. He hastily untied the tourniquet he always kept fastened around his waist.

"I'm going to put a tourniquet around the top of your leg. I've got to stop the bleeding." Pulling her dress back further, he pulled the tourniquet tight where her leg joined her body. "I know that's uncomfortable, but I've got to do it." Constance grimaced with pain. He applied firm pressure on her leg above the wound while the intensity of the gunfire picked up.

"How…did you…see me?" she stammered.

"Oh, I just happened to be passing by," he said in a soothing tone. "I suppose God put me in the right place at the right time." He tried to sound calm to keep her from panicking, while his own heart pounded wildly. She bled profusely. He implored God to help him save her. Surely, God would not force him to watch her bleed to death.

2:30 p.m. Mountain Run, which meandered between the depot and the Yankees' position, overflowed its banks due to the early morning downpour. Davies led the Second New York forward in a column of fours north of the railroad tracks. The stream presented less of an obstacle there when they galloped towards the Confederate guns. The surprised gunners, unaware that their support had been withdrawn, realized they were trapped in an exposed position. Knowing it would be impossible to save two of his guns, Thompson yelled to his men, "Save yourself and your horses! Retreat!" He rode out alone to observe the enemy charge. The Federal commanding officer, overcome with excitement at seizing such a rich prize, rode fifty yards in front of his men. Thompson advanced towards him firing his pistol. After exchanging shots, Thompson's bullet struck a fatal blow. The officer tumbled from his horse, then Thompson grabbed its reins and retreated to safety in town.

Custer, standing in front of the Wallach house, recognized Davies' success. He must follow up immediately and race for the train. He personally led the First Vermont forward on a route similar to Davies, but farther north. He circled around west of town and burst onto Coleman Street. Custer, unquestionably brave, personally led the charge that turned down Davis Street towards the depot. The thundering horses trampled Harriet's body. When the Vermonters opened up on the train it began to back out, heading south. Their bullets hit the engine and cars, but could not stop a piece of machinery that size. The Rebels at the station fired back and dashed behind buildings for defensive positions. Custer felt his horse collapse under him. He jumped to the ground and returned the Rebel fire.

Constance trembled uncontrollably while she listened to the fierce battle. Ames knelt beside her, feeling some relief that the bleeding had lessened. Momentarily, Federal horsemen charged down Culpeper Street at the end of the grassy area to their right. Simultaneously, several dismounted Rebels fired on the Yankees from the alley to the left of Ames. Realizing they were caught in the crossfire, he fell to the ground and rolled over on top of Constance, attempting to shield her from the bullets. Even amidst her pulsing pain and dizziness, she felt the pleasant sensation of his muscular body protecting her and his warm ragged breath in her ear. Bullets ricocheted from the brick building beside them and plowed into the dirt. She cried out when she heard a bullet hit only inches from their heads. He stroked her hair with his left hand. "Don't be afraid," he whispered in her ear. "I'm not going to leave you." They lay entwined for several minutes, their hearts pounding in unison, listening to the bullets thud and whistle around them. After what seemed an eternity, the Rebels withdrew down the alley and the Yankees charged towards the depot. Chew's last gun opened up on the Federals at the depot, shaking the ground with the impact. "How are you doing?" Ames asked. He raised up on his elbow.

"Dizzy...spinning." She tried to focus on his face in the swirling chaos while her leg throbbed.

"That's understandable. You've lost a lot of blood. Just close your eyes." The ground shook again from the noise of the artillery. "I'm going to check your leg." He sat up and looked at the wound again, unhappy to see some continued bleeding. "You're doing fine. Just hold on."

Custer, remounted on Ames's wandering horse, organized his men again for a charge. Since the prize of the train had gotten away, he would have to be content with capturing the last gun. "Follow me," he yelled. "We're going to take that gun!" His men cheered, then burst forward over the tracks and claimed their reward. Shortly after Custer secured the area around the depot, Davies rode up and reported that the remainder of the village was under Union control. Lomax fell back a mile and a quarter to the high ground of Greenwood Hill where Stuart personally took command. Custer and Davies soon pursued him.

3 p.m. Ames concluded that the sound of the cavalry galloping out of town signaled the battle was moving elsewhere. "Miss Armstrong, I'm going to look for a doctor." She lay motionless, unresponsive, and white as a ghost. Fear knotted inside him. He jumped up and raced down the alley to East Street. Wounded soldiers lay everywhere along Davis Street. Sickened at the sight of Harriet's mangled, trampled body, he took his coat off and covered her as best he could. The buildings on both sides of the street had been badly damaged near the depot. Numerous wounded soldiers called out for help. He turned to see several ambulances rattling down Davis Street. "Thank God," he muttered, striding towards them.

"I've got a badly wounded lady nearby who needs a doctor," he said brusquely.

The doctor looked at him surprised. "Our men deserve my attention first."

With a thunderous expression, Ames threw his words out like stones. "We've killed innocent civilians in this useless assault to capture a train. I've attempted to keep this lady from bleeding to death. I demand that you look at her immediately!"

Sensing that the powerful soldier confronting him was like a volcano about to erupt, the doctor decided to cooperate. "Very well, take me to her."

After they lifted Constance on the ambulance, the doctor examined her wound. When he removed several pieces of shrapnel, she groaned, but remained unresponsive. After he sewed up the wound and wrapped a bandage around it, he turned to Ames, nervously pacing behind him.

"She's obviously lost a lot of blood. You saved her life by applying the tourniquet, but she seems to be a bleeder. She's very weak."

"What are her chances?" Ames's voice broke slightly as he ran his fingers through his curly hair.

The doctor looked down and paused. "She's weak and anything could happen. It's hard to say." He shook his head sadly. "If she's lucky and the wound doesn't get infected, I suppose she has a chance. There doesn't appear to be any damage to the bone. She needs to sleep, but the key is getting good food into her to rebuild her strength. That muscle is badly lacerated. I doubt she'll be able to walk for at least a month."

Ames nodded gravely in understanding. "She lives nearby. If you'll loan me a stretcher and one man, I'll take her to her home."

"Yes, that's agreeable. Now excuse me while I attend our wounded."

Stuart planted a new battery atop Greenwood Hill[i] and opened up on Davies and Custer when they approached. The Fifth New York mounted a charge only to be repulsed by canister from the artillery and snipers. Lomax sent the Confederates in a countercharge down the hill. Kilpatrick arrived to reorganize his men. Using different tactics, he dismounted the Fifth and Second New York, and sent them up the hill firing carbines. Custer soon arrived and led the First Vermont and Seventh Michigan in to support the New Yorkers. Custer, at the forefront of the action, heard a plunk and felt a sharp pain in his foot. "I'm hit," he called. One of his men rushed to his aid and quickly carried him off. The tremendous firepower of the Federals forced Stuart to fall back.

---

[i] Greenwood Hill was named for the 18th century estate which still stands on it. It is located on Route 15 a short distance south of the Virginia Department of Highways. The fighting took place near the current water tower.

5 p.m. Colonel Beale, commanding Rooney Lee's men, took a defensive position at the base of Pony Mountain. The hill, the location of a Confederate signal station, towered 500 feet above the surrounding ground. Buford, supported by Kilpatrick, galloped to the hill and unlimbered his artillery. The local civilians rushed to the safety of the cellar in the Inskeep house, at the northwestern base of the mountain. A severe fight broke out when the guns opened up. One shell crashed into the Inskeep house and killed and wounded several civilians huddled in the cellar.

Aaron Ames sat by Constance's bed and perused the pictures on the small table beside it. There was one of John Pelham, a lock of golden hair, and another of an attractive dark-haired soldier with a mustache and goatee. Who was that? Was he the one he had seen her dancing with in the street? He looked at her left hand and was relieved not to see a ring. She looked so fragile and delicate as she lay there motionless. Her dark thick eyelashes and eyebrows stood in stark contrast to her chalk white face and lips. He knew he risked court-martial for deserting his post, but he refused to leave her alone. From the noise of gunfire and cannonading in the distance, it sounded like the Federals had slowly pushed the Rebels south; but at what cost? Leaning forward he rested his head in his hands and prayed. The sound of voices in the back yard interrupted his communion. From the window, he observed the distraught family coming home with two older men. He hoped they had not seen the condition of Harriet's body, and decided to walk down the steps to explain to them about Constance.

He stepped out on the back porch, then took his hat off so they would recognize him. John Cole and George McDonald stared, alarmed to see a Yankee. Recognizing him, Sadie scowled. "Ya jist can't get rid of these damn Yankees. They keep comin' back."

Amanda, overcome with grief about her mother, tried to comprehend the situation and address him. "Captain Ames" she stammered. "Where's Connie?"

"She's upstairs in bed." He walked down the steps toward them. "Before I explain, let me express my deepest sympathy about your mother. I despise what happened today." He briefly described to them what had transpired and the extent of Constance's injuries. Amanda and Sadie rushed upstairs to her. Ames put his hands on the boys' shoulders. "I'm so sorry about your grandmother."

Hudson's eyes bristled with hate. "Damn Yankees," he snarled, then pulled away. "Got no right to kill old ladies."

"Come on, boys. Let's go inside," Reverend Cole said.

Ames turned and addressed George McDonald. "Did they see her body?"

"No, we found her first. We went back to the cellar of the rectory and informed the family. I wouldn't let Amanda see her."

"I laid my coat over her." Ames looked down at the yard plowed by shells. "I know they want to bury her at the farm. Are there any coffins available?"

"Not unless we tear something down to make one." McDonald appraised the handsome Yankee. "We carried her to my newspaper office across the street. I don't have a horse or wagon to get her to the farm."

"Ah, so you're the newspaper editor. I've heard about you. I've got to report back to my command before I get court-martialed. I'm due a week's furlough. If I can get permission, I'll return and help with the burial. I'm deeply concerned about Miss Armstrong. She's in critical condition."

McDonald's face fell. "She's a favorite of mine. I'd hate to lose her. I've also heard about you. I suspect you risked your life to save her today. Thank you."

Embarrassed, Ames replied, "She saved my life once, too. Please tell Mrs. Yager that I'll return as soon as possible."

6 p.m. With the Confederates driven off, a Union signal station went into operation on Pony Mountain. Warren had marched the II Corps of infantry to Brandy Station and halted until he received word the Confederate signal station was shut down. He did not want Lee to be aware of the presence of infantry. With the report that Buford had taken Pony Mountain, he ordered Webb's brigade to march forward and occupy the town.

Ames wandered around the activity at the depot trying to obtain a horse. He observed several ambulances bringing injured to a temporary hospital in the courthouse. Startled, he watched two members of Custer's staff riding beside an ambulance. He walked closer, then recognized the familiar golden curls of the general. "General Custer," he called, walking alongside him, "I hope you're not seriously injured."

Custer looked up at him and smiled. "No, just a little foot wound. Ames, where in the hell have you been?"

"I've been attempting to save the life of Constance Armstrong," he answered with worry in his eyes. Custer listened to him spellbound while he briefly related the events of the day. "All of this death and destruction over a supply train that got away. Makes you wonder."

"You were brave as hell, but you know you could be court-martialed," Custer observed.

"I understand that, sir, but what would you have done if Libbie had been lying in the street like that?"

"I'd have done the same thing. I hope your lady friend recovers. I'll see that you get a coffin for her mother. By the way, we captured three of their guns. I bet Stuart and Beckam are smarting with humiliation."

"Thank you, sir," Ames said relieved. "Capturing the guns was a major prize." He paused, consumed with thoughts of Constance. "I'm due a week's furlough and would like to take it now so that I can help her family. I've also lost my horse. Don't know what happened to him."

Custer laughed. "I grabbed him after I was dismounted. You can have him back. I'm going home for three weeks to recover and win the fair Libbie. Give me a piece of paper," he said to one of his staff. "I'll write out permission for your week's furlough. You'll have to take this to Colonel Sawyer, who's in command in my absence. If he feels he can spare you, you can take off. You can get a ride to the front on an ambulance."

Ames smiled broadly and shook Custer's hand. "I'm most appreciative. I trust that you'll return to us healthy, happy, and engaged." Union infantrymen marched into town.

Next day, September 14, 1863: Armstrong town home

"Look at those sorry bluebellies marching through our town," Granny said to Lucy and Amanda, who sat in the parlor. "Murderers of civilians, that's what they are!"

"I...I'm so distraught, I don't know what to do next." Amanda wiped her eyes. "Poor

Connie is just barely hanging on and I'm not sure how to bury mother at the farm. If Lieutenant Ames doesn't come back, I guess we'll have to bury her at Saint Stephen's and move her later."

"Well, I know what I'm going to do. I'm going to vent my wrath," vowed Granny. She pulled a chair in front of the open window to the street. "You sons of bitches!" she yelled at the passing Federals. "You dirty rotten sons of bitches!" Lucy and Amanda shrugged their shoulders helplessly at each other.

"Let her alone. It's the only way we can fight back," Lucy whispered. Granny spent the entire day cursing the Yankees while they marched by. Several soldiers later wrote in their diaries about the insane, deranged old lady who had damned them.

Late in the morning, Ames entered the outside kitchen. He had waged a fierce argument to get permission to leave the front where the Union cavalry sparred with Lee's infantry, well entrenched across the Rapidan.

Sadie looked at him suspiciously when he placed a sack on the table from which emanated a cackling noise. "Where'd ya steal those chickens?"

"I bought them from Mrs. Anne Stringfellow. We were camped near her house. I told her I needed nourishing food for Miss Armstrong, and in our conversation she revealed her close friendship with the family. She was heartsick at the news of Mrs. Armstrong's death. How is Miss Armstrong?" he asked with lines of concern on his face.

Sadie's dark eyes filled with fear. "She's jist barely hangin' on. She sleeps most of the time. Can't git her to eat much."

Ames looked down so she could not see his eyes watering. "I've watched men die from loss of blood. They slowly fade away. We can't let her do that. She's got to eat to rebuild her strength. What do you have to put with these chickens to make soup?"

"Potatoes and onions is all."

"Make up a pot of soup and cut everything in small pieces. No one else is to have any of it. When it's ready you must force her to wake up and eat some. I'm going to take Mrs. Yager and the boys to the farm to bury Mrs. Armstrong. You must make her eat while we're gone. Do you understand?"

"Yes'r," Sadie said grudgingly. She resented him ordering her around, but his determination to save Constance impressed her.

"Lieutenant Ames, I'm most appreciative of your help today," Amanda said when they returned in the darkness from the burial. "And I haven't thanked you properly for sparing my husband's life at Brandy Station. I'll be forever grateful to you."

"I consider you my friends." Ames opened the back gate for her. "I trust he would do the same for me."

"Yes, of course he would." Union soldiers and creaking supply wagons along Cameron and East Streets distracted them.

They entered the brick kitchen and Ames addressed Sadie. "How is she? Has she eaten?"

"A little. I can't keep her awake long." Sadie's voice betrayed her fear. She stirred the large pot of soup on the iron cook stove. "We got company. There's some of those blue fellas in the house. Say they need it for headquarters."

Amanda sank onto the bench beside the trestle table. She dropped her head in her hands and muttered, "What next? I don't think I can handle this."

"Are we going to have to live with Yankees, Momma?" Hudson snuggled beside her. "I don't know," she whispered.

Ames sat down across from her, understanding her plight. "I'll talk to them and see that you're treated well. However, Miss Armstrong's survival is the first priority. We must see that she eats. That means waking her every few hours and feeding her. May I have your permission to do that?"

Amanda was emotionally and physically drained. Ready to have the burden of responsibility removed from her shoulders, she acquiesced. "Yes."

"Sadie, pour a bowl of soup and take it up to her room." He stood up and stretched. "I'll be up in a minute. First I need to speak to the soldiers in the house."

"If they will allow me to continue running the bookstore, I can earn enough money to buy food," Amanda said weakly as he walked towards the door.

"Miss Armstrong, Miss Armstrong, you must wake up." Ames shook her shoulders gently. The deep masculine voice penetrated her consciousness. Her heavy eyelids felt as if they weighed a ton. She did not have the strength to open them. "Miss Armstrong, it's Aaron Ames. Open your eyes." She felt her head being moved back and forth on the pillow. Mustering all of her strength, she slowly cracked her lids. She tried to focus on the face leaning over her in the spinning room, recognizing the curly brown hair. "I'm going to prop you up." He placed a pillow behind her and his strong arms pulled her up. She had to fight to stay awake. She wanted to drift away again.

"Sadie made you some delicious soup." He poked a spoonful into her mouth. She collected all of her strength to chew it. "You have to eat to regain your strength." He poked another spoonful into her.

Feeling exhausted after she chewed and swallowed it, she mumbled, "Too tired."

"I know how exhausted you must feel. Force yourself to stay awake," he insisted, then gave her more soup. "I risked my life by riding through gunfire and cannonading to save you. You can't give up and die on me now, damn it! I won't let you!" he said forcefully as he shook her. She worked to eat the soup, seeing the intense concern in his eyes. "You're a fighter. Hang on." He gave her more soup. She mustered all of her will power to continue looking into his hazel eyes. "That's good," he whispered tenderly with a smile before he gave her another spoonful. "I'm going to wake you up every two hours to make you eat." He wiped the soup from her face with a napkin. "So you'd better get used to it."

The weight of her eyelids pushed them down. "Don't drift off," he ordered. "Not until you've finished this soup. He took his hand and moved her face back and forth. "One more spoonful. You can do it." She ate obediently, gazing at him, trying to comprehend why he was here. He held a glass of water to her lips and she drank.

"Too tired." Her eyelids floated downward.

"I'm proud of you," he said while she drifted off. He pulled the pillows away and laid her down flat again. She had responded to him. That was encouraging. He leaned forward in the chair and yawned. Digging the grave with Billy's help had been exhausting and he had gotten little sleep last night. He closed his eyes and dozed for a few minutes.

He jumped as Amanda and Sadie entered the room. "How'd she do?" Amanda asked.

"She ate almost the whole bowl."

"Good Lawd! That's twice as much as she ate for me!" Sadie exclaimed.

"It's encouraging." Ames stood up and stretched his large frame. "She needs milk and eggs. Where can we get them?"

"We may be able to buy eggs," Amanda said. "John Minor Botts is one of the few farmers who still has milk cows."

"I'll ride out to his farm tomorrow and buy milk." Ames paced restlessly. "I'd like to sleep here on the floor tonight so I can wake her up to feed her. I've talked to Major Wilkins and he's agreed to let you occupy two bedrooms and continue running the bookstore. His staff will utilize the remainder of the house. I know this will be unpleasant for you, but considering that you haven't taken the oath, it's a generous arrangement."

"We'll attempt to get along with our unwelcome visitors," Amanda answered controlling her wrath. "Now, if you'll excuse us, Lieutenant Ames, we need to check her wound." He nodded, walked out into the hall, and closed the door.

"Miss Amanda, it jist ain't proper for him to stay in here with her tonight," Sadie argued. They pulled the sheet back and examined Constance's leg.

"He got her to eat more than either one of us. Proper or not, if he can save her, he stays," Amanda said sternly, asserting her authority. "There doesn't seem to be any bleeding. It's a little red, but it doesn't look too bad." She wrapped a fresh bandage around the leg and pulled the sheet back up.

"It still ain't proper," Sadie grumbled.

Next day, September 15, 1863: Armstrong town home

"Miss Armstrong, wake up." Constance heard the familiar deep voice. She forced herself to open her eyes, hoisting her heavy-laden eyelids slowly. "Wait until you taste what I have for you." His large hands lifted her shoulders and he propped her up. "I paid a visit to the Botts farm and purchased some milk and eggs." He lifted a glass of thick white liquid to her lips and she drank slowly. "Miss Mary Minor Botts said she would be more than glad to do anything that would help you recover. She claims you're the only person in Culpeper who's been nice to her."

She pushed the glass away. "It's good," she said weakly. "Let me...rest."

"Sadie and I whipped this up for you. It's eggs, milk, and sorghum." He watched her drifting off. "You can't go to sleep yet. Here, drink some more." He gently shook her and lifted the glass to her lips. She drank staring at his square jaw, high cheekbones, and dimpled chin. Everything about him evidenced strength, prowess, and masculinity. He was even more stunningly virile than she remembered. Feeling the heart-rending tenderness of his gaze, she would do whatever he asked. "Congratulations! You drank it all," he exclaimed, then took the glass away.

"Thank you," she mumbled with a slight smile before she closed her eyes.

Four days later, September 19, 1863: Stuart's headquarters

Robert Beckam's stomach churned with anxiety when he rode up to Jeb Stuart's headquarters at Brampton, an estate in Madison County near the Rapidan River. He had been notified of the battle at Culpeper while in Fredericksburg, but knew few details. He walked into Stuart's tent and saluted. "Major Beckam, welcome back," Stuart said. "We've needed you here."

"I regret I was away when the battle occurred, sir. Can you give me any details?"

"We were outnumbered two to one. A battle raged at the depot because we needed to get our last supply train away. They shelled the town," Stuart said disgusted.

Visibly shaken, Beckam asked, "What about the civilians. Were any hurt?"

"We don't know for sure, but from my observation of the action I believe there must have been some injuries. Not only that, we lost three of your guns."

"What!" Beckam said enraged. "That's a humiliation. I wouldn't have let it happen!"

"Probably not, but we can't change it now. Meade is probing our position and we fear an attack. I need you to be vigilant."

"Of course, sir. As you may understand, I'm most anxious for news about the civilians of Culpeper. Where's Stringfellow?"

"He's scouting behind their lines. If he returns with any news, I'll send him to you. I understand your concern."

"I appreciate that sir. I'll assess the situation here immediately." Beckam seethed when he stepped outside into the warm fall sunlight. Culpeper and the woman he loved were in the hands of the enemy, and there was nothing—absolutely nothing—he could do about it. On top of that, he bore the disgrace of losing three guns. Fate had not been kind to him. He wanted to retaliate, and the sooner the better.

Sadie's kitchen: "I'm very much encouraged," Ames said to Sadie, beaming. "She's much more responsive and awake today. I believe she's out of danger."

"I hopes you's right." Sadie dished up a bowl of beef soup. "She told me this mornin' how ya dashed into the battle to save her. You's saved mah dearest chile, so I'm gonna try to be nice to ya." She stared at him intently, her dark eyes still shooting sparks. "But that don't mean I like ya. The only reason we's letting ya spend so much time 'lone with her is 'cause Miss Amanda has to work in the bookstore and I's got to cook for them damn Yankees in there. She ain't got no Momma or Daddy no more, so I's got to look out for her." She stepped closer to him and shook her finger in his face. "If ya does one thing improper or lays a hand on her, ya gotta deal with me! Ya understand?"

Ames backed off a few inches in self-defense. "You've made yourself clear, Sadie. I can assure I have not, nor will I, do anything improper. I'll sleep in the cabin with Billy tonight if that makes you feel better. Tomorrow I report back to camp." He picked up the tray with the soup and hurried out.

Constance opened her eyes in eager anticipation when she heard the sound of his boots on the bedroom floor. "How many days have you been here?" she asked. He set the tray on the table.

"Six." The glow of his irresistible smile warmed her while he helped her sit up. "It's wonderful to see you awake and talking."

"Thanks to your good care." She spied the bowl of soup and reached over to take it herself, but he pulled it out of her reach.

"Now, Miss Armstrong," he said in a high feminine voice with his hand on his hip. "You know I can't allow you to feed yourself and spill that soup all over you. Why, then I'll have to clean up the mess!" he concluded, batting his eyelashes.

She erupted in laughter at his hilarious imitation of her. "Surely, I didn't sound like that! Was I that bossy?"

"Yes, you were!" He sat on the bed, so close that she felt the heat from his body and smelled the masculine scent on leather. He picked up the soup. "But the tables are turned now, and you have to do what I say. Open up."

She smiled when he poked the soup in her mouth. "Um, that tastes like beef. Where did you get that?"

"I have my sources. The railroad has reopened to Washington and there are at least eighty thousand soldiers here now. Supplies are much more readily available."

She continued to eat the soup with a frown on her face, hearing cannon fire occasionally in the distance. "I'm not sure I wanted to know that depressing news. What's happening? Where's the fighting?"

"Meade is feeling out Lee's strong defensive position in the hills across the Rapidan. I'm not sure what will happen. Don't you worry about it. Your job is to get well."

"I should. You've given me enough milk and eggs to make me moo and cackle." Ames chuckled and enjoyed watching her captivating smile. "That's a quote from my good friend, Frank Stringfellow."

"Stringfellow attempted to capture one of our generals recently. He and Mosby are giving us a fit by attacking our supply lines. Numerous parties are hunting them down."

"You'll never catch the Gray Ghost," she stated defiantly. "He and Frank are both too smart for you."

"Ah! You're combative again. That's a sure sign you're recovering. We captured John Hunt Morgan and his men, didn't we?"

"And the South is enraged at your humiliating treatment of them—shaving their heads and putting them in a penitentiary like common thieves. Facial hair is a symbol of manliness to us." She moved her shoulders back and forth against the pillows and grimaced.

"What's the matter?"

"My back is itching. It's driving me crazy. I guess it's from being in bed so long." She rolled over on her side. "Please, will you scratch it?"

Ames willingly complied. "Oh," she sighed. "That feels so good. Along the shoulder blades." Every ounce of her body tingled at the touch of his warm fingers.

He moved his fingernails up and down her shoulder blades. "We've got too many men searching for those horse thieves and renegades. I guarantee you, we'll catch them sooner or later."

"Would you like to bet?"

"Absolutely. What do you want to wager?"

She moved her back against his hands, making sure he got the itch spots. "How about an hour of back scratching for each one, Mosby and Frank."

"I accept!" His laughter was deep, warm, and rich. "That means you're going to owe me two hours of back scratching."

"Well, ex-cuuuuse me!" Sadie said sarcastically when she opened the door and glared at Ames. "Didn't ya understand what I done told ya?"

Ames stood up and confronted her. "She asked me to scratch her back. I haven't done anything wrong."

"That's a likely story!" Sadie huffed, then stood with her hands on her hips.

"It's true, Sadie. I did ask him to scratch my back. Don't be upset," Constance said weakly when she rolled back over. "Please, I'm too tired for an argument."

"I'll see you later," Ames said to Constance.

He walked past Sadie, too elated over Constance's improvement to let the Negress dampen his spirits. He went to the bedroom where the boys spent most of their time. Realizing they detested the Yankees in the house, he thought they would welcome the opportunity to get out. "Anybody interested in riding on my horse?" he asked the two of them.

Hudson jumped to his feet and David tumbled off the bed. "Do you mean it?" Hudson asked excited.

"I'm going first!" David cried, then raced past Hudson into Ames's arms.

That night, Ames and Amanda sat by Constance's bed. "Lieutenant Ames, we haven't thanked you for helping us keep the bookstore open," Amanda said

"I'm not sure I understand what you mean." He looked at Constance, his eyebrows raised.

"I used the check you sent me to buy inventory from a supplier in Baltimore. Without that Federal money we couldn't have made the purchase. Our sources in Richmond are drying up."

"I see. I'm delighted you made such wise use of the money."

"With all the soldiers camped close by, I've been overwhelmed with business," Amanda related. "I believe we should purchase more books and newspapers as soon as possible. I have a hundred dollars in cash. Would you be willing to write a check for that amount to our supplier, if I give you the cash? With the railroad re-opened we should be able to get a shipment quickly."

"Yes, of course." Ames reached into his pocket for a checkbook. "I'd be glad to loan you some money if you need more."

"Oh, no," Amanda said proudly. "We'll pay our own way. I'll soon repay you for the food you've purchased for us." She handed him the money and he gave her the check.

He placed the items in his pocket, then turned towards Constance. "I'm returning to camp early in the morning."

Her face fell. "I hate to see you go. I can't thank you enough for all that you've done for me. How were you able to get away for so long?"

"I was due a week's furlough. I'm a lieutenant now, serving on the staff of my cousin, General Custer. I'm proud to be associated with him. I believe he's the bravest and finest cavalry general in our army. That's why I'm wearing the red necktie." He motioned towards his tie. "It's a source of pride for our brigade to wear a tie like our esteemed general. But I'm digressing. He was kind enough to grant me permission to use my furlough. However, I had to do some fierce arguing to convince our temporary commander to allow me to leave at such a critical time."

"I'm thankful he consented," Constance said weakly. It became apparent to Ames that Amanda had no intention of leaving him alone with her. Sadie had undoubtedly related his alleged indiscretion.

He stood and bowed to both of them. "Ladies, I must bid you good night."

Constance slowly reached her fingers out towards him. When his fingers grasped hers, he felt as if a lightning bolt had surged through his body. Their eyes locked in an intense stare that said everything neither could verbalize.

Amanda cleared her throat. "Good night, Lieutenant Ames. Thank you again for all you've done."

"Will you come back?" Constance asked, her eyes infinite pools of appeal.

"Yes, you can count on it. But I don't know when. Meanwhile, I want you to behave yourself and be a model patient. I expect to get a good report when I return." He kissed her hand gently and turned towards the door.

"I'm too weak not to behave. Good night, Lieutenant Ames."

Next night, September 20, 1863: Constance's bedroom

"Lawd have mercy! There ain't never a dull minute 'round here!" Sadie bustled into Constance's room and closed the door behind her.

Amanda, reading with Hudson, looked up alarmed. "What's wrong?"

Sadie's eyes were opened so wide; it looked like they were about to pop out of her head. "Ya wouldn't believe me if'n I told ya!" She rushed to the drawn curtains at the window and peered out into the darkness. "I done tried to talk him outta it." She looked out of the window over the roof of the back porch.

"Who, Sadie?" Constance asked when Sadie raised the window. Constance sat with her mouth open while the legs and then the body of a soldier in a Union uniform climbed through the window. He turned towards her with that familiar boyish grin.

"Frank!" she gasped. "What are you doing here? The house is full of Yankees!"

"I had to see you," he said softly, then sat down on the bed and hugged her. "Mother learned through a Lieutenant Ames that you had been critically wounded." He kissed her on the cheek. "I had to see you for myself and know that you were recovering."

"Oh, Frank! I'm so glad to see you, but you've risked your life by coming here!" Tears brimmed on her eyelids.

"I risk my life every day. We're all incensed by the needless bombardment of the town and the civilian deaths. Mother is broken hearted about Harriet. She sends her deepest sympathy."

"Frank, what can you tell us about our men?" Amanda pleaded.

"Robert and Alex are frantic about the two of you. They asked me to check on you. Lee has a strong defensive line. I suspect that if Meade does not attack him, he'll take the offensive."

"Tell them that we've survived. Constance is slowly regaining her strength after a severe blood loss. I'm making good money at the bookstore. I don't want them to try anything dangerous. We'll be fine until they return."

"I'm relieved to know that." He looked at Constance's pale face. "You're a strong lady. I knew you would hang on. They'll never get the best of us. We have a will of iron."

They all froze at the sound of loud knocking on the front door. Sadie cracked the door to the hall, and they listened to one of the soldiers playing cards in the parlor walk to answer it. "Sir, we've been informed that Frank Stringfellow, the Confederate scout, is in the house," the arriving soldier said. Stringfellow sprang up from the bed and motioned Amanda to the window.

"Look out and see if there are any soldiers in the back yard," he whispered. She rushed to the window and cracked the curtains to peer out.

"Yes, I can see several," she answered in panic.

"Then I've got to hide." Stringfellow's eyes darted around the room. "Sadie, go downstairs and delay them as long as possible. Help them search the other bedrooms first."

"Lawd, help me!" Sadie shuffled out the door.

"Why don't you get in the bed with Aunt Connie?" Hudson whispered wide-eyed.

Stringfellow looked at him thoughtfully and took off his hat and boots. "Quick Hudson, run up to the attic and hide these. Connie, move over to the edge of the bed."

They heard Sadie downstairs. "Yas'r I knows Mista Stringfellow. He came to the kitchen a little while ago looking for something to eat. I gave him a piece of bread and shooed him on away from here. Told him not to hang 'round here and git mah ladies in trouble. He done left."

Stringfellow threw the sheet back and slit the edge of the feather mattress with his knife. "When I get in here, I want you to cover the mattress back up," he whispered to Amanda. "Connie, I'm going to squish down in it as much as I can. You roll over on top of me."

"If ya'll wants to come upstairs an' search the bedrooms, I'll help ya look for that rascal," Sadie told the soldiers who started up the steps.

Hudson raced back into the bedroom, avoiding the soldiers by using the back stairway. He watched Stringfellow crawl inside the feather mattress and lay down on his stomach with his hand over his face. He squirmed to work his way down into the feathers. Hudson pushed him down and pulled the mattress cover back over him. Her heart pounding, Amanda quickly tucked the sheet back in and pulled up the covers.

"Did y'all look under the bed?" they heard Sadie ask the soldiers searching the boys' bedroom.

"Roll back over, Connie," Amanda whispered. Constance felt Frank under her, but she covered him as much as possible. Her breath caught in her throat and her heart pounded. Amanda pulled a throw rug over the feathers on the floor, and dashed back to her chair. She was reading to Hudson when the soldiers entered the room.

"Excuse me, madam, but we have to search this room," one of the soldiers said rudely.

"My sister is very ill, as you can see," Amanda replied sharply. "I resent this intrusion. Please be brief."

The soldiers looked behind the curtains, peered out on the porch roof, got down and looked under the bed and in the cedar chest and wardrobe. Constance held her breath while she watched a small feather float daintily through the air. Stringfellow pushed his index finger against his nose to avoid sneezing, but the dust of the feathers nearly suffocated him. They had better leave soon.

"Sorry to disturb you." The soldiers walked to the hall.

"Ya got one more bedroom to search," Sadie told them.

Constance and Amanda both heaved a sigh of relief. Rolling over, Constance whispered to the mattress, "Frank, are you all right?" She heard muffled gagging. Amanda and Hudson rushed over and pulled the sheet and mattress-cover back, until they found his head. He lifted it up, gasping for air.[ii]

[ii]There is no evidence that Stringfellow ever hid in a feather mattress, thus this episode is fictional. However, Tom Hines, another famous Confederate agent, did accomplish this feat.

"Air!" He blew the feathers away from his nose.

"I don't think you should get out yet. They're still in the house," Constance whispered. She wiped the feathers from his face.

"Just give me air."

After about ten minutes, they heard the front door close and the remaining Yankees return to their card game. "They done gone now," Sadie bragged when she returned.

Stringfellow emerged from the mattress covered with feathers from head to toe. "Frank, you look like a snowman." Constance laughed quietly. Amanda and Sadie brushed the feathers off while Hudson went to the attic to retrieve his hat and boots. "You always make me laugh," Constance giggled.

"I know how to cut a shine, little sister." He brushed the feathers from his hair, turned to Sadie with a big grin and hugged her. "Sadie I love you."

"Don't ya ever make me do nothin' like that again, Mista Frank. An' look at the mess ya done made." She tried to sweep up the feathers.

"Somebody betrayed me," he mused, pulling on his boots. "It had to be someone who recognized my face—a citizen who has turned their allegiance to the North—a traitor."

"I can't imagine who would do such a thing," Amanda said.

"Nevertheless, I can't be seen here again without a disguise. Check the back yard now." He motioned Amanda to the window.

"I don't see anybody. I think it's safe."

He hugged them all and disappeared into the night.

"I'm exhausted," Constance sighed. "That's enough excitement for one night."

Four days later, September 24, 1863: Near Mitchell's Station

The cold rain pelted Stringfellow in the face as he and his two companions crouched in the bushes observing the Union camp around Mitchell's Station. "They're pulling out. No doubt about it," he whispered to John Frazier of Spotsylvania Court House and James Farish Hansbrough who lived nearby.

"Looks to me like they're heading north. What do you make of it?" Frazier asked, then shook the rain from his hat.

"I'm not sure I understand the significance," Stringfellow replied. "Maybe they're going to Tennessee since we whipped them at Chickamauga. Or could be there's more draft riots. One thing's for sure. After four days of scouting, we've got something important to report."

"I'd estimate at least two corps are pulling out," Hansbrough surmised.

Stringfellow nodded his head in agreement. "Yep. Frazier, take that information to the nearest picket and see that it gets passed on to General Lee immediately. We'll wait for you here."

Late that night, Frazier returned to his comrades. "The information is on its way. I saw the courier gallop off," he reported.

"Good," Stringfellow said relieved. "Now I suggest we find a place to get some shut-eye." The scouts had gotten little sleep in four days.

"Agreed." Hansbrough yawned. "Let's go to my house and get out of the rain."

Stringfellow pondered the situation. "I don't think that's wise. The Federals make periodic checks of the houses near their camps. I think we're safer right here in this pine thicket. I know the ground's saturated, but if we lay some pine boughs over the exposed roots of that big oak tree, we'll sleep like babes."

The three scouts set to work preparing their bed. They spread a blanket over the boughs, sprawled out and spread two more blankets over them. "I'm a light sleeper. We'll move out before dawn," Stringfellow told them as he took off his boots and hat. He closed his eyes and immediately drifted into a deep sleep.

When he opened his eyes, the sun was high in the sky. He had an instinctive feeling that danger surrounded him. The blanket was suddenly drawn away from his face and a sarcastic voice said, "Get up Johnny Rebs. We'll give you a better place to sleep than out in the rain."

Instantly awake, Stringfellow squinted his eyes and assessed the situation. Four Yanks stood over him with guns pointed. One false move and he'd be riddled with bullets. He'd made up his mind never to surrender. It was an ugly, depressing situation. Maintaining his coolness of mind, he suddenly came up with a ruse. He closed his eyes again, pulled the blanket back over his shoulders, rolled over and muttered in a sleepy voice, "Go away and let me sleep, will you!"

The amused Yankees burst out laughing. He cautiously moved his hand under the blanket to the pistol in his belt. Slowly, he extracted the gun, placed his hand on the hammer, and noiselessly cocked it. He felt Hansbrough doing the same thing. Tiring of the mirth and comedy, a Yankee reached down and jerked the blanket off of the three Rebels. Instantly, Stringfellow fired into his breast. The large man collapsed on him, bleeding profusely. The rest of the squad leveled their guns at Stringfellow, but their bullets plowed into their collapsed companion. Hansbrough rolled out from under one side of the body, while Stringfellow emerged from the other side. When Hansbrough shot one of the Yankees, he fell backwards firing his gun. The bullet struck Frazier in the head, killing him instantly. The other two Federals dropped their empty guns, and raced back to the camp, now in an uproar.

"Run for your life!" Stringfellow called to Hansbrough. "I'll meet you at the horses!"

Within seconds a large party of angry, vengeful Yankees charged forth from the camp. In his stocking feet, Stringfellow sprinted to the right through the woods. He ran as he had never run before. Even though he was in his Confederate uniform and could not be considered a spy, he realized that the angry mob would kill him in an instant. He ran breathlessly, knocking down limbs or anything that got in his way. There was little undergrowth in the pine forest, no good place to hide. He heard the enemy closing in on him from all directions. Flying as fast as his legs would carry him, he resolved not to let them hunt him down like a wild animal. His eyes darted around him, searching for a loophole of escape. There had to be a way to extricate himself from the trap. He wouldn't let hopelessness overwhelm him. This was a contest for life and death. He paused gasping for breath, and listened to his pursuers, closing in fast. No matter how fleet of foot he was, they would soon overtake him.

Darting forward again, he suddenly found himself in a small open field. In the middle was a cluster of pines, one of which had recently fallen. Panting, he dashed forward and concealed himself in the bushy top of the fallen tree. He loaded his pistols and grimly waited for the foe to discover him. If necessary, he resolved to fight and die. Within moments, four Federals searched the area. They walked nearly within reach of him, and one muttered, "Dirty killer. If I catch him I ain't takin' him in." He walked so close, Stringfellow saw his face and could reach out and touch him. His leg cramped while he watched them search for him, and then finally move away. Not believing his good fortune, Stringfellow slowly emerged from his hiding spot and rubbed his cramped leg and aching feet. Suddenly, a concealed Yank who had lingered behind, hollered, "Here he is!"

Gasping, Stringfellow sprinted forward through the field. Hearing them close behind him, he put forth his remaining strength and darted back into the woods at full speed, the ardor of the chase hotter than before. Panting, almost worn out, he debated whether to turn and fight and die. Desperate, he came out into a field again and dashed across a steam. With a raging thirst, he could not resist stooping down for a drink of cool water. Hearing them almost upon him, he threw himself into the dense undergrowth that skirted the stream. Hastily, he drew brush and tree roots over him and had no sooner disappeared from sight, than the enemy arrived. "Look, there's his knee print in the sand. He can't be far off. We've got him now!"

Soon soldiers filled the field, beating the bushes, hunting for their quarry. Systematically, they searched every hiding place. Lying on his back in the dense jungle with a cocked pistol in each hand, the exhausted scout listened to the search. A man walked down the streambed within a foot of him. If he had to fight his way out, Stringfellow determined to kill as many Yankees as possible in the process. He listened to their stomping feet and curses. One peered into the very bushes over his head. The scout tightened his grip on the triggers, but breathed easier after the man moved away. The search went on for over an hour before the Yankees became resigned to the fact that their prey had eluded them. Stringfellow could not believe his good fortune, and thanked God for his deliverance. At nightfall he safely made his way back to his horse, Hansbrough, and the Confederate lines.[1]

Four days later, September 28, 1863: Sadie's kitchen

"Momma, I'm back!" Joseph announced happily when he entered the brick kitchen.

Sadie spun around from the cook stove and threw her arms around him. "Honey chile, I done worried mahsef to death 'bout y'all. I was afraid y'all was in New York when all those black folks was killed."

Joseph kissed her on the cheek and stared at her. "Ya look thinner, Momma. Have ya been sick?"

"No, jist a little run down. Times been hard 'round here. But come on and sit a spell and tell me everythin'."

Joseph sat down, relaxed, and began his story. He was so glad to be back in Culpeper and oh, how he missed their good life on the farm. When he went with Pope's army, it was nigger do this and nigger do that. They treated them like dirt...not nearly as good as Judge Armstrong. But he knew if they had stayed on the farm, they would have starved to death. He had watched the Yankees destroy all the crops, fences, and livestock as well as tear down the deserted houses and cut the trees for firewood. Like a swarm of locusts, they swept everything away. Selene had gotten tired of living in a tent so they went into Washington, hopeful that Joseph could find a job. No such luck. They found that town a terrible place of muddy streets packed with soldiers and whorehouses.

Thousands of so-called freed slaves lived in hovels, practically starving to death for lack of work. He never wanted to live in a big filthy city because he loved the land and the outdoors.

So they returned to the army working for the cavalry this time, and had been treated a little better. Selene did laundry, but the kids were always sick. They expected another baby in a month. He assured Sadie that if their camp moved closer to town he would bring her grandchildren to visit. He promised her that he would never fight against their people, even though the Yankees constantly pressured him to do so.

Sadie and Joseph looked up startled when Aaron Ames entered the kitchen and plopped a sack on the table. "I brought you some coffee, sugar, and cheese."

"Mah goodness, real coffee! We can sure use that! Do ya 'member mah Joseph?"

Ames eyes registered recognition. "Of course, the famous captor of chicken thieves. I thought you looked familiar." He stared at Joseph intently. "Have I seen you around camp?"

"Yas'r. I'm working for Ginnel Custer. I thought I'd noticed ya one day, but warn't sure it was you. "

Ames smiled and looked at Sadie. "Tell me, how is our favorite patient?"

"She's improving slowly," Sadie answered with some concern. "She's still weak and gits tired easy."

"Has she been getting up and walking?" His voice tingled with anxiety.

"A little, but she says she gits dizzy and tired. Miss Amanda and I've been so busy, we ain't had much time to help her."

"Well, Sadie, since you're the person in charge around here now, I'd like your permission to visit her and help her walk," Ames said politely.

Flattered, Sadie became slightly puffed up with her new authority. "I'm glad ya understand the situation 'round here, Lieutenant Ames. Ya has my permission. I'll go up with ya and git her out of bed," Sadie declared in a very dignified manner. "Joseph, ya wait here for me."

Ames nodded to Joseph. "I expect I'll see you again at camp."

"Yas'r, Lieutenant Ames, I look forward to that," Joseph replied with a broad smile.

"Miss Constance, ya can't lay in that bed all day. You's gotta git up an' walk, an' I've got jist the person to make ya do it," Sadie ordered when they walked in the room.

Looking up from her book, Constance's spirits soared at the sight of Aaron Ames's tall muscular body behind Sadie. "Why, Lieutenant Ames, you did come back after all!"

"Yes, and I believe it's a good thing. I hear you've become quite lazy." Sadie helped her into her robe.

"How dare you even insinuate that," Constance retorted, slipping her feet into the slippers Sadie held for her. "You have no idea how useless I feel. I'm terribly frustrated that I'm dizzy and tired every time I stand up." He took her arms and steadied her; she stood, blinked her eyes, and waited a minute. "I have to let the dizziness pass."

"You lost a lot of blood. The dizziness is to be expected," he said soothingly.

She took his arm and leaned against him, blinking, her flesh prickling from the contact. "I'm ready now." She stared up into his compelling hazel eyes. "Forward, march. But take little steps."

She stepped forward slowly, wincing when she put her weight on the injured leg. "It's still painful. The back of my leg is so tight I can't bend it."

"That's normal." He took small steps beside her. "The doctor said it would be a month before you could walk normally. It'll become a little easier each day. Trust me."

Sadie watched the two of them slowly edge around the room. "That's real good, Miss Constance. I'll go fix y'all some coffee—real coffee!" She walked out, purposely leaving the door open.

"Real coffee?"

"Yes, I brought you some. The army finally got paid." They slowly shuffled across the floor.

"Is that why there's been so much noise and drunkenness in the streets? I've never heard such a ruckus. I've barely gotten any sleep the last two nights."

"Yes, I'm afraid the conscripts who've recently arrived are the dregs of the earth. Their conduct is deplorable. Would you like to walk up the hall?"

"I'll accept that challenge." They made their way into the hall, hearing the voices of the soldiers downstairs. "I'm so sick of being surrounded by bluebellies. It's humiliating to be cooped up in two rooms in our own house, while they lounge around downstairs. We've been taking our meals on the little table in my room so Amanda has as little contact as possible with them. I have few visitors because most of my friends are afraid to go out of their homes. I understand pillage and plundering is prevalent throughout the county. Our army behaved like gentlemen in Pennsylvania."

The two of them tediously crept back up the hall. "I'm ashamed to say it's happening," he admitted. "How are you doing?"

"I'm growing tired. How I yearn for energy. I need to help Amanda. She's working extremely hard."

"You've got to get well first." He guided her back into the bedroom. "Do you feel up to a game of chess? Perhaps I have a chance of beating you in your weakened state."

Her voice rang with laughter. "I'll play if you promise not to gloat should you defeat me." He helped her into one of the ladder back chairs by the small table. "The chess set is up there on the shelf."

When he reached up for the box, he noticed the books on her bed. "Looks like you've had lots of time to read. What are you reading now?"

He sat down across from her and thought he detected a small tinge of color on her pale cheeks. *Romeo and Juliet.* He put the pieces in place. "It's a beautiful love story, but I anguish over the tragic ending."

He looked up abruptly, his eyes studying her with curious intensity. "Did you remember that it's my favorite story?"

"Yes," she said softly, then dropped her eyes to the chessboard. "You go first." He paused for a moment and made his move. She quickly did likewise. "It's been nine days since I've seen you. I've heard quite a bit of cannon fire. Please tell me what's happening."

"We're camped on the Robertson River near Madison Court House." He slid a pawn forward. "On the twenty second we undertook a reconnaissance in force into Madison County to learn of roads, bridges, and Confederate troops. Stuart, of course, rode out to confront us. We had a very spirited engagement and maneuvered to surround him near a place called Jack's Shop. I was positive that we would capture the great Jeb Stuart and a large portion of his cavalry," he said quite animated.

"But?" she said with her eyebrows raised.

"But, he managed to fight his way out. In a fierce and gallant charge, the Rebs cut their way through our lines and escaped. They even managed to carry off their guns. I have to admire their resourcefulness and willingness to fight in what appeared to be a hopeless situation. I didn't believe it was possible for them to escape."

"I'm not surprised." Her lips curved up slightly and she made her move. "Jeb Stuart and his men are much too clever for you. Look what happened to you at Chicamauga."

"That was an unfortunate setback, but now that we control the Mississippi, we'll eventually prevail." He moved a rook. "The situation here remains uncertain. I believe Meade will attack soon."

"I hope a massive battle doesn't take place here." She contemplated the board for a minute and moved. "I've had a lot of time to think and reflect during my confinement. My mind is clearer now than when you were here before. Amanda told me how you buried Mother. I'm deeply grateful." He looked at her sympathetically while she stared at the beautiful oil painting on the wall. "She painted that landscape, you know. My mother was a very talented lady. She created beauty wherever she went, whether it was through her paintings, her music, her floral arrangements, or simply her lovely appearance and countenance," she continued, her eyes glistening with tears. "I'm suffering…terrible guilt now that she's gone," she whispered, her voice breaking.

He reached across the table and covered her hand with his. "Why are you feeling guilty?"

"Because so much of the time we seemed to have a battle of wills. She was a traditionalist and I always wanted to rebel and do things my way. But that doesn't mean I didn't love and respect her. I'm afraid though, that she thought I didn't love her. You see," she sobbed with tears sliding down her face, "there were so many times when I could have thrown my arms around her and said, 'I love you, Mother', and I didn't do it. And now…now she's gone. It's too late." She wept softly.

He took her hand in both of his and caressed it gently. He longed to hold her, but feared Sadie would appear at the door at any moment. "Don't be so hard on yourself. We're all guilty of not expressing our love to the people we care about most."

She intertwined her fingers with his, feeling the strength and warmth of his grip. "Amanda and I blame ourselves for her death. We were insane not to go sooner to the rectory cellar. I suppose we just didn't believe the Yankees would shell the town. Mother died a terribly brutal death."

"Hindsight is a wonderful thing, but you can't change what happened. It wasn't your fault. I believe she died instantly from the first shell, if that's any consolation. But the loss of a mother is always difficult to bear. I can understand your feelings. My mother's health is failing, and I doubt that I'll ever see her again."

She looked at him alarmed. "You used your furlough to take care of me instead of going home to see your mother? Why?"

"Because as much as I'd like to see her, I didn't believe my going home would save her life. I thought that by being with you, I could save yours." He kissed her hand tenderly.

"And you did," she whispered softly while leaning forward over the table, her eyes piercing the distance between them. "Not only did you risk your life to save mine, but then you refused to let me die. I knew every time I opened my eyes that you would be there and you would encourage me—make me eat. But most importantly, you gave me the will to live." Her eyes flooded with tears again.

He withdrew his hand abruptly when he heard Sadie stomping down the hall. "Now look what I brung ya," she said, placing a tray on the table. "Coffee, bread, and cheese!"

"Oh, that looks wonderful!" Constance said, regaining her voice. "This is a feast. I've longed for coffee for months. How we used to take the smallest things for granted."

"How'd she do?" Sadie asked Ames after she poured the coffee.

"Marvelous! I expect her to be running in a week." He cut the cheese and offered Constance a slice. Hudson and David raced down the hall to find the source of the inviting aromas.

"May I have some?" Hudson asked Ames while he stared hungrily at the cheese.

"Of course." Ames pushed chairs back for the two boys, who joined them at the table. "It's like a picnic."

"I want to go riding," David begged before he stuffed a piece of cheese in his mouth.

"I'm afraid I don't have time for that today. At the moment, I have to finish this chess game." He stared at the board thoughtfully and moved a knight.

"We'll help you." Hudson leaned over the board. Constance looked at Aaron and chuckled.

About thirty minutes later Ames said proudly, "Checkmate!"

"Aunt Connie, he beat you," Hudson yelled.

"I've been sick," she said defensively. "I dare you to gloat." She cast a challenging look at the Yankee.

He leaned back in his chair, clasped his hands behind his head, and laughed heartily. "After the defeat at Chicamauga and Stuart's escape, I needed a victory."

She wanted to taunt him about Frank hiding in her mattress, but knew that would be risky. All they needed was to be arrested for harboring a spy. "I know something that you don't know," she said in a teasing manner. "You passed up the opportunity to capture two of our most important generals. You probably could have ended this war."

He leaned forward, eyeing her suspiciously. "Oh, I did, did I? And who did I fail to capture?"

"Lee and Ewell," she answered innocently. "I watched you from the cupola at Beauregard at Brandy Station. I saw you spare Alex."

"I'm not sure I'm gullible enough to believe this. What color was my horse?"

"Black."

His jaw dropped and his eyes narrowed speculatively. "That's true, but what's it got to do with capturing the generals? It was a cavalry battle. They weren't there."

"Oh, yes they were," she said with a tone of confidence. "They were inside the house when you and your companions rode up in front of it. I watched you. You had a few prisoners with you, and then you rode off in the direction of Auburn. The two of them were in the house for the taking. You passed up a golden opportunity."

Astounded, he assessed her for a long moment. "You're serious, aren't you? They really were in that house?"

"I swear it," she answered in triumph. "Think what a hero you would have been."

He shook his head in disbelief. "You're making me feel like a fool."

"Oh, no. Like you said, hindsight is a wonderful thing. I just had to put you in your place. Couldn't let you get too arrogant over your victory."

"Lieutenant Ames, don't let her taunt you any longer," Amanda said from the corner where she was sewing. "We southerners truly are hospitable people. Won't you stay and have dinner with us?"

"I appreciate your kind offer." He stood up. "But unfortunately I must return to camp. It's a long ride."

"But you've been here such a short time. Must you leave so soon?" Constance's eyes caught and held his.

"Regretfully, yes."

When she attempted to stand, he took her arm to steady her. She wrapped her arm around his. "I'm not as dizzy. I feel much steadier. It seems you have a miraculous healing touch."

He took small steps with her towards the door. "I took lessons from you, remember?"

David wrapped his arms around Ames's leg, clinging to his trousers. "Please let me ride your horse."

"It seems I have competition for your attention," Constance chuckled when the three of them reached the doorway.

"David, leave Lieutenant Ames alone," Amanda ordered. "I'm sorry, but he misses his father."

"Tell you what, David, if you walk down with me, I'll let you sit on my horse for one minute." The four-year-old shrieked with delight.

Constance slipped her slender fingers into the large hand of the handsome Yankee. "You must come back. I demand a rematch."

"I expect you to be fully recovered. No excuses for illness next time." He kissed her hand and then reached down and took David's hand. Constance winked at him and the two new buddies disappeared down the hall.

15

Lee's Last Lunge: The Bristoe Campaign

October 3 - November 2, 1863

"I am convinced that I made the attack too hastily, and at the same time that a delay of half an hour, and there would have been no enemy to attack."
General A. P. Hill, C.S.A. after Bristoe Station

Five days later, October 3, 1863: Clark Mountain

Robert E. Lee, A. P. Hill, Dick Ewell, and Jubal Early completed the arduous trek to the peak of Clark Mountain on a crisp, clear, early fall day. Lee, having recently suffered another attack of angina, realized his strength had been sapped. Nevertheless, he remained determined to mount an offensive against Meade. The Confederate high command surveyed the imposing camps of the enemy in Culpeper through their field glasses.

"Gentlemen," Lee began as he paced. "I have received information from General Stuart's scouts and our friends along the railroad in western Virginia that General Meade has transferred two corps to Tennessee following our recent victory there. His strength is now around 75,000 while we have roughly 45,000. I had hoped for the return of General Longstreet from Tennessee before mounting an offensive, but it appears that will not happen any time soon. I believe we must move now for many reasons." The three generals listened attentively, with expressions of anticipation on their faces. "First, we must not allow Meade to transfer any more troops to Tennessee in order to protect our position there. If we can push him back towards Washington and apply pressure, he will not weaken his forces here. Second, we will be able to again take control of several of our counties that are suffering greatly from Union occupation." Powell Hill nodded enthusiastically. He detested having Culpeper under Federal control. "Third, we have recently received supplies for our North Carolina men from the blockade runner Ad-Vance. The next ship is not due for months. There is still grass for our horses. After heavy frost that food source will no longer be available and our poorly clad men will have to fight in worse weather conditions. The roads are in relatively good condition now. Also, the troops subduing the draft riot in New York will be returning soon. Meade is having problems with his newly drafted men. Desertions are high and executions take place every day in their camps. I sense that the morale of our men has taken an upturn. Do you agree?"

"Absolutely," Hill reiterated. "They are rested and encouraged after Chickamauga."

"They're hankering for a fight," Ewell added while Early nodded his head.

"Good." Lee turned and pointed to the west in the direction of Madison Court House. "We will move around to Madison and proceed in an arc to turn Meade's right and initiate battle in a place advantageous to us. General Ewell, your men will move in an inner arc, and General Hill you will move in an outer parallel arc closer to the mountains. General Stuart will screen your movements."

"The area we'll be traveling through is rough country with few good roads," Hill questioned. "It will be difficult to move rapidly."

"It will be a challenge," Lee agreed. "You'll have to equip a brigade of your men with axes to cut your way through forests when necessary." Hill nodded thoughtfully.

"Who will remain in our lines to hold Meade's attention?" Ewell asked.

"I propose to leave Fitz Lee's cavalry, Johnson's brigade from General Ewell and Walker's brigade from General Hill south of the Rapidan near Raccoon and Morton's Fords." Doing a little mental arithmetic, the other generals realized that was only about 7000 men. Meade could easily destroy them. Noting the concern on their faces, Lee stated, "There is great risk, but we must rely on Meade's timidity. If he learns of our movement, I believe he will retreat towards Washington. Hopefully, we can cut him off. Secrecy and speed are critical to this campaign. Begin now moving your wagons and sick men to the rear. We will march on the eighth."

Dolly placed Powell's hand on her rotund middle. "Did you feel that?" She snuggled up next to him under the covers.

"Yes, this baby kicks vigorously. Sweetheart, there's something I must tell you." He kissed her on the forehead."

"I don't like the sound of your voice. A battle is imminent, isn't it?"

"Yes." She observed the intense excitement in his eyes. "Lee is going to take the offensive. It's a daring move, but I believe we can be successful. There's nothing I want more now than a victory. We have a chance to sting Meade badly. We can retaliate for Gettysburg and the devastation his army has wrought in Culpeper."

"But you're greatly outnumbered and our men are poorly clothed. Thousands still need shoes."

"True, but we have our fighting spirit back. We may never have an opportunity like this again." His voice rose with excitement. "Lee is trusting me with the most difficult assignment. I've got to move my men further and faster. He told me that he would travel with Ewell. He knows if the opportunity presents itself, I will take the initiative and Ewell will not. I desperately want the chance to catch the enemy when they're vulnerable and hit them hard!"

"I understand, darling. But, remember, you're only human. When are you leaving?"

"The eighth." His lips feather-touched hers. "I hate leaving you with the baby due so soon. Anything could happen here. I don't want to endanger you. I believe it's best for you to go to Richmond and have our child there. My love and prayers will be with you."

Three days later, October 6, 1863: Meade's Headquarters

General George Meade looked up from the desk at his headquarters at the Wallach house, where he had enjoyed a pleasant stay with the Union sympathizers. Lovely young Nannie had charmed his staff with her piano playing and singing, and to add to the gaiety, several of his regimental bands had serenaded the family and his guests.

"Sir," the young soldier said as he saluted. "I'm reporting from our signal station at Pony Mountain. The signals sent by the enemy on Clark Mountain indicate a Confederate offensive is imminent."

Meade's jaw dropped and his face registered shock. Cryptographers had unlocked the key to the Confederate's secret code. However, this information seemed incredible. "You are positive this information is correct?"

"We are absolutely positive, sir."

"Very well. Thank you and keep me informed of any new messages or troop movement." Meade pondered the situation after the soldier departed. Perhaps Lee was withdrawing or sending troops to Tennessee. He could not accept the fact that Lee might be preparing to attack him.

Two days later, October 8, 1863: Madison Court House

"Place your guns on this knoll," Robert Beckam commanded his men who prepared to make camp for the night at the small town of Madison Court House. Beckam drank in the beauty of the Blue Ridge Mountains framed by a crimson sunset. Stuart had reached the town, which would be the launching site for Lee's offensive. Hill and Ewell followed behind. Stringfellow had sent Beckam a message reporting Constance's apparent recovery after her critical wound. Looking north in the direction of Culpeper, he longed to see her. Fury burned inside of him as he visualized retaliating against the enemy for their fiendish deed. The only thing standing between him and Culpeper was the camp of Kilpatrick's cavalry on the north side of the Robertson River.

George Armstrong Custer listened to his band play "Hail to the Chief" with surprise and delight when he returned to camp after his three-week furlough. Custer, the only Union cavalry general with a band, refused to be outdone by Jeb Stuart and his traveling musicians. He tipped his hat to his men who greeted him with three cheers. "Gentlemen, I thank you for that warm reception." He dismounted. "It's good to be back. I trust you have been busy in my absence."

"It's been boring," one of his staff officers complained. "Nothing but picket duty for ten days. We had some horse races for fun."

Custer worked his way through the crowd shaking hands in the twilight. "Lieutenant Ames, we must talk later," he said to his cousin. "I'll send for you when I've finished with official business."

"Welcome back, sir. I look forward to that."

Ames entered Custer's tent around midnight. "Have a seat, cuz," Custer said warmly. "I'm exploding with joy and I must share it with someone I can trust. I've captured the heart of my true love! The beautiful, wonderful Libbie has agreed to marry me!"

"Congratulations, sir." Ames shook his hand. He had never seen a happier or prouder man than Custer on this evening. He pulled two cigars out of his pocket, handing Custer one. "This is cause for celebration. Share your tactics with me. I need some inspiration."

"Tenacity!" Custer lit his cigar and leaned back in his chair, his blue eyes sparkling. "I never gave up. I hadn't seen her in five months. We had been corresponding indirectly through a mutual friend since her father forbade her to write to me. When I returned as a general this time, the town welcomed me as a hero. A group of young men planned a party in my honor and the newspapers interviewed me. I felt confident that I could offer her a more acceptable future as a general rather than a mere captain. She agreed to see me. We strolled together and went to church together, and then she attended a masquerade party given in my honor. We danced until the wee small hours of the morning. When we returned to her garden I showered her with kisses and proposed again. She accepted!" He pounded the desk with his hand. "I am the most fortunate of men!"

"I share your joy. Have you set the date?"

Custer became serious. "No, I still have to overcome the obstacle of her father. I didn't have an opportunity to address him, since he avoided me most of the time. I'll ask his permission in a letter. I understand his reluctance to give up his beautiful only child." He stroked his long blonde mustache thoughtfully. "I must admit I do fear he has an unfounded prejudice against me. But, surely he values his daughter's happiness. If she tells him herself of the depth of our love, he must eventually consent."

"I'm sure your persistence will ultimately win him over. You haven't suffered a defeat yet."

Custer chuckled. "Thank you for your encouragement. Now, tell me of your Miss Armstrong. I hope she has recovered?"

"She's slowly regaining her strength. I almost lost her," Ames said softly with pain in his eyes. "I believe my being there and acquiring proper food for her saved her life. I'm indebted to you for the week's furlough."

"I'm glad it made a difference," Custer replied leaning forward. "Surely, she must be in love with you, after all you've done. How could she resist?"

Ames smiled, then puffed on his cigar. "I used your technique. I told her *I love you* a thousand times with my eyes. I believe she does have feelings for me, but I don't know if her affection will overcome the fact that I'm a damn Yankee. Both of her parents have died brutal deaths at the hands of our army. I can understand her bitterness and hatred." He shook his head and then gestured with his large hands. "On top of that, I've got stiff competition."

"Who's your competition?"

"She was infatuated with or perhaps in love with John Pelham."

Custer whistled softly. "Pelham was one of the finest and best-liked men I've ever known. I mourned his tragic death. He's only been dead, what…seven months? His memory will be tough to compete with."

"According to her nephew, she's now romantically involved with Pelham's successor, Robert Beckam, who has known her since before the war."

"Um," Custer grunted. "You're competing with a high-ranking Rebel. I know nothing but good things about him from West Point. You do like a challenge, don't you?"

Ames smiled with determination. "It appears that way. I certainly never expected to lose my heart while marching through Culpeper. But it's happened…and there's no turning back," he said with a tone of wonder in his voice.

"Nobody ever gave me a prayer of winning the hand of Libbie Bacon. Perseverance is the answer. If she's the woman you love, don't give up until she's yours."

* * *

Next day, October 9, 1863: Morton's Ford

Alex stared at the thin line of men left in the fortifications at Morton's Ford. "If Meade comes after us we haven't got a prayer," he muttered to a fellow Ranger.

"Old Marse Robert will keep him guessing too much. Meade ain't got the guts to attack us."

General George Meade dismounted his horse at the top of Cedar Mountain. Reports of Rebel troops massing at Madison Court House had been filtering in for two days. He wanted to take a look for himself. "Here you are, General Meade." A signalman motioned the general towards a powerful telescope.

Squinting, Meade stared through the telescope focused on the upper Rapidan. "There they are all right." He watched ragged gray soldiers crossing the river and scrutinized an ambulance slowly crossing the stream. Little did he know that it contained Robert E. Lee, who was too weak to ride his horse. Meade then moved the telescope towards Madison where he saw camps of Confederate soldiers. "They are definitely massing." Meade pondered the situation. Lee was either retreating from the Rapidan or making a flank movement against him. He was beginning to give credence to Pleasanton's theory that the Confederates were abandoning Virginia and sending their army to Tennessee. Lee would fall back to Richmond to cover the evacuation of the government. Meade decided to order Buford to cross the Rapidan at Germanna Ford in the morning and reconnoiter the Confederate lines around Morton's and Raccoon Fords. If they were as weak as he assumed, he would order an attack. Meanwhile, he would have his men prepare five days rations and arrange the rest of his troops to meet a possible assault from Lee.

Next day, October 10, 1863: James City

6:30 a.m. Custer and his staff looked up from their morning coffee when they heard gunshots in the direction of Russell's Ford on the Robertson River. "Sounds like an enemy attack." Custer jumped up. "We know their infantry is on the move." A courier soon rode up confirming the attack by Stuart.

8 a.m. Marching since 5 a.m. from Madison, Hill felt his men deserved a brief rest. "Order the men to halt for a ten minute break," he told his chief of staff while his men arrived at Criglersville. He knew that as he turned his men north, the roads would deteriorate from bad to terrible. The intermittent rain would make the already soft ground harder to traverse. He had to pass through hilly, rough country, interspersed with streams. He heard his Pioneer Corps chopping trees ahead of the infantry. He would split his men into two columns to pass on either side of Mitchell's Mountain for the difficult, slow march.

9 a.m. When Jeb Stuart arrived at James City, he placed his men on the ridge immediately south of the hamlet located between two parallel ridges. "Have Major Beckam unlimber the guns," he ordered. Davies, of Kilpatrick's command, faced him on the next ridge to the north. Stuart had sent a handpicked band of men to scale

Thoroughfare Mountain and shut down the Union signal station. This assignment was completed in short order. Beckam's guns opened up with deadly accuracy, sending a shell that hit close to General Davies. The artillery duel and skirmishing continued most of the day. Stuart succeeded in holding most of the Union cavalry at bay, thus screening the movement of the infantry. Unfortunately, the First West Virginia scouted on the Union right and observed the movement of Ewell's troops towards Griffinsburg.

About the same time, John Buford crossed his cavalry at Germanna Ford, eighteen miles east of the fighting at James City. He knew nothing of Lee's offensive or the engagement at James City.

Noon: Meade, at the Wallach house, carefully monitored the incoming dispatches, concluding that the Confederates were moving towards his right, either to advance to the Shenandoah Valley or attack him. He shifted his II Corps to Stonehouse Mountain, west of town, to meet the advancing Rebels. On their arrival to the mountain, the engineers rapidly leveled trees to create an open field of fire. By late afternoon, Meade had three fifths of his infantry and one third of his cavalry between James City and Stone House Mountain, facing Lee's flanking columns.[1] He had called off the attack scheduled for the morning on Lee's remaining men at Morton's and Raccoon Fords. Buford did not know of the change and would have to fend for himself.

4:30 p.m. Dust flew as couriers rapidly galloped off from the Wallach house with new orders for all corps commanders. Meade watched them, confident of the correctness of his last minute decision not to fight Lee in Culpeper. Instead, he would flee to safety across the Rappahannock, a much better defensive position. All units were ordered to begin withdrawal to the north side of the river at 3 a.m. the next morning. His headquarters would be established at Rappahannock Station.

Nightfall Ewell's weary soldiers broke camp at Griffinsburg on the Sperryville Pike, while Hill's men stopped at Woodville and Slate Mills. The day's movement had been slower than Lee anticipated.

Next day, October 11, 1863: Culpeper Court House

3 a.m. Constance rolled over in her sleep, restless. She dreamed she heard noises, men's boots on the wooden floors, the creaking wheels of wagons, hooves on the streets, men marching. She slowly opened her eyes and listened. The soldiers in the house yelled at each other. "Pack up everything. Meade's ordered a withdrawal."

"Amanda." She poked her sister. "What's happening?"

Amanda rolled over and blinked at her. "It sounds like the army is on the move," she whispered. "Do you think they're going to attack Lee?"

"No." Constance limped over and peered out the window. "I heard one of them say they were withdrawing. East Street is full of wagons and soldiers."

"That's too good to be true!" Amanda joined her at the window. "Our prayers are answered if they truly are leaving. But why?"

"It could simply be a feint or a maneuver. The other answer is our army is approaching or flanking them." She gripped Amanda's hand. "We could be caught in a great battle. These two armies may fight here today."

Amanda put her arms around her trembling sister. "You've been through such a terrible ordeal. We've got to pray for deliverance. We will survive."

Dawn A scout galloped up to Jeb Stuart in the morning mist at his camp at James City. "The enemy has withdrawn, sir," the horseman reported breathlessly. "There's no sign of them in front of us."

Stuart pondered the situation. Turning to his subordinates, he commanded, "Young, keep your brigade here to cover the rear of the army and move forward towards Culpeper. Gordon, I'll accompany you and Beckam's artillery towards Griffinsburg where we'll unite with Funsten and precede the infantry into Culpeper."

7 a.m. John Buford sipped his coffee at his camp behind the Confederate line south of Morton's Ford. Unaware of Lee's flanking movement or Meade's withdrawal, he prepared to attack, assuming he would receive infantry support on the opposite side of the line. The hero of Gettysburg for holding the high ground on the first day, he was one of the Union's most capable cavalry officers. He turned, surprised to see a Union courier galloping up at top speed. Jumping from his horse, the courier handed him a message. "Thank God, I found you in time!"

Buford studied the message. Meade's withdrawal of the army had been underway for four hours. He was on his own and would have to fight his way through the enemy's line in order to join the retreating army as soon as possible. "This certainly changes the situation," he said to his staff. "We'll drive them out of their defenses at Morton's Ford and fight our way back to our army. By attacking from the rear, we'll have the element of surprise. I'm not leaving the artillery, so we'll need an assessment of conditions at the ford."

Guns cracked and the dismounted cavalrymen fought to take control of the Confederate trenches. Shortly, an officer reported back to Buford, "The road on both sides of the ford is in terrible condition, sir. It's not passable for artillery. We've taken control of the fortifications."

"Then we'll make it passable," Buford ordered. "Start a crew cutting trees for a corduroy road. We'll grade if necessary, but we've got to work fast. The Rebels will be sending reinforcements shortly."

Alex leaped off his horse and joined the dismounted Rebels firing at the Yanks at Morton's Ford. He aimed carefully and watched a bluebelly fall. "We'll run them out of there," he yelled to a fellow Ranger. Bullets whizzed past him during the intense fight. Due to Buford's superb leadership, the Federals managed to pass their guns over the ford and extricate themselves from a perilous situation.

"Mount up and prepare to charge," Fitz Lee ordered. Alex jumped on his horse and formed up with his comrades. It would be a running battle all the way to Stevensburg.

8 a.m. Aaron Ames paced restlessly at the temporary headquarters of Kilpatrick's division on the edge of Culpeper Court House. Frustrated by Meade's withdrawal, he realized they would be guarding the rear of the army. He watched Kilpatrick, Custer, and Davies conferring under a large oak tree. A courier rode up from the road to Sperryville. Moving closer, Ames heard him report, "The First West Virginia is confronting enemy cavalry on the pike to Sperryville. I'd estimate about fifteen hundred men, under General Stuart, we believe."

Kilpatrick turned to Davies. "Send the Fifth New York to reinforce."

Ames realized that if the Rebels arrived before the infantry had withdrawn from the town, a battle would ensue, thus endangering the civilians. He wanted to warn Constance, but felt he could not leave camp at this time. If danger came closer, he would go regardless of the consequences.

10 a.m. General George Meade met his provost marshal, Marsena Patrick, on the streets of Culpeper. Determined to withdraw his army in an orderly manner with all supplies, Meade approached the officers supervising the removal of stores at the depot. "Damn it, men, can't you move any faster?" he shouted. "Those rebel bastards are going to be on us soon. I want every last barrel loaded quicker than hell!" Moving a massive army with 27,000 supply wagons was no easy task.

"They're working as fast as humanly possible, sir," Patrick answered.

Numerous happy civilians milled around watching the Yankees run. Unable to control her tongue, Granny Ashby shouted, "General Lee is a gentleman. He doesn't cuss. Hope you Yanks know the way to Manassas. You should by now. Yes, sir, you're on your way to Third Manassas," she taunted.

Meade whirled around furious. "Quiet that woman," he ordered an officer.

The officer stalked up to Granny who squinted at him and shook her cane. "Madame, we'll have to arrest you if you can't remain silent."

"And then what will you bullies do? Shoot an old lady? I'm not afraid. I'm a Christian. I'll just die and go to heaven!"

"Sir, I must apologize for my grandmother." Lucy ran up and grabbed the old lady's arm. "She's somewhat senile." She dragged the furious woman away and whispered, "Granny, you've got to watch your mouth."

"These Rebel women are she-demons," the officer muttered.

11 a.m. When Jeb Stuart rode with his 1500 cavalrymen towards Stone House Mountain, he spotted the rear guard of the Third Corps infantry retreating almost parallel to him. He became fired up with the prospect of capturing the whole party. "Prepare to charge," he cried to the Twelfth Virginia. The Virginians charged forward, but the infantry turned and poured a volley into them. However, since the horsemen were in a depression, the balls flew harmlessly overhead. Throwing off their knapsacks, the Yanks fled in panic. Only an impassable ditch saved all of them from capture. In an enveloping movement, Stuart managed to capture several hundred men before he moved forward towards Culpeper.

At about the same time George Meade and the rear guard of the Army of the Potomac departed from town. Kilpatrick then became the senior officer in command. Hearing the gunfire on the turnpike to Sperryville, he realized Stuart must be near and determined to set up his artillery to defend the town.

"Lieutenant Pennington, I want you to move your artillery to the hill at the Wallach house and prepare for action," Kilpatrick ordered. Aaron Ames tensely watched the guns limber up and creak forward.

Noon: Ames and Custer looked through their field glasses at the Rebels in the tree line beside the pike, on a ridge west of the cemetery and Mountain Run.

"Saddle up, men," Custer ordered. "We're to move through the town and protect the artillery."

"Sir, may I request five minutes to ride ahead. I'll join you when you pass through town," Ames implored.

Custer stared at his cousin. "Five minutes, and you'd damn well better be there loverboy."

Ames bounded on his horse and charged ahead. "Thanks!" he called when he galloped by the general. He raced towards the Armstrongs' house through the jubilant citizens who lined Coleman Street. He saw Amanda and the boys on the front porch when he tied his horse.

"I must warn you that a battle may take place soon." He straddled the steps two at a time. "Please find shelter this time."

Amanda grabbed the boys' hands. "I can't thank you enough for all that you've done for us." David hugged his leg.

He nodded quickly. "Where's the patient?"

"She's in the bookstore," Amanda said with a slight smile. "She's slowly getting stronger."

He opened the door and dashed inside. Constance whirled around when she heard his boots on the wooden floor. She stared at him unable to speak. Finally, scarcely aware of her own voice she blurted, "I...hoped you would come."

She felt the solid strength of his arm when he pulled her into the corner where they were not visible from the windows. Her heart hammered in her ears; his nearness overwhelmed her when he rested his hands on her midriff. "I...I...don't know how to thank you," she stammered.

He put his finger to her trembling lips to silence her. "I only have a few minutes. I want you to be quiet and listen to me. First, you must go immediately to a safe cellar. The artillery may open up soon. Promise me you'll do as I say. I can't be here to save you again." She nodded and his steady gaze bore into her in silent expectation. "I don't have time to tell you all that is in my heart," he said softly, his hands slowly moving over her back. "You must realize how important you are to me. I promise you that as long as there's breath in my body, I'll come back." He clasped her body tightly against his well-built frame and kissed her firmly. A delicious shudder heated her, set her aflame, when she felt the strong firmness of his full sensuous lips against hers. She couldn't get her breath as the passionate shock of him raced through her body. He pulled away and lifted her chin until their eyes met. "Wait for me."

Too filled with emotion to speak, she nodded her head affirmatively. He grabbed her hand and pulled her down the hall and outside. "Go!" he ordered, then mounted his horse. Custer's band marched up Davis Street playing "Yankee Doodle," much to the irritation of the civilians. Constance hobbled towards the courthouse disoriented while she watched him gallop forward to join his comrades.

"Good riddance," the people yelled shaking their fists at the damn Yankees. "Have fun at Manassas, boys!" Swimming through a haze of conflicting feelings and desires, Constance could not hold back her tears. She stumbled towards the rectory.

Jeb Stuart rode forward with his men from the tree line into the vale, and the Federal artillery opened up. His horse reared as shells crashed into the line. Realizing it was folly to advance under the intense fire, he shouted. "Fall back and regroup!" Riding into the safety of the trees, he ordered, "Have Major Beckam bring up the artillery!"

Robert surveyed the situation through his field glasses from the ridge while the guns slowly advanced through the rough terrain. He saw the Federal guns in position on the hill east of town at the Wallach house. So far, their shells had passed over the town, doing no damage to the village. He must get the range and caution his men not to allow their shells to fall on the town. Surveying the streets, he was relieved to see few citizens outside.

1 p.m. "Fire!" His guns belched towards the Yankees. Seeing his position, the enemy quickly returned vigorous fire. Shells whizzed overhead, and a tree limb crashed down on Robert who rode between his guns. Unhurt, he encouraged his men. "Let them have it! Revenge for the people of Culpeper!"

While the artillery held the attention of the enemy, Stuart advanced into the town where he engaged the rear guard of Davies' brigade. The Rebels raced down the streets after the retreating Yankees. Guns cracked and the dismounted Federals fought back in a brief but vicious street fight.

Constance and Amanda huddled together in the crowded cellar of the rectory, listening to the gunfire. The ground shook from the artillery. "I hope our boys are beating the hell out of them," Granny muttered. The stagnant close air amongst the nearly one hundred crowded townspeople made it difficult to breathe.

After skirmishing for about thirty minutes with Kilpatrick's men east of town, Stuart, outnumbered two to one, decided it would be foolish to assault such a strong position. He heard the sound of artillery in the east and surmised Fitz Lee was approaching. Stuart devised a better plan. "Fall back to the town!"

Pleasonton and Kilpatrick watched the Rebels retreat through the town, suspecting Stuart was up to something. "He's going to reappear where we least expect it," Pleasonton said to Kilpatrick. "He's probably circling around to cut off our retreat."

"Shall we start moving?" Kilpatrick asked.

"Yes, have Custer march on the left of the railroad tracks and Davies will move on the right. Keep your eyes open. They'll try to cut us off."

Jeb Stuart's cavalry galloped north to Chestnut Forks (Catalpa) and then turned east on back roads attempting to reach Brandy before the Federals. Robert limbered his guns, then looked wistfully at the town. He had hoped to see Constance, but it was impossible now. It would be a challenge for his artillery to keep up with Stuart's blistering pace.

2 p.m. Stuart galloped through the open fields in front of Auburn while an imposing column of Union cavalry trotted parallel to him along the railroad tracks. The enemy had divined his intent to merge with Fitz Lee at Brandy and cut off their retreat. Now, they raced for the high ground of Fleetwood Hill. Raising up in his stirrups, Stuart spotted another line of blue cavalry under John Buford moving from Stevensburg towards Brandy. Concerned, he raised up in his stirrups again and caught sight of Fitz Lee's gray soldiers hotly pursuing Buford. "That's Fitz!" he yelled. Stuart knew his horses were too tired to outrun Kilpatrick. He'd have to slow him down.

When he approached the Botts mansion, his men drew within shouting distance of Custer's men. A few could not resist taunting the enemy and firing at them. Squelching the bravado, Stuart lined up the Twelfth Virginia and First North Carolina on the ridge near Auburn. With a Rebel yell and sabers glistening in the sun, they charged forward engaging the rear guard of the Yankees, thus opening the fourth battle at Brandy Station. Ames, riding behind Custer, saw the enemy horsemen advancing. Their assault and sniping at the rear guard did have the desired effect; it slowed the advance of the Yankees.

When John Buford reached the higher ground at Brandy, he caught his first glimpse of Kilpatrick's advancing columns. Fitz Lee also realized Kilpatrick was advancing and daringly interposed his division between Kilpatrick and Buford. Stuart continued to send in charges against Kilpatrick's rear. In turn the Second New York countercharged.

Fitz Lee's horse artillery opened fire on Kilpatrick, whose artillery quickly returned the favor. With shells crashing around them, Pleasonton, Kilpatrick, and Custer conferred. "They're in front of us and behind us," Pleasanton stated. "In essence we're surrounded."

"I propose we cut an opening through their line to the river," Custer said.

"We've got to charge and break through to unite with Buford," Kilpatrick agreed.

Pleasanton nodded. "Prepare your men for the charge of their lives."

When Custer rode up to his regiment, he detached the Sixth and Seventh Michigan to attack Stuart and formed the First and Fifth Michigan in columns. Spurring his horse to the front, he shouted, "Draw sabers!" The clank of metal resonated down the line. Custer took off his hat and handed it to an aide so his men could see his long golden hair. "We are surrounded," he shouted above the din of battle. "We have to open the way with the saber. Boys of Michigan, there are some people between us and home; I'm going home. Who else goes?"[2] The soldiers responded with three lusty hurrahs. Ames's voice could be heard above the others. Determined never to return to prison, he was anxious to fight his way out, relying on Custer's flawless leadership.

"Strike up the band!" Custer cried to his musicians who immediately played "Yankee Doodle." The song, his call to arms, always incited fierce enthusiasm in the men. Ames, to the left and slightly behind his cousin, heard the boy general cry, "Forward!" The regiment started to trot forward, Custer and his staff leading the way with their new battle flag flying high in the breeze. Turning in his saddle, Custer admired the forest of drawn sabers while they advanced in the sunlight. "I never expect to see a prettier sight!"[3] he yelled.

"It's a magnificent charge!" Ames cried back to him.

When they moved to within forty rods of Fitz Lee's line, Custer shouted, "Charge!" Bugles sounded and the Yankees screamed fierce battle cries. Surging forward they smashed into the Rebel line like mad men. The field became a melee of smoke and jabbing sabers, making it difficult to tell friend from foe. Fitz Lee's line was hit in the

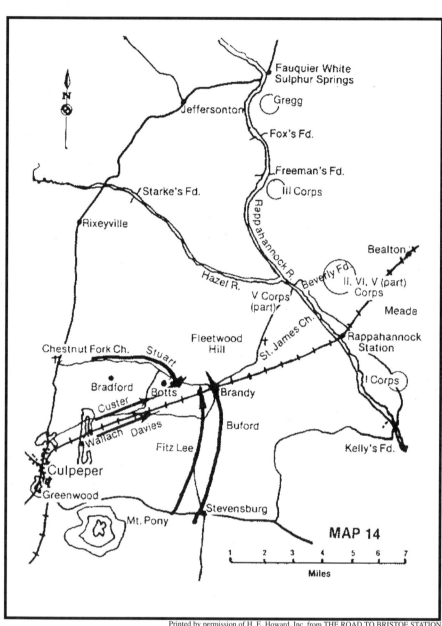

Inside image - labels: Fauquier White Sulphur Springs, Gregg, Jeffersonton, Fox's Fd., Freeman's Fd., III Corps, Starke's Fd., Rixeyville, Rappahannock R., Bealton, Hazel R., Beverly Fd., II, VI, V (part) Corps, V Corps (part), St. James Ch., Meade, Fleetwood Hill, Chestnut Fork Ch., Stuart, Rappahannock Station, Bradford, Custer, Botts, Brandy, I Corps, Wallach, Davies, Buford, Fitz Lee, Kelly's Fd., Culpeper, Greenwood, Mt. Pony, Stevensburg, MAP 14, Miles

Printed by permission of H. E. Howard, Inc. from THE ROAD TO BRISTOE STATION

The Fourth Battle at Brandy Station

front by Kilpatrick and in the rear by a portion of Buford's men. At the same time Stuart worked havoc on the left flank and rear of Kilpatrick's Corps, adding to the indescribable confusion.

Ames's horse reared after he jabbed at a Rebel coming at him from the left. Amidst the smoke, he saw Custer's horse tumble. The blonde-haired general rolled to the ground and soon jumped to his feet, firing at the enemy. Ames bore down on a Confederate and smashed him across the chest with his saber. After the Rebel tumbled to the ground, Ames quickly maneuvered to grab the reins of the horse. He dashed forward into the smoke and discovered Custer still shooting at the enemy. He tossed the reins towards Custer, who grabbed them and immediately mounted up. Smiling at his benefactor, Custer yelled and motioned his men forward toward the opening being cut in the Confederate line. Before the Yankees poured through it, the Rebels counter charged to seal the breach. Alex rode into the confusion, wielding his saber. He jabbed a Yankee and rushed forward when the Rebels merged to seal off the escape route of the enemy.

Ames fell back and yelled at a group of comrades to follow him. They charged into the Rebels and the impact of the assault sliced open the escape route again. Fighting fiercely, he watched the artillery, wagons, and ambulances move forward towards safety. Several ambulances overturned, throwing wounded men to the ground where the stampede trampled many helpless men to death. Suddenly, Ames felt his horse fall to its knees. Thrown to the side, he immediately rolled over to avoid being trampled by a charging horse. Pulling himself to his knees, he drew his pistol. In an instant he whirled around to fire on a Rebel bearing down on him from the rear. His bullet struck home and the soldier fell to the ground. Ames raced after the horse but was unable to catch it. In a desperate situation, his adrenaline pumped while he ran forward into a cloud of smoke and finally overtook the horse, trapped among several wagons. Panting, he dodged in and out until he managed to grasp the reins. Instantly, he threw his athletic body on its back and spurred towards safety.

The successful heroic charge allowed the majority of Kilpatrick's men to join Buford, who had wisely placed his artillery on Fleetwood Hill. By having control of the high ground, the Federals had guaranteed themselves safe escape across the river. Stuart charged and attempted to outmaneuver them, but was unable to secure the victory he so ardently sought. It was a draw. With 11,000 men engaged, this battle had rivaled the June ninth fray with intensity and bravery on both sides. Stuart had to be content with successfully shielding the movements of the infantry and capturing 555 prisoners.

Mid-afternoon: "Fresh air at last!" Constance muttered to the townspeople emerging from the cellar into the sunlight.

Hudson and David raced around the yard of the rectory burning off pent-up energy. Listening to the gunfire in the distance, Amanda turned to Constance. "I believe the fighting is at Brandy Station again. Thank God poor Fannie fled south to Nelson County."

Shortly, Reverend Cole, George McDonald and the other elderly men returned. "It's safe to go home now," Cole announced to the women and children. "Culpeper is in Confederate hands again!" A boisterous cheer went up from the crowd. "A few of our cavalry and infantry have arrived and removed the wounded and dead from the street fight. I'm also happy to report that the shelling did little damage to the town. Thank God, they shot over us!"

The inhabitants walked through the streets and cheerfully greeted their ragged liberators in a joyous celebration. However, those who had taken the oath in order to buy food wondered how they would fare with the Rebels in control again. Constance and Amanda hurried up Davis Street to hear loud cheers coming from the direction of the courthouse. "Lee! Lee! Lee! Long live Lee!"

"It's General Lee!" Hudson raced towards the beloved commander. A large and exuberant crowd gathered around the general, seated on Traveller. For the first time in two days he had mustered the energy to ride his horse rather than travel in a wagon. The warm welcome of the people of Culpeper lifted his spirits. The crowd rushed forward to touch him and shake his hand.

Wielding her cane, Granny pushed her way through the crowd. "Com'n through!" Reaching the commander, she squeaked, "General Lee, I think you should know that some of our people have been too friendly to the enemy. In fact, several ladies attended parties at General Sedgwick's headquarters." She pointed her cane at three young ladies in the crowd. "That one and that one and that one went!"

The accused ladies froze in fear while General Lee gazed at them. The crowd waited breathlessly for his verdict. "I know General Sedgwick very well," Lee said smiling slightly. "It is just like him to be so kindly and considerate, and to have his band there to entertain them. So, young ladies, if the music is good, go and hear it as often as you can, and enjoy yourselves. You will find that General John Sedgwick will have none but agreeable gentlemen about him."[3] The crowd smiled and the accused relaxed, thankful that Lee would not seek retribution.

Even Granny could not disagree with the gentlemanly Lee. "Our general is a true gentleman. He doesn't curse like Meade."

Next day, October 12, 1863: Rixeyville

10 a.m. Aunt Martha looked up from her sewing when she heard the gunfire. The first Confederate cavalry she had seen in weeks had ridden by a short while earlier. Still mourning the recent death of her husband, she remained convinced that the constant fear and harassment by the Union horsemen had caused his heart attack. She walked to the front porch and gazed across the horizon towards Culpeper. "Lord have mercy, Susie," she called to her faithful servant. "It's the most beautiful sight I've ever seen." The small black woman rushed outside to join her. They watched column after column of gray soldiers marching on the Warrenton Turnpike with battle flags blowing in the cold morning breeze. "Look at them! Thank God, it's our boys at last…thousands of them. They've come to save us!"

Ewell's Corps, accompanied by Robert E. Lee, edged northward in an attempt to turn Meade's right flank. At the same time, A. P. Hill advanced in a parallel course towards Amissville. The cavalry leading the advance had run into stiff enemy resistance around Jeffersonton.

Noon: Hans and Marta Yager huddled in the cellar with their daughters while the Confederate cavalry sparred with the Yankees, who held firm control of Jeffersonton. "Don't be afraid," Hans said. "Our men are fighting to liberate us." He cautiously moved to the one window with a view of the hill behind his store. "The Yankees are swarming on the hill around the Baptist Church. They're everywhere. The stone wall is protecting them."

"Oh dear God, please let our men be victorious. Release us from this reign of terror," Marta prayed.

When Lee and Stuart approached the hamlet, Colonel Mortimer Ball of the Eleventh Virginia met them. "The Yankees have reinforced their units in the village and are giving us stiff resistance. We can't take the town with so few men."

Frustrated, Lee said, "The infantry are bottling up at Rixeyville. We must move forward to the river as quickly as possible. General Stuart, bring up the rest of Funsten's brigade and clear the way."

2 p.m. Stuart's cavalry roared into Jeffersonton from three directions. One group circled around and struck by way of the Jeffersonton Academy against the Union right at the church. Another assaulted from the front while others attempted to cut off retreat from the rear. They fought intensely and the Federals attempted to withdraw across the river to Fauquier White Sulphur Springs. Cautiously peering out of the window amidst the clattering gunfire, Hans watched the blue soldiers being dislodged. "We've got 'em on the run! Looks like our men are rounding up several hundred prisoners!"

"God be praised," his wife replied in tears. "I pray Alex is safe."

Tom Rosser, the Fifth Virginia Cavalry, and one piece of artillery had been left on Fleetwood Hill to picket the Rappahannock while Stuart and Fitz Lee covered Ewell's advance towards Jeffersonton, some eight miles to the northwest. Rosser stared with disbelief at the spectacle confronting him on the plains of Brandy. A wave of Union infantry four miles wide led by Buford's cavalry advanced towards his small force. "Holy shit!" cried one of his aides. "Look at 'em coming. Why would they retreat one day, only to turn around and attack the next?"

It made no sense to Rosser, who knew he could only hope to slow them down or trick them. He sent word to Colonel Young in Culpeper to bring all his men and artillery to support him at Afton.

A few members of the advancing Union infantry stopped to bury their dead from the preceding day's battle, irate to see most of them stripped stark naked. Unsure of the location of Lee's infantry, Meade had sent over half of his command forward on a reconnaissance in force towards Culpeper Court House to engage the enemy. Rumors still circulated that Hill had been sent to Tennessee. Meade needed the answer to that question.

3 p.m. Amanda looked out the window of the bookstore at the Confederate horsemen riding by. "What do you think it means?" she asked Constance.

"Maybe nothing, but we'd better see what we can find out." She walked onto the front porch and yelled to the Rebels, "Can you tell us if we're in danger?"

"Could well be," a soldier called back. "We hear a large enemy force is advancing towards the town."

"On, no, not again," Amanda moaned. "Just when we thought we were free."

"We should prepare to go to the rectory at the first sound of firing," Constance said resolutely.

Sunset: Rosser and Young boldly spread their small numbers and six pieces of artillery out along a high ridge near Afton. The dismounted Rebels and their artillery opened up a severe fire against the advancing Yankees. Convinced he faced a formidable force, Buford refused to advance further in the night. The Confederates built extensive campfires and marched their band from point to point behind the lines to give the impression of a larger force. The gallant rebels spent an anxious night fearing an attack and rout in the morning. Nevertheless, they courageously held their position.

Late evening: Numerous town residents huddled together for warmth in the cold, clammy rectory cellar. "It sounds quiet out there. Do we dare go home?" Amanda asked Constance.

"I'm so tired," Constance said with a yawn. "But anything could happen. I think we should stay here."

"Mommy, I'm hungry," David whined.

"When will it all ever end?" Lucy mused. "We've been stripped of almost all food. Meade's army withdrew without leaving anything behind. "

"I bartered for quite a bit of food while the Yankees were here," Amanda said. "Food was more valuable to me at the bookstore than money. I'll gladly share."

"That's extremely generous of you," Reverend Cole said. "Some of us may have to accept your offer. Hopefully, food will come in by rail from Richmond soon."

"Meanwhile, we do what we must to survive," Granny added.

"Well, let's try to get some sleep and pray the Yankees don't occupy the town again tomorrow." Lucy stretched out on the dirt floor.

Next day, October 13, 1863: Culpeper Court House

Dawn: "It's safe to come out now," Reverend Cole told the townspeople, who had slept in his cellar. "A soldier just informed me that the Yankees fled during the night. It appears our men duped them into believing a large force protected the town."

After finally learning during the night that Hill's Corps was located at Amissville, Meade recalled the half of his army searching for the missing Rebels at Culpeper. Afraid Hill would cross the mountains and explode behind his army as Jackson had done at Second Manassas, Meade began withdrawing his army north along the railroad tracks. In the early morning light, Ewell and Hill marched towards a junction at Warrenton.

Dusk: Robert Beckam rode forward with Stuart, Funsten, and Gordon to the crest of the hill near the little village of Auburn in Fauquier County. His heart raced at the sight of a long line of Union infantry on the road before him, stretching as far as the eye could see. Behind the Confederates lay Catlett's Station on the Orange and Alexandria Railroad, where they had just observed a similar column of Union infantry moving northward. Stuart and his 3000 horsemen were trapped between the two massive columns of Yankees, and would be unable to unite with Robert E. Lee at Warrenton with their reconnaissance report. It was as perilous and desperate a situation as Stuart had faced in the war.

"If we leave the artillery and the wagons, we might have a chance of fighting our way through them," Gordon suggested.

"We absolutely cannot afford to leave seven guns behind," Beckam argued.

"No, I'll only desert the guns and wagons as a last resort. Fighting our way out would cause the unnecessary sacrifice of countless lives." Stuart's keen blue eyes scanned the horizon around him. "We can hide in this small vale of pines behind us. With darkness coming on, the hills on each side will shield us from their view. However, the slightest noise will give us away. The men must be cautioned to subdue their animals using any necessary measures." Staring Beckam in the eye, he continued, "Major, line your guns up behind the crest of this hill and be prepared to move them into action at any time."

Beckam nodded and rode to his batteries. He personally supervised the positioning of the guns making certain it was done as quietly as possible. Staff officers supervised the gathering of the men into the pine thicket. Within minutes, horsemen, artillery, and wagons were sheltered in the darkness between the hills, which kindly hid them from the view of the enemy. Another hour of daylight would have caused their sure destruction. His guns were positioned within 300 yards of the road where he heard the tramping feet of the enemy. He listened to the Union officers call out their orders and even heard the voices of their men in conversation.

Alex stroked the nose of his horse, trying to keep it calm, realizing this was the tightest spot Stuart had ever been in. His thoughts turned to Amanda and the boys. If he could just visualize making love to his beautiful wife and hugging his boys, he could endure this endless anxious night. He had great confidence in Stuart and respected Robert's ability with those guns. If Robert had to blast their way out, he knew he would do it right. His admiration and respect for Robert grew deeper every day. Nothing would please him more than welcoming him as his brother-in-law.

10 p.m. Robert watched six volunteers dressed in captured Federal uniforms depart to reach General Lee in Warrenton. Each was instructed to take a different route and to inform Lee of their entrapment. If Lee would attack in the morning, the cavalrymen could make their escape. Surely, one of the men would penetrate the hordes of Yankees and reach Lee safely. His heart stopped when he heard one of the mules on the supply wagons bray. Watching the ridge, the hostile feet continued to tramp along with the clanking wagons. Thank God, the noise of the wagon train drowned out the braying mule. Bone tired, Robert sat on the ground and leaned against a tree. He closed his eyes, but knew that sleep would be impossible on this tense night. As usual, his thoughts turned to Constance. His lips drew into a smile at the thought of embracing her. She was the only woman he wanted, and he steadily grew more confident that she would one day be his.

Next day, October 14, 1863: Warrenton

5 a.m. Robert E. Lee watched Ewell's troops march in the direction of Auburn. Miraculously, all six of Stuart's couriers had reached him, causing him to spend a sleepless night worrying about his cavalry general and his men. Lee's first priority for the day was to accompany Ewell and quickly rescue Stuart. Second, he must cut off Meade's retreat and engage him today. If Meade reached the safety of the Union fortifications at Centerville before Lee attacked, the campaign would be over with no gain. A. P. Hill's men marched north on the Warrenton Turnpike to search for Meade.

* * *

Robert listened to the clattering of the passing Union wagons. Restless, he knew dawn would surely bring on an engagement. Having conferred with Stuart several times, he was fully aware that he would have to blast their way out when daylight revealed their position. The burden rested squarely on his shoulders. The performance of his guns, the key to the escape, had to be executed flawlessly. He held the fate of 3000 men in his hands.

6 a.m. Beckam's men slowly and soundlessly pulled their guns into position on top of the ridge. The fog hung over the road and valley but was thin enough in spots for them to see unsuspecting Yankees preparing breakfast. Men milled around their camp-fires with their arms stacked. Some had taken their shoes off and relaxed on the ground. Robert moved silently among his men making sure the guns were aimed carefully and cutting the shell fuses precisely.

Alex felt his heartbeat quicken with the suspense. He loaded his gun. Their moment of discovery would surely come soon. Each man prepared to attack.

6:30 a.m. Stuart heard gunfire from the northwest and assumed Lee was coming to his rescue. After the fog lifted, he could delay no longer. He nodded to Beckam, giving him permission to open fire. Instantly, Beckam's guns blasted double canister into the stunned Federals drinking their coffee. One shell exploded killing and wounding seven men in the Fifty Second New York. Horses reared and stampeded. In the wild confusion some officers commanded their men to "fall in" while more fast-thinking leaders made their men lie down.

Within a short while the Yankees recovered, and a regiment moved towards the guns. "Let them have it!" Beckam yelled. His guns raked them with canister. They soon fell back behind the crest of a hill. Not to be deterred, the Yankees moved their artillery into position to assault Beckam's guns. When the shells crashed among them, Beckam ordered his men to, "Hold fast!" The ground shook while Beckam's seven guns engaged in a deadly and uneven battle with twelve Union guns.

A courier dashed up to Beckam shouting, "General Stuart says fall back to a protected position!"

"Limber up, men!" Shells shrieked around him. Several of his men were wounded, but the Rebels hastily moved their guns to safety and rescued the wounded amongst heavy artillery fire.

Stuart observed the enemy moving towards his left flank, his escape route. He ordered Colonel Ruffin and the First North Carolina to charge the position. With a vigorous charge the North Carolinians checked the Union advance allowing Stuart's wagons, artillery, and cavalrymen to dash through at an opportune moment and make their escape from a perilous situation. Assistance from Lee and Ewell did not reach them in time.

Mid-morning: A. P. Hill examined the still smoldering campfires with Federal knap-sacks, coats, and personal items littering the ground. "Looks like the Yanks just left in a big hurry," one of his staff officers commented. Hill nodded and contemplated the situation. The devastation and smoldering buildings he had observed on the morning's march incensed him. He preceded Ewell and Lee in the march towards Bristoe Station with hopes of cutting off Meade's retreat. All signs indicated he was gaining on the rapidly fleeing foe; thus his desire to attack increased. Unfortunately, he only had a small and inadequate group of cavalrymen with him to send out on reconnaissance.

"Order the cavalry to push forward towards Greenwich and see what they can turn up." He mounted his horse and his exhausted footsore infantrymen marched by. "Pick up the pace!" he called out. The signs of their quarry seemed to boost the morale of the men who marched faster.

"It's like a fox hunt," one of them said. "We'll catch them, General Hill!"

Within thirty minutes a cavalryman rode up. "We've taken a few stragglers and prisoners, sir," he reported. "They claim to be from French's Third Corps."

"How far away are they?" Hill asked.

"We made contact with their rear guard, but they're moving fast. They're maybe two miles ahead of us. Unless we pick up the pace, they'll pull away from us."

Hill rode back to his staff and issued orders for all brigades to close up and move on the double quick. Having heard firing in the direction of Auburn through most of the morning, he suspected that Ewell had been slowed down there while attempting to rescue Stuart.

1:30 p.m. Hill's pulse quickened at what he observed from a hill a mile and a quarter north of Bristoe Station. Looking down and to the east, he clearly spotted Union soldiers resting in the fields beside the shallow stream called Broad Run. After torturous days of struggling through wretched roads and chopping through forests, finally he had the quarry in sight! The stream lay directly in front of him, and the railroad and Bristoe Station were to his right. He believed he was observing the rear of the retreating army, the Third Corps. If he waited for Ewell and Lee to arrive, there might not be any enemy to attack. Safety and the entrenchments at Centerville were only ten miles away. Heth's Division was up, but the rest of his men remained strung out along the road. He wished he had Stuart to scout ahead, but Stuart was still with Ewell and Fitz Lee was off, heaven knows where, skirmishing with Kilpatrick. He resolved to seize the moment and move his men into lines of battle.

2:45 p.m. The intensity of the battle picked up while Hill's men advanced towards Broad Run. Suddenly, thousands of Union soldiers emerged from behind the railroad cut to the Rebel's right. Where in the hell had they come from? Warren's whole corps, moving north, had intercepted the Rebels and caught them in a deadly crossfire. Sick at heart, Hill realized he had moved his men into battle too hastily. Efforts to reinforce and withdraw his men could not halt the disaster. Confederates dropped like flies while their casualties mounted.

Nightfall: A gentle rain fell on the writhing soldiers that covered the bloody battle-field. The lines of the two armies lay so close together, retrieving the injured became a dangerous process. Their screams and groans pierced the black night. Robert E. Lee felt bitter disappointment at the disastrous scene confronting him.

Hill desperately attempted to explain the events of the day to the man he admired and respected so intensely. "I am convinced that I made the attack too hastily, and at the same time that a delay of half an hour, and there would have been no enemy to attack. In that event, I believe I would have equally blamed myself for not attacking at once.[5] I accept full responsibility."

Lee rebuked him, saying, "You made a great blunder."

Bristling at the retort, Hill asked, "What are your orders now, sir?"

"Well, general, you must have your Pioneer Corps bury these unfortunate dead," Lee answered curtly. Sensing the pain in this young general he valued above all others, Lee struggled to control his temper and his disappointment. After all, he had told Jefferson Davis he could send any of his officers to Tennessee except Hill. Putting his hand on Hill's shoulder, he said calmly, "Let us say no more about it."[6]

In the black moonless night, each Union soldier placed his hand on his cup and canteen to keep it from rattling, and silently escaped into the darkness to Union fortifications. Lee's last offensive came to a grinding halt.

A week later October 21, 1863: Culpeper Court House

Down on her hands and knees, Amanda scrubbed the mud stains on the Oriental rug. Constance fumed at the Yankees' lack of respect for their home while she dusted the badly scratched dining room table and stared at the depleted, chipped supply of dishes. "Amanda, I'm greatly concerned about Sadie. She's lost a lot of weight and I think she's working much too hard."

Amanda stood up and stretched, putting her hand in the small of her back. "We're all working too hard."

"But she's remained extremely loyal to us. We can barely provide her with enough to eat. I'd like for her to understand how much we appreciate her. Now that we have three extra bedrooms again, I thought perhaps…well, I was wondering if you would consider letting her move into the house with us?"

Amanda's jaw dropped. She spun around to confront her sister. "Servants don't live in the house! What would the neighbors think?"

Constance stood her ground with her mouth set in determination. "I don't care what the neighbors think. She's so lonely without Abraham, and Billy drives her to distraction. He's always hanging around staring at her. She's a member of our family and I love her dearly."

Amanda threw up her hands in surrender. "I know how much she means to you. If it's that important to you, go ahead and let her move in. Only, don't put her in mother's room. I can't handle that."

Constance smiled and wrapped her arms around her sister. "Thanks Mandy. I love you. You were so strong while I was recovering, keeping the bookstore open."

Amanda moved her hands across her sister's back. "I don't feel strong at the moment." Soldiers drifting into town had reported that the Confederate army had crossed the Rappahannock back into Culpeper. "I'm frantic about Alex." She pulled away and picked up the pail of water. "I've got to keep busy or I'll go crazy."

"Listen." Constance held up her hand. "It sounds like a train coming in. Maybe we can get some food. Even better, perhaps there are finally papers from Richmond. I'll go down to the depot and investigate."

Constance hobbled slowly through the cold drizzle, detecting much activity at the train station. The local citizens descended on the area in search of food, but in addition she saw hundreds of soldiers. Holding her umbrella to shield her from the raw rain, she pushed her way through the crowd to observe several hundred Union prisoners herded together and guarded by Confederate cavalrymen. Stripped of their hats, coats, boots, and any item of value, the captives, soaked to the skin, shivered in the forty-degree weather while mud oozed through their toes. Greatly concerned that many of them wore red ties, she moved closer and examined their faces. Not discovering the familiar ruggedly handsome face, she pushed forward and asked, "Were you with General Custer?"

A soldier turned his mud-caked face towards her and answered proudly, "Yes, ma'am. The Wolverines...the finest brigade in the cavalry."

"Do you know Lieutenant Ames of General Custer's staff?"

"I think he's the big fellow." The prisoners were shoved forward.

"Is he well? Is he alive?" Constance moved along beside them.

"Don't rightly know, lady."

"Connie! It's Alex! Over here."

She searched the crowd for the source of the voice, until she spied Alex on his horse about twenty feet away. Waving, she pushed towards him. He dismounted and hugged her. "You gave me a real scare. Thank God, you've survived. Frank told me you were recovering."

She stared at his filthy face and clothes. "Amanda's been gallant through it all. She coped with Mother's death and kept the bookstore open while I recovered. You should be proud."

"I am. I hate the way you've suffered. But, we've retaliated. These sorry rascals were captured two days ago at the Buckland Races," he bragged, motioning towards the prisoners. "We trapped Kilpatrick's men between Stuart and Fitz Lee. You should have seen them run. What a stampede!"

The lines in her face registered concern. "Were casualties heavy?"

"Not on our part. Don't worry, Robert's fine. We gave Davies a fit, and Custer was hit hard too. Unfortunately, most of his men got away. That dang Custer fights like a demon."

The tension melted from her face. "That's good news. Let's go home and get out of this horrible rain."

Two days later, October 23, 1863: Armstrongs' parlor

Jeb Stuart strutted in the Armstrongs' parlor, holding a handful of letters over his head for his staff and guests to see. "These are the scandalous love letters of General Custer, captured from his command wagon at the Buckland Races," he announced jubilantly. "I fear they're unfit to read to you with our fair ladies present. However, with some censoring, I imagine the Richmond papers will publish them. I'm sure the exposure of his lust will be an embarrassment to the boy general." His boisterous laugh filled the room. Stuart was in his element again. His cavalry had performed extremely well in the Bristoe campaign, thus redeeming his sagging reputation.

Clapping, John Esten Cooke said, "General Stuart, the rout of the enemy at Buckland was the most complete that any cavalry has suffered during the war."[7]

"Meade won't give us any more trouble this winter. We pushed them back and destroyed over twenty miles of railroad track. Our men are building cozy log cabins and preparing to spend the winter in dear old Culpeper," Stuart boasted. "You, the good people of Culpeper have had your land laid waste and still remain defiant. You have a will of iron. There is no submission in you. I've told my friends in Patrick County that they have suffered nothing compared to Culpeper. So, I ask you good Rebels of Culpeper, to join me in celebrating The Buckland Races and the birth of my daughter, Virginia Pelham. Sweeney, let's have some music!"

The musician tuned up and Stuart joined Constance, Robert, and Stringfellow. "Miss Armstrong, it's a pleasure to see you looking well after your wound." He leaned forward and kissed her on the cheek. "Let me extend my deepest sympathy for the cruel death of your mother."

"Thank you, General Stuart. It's wonderful to have you back."

Hudson, standing nearby, announced, "It was a Yankee who saved her."

Constance felt her face glowing. The men looked at her perplexed. "It's true, a Yankee soldier saw me fall and carried me to safety."

"Then I'm thankful that there are some noble gentlemen in the Union army." Robert put his arm around her. "Although somewhat jealous," he whispered in her ear.

Stuart looked at Stringfellow, thinner than ever. "Stringfellow, I trust you've recovered from your illness. You were sorely missed on the campaign."

"I'm feeling much better thanks to my mother's care, but I deeply regret that I couldn't be with you," Stringfellow said with a despairing look. "I can't help but believe that if I had been there to scout, General Hill would have been better informed. Things might have turned out differently."

"Perhaps, perhaps," Stuart replied thoughtfully. "But that's in the past." He moved into the center of the room. "Gather around, it's time to sing!" When the guests moved towards the piano and Sweeney, Robert watched Constance acutely. Pale and thin, she greatly concerned him. She seemed distant, not as vivacious as usual.

"Alone at last." Robert put his arm around her on the sofa. "I thought they would never leave." He pulled her against him as his lips moved against hers, kissing her, consuming her. "You don't know the agony I've gone through, knowing you were hurt and that I couldn't get to you." He gripped her tighter, moving his lips over her neck. "I've suffered such guilt for not being here when you needed me."

She pulled back and traced her fingertips over the dark bruises and scrapes on his face. "You have nothing to feel guilty about. Look at you, all bruised and limping after having your horse shot out from under you. We must both be thankful we're alive."

"That's true." He traced his fingertips over her arm. "I'm afraid I'm not as ecstatic about the situation as General Stuart. We lost hundreds of horses and our infantry accomplished nothing. Unfortunately, General Hill lost a lot of men at Bristoe Station while doing little damage to the enemy. We've practically starved eating nothing but cornmeal and bacon. It galls me to see the empty cans the Yankees left behind in their camps; they've had vegetables, condensed milk, lobster, oysters, fruit, and food we only dream of."

"I know. Even though we've had money to buy food, little has been available. I, too, am sick of corn meal." She grimaced. "Do you think you'll be here for the winter?"

"I hope so. There's no place I would rather be than here with you." He kissed her again. He sensed she wasn't responding with her usual enthusiasm. "Connie, is something wrong? You seem to be...distant."

She stared into his sincere dark eyes. He was the logical choice for her. Everybody said so. The army was back and would be here for the winter. It seemed like old times again. He had never reprimanded her for her involvement with John, and had remained loyal to her when she didn't deserve it. She must suppress her feelings for Aaron Ames. After all, he was the enemy. The memory of the passion aroused by his kiss would eventually fade. It might take time, but she would forget him. She couldn't hurt Robert.

"Rob, forgive me. I'm still dealing with Mother's death. It's been a harrowing experience. After losing both of my parents so close together, I suppose I've pulled back into a shell. I'm afraid to care for anybody just to have them taken away from me. It all scares me and makes me feel empty inside. Be patient with me." She laced her fingers with his.

"I can understand that." Yet, the question hammered at him...was she telling him everything?

"Perhaps, if you could take me out to the farm to visit her grave... it would help me." She laid her head against his shoulder.

Nine days later, November 2, 1863: Hill's camp

A lonely figure, Powell Hill rode through his camp in a black cape to protect him from the cold rain. He observed the neat rows of log huts his men had hastily constructed for protection from the elements. Red Virginia clay outlined the gray rough logs as lazy spirals of smoke emerged from the clay-lined log chimneys. Lost in his solitude, Hill continued to admonish himself for Bristoe Station. Normally congenial and outgoing, he would never be the same again. The Richmond papers had shown no mercy, placing all responsibility for the defeat on his shoulders. He longed for the days when he had commanded a brigade and was allowed to go into battle beside his men. That was what he did best. The awesome responsibilities of corps command left him isolated. He winced at the never-ending pain from his kidneys. At least today he had strength enough to mount his horse.

He could bear it all if only Dolly, wonderful, beautiful Dolly was here. She and Russie were the light of his life. As soon as the baby arrived and Dolly was strong enough, he would bring her to Baptist's house in Culpeper. He pondered that scenario. Would it be safe for them to come? Lee's army held a strong defensive position on the south side of the Rappahannock. Would Meade be content to pass the winter without hitting one more blow? He was not sure.

Hill noticed a large group of civilians gathered around his cabin headquarters when he rode up. "Greetings General Hill," John Starke, Sr. said cordially after Hill dismounted. "Culpeper's home guard has come to offer you our services. You're our most important citizen. We have sixty men ready to serve as your escort and body guard."

Hill shook hands with Starke and George McDonald. Embarrassed by the attention and still smarting from Bristoe Station, he replied, "I have no use for an escort. Besides, I think your sixty able-bodied men could render better service to the county by joining the ranks of some infantry regiment than by acting as body guard to any general."[8]

Hurt by his rebuff, the local men nodded and mounted their horses. "You know where to find us if you need us," McDonald said before they rode away. Hill chastised himself again and walked towards his cabin. He should not have appeared rude to his friends and neighbors trying to support him. The warmth of the fire cheered him once he was inside the cabin where several members of his staff worked.

"Any messages?" He held his hands in front of the shooting flames.

"Only one." His nephew, Frank Hill, handed him a telegram.

Powell Hill beamed, then announced proudly, "Dolly had a girl yesterday! We've named her Lucy Lee in honor of my favorite sister and our esteemed leader."

"Congratulations, sir!" His staff members applauded and slapped him on the back.

Shaking his hand, Major James Field, chief quartermaster, pulled several cigars out of his pocket. "I've been saving these for this happy occasion," he laughed and passed them around. "And, I have another surprise for you, General Hill. Come over here." He motioned to the corner. "Lift up the blanket." He pointed to an object concealed under an army blanket.

The removal of the blanket revealed a rough-hewn cradle. "It's beautiful," Hill said deeply touched. "I can assure you we will put it to good use."

"Your men have been working on it for several weeks. They present it to you as a token of their deep affection and esteem."

"It's a gift that Dolly and I will always treasure," Hill said fighting back tears. "Thank you all."

16

The Return of the Locusts

November 7, 1863 - December 3, 1863

Love is a smoke rais'd with the fume of sighs;
Being purg'd, a fire sparkling in lover's eyes;
Being vexed, a sea raging in lover's tears:
What is it else? A madness most discreet,
A choking gull and a preserving sweet.
Romeo in *Romeo & Juliet* by William Shakespeare

Five days later, November 7, 1863: Armstrong town home

Constance lifted her hand from Sadie's forehead and looked at Amanda with fear in her eyes. "She's burning up; she's so congested she's having difficulty breathing."

After listening to sporadic gunfire all afternoon, Amanda paced the floor of the front bedroom. "Unfortunately, there's not much we can do for her. I wish we had some chicken broth or food. We can put a kettle of water in the fireplace. The steam might help her breathing." The sound of cannon fire in the distance made her jump. "Those were cannons. Now it's starting to sound serious."

Constance placed a cool cloth on Sadie's forehead. "Let's hope it's only a skirmish or cavalry engagement. Surely, Lee's lines are strong."

"I can't help but worry. From one minute to the next, our lives are being turned upside down."

Next day, November 8, 1863: Armstrong town home

Constance awoke to the sound of creaking wagon wheels. Adjusting her eyes to the dawn light, she slipped her feet into her slippers, put on her robe, walked to the fireplace, stirred up the coals, and threw several logs on. She crossed the frigid hall to Sadie's room and rekindled her fire. Staring into the morning mist, she observed wagons and ragged Confederate soldiers slowly moving up Coleman and Davis Streets. Alarmed, she wondered if the army was retreating. She felt Sadie's scorching forehead and discovered her nightgown and bedding were soaked with sweat. "Sadie, you have to drink." She lifted her servant's head and Sadie gulped a little of the water. "Sadie, can you hear me?"

"Yas'm" she groaned weakly. "I's so hot."

Constance wiped her face and hands with a cool cloth. "Don't worry, I'm here. I'm going to take care of you."

Amanda ran into the room wide-eyed. "What do you think is happening? Surely our army isn't deserting us!"

"Some of them are definitely on the move. I'll get dressed and see what I can find out. Sadie's not getting any better." Her voice drifted into a hushed whisper.

The snow blew into the faces of Constance and George McDonald while they observed the mass exodus. He said, "From what I can gather, the Yankees surprised our bridgehead at Rappahannock Station. They captured most of the men and have crossed the Rappahannock."

"Isn't Lee going to fight?" she asked in disbelief.

"It's a humiliating disgrace!" a soldier cried. "Retreating like this!"

"Lee appears to be retreating behind the Rapidan again." McDonald's voice tingled with fear. "That means the Union army can't be far behind. I, for one, cannot tolerate the thought of spending the winter with the enemy. They'll arrest me sooner or later. They eventually get all the men on some trumped-up charge."

"What are you going to do?"

"I'm going to go pack my bag and fall in beside our men. I'll serve in the medical corps. At least I'll be helping our cause instead of putting up with Yankee insolence and insults."

"I don't know what we'll do. Sadie's too ill to travel."

"You'd be insane to stay here. For God's sake, get out while you can!"

"I can't leave, at least not now." She watched townspeople rush about frantically.

"I'll leave you a key to my office. If you can earn some income from the printing press, use it. I pray you'll survive the ordeal."

Robert fired his guns from Fleetwood Hill at the hordes of Yankees. It was his responsibility to slow them down and protect the withdrawing infantry. If Meade pushed hard, he could do severe damage to Lee's army. Stuart's men were positioned at the base of the hill for a charge. Robert prayed that Constance would get out. His responsibility was too great for him to leave his guns. He had sent a note to Alex begging him to get the women out.

"Those guns sound close," Amanda cried. "We've got to leave. I can't bear the thought of being surrounded by Yankees again. I wonder where Alex is."

"He'll come if he can," Constance reassured her. "The only way to leave is on foot in the snow. Are you willing to do that?"

"Yes! Yes! Anything to get away from them. Let's go pack a bag and go!"

"Amanda, there's no way that I'm going to leave Sadie. She's too ill to travel and we can't move her."

"We can ask John and his family to look after her. Please, Connie, we must go immediately. The Yankees could be upon us any minute. The town may be under fire!"

Constance wrung her hands while she paced the floor in the parlor, trying to steady her erratic pulse. "John and Susie have six kids and live in a shack. I can't trust them to take proper care of Sadie. I think you and the boys should leave immediately. The three of you need to be with Alex this winter. I'll stay until Sadie is better, and if I can travel through their lines, I'll join you in Orange."

Amanda stared at her dazed, blinking in bafflement. "Connie, I can't leave you behind. You have to come with us!"

The two boys ran into the room, each with a coat on and carrying a satchel. "We're ready, Mother," Hudson shouted. Amanda looked at her sister, standing firmly with her arms crossed.

With tears in her eyes, she begged, "Connie, don't make us leave you behind. I'll never forgive myself if anything happens to you."

Constance hugged her sister tightly. "Don't worry about me. If I can keep the bookstore open, I'll make enough money to feed us for the rest of this horrible war. I can take care of myself. Now, come, and I'll help you pack."

Constance knelt in the snow to embrace the boys. "Give me a kiss. I love you both."

"We love you, too, Aunt Connie." Hudson answered, then he hugged and kissed her.

"Don't worry, we'll take good care of Mother," David said as he gave her a big hug.

The snow blew thickly in front of her when she stood up to face Amanda. Both sisters became too choked up to speak. Clinging to each other tightly, each feared they would never see the other again. "You know how much I love you, Mandy," Constance finally blurted out. Her composure was a fragile shell around her.

"Of course I know," Amanda sobbed softly. "We'll pray for you. We all love you."

"You must go." Constance kissed her on the cheek. Looking one last time into her sister's tear-stained face, Amanda took the boys by the hand and walked towards the courthouse. Constance watched them trudge through the few inches of snow and slush churned up by the retreating army. None of them had proper shoes or gloves. She waved and blew them a kiss when they turned towards her one last time before melting into the mob of refugees and soldiers. Wiping a tear from her face, Constance doubted that they would reach the Rapidan before nightfall. How would they survive the frigid night? She hoped there would be enough houses and barns to house this fleeing mob. She glanced towards the Virginia House and saw Millie Payne waving from the window.

Constance entered the tavern room. "I assume you are all staying."

"Oh, yes." Millie wiped a window table with a rag. "We have no other place to go and mother insists that we'll make good money while the Yankees are here. All we have to do is tolerate the horrible creatures."

"I'm feeling rather lonely right now. May I sit down and visit?"

"Of course, Constance." Millie pulled out a chair for her. "I haven't talked to you in a good while. I'd love to visit."

A short time later Constance saw Alex from the hotel window. Dashing outside, she told him that his family had fled but she was staying with Sadie. Stunned, he informed her that Robert had sent him a note imploring him to get her out. None of his arguments convinced her to change her mind. He admitted that the Rebels had been taken by surprise and he considered this disgraceful retreat the saddest chapter in the history of the valiant army. There had been miserable management. He hugged her sadly and dashed off to protect the retreating army.

Next day, November 9, 1863: Armstrong town home

"Sadie, you've got to try to eat." When Constance lifted her head, Sadie cracked her eyes slightly and coughed a painful, hacking cough. She swallowed a little oatmeal and then closed her eyes again. Constance put her ear against her servant's chest and listened to her loud labored breathing. "Sadie, I'm here for you." She pulled the covers up over Sadie's scorching body.

Constance sighed deeply while she looked out the front windows at the sun glistening on the rapidly melting snow. She watched several Union cavalrymen climb the steps to the Virginia House and wondered how long she would be left alone.

Late in the afternoon, she heard the loud banging on the front door. Her heart pounding, she went resolutely forward to answer it. "Good afternoon, madam," a heavyset officer in his early fifties said. "I'm Major Bennett of the First Corps Infantry. I require your house as living quarters for my officers. How many bedrooms do you have?"

Incensed by his audacity, she curtly replied, "Six."

"That should do." He swaggered brazenly into the hall. "Show me around."

"Very well," she said icily, "since I appear to have no choice in the matter."

"You're an uppity Rebel." He slowly appraised her from head to toe. "We'll get along just fine if you cooperate. Have you taken the oath?"

"No, and I don't intend to," she shot back. "Now, if you'll follow me, I'll show you the downstairs. There are two offices which you may use." Smiling, Bennett and his men followed her. "I operate a bookstore in the front room. It's my only source of income."

"I'd be more inclined to let you continue your business if you'd take the oath," Bennett said sarcastically.

"If I took the oath it would be a lie. Which government I'm loyal to has nothing to do with the books and papers I sell. They come from Baltimore, so you should be happy with the selection."

"We'll have to see about that." After showing him the downstairs, she took him upstairs. When they entered Sadie's bedroom, Bennett's mouth dropped at the sight of the Negress in the bed. "What is that filthy wretched nigger doing here?"

"She's not filthy," Constance answered enraged. "She's my faithful servant and is gravely ill."

"I can't bring my men in here as long as there's a lazy, dirty, nigger in the house. Get her out of here!" Bennett ordered shaking his fists.

This was more than Constance could handle. "She's a free woman and has more right to be here than you do, sir! I'll thank you not to insult her!"

"In Illinois, where I come from, we passed a law prohibiting free niggers from coming into our state. We don't tolerate these people. What I say goes. We're moving her out. Don't you have any slave quarters?"

"There's a cabin out back." Constance shook with rage.

"Roll her up in that blanket and carry her out," Bennett ordered his men. "Miss, you'll have to wash these sheets before we can use this bed."

"I will not do your laundry!" Her withering glare burned through him. "There are plenty of laundresses in town you may hire." She rushed over to Sadie while the men roughly bundled her up. "Don't worry Sadie, I'm with you." Fortunately, Sadie seemed oblivious to her rude eviction from the bedroom.

Once Constance got a fire started in Sadie's cabin, she paced the floor venting her wrath. "Dirty hypocrites!" she muttered. "Sons of bitches. That's what they are. I'll live out here with Sadie rather than stay in the same house with those bastards." For the first time, she fully analyzed the cabin. Abraham had put down a plank floor after they were freed. Single beds lined the two outside walls of the small frame dwelling. A large armless rocking chair sat in front of the fireplace and a pine table nestled between the two beds. Sadie's treasured Bible lay open on the table beside a candleholder, Abraham's fiddle, and a wash basin and pitcher. Clothes hung on pegs around the walls. The most prized possession, Sadie's hand woven brightly colored rug, covered most of the floor. It was sparse but comfortable. Constance determined that she could survive here. If it was good enough for Sadie, it would have to be good enough for her.

She lit the candle in the fireplace, pulled the three-legged stool from under the table and placed it by Sadie's bed. Sitting down, she took the hand of her beloved servant in both of hers. She contemplated the wrinkled brown skin on the tops of Sadie's hands. These hands had given so much love and service to her and her family. Turning Sadie's hand over, she felt the smooth whiteness of the palm. She never could understand why Sadie's hands were so light on the palms. It was as if the color had worn off. Leaning her cheek against Sadie's hand, she began to pray that God would help Sadie get well. Sadie was all she had left to cling to. A sense of loneliness and isolation overwhelmed her.

She felt a tear trickling slowly down her cheek. "Sadie you must get better. I need you. You know how much I love you." She paused to sniffle and wipe her face. Placing Sadie's hand against her cheek, she continued, "I'm surrounded by thousands of Yankee soldiers. Please don't leave me alone to fend against all those damn Yankees."

Sadie slowly cracked her eyes. "I ain't gonna leave ya...'lone, baby," she whispered. "Not with all them...Yankees 'round."

"Oh, Sadie!" A cry of relief broke from Constance's lips, then she leaned over and kissed her on the cheek. "Thank God! Do you feel better?"

"I aches all over an' I's so tired," Sadie answered with a cough.

Constance lifted her head and gave her some water. "The house is full of Yankees. I knew you wouldn't desert me. I'll get you something to eat."

That night Constance rolled over on the small straw mattress trying to get comfortable. This rope bed was a far cry from her soft feather mattress. She closed her eyes, but sleep would not come. No matter how hard she tried to suppress them, the same visions confronted her, pure and clear. She saw Aaron, scooping her up in the street, dashing to safety. She felt his powerful body on top of her, shielding her from the bullets. He sat ceaselessly by her bed, feeding her, encouraging her, loving her with his eyes. With a shiver of vivid recollection she relived the excitement, the smoldering passion of his kiss. The harder she tried to ignore the truth, the more it persisted. He had left a burning imprint on her and she now accepted the fact that she could never forget him. Even though he was the enemy, she owed her life to him. Somehow he had become a part of her. Where was he? Had he been killed at Buckland? Was he wounded? She tossed and turned, praying for his safety.

Next day, November 10, 1863: Sadie's cabin

Constance watched the rays of sunlight dance against the wall from the one window in the cabin and listened to wagons clattering in the street. She had not ventured forth, but obviously the Yankees occupied most of the buildings in town. She placed two more logs on the fire and resumed her vigil beside Sadie. Firewood and food were dwindling away. It would be necessary to make provisions for their survival soon, but she had not opened the bookstore because of her attention to Sadie. She took her patient's hand while she slept. Sadie seemed to feel a little cooler and had been responsive several times during the day. She heard a gentle tapping on the door, then her heart hammered wildly. "Come in," she said apprehensively.

She recognized the tall, broad-shouldered silhouette of Aaron Ames against the sunlight when he entered and closed the door behind him. He leaned against the door and stared at her a minute, allowing his eyes to adjust to the darkness of the cabin. Her hair was pulled back from her high forehead in a large barrette, allowing soft curls to fall on her shoulders. His eyes searched hers for some sign of her feelings. "I…I was afraid that you had fled," he said softly.

When she stood up to face him across the room, the gathered skirt of her plain homespun dress fell to the floor from her tiny waist, cascading over the soft curve of her hips. He admired her hourglass figure and watched her firm, high breasts move up and down slightly as she breathed heavily. Her wildly beating heart the only audible sound, Constance finally found her voice. "Sadie is…critically ill. I had to stay…and care for her. Amanda and the boys left." His hair was longer. It fell to his shoulders framing his manly face. His large hands hung restlessly at his side.

"I see." Obviously disappointed at her response, he looked down for a moment, and then raised his head to stare back at her, an easy smile playing at the corners of his mouth. "Well, God bless Sadie."

"When I heard about the rout at Buckland, I feared for your life." A shiver of wanting surged through her, compelling her to take a step forward. "Thank God you're safe. What took you so long?" Her eyes radiated affection. She took another step towards him.

Encouraged, he replied, "Jeb Stuart," then took two long strides, met her in the center of the room, and engulfed her in his arms. She lifted her face towards him to meet his potent kiss. Seized by the passion of his embrace, her arms encircled his broad shoulders. When his large hands moved over her body, she returned his caresses with reckless abandon and thrust her fingers through his thick hair. His full sensuous lips covered hers hungrily with demanding mastery. Then his thrusting tongue forced her lips open and explored the recesses of her mouth, causing explosive currents to race through her. The frenzied physical release of their pent-up desire sent her senses reeling, skidding out of control. Feeling every inch of her body arched taut against his powerful frame left her weak. Frightened by the passion raging within her, she finally tried to pull away from him, but his strength overwhelmed her. "Aaron," she gasped breathlessly. "You've touched my heart deeply…but we must…stop. I fear you'll think…I'm a lady with no morals."

He pulled back, his wide shoulders heaving, and searched her eyes. "I don't think that. I've longed to kiss you for…over a year now. Forgive me…if I got too carried away…with my affection."

She took a deep breath, fought to calm the fire consuming her, to regain her fragile control, to force her mind to form a logical thought. "We must try…to talk. Please sit down." She motioned to the large rocking chair in front of the fireplace. He released her reluctantly and took his seat. She pushed her hair back over her shoulders, trying to organize her frenzied thoughts. "I'm not sure how to explain my feelings to you. You've touched my heart in a way that I never believed possible. When you kiss me, my heart cries, yes," She paced in front of him, her brain in tumult. "But then my mind says, no. We come from two different worlds and our worlds are at war. You fight for an army that I hate bitterly, an army that has brutally killed my parents. You're here to kill my friends and destroy my beautiful homeland."

He watched her silently with a closed expression while she stalked around him and continued, "I can't give you false hopes. Our relationship has no future. I can make you no promises. You must understand that," she blurted, scarcely aware that her voice faded away.

"I'm not asking for any promises." His hand shot forward and grabbed her arm. Instantly, he pulled her down onto his lap, and cradled her in his arms.

"Oh, Aaron!"

"Trust me. I promise to be a perfect gentleman. We have a few precious moments alone together, without Sadie breathing fire and brimstone down my neck, and I refuse to waste them debating the insanity of this war." He took her hand and placed it on an area of his scalp where the hair was matted with dried blood.

Concerned, she felt the hard ridge of scar tissue below. "What happened?"

"A bullet grazed my scalp a few days ago. My head could be blown off tomorrow, and from your experience, you certainly know how fleeting life is. Every minute is to be cherished." He planted a kiss in the palm of her hand and then turned it over kissing the top. He held her hand against his lips, kissing each finger, one by one. "Constance…may I call you, Constance?"

"Of course." She rested her head against his muscular shoulder.

"It's a beautiful name that certainly fits you. You're strong, resolute, and persistent. I'll always call you Constance, not Connie. Your nickname will be Reb." They both chuckled together and the twinkle in his eye melted her. "I admire your courage and your spirit, even though we disagree on many subjects. Our differences are small compared to the deep affection that binds us together. Your compassion saved my life, but by doing so you also captured my heart. I tried my best to forget you when I left here. I even enjoyed the company of many lovely ladies when I went home. Constance, you always lurked in the shadows of my mind. I couldn't rid myself of your memory." He twirled a ringlet of her silky hair in his fingers.

"I don't deserve such devotion." She slid her hand over his bulging firm forearm to his shoulder. "But if what you say is true, then why didn't you answer my thank you letter for the check?"

"Because your letter was formal and full of bitterness over your father's death. I felt it would be futile to try to reach you through letters. It seemed like a lost cause. You gave me no hope when I left. I determined to wait until I could see you in person." He rocked the chair slowly as his eyes caught and held hers.

"But I assumed you were dead or that some northern lady had won you. Then when I saw you at Brandy Station, I knew you were alive. Rooney Lee told me how popular you were with the ladies, so I was certain one had snared you."

His broad smile lit up his face. "You actually asked Rooney about me? I can't believe it. I'm flattered."

"Well, I was only inquiring about a mutual friend," she said with a teasing smile.

"Constance, look into my eyes and tell me what you see."

"I see warmth, affection, compassion, integrity and...um...passion."

"When you look at me, I don't want you to see a Yankee. I want you to see a man who loves and treasures you above all others. Can you do that for the next few minutes?"

She traced her fingertips tenderly over his cheeks, his bushy eyebrows, and his lips. "At this moment, I see a man who risked his life to save mine and then nursed me back to health, giving me the will to live. I believe I'm looking into the eyes of the bravest, most desirable man on the face of the earth." Their lips moved together softly, tenderly. This time their caresses were leisurely and controlled. Gradually trusting him, she relaxed and enjoyed his shivery, slow, drugging kisses.

Sadie awoke from her deep sleep to the sound of strange smacking noises. She looked around the dimly lit room. The only light emanated from the coals in the fireplace. She saw the back of the rocking chair with a pair of cavalry boots below. Constance's legs dangled off to the side. After listening to a sigh of delight, she cleared her throat and said, "Ex-cuuuse me, what is goin' on here?"

Constance jumped to her feet and rushed to Sadie's bedside. "I didn't know you were awake."

"Obviously!" Sadie glared at Aaron when he stood over her. "I kin see I'm gonna have to git well quick to keep things straight 'round here."

Aaron smiled at Sadie politely. "It's good to hear your voice again, Sadie. Things are back to normal now." He turned towards Constance and whispered, "I'll be in the kitchen."

"Whew! Did I get an earfull," Constance said when she entered the kitchen. "She must be recovering."

"I knew she would live to harass me again," he replied from the bench at the trestle table. "I spoke to Major Bennett when I arrived. He's not easy to deal with. You're going to have to stay on his good side to keep the bookstore open."

"His good side? Do you know what that hypocrite did?" She spat out the words contemptuously, then slammed a pan on the stove. She related the story of Sadie's eviction while she cooked some grits and fried a few pieces of bacon. "How can you condone such actions?"

"I can't, but he's in control and he's in your house. I don't like it any better than you do. He can close the bookstore if you make him mad, and then what will you do? Just don't cross him!"

"My blood boils every time I think about it," she answered stirring the grits, "but I'll stay out of his way. By living with Sadie, I don't have to see him. I'll even enter the bookstore from the outside to avoid him."

"He'd be a lot more agreeable if you'd take the oath."

"Take the oath?" she cried in dismay. "I will never be coerced into taking the hated oath." She stormed to the other side of the table, her eyes glaring as her nostrils flared. "It would be an act of treason, like selling my birthright. I will never take the oath of allegiance to a government that imprisons dissenters and is controlled by the military. My father's last words to me were, *Fight tyranny!* I will do just that until I take my dying breath. Don't ever suggest it again, Aaron. I will <u>never, never, never</u>, take the oath!" She pounded her fists on the table.

He reached across the table and grabbed her fists. "Constance, I'm glad to see your spirit back, but you've got to be reasonable about this. You're in a dangerous situation. How are you going to buy food?"

"I'll starve to death before I take the oath, and so will my friends and neighbors. Our will cannot be broken!"

"I believe you're serious," he said soothingly while he moved his hands over hers. "Do you have money to buy food?"

"Yes, I have some money." She sank onto the bench and leaned across the table gripping his hand until their lips practically met. "Aaron, I know this is a lot to ask, but will you make the purchase for me? That way I can keep my integrity against this cruel demand."

He studied her imploring eyes, weighed the question, and nodded his head. "I can't let you starve. You'll need firewood, too."

"That's true. Of course we have no way to haul any. Billy's still here. He can split it."

"The trees are rapidly disappearing because our men are building huts. We have one good supply near our headquarters at Stevensburg. I'll have Joseph cut a load and bring it to you."

"Oh, Aaron, that would be wonderful! Is Joseph well?"

"Yes, his family is with him. We're at Clover Hill."

"That's John Barbour's house. He was one of father's closest friends. I hope you've treated the family well."

"General Custer has been accommodating. He's using the upstairs while a tenant family, the Tripletts, occupy the downstairs. The Barbours have fled."

After they had eaten, he rose to leave. "When will I see you again?" she asked. He swept her weightless into his arms.

"In a few days, I hope." His eyes bathed her in admiration. "Perhaps I can take you to church on Sunday?"

She dropped her eyelids pensively. "Don't take this personally, but I'd rather not… be seen… in public with you. My friends would ostracize me. I need my friends. Please try to understand."

He looked like a wounded puppy. "It's not as if I'm a criminal. This county is overrun with Yankees. You won't be the only young lady escorted by one."

"Perhaps, but I need time to consider the situation. I know this is difficult for you to understand. Be patient." She lifted her begging eyes to his.

His heart melted when he looked into the smoldering depths of her eyes. "You've made me the happiest of men today. We'll take one day at a time. I'm not going to push you." Kissing her was heaven. He suspected a woman of such spirit would also possess great passion. The fact that he had been able to unlock her senses and now felt her passion matching his own exceeded his wildest dreams.

"Aaron, I do believe you're a gift from God. Without you I couldn't endure life in a Yankee city."

* * *

Joseph entered the cabin to see Sadie slumped in the rocking chair. "Momma?"

Sadie cracked her eyes and her mouth turned up in a smile. "Come here an' give me a kiss, son," she whispered weakly.

He kissed her on the cheek and pulled up the stool. "I hear ya been real sick. How ya feelin'?"

"I's so weak, but Miss Constance has takin' real good care of me," she said with a cough. "How's the fam'ly?"

"We's livin' in a tent at Clover Hill. I built us a chimney, so it's warm. The baby died 'bout a week ago."

"Oh, no!" Sadie's eyes filled with sadness. "The misery never ends, does it? How much longer will this war last?"

"Only God knows, Momma. We's so sick of it. Ya should see the way the Yankees is choppin' down all our trees for firewood and huts. There's thousands an' thousands of 'em swarming everywhere like locusts. An' they're tearin' down all the abandoned houses for the wood an' even takin' the bricks for their chimneys. Ain't gonna to be nothin' left when they get through. I brung y'all some firewood. Lieutenant Ames is gonna see y'all are taken care of."

Sadie nodded and rocked slowly. "I ain't got no use for no Yankees, but that man sure is crazy 'bout Miss Constance. I 'spect we should be thankful to have a friend like him."

Constance smiled while she looked out the kitchen window at Joseph and Aaron stacking the wood. Walking back to the iron cook stove, she put in a few more pieces of wood. "Is it hot enough, Sadie? Tell me how to fix this food."

Sadie stared at the canned food and ingredients Aaron had procured. Leaning back in her chair, she mumbled, "Lawd, what are we gonna do with this stuff?"

When the four of them finally tasted Constance's concoction, they ate quietly. "The cornbread is good," Aaron said with a twinkle in his eye. He and Constance faced Sadie and Joseph across the table. "The stew is …um…interesting. I've never had any quite like it." The two Negroes both rolled their eyes and laughed.

"Well, I didn't have all the ingredients I needed," Constance said defensively. "After all, I'm new at cooking."

"It's a good thing you have a bookstore to run," Aaron said in a casual, jesting way. "You'd never be able to make a living as a cook."

"Well, it serves you right, Mr. Yankee. If you had let us secede in peace, you wouldn't have to eat this terrible concoction. You must pay for your sin."

"But you forget, Reb, that secession is illegal."

"Illegal, my foot, Aaron Ames. When Virginia ratified the Constitution it was with the provision that she could withdraw if the government did not serve the people. There's nothing in the Constitution about perpetuity. That's what made the Articles of Confederation so unpopular. None of the states wanted permanence in the law. These so-called United States were an experiment. It's funny that the New England States didn't consider it illegal, when they met in Hartford to discuss seceding from the Union in 1814. Why is it suddenly illegal now?

"Because we must preserve the Union," he answered, growing serious.

"Balderdash! What you're really saying is, be my brother, or I'll kill you. Unite with me, or I'll exterminate you!" Her eyes blazed with defiance. "Whatever happened to the consent of the governed?"

"We can't allow this nation to splinter. How would we defend ourselves against European powers? If we allowed a state to secede every time they were unhappy with a law, we'd be a weak nation." He took a mouthful of stew and glared back at her.

"That's a ridiculous excuse for waging a war of aggression. We aren't concerned about an attack from Europe. We're too busy trying to defend ourselves against your desire to destroy us. John Pelham told me that the textbooks used at West Point taught the legality of secession and even outlined the proper way a state should go about seceding. Why would a northern school teach such a doctrine, if it's illegal?" She lifted her chin, refusing to back down.

He shrugged his shoulders. "Even if it's legal, our countries could never exist side by side in peace. The difference between slave and free economies would bring us to violence."

"That's because you would use your industrial might to conquer us. We have no desire to control you. We're an agricultural people who love the land, and want to live on farms. You're determined to take away our way of life. Can't you understand that we don't want to be industrial and live in huge filthy cities like you? Slavery isn't the issue. You could have bought the freedom of every slave with what this war is costing.[i] Our strongest loyalty is to our states, not the Federal government. When our men say they're fighting for their country, they mean their state. Our state is our country."

"Constance, I don't understand how your loyalty to your state can be greater than your loyalty to your country," he argued while he ate his cornbread. Joseph and Sadie sat spell bound, watching the sparks fly.

"That, Aaron, is because you were not by the grace of God born a *Vah-gin-yan!*" she said dramatically. "You must realize that *Vah-gin-ya* gave birth to this nation, and not vice-versa. It was our leaders who wrote the Declaration of Independence and the Constitution, and who led our nation in its earliest days. We have been citizens of these so-called United States for eighty-four years, but there have been *Vah-gin-yans* for over two hundred and fifty years. It was *Vah-gin-ya* who worked tirelessly to negotiate a compromise between North and South. We were drawn into this war by your president's illegal call to arms. Our men are proud to live and die as *Vah-gin-yans!*"

"I must admit, that was a stirring speech," he said, admiring her spirit. He took her hand under the table. "I mourn for poor old Virginia. I know I didn't pronounce it right. You'll have to teach me the drawl. Her fighting men have shed their blood on her soil, her women and children are starving and outraged, her fields and towns have been desolated. She has borne the brunt of this terrible war for her southern sisters. No one can deny that."

"We still have our honor and our spirit. You can never destroy that. Now," she said in a conciliatory voice, "what do I owe you for the food?"

---

[i] A Harvard economist, Claudia Goldin, calculated recently that less than half the money the North and South spent on the war would have paid for the freedom of all the slaves and given each 40 acres of land and a mule.

He stared at her thoughtfully, moving his fingers lightly over her hand. "You don't have to pay me."

"Of course I do, Aaron. I won't accept charity. I can support myself. I am, after all, a proud *Vah-gin-yan.*" She stood up and collected the dishes. "Besides, I don't want anyone to suggest that I'm a kept woman."

"That's the truff," Sadie said, then pulled herself up. "All this arguin' has done wore me out. Come on, Joseph. Help me back to mah bed."

"We'll head back to camp as soon as I help Constance with the dishes," Aaron said. Joseph nodded and helped Sadie out the door. Aaron's eyes rested on Constance. "You owe me thirty dollars."

She handed him a bucket when he stood up. "I'll get it while you draw some water." He leaned forward and brushed his lips against hers.

When he walked back towards the kitchen from the well house, he stopped at the window and admired the beauty of her image reflected by the flickering candlelight. Rapping gently on the windowpane, he got her attention. She curiously walked over to the window. He knelt on one knee and said with a dramatic flourish, "But, soft! What light through yonder window breaks? It is the east, and Constance is the sun!"

Giggling, she blew him a kiss. "Aaron, Aaron, wherefore art thou Aaron? Bring that water in here immediately, you hopeless romantic!"

"Pour it in this pot," she ordered when he entered, pointing to the stove. She placed the money in his hand. "Thank you for the food and wood. I don't know what I'd do without you."

"Let's hope you don't have to find out." He wrapped his arms around her midriff.

Her heavy lashes flew up as she studied him. "I'm surprised you still want to hold me after my outburst."

He moved his hands tenderly over her shoulders. "I enjoy our discussions…our bantering. You need to get your feelings out and I admit you make me look at things differently. You know if it was within my power, I'd make all the pain and devastation disappear." He kissed her on the forehead and eyelids. "Besides, the best thing about a fight is making up."

"When you touch me, all of our differences vanish in the wind." The touch of their lips rekindled the fire of their passion.

Six days later, November 21, 1863: Bealton Station, north of the Rappahannock

Frank Stringfellow, John Mosby, and seventy-five partisans huddled in the woods near Bealton Station, a railroad stop nine miles southeast of Warrenton, while the cold rain fell in torrents. They watched the activity at the cavalry and infantry camps pitched around the depot. Expecting an intrusion by Mosby, the cavalrymen had erected a log barricade around their campsite. Mosby was anxious to make a big hit on some of Meade's supply wagons. It had been a lean few weeks, and Jeb Stuart had ordered Stringfellow to assist in the effort. After several vigilant hours in the chilling rain, they finally spotted their quarry approaching. Five wagons escorted by thirty Yankees moved slowly from the north towards the station. "I'm going to divide our men into two groups. One to hit from the front and the other from the rear. You go with one and I'll command the other," Mosby whispered to Stringfellow.

392

When the Rebels stormed out of the woods, the surprised Yankees fired back and many fled. Riding up close to several, Stringfellow, carried away in the excitement, hollered, "Here's one from Stringfellow and one from Mosby!" as he fired his gun. One Yankee fell, but the others made their escape, fully aware of the identity of their assailants.

"Grab the wagons!" Mosby ordered while his men took the reins of the horses. Unable to get all of the wagons, they loaded many of the valuable medical supplies into their saddlebags. Dashing away when the alarm sounded at the depot, Mosby ordered his men to disperse into small groups. All escaped safely.

Two days later, November 23, 1863: The bookstore

Half a dozen soldiers milled around the bookstore when Anne Stringfellow entered. "Anne! How wonderful to finally see you again!" Constance said.

"My dearest Constance." Anne embraced her. "Words cannot tell you how I've grieved for your mother. No one can fill her place in my life."

"Thank you Anne." Constance clung to the little lady. "She loved you dearly. How were you able to get to town?"

"Uncle George brought me. We have one half-lame mule that neither army has taken. The poor animal managed to pull a wagon. The Yankees are everywhere. Their tents and huts cover the horizon in every direction." Lowering her voice to a whisper, she continued, "I refuse to let them run me out of my home. I told Frank to burn it to the ground if the Yankees ever occupy it. Frank sent me to see you," she said ever so softly.

Constance motioned her behind a bookcase in the corner. "Have you seen him recently?"

"Yes," Anne whispered with her eyebrows raised. "He needs information on the enemy's troop strength and locations. He especially needs to know if troops are coming in or leaving the county. We have a communication system." Constance listened intently, with surprise on her face. "He can see our house from the Rebel picket lines across the Rapidan. If I hang a green cloth on the clothesline, that means troops are coming in. A red one means they're leaving. White signifies that there is a message hidden under the duck rock."

"The duck rock? Our favorite hiding place on the river?" Constance whispered with a slight smile. "I should have known."

"It's very dangerous, but are you willing to help us? Being in town, you're very aware of the situation," Anne said setting her mouth in determination.

Constance only hesitated a second. "I will do whatever I can for our cause. How will I communicate with you?"

"Frank may send some of his scouts to make contact with you. Otherwise, you'll have to visit me at The Retreat. I know that's difficult for you."

"Yes, I have no means of transportation. Tell Frank that I'll keep my eyes and ears open at all times. If he can have someone reach me, I'll pass on whatever information I have."

"Good. Frank knew he could count on you." Raising her voice to a normal level, Anne said, "It's been wonderful seeing you again Constance, but I must go now."

"I've enjoyed your visit, Anne. Please come again soon." When they walked out from behind the book stack, Constance spotted Aaron browsing across the room.

He turned towards them and smiled. "Mrs. Stringfellow, I trust you're well," he said, then he bowed to the two ladies.

Anne stared at his face, and then smiled with recognition. "Oh, yes. You're that nice Lieutenant Ames who brought my chickens to Constance when she was injured. Your concern is greatly appreciated." She glanced at Constance with a questioning smile. "I'm delighted to see her looking so healthy and radiant again."

"Yes, thanks to Lieutenant Ames's kindness, I've finally regained my strength," Constance said. He laid a book on the desk and pulled out a dollar bill. "Good-bye, Anne." The little lady strutted out through the Yankees.

"*Leaves of Grass*," Constance said with her eyebrows raised. "Mr. Whitman has stirred up quite a controversy with some of his poems. There are those who consider them rather scandalous. I'm not sure that was his intent."

Aaron leaned against the desk with a broad grin. "Scandalous? I know I'll like it. You should discuss it with him sometime."

"What do you mean?"

"He's here you know, with the army. He serves as a nurse. I suspect he'll visit the best bookstore in Culpeper sooner or later."

"Indeed! I'll look forward to that. Business has been quite brisk. Now that the railroad is fully operational, I've telegraphed Baltimore for another shipment of books and writing supplies. I've also got money and a list to buy more food, if you're willing to make the purchases for me."

"Perhaps I could be persuaded," he teased while he ran his fingers over her hand. "It's rewarding to see the color back in your cheeks."

"I've regained my energy again, since I've been eating well. It's amazing what good food does for one's morale. I'd forgotten what it was like not to be hungry all the time. You will stay for dinner, won't you?"

"Depends on who's cooking." His mouth quirked with humor.

"Very funny! You'll be relieved to know that Sadie is strong enough to cook again. But, don't be so smug, Yank." She poked a newspaper under his nose. "Read this and weep!"

He stared at the headline in disbelief. "John Hunt Morgan escapes from prison. That's a disgrace. I can't believe it!"

"You can't keep our men down. They're too determined to resist subjugation. These brave souls dug a tunnel under the walls of the prison with a spoon. How's that for Rebel ingenuity?"

"He can't get far. They'll catch him soon. It's only a matter of time. Mosby and Stringfellow hit some of our supply wagons a few days ago. Massive efforts are underway to bring them in. There's even a reward. We can't tolerate the damage done by those renegades any longer. Their days are numbered."

"Frank's like a brother to me. I'd never forgive you if you harmed a hair on his head. He's only guilty of one thing, trying to rid his homeland of thieving Yankees."

"You've got to understand something, little Miss Reb. When bullets are flying, we don't have time for introductions. If my life is on the line, I fight to live."

Her expression softened, and she took his hand. "I understand that, Aaron. If there's one thing I want, it's for you to survive this terrible conflict. You spared Alex when you had the opportunity, and I appreciate that. I would hope you would do the same for

Frank. He's very dear to me. You'd be quite fond of him, if you had the chance to know him."

"Perhaps." He squeezed her hand. "Now I have to do my marketing."

Constance looked across the trestle table to see Sadie's eyelids droop. Aaron lightly moved his fingertips over Constance's hand under the table while she contemplated the chessboard. After making her move, she slipped her shoe off and ran her toes up and down his cavalry boots. He gave her a wicked glance, but attempted to concentrate. Finally moving, he placed his hand on her knee and squeezed it while they shared an intense physical awareness of each other. Her lips turned up in a slight smile when she made her final attack. "Checkmate!"

"Humph!" he scowled. "I believe you used unfair tactics, Reb."

"Now, don't be a spoilsport, Yank."

"Lawd, it's mah bedtime. I can't hold mah eyes open." Sadie yawned and stood up. "Now, Miss Constance, it's time for ya to come to bed too," she ordered, glaring at Aaron.

"I'll be there in five minutes, Sadie, I promise."

"If ya ain't there in five minutes, I'm comin' to git ya! Ya understand?" The old black woman walked to the door and shot daggers at Aaron one more time.

"I understand."

"Good night, Sadie. Thanks for the best meal I've ever eaten," Aaron said.

The instant he heard the door close, he stood up, grabbed her arm, and pulled her into a dark corner. "Don't you know you're driving me crazy." His lips came coaxingly down on hers. Giving herself freely to the passion of his kiss, her emotions skidded and whirled. Touching him excited her in a way she never dreamed possible.

"I've missed you," she whispered.

"I can't get away as often as I'd like." She felt the heady sensation of his lips against her neck. His lips recaptured hers, more demanding this time as he crushed her against him. "Five minutes isn't nearly long enough," he finally muttered, "for me to love you."

"I know…but I have to live with her," she said breathlessly. "I'm almost…afraid to be alone with you long." She buried her face in his neck and breathed a kiss there.

He slowed down the tempo of his kisses. "Sorry…I want you to trust me."

She stared up into his hazel eyes, lit from within with a golden glow. "I do. You've given me so much to be thankful for in the midst of this wretched war. Lincoln's day of Thanksgiving is three days away…let's spend his holiday together."

He cupped her face in his hands. "There's nothing I'd like better. But I can't promise it. I have the feeling something may happen. If I don't come, it's because I can't."

"What do you mean? Is there going to be a battle?"

"I don't know, and if I did I wouldn't tell you." His lips moved across her forehead. "Don't you trust me?"

"Not with any information I don't want the whole Rebel army to know."

"Aaron! I'm only concerned for your safety." She raised up and kissed him on the chin. A loud knock on the door interrupted them.

He groaned. "That's the shortest five minutes of my life."

* * *

Two days later, November 25, 1863: Morton's Ford on the Rapidan

Aaron shivered in the cold wind while he rode along the cavalry line a mile north of the Rapidan at Morton's Ford. "Have the men spread out and build fires," he ordered. "We want to give the impression of a large force." Soon Custer's band played and marched from place to place. When he finished his rounds, he wrapped himself in a tarp and attempted to sleep on the cold wet ground. Meade's army had advanced to the Rapidan and was prepared to attack Lee the following morning. The heavy rain and mud had delayed their assault for two days. Aaron realized that Lincoln and the newspapers had prodded Meade to take one last crack at Lee before winter set in. Nevertheless, he considered this assault in wretched weather against a well-entrenched foe total insanity.

Next day, November 26, 1863: Morton's Ford

Custer, commanding the Third Division due to Kilpatrick's absence because of his wife's death, had his men positioned to cross at Morton's Ford. They were to serve as a feint while the bulk of Meade's army crossed down river. When the cannons opened up from Meade's crossing, he turned to his men and ordered, "Forward!" The band played while the Union horsemen splashed into the frigid river. Aaron rode close behind Custer. Suddenly, thirty Rebel guns opened up on them. Cannon balls immediately burst among the horsemen, slowing the crossing. Saturated with cold water, Aaron cringed when a shell splattered only a few feet from him. He raced his mount up the slippery south bank, ducking the dirt spewing around him. "Keep moving!" he shouted to the men. Though many fell from the artillery fire, the majority crossed successfully. Soon the Rebels realized Meade's intent and pulled back, thus relieving Custer's men from the fierce barrage.

Frank Stringfellow watched the artillery fire from the Rebel trenches, sick at heart. Although unable to see The Retreat from his position, he knew too well that it lay directly in the line of fire. Shells had to be bursting around it. Overcome with concern for his mother, he couldn't comprehend her stubbornness. Why hadn't she left?

By sunset it was obvious that Meade's assault had stalled. Although his troops were on the south side of the river, Lee had seen his intention from Clark Mountain, and had expertly moved his troops to the hills around a stream called Mine Run. He held a powerful defensive position.

Culpeper Court House: "This is a heck of a way to spend our Thanksgiving," Granny complained to the ladies gathered around her dining room table. They listened to the cannon fire to the south. "Too bad we couldn't gather before Lincoln's designated day."

"We must be thankful that we're not surrounded by dreadful Yankees for the first time in three weeks," Mildred Hill said after she heaped sweet potatoes on her plate.

Lucy nibbled on pieces of cornbread and ham. "I pray that Lee repels the assault. But then, will the enemy come back here?"

"I hope not," Granny said bitterly. "I'm tired of being cooped up in two rooms while they enjoy our house."

"They watch us insolently and then attempt to make passes at us. They're a bunch of womanizers. What self-respecting southern woman would be seen in public with one of them?" Jane asked, then cast her eyes towards Constance. "Surely, Constance, you're concerned for Robert's welfare in this battle?"

"Naturally I am," Constance replied coolly. "I pray for all of our men."

"Thank you for bringing the corn bread and sweet potatoes. Where did you manage to get them?" Lucy asked.

"I'm making some money in the bookstore, so I had a kind Union soldier buy them for me. I'll never take the oath!" Constance said defiantly

"How convenient," Jane said. "That wouldn't be the handsome soldier who saved your life, would it?"

"Yes, he's been very kind." Hostility flashed in Constance's eyes. "We must all be broadminded enough to realize that there are some good Yankees as well as some bad Rebels."

"Constance is correct," Mildred Hill said. "If their army stays here all winter we'll all have to rely on the benevolence of their soldiers to survive. We have no choice."

After finishing her meal, Constance stood and excused herself, using Sadie's recent illness as an excuse. She let them all know that she had stayed in Sadie's cabin rather than live in the house with the Yankees. Mildred decided to walk with her saying she knew Constance must be terribly lonely without Amanda and the boys.

When they bade Granny goodnight on the front porch, a bright glow in the evening sky caught their attention. "That looks like a fire in the direction of Brandy Station," Mildred observed.

"That doesn't make sense. That's where they keep their supplies. The Yankees wouldn't be burning their own wagons," Constance said perplexed.

"But Mosby would!" Granny laughed slapping her leg. "I guarantee you, it's Mosby!" Granny was correct.

A sense of guilt overwhelmed Constance after she left Mildred. She pondered her ceaseless, inward questions. In reality, she wanted the Union army to spend the winter here, but could never reveal her true thoughts to her friends. For the first time in a year, she ate well and felt healthy and alive again. But that was not fair, since Amanda and the Confederate army probably lived on the verge of starvation. A tumble of confused thoughts and feelings assailed her. Aaron's love had been an awakening experience and at times she questioned if what she felt for him was love or lust. Could she ever make her friends understand that she could love a Yankee and still remain loyal to their cause? And what about Robert, wonderful, loyal Robert? The heavy burden of guilt and lone-liness weighed her down. For the first time in her life, she did not know who or what was right. Nothing made sense. She was certain of only one thing—she could no longer deny her compulsive need for Aaron's touch.

Four days later, November 30, 1863: Behind the Confederate lines

The mercury dipped towards zero. "We'll have to 'spoon' if we want to survive tonight," Stringfellow said to his companions in the Confederate trenches. The poorly clad soldiers wrapped their arms around each other and lay in a line, hoping the combined body heat would keep them alive.

"Stringfellow, you ain't got enough meat on you to keep anybody warm," one complained.

"Yep, but I can outrun a hundred Yankees. Can't believe Meade hasn't had nerve enough to attack."

"We've dug such strong fortifications, we'll slaughter them if they try to come up these hills. I wish they'd come on!" one soldier said angrily.

"I hear old Marse Robert is going to attack in the morning," Stringfellow replied. "We'd better get some shuteye. Sure wish I was hugging a pretty girl instead of you ugly varmints."

Next day, December 1, 1863: In front of the Confederate trenches

The Confederates silently crept down the hill in the early morning drizzle, only to discover that the enemy had fled during the night. Lee's quarry had escaped him.

Stringfellow wasted no time moving towards the river and crossing. He encountered no Yankees on his trip to The Retreat. His heart pounded while he crept up to his home. His mother's cherished flower garden, once a spot of beauty, had been plowed with shells. His worst fears were realized. Holes gaped in the house where it had been hit several times. A portion of the dangling front portico creaked in the wind. The eerie silence gave him chills. He crept cautiously around the house, listening for sounds of human occupation. Hearing and seeing nothing, he slowly mounted the familiar front steps and walked inside.

He involuntarily took a deep breath at the horror confronting him. Papers, knapsacks, and bloody rags littered the once stately halls. Some morbid Yankee had drawn a crude face in blood on the wall. The fireplace contained the remnants of the smashed furniture. Filled with rage, he slowly climbed the stairs. The mud and ashes ground into the polished floor of the landing indicated a sentry had been there. He surveyed the upstairs bedrooms, and found everything in order, except in his mother's room. Bloody bandages lay in a pile on a chair and the unmade bed evidenced bloodstains. He felt tears welling in his eyes. His mother obviously had been wounded and the Yankees had taken her away. He didn't know how, but he would have to find her.[1]

Next day, December 2, 1863: Confederate cavalry headquarters

Stringfellow returned to his tent depressed. For two days he had ridden wildly along the Rapidan, searching for clues to his mother's whereabouts. Unsuccessful, he gave up at nightfall. He entered his tent to find a sentry waiting for him. "I've got a message for you."

"News of my mother?" Stringfellow asked eagerly.

"Yep. An old Negro came into our lines today. He surprised us so we almost shot him. Said to tell you your mother had been wounded in the foot and has been taken to Summerduck. She's doing fine and is being cared for by a Federal surgeon."

Stringfellow heaved a huge sigh of relief. "Thank God!"

"The Yanks told her she could leave as soon as she was well enough to travel. The rest of the family has passed through the lines and are with friends. The old darkie wanted you to know that he and Aunt Felicia are taking good care of the missus."

"I can't thank you enough." Stringfellow shook the sentry's hand.

Jeb Stuart stared at Stringfellow, stunned. "You want to do what?" he yelled. "That's the most foolhardy thing I've ever heard. You have little chance of success. That house is surrounded by a regiment of Union soldiers."

"I understand the risk, sir," Stringfellow argued with fierce determination. "I'm experienced and creative. I've got to see her!"

"I don't care how daring and imaginative you are," Stuart said angrily while he paced up and down. "You're too valuable to me. I can't allow you to throw your life away."

"But my mother is the world to me, sir. My father died shortly after I was born. She's been both father and mother to me. I have to see her and let her know I care." Tears glistened in his steel blue eyes.

"I can understand your concern." Stuart stared at him stonily. "But you've done a lot of damage to those people over there. You know if they get their hands on you, they'll shoot you as a spy. Don't you realize they've probably done this to set a trap for you?"

"It has occurred to me, sir," Stringfellow admitted without flinching.

"And you still want to go?"

"Yes, with your permission, sir."

"I believe you'd go even without it," Stuart said coldly. A twinkle gradually came into his blue eyes. "Well, we can't have that." He sighed and held out his hand. "Permission granted, reluctantly." Stringfellow shook his hand energetically. "There's a General Casey over there I need to know more about," Stuart continued. "See what information you can pick up, and bring it back. I order you to bring it back!"

"Yes, sir!" The scout grinned and saluted.[2]

Madden's Tavern: Jack Madden grimaced when he heard another tree crash to the ground. "The way they're goin' there ain't gonna be a tree left standin' on our three acres of woodland," he complained bitterly to his father.

Willis Madden stared out of his front window at the thousands of retreating blue soldiers that covered the landscape on both sides of the road. In the twilight he watched them build campfires to cook supper, his fence rails and trees providing the fuel. He watched forlornly while they slaughtered four head of his cattle and prepared them for cooking. "Their officers are standin' there watchin' them destroy everythin' I've got. They ain't even tryin' to stop'em! Why in the world did they have to camp here?" he protested angrily.

Jack walked forward and rested his hand on the old man's shoulder. "They cover the horizon like a cloud of blue locusts, destroyin' everythin' in their path." He shook his head after another tree tumbled to the ground.

"I ain't taken sides in this fool war, but dang if both sides ain't taken me," Willis muttered.

Next day, December 3, 1863: Custer's headquarters

Thankful the weather had moderated, Aaron thought it almost felt warm when he and Custer drank their morning coffee around the campfire at Summerduck. A camp of

Federal soldiers surrounded the beautiful estate of Reverend Thornton Stringfellow, Frank's uncle. "Well, this was the greatest batttle that was never fought. What do you think will be the result of Meade's decision to withdraw?"

"He may be replaced," Custer answered thoughtfully. "But between you and me, I think he did the right thing. Too many lives would have been lost to no avail. We lost enough men as it was. Allowing some of our pickets to freeze to death is a disgrace."

"I saw infantrymen with their names pinned on their backs, ready to fight. That's inspiring. I know I wouldn't want my life thrown away so foolishly. Life is too precious to me now."

"You sound like a man in love, cuz." Custer sipped his coffee. "I understand. I feel the same way. Now that I've finally gotten Libbie's reluctant father to grant permission for us to marry, she wants to wait a year or two. I want her right now! There are women to have fun with and women to marry. They aren't the same thing. I admit I've had my fun. All I want now is to take her as my wife. I won't wait a year!"

"I wish you luck and I agree. I certainly don't claim to be a saint, but surprisingly, other women don't appeal to me now. Constance is the only one I desire, and she's driving me crazy." Aaron stared into space with a glint of wonder in his eyes. "There's something I have to tell you." He looked his cousin in the eye. "Stringfellow is like a brother to her. I'm not comfortable with the underhanded way we're trying to lure him here to see his mother. I'd rather not be a part of it."

"I hope your lovely Rebel isn't causing you to question your loyalty or commitment. Stringfellow's a renegade who has to be stopped. I hate to suggest this, but she may be using you. After all, you're buying food for her. She could well be a spy," Custer suggested with his eyebrows raised.

"I suspect every Rebel woman behind our lines is a spy of sorts. None of us accused you of disloyalty when you called a cease-fire to protect the life of your friend, Tom Rosser. We all realized he was in an exposed position, and that he was your friend. I'm not about to tell Constance anything she shouldn't know. Besides, how else is she supposed to get food? It's ridiculous to coerce these proud people into taking the oath."

"I'm afraid you've got me. I can't argue any of those points. Of course I don't want to see any of my southern friends killed. I don't question your loyalty, Aaron. You fight like a demon in battle. I need someone of your strength fighting next to me." Custer paused thoughtfully. "If you'd rather not wait here to watch us catch Stringfellow, perhaps you'd like to take a reconnaissance party across the river and see what our Rebel friends are up to. We need information."

"Yes, I'd gladly accept that assignment," Aaron said appreciatively before the rest of the camp began to come to life.

Just before dusk, Stringfellow placed *The Life of Stonewall Jackson* in his saddlebag. He intended to give the book, written by his friend, John Esten Cooke, to his mother. He mounted his horse and rode forward, contemplating his strategy. Under the cover of darkness, he would cross the river and penetrate the camp around Summerduck. He carried a Union jacket, which he would wear to blend in with the enemy soldiers.

He rode carelessly towards the river, not expecting any danger while he remained on the south side. The sound of galloping horses behind him did not alarm him, until he turned around to see enemy soldiers within a hundred feet of him. Dismayed, he realized it must be a Federal cavalry detachment returning from a raid. "Halt!" one of them cried. They fanned out to cut him off from the woods. With capture and certain death behind him, he had only one alternative. He must ride hard and fast towards the river and enemy lines. Perhaps he could give them the slip.

Spurring his horse, he bent low in the saddle and his mount surged forward. The Yanks commenced firing. Bullets whistled by him, but he felt his horse gradually pulling away. He thought he had a chance, and spun around to fire a few shots at his pursuers to deter them. Fortunately, the nearest Federal threw up his hands and pitched from his saddle when one of Stringfellow's bullets hit home. The others pulled up slightly and the gap between opponents widened. The road twisted downward until Stringfellow glimpsed the uncertain safety of the river looming before him.

Almost to the dark river, he heard the thud of a bullet striking home. His mount lurched, and then slipped slowly to its knees. Stringfellow kicked his boots out of the stirrups, hit the ground on his feet, tumbled forward and rolled almost to the water's edge. He overheard the Federals shouting behind him, confident of his capture. At this point, he couldn't disagree with them.

He kicked off his heavy boots and ripped off his jacket. Taking a deep breath, he made a headlong dive into the water. The shock of the frigid water took his breath away. He swam frantically under water, staying down until he felt his lungs would burst. When in midstream, he was forced to make his way cautiously to the surface.[3]

Aaron reached the riverside first. Seeing his quarry dive in, he sprang out of his saddle with his revolver pointed towards the river. He saw the head emerge in the middle of the stream, then peppered the water with bullets. The Rebel threw both of his hands up into the air, indicating he had been hit, and then sank below the surface.

"You got him, Lieutenant Ames!" another soldier cried after he rode up. "There's no way he could survive in that frigid water anyway."

Ames lowered his gun while his eyes scanned the surface of the river. One of his men gathered up Stringfellow's boots and coat, while another searched his saddlebag.

"Congratulations, Lieutenant Ames! You just shot the famous Frank Stringfellow!" A soldier handed him a book opened to the flyleaf.

Ames spun around reeling in astonishment. His eyes fell on the inscription in the book, *To my good friend, Frank Stringfellow, John Esten Cooke.* He gawked in disbelief, then his stomach churned spastically. He felt as if a giant stone was lodged there, and that the only way he would get relief would be to throw up. Attempting to maintain his composure in front of his men, he ordered them to mount up. Waves of nausea and overwhelming guilt plagued him when he swung into the saddle. Fate had dealt him a cruel blow. He had done exactly what he had hoped to avoid.

17

Blue Christmas, Happy New Year

December 3, 1863 - February 16, 1864

My only love sprung from my only hate!
Too early seen unknown, and known too late!
Prodigious birth of love it is to me,
That I must love a loathed enemy.

Juliet in *Romeo and Juliet* by William Shakespeare

December 3, 1863 (con't): The Rapidan

Stringfellow clung to the north bank of the Rapidan with his nostrils just above the water. In the gathering dusk he glimpsed the Federals packing up his boots and coat. Growing numb, he felt his blood turning to ice. Would they never go away? After a few endless minutes, the bluecoats finally rode off. Struggling, he stiffly pulled himself up the bank and out of the frigid water. He shivered so violently that his body jerked and twisted convulsively. Realizing he could only survive a short time in his wet clothes, he determined to head towards the enemy in the hope of confiscating dry attire.

Smelling smoke, he saw a slight haze coming from the woods to the east. He stumbled in that direction, forcing his half-frozen legs to move. Unable to feel the ground beneath his numb feet, he stopped momentarily to massage his feet, and then moved determinedly forward. Gradually the coldness gave way to the pain of a thousand needles. After his circulation increased, the needles eventually stopped jabbing.

When Stringfellow caught a quick glimpse of canvas in the woods ahead of him, he dropped flat to the ground in the underbrush. At that exact moment a sentry marched around a tree not ten feet from him. Holding his breath, he waited until the Federal turned around and marched away whistling. The scout cautiously moved forward towards the encampment on his hands and knees. When behind the last row of tents, he spotted the soldiers lined up in the center of the encampment to receive their evening meal. The aroma of hot food and coffee made him salivate.

A pennant waved in the cold breeze above a tent in the center of the line. Seeing no movement behind its canvas walls, the scout crept towards it. This was the headquarters tent; who could better supply him with dry clothes than the general? He placed his ear against the canvas and listened intently. Hearing nothing, he took a deep breath and silently worked one of the tent pegs loose, lifting the edge of the tent just enough to see inside. Fortune was with him! Stringfellow wriggled his way under the canvas into the empty tent.

A lantern cast soft light around the tent. Being careful not to cast his shadow on the front of the tent, he searched the general's trunk. When he tried on the general's coat, he discovered it was about four times too big for him. As much as he would like to impersonate a general, this simply wouldn't work. He threw the coat back in the trunk with disgust, and wondered how the general even managed to mount a horse. Next he threw back the mattress of a cot to discover the uniform of a reasonably sized aide. Now all he needed was a pair of boots to complete his outfit. The scout felt somewhat cheated when his search revealed none. Surely, a man of the general's status could afford more than one pair of boots. "Good evening, sir," he heard a sentry say. The good general must be approaching. Sweeping the papers off his desk, Stringfellow quickly exited by the way he had come.

After he had safely passed the pickets, he stopped in the woods and changed into his dry clothes. Ah, how wonderful the warmth felt! His whole outlook changed to strong optimism. He cut up his pants and used them to bind his feet. Reasonably warm, he headed through the woods towards his mother at Summerduck.[1]

Custer looked up from the campfire when his cheering comrades galloped into camp. "We got him! We got Stringfellow!" one of them shouted. He dismounted and rushed towards Custer, handing him a book. The soldier opened it to the flyleaf, and Custer held it close to the fire in order to read the inscription. "We chased him to the river and then he jumped in. Lieutenant Ames was the first one there and he shot him in the river. No way he could have survived!"

"Then congratulations are in order," Custer said. He searched for Ames, who was nowhere to be seen.

Ames walked through the darkness to his tent and confronted Uncle George and Aunt Felicia, the faithful old servants of the Stringfellows. "Is it true, what they're yellin'?" Uncle George asked him with tears in his eyes. "Is Mista Frank really dead?"

"I'm sorry. I'm afraid it's true," Ames replied.

"Oh, Lawd! Not Mista Frank!" Felicia buried her head against George's chest, sobbing. "I done raised that boy."

"How in the world we gonna tell the Missus. It'll kill her." George attempted to comfort his wife.

Aaron tried to swallow the lump that lingered in his throat. "You don't have to tell her. One of our men will do that."

"Lieutenant Ames," he heard Custer call. "I need your report."

When Custer joined him in the shadows, Aaron tried to find his voice. "I'm sorry sir. I needed a few minutes alone. What the men have told you is true. May I speak to you in private, sir?" He motioned Custer farther away from the others.

"Certainly." Custer followed him. "You're to be congratulated. This feat will bring you fame and a promotion. You're a hero."

Aaron spun around to confront Custer with fury in his eyes. "I have no desire for fame nor will I accept a promotion because of this! It means nothing to me. You must understand that Constance is the only person I want to be a hero to. I'm afraid she'll never forgive me for what happened today!"

"You're overreacting," Custer said. "You were only following orders. You ordered him to halt. He didn't. Your orders are always to shoot to kill in such circumstances."

"I'm sick of the needless killing. And now I am *out of her favor, where I am in love*, to quote Romeo."

"What she doesn't know won't hurt her. I doubt that she'll ever find out about this unless you tell her."

Aaron looked at him thoughtfully and shook his head. "Everybody in this camp knows what happened. You know how these things spread through the army. It will be more damning for me if she hears it later through somebody else. I don't want a relationship built on lies and deceit."

Custer placed his hand on his cousin's shoulder. "Come and get some hot food. It'll help you get a better perspective on things. We'll be returning to Clover Hill tomorrow."

"I have no appetite. I simply want to go to my tent and be alone."

Stringfellow stopped in the moonlight and placed the sentries around Summerduck. He watched the Yankees lolling around the campfires encircling the house. When a friendly cloud swept across the moon and cast a large shadow, he crept up to the detached kitchen. Raising his head slowly, he peered inside the window to see Aunt Felicia and numerous Yankee soldiers. The old lady hobbled towards the window carrying a lantern and Stringfellow softly scratched on the glass. Aunt Felicia moved the lantern so that the light fell directly on the scout's face. Screaming, she cried, "I've seen a ha'nt!" The lamp crashed to the floor, causing a commotion.

Stringfellow dropped below the window, then dashed to the corner of the building. He walked leisurely towards the group of men around the fire and sprawled on the ground as if he belonged. Soldiers rushed from the kitchen. One came towards the campfire and asked, "See anybody come this way?"

"Ain't seen a soul," a soldier replied. "What happened?"

"Oh, the old nigger lady thinks she saw a ghost. Dropped the lantern and almost set the place on fire."

The soldiers around the fire laughed. "You know how those people are. They're always seeing ha'nts!"

Stringfellow lay there calmly waiting for things to settle down. He watched the kitchen door until Uncle George emerged with a bucket. Not wanting to alarm him, he followed the old man down the hill towards the spring. When the Negro bent down to fill the bucket, the scout walked up softly behind him. "George, don't whirl around. There's nothing to be alarmed about. It's Frank, and I'm not dead."

Shaking, the old man turned around and took a deep breath. Finally, he said, "Is that really you, Mista Frank?"

"Yes, of course it's me."

"They told us they done shot ya in the river. That's why Felicia thought ya was a ghost. Ya ain't really, are ya?"

"No, no," Stringfellow answered, trying to control his smile. "Those Yankees aren't as good shots as they think. Look George, I need to get into the house to see mother. How is she?"

Slowly recovering his control, George answered, "She's all right, but we ain't told her 'bout ya bein' killed. But Lawd have mercy, Mista Frank, the house is fulla those blue people."

"I know that George, but here's what I need you to do. Go back to the kitchen and tell Felicia that I'm no ghost, but if she screams like that again, I may be. I need her to bring me an old dress and a bonnet with a wide brim. My life is in her hands, so she'll have to be careful."

"Yas'r, Mista Frank. She'll do it if I can convince her ya ain't no ghost." Stringfellow moved into the shadows and waited by the spring while the old man walked back up the hill. Shortly, Aunt Felicia, cool and composed, came to him. He hugged her and quickly put on the dress and bonnet, rolling up his pant legs so they wouldn't show.

He looked into the old woman's eyes. "What we're about to do is dangerous. It could get us both killed. Are you willing to try?"

Aunt Felicia said resolutely, "Yas'r. I'll die when the good Lawd takes me."

"When we go up to the sentry at the front door, you tell him that mother is worse tonight and you need help with her. If things go wrong, get out of the way. I'll have to kill the sentry and make a break for it. If they question you later, tell them I forced you to do it. Understand?"

The two of them walked up the hill to the house. Stringfellow kept his head down and his hands behind his back when they presented themselves to the guard at the front door. Eyeing them carefully the sentry asked, "Who's with you, old woman."

Aunt Felicia played her role like a professional, explaining that she needed help with the missus. The unsuspecting sentry allowed them to pass. The scout felt the Yankee's eyes boring into his back while he walked down the hall, fully expecting a command to halt at any moment. Unmolested, they went up the stairs and entered the bedroom. Stringfellow found his mother asleep in the bed. Tears came to his eyes, as he looked at her in the low light shed by the lamp. She looked tired and so much older than he remembered. He took off the bonnet and dress and put them in the closet. Aunt Felicia smiled and left them alone.

Tiptoeing over to her bed, he pulled up a chair and gently shook her. Her eyes opened immediately and she was alert. A stern look came over her face when she saw him. "Frank! Coming here is the craziest thing you've ever done! Don't you know they've set a trap for you?"[2]

"I love you, Mother." He kissed he on the cheek. "I had to see you. Nothing could keep me away."

Tears came to her eyes and she reached out to hug him. "My darling son," she said her voice breaking. "You know how dearly I love you. I'm overjoyed to see you!"

They talked for hours into the night. She explained that she had been walking in her garden doing her normal work during the battle when a bullet struck her in the foot. The Yankee surgeon who operated on her had been a gentleman. He showed her the missile and called it a Minie ball, a type of bullet used only by the Confederates. She, of course, refused to believe that one of her own people had wounded her. Stringfellow smiled but did not argue with her. She revealed to him the details of her trip to Constance and her willingness to help him. He commented that he would contact her if necessary, but would be careful not to endanger her. She added that she had seen that Yankee, Lieutenant Ames, at the bookstore and wondered if a romance was brewing between the two of them. Frank said it didn't matter. He knew he could trust Connie with his life. When they were both exhausted, he rolled up in a blanket on the floor, and the two of them went to sleep.

Next day, December 4, 1863: Summerduck

The knock on the door awakened them. "Doctor's here, Missus," Felicia called. Stringfellow threw the blanket on the bed and concealed himself in the closet.

"Tell the doctor he may come in," Anne replied after Frank closed the closet door.

Stringfellow heard the masculine voice ask, "How are you this morning, Mrs. Stringfellow?"

"Oh, I'm feeling much better, Doctor."

A chair scraped across the floor and there was silence for a few minutes while the doctor examined her wound. "Your foot is healing very nicely. I believe you'll be able to travel through our lines and join your family in a few days. I know you'll be happy to get among your own people."

"Oh, yes," Anne answered with a slight note of amusement in her voice. "I'm anxious to see my son, Frank."

"I see," the doctor said pensively. He paused for a few moments reluctant to break the news to her. "Well," he finally said clearing his throat. "I can't delay this any longer. I'm afraid I must tell you."

"Tell me what, Doctor," she asked innocently.

"Mrs. Stringfellow, I'm very sorry, but I have bad news for you. Your son, Frank," he said kindly, groping for words, "the scout…he has been captured. He is," the surgeon's nerve failed him.

Anne laughed softly. "Oh, Doctor, I've heard that so many times I don't worry about it any more. My son can take care of himself."

"I'm afraid that's not the case this time. You see, madam, he's been shot and killed."

Anne took a deep breath, and asked apprehensively, "Are you quite sure about that?"

"Positive, madam," He went on to relate the details of how Stringfellow was shot in the river.

Her voice shaking, she asked, "Have you recovered his body?"

"No, but we will soon. There is absolutely no doubt that your son is dead. If it is any comfort to you, he died a brave death."

"I'm sure that he would. But until I see his body with my own eyes I won't believe that he's dead. My son has the habit of showing up when and where you least expect him, Doctor." Stringfellow chuckled at his mother's acting skills.

The doctor sighed and shook his head. "Have it your way. But, perhaps this will convince you. We have his coat and boots and he was bringing this book to you."

"My son was bringing that book to me? May I have it, Doctor?" For the first time, Stringfellow could detect a true strain in his mother's voice.

The scout stayed and helped nurse his mother for several days. The Yankees suspected nothing, but commented on how much food the little old lady consumed. Stringfellow slipped out of the house one night and made his way back to cavalry headquarters several days later. He presented Stuart with several newspapers and the papers from the general's tent, which turned out to be the payroll from General Casey's division. Thus, the Confederates gained an accurate picture of his forces.[3]

Constance labored over the ironing board while Sadie prepared dinner. The knock on the kitchen door startled them. "I'll get it." Eager with anticipation, Constance set the iron down and rushed through the dark pantry alcove to the door. Opening the door, a cry of relief broke from her lips at the sight of Aaron's tall form. "Aaron, I've been frantic about you!" When he stepped inside and closed the door, she threw her arms around him and met his kiss eagerly.

"I've missed you terribly," he whispered between devouring kisses. "You were never out of my mind." After a few minutes, Sadie cleared her throat loudly.

"Come and tell me about the battle." Constance took his hand and led him out of the alcove. He nodded to Sadie and smiled.

"It was a cold miserable campaign," he began as he lowered his exhausted body onto the bench at the trestle table. "Your army dug in and held a strong defensive position in the hills around Mine Run. We learned something that was no surprise to me. Lee is as formidable an opponent on the defense as he is on the offense. Basically, our men died in vain. Nothing was accomplished."

"God answered both of my conflicting prayers." Constance placed the cool iron on the stove, picked up the hot one carefully with a cloth, and continued ironing. "I prayed for your safe return and the success of our troops. What do you think will happen now?"

"Who knows?" He moved his hands restlessly together. "There are all sorts of rumors that Meade will be replaced and Lee will attack. Perhaps nothing will happen and we'll spend the winter here in peace and quiet."

"Major Bennett has rudely ensconced himself in our house again. If your army spends the winter, there won't be a tree left in the county."

"I understand," he said quietly. She finished ironing the dress and folded the ironing board up. After she hung the dress in the alcove, she looked over Sadie's shoulders. "How long until dinner is ready?"

"Oh, not too long."

"Good, I'll set the table." She collected the dishes and eyed Aaron across the table. He seemed distant and upset. "Aaron, is something wrong? Are you feeling well?"

When he looked up at her, she observed the lines under his eyes and several days' stubble of beard. "I'm tired," he answered, pausing in thought. Building up his nerve, he continued, "There's a matter that weighs heavy on my heart. I'm not sure it's wise for me to reveal this matter to you, but at the same time I feel compelled to always be open and honest with you."

She placed the plates around the table slowly. Looking at him perplexed, she answered, "Of course I want you to be honest with me."

He rubbed his hands over his eyes and leaned forward on the table. "Yesterday, I took a party of cavalrymen back across the Rapidan on a reconnaissance mission behind Rebel lines. We left from Summerduck near Raccoon Ford."

"Yes, I know where that is," she said apprehensively while she arranged the silverware on the table.

"I'm sure you can understand the danger involved in such missions." She nodded her head in understanding. "When we were returning, we encountered a lone Rebel riding ahead of us. As we closed in behind him, I ordered him to halt. He spurred his horse in an attempt to escape."

"Well, what did you expect him to do?" she asked in frustration.

"We gave him an opportunity to surrender," he continued in a resigned voice. "When he fled we were forced to fire on him. Those are our standing orders. When a man does not surrender we are to shoot to kill." She gazed at him with reproachful eyes. "He turned around and fired back at us, killing the soldier riding beside me."

"I'm thankful he didn't hit you," she said softly.

"We shot his horse out from under him as he approached the Rapidan. He jumped out of the saddle, pulled off his coat and boots, and dove into the river." She backed up against the wall, her hands trembling. "I was the first one to arrive at the riverside, and I saw his head emerge in the middle of the river." He looked up at her with tears in his eyes. "I fired at him several times…he threw his hands up and sank to the bottom."

"It…it was…Frank, wasn't it?" she said in a broken whisper.

"Constance, I'm sorry—you've got to understand—I didn't know who it was," he emphasized in a voice full of entreaty.

"You…you killed Frank!" she sobbed as the cup and saucer in her hands slipped downward and smashed against the brick floor. Something inside her snapped and her features contorted with shock and anger. "You murdered him!" she screamed. "You didn't have to shoot him. You could have captured him. But you murdered him!"

He stood up and faced her across the table, bitterly hurt by her accusation. "Even if we'd captured him, he'd have been executed for being a spy within a matter of hours."

"I thought you were different!" she yelled hysterically through her tears. "I thought I could trust you. But you're just like all the rest. You're just another murdering Yankee!"

His pride badly wounded, he could no longer control his temper. "If I'm a murderer, then so are you. You beat a Yankee to death and it wasn't even in self-defense." His voice was cold and lashing. He shook his finger at her with a fiery, angry look that was unfamiliar to her. "You're just another stiff-necked, proud, haughty, *Vah-gin-yan*. You think you're always right—that you're superior to everybody else in the world. You won't even listen to the other side of the story!"

"I believe, Lieutenant Ames, that we've both paid our debts to each other. I have nothing else to say to you." Her accusing voice stabbed the air as she shot him a hostile glare through her tears. "Please leave."

"I'm on my way out!" He slammed his hat on his head while his furious gaze swung over her in a prolonged moment of deafening silence. He took several steps towards the door, then swung around and said, "I have the sudden urge to read *The Taming of the Shrew.*" When he reached the dark alcove, he turned and looked at her one more time. This time the fury in his eyes melted into pain. *"O, I am fortune's fool."*

The door slammed, then she covered her face with trembling hands and gave vent to the agony of her loss. She recognized the line Romeo had uttered after killing Juliet's cousin, Tybalt.

Sadie hurried over to her and encircled her with her arms. "It's all right, baby."

"Of all people, why…did he have to kill Frank?" Constance gasped between sobs.

Ten days later, December 14, 1863: The bookstore

When Constance heard the loud commotion in the hall, she walked to the door of the bookstore to investigate. Soldiers stacked countless trunks and hatboxes, while a plump middle-aged lady supervised. "That pile belongs to Maureen. She'll take the smallest bedroom upstairs while I, of course, will be with Major Bennett." The soldiers picked up several of the trunks, and a tall auburn-haired lass in her twenties followed them down the hall to the back stairway.

The round-faced lady appeared expensively dressed in what Constance considered a gaudy outfit of bright burgundy with gold trim. Her curls fell from under her hat and only made her elephantine face look fuller. She noticed Constance's plain homespun dress and shot her a condescending look. "You must be the poor little waif who runs the bookstore," she sniffed haughtily.

"I'm Constance Armstrong. I own this house."

"You're an uppity little Rebel, I hear. I'm Mrs. Bennett and I'll control the running of the house and kitchen now that I'm here."

Trying to control her fury, Constance replied, "You may use the house however you wish. I will not interfere. However, my servant has control of the kitchen."

"We're not eating anything your nigger cooks. I've brought my Irish maid to prepare our meals. You and your nigger may use the kitchen before 7 a.m. and after 6 p.m. The rest of the time it's ours," Mrs. Bennett stated smugly with an air of superiority. "Since you're living in the slave quarters with your nigger, I don't want you to enter any room in the house except your little store. We can't have the rest of the house contaminated. If you give me any trouble, Miss Armstrong, I'll have my husband shut your store down."

Constance gritted her teeth to keep from grabbing the colossal old hag around the neck and choking her to death. "You've made yourself clear, Mrs. Bennett. I do hope you'll be comfortable in my parents' bedroom. I trust that their ghosts will not disturb you."

"Ghosts?" Mrs. Bennett sneered with her thin eyebrows raised.

"Yes, their ghosts have been very active in that room and they hate Yankees. My father died of pneumonia while falsely imprisoned by your army and my mother was shot by artillery and trampled to death when your army invaded our town. You can understand that their ghosts might seek revenge against Yankees."

"I don't believe a word of it," Mrs. Bennett snorted, then she waddled down the hall.

Sadie paced in front of the fireplace in her cabin. "I been cookin' in that kitchen all mah life, an' now they say I can't come in it? Damn Yankees!"

"I don't think I can tolerate that witch the rest of the winter," Constance complained while she rocked in the rocking chair. "We've got to figure a way to get rid of her."

"How we gonna do that? If we harm her, they'll hang us!"

"There's got to be a way," Constance said in deep thought. "It's you and me against them, Sadie."

Next day, December 15, 1863: The depot

The cold bitter wind chilled Constance to the bone while she waited with the crowd at the depot for the train to arrive from Washington. Expecting a shipment of newspapers, she would not allow her eyes to meet those of any of the Yankee soldiers gawking at her. She had no privacy. Their eyes followed her wherever she went. These last ten days had been the longest, saddest days of her life. The thought of Frank's death left her bereft and desolate. Without the anticipation of Aaron's visits, life had become pure drudgery. She had to force herself to get out of bed each day and now, she had the added vexation of Mrs. Bennett. Her life was a bitter battle. No matter what, she must keep the bookstore open. That money might be her salvation in the future.

The halted train discharged mountains of black smoke while many soldiers and a few women disembarked. Everybody knew the soldiers traveled to Washington for female entertainment among the streets lined with brothels. She jumped back reflexively at the shock of seeing Aaron's tall frame among the passengers. Instantly, she ducked down behind a pile of crates. Why had he been to Washington? Had she lost him to another woman already? A man with such potent magnetism was too desirable to remain lonely long. The thought froze in her mind. Their relationship seemed doomed, and yet she had to fight her overwhelming need to be close to him. She peered out to watch him mount the horse brought by one of his men. Too proud to cry out to him for forgiveness, she blinked back tears and felt the nauseating sinking of despair while she watched him ride away.

Next day, December 16, 1863: The bookstore

Constance smiled at Mary Minor Botts when she entered the bookstore. "Miss Botts, I want to thank you for selling milk and eggs to Lieutenant Ames when I was ill. I owe my recovery to you."

"I'm delighted to see you looking so well, Miss Armstrong. That handsome Lieutenant Ames seemed most concerned for your welfare. You're a fortunate lady indeed. Do you see him often?"

"I'm afraid I haven't seen him for a good while." Constance's face fell. "I hope your father didn't suffer ill health while he was in jail in Richmond."

"No, he's most happy now and is enjoying the company of all of the Union officers. We have parties and gatherings at our house almost every night. Unfortunately, I'm too sad to enjoy all of the merriment."

"And why is that? A lovely young lady like yourself should be the center of attention."

Mary's eyes flickered with pain. "A Union officer, Captain Hoxie, has won my deepest affection. A few nights ago I was talking to him in front of our house while a party went on inside. Suddenly, from out of nowhere, two horsemen rode up and demanded his surrender. Shocked because they were in Federal uniforms, he asked, 'Surrender to whom?' One of them pointed a revolver at his head, and he decided debate would be futile. He handed them his sword and they ordered him to mount behind one of them, threatening him with instant death if he attempted to escape. At the same time, a regiment of infantry advanced towards us. I do not know if they were afraid to shoot or didn't comprehend what was happening. At any rate, my dearest soldier was carried off without a shot being fired. I fear he is now in a Confederate prison. These Rebel scouts, dressed as Yankees, have infiltrated the county and scour the countryside for lone soldiers. None are safe unless they travel in groups."

"That's an incredible story," Constance said sympathetically. "None should have to suffer the hardships of prison. I hope your soldier will return safely to you."

"I appreciate your sympathy. He's my true love. Meanwhile, I believe I'll have many hours to read. Do you have any new books?"[i]

"Oh yes." Constance led her to the bookshelves. The two women browsed and enjoyed each other's company for a good while.

When five o'clock arrived, Constance put on her coat and locked the bookstore.

She walked through the light sleet to the Virginia House. The eyes of the soldiers looked at her expectantly when she entered the tavern room. Not wanting to return their stares, she scanned the room for Millie. The plain young woman waved to her from behind the bar. "Hello, Constance!"

"Millie, I must tell my woes to someone," Constance said softly, then leaned against the bar.

Millie eyed her with concern after she served a beer to one of the soldiers. "What's happened now?"

Constance related her situation with Mrs. Bennett and her Irish cook.

"What a bunch of hypocrites!" Millie said furiously. "I believe the condescending wives are worse than the soldiers. They treat us all like hired help."

"Sometimes I think my anger will consume me," Constance whispered. "At any rate, I was hoping that your mother might hire Sadie to cook here during the day. She's feeling better now and needs to keep busy."

"That's a possibility, but you'll have to ask Mother. At the moment she's in the other room being interrogated by some soldiers. They think she's a spy."

"Do tell?" Constance said shocked. "Are we all under suspicion?"

"I believe so. They've quit letting Rebel ladies pass through their lines to Orange because they believe we're all spies. So, we're trapped here, whether we like it or not."

"I didn't know that. We have no choice but to make the best of the situation."

"I agree. You know, Constance, most of these men are the scum of the earth…conscripts and bounty hunters. But, I must confess I've met one very nice soldier from Delaware who's a gentleman. I'm enjoying his attention. Please don't say anything about this to our friends."

"I won't," Constance replied with a smile. "I know that there are many good men in the Union army."

"How many of our men will return? The prospects of spinsterhood are depressing. I don't want to spend my life alone."

The door to the family quarters opened and several Union soldiers filed out. Constance walked inside to confront an irate Mary Payne. "Everybody wants to know my loyalties," the little lady complained. "I hate this war and I have no loyalties. Both sides suspect me, and both sides want me to work for them!"

Constance told her she understood and then explained Sadie's situation. Mrs. Payne agreed to hire Sadie, whose reputation as a cook was well established in the town.

Constance rolled over in her bed and took her pocket watch from the table. She held it up so that the light from the fire revealed the time to be almost midnight. Quietly, she pulled back the covers and sat up on the bedside to put on her shoes. She tiptoed towards the door and pulled her arms into her coat. Slowly, she cracked the door and slipped outside into the moonlight. Waiting for her eyes to adjust to the darkness, she scanned the dark windows of her house. Hopefully, everyone was asleep. She slunk to the back door and silently opened it with the key in her pocket. Thank God, the door didn't squeak. Once inside the hall, she slipped her shoes off and then crept silently up

---

[i] Mary Minor Botts married her captain at the end of the war.

the steps in her stocking feet. She paused as a step squeaked slightly and listened. She only heard the sound of snoring.

When she reached the top of the steps, she cautiously tiptoed to the door of her parents' bedroom and put her ear against the door. Good! She heard two people snoring loudly. She grasped the handle and pulled it towards her so the door opened quietly. The firelight revealed two rotund forms in the bed. She prowled around the room picking up a brush from the bureau and a necklace and picture of the Bennetts from a table. Putting the items in her pocket, she reached her fingers to one of the locks on a window. She turned the lock and then slowly raised the window about half way, to allow the cold air to flow into the room.

Quickly, she skulked back down the stairs and raced into the dining room where she placed the necklace on the table. Then she moved to the hall and laid the brush on the hall table. In the parlor, she slipped the photograph out of the frame and tore it up. The pieces fell to the floor and she placed the frame on a table. Without hindrance, she locked the backdoor and fled to the safety of her bed with no one learning of her nocturnal expedition.

Next day, December 17, 1863: The bookstore

"Good morning, Mrs. Bennett," Constance said politely. The beefy lady swayed into the bookstore in a dress much too frilly for someone her age. "May I help you?"

"Miss Armstrong, some very strange things occurred last night." Her beady eyes narrowed with suspicion. "Several items were removed from my bedroom."

"Oh!" Constance faked shock. "I do hope nothing was stolen and that you weren't harmed. I must apologize for my parents."

"Still sticking to the ghost story, huh?"

"I can assure you, it's no story. I've seen images of both of them in that room. Usually, they do playful things with me, but I'm concerned that they might do something harmful to you," Constance said with complete sincerity. "You weren't injured, were you?"

"No, and I don't expect this to happen again. Do you understand me?"

"Of course I understand you, but it's out of my control. I have no influence in the supernatural world."

"Balderdash!" the old hag snorted with her nose in the air. She allowed her eyes to roam around the bookstore.

"Perhaps you need something to read to keep your mind off of what happened." Constance placed a Harper's magazine in front of her. "I'm sure a lady of your status would enjoy seeing the latest fashions."

"Yes." Mrs. Bennett flipped through the magazine. "This war has made my husband a very important man. I must maintain the proper image. We'll be in total control as soon as we've conquered all of you uppity Rebels."

"And what will you do with the slaves when you're in control?" Constance asked calmly.

"Oh, we'll either send them all back to Africa or leave them here for you Rebels to take care of. We certainly aren't going to allow these black Sambos and their pickaninnies in Illinois. Good day, Miss Armstrong." She pranced out without paying for the magazine.

Eight days later, December 25, 1863: Sadie's cabin

A permanent sorrow and sense of aloneness weighed Constance down while she listened to Sadie read the Christmas story. Fragrant aromas of roast turkey and other delicacies drifted through the air from the kitchen to Sadie's cabin. She stood up and put one of their few remaining logs on the fire after Sadie concluded her reading.

"You read that beautifully Sadie. I'm quite proud of you." Constance sank back down in the rocking chair, her eyes growing moist. "Never did I dream that Christmas could be so blue. Without family to share it with, it has no meaning. On top of that, there's the added insult of having to listen to the damn Yankees singing carols and playing my piano," she hissed as strains of *God Rest Ye Merry Gentlemen* reached her ears.

"An' smell the food they's cookin' in mah kitchen." With fire in her eyes, Sadie took Constance's hand. "We's got each other. I know ya loves me, Miss Constance, an' that ya stayed here 'cause I was sick. But, I think ya needs to be honest an' admit that mah sickness wasn't the only reason ya stayed."

Constance arched her dark eyebrows. "I would never have deserted you. I don't know what you mean."

"I means ya stayed 'cause of your feelings for Lieutenant Ames. Otherwise, why did I wake up to hear all those smackies? Jist be honest with me an' yourself!"

Constance's mouth curved in an unconscious smile. "I admit it. I was hopeful he'd return, but I'd have stayed with you regardless."

"That's more like it," Sadie said with a satisfied grin. "You's had the longest face I's ever seen for the last three weeks, an' I'm tired of lookin' at it! Now don't git me wrong, I ain't got no use for no damn Yankees, but that man wouldn't have done what he did for ya, unless he was crazy or in love, or both! Ain't ya got sense enuff to know when a man's in love with ya?"

Constance couldn't hold back the tears welling in her eyes. "Oh, Sadie, there's a battle raging in my mind. I don't know what's right any more. Why does he have to be a Yankee and why did he have to kill Frank?"

"Only the good Lawd kin answer that. I knows how much ya loved Mista Frank an' how you's mourning him. But, Lieutenant Ames didn't have to tell ya he killed him. He was honest with ya. How'd ya have felt if'n he hadn't told ya an' ya heard it from somebody else?"

"Betrayed. Like I couldn't trust him."

"War makes good people do bad things. What if Mista Frank had shot him? Could of happened jist as easy. Would ya have forgiven him, if'n he didn't know who he was?"

"Yes." Constance wiped her eyes. "And I'm sure Aaron didn't know who Frank was."

"What really matters is what's in your heart. Are ya in love with him?"

"Yes," she stammered in a tear-smothered voice. "I never wanted to love a Yankee, but I do love him. He's captured my heart in a way I never believed possible. But, I'm afraid I've lost him. I hoped he would come back, but I don't think he ever will."

"Now ya listen to me, young lady." Sadie shook her finger. "You's got to swallow your pride an' tell him you's sorry an' that ya forgive him for Mista Frank. You write him a letter an' send it by Joseph next time he comes, an' I bet Lieutenant Ames will be here quicker than a duck can jump on a June bug! Trust Sadie."

"Oh, Sadie, I hope you're right." Constance stood up and threw her arms around the old woman. "I'll write him a letter right now. I can't believe you're taking up for Aaron. He thinks you hate him!"

Sadie patted her on the arm. "Let him think I hates him. If'n he comes back, I'm gonna have to put the fear of God in him to protect your virtue. Besides, I wants to see ya happy, chile. Now, how much longer before I kin git in mah kitchen an' cook our Christmas dinner?"

"About half an hour." Constance sat down at the table.

Constance heard the door close in the dark pantry alcove while she placed the plates on the trestle table. "Momma." Joseph emerged from the shadows. "Merry Christmas!"

"Lawd, son." Sadie hugged him. "It's Christmas, but there ain't nothin' merry 'bout it."

Constance's face fell when she realized he was alone. "You're by yourself?" she asked with a note of sad resignation.

"Yas'm." Joseph warmed his hands over the cook stove. "It's startin' to snow."

"Joseph, I have a letter I want you to take to Lieutenant Ames."

He walked around the cookstove and slowly took the letter from her, placing it in his pocket. "I'll do mah best, Miss Constance, but I don't know…if I'll be able to git it to him."

"What do you mean?" she asked concerned.

Joseph shifted from foot to foot, looking at the floor. Finally, he glanced up at Constance with sad eyes. "I'm sorry to have to tell ya this, Miss Constance, but he went out on a scout yesterday, an' some of our boys tried to capture him."

"Go on." Constance grabbed his arm while her heart hammered against her ribs. "What happened?"

"He got away an' made it back to camp, but…." Joseph stopped, unable to finish.

"But what?" Constance screamed shaking his arm.

"He got shot in the stomach real bad. It don't look good."

"Oh, God, no!" She put her hands over her face and uttered a low tortured sob. Sadie rushed to her and gathered her in her arms.

"He was too weak to write, so he dictated this letter to a friend an' asked me to bring it to ya." Joseph handed her a letter. Her hands trembled, so Sadie opened the envelope for her. Brushing away tears she finally focused her eyes and read:

My dearest Constance,

I do not know how many more breaths I will take on this earth, and I feel compelled to communicate my true feelings to you. I love you more deeply than I ever dreamed possible. I came back to this terrible war not only out of patriotism, but because I thought you would need a friend on the other side. I wanted to be here to protect you. When I saw that the town would be shelled, I volunteered to ride ahead and sight for the artillery. That's why I was close enough to see you when you fell, and with God's help was able to save you.

I have suffered deep guilt and regret over Stringfellow's death. His mother was wounded in the battle, and our cavalry camped around the house where she was recovering, in the hope of luring him there and capturing him. I felt it was an underhanded

414

scheme and requested not to be a part of it. Ironically, in an effort to avoid him, I went on a scout across the river and encountered him. I realize it was a mistake for me to tell you what I'd done, but I didn't want our relationship to be based on lies and deceit. It was my dream that we would always be open and honest with each other, communicating our innermost thoughts. I suppose I hoped that if you could forgive me, it would help eliminate my gnawing guilt. That was too much to expect, since he was so dear to you. That you will forgive me, my darling Reb, is my last wish.

Farewell, my love,

Aaron

Sadie handed Constance a handkerchief and she wiped her face. Still shaking, she turned to Joseph and whimpered, "You must take me to him at once."

"But Miss Constance," Joseph protested, "he might not be alive when ya git there. It's freezing an' it's startin' to snow."

"Joseph," she sobbed hysterically, then jumped up and pulled on his arm. "You don't understand. I've got to tell him how much I love him. Maybe there's a chance I can save him. You must take me!"

"All right, Miss Constance," he said reluctantly. Constance raced towards the alcove to get her cape. When she entered the shadows, a large hand reached out and grabbed her arm.

"Oh!" she cried with shock. She felt the muscular arms around her and then the warmth of those full sensuous lips against hers, kissing her tears away. Was she dreaming? "Aaron?" She threw her arms around him, returning his kisses. "You're not wounded?" A warm flood of joy surged through her.

"Only in my heart," he answered softly, then consumed her with his kisses.

Then the shock of what he'd done hit her. "You tricked me!" She tried to pull away.

"No, I didn't." He pressed her close against his well-muscled chest, refusing to let her go. "I don't know how many more breaths I'll take on this earth. We lost three precious weeks in a stalemate, each one of us too proud to apologize."

"But you made me think you were dying. How cruel!" she said with a pout, enjoying the security of his protective arms around her.

He held her firmly against him, stroking her hair. "I'm not going to let you run from your feelings. You said you loved me; I heard you. Would you only admit it because you thought I was dying?"

"Well, there was no obligation, no commitment." She tried to focus on his eyes in the darkness.

"Constance." He took her face in his hands. "I ask no commitment from you. I'm going to be here for the rest of the winter. Shall we ignore the beautiful, deep love we feel for each other, or enjoy it?"

Her resistance faded away. "It would be a lot more fun to enjoy it." She stood on her tiptoes and kissed him gently. "There has been no sunshine in my life since you left. I didn't want to love you, Aaron. I tried hard not to fall in love with you, but then you dashed back into my life like a knight in shining armor. I do love you deeply… completely." She traced her finger around his lips, "And I never thought I'd say this to any man…because I'm so independent, but…I…I need you."

His whole face spread into a dazzling sensuous smile. He hoisted her up above his head, and then slowly lowered her as her lips met his. After several minutes of sighs and heavy breathing, Sadie could no longer control her tongue. "Sure is gettin' steamy in here!" she said loudly.

"Whew! Ain't it though!" Joseph laughed. "I'm ready to eat those oysters, blueberry pie, an' yams we brung."

"Oysters?" Constance asked as their lips parted.

"Yes." Aaron took her hand and they emerged from the darkness. "And I'm starving."

"Joseph, I can't believe you were an accomplice to this cruel deception," Constance scolded.

He smiled sheepishly. "Jist tryin' to keep everybody happy, Miss Constance."

"I've missed you, Sadie," Aaron said with a broad grin.

Sadie's lips turned up slightly in a smile, and then her usual scowl returned to her face. "Ya jist 'member who's boss 'round here an' we'll git along fine, Lieutenant Ames."

He nodded dutifully, and then turned to Joseph. "I want to read my letter." Joseph handed him Constance's letter; he sat down and read it near the candle, his eyes growing moist.

Constance linked her arm through Aaron's while the two of them embarked on an after dinner walk through town. The cold wind made them draw close together while they listened to the raucous laughter of the Union soldiers occupying every building. She told him of her past Christmas celebrations, the traditional caroling with her family and her sense of loneliness this year. He related the joys of ice skating, sleigh riding, and a Maine Christmas, and then bragged about the cozy log hut he and five others had constructed for their winter quarters. She narrated the capture of Mary Minor Botts's captain and expressed her concern for him riding alone to visit her. He admitted that the Rebels lurked everywhere and agreed to travel in daylight or with a group of soldiers.

He described for her the racetrack that Custer had built at Clover Hill and the diversions of military life: racing, debate clubs, reading, gambling, singing, and even balls where half of the men dressed as women. He admitted he had succumbed to all the vices without her good influence. He laughed over Custer's blissful euphoria when his darling Libbie agreed to marry him on February ninth. Even though all of Custer's staff would attend the gala wedding in Michigan, Aaron promised that he would not leave her for a week.

She vented her wrath over Mrs. Bennett's condescending treatment of her and her blatant racism. They both agreed they were deeply touched by the other's letter and decided to write to each other every day they were apart, so that they would know and share every detail of their lives.

Constance stopped and stuck out her tongue to catch a snowflake. "Aaron, there's something I must ask you," she said apprehensively. "Did you ever find Frank's body?"

"No," he responded with a tone of sadness. "But the Rebels could have fished it out. His mother, poor woman, refused to believe he was dead unless we could show her a body. She's nearly recovered from her wound and is staying with friends in Orange now."

"I'm glad to hear she's doing well. The pain of Frank's death gnaws away at my soul. I, too, can't give up hope that he's alive. I know how well he swims under water."

"I hate to see you build up false hopes. There's nothing I'd like better than to hear he's alive, but I don't believe it's possible."

She walked silently for a minute staring at him. "I saw you get off the train from Washington. I suspected you had gone there to meet another woman and was afraid I'd lost you."

"Actually, I did meet another woman," he answered in complete seriousness.

Her face registered concern. "At least you're honest. I admit it. I'm jealous."

"She's quite lovely and about your size. I know you'd like her." His eyes twinkled with merriment. "I met my sister and two of my brothers. Since I used my only furlough to take care of you, I couldn't go home for Christmas. They were kind enough to come visit me."

"Aaron, you're such a tease! But, I feel guilty because you couldn't go home for Christmas. I'm glad you at least got to see some of your family."

"Yes, we had a delightful visit." They walked along silently for a few minutes. "Speaking of visits, Sunday is the best day for me to visit you. And if I can manage it, I'll try to get away one other day during the week."

"That gives me something to live for." She paused for a minute in thought. "I want you to take me to church on Sunday."

He looked at her intently, then opened the back gate. Deeply touched by her concession, he responded, "I'd be most honored to accompany you. I want to share my faith with you, but are you certain you're ready for this?"

"Yes," she said with conviction. "We worship the same God, accept the same Savior, and are both Episcopalians. I believe that God sent you to me. Nothing should keep us from worshiping together." She turned and faced him in the shadows of the boxwoods, taking both of his hands in hers. "Aaron, I've had lots of time to think and search my heart these last three weeks. I've concluded that you're the most important person in the world to me. I'm proud to be seen with someone of your integrity. I realize my friends will shun me, but I hope that I can eventually make them understand that it is possible for me to love you and remain loyal to the Confederacy."

"You've just given me the most marvelous Christmas present imaginable." He pulled her close and his lips parted hers in a soul-searching message. "Um," he sighed as a few snowflakes tickled their faces. Finally releasing her, he reached into his pocket and pulled out a tiny wrapped package. "Merry Christmas." He placed it in her hand.

"Do you mean you got me a Christmas present, even while you were banished?"

"I suppose I'm an eternal optimist. Remembering the passion of your kisses gave me hope for reconciliation. My sister, Abby, helped me pick it out in Washington. She's a hopeless romantic like me. The rest of my family disapproves of our relationship. They're convinced some southern Jezebel has cast a spell over me."

Giggling, she walked towards the soft light radiating from the kitchen window and lifted the lid. Inside she saw a dainty gold chain with a small gold heart dangling from it. It would be improper for her to accept such a gift, but who cared about proprieties any more, she rationalized. She lifted it up to the light, turned to him, and took his hand. "Oh, Aaron, it's a beautiful bracelet. Put it on for me."

She pulled back her glove and sleeve and he worked clumsily with his large hands to hook the bracelet. "There!" he said after he finally hooked the clasp. "Now you're wearing my heart on your sleeve. Treat it gently."

Aunt Martha yawned before she picked up her knitting and settled into the easy chair by the fire. The life of a spy was exhausting. Every morning she rose early to bake her pies, which she then sold in the camps of the Union soldiers. Always keeping her eyes and ears open, she later passed information on to the Confederate scouts who frequented her house. A born extrovert, she loved the company of the soldiers who hid out at her home. Many times, such as tonight, she entertained old friends from the Little Fork Rangers, who scouted the area and visited their families. Sleeping soundly upstairs were Isaac Lake, Hill Jefferies, Art McCormick, and Silas Newsome. She clicked the knitting needles together with her nimble fingers and heard her safeguard, Private Williams, riding his horse around the house. He was such a nice young man, even if he was a Yankee. She had befriended him, fed him royally, and quickly won his allegiance. He never reported the nocturnal comings and goings at her house to his army because his sympathy for her caused him to turn a blind eye. But still, she wondered, how long would her activities remain a secret? Could she trust her neighbors not to inform?

She cocked her gray head at the noise in the distance. It sounded like hooves, lots of hooves, moving closer to her. Throwing her knitting aside, she dashed to a window. She spotted several hundred horsemen coming up over the hill. Instantly, she puffed her way up the stairs and dashed into the bedroom. "Wake up! Yankees!" she gasped, her heart pounding wildly.

The Rangers sprang from their beds, then pulled on their boots and guns. McCormick peered out of a window. "Dang it! It's a powerful bunch of 'em!"

"The house is surrounded, Rebels," a Yankee yelled after guns fired into the air. "We know you're in there. We demand your surrender,"

"I ain't goin' to prison. I say we can shoot our way out," Newsome said through gritted teeth.

"I'm with you," Lake vowed.

"No!" Aunt Martha cried, her voice high and hysterical. She grabbed his arm, bursting into tears. "Please, I beg you, surrender. I…I'm an old widow…they'll burn my home…in reprisal."

The four soldiers stared at each other and then finally began unbuckling their guns. Although they detested the prospect of prison, they wished no harm to come to the loyal old lady.

"Don't shoot! They're coming out to surrender!" she shrieked through the open window.

Five days later, January 30, 1864: Sadie's cabin

Sadie awoke to a blood-curdling scream. "Miss Constance, did ya hear that? Sounded like it came from the house!"

Constance rolled over and wiped her eyes, trying to focus in the dawn light. Another high shrill shriek pierced the air. "I think our good friend, Mrs. Bennett, has had another visit from a ghost." She smiled wickedly and rolled back over. "You'd think it would be enough to scare her and that vicious Irish maid away from here!"

"I can't stand 'em much longer," Sadie said furiously. "That maid follows me 'round harassing me, callin' me stupid dirty nigger. She won't let me keep any food in the kitchen. I have to carry ours in an' out every day. What'd ya do to her this time, Miss Constance?"

"Oh, I dripped blood all over her dress." Sadie laughed and she pulled the covers back over her head.

Constance snuggled into the drowsy warmth of her pillow while her mind drifted into daydreams. Tingling, she burned with desire at the memory of Aaron's hands moving gently over her body. The two of them constantly sought new and creative ways to show their love through touching. Under Sadie's ever-vigilant eye, their passion had been kept under control. The little time they spent alone was ecstasy. Fortunately, he respected her. When she asked him to stop, he did.

Sometimes, he arrived on Saturday afternoon and spent the night in Billy's cabin. Then they had all day Sunday together. Reverend Cole had greeted him politely at church, while most others stared at him coldly. When Aaron commented on the empty belfry, Constance coolly explained that the church had donated the bell to the Rebels to melt for bullets. The Ashbys snubbed her on the street, crossing to the other side when they saw her coming. Millie Payne remained her only friend. Nevertheless, the warmth and exhilaration of Aaron's love overshadowed the pain of rejection. She had gained weight in the right places and never felt better. The news of John Hunt Morgan's triumphant reception in Richmond had buoyed her spirits and those of the Confederacy. If she could get rid of Mrs. Bennett, life would be good again.

Four days later, February 3, 1864: Sadie's cabin

"Yes, of course there's risk, Sadie. But otherwise we'll have to tolerate her the rest of the winter," Constance said, then put on her coat.

"I can't stand her no more. I'll do it!" Sadie declared wrapping a shawl around her worn dress.

"Maureen's in the kitchen. We'll go up the back steps and check all the bedrooms to see that the soldiers are out. Mrs. Bennett's always the last one to get up. Your job is to instantly unwrap the wire and hide in the cellar until the excitement is over." The two women casually walked across the yard, watching to be sure Maureen couldn't see them out of the kitchen window. They darted behind the large boxwood beside the house and pushed open the wooden door to the shallow cellar. Constance climbed in first and Sadie followed. Letting their eyes adjust to the darkness, they crept across the dirt floor to the back stairway. Constance cracked the door and listened to the soldiers upstairs in her father's office. She silently moved up the narrow enclosed stairwell to the second floor. Seeing no one, she crept from one bedroom to the next to find each one empty. As she expected, the door to her parents' room remained closed. She knelt down at the top of the main stairway and wrapped a fine wire around the posts on both sides, about three inches above the floor.

She motioned Sadie to stand flat against the wall around the corner. Sadie plastered herself against the wall, her eyes bulging. "Remember, you've got to act fast," Constance whispered before she turned and fled back down to the cellar.

Sadie stood motionless for almost twenty minutes until she heard the bedroom door open. Her heart pounded while the heavy footsteps trod towards the stairway. The instant she heard the first thud, she sprang around the corner, unwrapped the one end of the wire that remained attached, and flew down the back stairs to the cellar. Panting, she reached the cellar almost as soon as Mrs. Bennett crashed to the foyer.

Constance looked up from her desk nonchalantly when she heard the loud crash and the commotion of the soldiers running through the house. Fortunately, there were several soldiers in the bookstore, including one of Major Bennett's staff, giving her an airtight alibi. Alarmed, he raced out of the bookstore into the main portion of the house. Constance casually moved towards the window to the street. Shortly, her lips turned up in a satisfied smile while she watched Sadie race across the street into the Virginia House. They had done it!

Without remorse, she watched an ambulance arrive. The attendants carried Mrs. Bennett out and Maureen and Major Bennett accompanied her to the corps hospital. The officer came back into the bookstore visibly shaken. "Mrs. Bennett took a terrible fall down the steps."

"I'm so sorry." Constance turned around with a look of concern. "I do hope she's not seriously injured."

"It's hard to tell. She's unconscious. The Major mumbled something about a ghost pushing her. Does that make sense?"

"I'm afraid it does," Constance answered quite sadly. "I warned them that my parents' ghosts haunted this house."

Five days later, February 8, 1864: The bookstore

Constance shifted uncomfortably in the chair behind her desk. The lecherous stares of the officer browsing made her furious. She felt him undressing her with his eyes. An unattractive man in his late twenties, he possessed a straight mouth formed by two thin lips below a large nose, which flared at the nostrils. He pulled two books from the shelves and swaggered up to the desk. With an insolent smile, he said, "I'd heard that this bookstore possessed not only the best selection of books but the most beautiful proprietress. Allow me to introduce myself. I'm General Judson Kilpatrick."

"Will this be all for you today, General Kilpatrick?" She picked up the two books.

Raking her with his eyes, he responded, "I'd be pleased to form a friendship with a southern belle as lovely as yourself, Miss...uh..."

"Armstrong," she answered acidly. "That will be one dollar."

He handed her the money, still ogling her. "I'm headquartered at Rose Hill at Stevensburg. In an attempt to bring some warmth to this frigid winter encampment, I'm holding a ball next Saturday. I'd be honored if you would attend. Your loveliness would add much to the festive evening."

She turned a cold eye on him. "Thank you for your invitation, but I have other plans."

"You should not reject my proposal so hastily, Miss Armstrong. A man in my position could be very helpful to a Rebel lady attempting to survive."

Constance pursed her lips in suppressed fury, then heard footsteps in the hall. Over-joyed to see Aaron walk through the door, she broke into a radiant smile and rushed towards him. Aaron saluted Kilpatrick, then kissed her hand. "I'm Lieutenant Ames of General Custer's staff, sir."

"Ah, yes," Kilpatrick said. "I thought all of his staff went to the gala wedding?"

"Yes, that's true. Today is the good general's last day of bachelorhood. I had a compelling reason to remain in Culpeper." He smiled at Constance and slid his hand around hers.

"I see. I was trying to convince Miss Armstrong to attend the ball I'm holding at Rose Hill next Saturday. I'd be honored if you'd escort her."

Aaron looked at Constance with questioning eyes and she said, "That's kind of you sir, but as I said, I have other plans."

"The invitation stands if you change your mind." Kilpatrick walked to the door.

"Good day, sir," Aaron said.

Aaron turned and hugged Constance after Kilpatrick was out of earshot, and laughed. "It's a good thing I arrived to save you. He's a notorious womanizer. Everyone's snickering over his relationship with his two Negro cooks."

"Never have I had to endure such lewd stares," Constance fumed. She walked to the door, pulled the key from her pocket and locked it. "Time to close shop. He makes you look like Sir Lancelot!"

Aaron laughed, pulled her close, and kissed her. Then he bitterly expounded on his feelings about Kilpatrick. "I detest that man! He followed right into Stuart's trap at Buckland. It's only because of Custer's wariness and sixth sense that I survived. He's a vainglorious braggart who will endanger his men carelessly in any effort to further his career. That's why the men refer to him as Kil-Cavalry."

She leaned her head against his chest. "I don't like having you under his command. I heard the cannons firing day before yesterday and worried about you. What happened?"

He took her hand, walked behind the desk, snuffed out the candle, and sat down. Pulling an envelope from his pocket, he said, "Here are my promised letters. Now come here, my little Rebel, and I'll tell you about it." She sat on his lap and snuggled against him. "Ah, this is so much more delightful than being out in the cold on picket duty. That's where I've been this week, trying not to freeze to death while riding the twenty-five-mile picket line along the Rapidan."

"The weather has been the coldest I can remember." She tenderly moved her hand over his arm and shoulders. "Were you involved in the fighting?"

"No, thank God. From what I can gather, General Hays led the Third Division to Morton's Ford. They crossed the river and were soon met by heavy artillery fire. Severe fighting took place around the Buckner house and Jeremiah Morton's house. The artillery pinned down our men for a while. Nothing was accomplished. They re-crossed the river during the night. We had about 250 needless casualties."

"Jeremiah Morton is one of the richest men in the Confederacy. I wonder how he feels about secession now?" Constance mused. "But why would you suddenly attack at this time?"

"It makes little sense. One rumor I heard was that General Benjamin Butler was moving from Hampton towards Richmond in an attempt to free our prisoners, and this was a diversion. Over 12,000 of our men are packed into a prison that can handle at best 3000. They're starving to death and dying of disease at a staggering rate. One report said 500 deaths in a month. The families of the prisoners, who are crying for their release, assail Lincoln daily. He made a desperate attempt which I'm sure has failed. Any way you look at it, it was a waste of lives."

"Lincoln is to blame for the suffering and deaths of all the prisoners on both sides," she said with fire in her eyes. "He's the one who stopped prisoner exchange, thus forcing this inhumane situation. We hold more of your prisoners and offered to make an even exchange, which he refused. I can assure you, your prisoners are being fed as well as our army. We have little food because of your blockade. You have no excuse for starving our men, except cruelty. Not only that, our men are freezing to death in prisons in Delaware and on the Great Lakes. I can assure you that when the figures are known, the death rate will be higher among our men.[ii] Lincoln and Lincoln alone is responsible for this inhumanity of man to man!"

"No one deplores what's happening to the prisoners more than I do!" he said brusquely. "I've been there and seen the lice, the rats, the excrement and men dying in filth. I believe my chances of survival are better on the battlefield than in prison. We've got almost as many of your men in prison as you have on the battlefield. That's why Lincoln won't release them. Meanwhile our men are suffering and dying. It's a cruel political decision."

She pulled back and glared at him. "He knows our men, if released, will fight his tyranny with a vengeance. Yours will desert this unjust war. Look at the thousands of your men who have bought their way out of the draft.[iii] You have two and a half times more men than we do, and yet you cannot and will not defeat us on the battlefield like men. Instead, you'll starve us to death. Mark my words!"

"It's the lack of patriotism by those who refuse to serve that has prolonged this war. I'm fighting to see it ended as soon as possible and the Union restored. All men should be free, black and white. I'm fighting for human rights. I know you assert that we could have purchased the freedom of the slaves, but I don't believe those hotheads in South Carolina will ever give up slavery without a war. If it becomes a war of starvation, I will no longer fight," he declared returning her glare.

"If those are your true beliefs, I admire them Aaron. Thanks for letting me vent my wrath and not dominating me." She leaned her head back against his shoulder.

His lips turned up in a smile. "Even if I could dominate you, I wouldn't. It's your fire and intellect that excite me. The free interchange of thoughts makes our relationship stimulating. I've courted numerous beauties who were anxious to please me at every turn. I always grew bored. You'll never bore me."

Her hand smoothed his curly buckskin hair back from his face. "I've been suspicious of your conquests with other women. I can tell by the way you touch me that you're far more experienced in the gentle art of making love than I."

His lips softly brushed against hers. "I've never claimed to be a saint, but you must believe that I haven't touched another woman since you first kissed me."

"Havin' mah kitchen back is wonderful!" Sadie boasted while she stirred the stew.

"Do you mean Mrs. Bennett is gone?" Aaron said from the table.

"The poor old round lady tumbled down the stairs and broke a leg and an arm. She's gone back to Illinois. We can't believe our good fortune!" Constance said with a wicked

---

[ii]According to figures released by the U.S. government in 1866, of the 270,000 Yankees held in Rebel prisons, 22,576 died. (8.3%) Of the 220,000 Rebels held in northern prisons, 25,436 died. (12%). The death rate of Rebels was almost **50% higher**.

[iii]86,724 northern men bought their way out of serving in the army.

grin. "I've convinced the soldiers to take their meals at the Virginia House, so Sadie and I have complete privacy now."

"Congratulations! This calls for a celebration." He watched Constance put the plates on the table. "You know, in January the Third Corps had a lavish ball at Sunnybright near Brandy. Our Second Corps will not be outdone. Plans are underway to build a gigantic ballroom on Cole's Hill. Lumberjacks and carpenters are already getting the work underway. Hundreds of ladies and dignitaries from Washington have been invited. It will take place on Washington's birthday and will be the grandest event of this winter encampment. Since I'm on General Custer's staff, I've been invited. I'd be honored to escort you, my beautiful Rebel."

"Oh, Aaron," she said softly after she sat opposite him. "I wouldn't be comfortable socializing with so many Yankees. It's one thing to go to church and be seen around town with you, but to go to an event like that seems like treason. I'm sorry."

"Nonsense! You don't have to take the oath to attend. There will be other southern ladies there," he argued. "Besides, you need to dance and have fun. You can have the last laugh knowing the U.S. government is paying the bill."

"You's young, Miss Constance. Enjoy yourself! How long has it been since ya danced?" Sadie asked.

"No, I'd feel too guilty. Besides I know I'd say something to embarrass you, Aaron."

"I'd never be embarrassed to be with you. You're passing up an enjoyable evening. But if your answer is definitely no, then I'll ask someone else. I refuse to miss this event."

She scrutinized him to determine if he was joking. When she realized he wasn't, she answered. "That is your privilege." He said nothing. She walked over to the pine cabinet and got the utensils from the drawer. She placed them around the table and then stared at him quizzically. "Who will you ask?"

He rolled his eyes in thought. "There are several ladies in Boston who would welcome the opportunity to attend this gala ball."

She strolled to the stove, poured two cups of coffee, set one in front on him, and then positioned herself opposite him. Momentarily lost in her own reveries, she traced her finger around an invisible pattern on the table. Aaron cleared his throat in the deafening silence, gave her a narrowed glinting glance, his face closed as if guarding a secret. He knew he had her backed into a corner, but he refused to give in. He must force her to enter and understand his world if there was to be any future in their relationship. The silence loomed between them like a heavy mist, making her uncomfortable. Her nerves tensed while she sought a compromise and a way to save face. After sipping her coffee quietly for several minutes, she looked into his eyes with triumph and said, "I suppose I should celebrate the birthday of a distinguished *Vah-gin-yan*. After all, Washington was the first Rebel and leader of our first revolution."

Aaron's laughter was a full-hearted sound. He loved their gentle bantering, her subtle wit. He reached across the table and took her hand. "I agree. You're only being a loyal *Vah-gin-yan.* I can actually say it correctly now."

Constance chuckled. "But what will I wear? All of my dresses are out of style. I don't want to stand out like a sore thumb!"

"You'll look beautiful regardless of what you wear. But if you want a new dress, I'll have my sister send you one. She's about your size."

"I will not take charity, Aaron. You know that. I'll pay for the dress myself." She looked at Sadie and giggled. "Actually we could use some new unmentionables too, plus shoes."

"Lawd, ain't that the truth." Sadie poured the stew into bowls.

"I've got enough money to make the purchases. I'll only accept them if she sends the bills along." She squeezed his hand. "I suppose God will forgive me for having a little fun during this horrid war. Sadie, we'll make a shopping list after dinner."

Eight days later, February 16, 1864: Stevensburg

Stringfellow and two companions waited silently in the woods near Stevensburg for the cover of darkness. Near Second Corps headquarters, they intended to work their way into the numerous Union camps in the vicinity and see what information they could pick up. The scouts always searched for opportunities to capture a "bluebird" or two. Shivering as the last rays of light faded, they heard a horse moving towards them on the frozen road.

"Sounds like only one," Stringfellow whispered. "Could be a courier. Let's see."

The three scouts quietly moved down the road and fanned out in three directions. The unsuspecting Yankee jogged around the bend straight towards the Confederates. When he was abreast of them, Stringfellow gave the signal, and the Rebels leaped their horses into the road. The shocked Federal wheeled his horse around, but one of the scouts grabbed the bridle. When the Yank reached for his revolver, Stringfellow leveled his carbine in his face. The prisoner hastily raised his hands.

"Good evening, captain," Stringfellow said cordially. "You seem to be riding south. Allow us to act as your escort." He motioned to one of his men who took the bluecoat's arms.

"You damned rebel bushwhackers!"

Stringfellow smiled and shook his head. "We're regular soldiers from General Stuart's command. You're now a prisoner of war."

The angry captain protested. "You're crazy if you think you can get away with this! We're in the middle of a multitude of Union camps."

"I'm well aware of that, but we'll make it just the same," Stringfellow responded calmly. With a note of hardness in his voice, he ordered, "Bind his hands and gag him good."

The sleet pelted them on the cold windy ride. The group had several encounters with enemy scouting parties. Once a cavalry detachment rode so near that the scouts heard the creaking leather of their saddles. Stringfellow pressed his carbine against the captain's head while his men held the nostrils of their horses to keep them from snickering. In a few moments the enemy party passed. When he was sure they were safely out of the way, the scout gave the signal to move out.[4]

One of the men rode forward to locate a safe crossing on the Rapidan. When he reported back, the others followed him into the frigid water. Their legs grew numb, but their circulation quickly increased as hostile bullets peppered the water behind them. "Keep riding," Stringfellow ordered grimly. They spurred their horses up the bank and fled to the safety of the woods.

Later that night Stringfellow warmed his hands in front of the fire at a house used as a Confederate picket post. He wondered about the captain he had captured. Why was he riding alone? He could be a courier, but they usually rode with several other men. One of his men entered the room and turned his palms towards the flames. "We searched the prisoner sir. This is all we found." He handed a piece of paper to Stringfellow.

The scout tilted the paper to read it with the light from the flickering fire. "Um!" he grunted in surprise. It was a pass through Federal lines made out to Miss Sallie Marsten, a young lady whose family he knew well. One of her brothers had been killed at Williamsburg and another was missing in action. Undoubtedly, the Marstens were loyal Confederates. There must be a logical explanation.

"I need to have a little chat with the prisoner. Bring him in."

When the Federal captain was ushered in, Stringfollow told him, "Have a seat. Make yourself comfortable."

"I'd rather stand," he answered curtly.

"Very well." Stringfellow folded the pass in his hands. "What were you doing riding south with this pass in your pocket?"

"I don't have to answer your questions. It's none of your business."

"That attitude isn't going to help you, captain," Stringfellow said brusquely. "We'll find out the truth one way or another. How do you know this lady?"

The officer hesitated and shifted from one foot to the other. "She rode into our lines a while back, seeking information on her missing brother. She thought we might have captured him. I tried to help her without success."

"Why were you taking her a pass?"

The color rose in the captain's face. "I...I felt sorry for her. Seems like she's had a pretty tough time, and I wanted to take her mind off her brother. We're having a gala ball soon, and I thought she might come."

Stringfellow's eyes twinkled as he smiled. "You must have thought quite highly of her to risk going through our lines."

"I'd have made it, if it hadn't been for you renegades. What's going to happen to me now?"

"You're on your way to prison. If you're lucky, you'll survive."

The captain shook his head with a long face. "If I write to her in your care, will you see that she gets my letters?"

"Certainly." Stringfellow stood and the two men shook hands.

Stringfellow sat down and gazed into the flames. A plan slowly formed in his mind. It would require a trip to the Marstens' in the morning.[5]

18

Dance, Stringfellow, Dance!

February 17, 1864 - February 28, 1864

"I had a great time." (signed) John Mosby
Note written on the wall at the Union Washington's Birthday Ball, Stevensburg

---

Next day, February 17, 1864: The bookstore

Constance glanced up from her desk to see Aaron lounging casually against the doorframe. "Sakes alive, Aaron, you got your hair cut!"

"Yes, I decided that since I'll be escorting the fairest of ladies to the ball, I should no longer resemble a shaggy dog. Actually, I was copying Custer, who had promised not to cut his curly golden locks until we won the war. However, he acquiesced to Libbie and had them shortened for the wedding." He kissed her hand.

"You're powerful handsome regardless of the length of your hair," she said with a coy smile. "I rather liked it long."

"I'm delighted you feel that way, fair damsel. Your chariot awaits you," he replied with an irresistibly devastating grin as he motioned towards the window.

Curious, she traipsed to the window and gazed at the six cavalrymen surrounding a gilt trimmed carriage with silver harnesses. "I recognize that carriage. It belongs to Blucher Hansbrough. You stole it from him!"

"Now calm down, little Reb. We have generously supplied his family with food so…he…um…loaned it to us."

"Unhuh …it's another bit of booty for you Yanks to cavort around in."

Ignoring her jibe, he continued, "General and Mrs. Custer are arriving today and we've come to escort them back to camp. However, they aren't due until this afternoon. Since it's only ten o'clock, I've come to persuade you to ride to Brandy with me so we can have our pictures made. There's a photographer working there."

"Honestly, Aaron, you come up with the wildest schemes. Loaned, my foot! I'm not about to be seen riding in a confiscated Confederate carriage." She turned towards him with her chin set in a stubborn line.

He glanced at the two other soldiers browsing in the store and clasped her hand. "Your dress has arrived at Brandy and we must pick it up. I don't know when we'll have another opportunity to ride in a carriage. Let's enjoy it. When was the last time you rode in a carriage, Reb?"

She smiled with an air of pleasure, appraising him. He did look quite distinguished with his hair cut. "I haven't ridden in or on a carriage since that day you safely escorted us to town. I must admit, I would treasure a tintype of you, also. But, I'm embarrassed to be seen surrounded by Union cavalrymen."

He leaned towards her until she felt his warm breath in her ear. "We'll draw the curtains so you can't be seen. I've got a fierce hankering to hold you close. Now, lock up the store and let's go!" Her resistance dissolved. At the thought of his touch, she felt blissfully happy, fully alive.

The two of them became quickly entwined in a frenzied embrace while the carriage jostled through the town streets. Her body craved his hands, and they fully utilized this rare interval of privacy to touch and love each other. Their closeness was like a drug, lulling them into euphoria. When the carriage finally came to a stop after almost an hour's ride, it seemed as if they had only been alone for minutes.

Stacks of boxes and supplies confronted her as far as the eye could see after he helped her from the carriage. Hundreds of wagons were arriving and being loaded in the constant flurry of activity. He explained that several rail sidings had been constructed for the trains at this main supply terminal for the army. Thousands of recently arrived cattle mooed in the corral enclosure. She complained about the smoky fog darkening the sky in every direction, obviously caused by the thousands of fires built by the Union soldiers. Beautiful Culpeper had become a filthy Federal city, she observed bitterly. He appeased her by purchasing ham, bread, and a bottle of wine from a sutler's wagon. They soon consumed their lunch from a makeshift table of crates. For dessert they had fudge, a delicacy she had not tasted in three years.

Next they went to the photographer's tent. Aaron demanded that her hair be down and even brushed and styled it for her. The photographer took two poses, one full-faced and one profile. Aaron posed likewise. She lifted his hat and fluffed his hair. He insisted that they have a picture made together. Somewhat embarrassed, she deemed it improper because they were not married or engaged. He eventually won the argument by tactfully agreeing to show it to no one. Thus, they posed with her seated, him standing behind her, his hand on her shoulder.

Then they strolled to the shipping office, located two large cartons from his sister, and placed them on the carriage. He took her on a walking tour of the rest of the massive facility, pointing out the office of the U.S. Christian Commission, and explaining that the delegates were leading a dramatic religious reawakening. The Commission provided materials to construct chapels in the individual camps. He bragged about the one he had helped build at Clover Hill. They walked to the edge of the railway buildings where her eyes scanned the vast sea of log huts and stables joined by corduroy roads. Laid out in systematic precision by regiments, the camps had sprung up on once-beautiful farmland. Not a tree graced the vista dominated by desolate stump lots and mud. He pointed to his right, towards a knoll just north of Fleetwood Hill where Meade had established his headquarters. Aaron explained that Meade had chosen tent headquarters while most of the other officers lived in houses. Provost Marshal General Marsena Patrick, headquartered with Meade, had struggled to protect the citizens of Culpeper from wanton destruction.

He next pointed to Beauregard, the principal hospital of the army, explaining that each corps also had its own hospital staffed by the efficient U.S. Sanitary Commission. Thus disease had been well controlled. She marveled at the luxuries available to the Yankees that the Confederates wouldn't dare dream of. He elaborated that doctors used one tent beside the hospital complex to brand a D on the right buttocks of deserters. Although a gruesome practice, it was more lenient than the usual death by firing squad.

He laughed about the way John Minor Botts had manipulated the army into protecting his farm and interests. A soldier dared not touch his sheep or cattle knowing full well they would be reported to Marsena Patrick. However, it seems a soldier assigned to "safeguard" his farm had convinced one of the Botts daughters to surrender the citadel of her affection. Her expanded waistline had caused considerable gossip. Shocked, Constance wanted to know which daughter, but Aaron was not sure of the scandalous daughter's identity.

They strolled back to the photographer's tent and laughed at their pictures. He picked out frames for each and the photographer placed them in the frames. "These will be my most valuable possessions," Aaron said above the train whistle. "I'll hang them on my cabin wall and carry them with me on the campaign." He took her arm and looked down at her thoughtfully. "I realize what you've seen today may be somewhat overwhelming for you. However, I believe you'll like Autie and his bride. Try to be open minded. She's twenty two and away from a very comfortable home for the first time. I'm sure she would enjoy the friendship of another woman while she's here. She was valedictorian of her seminary class. You two intellectuals should have much in common."

"Autie? I've never heard you call him that. I'll try to extend some southern hospitality to her, although it's difficult under these unpleasant circumstances."

"Yes, his name is Armstrong, but Autie's his nickname. Our mothers are half-sisters. We were pen pals as children but never met until the Gettysburg campaign. You know how fond I am of him. Even though he's just twenty four, he's the most capable cavalry general in our army. At least since the untimely death of John Buford."

"With a name like Armstrong, we must be distant relatives also," she chuckled.

After the train ground to a halt, the couple waited with the rest of Custer's staff until the newlyweds disembarked. The soldiers saluted and broke into cheers. Custer, all smiles, shook hands with his men. The other officers greeted Libbie warmly because they had all attended the wedding and reception. When Aaron introduced Constance, the general bowed politely with a twinkle in his blue eyes. "Miss Armstrong, I've heard many fine things about you. It's a pleasure to meet the lovely lady who kept my cousin away from our wedding."

Constance felt the rising color in her cheeks. "Thank you sir, and congratulations to the two of you. I wish you every happiness."

Aaron bowed politely to Libbie and kissed her hand. "Welcome to Culpeper, Mrs. Custer. I hope knowing another young lady your age will make you feel more at home here. Constance has a well-stocked bookstore that I thought you might like to visit."

The petite young lady with brown hair piled in curls on her head smiled radiantly. With large eyes and a high forehead, in many ways she resembled Constance. Immaculately attired in a navy dress with brass military buttons and trim, she represented the picture of fashion. "Lieutenant Ames, Autie has spoken warmly of you. I'm delighted to finally meet you and Miss Armstrong."

"Now men," Custer said mirthfully. "I went to the West to gain a new command, but believe I have returned with a new commander!"

Everyone laughed and Libbie blushed. "He's in complete control," she countered. "Otherwise I wouldn't be here on the front. But, I'd live in a tent if necessary to be with my general."

While the staff loaded their trunks on the carriage, Aaron whispered to Custer, "I hope you don't mind going back through Culpeper, sir. I have to drop Constance off and deliver a dress my sister sent her to wear to the ball. I thought perhaps Mrs. Custer might enjoy visiting her bookstore."

"Yes, that's an excellent idea. It'll give the two of them time to get acquainted. It's amazing how closely they resemble each other. I believe we've found the two most beautiful ladies in the world."

After they climbed into the carriage, Libbie expressed surprise at all of the military supplies surrounding the station. She gazed at the endless camps while the carriage rattled towards Culpeper. "This is a whole new world to a city girl from Michigan. It's as if I've been transported to Mars."

Constance asked them to tell her about the wedding, thus prompting Libbie to begin a long dissertation. They had been feted by Monroe society at various teas and receptions prior to the wedding. The town embraced Autie as its most famous son. The First Presbyterian Church had been filled almost to suffocation, forcing some of the cavalrymen to stand along the walls. Autie had been dashing in full dress uniform, and she had worn a gown of white silk with deep points and extensive trail. Her veil floated back from a bunch of orange blossoms fixed above the brow. Her father believed it to be the most splendid wedding ever to take place in the state. Three hundred people attended the reception held at her home. The wedding gifts had been magnificent: a silver engraved dinner set from the First Vermont Cavalry, a seven-piece silver tea set from the Second Michigan Cavalry, etc., etc. They had traveled to Cleveland and Rochester and journeyed down the Hudson to West Point, one of the loveliest places she had ever seen. Everyone was delighted to see Autie, and he was thrilled to return to the place he loved so well.

Custer quipped that he should have loved it, since he had so much fun there. That was evidenced by the fact that he held the record for the most demerits and was last in his class academically.

Then, Libbie continued, they went to New York City and Washington, where many dignitaries entertained them.

Constance and Libbie stepped down from the carriage in front of her house. "I can assure you, Mrs. Custer, that this was once a beautiful town."

"My, what a melancholy looking place," Libbie observed. "War does terrible things."

Constance unlocked the bookstore. "Undoubtedly," she agreed as they walked in. In the dim late afternoon light, she lit several candles. The two women enjoyed browsing and discussing books. They soon discovered how well read they both were, and it formed a bond of friendship between them. Libbie expressed sympathy to Constance over the loss of her parents. She confessed that her mother had died when she was twelve and she had felt quite lonely when she was sent away to school. By the time the two men returned from unloading Constance's crates, Libbie had selected three books for purchase

"I'm not sure if I'll see you before the twenty second," Aaron told Constance. "The dance will go on until the wee hours of the morning. Most of the women will be staying at camp. Can't I persuade you to do likewise?"

Constance looked troubled. "I wouldn't feel comfortable."

"Nonsense. You can stay in the house with us," Libbie insisted. "We'd love to have you. I'm sure there will be many other women."

"That's most kind of you, Mrs. Custer. Let me give the matter thought." She smiled at Aaron who kissed her on the cheek. Then she bade them all goodnight.

Constance lifted the pale lavender moiré dress out of the box. "Oh, this is beautiful!" she gushed to Sadie. A note drifted to the floor. Picking it up, she read it and smiled. "It's from Aaron's sister. She said she's only worn this dress once, and that I may borrow it and return it to her for no charge. That's a very generous offer."

Sadie unbuttoned Constance's plain homespun dress. "Well, let's see it on ya!" Constance stepped out of her dress and pulled on a hoop. Then Sadie helped her carefully slip the moiré over her head, placing her arms in the dropped puff sleeves. Constance held her breath while Sadie buttoned it up.

"It's not too tight," she exclaimed relieved. Sadie fluffed the full skirt and felt the waist.

"We might havta take it up a little in the waist. You's so tiny!" She backed off and looked at Constance from a distance. "That color is beau'ful on ya, Miss Constance. Ya look like a queen!"

"Oh, I'm dying to see!" Constance held up a small mirror. "How I miss the big mirror in my room. I love the off-the-shoulder style and the skirt with scalloped festoons. It's the latest fashion. Look, she even sent ribbons to match." She pulled several ribbons of varying shades of lavender from the box. "I'll use these in my hair and put Aaron's gold heart on one to wear around my neck."

Sadie rummaged through the box containing removable collars and sleeves, unmentionables and shoes. "Lawd, how wonderful it'll be to have shoes without holes in the bottom!"

Constance sat on the bed and Sadie slipped the fancy dancing slippers with heels on her feet. Standing up, she said, "They fit fine. How's the length of the dress, Sadie?" Backing up as far as she could in the slave cabin, Sadie nodded affirmatively. "It's gonna be fine. Maybe an inch too long, but we don't wanna hem it if you's gonna send it back."

"It'll save me a lot of precious money. Let's leave well enough alone." She beamed while she whirled around. "Sadie I'm ecstatic at the prospect of dancing with Aaron, but I'm not comfortable at the thought of socializing with all those Yankees. He wants me to spend the night at Clover Hill after the ball. I'll only agree to it if you'll go with me. It'll give you an opportunity to see your grandchildren."

Sadie nodded thoughtfully and straightened the layered skirt. "I'd love to see mah grand babies. I'll be your chap'rone. Together, we oughta be able to stand them Yankees. I won't leave ya alone."

"Thanks Sadie, I love you!" Constance hugged her closest confidant exuberantly.

Four days later, February 21, 1864: The bookstore

"You're a day early," Constance said to Aaron when he walked into the bookstore. He smiled at her with that captivating grin that she loved so dearly. "The town's bustling with dignitaries and women. I heard there would be a meeting and speeches at the courthouse this afternoon. Let's go and see what the rhetoric is about."

"You go ahead and listen. I certainly don't want to hear a bunch of hotheaded politicians bragging about subduing the Rebels," she insisted while he kissed her hand.

"Come now, Reb. You're too much of a political observer to miss this. I saw several women entering the building. Don't you want to hear the enemy's propaganda?"

"That's exactly what it is, propaganda! It's all a vicious plot to stir up hatred to destroy us. I'd like to debate all of them," she sputtered furiously.

He moved his fingertips over her hand. "You'd be a formidable opponent. Come with me so I can watch you put all those danged politicians in their place!"

Her lips turned up in a slight smile of defiance at his challenge. "You're teasing me, Yank. But you've aroused my curiosity. I'll go and observe, because one of these days I intend to write a book that tells the truth about this unjust war."

Curious enlisted men and officers packed the courthouse. With standing room only, the couple pushed their way along a wall to a place of observation. Several women dotted the onlookers and many officers in rich glittering uniforms sat on a platform in the front. Constance's thoughts drifted back to the first meeting she had attended in this same building over three years ago, when secession had been enthusiastically approved. None of them dreamed it would ever come to this.

Senators Chandler of Michigan and Wilkinson of Minnesota spoke first. They proclaimed the glory of preserving the Union and praised the brave fighting men of their great army. Several other politicians and generals evoked enthusiasm from the audience, but it took the fiery address of Judson Kilpatrick to bring the crowd alive. The cocky 5-foot, 7-inch wiry general paced the platform. With a long thin jaw, thin sandy sideburns to his chin, and a prominent nose, his appearance was almost comical. Yet his swaggering loud voice and impressive oratorical skills had mesmerized the audience. In conclusion, he hinted that something grand was about to happen and that he would play a major role in the accomplishment. The crowd cheered wildly.

"There's no doubt that Kilpatrick has political ambitions," she said to Aaron after they left the meeting.

"That's what scares me," he answered perturbed. "I'm sure he fancies he will one day be president. He'll do anything to advance his reputation and fame, regardless of the consequences to his men. I don't feel happy having my life in 'Kill's' hands at the moment. Who knows what kind of a crazy scheme he's cooked up."

"He made it sound as if something will happen soon. What could he do in this terrible winter weather?" She linked her arm through his.

"I'm afraid to guess," he said solemnly. "He's having a huge dinner at Rose Hill tomorrow night prior to the ball to impress all of the visiting dignitaries. We've been invited. What do you think?"

"That's the last place I want to be. Aaron, I'm going to this ball for only one reason, to dance the night away in your arms. Please don't expect me to spend any time socializing with these other Yankees."

He smiled down at her. "I appreciate your concession. We'll have dinner at Clover Hill. Will you spend the night?"

"Yes. Sadie's coming with me. She can stay with Joseph and his family."

"Good. There will be a grand review the following morning. I have to participate. I know you don't want to go."

"Absolutely not! I refuse to watch you parade your military might on our fields! I'll stay at Clover Hill until you can bring me back to town."

They stopped in front of her house and his eyes bathed her in admiration. "We're going to enjoy a marvelous romantic evening despite our political differences. Trust me. I admire your courage to attend. You'll outshine all the Yankee ladies."

"The dress is beautiful," she answered smiling broadly. "I can't wait to wear it."

"I'll pick you and Sadie up tomorrow at three, my lovely Rebel. I'm counting the minutes." He leaned over and kissed her on the cheek.

Next day, February 22, 1864: The Marsten home in Orange

Sallie Marsten giggled while Stringfellow took off his shirt and rolled up his pants legs. "My party dress is altered to fit you perfectly, Frank. I still can't believe you're going to the ball in my place."

Stringfellow placed two derringers in his pants pockets. "Somehow I feel more secure having these along."

"First we have to put on the hoop," Mrs. Marsten said. He lifted his arms and they slipped the hoop over his head. Tying it at the waist, she continued, "I've padded this high neck dress in the right places so it won't be too obvious what nature didn't give you."

Stringfellow laughed and they lifted the dress over his head. "That was thoughtful of you." After they moved the pink brocade dress into position, he asked, "How does it look? I'm not sure pink is my color."

Sallie laughed uncontrollably "Frank, you're positively beautiful! Pink is divine on you." They buttoned up the dress. "Look at yourself in the mirror. You have a fashionably slim waist."

Stringfellow loped across the room, stuck his chest out, and admired his image. "I'm prettier than I thought!"

"Oh, but we must coach you in the art of femininity," Mrs. Marsten insisted. "If you walk like that, you won't fool anybody. You've got to take short dainty steps and raise your voice several notches."

The scout walked slowly across the room, attempting to look dainty. "Is this the way, madam?" he asked in a high voice.

"It's better Frank, but this will take some time. Sit down while we work with your hair and powder your nose. Then we'll give you more lessons in primping, sitting, and flirting. Remember, it'll be more difficult to fool the women than the men," Sallie said. He dutifully sat down in front of the mirror.

Mrs. Marsten brushed his shoulder length hair and then pulled it up in the back. "I'm going to add a few of my hair switches around the face to make it fuller," she explained, then pinned the curled switches in place. "The color is almost perfect."

"Just be sure to pin them securely," Stringfellow said. "I don't want my hair to fall out in the middle of a dance."

"I still feel badly about that nice Yankee captain being in prison," Sallie mused. "I'm touched that he attempted to bring me that pass. I did like him, but I'd never have considered going to a Yankee dance. You'll probably be the only southern girl there, Frank."

"This is the craziest thing I've ever done." He stood up, gathering his skirt. "Now, show me how to walk. My life depends on it."

After over an hour of practicing, Stringfellow decided to make his royal descent down the curved stairway. With his head held high, he gracefully descended the stairs without attempting to see his feet below the wide skirt. Dave Marsten, who had know him for years, laughed so hard that tears rolled down his face. "Frank Stringfellow dressed up as a girl. What in God's name is this war coming to!"

"Father, dear," Stringfellow said in a high voice, "Show me to the buggy. It's only proper that you accompany me to the river."

Still laughing after they walked outside, Marsten turned to help the scout climb into the seat. Ignoring his help, Stringfellow climbed awkwardly into the buggy. "Let's don't carry this too far, Dave," he said laughing.[1]

Clover Hill: "I can't believe that this is the farm of John Barbour, that I knew so well," Constance observed when the ambulance approached Clover Hill, surrounded by a sea of huts.

Aaron pointed to the large racetrack on the left of the house. "That's where Kilpatrick and Custer race their finest thoroughbreds. Many an hour has been whiled away betting and cheering the horses. We've got about a half-hour of daylight left. Would you like to see the infantry camps?"

Constance looked at Sadie who shrugged in agreement. "We may as well see it all," she answered, thankful to delay her entrance into Yankee society. The ambulance jostled east towards Hansbrough's Ridge. She noticed Yankee camps surrounding Salubria. "Who's at Salubria?"

"General Davies has his headquarters there. It's probably a good thing, because the house has been protected. Our men call it The Fort. It's one of the few brick buildings that hasn't been torn down."

"I'm appalled at the way they destroyed Stevensburg Baptist Church," Constance observed bitterly. "Took it apart to get the bricks for their chimneys."

"That's a wicked sin," Sadie grumbled.

When they reached the tip of Hansbrough's Ridge, Aaron turned the wagon onto a narrow road on the crest of the ridge. Neat, precisely laid out rows of huts spanned both barren slopes of the ridge. "This is a wonderful defensive position with extensive visibility in both directions. The men have dug a line of outer trenches on the lower slope and another line of inner entrenchments to protect the hospital and fort on top."

Spirals of smoke drifted lazily from the hundreds of stone chimneys. "The view of the sunset is spectacular," Constance said. "Too bad this beautiful spot has been marred by the trappings of war."

"True. The cemetery at the base of the hill is filled with those who've died from disease and the many executed deserters. It's a terrible spectacle to watch. The large building ahead of you is the Second Corps Hospital." Aaron pointed to the rectangular log structure, then pulled the reins to stop his horse. "General Hancock has his headquarters at the Hansbrough's which is on a knoll in that direction." He pointed northeast.

"Yes, I'm familiar with the house," Constance answered. "Where's the ball?"

Aaron turned the ambulance around and started back. "It's in an enormous new plank building located in the valley between this ridge and Cole's Hill, a short distance north. We need to return now for the wonderful dinner that the Custers' cook, Eliza, has prepared for us. Custer also declined Kilpatrick's party. He seems preoccupied with concern about the rumored upcoming event."

"I'm worried about you." Constance looped her arm through his.

"We mustn't let anything mar this enchanted evening. You're a vision of loveliness. I'm anxious to show you off."

Stringfellow turned his plan over and over again in his mind. He couldn't find any flaws in it. He had a pass through Confederate lines plus the captured pass to get him through the enemy's lines. If luck was with him, it should work. When they stopped at the forward Confederate picket post at the river, he handed over his pass. The shocked picket studied the pass for a minute and then turned and spat on the ground in disgust. "Can't believe a respectable Rebel lady would go to their damn ball," he mumbled. He waved his hand motioning the buggy forward, and then turned and stormed away.

Dave Marsten climbed out of the buggy and untied his horse from the back. When he swung into the saddle, he said loudly, "Remember, Sallie, we don't expect you to stay too late!"

Stringfellow drove the buggy across the river, putting his feet up on the dash to keep from getting wet. His stomach churned in spasms. He felt insecure penetrating enemy territory without a horse under him and a gun in his hand. If his disguise was discovered, he was a dead man. For a moment, he considered turning back. But, it was too late. When he came up the north bank, a picket rode out of the woods and stopped his horse in the path of the buggy.

"Hold up, madam." He rode close and looked curiously at the young lady. "Why are you here?"

"Why I'm on my way to meet a friend in your army," Stringfellow said in his feminine voice. "He invited me to the ball tonight."

The soldier eyed "her" suspiciously. "Do you have a pass?" Stringfellow nodded yes and pulled out the pass from his purse to show him.

The Yank waved his hand. "Keep it. Follow me. I've got to take you to the lieutenant." Stringfellow followed the picket about a mile to a house located in the middle of a field. The soldiers, warming their hands around the glowing fire, curiously watched the buggy stop and the picket dismount. He walked to the side of the buggy, and held out his hand. Feeling a little foolish, Stringfellow graciously accepted his assistance. The picket escorted him into the house and explained the situation to the young lieutenant. The officer studied the document thoughtfully under the lantern on his table. "Usually, Miss Marsten, you Rebel women wouldn't dirty your shoes with us Yankees. What makes you different?"

"Why, lieutenant, the captain was most thoughtful while assisting me with information about my missing brother. He took a terrible risk to bring me that pass. Naturally, I just had to come," Stringfellow explained sweetly.

"Naturally," the officer replied with a slight smile. "I believe he was foolish myself. I assume he'll be waiting for you. I won't detain you any longer. One of our men will escort you to the ball." He stood and walked Stringfellow to the door, resting his hand on the scout's arm. "Miss Marsten, I may come to the ball later myself. I hope your captain will allow me to dance with you."

"Oh, yes, I'm sure he will," Stringfellow said flirtatiously, remembering to lower his eyes. "You have been most kind."[2]

While their carriage neared the site of the festivities, Aaron explained to Constance and the Custers, "The carpenters and lumberjacks have been working for over a month to construct our Palace of Pleasure. It's a wonderful diversion from the mud and misery of camp."

"You'll have the opportunity to meet many dignitaries tonight, little wife," Custer said affectionately to Libbie. "Vice-president Hamlin, the governor of Rhode Island, a large delegation from the British Embassy, and numerous senators and Supreme Court Justices will be here. They arrived this afternoon on a heavily guarded train. Let's hope Mosby doesn't embarrass us by making an unwelcome intrusion on the festivities."

Constance smiled with a twinkle in her eye. "I suspect, General Custer, that I will not be the only Rebel enjoying the ball. Our men never miss an opportunity for merriment."

Everyone chuckled. "I never dreamed camp life could be this exciting," Libbie said. "I have much to learn about military protocol. I'm amazed to watch mature officers reporting to my merry boy of a husband. Autie, do they obey you? I wouldn't if I were them."

"Yes," Custer replied laughing, "and remember my gypsy wife, that you can be punished for insubordination. There are rules for camp followers." He turned towards Aaron and continued, "Cuz, I must confess that commanding a brigade is far easier than commanding a wife."[3]

Chuckling, Aaron said, "I appreciate those words of wisdom and warning, sir. I believe we've arrived." Soldiers helped them disembark and escorted them up the lantern lit walkway. The size of the 90-foot by 60-foot building with a soaring canvas ceiling amazed Constance. Hundreds of candles installed on circular chandeliers and Chinese lanterns cast a mellow, romantic light over the interior that smelled of fresh cut pine. Aaron helped her out of her cape while she stared at the multitude of flags that draped the walls and ceiling. "Every regimental and headquarters flag of the Second Corps is on display tonight," he explained. "They've lost 19,000 men but take pride in the fact that they've never lost a flag." Evergreens, sabers, drums, revolvers, rifles, and bayonets completed the decorations. "We'll take your capes and return shortly with refreshments." Aaron and Custer walked towards the center of the room.

Libbie watched her husband in adoration. "He's my bright shining star," she whispered to Constance. "If loving with one's whole heart is insanity, then I confess I'm a candidate for the insane asylum. Never did I dream the marriage bed would hold such sensuous delight."

Surprised at her revelation, Constance smiled and whispered, "Your love and devotion are obvious. General Custer's exuberance and zest for life are inspiring." They watched the lavishly dressed guests stream into the huge hall until Aaron and the general returned with glasses of punch.

After she accepted the crystal cup, Aaron offered his arm. "Allow me to show you the romanticized display of army life at the end of the room." He bowed to the Custers. Constance took his arm proudly. She thought him the picture of manliness as the rich outlines of his shoulders strained against the fabric of his neatly tailored uniform with red tie. The brass buttons across his broad chest and polished cavalry boots sparkled in the soft light. She admired his trimmed horseshoe mustache and wavy honey brown hair brushed back neatly from his face. His powerful presence was even more compelling in a crowd.

"Camp has never looked this good," he quipped while they examined the spotless white tents, stacked rifles, a campfire with gleaming kettles, and two small cannons.

"The brass on those cannons is so shiny, they look like they've just arrived from the factory," she observed with a smile. "You and I both know that war is gruesome filth. But, perhaps this display will impress the naïve northern women."

"You stand shoulders above all of them," he said softly. He studied her face, seeing both delicacy and strength. "Hold your head high, because you've endured it all with a bold courage that they don't even comprehend. They cannot match your beauty. You look like a queen in that dress, but it's the beauty of your soul that shines brightest. I love you for wanting to be with me enough to come here tonight."

"Aaron, I'll never pass up an opportunity to dance in your arms." She slipped her hand in his. "You've become the center of my life. Therefore, it's only proper that I should try to understand your world."

They became aware of several soldiers standing behind them and turned around to confront Judson Kilpatrick and his entourage. Eyeing her lustfully, Kilpatrick smiled with recognition. "Can this lovely enchantress be the proprietress of the bookstore? Lieutenant Ames, you're a fortunate man."

From Preston, Tenth Cav., N.Y.S. Vols.

General Judson Kilpatrick, U.S.A.

"Yes, I agree sir." Aaron stared at the young, tall, slender colonel with reddish-blond hair and a thin goatee who accompanied Kilpatrick. With a crutch under one arm, he obviously had an artificial leg.

"Allow me to introduce Colonel Ulric Dahlgren," Kilpatrick said.

Aaron saluted. "It is good to see that you've recovered from your Gettysburg wounds."

"Thank you. I've escaped from the jaws of death and am thankful to feel robust again." Dahlgren looked at Constance. "And who is this lovely lady?"

"This is Miss Constance Armstrong," Aaron said.

Bowing formally, Dahlgren inquired, "And where are you from Miss Armstrong?"

"Culpeper is my home," she answered calmly.

"Ah," Dahlgren said with a smile. "Am I to assume that since you're here tonight, that you've taken the oath?"

Constance held her head high. "No, I'm here to celebrate the birthday of a great *Vah-gin-yan*. Washington was the leader of our first revolution and a true Rebel. We honor his memory as we fight for those same freedoms today."

"I see," Dahlgren said with a charming smile. "I won't attempt to debate you." The notes of a waltz drifted through the air.

"Please excuse us," Aaron said. "We don't intend to miss a single song."

"Lieutenant Ames, I hope you'll allow me at least one dance with Miss Armstrong," Kilpatrick asked.

"Perhaps, one, sir."

Aaron guided Constance to the dance floor. With his strong arm against her back, she moved effortlessly with him. His movements were swift, full of grace and virility. He observed the eyes of numerous soldiers watching her while they glided across the floor. With her dark lustrous curls piled high on her head, and her hourglass figure, she was a vision of beauty. "You handled that well," he said.

"I don't intend to mar your evening by causing any unpleasantness. But I won't deny my loyalties."

"No, I don't want you to. I wonder why Dahlgren's here? He's only about twenty one and probably the youngest colonel in the army. His father is Rear Admiral John Dahlgren who commands the Union fleet off Charleston. He's quite influential with Lincoln and the powers in Washington. Dahlgren obviously isn't here to dance because of his leg. I fear he's involved in whatever Kilpatrick is conjuring up. Dahlgren's name will bring more fame and attention to his endeavor. It all makes me uneasy."

"Aaron, let's not spoil a moment talking about the likes of Kilpatrick," she said while they moved in unison. "I'm not surprised that you're a marvelous graceful dancer. I can anticipate your every move. This is pure heaven!"

Stringfellow entered the ball, looked around at the nearly three hundred ladies, and assumed they had come from cities like Washington, New York, and Philadelphia. Taking small dainty steps around the edge of the room, he wondered if he would be the only "southern lady" present. He took a seat beside some women sitting primly against the wall. One of them said, "Just look pretty and smile. There are more of them than us. You're sure to catch one in a minute." He sat inconspicuously and listened. He heard another lady explain that she was meeting her boyfriend for the first time in a year. His corps, which had been in the West, had recently returned to northern Virginia. Now she could come down from Washington to see him. Stringfellow made a mental note to check the intelligence records to see if this troop movement had been reported to Lee.

The scout felt the admiring eyes of several soldiers assessing him. When he looked up, his eyes met those of a chunky major who smiled and bowed politely. "Pardon me, madam. May I have the honor of dancing with you?"

"Oh, I'm so sorry, sir, but I'm waiting for my escort," Stringfellow said sweetly.

"I'm sure he won't mind if I entertain you until he arrives." The major held out his hand. Stringfellow realized there was probably no way he could avoid dancing. Nervous sweat trickled down his back while they walked to the dance floor. A determined but clumsy dancer, the major shoved and pushed Stringfellow, who attempted to smile. He winced after the major trod on his toes repeatedly. Finally, they developed something akin to rhythm.

Smiling at him flirtatiously, the soldier inquired, "Where are you from madam? You seem to have an accent like some of these Rebel women."

"Yes, that's true. You see I'm from Baltimore. We're all wondering when this horrid war will end. When do you think Meade will finally move, major?" Stringfellow inquired batting his eyelashes.

"Meade's no fighter! He got lucky at Gettysburg. Let me tell you something in confidence, my dear." Stringfellow felt his breath on his ear. "When this terrible winter weather ends, we'll move against Lee. This time we'll have a real fighter lead us. I can assure you the war will be over by summer."

"Why, major, what wonderful news." Stringfellow traced his fingers over the back of the soldier's neck. "I don't suppose…oh, no, of course not. I couldn't ask you to divulge a military secret," he said dropping his eyes.

The major winked knowingly and pulled Stringfellow closer. "The news will be out in a few weeks. I've just returned from our capital and a friend of mine in the War Department says it's all set. When the news breaks, you'll have to _grant_ that I was correct." He laughed at his cleverness.[4]

Stringfellow giggled. "Major, you're such a tease." The music ended and they walked to the lavish food table where the scout indulged in the delicacies; pleased with the information he had extracted from his clumsy partner. If the major was correct, that must mean U.S. Grant, who had raised some much havoc in the West, was coming to Virginia. When he looked up, he thought that he saw a familiar face in the crowd. That dark haired beauty in the lavender dress looked like Constance. Someone moved into his line of vision, then the major insisted on one more dance. Stringfellow reluctantly consented and they moved back on to the crowded dance floor. While they circulated, his eyes caught sight of her again. Yes, it did look like Connie!

Aaron smoothly whirled Constance around and her eyes fell on a familiar looking lady in a pink dress. Where had she seen her before? She must be a southerner. Somehow she just couldn't place her. She turned her head to get a better view. "Is something wrong?" Aaron inquired.

"No. I see a familiar lady, but I can't place who she is." She leaned her head against his shoulder thoughtfully. Perhaps, it wasn't that she knew the lady, but simply that she reminded her of someone—but who? Suddenly it hit her like a flash. She looked like— Frank! Her imagination must be playing tricks on her. She searched the crowd again for another glimpse.

After the music ended, the major hinted to Stringfellow that he would deem it an honor to show "her" his quarters. When "Sallie" declined gracefully, the Yankee walked away seeking another conquest. Stringfellow slowly edged through the crowd towards Constance. She must be with that Yankee who had saved her life. Regardless, he knew he could trust her. Perhaps she could give him more meaningful information. "Miss Armstrong," he called in his high voice when he saw them nearby. Constance whirled around, her eyes bulging and her heart hammering.

"Miss Armstrong, you may not remember me, but I'm Sallie Marsten from Orange. I wanted to let you know that I've seen your sister, Amanda, and her boys, and they're well." Stringfellow winked at her.

Her heart leaped with joy and she tried to maintain her composure. She stammered, "Yes…I knew you looked familiar, Miss Marsten. Allow me to introduce Lieutenant Aaron Ames."

Aaron bowed politely. "It's a pleasure, Miss Marsten. What brings you to our ball?"

"Well, a kind Yankee soldier helped me with information about my missing brother. He was quite taken with me, and bravely brought me a pass for tonight. I could not refuse his kindness. I'm delighted to see another southern lady here." Stringfellow looped his arm through Constance's. "Would you excuse two old friends, Lieutenant Ames, while we go…um…powder our noses?"

"Certainly," Aaron said with a broad smile. Constance squeezed his hand and then hurried off with "Sallie." Her heart pounded wildly while Stringfellow led her across the room to the door outside. The cold night air shocked them when they walked out into the darkness. Stringfellow pulled her around the corner of the building.

"Frank, is it really you?" she whispered.

"Don't you think I'm beautiful, Connie?" He hugged her.

"You're the most gorgeous creature I've ever seen. I thought you were dead! I've mourned you, but I never gave up hope. Aaron believes he shot you in the river. He was overwhelmed with guilt when he found out who you were," she gasped as she held him.

"You mean he's the one? Ha! Your Yankee's not as good a shot as he thinks. I swam underwater to the bank and waited for them to leave. Then, dressed as a servant woman, I snuck into the house where they had mother and spent three days with her."

"Frank, you're incredible! You've restored my faith and hope in the Confederacy."

"Stand close so we don't freeze to death." He pulled her to him. "I don't know how you women stand these blasted hoops." She stood still while a soldier walked by. "Now, tell me about your Aaron."

"He saved my life. He's captured my heart, Frank. But, I still remain loyal to our cause. I'm sick of watching these impudent Yankees parade in their splendor. Tell me about our men and Amanda."

"Amanda and the boys are fine. Don't be discouraged because they outnumber us. Our will remains strong. Every one of our men is prepared to defend our land with their lives. Not only that, the Copperheads are planning to rise up and join us. John Hunt Morgan's triumphant reception in Richmond has buoyed our spirits. Opposition to Lincoln grows stronger each day. Civilians march on the White House, demanding that he resume prisoner exchange again."

"You give me courage to resist them. I won't even ask why you're here dressed as a girl. Tell me what I can do to help our cause."

"Knowing the enemy's intent prior to their action is imperative. That's the only way we can win with smaller numbers. Have you heard anything about Grant taking command?"

"No, but Kilpatrick hints that something grand is about to happen and that he'll play a major role in the triumph. I'm sick of his boasting. I heard him speak at the courthouse. Also, Ulric Dahlgren is here—Aaron assumes to ride with Kilpatrick."

"That means there's going to be a cavalry raid. We need to know their intent. If you learn any more details, you must get the information to me."

"But how Frank? How can I do that?"

He thought for a moment while they listened to the chatter of the ladies in line to the necessary. "If you can get a message to the duck rock and hang a white cloth, I'll see it. I know that's risky. The safest way to travel is west of Pony Mountain and then through the fields. My men also check in regularly at your Aunt Martha's house. She dresses as a peasant and sells pies to the Yankees, thus picking up information."

"Aunt Martha's a spy! Bully for her!"

"I may have some of my scouts make contact with you at the bookstore, but I can't predict when that will be. It's important that the Yankees continue to think I'm dead. It takes the heat off. I'll tell your family not to worry about you."

"Let them know that I'm making good money at the bookstore."

"Do you have anything to write with in your purse? I want to leave our hosts a thank you note."

Constance giggled. "Here's a pencil" He scribbled on the wall in the darkness. "What did you write?"

Stringfellow chuckled. "I had a great time, John Mosby."

Constance couldn't control her laughter. "Frank, you're too much. You lift my spirits!"

"Now come and guard the door to the necessary for me. I don't want any of these ladies to walk in and realize my anatomy is different from theirs."

Aaron admired her proudly as she carried herself confidently across the floor, head held high. Although delicate, her proportionately broad shoulders accented the slenderness of her waist. Disturbed, he spotted Kilpatrick moving to intercept her. She attempted to avoid him but he pursued her relentlessly. "Miss Armstrong, I was promised the honor of one dance."

She hesitated while he held out his hand, but decided she may as well get it over with. Perhaps she could extract some vital information from him. "It would be my pleasure, General Kilpatrick." She gave him her hand.

He guided her into the center of the dance floor and pulled her much too close, his eyes straying down the bodice of her dress. "Allow me to say, Miss Armstrong, that you're the most comely lady here tonight. I was honored to see you at the meeting at Town Hall yesterday."

"You're an extremely gifted orator, sir. Surely, politics must be in your future." She tried to maintain her distance from him.

"I believe that after I've won fame in this war, it will be easy for me to be elected to high office. I've always aspired to be a leader in our great country." He moved his hand suggestively across her back.

"You intimated that you will soon be involved in a grand military action. I am of course curious of your great endeavor." She stared into his eyes with an alluring smile.

His wide mouth moved into a haughty grin. "You're a temptress, Miss Armstrong, but you're still a Rebel. Let me simply say that soon I'll be marching on the streets of Richmond and this war will be over."

"Oh, I've heard so many Yankees make that boast over the last three years. My reply to you is the same as to the others. The only way you will get to Richmond will be as a prisoner of war."

He laughed heartily. "You're an intelligent woman. Surely you've realized that the South cannot hold out much longer and will be left in smoldering ruins. After all, you've attached yourself to a Yankee, which is a wise decision for your future. However, a mere lieutenant will not be able to provide for you like a general. You need a man who's a rising star. Someone with a promising future. Think about it Miss Armstrong. I would welcome your affection. You could live lavishly."

Fury almost choked her. She looked over Kilpatrick's shoulder at Aaron who had moved towards them protectively. She turned her mouth down in a grimace and then mouthed the words, "Save me!" He smiled and nodded to her. She stared up at the general and said coldly, "You must accept the fact that I'm in love with Lieutenant Ames. He saved my life when shrapnel hit me at the Battle of Culpeper Court House. I want to thank you for bringing us together."

Kilpatrick raised his eyebrows in surprise. "Love can't provide money and prestige. But I don't understand how I brought you together."

"Because you, sir, were the brutal, unmerciful, ambitious general who ordered that the town and innocent civilians be shelled. You murdered my mother and God will see that you burn in hell for your sin!" He pulled back from her, his eyes blazing with indignation. The music stopped and Aaron immediately reached their side.

Kilpatrick handed him her hand and sneered contemptuously, "You may have your sharp-tongued shrew back," before he swaggered away.

Aaron arched his thick eyebrows in mocked surprise. "Am I to assume that you insulted the good general?"

"He tried to proposition me into joining his harem. I had to put him in his place."

Aaron wrapped his arms around her and kissed her on the neck. "I'm proud of you Reb. You got rid of him and now I won't have to challenge the bastard to a duel. How about some champagne?"

She giggled. "What a marvelous idea, my love. I won't leave your side again. Let's celebrate! I'm ecstatic at seeing another southerner and learning Amanda and the boys are well."

Stringfellow swallowed another oyster, then decided he had consumed enough food for a delicate young lady. Turning towards the exit, he confronted the slender lieutenant from the picket post.

"Madam," the lieutenant said. "Allow me to escort you outside."

Stringfellow eyed him warily. "Why, that's most thoughtful of you lieutenant. You see my escort never showed up and I was about to return home."

The Yankee took Stringfellow's arm forcefully and guided him outside. The silver rays of moonlight lit the surrounding sea of buggies and carriages. "You know as well as I do why your escort didn't come. He's probably in prison." The soldier guided Stringfellow away from the crowd. When out of earshot of the others, he suddenly stopped and said, "I don't know what your game is lady, but you're in trouble. I checked up on your captain and found out that he's been missing for weeks. How do you explain that?"

Stringfellow thought coolly. Obviously the Yank hadn't penetrated his disguise. "I'm shocked!" he began earnestly. "All I know is that he brought me the pass and promised to meet me. I don't know what happened to him, unless our men captured him when he returned from my house. I pray that's not the case."

"I don't believe that story, lady. I think you had him bushwhacked and you're here as a spy!"

"Why, Lieutenant," Stringfellow said aghast. "If you think I'm a spy, why didn't you have me arrested inside at the ball?"

"I—well, that is…" the officer started.

"I'll tell you why," Stringfellow said coyly. "It's because you, sir, are a gentleman. You don't believe I'm a spy. I can't tell you how much I appreciate your trust," the scout said softly, then took the officer's hand. "I'll make it up to you."

The lieutenant moved forward and put his hands on Stringfellow's shoulders. The moonlight made his eyes glow while he perused Stringfellow lustfully. The officer took a deep breath and moved his lips towards Stringfellow's. The scout giggled and stepped back.

"Now, you handsome man, if you'll just turn around and close your eyes for one moment, I'll show you how very much I appreciate your kindness."

The slender young officer smiled with a gleam in his eye and turned around dutifully. He listened to Stringfellow's skirt rustling while the scout reached into his pockets and pulled out both derringers.

"I'm ready. You can turn around now, Lieutenant," Stringfellow whispered softly.

When the officer turned around he didn't see the derringers in Stringfellow's hands. His smile turned to a look of puzzlement when he realized "Sallie" was still fully clothed. "But, I thought…"

"In this cold weather," Stringfellow said insulted. "Why, young man, shame on you!" He lifted the derringers until the moonlight glistened on them. "I hate to tell you this, sir, but I'm a scout for General Jeb Stuart and you're my prisoner. If you move or cry out I can assure you, I'll kill you instantly," Stringfellow said in his normal voice.

The young officer stared at him in disbelief. "What is this madam? Have you lost your mind?"

"I'm no madam, but I can't prove it to you at the moment. Now, we're going to walk to my buggy, get in, and ride out of here to the river. At the picket post, you will say that you're seeing me home safely. This derringer will be pressed into your ribs." Stringfellow poked the officer with the gun. "If you make one false move or say the wrong thing, I will kill you instantly, even if it means I die too. Now get going."

The shocked lieutenant walked forward with his shoulders stooped. When they found the buggy, Stringfellow untied his horse and prodded the officer into the seat. They drove silently down the road until they reached the picket station. "Now, your life depends on what you say and how you say it," the scout cautioned, then poked the gun into his captive's ribs.

The picket called to them to halt, and rode up to the buggy shining a lantern inside. Spying the lieutenant, he came to attention and saluted. Stringfellow handed him the pass and jabbed the officer in his side. "I'm seeing the young lady safely home. I'll return shortly," he said meekly. The picket gave them a knowing grin and motioned them forward. "Have fun, Lieutenant, and watch out for them Rebs."

When they reached the river, the captive realized he was indeed on his way to prison. Desperate, he whirled around and struck Stringfellow with his fist. The swift blow in the face almost knocked the scout out of the buggy. Grabbing the side of the door, he regained his balance. Quickly, Stringfellow raised the derringer and clubbed the Yankee across the head. It took several hard blows from the small gun to render him unconscious. After crossing the river, the buggy soon reached the nearest Confederate post. Stringfellow leaped out in his gown and pulled the switches from his hair. To the amazed sentry he said, "Frank Stringfellow, scout, reporting with a prisoner."

The dazed Federal sat up, stared at him, and then slumped back into the seat. "My God, how did this ever happen to me." He put his hands over his face.[5]

Clover Hill: Constance giggled when the two of them entered the dimly lit hall at Clover Hill. "I'm still giddy. I can't believe we were the last ones to leave."

"You're the one who drank five glasses of champagne and insisted that we dance every dance," he chuckled. Then he untied her cape and let it fall from her shoulders. "I knew you'd had enough when you told the vice-president that Lee was the greatest general alive." He trailed his fingertips lightly over the white skin exposed by her off-the-shoulder dress.

"Well," she said with a little pout, sticking her lower lip out. "He agreed. It's your fault for letting me drink that much. I've never had champagne before. Oh, but we had such a marvelous time!"

"That we did, my beauty. You stole the show." Their mouths melted together. Leaning against the wall, she absorbed the full force of his powerful body against hers while their tongues moved together playfully. His lips seared a path down her neck and across her bare chest, setting her on fire. "I want to kiss every inch of you," he whispered.

She took a deep breath and sighed, "Um...yes." His nearness made her senses spin.

He stood up and placed his thumbs together in front of her navel and moved his hands around her waspish waist until his index fingers met. "Your waist is so small I can encircle it with my hands. You're...the picture of fashion...I've never wanted a woman as much as I want you". He contemplated her and breathed unevenly. "However, I make it a practice not to seduce intoxicated southern ladies."

She wrapped her arms around his neck and nibbled his ear. "I know after tonight, that my love for you...knows no bounds. Don't tease me...about being tipsy."

He crushed her against him as his tongue sent shivers of desire racing through her. Reluctantly raising his mouth from hers, he gazed into her eyes. "Constance, it's three o'clock in the morning. I love and cherish you. Now, go upstairs before I lose control. You'll be clear-headed in the morning." He turned her around and gently pushed her towards the stairs.

Weaving, she clung to the handrail for support and murmured, "Good night, my handsome Yankee." When she reached the bedroom she shared with three other ladies, she realized that as the last to arrive, she had been relegated to the pallet on the floor. She held on to the bureau for balance, slipped out of her dress, and then stretched out on the makeshift bedroll. When she closed her eyes, the room spun and she heard noises emanating from the Custers' bedroom next door. She rolled over and put her ear near the spinning wall. The bed squeaked while she overheard Libbie moan and cry out in ecstasy. How she envied them their passionate lovemaking. Closing her eyes again, she ached for Aaron and the fulfillment of his love.

Next day, February 23, 1864: Clover Hill

Constance's head pounded when she finally emerged from the bedroom. Libbie greeted her in the hall and insisted on showing her the calico curtains that the other officer's wives had hung around the four poster bed in their bedroom. She laughed at how all the men referred to headquarters as "The Honeymoon Cottage." Then she extolled the virtues of Eliza, the Negro servant who had come into Custer's camp at Amissville. Eliza managed the cooking and running of the household and catered to Libbie's every whim. Autie told her that as his wife, she was not to lift a finger.

They went down to the dining room for an elaborate breakfast of bacon, eggs, biscuits, and sweet rolls. Constance felt like an outcast with all of the Michigan officers and their wives until Aaron arrived. She listened to Custer's band playing outside while the soldiers prepared breakfast for the other ladies, who had slept in tents. She ate little and was relieved when Aaron took her outside to see his hut and the chapel.

The day was bright and almost warm while they walked across the corduroy road to his hut. He explained in great detail how they had dug a deep foundation for the twelve by twelve structure to keep the floor dry and then dragged the logs to the site to form the walls, and daubed red mud between them. The junior grade officers had the privilege of installing the luxury of a wood floor. The Sanitary Commission had provided the canvas roof. Their greatest achievements were the fireplace and chimney constructed of green logs lined with red clay, and the pit in front for the bean pot. It was there that they did most of their cooking. She peeked inside and greeted his other five hut-mates.

Then they strolled across camp to the small primitive chapel. He had helped carve the cross on top and assured her that he attended prayer meetings during the week. The inside contained a rough altar and rows of half log benches. They went outside to see the companies forming for the grand review to be held on a level field below Cole's Hill. She convinced him that she would be fine until he returned and blew him a kiss when the impressive company rode off.

With her hand over her eyes, she scanned the camp for some sign of Sadie. She spotted two small huts set a distance away from the others with several Negroes milling around a campfire. Walking through the mud towards them, she soon recognized Sadie and Joseph with two children. Selene, fearful of Constance's wrath over her stolen clothes, stayed in the hut. Sadie proudly introduced her to her new granddaughter, Mary, balanced on her hip. Constance told them what a wonderful time she had at the ball and that she had met another southern lady. They were elated to learn that Frank was alive. Constance told Joseph that she'd heard Kilpatrick bragging about some big raid he was about to make. She emphasized that they must keep Frank informed. Joseph said the cavalrymen had been checking and re-shoeing the horses plus getting them fed up good. He didn't know where they were going, but Custer seemed nervous. Constance urged him to keep his ears open and see if he could get any information out of Eliza. She made him promise to ride to town at once and inform her of any news he obtained. Sadie rolled her eyes skeptically at the whole scheme.

Constance decided to walk to Aaron's hut to read until he returned. When she entered the warm hut, she stood still a few minutes for her eyes to adjust to the darkness. She placed another log on the fire and lit a candle. A small table with four stools stood next to the fire, and three sets of bunk beds lined the walls. She recognized Aaron's lower bed by the two pictures of her hung on the rough log walls. True to his promise, the picture of both of them was nowhere to be seen. She sat on his bunk and tenderly moved her hand across the wool blanket. She felt that by being there she could some-how absorb him and his world. He lived a far more sparse existence that she did in Sadie's cabin.

Suddenly, guilt overwhelmed her. He had given her so much and done everything possible to help her endure the Union occupation, and yet his world was mud, misery, danger and death. She hadn't been sensitive enough to the inner turmoil he must also be suffering. He had lived in her world, but she was a stranger in his. He had the ability to penetrate her innermost thoughts, and she desired to do likewise. She reached down and picked up the pile of books by his bunk: his well-worn Bible, *The Works of Shakespeare, Leaves of Grass*. Then there was the neat bundle of her letters. Each day her love for him intensified, and after her shameless behavior last night, she loved him more dearly for not taking advantage of her. She vowed never to drink champagne again. She had to pour out her love to him. That's what she'd do! She'd sit down and write him a love letter expressing her desire to absorb and understand his world.

Five days later, February 28, 1864, Sunday: Coleman Street

6 p.m. Constance stood in front of her house watching the soldiers march through town with their band playing. Obviously they wanted to be seen and heard. Evidently, Kilpatrick's plot was unfolding. "What unit are you?" she called to the marching columns.

"Sixth Corps, General Birney," a soldier called back with a flirtatious smile.

She pulled her scarf over her head in the brisk wind and walked down Cameron Street contemplating the situation. Aaron must certainly be involved in the offensive, since it was Sunday and he hadn't shown up. She walked through the gate towards the kitchen and detected a form moving towards her in the darkness from the stable.

"Miss Constance, it's Joseph." His face emerged from the shadows.

"Joseph!" She gathered her skirt and dashed up to him. "Do you know what's happening?"

"I's got a good idea. Come on inside an' I'll tell ya what I done heard."

After they were inside, she pumped him for information. He told her Custer and about 1500 men had ridden off in the afternoon singing and making all kinds of racket. Miss Libbie seemed powerful agitated to see the general go, although Eliza tried to comfort her. Later, Eliza told him Libbie was upset because the men were going on a dangerous mission towards Charlottesville. She'd heard Custer complaining because Kilpatrick was using them as decoys to attract the Rebels, while he led a raid on Rich-mond. Then Joseph decided to ride over to Rose Hill to see what he could find out. Cavalrymen surrounded the house, drawing rations and preparing for a raid. He found Sam, the old servant who'd lived there for years, who said the tenant family living in the cellar had overheard Kilpatrick's boasting upstairs. The crazy general even rode his horse through the hall. Kilpatrick said he was going to free the prisoners, kill Jeff Davis and his cabinet, and he didn't care if he sacrificed Custer's life to do it! It would be worth it and it might end the war. They were leaving tonight.

"What?" Constance gasped. "So Kilpatrick really is crazy enough to go to Richmond! It sounds like he's sent Custer on a suicide mission in order to garner fame for himself." She slapped her fist into her hand. "Kilpatrick's burning ambition could kill Aaron. He's got to be stopped. If he frees the prisoners and kills President Davis, the South would be devastated. I must get a message to Frank!"

Sadie walked over to her with her hands on her hips. She reached her hands out and grabbed Constance by the shoulders. "Now, ya listen to me young lady, there ain't no way ya can get a message to him an' not risk your life. I forbid ya to do it!"

Constance held her ground with fire in her eyes. "I'm twenty one and I can make my own decisions. If I get a message to Frank, it could save Richmond and Aaron. The Rebels will know Custer's raid is a feint and not send all of their men after him. Richmond is lightly guarded. That's why forewarning is imperative." She pulled back from Sadie, walked to the alcove, put on her cape and scarf and picked up a lantern. "I'm going to the attic to see what kind of disguise I can come up with."

Constance stood up after pulling on her boots. The old servant frowned and assessed the outfit: an old pair of her father's riding pants and boots, a plain shirt, the blue uniform coat of the Union soldier who died in their house after Cedar Mountain, and a black slouch hat with no known origin. "Humph! Ya ain't gonna fool nobody."

"Don't be so negative, Sadie. It's dark outside." She knelt down and pulled up the loose floorboard that concealed her small pistol and a sheathed Bowie knife. Taking both items in her hands, she stood up and checked the gun. Seeing that it was loaded, she stuck it and the knife under the makeshift rope belt that held up her pants. She pulled the stool up to the small table, tore off a small piece of paper, and sat down to write:

F.

Custer's raid to Charlottesville is a feint. The real thrust of the movement will be led by Kilpatrick. He plans to free the prisoners in Richmond and kill President Davis and his cabinet. He's leaving tonight, February 28.

C.

She laid the note on the table and folded it accordion style so that the finished product was no more than a quarter inch wide. "Now, Sadie, I want you to braid this note into my hair. I need one long braid down the back to conceal it."

Sadie sighed heavily and then dutifully performed the task. "At least tell me where you's goin'." She platted the hair, placing the note in the middle.

"I'm riding to The Retreat to put the note under the duck rock by the river. Frank told me to leave it there, and hang a white cloth as a signal. Have you covered the note?"

"Yes, chile, your hair is thick. Lawd, that's a long ride an' ya gotta go through their lines. It's plain crazy!" Sadie tied a piece of yarn around the end of the braid.

"Now, put the braid on top of my head using the pins." Constance handed the metal hairpins to Sadie. When the braid was secure she stood up and pulled the sheet from her bed. After folding it, she walked towards the door, and said, "I've got to get a few things from the kitchen."

Sadie looked at her with tears in her eyes, her lower lip trembling. "I's gonna be a wreck till ya gits back from this crazy trip. I'll pray for ya."

Constance threw her arms around the old woman. "I love you, Sadie. I <u>must</u> do this." She walked out the door contemplating what other items she needed to take. Once inside the kitchen, she grabbed a small jar with a lid, several wooden clothes pins, and took from the drawer the 3-foot length of fine wire she'd used to trip Mrs. Bennett. Thinking it might come in handy, she wound it into a small coil and placed it in her shirt pocket. Time was of the essence. She must leave.

She pushed open the stable door silently while one of the horses snorted. After her eyes adjusted, she crept to the stall of a small black mare, stroked the horse on the nose for a few minutes to get her confidence, and then placed the blanket and saddle on her plus the bit and bridle. She searched through several saddlebags hanging on the wall until she discovered a compass. That would be helpful. Placing the sheet and the rest of her items in a saddlebag, she threw it over the mare and led her to the door. She pulled on her father's riding gloves, feeling his presence and spirit while she adjusted the gloves around her small fingers. When she peered out, not a soul was in sight. She led the mare onto East Street, and then swung into the saddle, patting the horse on the neck. "Come on, girl. We've got to be a team tonight."

The stars twinkled on the clear cold evening and a sliver of moon glistened in the sky; enough to give some light, but not too much to reveal her presence. Fate seemed to be with her. She felt that she would not be questioned until she had to cross through the picket line outside of the Union camp. Shivering in the cold wind, her eye remained ever vigilant and her heart beat rapidly. She contemplated the strong motives that had prompted her to take this risk. She hated Kilpatrick and certainly wanted to prove her loyalty to the Confederacy. Her father's spirit was with her; she seemed to hear him whispering, "fight tyranny!" But most importantly, she went in the hope that her actions might save Aaron's life. He was out there riding under these same stars. She wondered if he was thinking of her.

Aaron felt tense and uneasy while his horse galloped over the hills towards Charlottesville. Custer was leading them deep into enemy territory. Certain that their expedition was a feint for Kilpatrick, anger burned inside him when he thought of how carelessly his life was being risked. Jeb Stuart and half of the Confederate army could be pursuing them. He had to get his mind off of the danger. His lips turned up in a smile when he thought of Constance. At least he didn't have to worry about her tonight. The town was in no danger and he visualized her serenely nestled in her bed.

The moonlight outlined the ghostly figure of Ulric Dahlgren who anxiously watched the last of his 500 men splash across the Rapidan at Ely's Ford. Having easily captured the entire Confederate picket force, all was going according to plan. Confident that the Confederates were oblivious to his movements, he sent a courier to Kilpatrick with the news. Kilpatrick's men would be following him in short order. "Ride full speed to Spotsylvania!" he ordered his men.

The cavalrymen dashed into the night with Hugh Scott and Dan Tanner, Confederate scouts, joining the rear of the column. The two Rebels would ride calmly with the Yankees until they had an opportunity to break away. Then they would ride like hell to inform Wade Hampton, whose small force guarded Richmond, that the Yankees were coming!

The tall peak of Pony Mountain loomed before Constance. Several times she had hidden in the shadows when she heard other horsemen nearby. She determined to follow Frank's directions and travel on the west side of the mountain, not following a main road. If Kilpatrick's men, who were on the other side of the mountain, traveled east, she would not confront them. Custer had already passed by en route to Charlottesville. She put her head down into the bitter wind, and her hands grew numb. She understood the hardships soldiers endured daily. Pulling the compass out of her pocket, she held it until the faint moonlight glistened on the needle. She determined if she headed south through the open fields she would reach the river and then turn east.

After she had ridden several miles, she spotted the huts and tents of the Union camp on the horizon. Her pulse raced erratically. Getting through this camp and picket line would be the most dangerous part. It was after midnight and the camp appeared quiet. She rode up to the edge of a line of huts and dismounted. Pausing to listen, she heard only loud snoring. She pulled the horse's reins and moved quickly from one shadow to another. Suddenly, two men emerged from a hut, laughing and talking. She dragged her horse behind another hut and waited breathlessly, sure they would hear the deafening pounding of her heart. They passed by oblivious to her.

Finally, she reached the edge of the camp. She tied the horse to a pole and slithered forward on her stomach in the undergrowth, feeling the heavy frost against her face. Looking to her right and left, she finally caught sight of a picket through the tall grass, marching with his gun over his shoulder, whistling. She observed him for several minutes until he repeated his beat. Now that she knew the area he covered, she must pass as far down wind from him as possible. The strong wind would carry away the sound of her horse's hooves. She rushed back to her horse and bounded into the saddle. She rode forward slowly, keeping an eye on the picket. When he turned his back to walk in the opposite direction, she spurred the mare when he was out of earshot. They sprang forward at a gallop, flying over the field. Constance leaned forward, spurring her horse to go faster. They kept up the blistering pace while she glanced behind her to see if they were being pursued. Thank God! It looked like they had made it!

She allowed the mare to slow down to a trot and with the help of her compass, they soon approached the river. Constance could make out the dark hills on the other side of the Rapidan, but was unsure of her exact location. She decided to turn east before she got closer to the river. Union cavalrymen picketed the river line and she didn't want to encounter one yet. She strained her eyes for a familiar landmark. Nothing became obvious to her, but she remained confident she rode in the right direction. After a few minutes, she spotted a house in a grove of trees. It looked like The Retreat. After the horse trotted closer, she grew elated at the sight of the familiar house. Even in the faint moonlight she was sickened by the damage done by the cannon fire.

The hoot of an owl caused her to jump. Sweeping her eyes towards the river, she searched for the movement of a picket. Seeing none, she moved forward cautiously, finding her way towards the duck rock with no problem. She stopped her horse about a hundred yards away and contemplated the situation. If she waited to spot a picket, she might waste a great deal of time. She had to move quickly to return to town by daybreak. Resolutely, she moved forward slowly, scanning the horizon. When she reached the duck rock, she dismounted and tied her horse to a stump, listening to the sound of the rushing river behind her. She retrieved the small jar from her saddlebag, set it on the rock, pulled her hair down, and undid the piece of yarn. Unbraiding it, she ran her fingers through her hair until she pulled the message out. Hastily, she put the paper in the jar, screwed on the top, and placed it in the designated location under the rock. It was done! Without wasting a second, she twisted her hair into a knot and was about to pin it up when she heard a horse galloping towards her.

"Put your hands up or you're dead," a soldier yelled while he surged towards her. She spun around, causing her hair to cascade down her back. He was too close! She had no choice but to comply and slowly raise her hands. Panic rioted within her.

"Don't make a move." He dismounted with the gun pointed towards her. "What's the password and your regiment, soldier," he demanded as he walked closer. Her breath caught in her throat and black fright swept through her. The tall, heavy-set Federal in his mid-forties eyed her warily. When he spotted her long black hair hanging down her back, his lips turned up in a smile.

"Well, now, I don't believe you're a soldier at all." He reached to her chest and fondled her breast. Constance gasped, trying to move backwards, but the huge shoulder-high boulder prohibited her retreat. He spat some tobacco juice on the ground and lifted her chin towards the moonlight. "Aren't you the pretty one, though. There's only one reason a woman would be out here at night, and that's 'cause she's a spy."

"No, I'm not a spy," Constance managed to squeak out. "I'm trying to cross the river to nurse my sick brother in the Confederate army. That's all."

"Now, pretty as you are, I don't buy that story." He moved closer, wedging her between him and the rock. "Spies hang you know." He moved his hand around her waist, pulled out the gun and knife, and stuck them in his belt. "You're mighty heavily armed, sweetheart."

"I had to protect myself. Your rules forced me to sneak through your picket line," she said defiantly.

He slid his hand between her legs and she seethed with humiliation, unable to pull away from him. "You know if you was nice to me, I might be persuaded to take you back through our lines, and not turn you in for a spy." He leaned forward and kissed her. Her stomach churned from the taste of the tobacco juice.

She felt momentary panic while her mind jumped and raced, searching for a way out. Thought after thought flew through her brain in rapid succession. When she could finally pull away, she gasped, "If I do what you want, do you swear you'll release me?"

"You can count on it, sweetheart," he answered with an arrogant smile.

"Very well...back up and give me room to...take my pants off." He stepped back smiling; she sat down on the ground, pulled her boots off, then stood up and let her pants and pantalettes slide to the ground. He eyed her lustfully while she stood before him naked below the waist. "Now it's your turn," she said softly.

He hesitated for a minute, breathing hard, unable to believe his good fortune.

"Make up your mind," she muttered. The frigid wind swept goose bumps across her exposed skin. "I'm willing to please you to save my life."

That did it. He leaned against the rock and pulled his boots off. Then he slightly turned his back to her and unbuttoned his pants. Instantly, she jerked the coil of wire out of her shirt pocket, rapidly wrapping the ends around her gloved hands. When he leaned against the rock to pull one leg out of his pants, she sprung towards him and looped the wire around his neck. She jerked it tight with all of her strength while adrenaline surged through her body. "Ah! Ah!" he choked as she cut his breath off by pulling the wire tighter. He flailed his hands behind him to grab her, but was unable to do so since she was wedged between him and the rock. She felt the sharp pain of the rough rock scraping and gouging her bare buttocks. Mustering all of her strength, she grunted and pulled harder until he slowly slid down the rock. Wrapping the wire tighter around her aching fingers, she pulled furiously again until he went limp. She gasped for breath and held her position until she thought he was dead. She couldn't take any chances…had to be positive he was dead. Her mind spun and her eyes darted wildly around her. She spotted the knife and with a reflex action, grabbed it and sliced it across his neck. She cried in horror when the blood flowed profusely and the reality of her actions penetrated her brain.

Breathing spastically, she leaned against the rock again to regain her strength and felt a painful throbbing in her raw hindquarters. After her heart quit racing, still breathing hard, she retrieved her clothes and got dressed. Guilt-ridden, she glanced at the sickening sight of her blood-soaked victim. Surely, she had to give him some dignity. Struggling, she pulled his pants back up, fastened them, and put his boots on. Perhaps Belle Boyd was right. All is fair in love and war. After re-coiling the wire, she retrieved her gun, rushed to her horse, pulled the sheet and clothespins out of the saddlebag, and pinned the sheet in place over a low tree limb. Surely, Frank would see it in the morning. This whole escapade had to pay off. She tied the Yank's horse to a tree in the hope that Frank would retrieve him.

Springing on her horse, she dug her spurs in, forcing it to gallop across the fields. They had to move fast to get back by dawn, in spite of the burning pain caused by the saddle against her raw buttocks. The heavy moist air settled in the bottom causing fog to form in the low areas. She thanked God for being with her. The fog would make it easier for her to slip back through enemy lines.

Judson Kilpatrick's wide mouth moved into a broad smile while he watched the last of his 3500 men cross safely at Ely's Ford. Turning to his couriers, he said to one, "Inform General Meade that our crossing was a complete surprise. No alarm has been given. The enemy does not anticipate our movement." After the messenger dashed away he turned to a second courier. "Ride to General Pleasanton and tell him that I will double our bet of $5000 that I will enter Richmond successively," Kilpatrick commanded arrogantly.[3]

Next day, February 29, 1864: The Confederate camp

Stringfellow sipped his Confederate coffee restlessly in the dawn light. Aware of the enemy troop movements around Lee's flank towards Madison, he knew Stuart had been sent out to halt the intruders. However, Stringfellow remained suspicious that the real thrust might be in the other direction towards Richmond. His scouts were watching Ely's and Germanna Fords. A messenger galloped up to him. "Captain Stringfellow, a picket's seen that signal you told us to watch for. You know, the white cloth across the river!"

Stringfellow jumped to his feet. "Is it near my home?"

"I think so."

The scout moved towards his horse. "I'll need two men to ride with me. We're going over to investigate."

"Yes, sir. Jones and I'll go." They galloped off towards the river. The three men forded the frigid river, wasting no time. If there was a message, Stringfellow needed to retrieve it before the fog completely lifted. He headed directly towards the duck rock and spotted the sheet hanging in the tree limb. It had to be a message from Connie! She evidently had risked her life to come here. Splashing up the bank, his eyes scanned the horizon for a Federal picket. He dismounted and walked towards the rock in the morning mist. "My God," he muttered when he saw the blood-drenched body of the Yankee picket. Filled with a sense of foreboding, he reached his hand under the rock and pulled out the jar. Sure enough, he saw a message inside. He twisted the lid off the jar and unfolded the small piece of paper. So, Kilpatrick was going to Richmond to free the prisoners and kill the president! His suspicions were confirmed, but how in the name of God had little Connie killed that huge Yankee soldier?

"Boys, I know you aren't going to believe this," he said incredulously to the two soldiers who gawked at the body. "But a 5-foot, 3-inch girl did that."

"Bull! Ain't no way!" one of the soldiers exclaimed. Stringfellow pulled the sheet from the tree and folded it. "Look at how big that guy is!" The soldier knelt down and looked at the corpse closely. "There's so much blood, I can't tell what happened. She couldn't possibly have overpowered him. She must be one clever lady."

"I don't know how, either," Stringfellow mused. He mounted his horse and took the reins of the Yank's captured horse. "But this is vital information. Constance Armstrong is a heroine. Mount up. We've got to ride back fast to telegraph Richmond." The two soldiers shook their heads in disbelief. The boys back in camp weren't going to believe this one.

19

Grant Arrives

March 2, 1864 - April 24, 1864

Grant is "a drunken wooden-headed tanner."
Abraham Lincoln, 1861

Two days later, March 2, 1864: Sadie's cabin

Constance's whole body shook from her painful, hacking cough. Feeling her forehead, Sadie exclaimed, "You's still hot. Sakes alive chile, what did ya reckon would happen when ya spent the night out in the cold? Now roll over an' let me check your behind."

Constance groaned, rolled to her stomach, and Sadie lifted her gown up. "Am I going to be scarred for life?"

"You's still bruised an' swollen an' there's some big scabs. I 'spect most of it'll go 'way." Sadie wiped her with a wash cloth.

Constance cringed while Sadie helped her roll onto her back. "I'm proud that I did it, Sadie, but I'm worried about Aaron. Are you sure you heard correctly that Custer made it back to Madison?"

"That's what they said at the Vahginya House yesterday. Nobody seems to know nothin' 'bout that awful Kilpatrick an' Richmond. Now don't ya fret none. You's got to git yourself well." They heard a soft knock at the door.

Sadie ambled forward and cracked the door slightly, looking at the soldier in the darkness. "I have a letter for Miss Armstrong." He stuck an envelope into the door. "Tell her I'll be back in a hour if she wants to reply."

"Is Aaron wounded?" Constance lifted herself up in the bed.

"No, he's simply a bit under the weather," the Yankee answered politely. Sadie closed the door and handed the letter to her patient, who immediately ripped it open. Pulling the candle on the table closer, Constance read:

My dearest Constance,

I have a fever, a painfully sore throat, and I ache all over. Forgive me for sounding like a big baby, but how I long for your tender healing touch. I fear that three days hard riding in inclement weather has taken its toll on my normally robust health. However, I have returned safely from an extremely hazardous raid, and am thankful for that blessing.

On our diversionary foray we rode almost a 100 miles in 48 hours. The ice, snow, and freezing rain were less than enjoyable. I am happy to report that we returned with 50 prisoners, several hundred horses, and a Virginia flag without the loss of a man. We approached the Rebel encampment at Charlottesville on the 29th. The regiment which was sent ahead to scout surprised the enemy and captured 50 prisoners. The prisoners

452

reported that Fitz Lee held Charlottesville. After a brief artillery duel, we burned a mill and bridge on the Rivanna River and withdrew. We started north in a cold drizzle, which soon froze and turned the ground into a sheet of ice. All night long we skidded and stumbled on a course led by one of the prisoners who claimed to know a short cut. As the first rays of dawn lit the sky, it appeared we were being led west towards the snowcapped mountains instead of north. Sensing a trap, Custer dropped back with his main force and crossed the Rapidan at another ford. Sure enough, Stuart's cavalry lay in wait further up the river. When they discovered that we had slipped by them, they pursued us for a short while, inflicting a few wounds. I do not understand why half of the Confederate army did not swoop down upon us. It is a miracle for which I am most thankful.

Anger seethes inside of me as I contemplate the senseless risk of our lives for the purpose of diverting attention from Kilpatrick's force moving on Richmond. Little is known of their expedition as I write. I predict it will be a complete failure at the cost of many lives and horses. Rumor has it that Kilpatrick bypassed Meade and Pleasanton, and got direct approval for his raid from Lincoln. If this is the case, my estimation of Lincoln has dropped significantly. Only a foolish desperate man would grasp at straws and approve such a reckless scheme.

My thoughts were always of you. It was comforting for me to know that you were in no danger while I was gone. Hopefully, I will feel better within the week and I will come to you.

This pen cannot reveal the intensity of my love.

Aaron

Coughing repeatedly, Constance pulled back the covers and sat up. She placed her pillow on the stool and slid carefully over to sit on it. "Thank God he's safe," she said hoarsely; then she started to write. "Perhaps it's better that he not see me in my current state."

A week later, March 9, 1864: The bookstore

Behind her desk in the bookstore, Constance devoured the newspaper stories of Kilpatrick's failed raid. With wide eyes she read that Dahlgren had been killed and that papers taken from his body revealed orders to kill Davis and his cabinet. The South was outraged. New York papers placed responsibility for the raid squarely on Lincoln's shoulders. Hearing a customer, she looked up surprised to see her old friend. "Lucy," she said warmly. "I'm delighted to see you."

Lucy's thin, drawn face stared back, showing little emotion. "Constance, I want you to know that I don't hate you because of your Yankee gentleman friend."

Constance threw her arms around her and held her for a minute. "Oh, Lucy, thank you. That means so much to me." She pulled back to observe tears in her friend's hopeless eyes. "How are you surviving this winter encampment?" Lucy shook her head forlornly and stared at the floor. Concerned about her gauntness, Constance probed, "Do you need food?"

A tear rolled down Lucy's sunken cheek, then she looked up and nodded affirmatively. "We're starving to death, but Granny won't let us accept any food from the soldiers," she gasped softly. "I don't know if she'll accept food from you either."

"Then we won't tell her the source," Constance said defiantly. "I know many people are hungry. I'll gladly share what I have. You've been my lifelong friends."

Losing control, Lucy sobbed openly. Constance pulled a handkerchief from her pocket and gave it to her. "Thank you," Lucy mumbled. "Granny and Jane think you're a traitor...that you've treated Robert terribly. I believe you're simply...human."

"It is possible for me to love a Yankee and still remain loyal to our cause. I know that's difficult to comprehend. Come, let's go to the kitchen and get you some food." Constance put her arm on Lucy's shoulder. "I hope you'll tell others to come to me if they're in need."

When Constance returned to the bookstore she contemplated Lucy's revelation. She felt compelled to do all that she could to feed her friends. Once the Union army pulled out, which it would certainly do as soon as the roads became passable, she'd have no reliable source of food. It seemed prudent to purchase as much food as possible now with her existing money and silver. She paused to collect money from several soldiers who anxiously purchased papers to read about Kilpatrick, and then sat at her desk to write. Since Aaron hadn't come yet, she'd write him her thoughts. Surely he would help her. She pulled out a piece of paper. Another day without seeing him did not seem tolerable.

When she heard the footsteps in the hall, she glanced at the door. Aaron's eyes captured hers with a gaze as soft as a caress. "Aaron!" She bounded towards him. He encircled her with his muscular arms and brushed his lips against hers tenderly, disregarding the gawks of the soldiers in the bookstore.

"It seems an eternity since I've seen you," he said softly. "How've you been?"

"Frantic about you." Her fingers entwined with his while she pulled him towards the desk. "And a bit under the weather myself. I've had a terrible cough and had to close the store several days."

He sat on the edge of the desk and pulled her against him. "You've got to take better care of yourself. I have an excuse for getting sick, but you don't." He glanced at the headlines of the newspapers stacked on the desk. "Much has transpired since I last saw you."

"Grant has been named Lieutenant General and commander of all Union forces," she said while his hand moved gently down her back. "He's such a common-looking fellow and a known drinker. I don't believe he's any match for Lee."

Aaron smiled at her with his eyebrows raised in skepticism. "He's won battle after battle in the West. Lincoln even said he'd like to know what brand of whiskey Grant drank, so he could pass it on to his other generals. But, I agree with you. I'm dubious. He hasn't faced the likes of Lee yet. Rumor has it that he's conferring with Meade at Brandy today. Question is, will Meade stay or go?"

"On top of that, the papers are full of stories about Kilpatrick's fiasco. The enraged South believes Lincoln authorized the assassination of President Davis and his cabinet and the burning of Richmond."

"I agree that Lincoln authorized the raid, but I cannot accept the fact that he knew about the killing of Davis. That's simply southern propaganda. If it was authorized, Kilpatrick's the one responsible."

"Aaron you're being naïve," she sputtered, bristling with indignation. "Lincoln sent our old adversary John Pope to Nebraska to kill the Indians and then authorized the mass execution of thirty-eight redskins to appease the voters of Nebraska. You said yourself he was desperately grasping at straws to end this war. He's too unpopular to ever be re-elected. He'd agree to anything that would make him a hero, regardless of how dastardly the deed. He got caught this time ordering an assassination and now his life is on the line."

The corner of his mouth twisted with exasperation. "You're wrong Reb, but the problem is, no matter what's true, this war has been taken to a baser level of brutality. I bitterly resent the way my life was risked, but I must smile at the thought of Kilpatrick and his men being brought back to Washington by boat like a pack of old women. They had to skedaddle down the peninsula to Butler for protection."

Constance's lips curved into a satisfied smile. She felt that somehow her information had played a small part in the outcome of the event. "How I'd love to interview him right now. He lost three hundred and forty men and over five hundred horses. How do you think he'd explain that?"

Aaron chuckled. "I'm sure he'd tell you how much property and how many miles of railroad he destroyed and maintain that his raid was a success. In reality, he lost his nerve. He probably could have freed our prisoners if he'd persevered. He's a frothy braggart who's reluctant to fall on the battlefield. I can only hope that we'll soon be rid of 'Kill.'"

"Wouldn't that be wonderful," she exclaimed with merriment twinkling in her eyes. "It's a sunny, clear day today. Why don't we celebrate your return?"

"That's exactly what I had in mind." He traced his fingers tenderly up and down her arms. "The Custers are coming to town soon, and we're going on a carriage ride."

Libbie browsed in the bookstore. "Miss Armstrong, it was so painful for me to tell Autie good-bye when he rode off on that raid. For the first time I observed him going into battle, and it was far more difficult than I ever dreamed. Eliza comforted me and assured me that he always came back. Nevertheless, I was overcome with a feeling of bewilderment and terror in those strange lonely circumstances. I felt the Rebel family downstairs could only have feelings of hostility towards me, and I was uncomfortable staying there alone and unprotected."

"What did you do?" Constance pulled a book from the self and handed it to Libbie.

"I decided to go to Washington and wait for Autie's return. I was overjoyed when I received a telegram from General Pleasonton informing me that Autie had returned safely to Madison. A few days later he joined me in Washington and we resumed our honeymoon. His enthusiasm and energy kept me moving constantly from the theatres to restaurants, to visits with friends. The days passed all too rapidly."

"I must admit I envy your opportunity to go to the theatre. I haven't seen a good performance in years," Constance said. Libbie laid several books on the desk. "These should keep you entertained if you get bored at camp."

"Yes, but I haven't had time to be bored yet. Last night we rode in the lavish carriage to General Pleasonton's headquarters where he provided us with an extravagant six-course dinner. I'm so delighted that you can join us on a ride to the top of Pony Mountain." Libbie laid several dollar bills on the desk.

Constance smiled at the well-dressed, attractive woman. She couldn't help but like her. "You were thoughtful and kind to include me."

Constance glanced out the window of the carriage at the six cavalrymen escorting them. At least the Rebels were keeping the enemy on their toes, she thought. "General Custer, you're to be congratulated for returning all of your men safely. I, for one, am most appreciative." Constance squeezed Aaron's hand.

"Thank you, Miss Armstrong. We were fortunate to avoid one Rebel trap, but I'm surprised they didn't send a stronger force after us. I suspect the Rebels realized our true intent was Richmond. It was rumored all over Washington and even came out later in some of our papers." Custer said pleasantly.

"Our men do have a way of knowing everything," Constance replied with a curious smile.

"I'm afraid my image of military life has been shattered," Libbie said. "I was disturbed to learn that Kilpatrick confessed that he would willingly sacrifice Autie's life for the success of his vainglorious mission. I didn't dream that jealousy and heartless indifference to the lives of others existed in our army."[1]

"We all have great disdain for 'Kill,'" Aaron said, his mouth thinning with displeasure. "Let's pray that we're soon rid of him. I, for one, would trust my life in your hands any day, sir. Your mission was a success, and the public will soon acclaim your achievements."

"Thanks for your vote of confidence, cuz." Custer stroked his bushy mustache while the carriage came to a halt. "I believe we've reached the top."

A brisk breeze chilled them when they disembarked to gaze at the spectacular view in every direction. They stood for a few moments on the treeless mountaintop and watched the signalman swish his flags in the wind. Perched on a rock outcropping, he was visible for miles. "How do they understand what those signals mean?" Libbie asked.

"They have their own code, little wife," Custer answered affectionately. "It changes frequently."

The four of them strolled to the southeastern edge of the hill and stared at the smoke drifting from the Rebel encampment across the Rapidan. "My goodness, are we really looking at the wild fierce Rebels?" Libbie asked. "They're so close it frightens me."

"There they are. Their camps are all stretched out before you." Custer put his hand on her shoulder and pointed.

Constance had a lump in her throat while she gazed at her army across the river. Their number was so few compared to the Yankee camps, which covered most of Culpeper County. Tears came to her eyes at the thought of how hungry and cold they must be. "They aren't wild men," she said softly to Libbie. "They're simply brave men willing to fight to the death to protect their homes. You may annihilate us, but you'll never defeat us. Our will is too strong."

Aaron's glare burned through her and the Custers stared at her in disbelief. "Constance, please..." Aaron began.

"Let me finish," Constance interrupted. She lifted her chin, meeting his icy gaze straight on. "You're both honorable men and brave soldiers who are fighting for a cause you believe in. But you must obey your orders. Lincoln, by ordering Davis's assassination, has turned this into a brutal war of extermination and destruction. You'll destroy or steal everything that we possess and then you'll take away that which we treasure most...our land. Our money will be worthless and you'll buy our land for bargain prices or take it because we can't pay taxes. In your greed for more and more land you'll next exterminate the Indians and steal their land." She looked Custer in the eye coldly. "You'll be forced to obey the orders of your greedy imperialistic government."

"Constance, I believe we should take a walk," Aaron said abruptly, then he grabbed her hand roughly. He dragged her down the hill and into the trees.

"That was uncalled for," he scolded angrily when they were out of earshot. "They didn't have to invite you for a ride."

She planted her hands on her hips and tossed her head in defiance. "I spoke the truth. I was overcome with emotion when I saw our men. I couldn't help it."

"But you didn't have to be rude! They're good people who strongly disagree with your position. Couldn't you have waited and vented your wrath to me later? I'm used to it," he blurted with a heavy dose of sarcasm in his voice.

She had never seen him this way before. The hardness of his glare burned through her, frightening her. It wasn't her intention to embarrass him. "Poor Aaron," she said apologetically. She moved to him and put her arms around his waist. "You have to listen to so much anger. I'm sorry if I insulted them. They're quite likable and their love is inspiring. I suppose I can't help but envy Libbie. She's enjoying fulfilled love." The tense frown on his face gradually relaxed. "But she talks of six-course dinners while my mind is consumed with worry about how we'll keep from starving to death when your army leaves." She briefly related her encounter with Lucy. "I believe I should convert all of my cash and silver into food soon. There will be little to buy once your army marches."

He slowly moved his arms around her, pulled her head against his chest and said in a conciliatory tone, "You're compassionate and generous. I agree, it's wise to accumulate food now. I believe I can telegraph my sister to ship cases of food cheaper than we can purchase from the sutlers. I know we can provide cheap canned codfish and blueberries. How much money do you have?"

"About a hundred and fifty dollars." She looked into his forgiving eyes. "Plus quite a bit of silver buried in the cellar." She slid her arms around his neck. "I love you so intensely, Aaron, but my mind is swirling in turmoil. Forgive my outburst."

The breeze blew against them gently while he moved his lips over hers. She drank in the comfort of his nearness, releasing her hostilities to float away on the wind.

"Cuz, we've got to go!" Aaron soon heard Custer call in the distance.

"I think we lost track of the time." His lips touched hers one last time. "Now promise me, Reb, that you'll apologize."

"Um," she sighed when he finally pulled away reluctantly. "Very well Yank, I'll ask them to forgive my outburst."

Ten days later, March 19, 1864: The bookstore

Constance unpacked the carton of newly arrived *Harper's Weekly,* astounded to see a drawing of General Custer leading a cavalry charge during the Charlottesville raid on the front cover. She thought the illustration by Al Waud a wonderful likeness. "Is it closing time yet?" Aaron bounded energetically into the bookstore.

"Almost." She stood up to greet him. "What luck did you have with the silver?"

He leaned forward and kissed her lightly. "I took it to Brandy and negotiated with

457

the banker there. He finally gave me a hundred dollars. It's the best I could do." He pulled the bills from his pocket. "Do you want me to send it to my sister? She's found a good source for rice and canned condensed milk."

"Yes, that's wonderful. I've given away quite a bit of food this week. Townspeople are beginning to come by. I take their Confederate money to help them save face. I've written you several letters this week." She pulled a bundle from her desk drawer.

"Such treasures." He retrieved three envelopes from his pocket and handed them to her. "You'll never believe what happened to the Custers a few days ago."

"What?" She walked to the door and locked it.

"They were riding down Pony Mountain in the carriage when the horses were suddenly startled and bolted. When they went around a curve the door flew open and Autie was thrown out. Libbie screamed hysterically but managed to hang on until the driver got the carriage under control. It's a wonder they weren't both killed."

"Was the good general injured?" She leaned against him.

He put his arms around her and continued. "He hit his head and must have a concussion. He's been trying to carry on with work as usual, but isn't doing well. He's decided to take a furlough to Washington."

"I'm glad he wasn't seriously injured." Her lips turned up in a slight smile.

He arched one eyebrow and stared at her in accusation. "That's not a smirk on your face is it?"

"Why no," she laughed. "You know I wouldn't smirk because he was riding in a confiscated Confederate carriage. I won't even say it served him right. In fact, I'll send this magazine to him." She reached to her desk and gave him a copy of *Harper's*.

Aaron stared at the cover and whistled. "That looks exactly like him. He deserves the publicity." He laid the magazine down and looked at her. "Kilpatrick's back. His men got thrown out of Washington because they were so rowdy. The controversy over the Dahlgren papers has the whole country in turmoil. I can't believe Grant will leave him in command long. Autie's the best cavalry general we have. He deserves to be given command of the division."

"But he's so young." She snuggled against him. "Let's not talk war now."

Nine days later, March 28, 1864: Coleman Street

After six inches of snow and rain a few days earlier, Constance and Millie were delighted for the opportunity to get outside and walk. "Finally, there's a touch of spring in the air," Millie said as they attempted to cross Spencer Street, avoiding the muddiest spots. A large attachment of cavalry passed them, apparently escorting a wagon along Coleman Street.

"Yes, as soon as the roads are passable, the Yankees will be leaving. I have such mixed feelings about that. I hate the thought of telling Aaron good-bye; plus I wonder where we'll get food." Constance watched the wagon stop in front of the Rixey house, former home of Extra Billy Smith.

The two young ladies moved forward towards the throng. "I agree. My dear Yankee is talking of marriage after the war. I don't want to lose him. He's a wonderful man." The soldiers saluted the average-looking short man with light brown hair and beard, walking across the lawn towards the stately mansion. When he turned towards them briefly, Constance noticed the cigar clenched in his mouth and realized there were three stars on his shoulders.

"My word, that must be Grant! There's nothing impressive about him. His appearance is plain, almost slovenly." Several soldiers followed behind him carrying trunks. "Looks like he's moving in. Wouldn't you know he'd pick the most impressive house in town for his headquarters? He must relish the thought of taking over the former home of the Governor of Virginia," Constance observed sarcastically.

That night, Constance listened attentively while Sadie slowly moved her finger over the lines on the page and read to her the way she had night after night. Seated side by side at the trestle table, the two of them were absorbed in *Oliver Twist*. The old servant looked up from the book, bewildered. "Those poor waifs in London had a terrible life. Mah chil'en on the farm was much better off. We never had to worry 'bout havin' enough to eat."

They heard a soft knock on the door. "I wonder who that could be? It's late." Constance picked up a candle and walked to the door. She cracked the door a few inches and peered out. Holding the candle up, she distinguished the form of a Union soldier with a white beard and hair. "Yes?"

"Connie, it's Frank," he whispered. "Are you alone?"

"Frank! Oh, my God." She opened the door a little wider. "Only Sadie is here."

He slunk inside and closed the door. In the dim light, he looked convincingly like a little old man. "How do you like my disguise?" he asked, his blue eyes twinkling.

"I can't believe it's you. I only recognize your eyes. Where did you get the beard?" They hugged each other.

"I have connections in the theatre." He pulled back to look her in the eye. "You, my fair lady, are a heroine and the talk of our army. Your message helped us stop Kilpatrick. But how, in the name of God, did you kill that Yankee?"

Flattered, she blushed at this compliment. "Come sit down. I'll tell you all about it. Are you hungry?" She led him to the table.

"Silly question. Of course I'm starving. Sadie, I hope to have some of your cooking."

"Praise the Lawd, Mista Frank! You has returned from the dead!" Sadie said elated, then she got up and walked to the stove. "Of course I can cook somethin' up for ya!" Constance gave him a detailed blow by blow description of her trip to the duck rock. He marveled at her monologue, and then greedily consumed the food that Sadie placed before him.

"I'm still astounded at your courage." He ate the last crumb of bread and wiped his snowy beard. "Sadie, that was almost as good as the dinner I had with General Sedgwick." Constance rolled her eyes in disbelief. "Don't believe me do you? Disguised as a Yankee from a far regiment, I visited the good general at Farley. He graciously invited me to dinner. Then he was talkative enough to pass on vital information, which I immediately relayed to Stuart."

Constance shook her head, giggling. "Frank, I know better than to doubt you."

"Good! I'm here to solicit your help again. I was afraid to come to town without a disguise after what happened last time."

"Sadie and I believe Mary Payne informed on you." Constance picked up his plate.

"That's right," Sadie said. "I've seen Yankee soldiers come in an' talk to her quiet like, an' then give her money."

"Sounds like she works for whichever side pays the best." Leaning forward on his elbows, he stared at Constance intently. "We've got to know Grant's plans. It's imperative to the survival of the Confederacy. Where and when will the main thrust come? Which army will he march with? Will Meade retain his command? How many men will they have? Tell me, have you heard anything?"

Constance fully comprehended the seriousness of the situation. "He moved into the Rixey house today. I assume that will be his headquarters. I've heard nothing about Meade leaving, so he must be still in command." She massaged her forehead with her fingers thoughtfully. "Grant's right under my nose. There ought to be a way to penetrate his headquarters."

Sadie's eyebrows moved together in a frown after she adjusted the kerchief around her head and sat down beside Constance. "Now, Miss Constance, I don't want ya gettin' no wild ideas."

"There has to be a way," Frank mused to himself. He sat for a few minutes deep in thought, thumping his fingers on the table. "We need somebody inside that house to listen and look at his papers."

"Well, perhaps he needs to have some forms and papers printed. I could approach him, since I have the only printing press in town," Constance suggested.

"Hum." The lines of concentration deepened along Frank's brows. "That's a possibility, but I doubt he would let you print anything confidential. If it gave you access to the house, perhaps you could do some snooping. However, if he knows you haven't taken the oath, you'll be under suspicion. We need someone they'd never suspect."

They sat in silent thought for a few minutes and then, as if their minds worked in unison, both Constance and Frank turned and stared at Sadie. Sensing the implication of their attention, Sadie shifted her weight nervously. Finally, she looked up and confronted Constance. "I know what you's thinkin'. They'd never suspect me an' I kin read."

"Oh, yes, that's true Sadie." Constance's voice rose in animation. "You read beautifully and they think, foolishly, that all the Negroes are on their side."

Sadie sighed and gaped pop-eyed. "This could be dangerous work."

"You're right, Sadie," Frank said. "I don't want to put pressure on you to do something you're not comfortable with. However, you could provide a great service to our cause and keep us from living under Yankee rule."

Sadie thought for a minute staring at the floor. Slowly, she raised her eyes to earnestly meet Frank's. "The last thing I want is to have a bunch of Yankees like that Miz Bennett bossin' me 'round," she said defiantly. "I'll do it!"

"Bravo!" Constance threw her arms around the old woman. "I always knew you were a true Rebel."

Frank laughed at them. "You two are a clever and fearsome pair. I'm thankful you're on my side!"

"Lawd, Lawd," Sadie chuckled. "The things I let you two chil'en talk me into. So, how am I gonna do this, anyway?"

"You'll go there first thing in the morning and beg work from the great liberator army.

Tell them you can cook, clean, and wash clothes and that you desperately need money. I guarantee that they'll hire you," Constance said. Sadie simply smiled guardedly and shook her head.

"It's risky for me to come back to town to pick up intelligence from you." Frank explained scratching his uncomfortable beard. "I've got almost a hundred scouts working in the county. They'll make contact with you. There's a young fellow from Loudoun County, Channing Smith, who'll be placed in charge of this project. Of course they'll all be in Federal uniforms. If you're not sure of their intent, we'll use 'duck rock' as the code words."

Constance burst out laughing, revealing her beautiful smile. "Frank, you always lift my spirits. With resourceful men like you around, there is hope for our cause. We will do our utmost to gather vital information for operation 'duck rock.'"

"Don't be discouraged, Connie. If we can keep Grant from taking Richmond, Lincoln will never be re-elected. The North is ready for peace. Now, may I get a few hours sleep before I slink away?"

She hugged him and assured him that he was welcome to stay as long as he wanted. She and Sadie departed for the cabin to discuss the details of their mission. Constance cautioned Sadie that Aaron must not know she was working at Grant's headquarters. Any knowledge he had of their activities could incriminate him, should they be caught.

Thirteen days later, April 10, 1864: Sadie's kitchen

"Gin'el Grant smokes those smelly cigars all day," Sadie complained. "He's always walkin' up to Gorrells' to buy more. An' every mornin' I find a few glasses smellin' of spirits. He don't talk much. He sure ain't the gent'man Gin'el Lee is."

"But do you think anyone is suspicious of you?" Constance asked while she stirred the soup. "You've got to be careful."

"Oh, I knows that," Sadie said with a big grin. "I reads everythin' in his trash can an' listens best I kin when the door's closed. I tell all them Yankees how happy I am their army is here an' I jist keep smilin'. I saw a letter in his room to his wife, tellin' her she should sell her slaves. Kin ya believe that? His wife still owns slaves."

"Oh, I believe it. Nothing about the Yankees surprises me." Constance turned her head when she heard a knock at the door. She cautiously walked to the alcove and cracked the door.

"Miss Armstrong," a tall young soldier whispered. "I'm Channing Smith here to talk to you about operation duck rock."

"Oh, yes, Mr. Smith, please come in." Constance opened the door. "We were wondering when we'd see you."

"Thank you." The tall brunette soldier stepped into the light. He had a long, almost droll face. "Stringfellow said you'd have information for me."

"Yes, please sit down and join us for dinner. My servant, Sadie, has been working at Grant's headquarters. She reads well and is most reliable." Constance motioned him to the table. He smiled broadly at Sadie, who nodded with a new look of importance.

He ate greedily while the two of them revealed the facts that Sadie had discovered. The scout listened attentively and nodded his head in appreciation. He commended the ladies for their service and then penned the following letter to General Stuart:

General,

I send you the following information, which comes from a source perfectly reliable. I am indebted to a lady in Culpeper Court House, who is very prudent, vivacious, etc. and whose opportunities for hearing are good a she has been a good deal at Grant's Headquarters.

The sutlers, traders, and everything of the kind are ordered to pack up, and leave within ten days. All extra baggage has been sent to Washington, and all persons not connected with the army ordered to leave.

The Eleventh and Twelfth Corps have been ordered here and are daily expected. The three consolidated corps are estimated at 75,000 – 25,000 each. Meade is expected to have 100,000 men when all reinforcements come up.

Guards and deserters report a large number of artillerymen as having arrived.

Gen. Grant has been to Fortress Monroe to confer with Butler, but has returned to the army. I can hear of no road in construction to Germanna Ford. No fortifications about Court House or Stevensburg.

The roads are in shocking condition. Corduroy roads have been made all through their army. I will try to learn which way they will move. This can only be done from leakage from staff officers of Grant's. You can judge its merit. Desertions are very frequent. Forty said to have escaped the other night. They all confirm these reports.

This lady gathered the information by hearing confidential conversations of officers. You know her, but I am requested to give no name. I will do my best at watching, and will try and advise you at an early period of movement. I will go to Fauquier tomorrow to watch the railroads and will leave a man in Culpeper with instructions to notify you of any movement.[2]

Yours Most Respfly,
Channing M. Smith

"Ladies, please keep up the good work. We still need to know when the army will move and in what direction. One of my men will be in touch with you in few days." Smith stood to leave.

Two days later, April 12, 1864: The Culpeper Observer

Constance peered out the doorway of the newspaper building. "Aaron, I'm over here."

He climbed down from the loaded wagon stopped on Cameron Street by the kitchen. Hearing the clatter of the printing press, he called, "What are you doing? Are you back in the printing business?"

"Yes." She watched him walk towards her in the twilight. "I'm printing some forms for General Grant. Come into my office."

He stepped inside and closed the door. "You're a mess! You've got ink smudges all over you." He enfolded her in his arms and kissed her warmly. "I never know what you'll be up to next."

"I couldn't pass up the opportunity to make a little more money. He has his head-quarters in Extra Billy Smith's old house, so I decided to see if I could solicit some business. Fortunately, I got this temperamental old printing press to work. I've been working a few hours after I close the bookstore every day. It's exhausting." She leaned her head against his broad chest.

"You never cease to amaze me," he said above the din of the printing press. "Come outside and see the shipment of food I've got for you."

The number of crates piled on the wagon thrilled her. "This is wonderful, Aaron. Your sister has done a marvelous job!" She walked around reading the names on the crates, "Codfish, canned milk, rice, cornmeal, canned blueberries, flour, sugar, beans, salt. I must be dreaming!"

"I'll stack these in the kitchen while you finish your printing. It's a beautiful evening. Let's go for a walk after dinner." He lifted the first crate off.

"I'd love it. Have I told you lately that you're the most wonderful man on the face of the earth?" She strolled back across the street.

"No, tell me that and more later." He lugged a heavy crate towards the kitchen

The crates filled the pantry and were stacked to the beamed ceiling around the small kitchen when Constance and Aaron enjoyed a dinner of fish and rice. He cautioned her to bolt the doors and cover the windows to prevent theft of such a large cache of food. He then went into a long tirade about the army's disenchantment with Grant. The infantry was threatening mutiny since Grant reorganized five corps into three. The men resented being separated from their former comrades. It was like separating families. On top of that, he had brought in his cronies from the west to lead the cavalry. Sheridan had replaced Pleasonton; Torbet was given the First Division. Everyone was elated that Kilpatrick had been shipped west to Sherman.[i] Aaron vented his fury that Autie had not been given Kilpatrick's command. Instead it went to a less experienced officer, Wilson.

He beamed when questioned about Autie's health. Yes, he had returned to camp full of vim and vigor, but their drills of new cavalry tactics were ceaseless. The men collapsed into their bunks each night. He spoke scornfully of the new draftees who had arrived. They were nothing more than mercenaries who couldn't be trusted on picket duty and deserted at the first opportunity.[ii]

She studied every feature of his face imprinting it on her mind. Anxious to be able to touch him, she was elated when he finally said, "And now, Miss Armstrong, it's time for a short walk before I return to the agonies of camp."

Five days later, April 17, 1864: Armstrong garden

Beads of sweat glistened in the sunlight on the taut skin of Aaron's muscular shoulders while he turned over another spade of red dirt. The blood vessels bulged over his ballooning biceps when he jabbed the shovel back into the ground. Constance devoured him with her eyes from the edge of the garden, admiring the way the hair curled on his chest and trailed down his flat abdomen to his navel. She remembered how she had

---

[i] When Sherman offered Kilpatrick a role in his march to the sea, he said, "I know Kilpatrick is a hell of a damn fool, but I want just that sort of man to command my cavalry on this expedition." Sherman and "Kill" left a wide swath of Georgia and South Carolina in smoking ruins.

[ii] Desertions in the Union army reached 5,000 a month.

appreciated his physique while undressing him after Cedar Mountain. When questioned, he told her he had developed his muscles by rowing, lifting fishnets, and loading crates on the docks. Always involved in athletics, of late he had spent much time lifting logs to construct huts. Feeling her admiring stare, he paused and gave her a devilish grin. "It's not polite for southern women to gawk at Yankees without their shirts on."

She felt the heat in her cheeks and a smile of enchantment touched her lips. "Forgive me, handsome Yankee. But, I like what I see." She reached the dipper down into the pail of water and handed it to him.

He gulped it and wiped the sweat from his forehead where his hair hung in curls. He looked behind him to see Billy breaking up the clumps with a hoe. "He seems to always understand what needs to be done. I have the greatest sympathy for him. We arrived here together, and I think, there, but for the grace of God, go I."

Constance took the dipper from him. "I know somewhere there must be a wife and children waiting for him. It's a terrible tragedy. He wanders off sometimes for days at a time, but he always comes back. I wonder what he really knows or understands." Aaron resumed his labor, struggling to cut through the clumps of weeds that had overtaken the small garden beside the kitchen.

Unable to take her eyes off of him, she was thankful that he felt so secure and self-confident in his masculinity. Thus, her outspokenness and intellect did not threaten him. They both realized their time together would soon end but found it too painful to discuss. They had shared every detail of their past and present lives, but had a mute agreement never to mention the unmentionable—the future. Her mind swirled in a battle of conflicting emotions. She couldn't seem to face or accept the inevitable.

"I believe that's all I'll have time for today. Now I'll go to the stable and get some good manure." He leaned casually on the shovel, gazing at the small plot. "Do you think the Good Lord will forgive me for working on Sunday?"

"I pray that he will. Sadie and I greatly appreciate your mission of mercy. At least we'll have fresh vegetables this summer." She watched his powerful back when he moved towards the stable with easy grace.

Constance turned her nose up at the pungent smell of the manure the men shoveled on the freshly turned earth. Aaron laughed at her facial expression and teased her about being finicky while he and Billy worked the manure into the soil. To prove him wrong, she picked up the hoe, dug the rows, and planted the seeds.

Aaron scrutinized her, laboring in her old straw hat and homespun dress. She possessed more courage and energy than any woman he had ever known. She radiated a vitality that drew him like a magnet, and yet her strength did not lessen her femininity. He prayed she would have the ability to survive the trying times he feared might come. Marching forward and leaving her behind was the most difficult task he had ever faced. The thought of it gnawed away at his innermost being. When he paused and drank her in again, he felt as if his pounding heart would explode with love and desire. He would probably see her only one more time.

One week later, April 24, 1864, Sunday: Sadie's kitchen

Sadie was seated at the table reading her Bible when Aaron entered the kitchen. "Good morning, Sadie. I thought you'd be at church?"

"No sur. I's got a terrible cough, so I decided I'd best stay home. Miss Constance wondered where ya was, but she went without ya." Sadie looked up at him and coughed.

"I'm sorry you're not feeling well." He sank onto the bench across from her. "But I need to talk to you alone." He reached into his pocket, pulled out a roll of bills, and laid them on the table. "I've saved $125. I won't see you again before we march. I want you to hide it away until all the food has been eaten and it's your last source to purchase food. You are not under any circumstances to tell her where you got it. Do you understand?"

"Yas'r," Sadie answered slightly confused. "But why don't ya want her to know?"

"Because I know how proud and independent she is. She'd never accept it." He looked down at the table and then slowly raised his eyes to meet hers, his face coloring. "I want to marry her, Sadie. If she ever agrees to have me, it must be because she loves me, not because she feels obligated to me. Therefore, I want you to put your hand on that Bible and swear to me that you'll never divulge the source of that money to her, and that you won't give it to her until all of your other resources are gone."

"But, Lieutenant Ames, how am I gonna do that? What'll I tell her?"

"Now, listen Sadie. A woman who's clever enough to catch a chicken thief and can read as well as you do, is smart enough to figure out a way. So," he demanded, thumping the Bible with his finger, "put your hand on that Bible and swear it to me."

Sadie reached her right hand out and placed it on the Bible. "I swear it," she said solemnly. She stood up and took the money to the pantry alcove.

Aaron paced the room restlessly until she returned. "Since today is the last time I'll see her, I brought another horse. I'm going to take her on a picnic."

"What!" Sadie exclaimed shocked. "It ain't proper for the two of y'all to go off unchaperoned. No sur. Ya ain't gonna do it."

Aaron turned to confront the irate tall black woman. "She's almost twenty-two years old and is capable of making decisions for herself."

"Oh, no she ain't. She ain't got no momma or daddy to make her act proper. I'm the only one she's got to protect her." She picked up the large iron frying pan from the stove and stalked towards him. Aaron took a step backwards and found himself pinned against the wall. "Y'all is so much in love, I know what's gonna happen if y'all is alone," she lectured with the reds of her eyes glowing and the frying pan raised above her head. "What's she gonna do if ya dishonor her and she gets in the fam'ly way, an' you's killed? We don't need another mouth 'round here to feed." Aaron fully expected fire to flame forth from her nostrils when she breathed in his face.

"Sadie," he protested. "I'm trustworthy."

"You'd better be," she spewed forth, then stabbed her finger firmly against his chest. "'Cause when ya come back here, you's gonna have to put your hand on that Bible, an' swear to me that mah baby's virtue an' honor is still intact. Do ya understand me, Mista Yankee?"

"You've made yourself perfectly clear." He attempted to slide past her.

"And if ya can't swear it, you's gonna have to deal with me!" Sadie wielded the frying pan.

Aaron managed to slip away from her and darted to the door. "I'll wait for her outside," he said relieved to be out of her reach.

* * *

Constance scrambled through the carts on East Street in the warm sunshine when she saw Aaron waiting at the back gate. She paused to let an ambulance creak past her. "Aaron, I was worried about you when you didn't arrive in time for church." She collapsed into his arms.

He hugged her and kissed her lightly. "I couldn't get away sooner. It's been a week of frenzied activity. Yesterday Sheridan reviewed the entire cavalry outside of town, and Friday General Grant reviewed the Second Corps at the field below Cole's Hill. We drill and practice shooting for hours. There's too much preparation necessary and too little time." He paused and searched the depths of her enormous sapphire eyes. "Constance, this is our last day together. I will not be permitted to leave camp again."

She gasped when she heard the inevitable news, her eyes filling with pain. "I was afraid you'd tell me that…but it's a beautiful day. Let's enjoy it to the fullest."

"After some tall talking and bribery, I managed to borrow a horse from one of my hut mates. We're going on a picnic. I feel compelled to take you to Cedar Mountain and share my experiences there with you."

She reeled with unfettered joy at the thought of finally having some privacy with him. "I'd like that very much. I'll go get my riding gloves and tell Sadie."

"I've already told Sadie," he cautioned as he held her arm. "My ears are still burning from the lecture. She's in a foul mood at the moment."

Constance shot him a conspiratorial wink and nodded. "Thanks for the warning. I'll only be a minute."

The warm breeze made Constance feel airborne while they rode south past Greenwood. When they neared the Federal camp, she watched wagons being loaded. A few Yankees tore down their huts while others put up tents. Aaron explained that the army had to get used to sleeping outside again. Soldiers gawked at the couple who rode through the mud and stumps. At the perimeter of the encampment, Aaron stopped to address the soldiers at the picket station.

"Where are you headed?" a soldier in his thirties inquired.

"We're going to the Cedar Mountain battlefield. I'm Lieutenant Ames of General Custer's staff," Aaron explained while Constance endured the soldier's crude stare.

The officer shook his head and smiled slightly. "You must be aware that once you go outside of our lines you're open game for Rebel bushwhackers. We're not supposed to let any Rebel ladies pass through our lines."

"I'm not concerned about bushwhackers during the day," Aaron said coolly. "I'll take responsibility for seeing that this lady returns to our lines."

"Very well. But, remember you go at you own risk." Aaron spurred his horse and the two of them rode forward. "Have fun, Lieutenant," the soldier called behind them. They took the horses to a trot while they passed Val Verde. The blue mountains loomed on the horizon in the crystal clear air.

Aaron stopped at the intersection with the Mitchell's road. "It's important to me that I share with you what happened on that fateful day. Our artillery was lined up along this road. I spent most of the morning in that ravine," he said pointing, "sweltering in the sun. When the Confederates arrived they had sense enough to move their artillery up on the side of the mountain." He pointed towards the Slaughter's house. "That wise decision gave them the victory."

Constance followed his movements and understood the tactics. "I can see that our artillery would cover everything from that position. What happened next? I know the battle raged around that house, which belongs to my good friends, the Crittendens." She nodded towards the dilapidated house in the distance. "Show me where you fell."

"Follow me." He rode forward until he stopped his horse in the middle of an unattended field and dismounted. "This field was covered with dead and wounded men." He lifted her down from the sidesaddle. She took off her riding hat and followed him while he walked through the field studying the lay of the land. Finally, he took her hand and stood on a small knoll. "This is the spot. I'm certain of it. This is where I fell. The Tenth Maine was ordered to make a suicidal charge across this field while our comrades were retreating. The Confederates had taken a position in those trees and on that side of the field," he said with a glazed look of despair, pointing.

"My God, Aaron, you had no protection. You were caught in the cross-fire," she exclaimed with a hitch in her voice while she gripped his hand tightly.

"Men were falling in every direction." He gestured sharply with his hands. "I felt a pain in my left arm, but I continued to fire my gun. Then suddenly a shell exploded behind me and I was thrown forward with an intense pain in my...well you know where," he said with a slight smile. "I fell with such impact that my right arm was twisted. Then another man fell on top of me and I felt it snap."

She slid her arms around his waist. "Oh, Aaron, how you must have suffered."

He looked down at her long face and rested his arm on her shoulder. "It was pure hell! I'm determined that the bravery and sacrifice of the Tenth Maine must be commemorated. If I survive this war, I'll see that a monument is placed on this spot."

"Yes, I think you should. Those men can't be forgotten."

"Constance, the reason I brought you here is because I want you to understand how you saved my life, even before I reached your house."

She searched the depths of his eyes, confused. "I'm not following you."

He put his hands on her face and lifted it towards him. "When you defiantly marched out to meet us at the farm, I was impressed with your courage. But the beauty of your face overwhelmed me. Your huge deep blue eyes, long lush lashes," he said tracing his fingers around her eyes, "your turned up nose and delicate mouth," he touched each feature, "and your white china skin." The back of his hand caressed her cheek. "When I saw you that day at the train station crying after your father was sent to prison, I was filled with compassion and longed to comfort you. While I lay on this spot," he said pointing to the ground, "I was weighed down by the dead bodies piled on top of me. My body was riddled with pain, and the sun beat unmercifully on my face. I felt myself weakening from loss of blood and dehydration. I needed something to hang on to. Something to give me the will to live." Her heart melted as she saw the tears in his eyes. "Nothing seemed to help me until I saw the vision of your face. Then I knew I had to live to see your face again. If I could keep focusing on your face, I knew I would hang on."

"Oh, Aaron, this seems difficult to believe." She put her arms around his shoulders. "And yet I do remember you repeating 'face' when you were delirious."

His mouth molded over hers softly and then he held her head firm against his muscular chest. "All night long I listened to the cries and moans of the wounded. The sun beat on my face again in the morning. You had warned me about the wrath of A .P. Hill, and I witnessed it as he led the charge across this field. But that morning he heard my weak cry for water, and came to my rescue. I also witnessed his mercy."

"That sounds like Powell."

"Then he had his men carry me over to the edge of the woods and put me in the shade with two canteens." He led her across the field to the woods. "There," he said pointing, "is where I lay all day, watching the Rebels bury their dead in that ravine. I kept focusing on your face. Of course I was unconscious when they finally brought me to town. I don't think it was a coincidence that you found me and took me in. It was Divine Providence. God heard my cry and sent you to me to save me. When I finally came out of my delirium, I thought I was in heaven. There was your face. It was like a dream."

Tears trembled on her eyelids. "Perhaps God was using me. I only know that I was overcome with compassion when I saw you. I couldn't let you die after the kindness you had shown us."

"I fell in love with you, and even though I realized that you were infatuated with John Pelham, I couldn't get you out of my mind when I left."

"I'll admit that I admired your physique and thought you were the most desirable man I'd ever seen. You seemed like a man of integrity and I found myself enjoying your company. However, I pushed those romantic feelings to the back of my mind and denied them because you were a Yankee." She paused and caressed his bronze face. "You're right, I was infatuated with John. However, if you had been a Rebel, you'd have given him stiff competition."

"That's encouraging." He kissed her softly on the forehead. "I saw Pelham fall at Kelly's Ford. I could take no pleasure in the death of one so brave, but it did give me hope of winning you."

"I'll be honest with you and tell you that I loved John, but not as deeply as I love you. I was crushed by his death. I knew that I'd never love passionately again and what's more, I was afraid to let myself care about any one."

"I appreciate your openness. It wasn't a coincidence that I was able to get to you when you were wounded. I moved forward to sight for the artillery and to be close so I could see you, but it was with God's help that I saved you." His hands moved slowly down the length of her back.

"I completely agree with you, Aaron. I have never doubted that God sent you to me. It was a miracle and this time it was you who gave me the will to live." She moved her hands gently over his broad chest. "You touched me so deeply that week that you nurtured me. I fell hopelessly in love with you. You taught me the true meaning of love. It means giving of yourself unselfishly for the welfare of the other, even if it means risking your life." She pulled his rugged face towards her and kissed him again and again. "I never dreamed I could love so intensely, especially so soon after John's death. It's a miracle… that I can't explain. I'll always honor John's memory, but you'll never live in his shadow." She stared into the depths of his compelling eyes. "My love for you is infinite. You're the true love of my life."

"That means everything to me." His sensuous lips brushed over her neck. "I think I must be dreaming again. I don't believe it was a coincidence that Sadie was ill and kept you from leaving Culpeper. It was fate."

She smiled seductively with a twinkle in her eye. "Perhaps, but I would have stayed in Culpeper even if Sadie hadn't been sick. It would simply have been harder to come up with an excuse. You told me to wait for you, and I'd have done it regardless."

"Do you really mean that?" She nodded yes. "I brought you here to bare my soul to you, to tell you my innermost thoughts. I believe that God has brought us together for a reason. We were meant for each other."

She consumed him with her eyes. "I'm immensely touched by your revelations." Her lips turned up in a teasing smile. "And I believe we're both hopeless romantics."

He offered her a sudden, arresting smile. "May I suggest that we get out of the hot sun now, and find a cool spot by a stream for our picnic?"

"What a wonderful idea. We're not far from Crooked Run. Surely, there are few trees left to shade us." They moseyed towards the horses grazing in the field, their hips touching lightly.

"This looks like a perfect spot," Aaron proclaimed when they rode into a small level open grassy area beneath a large oak tree.

Constance viewed the mountain laurel and large bushes surrounding the bubbling stream. "It's beautiful!" she chirped after he helped her down. "Look at the ferns and lady slippers." The wooded canopy allowed small patches of sunlight to dance on the rapidly flowing water.

Aaron took the blanket from his saddlebag and spread it in the tall grass at the base of the tree while Constance picked flowers. "I've got cheese, bread, wine, and lemon pound cake baked by my sister." He placed the sack on the blanket, took off his hat and jacket, and motioned to her to sit down.

She removed her riding gloves and hat and positioned herself on the blanket beside him, arranging the folds of her skirt. Attired in a simple faded navy dress, she was glad she was not wearing a hoop. Hundreds of blackbirds and crows raised a loud racket in the trees above them. "It appears that we are not alone." She stared up at the noisy flock of birds. "One expects ants and flies at a picnic, but not intruders as loud as those birds."

He clapped his hands loudly, prompting the birds to fly out of the trees and flutter in all directions. While he spread the slices of cheese and bread before them, the flock settled back into the trees. "I don't believe my attempt to rid us of our unwelcome guests was successful." He uncorked the wine.

"That's because our land has been practically denuded of trees. There are few places for them to roost and the crows feast on the dead carcasses of horses and other live-stock." She took a bite of bread and cheese.

He poured the wine into two metal cups and handed them to her while he replaced the cork on the bottle. Taking one cup from her, he lifted it up and touched it to her cup. "To our love," he said as a toast, their eyes locked.

"It is a wondrous miracle. I'll drink to that." She sipped the wine, aching with an inner longing. "Aaron, tell me what you're feeling deep inside you about the impending campaign."

He ate and sipped the wine thoughtfully, attempting to control his burning desire. "I'm disillusioned with Lincoln and the way the war's been conducted. Grant's arrival has mustered little enthusiasm. Our army, though almost twice as large as Lee's, contains mostly conscripts and green soldiers. I'd like to think we would march straight to Richmond and end the war quickly. However, I'm afraid it's going to be a long bloody campaign. I have too much respect for the talents of the wily Lee and the fighting ability of his seasoned veterans." He picked up another piece of bread and cheese and ate. "I fully realize that any Rebel would shoot me in a instant to get my boots and the food in my knapsack. I've watched large groups of them being baptized in the Rapidan and know they're willing to die for their independence. The thought of those crazed, gaunt, hollow eyed soldiers charging out of the woods screaming the Rebel yell makes my blood turn to ice."

"Is there any way that I can convince you to stop fighting?" she questioned hopefully between mouthfuls.

"No, I'm too committed to the preservation of the Union and have intense loyalty to Autie. I'd never consider desertion or shirking my duty. However, I signed up for two years and can muster out in late June."

"Will you?" she asked anxiously.

He stared at her intently, weighing his answer. "I can't say. It depends on what transpires between now and then. I'm convinced that we'll eventually triumph and that our cavalry is now superior. The South is suffering from lack of horses. When my time is up, I suppose I'll have to wage a debate with my conscience to determine my future actions." He finished his wine. "Did you get enough to eat?"

"Yes," she said with an alluring smile. "Let's save the cake and rest of the wine for later."

He stood up and picked up the half-empty bottle. "I think I'll put this at the edge of the stream to cool."

She watched the movement of his athletic body with eager anticipation. He returned to the blanket, slouched opposite her, reached his hand to the back of her head, pulled off the net holding her chignon, then pulled out the pins. When her hair cascaded down on her shoulders, he took his hands and ran them through her silky locks. She stared at him silently, her eyes smoldering with desire. His hand moved to the back of her neck and under her chin, pulling her lips towards his. They kissed gently moving their lips softly together. She slid her arms around his neck and the intensity quickened. He lay down on the blanket and without any coaxing she was beside him. Constance burned at the contact of his muscular body against her. The passion of their kisses made the cackling of the birds fade further and further into oblivion. She parted her lips to the determined demanding thrust of his tongue. The heat of the sun beating on her fed the fire raging within her. Her fingers absorbed the texture of his tawny hair. Time stood still.

She felt the full force of his body after he rolled over on top of her. When he moved his hands over her body, she moaned with pleasure. His fingers caressed her, teased her, made her throb with excitement. She wanted to know more. Ready to surrender, she passionately returned his every caress.

Burning with a scorching heat, Aaron sensed that she would not stop him this time. With ragged breath, he finally rolled on his side and whispered, "Constance, marry me right now. We can ride into our lines and quickly find a chaplain." She slowly opened her smoldering eyes and looked at him shocked. His head was propped on his elbow just inches above her while his other hand rested on her abdomen. "Then we can consummate our love properly, without guilt."

She stared at him silently for a minute, unable to focus, to think. "Aaron, dearest Aaron. We said no promises…no obligation. Remember? As deeply as I love you, I…I can't marry you. At least, not now." The hurt and disappointment in his eyes tore at her heart. Breathing rapidly, she reached her hand up and unbuttoned his shirt. "But we can still…be intimate."

He hesitated, inhaled sharply as she pulled his shirt open and ran her fingers across his chiseled chest. He took her hand and kissed it, one finger at a time. His mind struggled to control his raging passion. Damn Sadie! Her tirade had penetrated his conscience. Struggling, he sat up slowly, looked down at her with eyes brimming with love, and said in a husky whisper, "Constance, I'm four years older than you are and I've sown plenty of wild oats. As passionately as I want you, you're too precious to me for that." He took a deep breath and brushed her hair back from her rosy face. "I will not dishonor you. When I take you, it'll be as my wife. Then you'll be mine and mine alone, forever." She was breathless—speechless—couldn't believe he'd given her the proper answer, didn't want to hear the right answer—not at this moment.

He took her arms and pulled her up. "Lean up against the tree," he ordered. She pushed backwards until her back was against the trunk of the large oak tree. He stretched out with his head in her lap. "Now, I'll have to behave myself," he said with a roguish grin. "You told me earlier that I was the true love of your life and yet you won't marry me. It doesn't make sense. You must share your innermost thoughts with me. I've bared my heart and soul to you and now you owe it to me to do likewise."

Her eyes grew misty as she stared down into his hazel eyes. "Yes, you're right. I must attempt to explain my turmoil to you." She tenderly moved her fingers over his face. "There's a war raging inside me between my heart and my mind. My heart tells me that you're the perfect mate for me. I know that I'll never love anyone else as intensely as I love you. You seem to know and understand my every desire, and what's more, you accept my flaws. Most importantly, you don't attempt to dominate me and actually seem to enjoy our heated debates. You respect my intellect. I've often wondered if I'd ever marry because of my independence. I questioned if I could love any man enough to surrender my property ownership and all rights to him. There's no doubt that I love and trust you enough to do that."

"So far, I haven't heard any problem. You know that I favor equal rights for women. I'm such a radical that I even believe women should be given the right to vote."

"And that makes you even more perfect." She moved her eyebrows together in consternation. "But, my mind tells me that I can never marry you as long as you fight for the army that's destroying my homeland. Our worlds are still at war."

"But the war will end and I'm not going to fight forever."

"That may be true. But, you've admitted that your family, except for your sister, strongly disapproves of our relationship. If you marry me, you may be disinherited, and I refuse to come between you and your family."

"Being disinherited won't stop me from marrying you. My family will love you as soon as they meet you. I'm certain of it."

"Aaron, I can never live in the North," she said bitterly. "I couldn't tolerate watching the gloating, wealthy people who've destroyed all that I have. The hatred and fury inside of me would explode and I'd be an embarrassment to you, as I was with the Custers. I don't want to be an albatross around your neck. You're bright and talented and you have a world of opportunity ahead of you if you go home after the war. I cannot stand in your way."

"I'm certain that your feelings will soften in time. Working together, we can achieve anything we want. I admit I've dreamed of taking you home. Of course our opportunities will be greater in the North," he pleaded. "Be open-minded."

"I'll never live in the North," she vowed with fire in her eyes, "and I can't ask you to return to this land of devastation. I believe that you've asked me to marry you out of the passion of the moment. When the war ends, I suspect you'll see things more realistically and I don't want you to feel any obligation to me. The problem is inside of me, Aaron. You're not the problem. You must understand that," she concluded on the verge of tears, her voice breaking.

"I believe our love is much stronger than the hate you feel. It will eventually prevail and we'll resolve these petty differences. But I wonder if you've told me everything. I suspect that your involvement with Robert Beckam is the real problem."

"No, Aaron," she said frustrated, "that has nothing to do with it. Let me try to explain." She paused in thought for a few minutes and continued to touch him gently. "I met Robert before the war and I have the greatest admiration and respect for him. He's a wonderful person. However, I realize now that I was never in love with him. He remained loyal to me even after my involvement with John. When he was given command of Stuart's Horse Artillery, I felt he needed my support with such an awesome responsibility. He seemed to need me and, I believe, hoped to marry me. I found myself growing fonder of him and hoped that I'd fall in love with him one day. He appeared to be the logical choice for me since I never hoped to love passionately again. But, then you came dashing back into my life and swept me off of my feet. Robert sensed my aloofness after the Bristoe Campaign. I tried to explain it using mother's loss as an excuse. I did everything possible to put you out of my mind. I kept telling myself that I would forget you eventually. I never wanted to hurt Robert. But now, I'm the one who is a prisoner of your love." She leaned over and kissed him softly, tenderly.

"Um," he sighed. "I'm delighted with that revelation. I'm sorry I pushed you, but I needed to be sure. We may not have resolved everything, but at least I understand your thinking better."

She reached around and picked up a piece of pound cake. "Dessert?" she giggled and then broke a piece off and put it in his mouth.

They laughed and teased together. She fed him two slices of the cake until bird dung splattered across his face. "Holy shit!" He bolted up and attempted to wipe it off with his sleeve.

Unable to control her giggling, Constance answered, "I don't think there's anything holy about it."

"I'm going to wash my face," he chuckled. "Besides, it's time to retrieve the rest of the wine." Constance stood up and stretched her back while she watched him saunter down the slight slope to the edge of the stream a few feet away. He knelt down and splashed water in his face and she surveyed the beautiful canopy of green around her.

Abruptly, her eyes froze on the glint of light reflected from metal in the bush several feet in front of Aaron.

"No!" she screamed as she lunged to throw herself between the gun barrel and Aaron. When the shot rang out, she felt a sharp sting caused by the bullet grazing her shoulder. Instantly on his feet, Aaron reached for his gun.

"Take your hand off that gun or you and the lady are dead," a soldier ordered. Two men in blue dashed up to him from the bushes to his left. Surveying the situation, he felt he could take them in a fair fight, but refused to endanger Constance. Seething, he slowly raised his hands. A third man appeared from the bush in front of Constance.

"What's the meaning of this?" Aaron demanded.

"We're scouts for Jeb Stuart and you're a prisoner of war." The man closest to Constance removed Aaron's gun.

"No, please, I beg you, don't take this man prisoner," Constance pleaded.

"No self-respecting Rebel woman would be out in the woods with a Yankee," the tall soldier snarled, then spat on the ground.

"Who commands this group?" she begged. When the tall man nodded, she continued, "I must speak to you in private. I have an urgent and personal matter to discuss with you." Aaron gaped in stunned silence. What was she up to?

"Very well," the tall soldier agreed. "Keep a close watch on him boys." He swaggered through the bushes to a spot out of earshot. "Now, what's this urgent matter?"

"My name is Constance Armstrong. I'm a close friend of Frank Stringfellow. He's like a brother to me. Do you know him?"

"Yep. Everybody knows Stringfellow."

Encouraged, she continued, "I've been spying for him and faithfully serving our cause. I risked my life to take a message to him about Kilpatrick's raid. In fact, I even had to kill a Yankee picket. At this very moment, my servant is working in Grant's headquarters. We're passing information on to Channing Smith. As a personal favor, I ask you to spare this man."

He eyed her suspiciously. "If what you say is true, how did you kill the picket?"

"He attempted to have his way with me. I choked him with a wire when he pulled his pants down, and then I slit his throat."

"Well, I'll be damned!" the soldier exclaimed slapping his leg. "You must be the one. We all wondered how you'd killed him. You're some tough lady, Miss Armstrong. But why do you want to save this damn Yankee?"

"He risked his life to save mine during the shelling of our town. He's an honorable man and very dear to me. You and I both know that one more man in prison isn't going to determine the outcome of this war. Take the horses and anything else you want, but please don't take him. I beg you," she pleaded with fervor.

The soldier understood the intensity of her plea. "Very well, Miss Armstrong. You've served our cause well. I'll agree to your request for mercy."

"Oh, thank you! You're a kindhearted man," she exclaimed with tears in her eyes.

When the two of them returned to the others, the leader said, "Strip out of those clothes, Yank. This lady has persuaded me not to take you in, but we're taking everything else." Aaron stared at Constance with questioning eyes. She smiled slightly when he took off his shirt. He sat down and pulled off his boots and socks while the other two scouts admired the horses. "Nether garments too," the leader ordered.

"Surely you aren't going to leave him without…any…you know…" Constance questioned.

"His are in better shape than ours, but we'll trade. Brown, you're the tallest. Come on over here and trade trousers with this Yank." When Brown approached, he motioned to Constance to turn around. She complied.

The leader shortly announced, "We're through, Miss Armstrong." She spun around to see Aaron standing in tattered patched pants five inches too short. The Rebels devoured the last two pieces of cake, rolled up the blanket, and mounted their horses.

"See you on the battlefield, Yank," they hollered as they rode through the woods with the two captured horses.

Aaron walked to her and moved his finger over the bloody tear in the arm of her dress. "Don't you know you could have been killed!"

"It's only a scratch. I didn't have time to think about it. I couldn't let them shoot you!" She wrapped her arms around his waist and pressed her lips against his hairy bare chest, his nipples. "Besides, now we're even."

He lifted her face toward him and kissed her repeatedly. "Damn it, Constance, we're not keeping score," he lectured while he kissed her neck. "Don't you ever do anything that dangerous again. You've proven your love for me above any shadow of a doubt." He paused and looked into the depths of her dancing eyes. "What I want to know is how you convinced them to let me go."

She smiled innocently. "I have friends in high places, and I used my feminine wiles." She enjoyed moving her hands over his naked torso.

"I don't think I believe that. Whatever you said had to be communicated in private." He slanted one eyebrow, eyeing her suspiciously. "You're a spy, aren't you?"

"Aaron, what you don't know can't hurt you. Your safety has always been my primary concern."

He frowned at her and shook his head. "Somehow, I'm not surprised. My first impulse is to turn you over my knee and spank you." His full lips turned up in a captivating smile. "But since your activities have kept me from rotting away in a filthy prison, I believe I'll thank God for your espionage instead."

She chuckled, reached into her pocket and handed him the small box that had once held the bracelet he gave her. "I have something for you to wear above the waist now that you've been stripped naked. I'm glad I didn't give it to you sooner. They'd have taken it."

He opened the box and pulled out a gold chain with a cross on it. "Um…it's a beautiful…appropriate gift."

"My great-grandmother gave it to my grandfather for protection when he left to fight in the Revolution. He always felt that it brought him home safely. I pray that it will do the same for you." She took the chain and hooked it around his neck.

Moving his fingers over the crucifix, he said, "I'm proud to wear an heirloom of your family. You know that my faith is strong. I don't fear death. I know I'm saved through the precious blood of my Savior. But… you've given me so much to live for. What I fear most is…separation from you." He kissed her on the forehead.

"I feel the same way." She slowly moved her fingers up his neck. Suddenly a thought struck her that made her eyes sparkle. "You know, Aaron, the scouts forgot one thing…the wine's still in the creek! Let's celebrate your escape from prison by drinking the rest of it."

Aaron felt the sun beat unmercifully on his head and shoulders while the two of them walked along the dusty road towards town. He winced when a sharp rock jabbed into his bare foot.

"Now you can understand the commitment of our men," she commented, holding his hand. "Many of them walked all the way to Gettysburg and back without shoes."

"Believe me, I admire the courage of the Rebels. However, our last day together hasn't turned out exactly as I planned it. First you refused to marry me, next a bird crapped in my face, and finally I was stripped of everything by a bunch of renegade Rebels."

"My poor darling," she murmured sympathetically.

"Never have I been so humiliated," he ranted. "You have no concept of the abuse and hazing I'm going to face. The loss of two horses is a terrible disgrace. I'll be lucky if I'm not court-martialed."

"You risked it all to share your experiences at Cedar Mountain with me. Take solace in the fact that our hearts and souls have never been closer."

"I'm willing to accept all of the humiliation of the day because you proved the depth of your love for me. Constance, won't you at least agree to an engagement?"

"I promise you that I'll wait faithfully for you until the end of the war. If you still want me, we'll discuss plans for our future. The word engagement implies obligation, and I don't want you to feel any obligation to me."

He stopped and looked down at her, frustrated. "Of course I'll still want you. I'm in love with you and as long as there's breath in my body, I'll return to you. I now consider us engaged."

"Very well," she conceded while taking his hand, "call it whatever makes you happy, but we still have many matters to resolve."

When they approached the picket station, the same officer was on duty. "Why, Lieutenant! Looks like a few Rebel bushwhackers paid you a social call. What did you do, hide behind your lady's skirt for protection?" he cackled. Constance felt Aaron's shame and embarrassment.

"Thanks for the ride," Aaron said after he helped Constance down from the wagon. Clad in a borrowed shirt and old tight boots, he opened the gate for her. "I've got to get back to camp and face the consequences. But first, I must tell Sadie good-bye."

When the two of them walked into the kitchen, Sadie picked up her Bible and thrust it in front of Aaron. He put his left hand on it and raised his right hand. "I, Aaron Adams Ames, do solemnly swear in the sight of Almighty God and Sadie Jordan that I have returned one Constance Rixey Armstrong safely, with her honor intact. I furthermore swear that I will return and marry her, if she will have me."

Sadie's face broke into a radiant smile revealing her large pearly teeth.

"What is the meaning of this?" Constance demanded irritated.

"I told you I'm no saint." Aaron took his hand off the Bible. "I simply didn't want to have my head bashed in by that frying pan." He pointed to the large iron skillet.

"Sadie, surely you didn't threaten him! How dare you interfere?" Constance scolded. Sadie hung her head in repentance and mumbled, "We jist had a little talk, that's all."

"Take good care of her, Sadie." Aaron rested his hand on the faithful servant's shoulder. The old woman looked up at him and smiled affectionately. Now that Constance was safe and he was leaving, she supposed she could be nice to him. "May the good Lawd watch over ya, Lieutenant Ames."

He took Constance's hand and led her outside. They both knew that this was their final farewell. Neither could speak. He stared down at her in the soft twilight. Her eyes filled with tears and her lower lip trembled. His vision became blurred as he watched a tear trickle down her cheek. He wiped the tear and caressed her face tenderly. She reached up, touched his face and then traced her fingertips over the gold cross. Unable to speak, she mouthed the words, "love you." He nodded and mouthed back, "me too." He felt a tear sliding down his cheek, then mustered all of his strength to do the unavoidable. What he had to do now was far harder than charging head on into Jeb Stuart's cavalry. He turned and walked away from her. Tears cascaded down his face while he staggered out the back gate and turned up East Street. He couldn't turn around and look at her, no, couldn't do that. If he did, he'd never be able to leave. He struggled to put one foot in front of the other. Concentrate...that's all he had to do...just keep putting one foot in front of the other...try not to think of her.

Constance rushed to the back fence and strained to watch him as long as possible. She leaned over the fence sobbing...caught one last glimpse of his broad back. When he was out of sight, she put her hand to her mouth, ran to the cabin, threw herself on her bed and wept hysterically. Sadie heard her from the kitchen and came to her. Rubbing her back, she said, "It's gonna be alright, honey."

Sobbing—gasping for breath, Constance blurted, "I'm afraid...I'll never see him...again."

Sadie continued to rub her back for a long while, but the sobbing didn't stop. "You's jist gotta cry it all out." She got up and left Constance alone in her misery.

20

If It Takes All Summer

April 20 – September 9, 1864

"I propose to fight it out on this line if it takes all summer."
Ulysses S. Grant, May 11, 1864, Spotsylvania Court House

Six days later, April 30, 1864: Grant's headquarters

Sadie's mind raced when she carried the tray into the stately hall of Grant's headquarters. Fully aware that Grant and Meade were discussing plans for the spring offensive behind the closed doors of the parlor, she contemplated a scheme to overhear them. Thus far, her vigilance had failed to answer the critical questions: when would the army move and in what direction? She smiled sweetly at the staff officers seated in the hall. "Good mornin' gent'men. It's a fine day today. I thought ya'll might be hungry so I brung ya some coffee an' biscuits." She set the tray on the oval Queen Anne dining room table. The tantalizing aromas drew the three soldiers into the room.

"I believe we could use some refreshment," one said. The three of them poured mugs of coffee and enjoyed the flaky biscuits. Sadie traipsed into the hall and with her back to the soldiers, took the pair of scissors from her pocket and cut a button off her faded calico dress. She nonchalantly threw the button on the floor and watched it roll towards the parlor doors. Immediately, she dropped to her hands and knees and crawled towards the doors, searching the floor.

The blood pounded in her throat while she crept across the oriental rug towards her destination. She recognized Grant's voice. "I understand your reluctance to get caught again in the wilderness area, but it is the closest route to our supply lines. It's the way we must go. My mind is made up. You will order the army to commence movement after midnight on the fourth."

"Then we will cross the Rapidan at Germanna and Ely's Fords," Meade conceded.

Sadie felt the eyes of one of the soldiers watching her suspiciously after she reached for the button. She stood up modestly holding the bodice of her dress together. "Sorry, one of mah buttons popped off," she explained as he stalked towards her.

Eyeing the button in her hand skeptically, he hesitated, and finally said, "I see. Move along now. We don't want you in this hall."

"Oh, yas'r. I's sorry. I didn't mean to do nothin' wrong," she said apologetically and fled to the back door. Once outside, she leaned against the door to catch her breath. Her heart pounding, she decided to hustle to the bookstore and give Constance this vital information. Amazed at her good fortune, Sadie maneuvered briskly through the crowd of soldiers towards her destination. Confederate scouts had been making contact with Constance daily in search of new information on the intended move of the Yankees. At last she had the answer for them.

Two days later, May 2, 1864: Clark Mountain

The burden of responsibility rested heavily on Robert E. Lee's shoulders. He stood for the last time on the summit of Clark Mountain with the commanding generals of the Confederate army, reflecting on the many treks he had made to this scenic mountaintop to survey the camps of his adversary. Only days before he had told President Davis that he hoped those people over there were not as formidable a force as they appeared to be. Davis seemed to comprehend the changes in the Federal camp and the buildup of their strength. Nevertheless, he still expected Lee to hold them off like he had done so many times before. From the reports of his scouts and his own visual appraisal of the camps, Lee estimated at least a 100,000 Federals would march to confront his 60,000 ragged veterans.[i] His eyes glazed over at the memory of the adoration expressed by his men when he recently reviewed the troops following Longstreet's return. They had pushed forward to touch him and his horse as if they were sacred. He knew these men were prepared to unflinchingly do his bidding.

He listened patiently while Longstreet, Hill, and Ewell pointed and debated the direction of the Union movement. Despite signs of activity in other directions, Lee ultimately asserted, "Gentlemen, it is my belief that the movement will be around our right by way of Germanna and Ely's Fords." Pointing dramatically for them, the distinguished general continued, "If so, it will be to our advantage. If we can attack them while they are still snarled in the wooded wilderness area, it will negate the superiority of their artillery. I expect the march to begin within two days. Have your men ready to move at an instant's notice."

Two days later, May 4, 1864: Front porch of the Virginia House

Constance and Millie Payne rocked in the chairs on the porch of the hotel, each holding handkerchiefs to their noses to avoid the dust stirred up by the gigantic migration. Neither had gotten much sleep the preceding night due to the ceaseless noise caused by the marching army after midnight. It now appeared that most of the Yankees had left town. Constance's emotions seemed out of control when she contemplated the sudden change in her life. Too depressed to eat since Aaron's departure, she prayed constantly for the success of the Confederate army and his survival. Although delighted to get back into her house again, she knew chances for earning money would be drastically reduced now, and little food would be available for purchase. The two young women wondered if they would continue to be social outcasts because of their Yankee beaus.

"I think most of them are gone now. I wonder if this is the end of the war for us? Will soldiers ever stop marching through Culpeper?" Constance mused.

Millie nodded. "I pray it's so."

"Look!" Constance nodded towards a group of horsemen riding towards them from Grant's headquarters. "It's Grant and his staff!" Mounted on his handsome bay, Cincinnati, Grant rode at the head of his staff. Attired in his best frock coat, a blue waistcoat, a black hat with a gold cord, and a blue-and gold silk sash around his waist, his appearance

---

[i] In reality, the Federal force finally numbered 118,700.

was more impressive than in the past. His face wore an expression of grim determination as he clenched a cigar in the corner of his mouth. His cold stare gave Constance a feeling of foreboding. "He looks like he'd butt his head into a brick wall," she whispered after he rode past them in the morning sun. "I believe I'll stroll down to the Rixey house to see if Sadie has finished her work there."

Constance arrived to find Sadie rummaging through the parlor. She held several pieces of partially burned paper in her hands. "I pulled these outta the fireplace soon as they left. I can't find nothin' else they left behind."

Constance took one of the pages and scanned it when they heard the sound of boots in the hall. Panicking, she and Sadie stuffed the papers under a chair cushion and turned anxiously towards four soldiers swaggering into the room, the brims of their hats concealing their faces.

"You two ladies are under arrest for being spies," one of the soldiers announced testily.

Constance's heart pounded wildly and Sadie gripped her hand in fear. They froze for several moments, listening to the ticking of the grandfather's clock, until the soldiers snickered. "And dang good ones, too!" a familiar voice said.

Finally realizing that her adversaries wore gray coats, Constance relaxed and giggled. "Frank, this is no time to cut a shine! What're you doing here so soon? Don't you know that Grant just left?"

"Indeed, I do. We've had the place staked out." He hugged her and kissed her on the cheek. "Excuse our little ruse. Did they leave us anything exciting?"

"Just these papers that Sadie pulled out of the fireplace." She retrieved the papers from under the chair cushion. Stringfellow read them quickly and then passed them on to Channing Smith, James Hansbrough, and R. H. Lewis.

"You ladies have done us a great service," Smith commented.

"Sadie, you've been a true Rebel. We're indebted to you for your brave service," Frank said affectionately. Sadie beamed proudly. "But, duty calls. We must ride ahead to catch up with Grant's entourage."

"Frank! That's too dangerous!" Constance protested.

"But it's also the best place to pick up vital information for Marse Robert. With our help, he'll stop Grant."

Constance's eyes met Frank's misty blue ones, twinkling with devilment. "Frank, please don't throw your life away needlessly. You're so dear to me." She wrapped her arms around his sparse body and held him for a minute.

"Thanks, Connie. I'll be careful." He winked at her playfully.

"We must be off. You ladies should hurry to the deserted Union camps to see what you can salvage. The other civilians are already scavenging in them," Smith said as the four scouts filed out the door. Constance followed them through the back door and waved her handkerchief until they disappeared down Coleman Street. With a lump in her throat, she wondered if any of these four intrepid men would survive.

Tears welled in Willis Madden's eyes while he watched the continuous flow of soldiers and wagons through his farm. The stifling dust formed a hovering cloud, distorting the view out of his windows. By midday, most of the army had trampled his farm en route to the two fords, sweeping away his little remaining food and fodder. At sixty five, he lived alone and depressed. His sons had fled to Alexandria to seek work, but he refused to leave the land he had labored so diligently to buy and make productive. His story was one of the cruel ironies of this unjust war. The very army that was supposedly fighting to bring freedom and justice to his race had ruined him.[1] His face twisting in anguish, he shook his head bitterly. For Willis Madden, there was no justice. He would survive by trapping game and farming, but the gnawing memory of his loss would cause him to die a broken man.[ii]

After finishing his lunch, Grant puffed on a cigar and chatted with his staff on the porch of a farmhouse overlooking Germanna Ford. He watched a steady flow of soldiers march across the pontoon bridges. In a good mood, he agreed to an interview by a reporter.

"General Grant, sir, how long do you estimate it will take you to capture Richmond?"

Grant blew smoke rings and answered calmly. "I will agree to be there in about four days."

The reporter gaped at him in stunned silence. The members of his staff, too, gawked in disbelief.

Realizing he had gotten their attention, Grant muttered almost as an aside, "That is, if General Lee becomes party to the agreement. But if he objects, the trip will undoubtedly be prolonged."[2] The staff and reporter burst into laughter, realizing the joke was on them.

Stevensburg: Stringfellow and Smith gazed out the window of a house in Stevensburg into the gathering darkness. Believing it would be safe to move on now, the four scouts thanked the Rebel family for harboring them safely for a few hours and resumed their ride towards Germanna Ford. In the darkness, a courier from Grant's headquarters rode up to them. Unable to discern their gray jackets, he innocently inquired. "I have a message from Grant's headquarters. Can you tell me the way to General Devens's cavalry command?"

"Certainly," Smith replied. "Go about a mile to Stevensburg, then go right about three miles and take a left at the first fork in the road."

"Thanks, I appreciate that."

"What's the headquarters news?" Stringfellow inquired.

"Gregg reported in that he has thus far seen no Rebels. He intends to press south with the Second Cavalry in the morning."

"We'll be in Richmond before those stupid Rebels figure out what's happening. Have a good night!" Stringfellow called to the courier.

The four scouts tried to muffle their snickers. "He'll spend the whole night looking for Devens's headquarters," Hansbrough chuckled.

"Yep, and at least we know what the Second Cavalry is up to," Stringfellow laughed. They trotted forward unmolested until they reached the pontoon bridge across the Rapidan. A brilliant white light on the south bank illuminated the way for them across

---

[ii]Willis Madden is buried in a grove of trees across the road and west of the Madden house, which is still a residence for his descendants.

the convenient pontoon bridges. "The Yanks were helpful to provide that light for us," Stringfellow quipped. The scouts saw several campfires when they clambered up the south bank. "Let's separate and investigate these encampments," Stringfellow ordered. "I'll take this closest one up the hill. We'll rendezvous at Parker's store on the Orange Plank Road in about two hours." The other three Rebels nodded in agreement and rode off in separate directions.

Grant shuffled the papers in his sparse headquarters tent until a staff officer walked in and saluted. "Sir, a scout has just reported that a portion of General Lee's army appears to be moving through the wilderness area towards us."

Surprised that Lee would have his army in motion so soon, Grant realized Burnside's Corps was stretched out along the Orange and Alexandria railroad from Manassas to Rappahannock Station. Contemplating the situation, he decided that perhaps it would be wise to order Burnside to join him at once. "Send a courier to General Burnside immediately. Order him to make a forced march until he reaches this place. Tell him to start his troops in the rear at once, and make a night march."

"Yes sir." The officer saluted and exited.

Stringfellow tied his horse to a tree and cautiously joined the group of Federals milling around. "Identify yourself soldier," a Yankee ordered.

Realizing his gray uniform was probably discernable in the faint firelight Stringfellow gave a ready reply. "One of General Stahl's scouts with a detail, on our way to the front." It was not unusual for Federal scouts to appear in camp wearing gray uniforms. General Stahl, a cavalry officer stationed in West Virginia, could feasibly be sending scouts to the front. He wasn't close enough to deny the information. Finding the explanation plausible, the Yankee stepped aside to let Stringfellow join the group. He threaded his way through the soldiers towards the large headquarters tent. With all the flags fluttering, it appeared to be the headquarters of an important general. Was it Grant or Meade? Crouching in the shadow cast by the large tent, the scout watched the soldiers moving and sitting around the flickering fire. A short man emerged from the tent and paused to light his cigar, his lighter reflecting the features of his face. It looked like Grant! A taller thin man walked up to him and saluted. He, too, lit a cigar and they ambled to the fire and sat on boxes. Stringfellow watched them clearly while the flickering campfire highlighted their profiles. Undoubtedly, it was Grant and Meade.

Seeing Grant's silhouette distinctly outlined in front of the flames, Stringfellow slowly pulled his pistol from the holster and cocked it. He lifted it in front of his face and took careful aim. With Grant squarely in his sights, beads of sweat appeared on his forehead when he attempted to pull the trigger. Somehow, he froze. Try as he might, his finger wouldn't move. His hand shook as Grant walked away into the shadows. He had lost the opportunity to kill Grant forever.[iii]

Shaken at his inability to act, he replaced the gun in the holster. What was wrong with him? Maybe he simply wasn't a cold-blooded murderer. Was he afraid to trade his life for Grant's? His lips twitched and he heard Connie's voice warning, "Don't throw your life away needlessly, Frank." He circulated back through the soldiers striving to overhear conversations. He picked up some talk of Burnside's Corps being ordered forward.

[iii] Stringfellow did have such an opportunity to kill Grant, but it ocurred later in the campaign.

At the appropriate hour, all four scouts arrived at the designated location. Stringfellow did not reveal his lost opportunity with Grant. A group of Union cavalry encountered the scouts when they rode through the woods towards their lines. "What cavalry is that?" a Yankee hollered in the darkness.

"Jeb Stuart's for all you know," Smith brazenly yelled back. Amidst the laughter they rode on undisturbed. Evidently it never occurred to the Union horsemen that they really were Jeb Stuart's scouts in their own gray uniforms.[3]

"It pays to be truthful," Smith chuckled to his comrades. Within hours they were reporting all the vital information they had learned about the distribution of Grant's army to Jeb Stuart.

Two days later, May 6, 1864: Armstrong town home

Constance pulled the needle through the patch over the rip in the divan. She glanced at Sadie, down on her hands and knees, scrubbing the red mud from the parlor floor. The Yankees had left the house a filthy wreck, but she refused to let it upset her. Elated to be back in her own house, she had enjoyed sleeping comfortably on her feather mattress. Her eyes fell on the stack of wool blankets and candles they had confiscated in the deserted enemy camp. Those items would come in handy later. Constance visualized the swarms of ravenous mountain people rummaging through the camp. Ragged rough-skinned men and women smoking pipes, they appeared gaunt and desperate.

She moved closer to her work, her eyes haunted by an inner pain. The mountain people had not bothered her nearly as much as the townspeople, who avoided her as if she had leprosy. Even though she had given food to many of them, she doubted they would ever accept her again. The pain of rejection was like a cold fist closing over her heart.

She looked up at the faint noise of guns in the distance. "Sounds like the two great armies have collided not too far away. I'm consumed with worry about Aaron."

"Ya been eatin' like a bird since he left. I think you's jist plum love sick."

"I feel empty without him, Sadie, as if part of me is missing." She tried to focus her attention again on her mending. She hoped Amanda and the boys would return soon. Perhaps their company would ease her loneliness.

Sadie stood up and stretched with her hands in the small of her back. She picked up the bucket and dirty cloth and plodded towards the kitchen to start supper. Constance sewed patches on the upholstered furniture for over an hour, while visions of Aaron drifted through her mind…his hazel eyes, the dimple in his chin, his bushy mustache, his muscular hairy chest. The clatter of running feet in the front hall shocked her from her daydreams.

"Aunt Connie, we're back!"

Constance jumped up before the two boys raced into the room. She dropped to her knees and wrapped an arm around each nephew. "Thank God you're safe! How I've missed you!" she blurted, then kissed each one. Both looked a little taller, but their dusty cheeks were sunken.

"We missed you too." Hudson hugged her. "It's good to be in our own house again!"

"Did you kill another Yankee, Aunt Connie?" David asked wide-eyed.

Amanda rushed into the room breathless. "Connie!" Constance sprang up and threw her arms around her thin pale sister. "We've prayed for you," Amanda whimpered through her tears.

"I hoped you were well," Constance sniffled. She looked into her sister's cow eyes. "Frank told me all of you were fine, which relieved my mind."

"And we hear you've served our cause nobly. You're a heroine, Connie. I even brought you a letter from General Stuart."

"What? I can't believe it!" Her mouth hung open in amazement, then she noticed Alex leaning against the doorframe. "Alex, what're you doing here? Are you ill?"

"No, No." He hugged her and kissed her on the cheek. "Amanda has persuaded me to transfer to Mosby's command since my three years are up with the Little Fork Rangers. This way I'll be closer to all of you." He stood back and scrutinized her from head to toe. "I must say that you look beautiful and healthy. I believe you've even gained some weight."

Constance suddenly felt guilty. "Yes, my health is excellent. I've been fortunate to make good money in the bookstore and purchase plenty of food. The four of you must be tired and hungry."

Amanda said, "We were amazed that the Yankees left so much behind in their camps. It was a challenge, but we carried what we could. It's all on the front stoop."

"Oh, there's so much to tell." Constance's voice rose in excitement. "But first boys, run to the kitchen and let Sadie know you're here so she can prepare a large dinner. Bring back something to drink." The two boys scurried past her. "Now, sit on the divan, the two of you, and we'll take turns talking. Amanda, you go first."

Amanda snuggled in beside Alex to tell her story. The Hume family had been kind enough to rent her and the boys a room. Orange had overflowed with refugees and families visiting the army. The common dedication to their cause bound them all together in close and supportive friendships. Food had been scarce, and they had all suffered from hunger but managed to survive and keep their spirits high. Dolly Hill had been most kind and invited her to visit in her house often. The two of them had grown devoted to each other. Dolly told her all about the trip she and Powell took to Richmond to witness her brother's triumphant return after his daring prison escape. Dolly reported that President and Mrs. Davis had adopted a little mulatto boy whom they knew was being abused. He lived in the White House of the Confederacy with them, enjoying the same privileges as their own children. Amanda and Alex attended the christening of the Hills' daughter, Lucy Lee, Robert E. Lee being the proud godfather. She and Dolly sang together frequently and enjoyed the many dances and concerts sponsored by the army. An enormous religious revival swept through the army, strengthening the men in their resolve to fight for their independence. She and Alex had been astounded when Frank wrote them about Constance's espionage and the killing of the picket. He cautioned them not to reveal Constance's identity in this escapade as it might endanger her. Amanda concluded with the sad news that she had suffered another miscarriage at the end of March.

Alex narrated that he had enjoyed having the boys so close at hand and had frequently taken them into his camp and allowed them to ride his horse. The biggest problem confronting the Confederate cavalry was lack of well-fed horses. Cavalrymen on the road today had reported a fierce battle underway in the thick underbrush of the wooded area near Chancellorsville. Alex felt the bloodiest days of the war were yet to come but hoped that if Lee could keep Grant from taking Richmond, Lincoln would not be re-elected. He intended to travel north in a few days to join Mosby. It would be a different and exciting kind of warfare and Alex vowed that he would never stop fighting as long as Yankees trod on Virginia soil. He vented his bitterness about the terrible changes wrought on the town and county by the Union occupation. Hundreds of buildings had been swept away and thousands of acres of farmland lay in ruins.

Then, he pulled a packet of letters out of his pocket and handed them to Constance, explaining that Robert had sent them. The Horse Artillery had been camped near Charlottesville and he had not seen Robert until late February when he brought the letters. Never had he seen a sadder or more depressed person than Robert when he revealed that he was leaving for Tennessee. Robert did not understand the reason for his transfer, but it appeared to be a promotion. Duty bound, he could not refuse the order. Robert hated leaving without seeing Constance or his family, and wondered if he would ever see them again. He confided to Alex that if he survived the war, he hoped to seek Constance's hand in marriage. Alex looked Constance in the eye and told her she could do no better than Robert Beckam.

Taken back by all of this, Constance thanked Alex for the letters. She wanted to shout joyously of her infinite love for Aaron, but suddenly it didn't seem appropriate. How would they react? Rather, she told them of her life with Sadie in the cabin, her refusal to take the oath, and Aaron's kind deed of purchasing food for her. They laughed when she explained how she and Sadie had gotten rid of Mrs. Bennett and listened spellbound to the tale of her trip to the duck rock. She concluded with a description of Sadie's activities at Grant's headquarters.

Sadie announced dinner, and they all rushed into the dining room. After they joined hands, Alex said the blessing: "Most gracious and loving heavenly Father, we humbly thank you for bringing us safely together once more as a family. Never again will we take for granted the simple blessing of gathering together around our own dining room table. Thank you for providing food to sustain our bodies. Help us to survive the famine, which has been caused by our aggressive and cruel enemy. Be with our brave army as it fights fearlessly for the God given right of self government. Give us the strength and courage to resist tyranny. We submit our lives to your will through the saving grace of our Blessed Lord Jesus. In His name we pray. Amen."

"Amen," they all repeated. Sadie dished out large bowls of bean soup .

The boys devoured their food voraciously. After several mouthfuls of soup, Hudson asked, "What are those lumps of white stuff?"

Sadie chuckled and explained that it was codfish shipped from Maine by Lieutenant Ames's family, and that they had food stacked clear to the ceiling in the kitchen. Constance elaborated that she had taken all of her profit from the bookstore plus the money from the sale of the silver and purchased as much food as possible. She admitted that she had already given quite a bit of it away to the starving townspeople.

Amanda said between gulps of soup, "You're right to share. We must all support one another. We couldn't have survived the winter without kind, generous friends. Don't eat so fast boys. You'll make yourselves sick."

"But we've been hungry for months," David protested.

"Just slow down," Alex said firmly.

"Aaron planted a garden for us before he left," Constance explained. "It should provide us with vegetables all summer. Surely the war will be over before winter."

Sadie set a large bowl of rice pudding on the table when the soup was gone. She dished it out into bowls and then topped it with blueberry sauce.

"That looks delicious," Hudson said with big eyes.

Sadie said proudly, "We's got canned milk and canned blueberries."

"Um, this is marvelous." Amanda savored a large spoonful. "Do you have sugar?"

"Yas'm. A little."

David rapidly devoured the whole bowl full. "More please?" he begged.

Sadie refilled his bowl and Alex cautioned him to slow down. In a very short time the entire cherished dessert had disappeared.

Alex leaned back in his chair and sighed. "I don't think I've been this full in six months." He stared at Constance thoughtfully for a minute. "Connie, it appears that Lieutenant Ames has been quite generous and kind to you."

"Yes, I could not have survived without his help."

"Exactly what was your relationship? Surely, you weren't seen in public with him?" Alex's voice was thick with insinuation.

Amanda looked sideways at her sister with concerned eyes. Constance paused for a moment and then turned a cold eye on Alex. "Yes, I was proud to be seen in public with the brave and honorable man who saved my life," she shot back defiantly. "If you want an honest answer about our relationship, he has captured my heart."

Alex leaned forward with a scowl on his face. "But you can't take this crush seriously. It's understandable that you'd allow him to buy food for you, but any thought of a permanent relationship is impractical."

"I believe I'm old enough to make my own decisions," she snapped indignantly.

"We'd never accept him and I doubt that his family would welcome you with open arms," Alex argued.

Trying to control her rage, Constance blurted, "You seem to have forgotten that he spared your life. You wouldn't be alive except for his mercy."

"I'm grateful for that and realize he's a man of integrity. Nevertheless, he's still a Yankee. You must forget him and your futile romance. You'd be foolish to destroy your chances with Robert."

Constance's face grew hot and pinched with resentment. "It's in God's hand. Who knows if any of the three of us will survive this horrendous war." She abruptly stood up to leave.

"Please, we're all exhausted and need to sleep. Let's not ruin our homecoming with any hostility," Amanda begged.

Constance wiped a tear from her face after she closed the door to her bedroom. Why did her life have to be so complicated? She didn't want her feelings for Aaron to come between her and her family. Didn't anybody understand? Deep inside, she exploded with joy over the beauty of her love and yet she had no one to share it with. God understood…maybe Sadie understood. Frustrated, she sat down at her desk and opened the letter from Jeb Stuart:

Dear Miss Armstrong,

Please accept my most grateful appreciation for the intrepid service you have performed for our army. Captain Stringfellow informed me of your daring effort to notify us of Kilpatrick's raid. Your information was vital to us as we stopped his audacious attempt to assault Richmond. The fact that you were forced to kill a Union picket confirms your bravery and unflinching loyalty to our cause. You are a true and noble daughter of the Confederacy.

Please express my appreciation to your loyal servant for penetrating Grant's headquarters and risking her life for our cause. The unwavering loyalty of your servants attests to the kind treatment they must have received from your family.

As I write this letter, my thoughts inevitably turn to the gallant Pelham. I know he would be proud of your valiant deeds.

With sincere appreciation,
J.E.B. Stuart

She carefully folded the letter and returned it to the envelope. This letter would be one of her most treasured possessions. She would have Hudson place it in the chest with the Minuteman flag in the morning. As much as she wanted to show it to the Ashbys and her other friends, she decided to wait. Union cavalrymen still guarded the railroad and who knew when contingents from their army might occupy the town again. It would be dangerous to reveal such solid evidence of her spying. The risk of arrest was too great. Eventually that letter might exonerate her in the eyes of her friends, but not now.

Her eyes fell on the stack of letters from Robert. She gently ran her finger over the string that bound them, but did not untie it. She couldn't bring herself to read them yet. Her heart ached over his sadness and depression at being transferred. Always honorable, he would never disobey an order. She didn't want to deceive or hurt him. It seemed cruel to confess her love for Aaron at such a desperate time in Robert's life. She sighed heavily and leaned back in her chair. Tomorrow she would write him a warm, newsy, supportive letter, but remain noncommittal about her feelings. It would not be easy, but that was the only viable solution.

Erupting with emotion, she turned her eyes to Aaron's pictures. She grabbed a piece of paper and pen, letting her love flow onto in. Communicating her emotions to Aaron helped relieve the tension and loneliness haunting her. Unsure how to get her letters to him, she considered giving them to the Union soldiers who guarded the railroad. Or she might resort to sending them to his sister in Maine to be relayed to him. They both realized it would be extremely difficult to communicate, but that didn't weaken her determination to try.

Three days later, May 9, 1864: Armstrong town home

Amanda contemplated her sister across the breakfast table and sensed that she possessed a beautiful new radiance. "Connie, Alex left last night so that he could travel under the cover of darkness."

Constance looked up from her oatmeal and smiled. "Yes, I hope that he'll reach Mosby safely."

"Now that he's gone and before the boys wake up, I feel the need to talk with you," Amanda said pensively. "I allowed Lieutenant Ames, Aaron, to nurture you back to good health because you seemed to respond to him. I never doubted that he was in love with you. Under such intimate circumstances, it would have been nearly impossible for you not to reciprocate his affection."

Constance leaned forward almost giddy as the words gushed from her, "Mandy! Thank God you've said that. I've wanted to scream from the mountaintops that I am in love, I am in love, with the most wonderful man on earth, but there was no one to share my joy with. I felt as if I would explode!"

"I understand. I didn't want to cross Alex. Don't be upset with Alex because of his disapproval. He's intensely loyal to Robert."

"I appreciate Alex's loyalty, but Aaron is in every way the perfect match for me...except for the fact that he's a Yankee. I didn't want to love him, it simply happened. Our love is a beautiful miracle, and I'm empty without him. We both firmly believe that God brought us together."

Amanda had to smile and chuckle at her sister's exuberance. "Your enthusiasm and devotion are inspiring. You remind me of myself when I became determined to marry Alex. Do you remember how strongly mother and father disapproved?"

"Oh, yes, I remember. They felt he was a social climber and that he wasn't good enough for their daughter. You pouted, you cried, but you refused to give in. I always admired your fierce determination to marry the man you loved."

"Connie, I want you to know that I understand your frustration and will always be here to listen to you." She paused thoughtfully and ate her oatmeal. "However, I must be honest and say that I believe the hurdles the two of you face are far greater than ours. You're enemies in a bitter conflict. Has he proposed?"

"Yes," Constance said more seriously. "I told him I could not marry him as long as he fought for the Union army and that I would never live in the North." Her face fell and she continued, "I can't ask him to give up a bright future at home to live in this waste-land. We truly are star-crossed lovers."

"What did he say?"

"That our love was stronger than our differences and that he considered us engaged. He promised to return to me as long as there was breath in his body and I pledged that I would wait faithfully for him."

"Oh, Connie, that's beautiful," Amanda said softly. "I pray that your dreams come true. I'll never object to your marriage."

Constance jumped up, ran around the table, wrapped her arms around her sister, and kissed her on the cheek. "I love you, Mandy. Your support means everything to me. Now, I'm going to the depot to give Aaron's letter to the Yankees on guard there."

Surprised, Constance observed a large group of ragged Confederate cavalrymen surrounding the depot in the morning fog. Obviously a change had transpired. Their eyes ranged freely up and down her body while she moved towards them with feline grace. "Mornin' ma'am," a tall blonde soldier drawled.

"Good morning gentlemen. What company are you?"

"Company B, Ninth Virginia Cavalry. You a loyal Rebel lady?"

"Yes, of course I am."

"We've cleared the enemy from the railroad and captured their supplies. We're picking up their stragglers as we move through the county. You are now rid of the hated enemy."

"That is good news, indeed."

An acne-scarred Rebel said with bitter resentment, "The damn Yankees insulted us by leaving a detachment of nigger soldiers to guard Brandy Station." One of his companions spat on the ground in disgust. "It's degrading for us to fight them…damn traitors to the South. We lined 'em up and shot every last one of 'em," he snorted contemptuously.

Constance's face glazed with shock. "You mean you murdered them all? Don't you understand they joined the Yankees because they were starving to death?"

"Don't see it that way lady. We ain't got enough food to feed 'em in prison anyway."

"Nevertheless, I don't believe two wrongs make a right. Good day, gentlemen." Her nose wrinkled in disgust, she pivoted around and hurried away. Would the atrocities never end? The poor colored people, in search of that illusive dream called freedom, had moved from serving one master to another. Unable to find work or food, their choices were limited. The Yankees put them on the front lines where they were slaughtered in droves. They were damned if they did and damned if they didn't.

Now that the Yankees had left, she pondered how to get her letter to Aaron. She would have to wait until another train came in from the north. Heaven knows when that would be. There were few people on Davis Street when she looked in the window of Stark's Mercantile. Old Mr. Stark nodded to her icily. The local residents bravely attempted to resume life as usual; court would reconvene in a few days and local elections were scheduled. Neighbor mistrusted neighbor, each one suspicious of the other's loyalties. In these perilous times it made more sense to be noncommittal.

When she reached Coleman Street, two ambulances confronted her. She heard the moans of the wounded. "Excuse me, lady," the old driver said. "I've got some bad hurt men from the battle. Do you know any kind souls who'll take 'em in?"

She nodded thoughtfully. "What can you tell me of the results?" She peered at the writhing bodies on the wagon.

"It was the most horrible thing I ever done seen. Thousands of bodies are strewn in the woods unburied. The rifle fire was so thick it caught the woods on fire. Many of the wounded burned to death."

Constance turned her head and gagged. Regaining her composure she asked, "Who won?"

The old fellow scratched his head. "I reckon ol' Marse Robert got the better of 'em. We thought they'd retreat like they always done in the past. But ol' Grant started moving on towards Richmond. The fighin' ain't over yet."

"I was afraid of that. The two great armies have crashed together like two mountain rams. Their horns are locked and now they'll fight to the death." Once again the harsh realities of war had been dropped on her doorstep. "I'll take two men into my house around the corner. Follow me, I'll show you."

Eight days later, May 17, 1864: The bookstore

Culpeper remained a no man's land without much communication from either north or south. Trains did not enter from either direction and therefore newspapers were rarely seen. Constance prayed daily for a letter from Aaron, but none had come. The bookstore had little business since few people had money and most boycotted her because of her rumored disloyalty.

A tear rolled down her cheek while she studied the newspaper Millie Payne had just dashed in to loan her, a paper a customer from Orange gave her. The South had suffered an irreparable loss—Jeb Stuart—killed at Yellow Tavern. Not only that, Longstreet had been wounded at the Wilderness and a bloody battle had taken place at Spotyslvania Court House.

Constance sat at her desk attempting to absorb the essential news provided in the Richmond paper. General Custer's men killed Stuart! Her mind raced. Was Aaron there? Did he kill Stuart? Was he alive? She stopped and blew her nose again trying to get a grip on reality. Stuart had been outnumbered three to one. She realized that no matter how valiantly the Confederates fought, they could not compete with those numbers. Her mind drifted back in time...how she had loved Stuart's gay laughter and zest for life. A more courageous and talented cavalry general never lived. Undoubtedly, his honorable name would be etched in history forever. She visualized Stuart reunited with John in paradise...both of them smiling, glowing in radiant white light, Stuart holding little Flora on his knee. She paused to wipe the tears from her cheek. Reading on, she saw the appalling death figures from Spotsyslvania. Grant's casualties far outnumbered Lee's. According to the Richmond paper the outcry in the North over the bloodshed was threatening Lincoln's presidency. His staggering unpopularity remained the only ray of hope for the cause of the Confederacy.

Five weeks later, June 22, 1864: Armstrong parlor

Constance rocked while her fingers moved nimbly darning socks. Her mind drifted to thoughts of Aaron. Although none of his letters had reached her, she had received one telegram from his sister informing her that he was alive and well. But that was three weeks ago, and since then the bloody Battle of Cold Harbor had taken place. Even of more concern was the report of a vicious cavalry battle at Trevillian Station on June twelfth. The Richmond newspapers reported that Custer had been surrounded and sustained heavy losses. She prayed for Aaron morning, noon, and night, but the agony of not hearing from him consumed her. She forced herself to concentrate and attempted to listen to the narrative Alex was spinning about his life as one of Mosby's Rangers.

In his element, Alex sprawled on the divan between his two adoring sons, who hung on his every word. He liked the life of a partisan and welcomed the change of living with families instead of in camp. He currently resided with the Edmonds family near Paris. The farm, located at the base of the mountains, enabled the partisans to quickly disappear into the hills when the Yankees came calling. When not in action, they enjoyed a life full of fun and socializing. Mosby sent out word for his men to assemble prior to a raid. He usually targeted Yankee supply trains. Without the consent and protection of the civilians, the Rangers could not function. Alex had been pleased to discover several Culpeper men among the command, including Robert Grayson.

Chuckling, Alex described how Robert Grayson, when wounded, had recovered in the cellar of Salubria while Federal General Davies occupied the upstairs. Next, he related a tale told by Mosby himself. Last winter a play was performed in Washington based on Mosby's Rangers. Mosby happened to express his desire to read the script in front of a group of men containing Frank Stringfellow. Undaunted, Stringfellow rode to Washington, saw the play, and returned to Mosby the next day with a copy of the script!

Amanda sewed contentedly during the storytelling. Color and fullness had returned to her cheeks and her face radiated joy again.

A knock at the door interrupted their laughter. Hudson raced forward to the hall. Stress lines on Constance's brow revealed her tension. She laid her darning aside. Hudson charged into the room and held a telegram out to her. Her stomach contracted in a tight ball; she could not force her hand to grasp it. He laid the piece of paper in her lap, and finally she lifted it up with a trembling hand. Her eyes could not focus on the shaking letters. Amanda knelt by her side and steadied the message:

Dear Miss Armstrong,

We have just received a letter from Aaron informing us that he survived the battle at Trevilian Station. He was, however, wounded in a lower limb, but assures us it is not serious. He is in a hospital in Washington. He sent me a letter to forward to you and begged me to advise you that he is on the way to recovery and loves you more than ever.

Abby

"Aaron's alive!" she blurted, her eyes moist with joy.

Amanda hugged her and kissed her on the cheek. "And even though he's injured, it doesn't sound serious. I'm so happy for you!"

"It means he won't be fighting again for a long time," Constance blubbered as tears of joy streaked down her face.

Alex's face flushed with indignation. "I can't believe we're celebrating the survival of a Yankee," he growled sarcastically. "I risk my life every day to kill those aggressors to our soil."

Constance sprang up and confronted him with a scorching stare. "How dare you ruin my exhilaration!" she shrieked. She clutched her hands into fists before she stormed out of the room.

Amanda shot daggers at her husband, then hurried after her sister. "Connie," she called from the back porch. "I apologize for Alex. Where're you going?"

Constance spun around in the middle of the weeds, her eyes still smoldering. "I'm going to Saint Stephen's to throw myself on the altar in grateful prayers of thanksgiving. I hope your cruel husband is gone when I return."

Two weeks later, July 5, 1864: The depot

The intense heat from the sun baked Constance while she strolled towards the depot. Occasional railroad service south had resumed on an unpredictable basis, but no trains came in from the north. A ragged, filthy soldier leaning against one of the dilapidated buildings nodded at her. She veered away from him. Deserters from both armies filtered through town on a daily basis. Always hungry, they presented a dangerous menace. They complained of being sick of the war, now a stalemate. Grant had Lee bottled up at Petersburg, and rumors abounded that Early was leading a small band of Confederates north down the valley towards Washington. She gave little credence to the rumors. Frustrated that she still had not received Aaron's promised letter, she made daily treks to the depot to see if any traveler from Warrenton had dropped off mail. The terrible system relied on the services of the few civilians who had horses. However, there was no other alternative, and she refused to give up hope.

Old Mr. Aylor, the former postmaster, smiled at her when she walked in. "You're in luck Miss Armstrong. An old fellow from Warrenton toted a sack of mail with him when he come down to catch the train to Richmond. Here's that letter you've been waiting a coon's age for!"

She clutched the heavy envelope to her bosom. "Thank you! Oh, a million times, thank you!"

Gasping for breath after sprinting home and up the stairs, Constance threw herself on her bed. Her chest heaving laboriously, she ripped the letter open and devoured the words:

June 17, 1864

Constance, my dearest,

My heart is exploding with love for you as I lie in this crowded hospital ward in Washington. I have poured out ardent prayers of thanksgiving to the merciful God who has allowed me to survive this bloodiest campaign of the war. The toll of death and misery is beyond comprehension. To put your mind at rest, I have received a clean wound in my left calf muscle, and expect full recovery in the near future. My separation from you has made one thing crystal clear to me; you are my world. I've received one letter from you and rejoice that Amanda and the boys returned safely. There is so much to tell you, I scarcely know where to begin.

I suppose, first I should give you a brief summary of the campaign. Lee has proven to be a more crafty and deadly adversary on the defense than he was on the offense. He hit Grant hard in the dense wilderness area, inflicting heavy casualties. Stubbornly, Grant moved forward pushing his army towards Spotyslvania Court House. Meanwhile, Sheridan made a raid in the direction of Richmond in an effort to get Jeb Stuart out in the open and destroy him. Stuart, facing three to one odds, pursued us. I must admit I admire the courage of the Rebels. You have probably heard of Stuart's death. Although I found him obnoxious and arrogant when I met him at your house, I must confess I mourn the death of such a brave and gifted general. Custer's men were aggressively involved in the battle and one of our men shot Stuart. Don't worry, it wasn't me. I will not reap your wrath for that deed. Stuart's death reiterates the supremacy of our cavalry.

We returned to hear of the terrible battle at Spotyslvania Court House. Learning our design, Lee won the race and erected a V shaped fortification. In charge after charge, dead bodies piled up in front of the bloody angle. After untold carnage, our efforts to break through Lee's lines failed.

Still determined to take Richmond, Grant moved around Lee's left in the direction of a crossroads called Cold Harbor. The intrepid Confederate Scouts learned our designs. In fact one of Grant's orders appeared in the Richmond paper verbatim the next day. Lee's men dug in and constructed impregnable earthworks. Then I witnessed the most terrible event of this war. Grant ordered a charge of those deadly fortifications. As our poor men moved forward, the protected Rebels unleashed waves of rifle fire, which sounded like sheets ripping. In less than ten minutes almost 7000 of our men were lost. It was not war. It was murder. Grant is referred to as "the butcher," a term I believe fitting. As I watched the senseless destruction of our men, something inside me snapped. I realized I could not continue to fight for such an army.

To pile on the agony, our wounded lay on the field unattended for four days. It was all due to the cruelty of Grant, who refused to admit he'd been defeated and ask Lee for a truce to attend his wounded. The cries of those helpless men still haunt me. Most were dead by the time help finally was allowed to reach them. Some had attempted to use spoons to dig protective trenches around themselves. I decided then, that when my enlistment was up in late June, I would resign. I cannot fight for a government that treats its soldiers so cruelly and allows prisoners to rot away and die by the thousands, when they could be exchanged. I'm sure you are ecstatic to hear this revelation.

Constance took a deep breath, and wiped a tear from her cheek. Aaron's decision was too good to be true. She turned her attention back to the precious letter.

I have mentioned that Lee's success was due primarily to the daring work of his vigilant scouts. And here's the other astounding news; I give full credit to none other than Frank Stringfellow! As unbelievable as it may seem, it appears Stringfellow lives! Your friend, Governor Extra Billy Smith, bragged in a Richmond newspaper article about the daring escapades of the Confederate scouts and listed them by name, including Stringfellow. In addition, one of our scouts who has seen Stringfellow before, claims to have glimpsed him in our camp. I will never comprehend how he survived in that frigid river, but I rejoice that I am exonerated from all guilt. It is one less obstacle to stand between us.

Our cavalry was then sent forward to make a raid on Trevilian Station. The Confederates seemed to know our design and we soon found ourselves surrounded by the fierce fighting men of Wade Hampton. Our situation was as desperate as any I have seen. Custer maintained his calm. Amidst frantic fighting he organized us for a charge to cut our way out. It was our only chance to avoid sure capture or death. When we began fighting for our lives, my horse suddenly collapsed beneath me. I managed to pull myself to my feet amidst the smoke, and ran after my comrades. Screaming for help, I knew I would be captured if left behind. Somehow, Autie heard me and ordered one of his staff to rescue me. With a grateful heart, I bounded onto his horse, and we fought our way out. In the melee a bullet penetrated my calf. It is a small price to pay for my freedom.

Unfortunately, when I lost my horse I also lost my most valuable possessions, your pictures and the letters you wrote me while in Culpeper. Those treasured items sustained me through the endless campaign and are irreplaceable. I will desperately miss those pictures, even though I continually conjure up visions of you in my mind.

Since I arrived at this hospital four days ago, I have had ample time to reflect and contemplate our situation. I want to share the many conclusions which have become clear to me:

First, I will not fight or kill again. The North is screaming in protest to the terrible carnage. It is my belief that Grant has lost close to 60,000 men in a month. That's as many men as Lee started with. Militarily, he is no match for Lee. If the election were held today, Lincoln wouldn't have a prayer of winning another term. I personally will vote for the Democratic candidate, probably McClellan. If peace is negotiated, granting the Confederacy independence, I can live with that. No men have fought harder or more courageously than Lee's Army of Northern Virginia. I'd love to see the expression on your beautiful face as you are reading this. I'm sure you're cheering, but please don't snicker.

However, I still have to live with my Yankee conscience, which will not let me walk away from the war. I feel a deep commitment to support the brave men who continue to fight for the Union and the abolition of slavery. After my experiences en route to this hospital, I have decided to volunteer in the field medical service. I will not risk my life to kill, but I'm willing to risk my life to save others and carry injured men from the field. It is my hope that I can save lives on both sides. We have to do more to alleviate suffering. I've always had an interest in medicine. This experience will help me determine the direction I take with my future. After much internal debate, I believe this is the correct moral decision for me. It's a compromise, my darling, but I pray that it is a compromise we can both live with.

I do not know what direction this war will take, but now that Grant has Lee under siege, I fear it will mire into a war of starvation. You know that I have always felt that this matter should be decided on the battlefield between men. However, since we have not been able to defeat your army on the battlefield, I fear the war will now be waged on the women and children through starvation. I strongly disapprove of such shameless tactics. My first impulse is to rush to your side as soon as I am well. But if the war rages on, that may be dangerous because of Mosby's men. I pray you will survive without me and that you will understand my moral obligation to serve in the medical corp.

My love for you grows stronger each day and I have contemplated the change in my personality since you captured my heart. You've made me a better person. Yes, I still have my vices of gambling, drinking occasionally, and enjoying a good cigar, but I believe I am less self-centered. You see everything came too easy for me. I had money, intelligence, reasonably good looks, and I could have anything or anybody I wanted. In romantic relationships, I'm afraid that I did all the taking. Life wasn't very fulfilling or challenging for me. Then I watched you giving of yourself, caring for me, doing all in your power to save my life, the life of an enemy. I knew I had to give back to you, to attempt to save you from the devastation that was to come. Giving my love to you has provided me with the greatest joy of my life. I suppose that is why I have decided to give again of myself to help the wounded.

As I contemplate our future, I realize that my world is where you are. Yes, I could return home after the war, and make an excellent living and have everything materially I wanted, but it would be empty without you, darling Reb. I understand your reluctance to live in the North among the people who have destroyed your world. If I had endured your losses, I would also be bitter. After much soul searching, I have determined to return to Culpeper when the war ends. I've spent so much time there, it seems like home. I'm actually getting used to the Virginia heat and do not believe I could endure a winter in Maine. Since I fought for the army which destroyed Culpeper, it is my moral duty to help rebuild it. Yes, we'll be poor, but we'll have the challenge of relying on our talents to build our lives together. I know I wasn't, by the grace of God, born a *Vah-gin-yan,* but with your tutorage I believe I can be a noble son of The Old Dominion.

You have once refused my proposal of marriage and injured my pride. Remember, I'm not used to rejection and do not wish to be turned down again. I hope that I have removed all obstacles to the union of our bodies and souls. If we are to wed, you must ask me. This will be your first, but I'm sure not your last, act of asserting your authority in our relationship. I'm optimistic that if I sit on your doorstep long enough, you will eventually marry me to get me off the street.

As I gaze at the homely nurses in this place I hunger for your touch. I eagerly anticipate the rapture of fulfilled love and marvel at the mystery of two souls and bodies melting together in exultation.

Yours for all eternity,

Aaron

P.S. I will be at home recovering by the time you receive this letter. Write to me there. I just had a nice surprise visit from Libbie. She sends her regards. Autie's star shines brighter than ever! She is furious that the Richmond papers have published her intimate love letters to Autie, which were captured at Trevilian Station. Admit it Reb, this time the Rebels are guilty of a great impropriety.

Tears of joy bubbled from Constance's eyes. A tide of exultation washed over her, then she felt airborne. Floating, drifting, she watched a fly buzz her face. Swatting, she giggled, "Go away, fly. You can't make me mad." Dizzy with glee, she rolled on her side and clutched the precious pages to breast. She laughed and cried simultaneously while the unfettered happiness within her worked its way to the surface. The fact that he was willing to separate from his family and live with her in Culpeper touched her so deeply she felt intoxicated. Still laughing, she wiped the tears from her face and reached for Aaron's picture. A hot wave swept over her body while she stared adoringly at his roguish eyes. She pressed the picture tenderly to her lips. Euphoric, humming, she danced to her desk and began writing to him.

July 5, 1864

Aaron, my dearest love,

Your letter has filled me with such euphoric joy that I am perfectly giddy. I laugh, I cry, and if you could see me you would say that I am crazy as a loon! A happiness that I never dreamed possible fills my body and soul. You, my darling, are my life and you make me complete.

I rejoice at your decision to quit fighting and join the medical corps. Yes, a thousand times yes, it is the morally correct thing for you to do. I fully support your choice to alleviate the suffering of others. You, self-centered? Balderdash! I do not believe you were ever that way. But, nevertheless, I love you for being compassionate and giving. Do not worry about me. Your garden is bursting with vegetables and we still have plenty of food. I will survive while you fulfill your moral obligation.

I hope that you are being completely honest with me about the extent of your wound. How I yearn to be with you to nurse you back to health. I trust that your family will fulfill that role. I'm afraid they will also consider you insane if you tell them you are returning to Culpeper when the war ends. Your willingness to give up your family and wealth for me has touched me so deeply that I weep. I do not deserve such a man. I cannot believe a Jonathan from Maine would cast his lot with a F.F.V. as poor as Job's turkey. But yes, you do have the potential to be a noble *Vah-gin-yan*.

I must caution you that you will confront much hostility here. Alex is violently opposed to our relationship. It has caused a breach between us. I try to avoid him as much as possible. Most of my neighbors still snub me because of you. I promise you this, if we cannot make a living here or endure the ridicule, I will go anywhere with you except to the North. We could sail away to a tropical island or go to Europe. It's fun to dream!

After you left, I was so depressed that I had no appetite. I'm withering away from the dull life without you. Now that I know you are alive and recovering, I will have a new zest for life. I'm living for you.

Praise God, Frank lives! I've known for some time that you did not kill him. This time, the joke's on you, my gullible Yankee. Sally Marsten, at the Washington's Ball, was none other than Frank in disguise! He was right under the nose of hundreds of Yankees! Because I was so elated to find him alive, I fear I celebrated by consuming too much champagne. He swam to the bank of the river and kept his nose above water until you left. Next, he snuck into a Yankee camp and got dry clothes and then went to Summerduck. Dressed as a servant woman, he went up to see his mother and spent several days with her. How I gleefully look forward the day when you will scratch my back for two hours, and I will reveal all!

Yes, I admit the Rebels definitely acted improperly by publishing Libbie's intimate letters. The night of the ball I slept by the wall to their bedroom. The sounds of their passionate lovemaking set my blood aflame. When I find you sitting on my doorstep, I assure you that I will look deep into your wonderful hazel eyes, and ask you that very important question as fast as greased lightning. I grow feverish with desire when I dream of the day we will become one. I can endure any hardship knowing that you will one day return to me.

I close with Juliet's immortal words: "My bounty is as boundless as the sea, My love as deep: the more I give to thee, The more I have, for both are infinite"

Eternally yours,
Constance

Six weeks later, August 18, 1864: The garden

Amanda ran her thumb along the inside of the green pod, popping the butter beans into the earthen bowl in her lap. Perspiration rolled down her back while she contemplated the half-full tan bowl. From her vantage point in the dilapidated gazebo, she watched Alex and the boys working in the small garden. David proudly pulled up a potato and clasped it in his stubby fingers. Alex looked up from his hoeing and smiled his approval at his five-year-old son. She felt a tug at her heart over the sight of her two rag muffins, knowing the war had robbed them of childhood frivolity. Already they appeared as serious, angry old men. She had tried to tutor them, keep them up in their schooling, and make life seem normal somehow.

Her sore thumb ripped another pod open. She paused as a wave of nausea swept over her. She had not intended for it to happen, did not want it to happen this soon, but there was no doubt, she was pregnant again. Her energy drained, she looked to her husband for strength. The sunlight set his auburn hair aglow while he talked with animated gestures to the boys.

Portions of his narrative drifted through her subconscious: Mosby raided Sheridan's supply trains near Berryville, captured 500 mules, 100 horses, 200 prisoners, 100 wagons, burned what they couldn't carry away, Alex brought prisoners to Culpeper, sent 125 head of cattle to Lee, killed Yankees who burned farms, Yankees retaliated by killing Rangers, revenge and blood, blood and hate, an eye for an eye. It went on and on and on. In the innermost part of her mind she thought what she did not dare speak; the Confederacy was doomed and the bloodshed useless. Thankful Alex had visited three times since he went with Mosby, she wondered if she could ever convince him to stop fighting. No, it was useless. A dark cloud drifted over her. She knew he would rather die than surrender.

Constance provided a ray of sunshine in her gloom. She radiated joy and exhilaration at a time when their world was crumbling. Amanda smiled inwardly at the picture of her fiercely independent sister madly in love. She had witnessed Aaron and Constance together, and understood how it had all happened. Try as she would, she could not make Alex understand. Her stomach churned at the thought of the tension between her husband and her sister. Uncomfortable even being in the same room, Constance retreated to her bedroom when Alex was home. Amanda found herself trapped help-lessly in the middle of the smoldering conflict between the two people she loved most dearly. Danged war! Was it going to destroy her small family too?

She ran her fingers through the cool green limas in the bowl. They felt good to her touch and would provide a nutritious meal. She must focus on her blessings. She strolled through the weeds, by the overgrown boxwoods, to the edge of the garden, and smiled dreamily at her three dust-covered men.

Three weeks later, September 9, 1864: Armstrong parlor

Amanda's throat constricted while she and Constance absorbed the two newspaper articles, one about Sherman taking Atlanta and the other reporting the death of John Hunt Morgan in southwest Virginia. The blood drained from her face. In a voiceless monotone, she said, "I fear Lincoln will be re-elected now. The Yankees can smell victory...taste the spoils of war."

Constance gave her a stricken look. "We can't give up hope. There are constant rumors that England and France are coming to our aid. And what about the support of the Copperheads?"

"Pshaw!" Amanda said bitterly. "Those rumors are silly pipe dreams. They'll all watch idly while we're annihilated."

Constance attempted optimism. "But Lee still holds out. The Battle of the Crater did the Yankees more harm that good."

Amanda leaned her head against the back of the sofa and closed her eyes. "I pray God will give our leaders the wisdom to admit defeat. No more of our men must die in vain," she whispered, her voice cracking. She had a vision of massive crowds filing by John Hunt Morgan's casket in Richmond. The entire South was weeping and wailing over the loss of its knightly son. She saw scorching tears flooding from the blue eyes of Dolly Hill who knelt by her brother's remains. Amanda cringed. She wanted to reach out and touch her dearest friend. Sighing deeply, she knew all she could do was write her a loving and compassionate letter.

21

Surviving Scorched Earth

September 20, 1864 – April 4, 1865

"Render the Valley of Virginia, such that a crow flying over will have to carry its own provisions."　　　　General U. S. Grant, U.S.A. to General Phil Sheridan, U.S.A.

"One hundred million dollars of damage has been done to Georgia; twenty million inured to our benefit, the remainder simple waste and destruction."
General William Tecumseh Sherman, U.S.A., following his march to the sea

---

Three weeks later, September 30, 1864: Armstrong back yard

Constance watched the corkscrew of apple peeling fall into the bucket after she twisted her knife. It had been a bumper year for apples and she was pleased with the yield she had brought back from the farm yesterday. By bartering canned codfish with the Gorrells, she had gained use of their horse and wagon for a day. Long-faced, she reflected on the neglected condition of Panorama. All of the outbuildings had been swept away except the brick kitchen.

The autumn sun reflected on David's coppery hair when he dashed up to the bucket and stuffed some peeling into his mouth. "Eat as much peeling as you want," Amanda said. "We can't let anything go to waste."

Constance waved her hand at the swarming flies and contemplated her pregnant sister's pallid face. Hopelessness about the war seemed to be sapping her strength. Just eleven days ago, Union cavalrymen had swept through the county and destroyed the railroad and telegraph at Rapidan Station, leaving Culpeper cut off from the south. On their return trip north, a group of Confederates marching from the valley towards Richmond skirmished with the intruders near Pony Mountain. Once again blood had been shed on their soil. Rumors abounded of wanton burning and destruction in the valley. Amanda was well aware that Mosby and his small band of men fought daily to halt the wanton destruction.

Hudson loped through the goldenrod towards them. He held his pail up proudly to display the pokeberries he had collected. "That's good," Amanda said. "Go into the kitchen and get the mortar and pestle from Sadie to crush them. They should give us a bottle of ink."

After Hudson wandered away, Amanda set the bowl on the table between the two of them. "I'm sorry, Connie, but I feel nauseated. I'm going inside to lie down."

"I understand. You go ahead. I can finish peeling these." David traipsed behind his mother into the house. Constance sliced her knife into another apple. Each day she grew more concerned about shortages. They had no ink, little paper, no soap, and their food would not last more than a couple of months. Her stomached knotted while she contemplated their future if the war did not end soon. She turned her thoughts to Aaron, the bright spot on her horizon. The two letters she had received from him since his return to the hospitals near Petersburg had lifted her spirits. He was her hope, her light-at-the-end-of–the tunnel, her reason for being.

The shadow of a man moving towards her interrupted her daydreams. When she looked up she could not recognize the Confederate soldier. He took his hat off and nodded to her grimly. She stared at his bearded face and eyes, noticing something familiar in his eyes. "Robert Grayson!" she said suddenly.

"Miss Armstrong," he mumbled with a despairing look. "I regret that I'm the bearer of sad tidings."

She swallowed dryly, her hands gripping the arms of the chair. "Alex?"

His face etched with sorrow, he nodded. "I'm sorry. He's dead."

Constance gave a startled gasp. "Oh, dear God, no! How?"

Grayson sat down in the chair beside her, leaning forward. "We hit a Union supply train near Front Royal. Didn't know a reserve brigade was following them. They came on us like a flock of birds when a stone is thrown into it. We scattered toward the mountains, but they captured six of our men, including Alex."

Constance gaped pop-eyed. "But if he was captured, he should be in prison?"

"The Yankees didn't follow the rules," he continued angrily. "They were furious about us getting their wagon train near Berryville and killing some of their men in retaliation for house burnings. Their soldiers screamed for blood. They took four of the prisoners and executed them in a lot behind a church. One of them was a seventeen-year-old kid who had ridden with us for the first time. The bastards shot him while his widowed mother begged for mercy."

Constance winced. "Was Alex one of the four?"

"Nope. He was one of the two they beat and interrogated to reveal the location of Mosby's headquarters. I'm proud to say neither one gave in. Alex died a martyr. They hung the two of them from a walnut tree, and tied a placard on them saying, 'This will be the fate of Mosby and all his men.'"

Constance shook her head despondently and wiped the tears from her face. "There's no end to the brutality."

"Mosby questioned the people in Front Royal. He believes General Custer is responsible and we will retaliate," Grayson declared vehemently.

"Custer?" she asked stunned. "I'm shocked he'd do such a thing." Grayson shook his head with a sneer. "Please, Robert, help me tell Amanda and the boys. I can't do it alone."

"Yes'm. I'll go with you. They need to know how bravely he died."

Constance and Grayson hustled into the kitchen where Sadie and Hudson were straining the berry juice. "The two of you must come inside to the parlor with me. There's some news we all need to hear together." Looking at her ashen, tear-stained face, both followed obediently without uttering a word. When they entered the parlor, they found Amanda stretched out on the sofa with her hand over her face, while David played in the floor with a wooden top.

"Mandy," Constance said softly after she leaned over her sister. "You need to wake up. There's someone here to see you."

Amanda opened her eyes slowly and tried to focus. She couldn't comprehend the situation. Constance lifted her to a sitting position. She looked around the room at the solemn faces while Constance sat beside her, with her arm around her. Her eyes froze on Robert Grayson. She stared at him for a minute and let out a low groan when she recognized him. Her face a study of desolation, she whispered, "Alex?"

"I'm sorry, Mrs. Yager," Grayson said hanging his head. "He died a brave and gallant death."

"No, No!" she wailed overcome with grief. She dissolved into tears while Constance tightened her arms around her. David tottered towards his mother and laid his head in her lap, whimpering.

Hudson's lips pursed with suppressed fury and his eyes moistened. When Sadie put her arm on his shoulder, he jerked away and muttered hatefully, "Damn Yankees."

Grayson shifted and reshifted his weight from foot to foot while the family unleashed their grief. Constance stroked her hand across David's head and rocked Amanda tenderly. "I know, I know," she kept whispering to her sister. After several minutes of hysterical sobbing, Amanda seemed to regain slight control. She looked at Grayson with blood-shot eyes, her face twisted in anguish. "How?" she stammered.

Grayson pulled up the rocking chair, and explained in detail the circumstances of Alex's death. When he concluded, Amanda whispered, "Can't believe…brave and honorable husband…hung like criminal…buried in Front Royal."

"We'll move him to the farm after the war, I promise you that, Mandy," Constance assured her. "Now, I think you should go upstairs and let me put you to bed."

Constance sat and talked with the boys for more than an hour after she got Amanda to bed. She urged them to always be proud of their father because he died a hero and martyr for their noble cause of independence. They must never forget his sacrifice. They were more important than ever to their mother and must give her their love and encouragement. David let his pain flow from him through his tears, but Hudson sulked in angry silence. She worried that his bitterness would consume him.

When she entered the bedroom, Amanda was still weeping. She sat on the edge of the bed and took her sister's hand, looking at the dark circles under her eyes. Amanda turned her bloodshot brown eyes towards her. "My fault…begged him to go with Mosby."

"Horsefeathers! You can't blame yourself. He could have been killed just as easily with Stuart. I…I think that if Aaron had been with Custer…he could have talked him out of hanging Alex." Constance squeezed her sister's hand.

"Couldn't say it in front of boys…his death useless, senseless…accomplishes nothing," Amanda whimpered.

Constance stroked her forehead gently. "He died a brave and noble death. You must all cherish that."

"Nothing to live for…can't go on."

"I know you feel that way at this moment, but you must go on. You have two wonderful sons who need you desperately and a daughter on the way. I'm sure of it."

"Don't know how to provide for them…how can I bring another child into…war-torn world?"

"God will show us the way. You must live for your children."

Amanda clung to her sister's hand as tears flowed down her cheeks. "Help me."

Chilled to the bone, Amanda pulled the wool shawl tighter around her shoulders and sat at her mother's desk in the parlor. With an acute shortage of wood and considerably colder weather on the horizon, she could not indulge in the luxury of a fire. Following Alex's death, the icy fingers of depression had gripped her soul. Night after night, she woke up, screamed, saw his lifeless body hanging from a tree, could not get to him, begged for mercy.

She jolted up straight and listened to the muffled sound in the distance. Was it her imagination or did she hear cannon fire again drifting over the mountains from the valley? Early's defeat October 19th at Cedar Creek had left the Shenandoah Valley in the hands of the burning marauding Yankees. She shuddered at the thought of the bread-basket of the Confederacy in flames—crops, barns, live stock, everything destroyed. The prospect of starvation this winter was staring them all in the eye.

She smiled slightly when she felt the flutter in her broadening abdomen. The baby's kick made her realize she still had something to be thankful for; her baby, an extension of Alex, was growing inside her. She took Dolly Hill's letter and laid it on the desk, turning to the backs of the pages. Fortunately, Dolly had not written on the backs. Her warm and compassionate letter of sympathy had touched Amanda deeply. Always at Powell's side, she and the girls were living in Petersburg. Having no paper of her own, Amanda dipped her pen into the homemade berry ink and wrote rapidly on the back of the letter, attempting to ease the pain of her loss by communicating to her closest friend.

Constance strolled into the room rubbing her arms for warmth, huddled into the rocking chair, and contemplated her thin angular sister. "Amanda, I'm afraid the war may drag on during the winter. We've got to attempt to trap or hunt for food," she said with a helpless gesture of her chapped hands.

Amanda gave her shivering sister a morbid look. "The bad news keeps striking like hammer blows. But, you're right. Perhaps some of the old men can show the boys how to build traps."

"Yes, I thought that might be a good project for Hudson. He needs to be busy …feel helpful…to work through his grief."

Amanda nodded glumly. "He's become sullen, withdrawn. I can't reach him. Maybe catching rabbits or squirrels will give him a purpose."

"He's smart as a steel trap. We'll give him a challenge." Constance blew on her fingers. "Keeping warm will be the other problem. Wood's as scarce as hen's teeth, and we have little money to buy any."

Amanda chewed on her bottom lip. "I hate to say it, but…we might have to chop down the magnolia tree."

Constance's face flushed with indignation. "Heaven help us! I hope not!"

The back door slammed and Sadie charged into the room, waving her hands wildly. "Lawd sakes alive! Ya ain't gonna believe what I done found!" Her voice rose high with excitement as she held a dirty mason jar in one hand.

Constance bolted from her chair and her eyebrows shot up in surprise. "What, in all creation, has got you in such a state?"

Sadie thrust the jar into her hand. "I was pullin' the turnips, when I saw the glass…started diggin'…thought what in the world…an' then I pulled this outta the dirt!"

Amanda peered over her sister's shoulder while she unscrewed the lid of the dirty jar. She gave a startled gasp when Constance pulled out a roll of money. "Dear God in heaven, it's money with value, Yankee money!"

"Now, don't that cap the climax!" Sadie said, with a Cheshire cat smile.

"I…I can't believe it," Constance mumbled. She unrolled the bills with shaking callused hands, then separated them on the table, counting. "This is a miracle. It's $125!" She scrutinized Sadie suspiciously. "It makes no sense."

"I reckon one of those boodles an' boodles of Yankees that was here buried it for safe keepin'," Sadie surmised with big eyes.

"But he wouldn't have forgotten that much money," Amanda argued.

"I betcha he done took sick or got killed in a battle. He's a gone coon, dead meat, an' we's got a pow'ful parcel of money!" Sadie's eyes glinted with excitement.

Constance shrugged her shoulders in a helpless gesture. "I…I…suppose it's possible. It's the most wonderful blessing a body could ask for. This God-send should get us through several months!" Amanda hugged her and they giggled like two little girls at Christmas.

Five weeks later, December 18, 1864: Amanda's bedroom

Amanda felt the baby's strong kick. She gazed out of her window at the gray sky, thinking it matched her mood. The distressing news of Lincoln's re-election and Sherman's brutal march from Atlanta to Savannah overpowered her. She tried to visualize the wanton destruction, a sixty-mile wide path of scorched earth with only chimneys left standing. Never in the civilized world had such catastrophic fury been wielded against helpless women and children. Rage burned deep inside of her at a foe that would resort to starvation to subjugate a people. But on the other hand, why hadn't Davis negotiated a settlement? Would they all be dead before the Richmond government admitted defeat?

Wringing her hands, she walked to the bed and pulled the threadbare patched sheets off. There was no soap to wash them, but she would boil them anyway. She dropped the sheets in a pile on the floor and stood in front of the fireplace warming her hands. At least they had been able to buy a big load of firewood, even though many items were not available at any price; candles, sugar, coffee, cloth, and most importantly salt. Since the Yankees raided Saltville in southwestern Virginia, the precious commodity was non-existent. No meat could be cured or food seasoned. Never again would she take those life-sustaining white granules for granted.

David stormed into the room and threw his arms around her legs, sobbing. "Mommy, the other boys won't play with me…call me a Yankee lover 'cause of Aunt Connie."

She led him to the chair, lifted him into her lap, and observed the wounded look in his eyes. "Not again," she muttered. "We know that what they're saying is a lie. You've got to be a big boy and ignore it."

"But I'm so tired of being left out." He buried his head in her bosom. She sighed and stroked his auburn hair. Enough was enough! How could they ridicule her son after Alex had died a martyr's death? She understood Constance's concern over revealing her spying activities, but good friends could be trusted. There was one person who would change people's minds. She resolved to pay Granny Ashby a visit.

Constance moved the feather duster lightly over the scratched table in the parlor and paused when she heard the shuffling of many feet in the hall. Granny Ashby scurried into the room followed by Lucy, Blanche, and Amanda. Granny cocked her timeworn birdlike face, looked up at Constance and squinted through her spectacles. "Amanda and I have had a long chat. Do you think you can forgive a crotchety old fool?"

Shocked, Constance shot her sister a questioning look. "You didn't...tell them?"

"Forgive me Connie, but I could tolerate the persecution no longer. Your friends won't betray you." Amanda moved to her sister's side.

"You can trust us with the secret of your brave deeds," Granny squeaked with crinkles around her eyes. "You know, Constance, a coon's age ago when I was young, I reckon if a young man as likely as your Yankee had taken a cotton to me...saved my life...I'd have done some sparking too!"

Constance laughed nervously. "Does this mean we're friends again? You don't think I'm a fallen woman...a traitor?"

"No. Forgive us for being such snobs," Blanche said. She and Lucy moved forward and hugged Constance.

"Jane's still peeved because of her jealousy over Robert," Lucy whispered.

Granny pushed her way through and joined in the embrace. "Now spin us a yarn about how you killed that Yankee picket."

"Oh, please, have a seat." Constance sunk into the rocking chair. "I'm proud of delivering the message, but not of having to kill. I regret the circumstances, but I'll explain it all to you."

After a detailed narrative of Constance's adventure, they all vented their horror at the recent wanton destruction wrought by the Yankees. The Ashbys admitted their food was almost gone and they had little gold left for purchases. Constance generously volunteered to share with them again. Granny vowed to lead a personal crusade amongst the townspeople to vindicate Constance of all charges of disloyalty. She would make her plea from a soapbox to anyone who would listen, preaching that a romance with a Yankee was not treason. Under no circumstances would she reveal Constance's activities as a spy.

When their guests departed, the two sisters contentedly settled in front of the fireplace to do their mending. Shortly, Hudson loped into the room and handed Constance a letter. She grabbed it eagerly, anticipating that it was from Aaron. Startled, she looked at Amanda with a furrowed brow. "It's from Mary Beckam." She opened it slowly, her eyes wide in alarm. She knew there had been fierce fighting in Tennessee. Her eyes scanned the page while her stomach tightened into knots.

Dear Miss Armstrong,

It is with the deepest grief that I must inform you of the tragic death of our beloved son, Robert, on December 5th at Ashwood, Tennessee. On November 29 as his artillery was pounding the enemy, a shell struck a large boulder and hurled a fragment of rock into his temple. My talented, amiable son now lies beneath the cold ground at St. John's Episcopal Church near Columbia, Tennessee.

Constance gasped for breath. "Robert...dead...died almost like John," she stammered.

Amanda's face fell. She spoke with little expression, "Another useless sacrifice to our cause. I wish I could cry for Robert. He was honorable and noble, but I'm empty inside. I...can't cry again."

Constance brushed away a tear and attempted to focus on the letter.

> We must find comfort in the words of General Stephen D. Lee, whose letter informed us of the heartbreaking news. "During the affair around Columbia your gallant and accomplished son, Col. R.F. Beckam, was mortally wounded while industriously and fearlessly directing the artillery firing against the enemy. He was one of the finest and best officers in the service. When informed of his death, General John Bell Hood commented that he was one of the most promising officers of his rank.[1] Personally, I found him to be an extremely nice and gallant young fellow. I mourn his loss with you."

> As a mother I must cope with the empty void, the unfulfilled dreams left by Robert's loss. He confided to me of his deep affection for you. We hoped that one day he would make you a member of this family. I pray that God will sustain you through these hard times in our land and that we may meet again when peace comes.[i]
>
> Your sincere friend,
Mary Beckam

Constance wiped her tears, sniffled, leaned her head against the back of the rocking chair, and closed her eyes. What a senseless waste of life. Robert, who only wanted to build, would never be able to use his creative talent. She pictured him handsomely attired at the ball, all the ladies rushing towards him to ask for a dance. Always loyal and supportive, he had played such a prominent role in her life. Her admiration and respect for him had not dwindled since Aaron stole her heart. The sharp stabbing pain of grief gnawed away at her. She would have to live with it. Sighing loudly, she determined to write a compassionate letter to his mother and return her pearl necklace.

A week later, December 25, 1864: Coleman and Davis Streets

Hudson molded the snow in his hands and hurled it against the brick wall of the courthouse. Furious at the rumors of Yankee cavalry under General Alfred Torbert ravaging the county, he wanted more revenge than throwing snowballs. He grunted, then watched another white missile splatter against the bricks. So this was the day for peace on earth and good will towards men. Humbug! Retaliation was what he sought and at nine, he considered himself old enough to fight. After he knelt down for another handful of snow, he noticed a lone rider approaching him through the six inches of snow on Coleman Street.

The teenage rider stopped his horse, and said, "Hello Hudson."

"Where'd you get that fine hoss, William?" Hudson stood up and admired the animal.

"I've had him hidden in Madison," William Nalle, who two years earlier had bravely gone to watch the Battle of Cedar Mountain, answered. "I've heard about the marauding

---

[i] Little is known of Robert F. Beckam's (originally spelled Beckham's) personal life, other than the fact that he never married. However, his impressive military record and high moral character make him a hero deserving our honor and remembrance.

Yankees and I'm on my way out to check on grandmother. Hope I'll nab a few Yanks."
He patted the gun on his belt.

Hudson raised his eyebrows in surprise. "Do tell? Take me with you!"

"Why, you're just a kid!"

"I've got a gun…can shoot good. I may be small, but I've got grit," Hudson argued, standing tall and sticking his chin out.

William scrutinized the long faced boy thoughtfully. His grandmother's house, Fairfield, was only a mile from Panorama. He had known Hudson all his life and found him to be a spunky kid. "I've got a mind to let you go along. Go get your gun, pard."

"Yes!" Hudson slapped his knee, then sprinted down the street, his legs pistoning wildly in the snow. If he could just sneak into Aunt Connie's room and get her pistol, he would be on his way to killing Yankees.

Several minutes later he dashed back breathing laboriously, pistol tucked in his belt. William held out his hand and Hudson climbed on the horse. He put his arms around William's waist. "Thanks partner. Let's go make dead meat of some Yankees! I can't wait to get outta this one-hoss town."

They had an uneventful ride until they rounded a curve in the road about two miles south of Rixeyville and spied about twenty Yankees riding towards them. "Halt!" one of the Yankees ordered after a shot rang out. William spurred his horse into the woods and galloped down a hill towards a ravine. The boys quickly dismounted, grabbed the reins of the horse, and hid in the snow behind some large rocks. Hudson's heart pounded wildly while the Yankees rode by on the road above them.

"I think we'd better hide here until candle lighting," William whispered. "It's too dangerous in the daylight."

Hudson blew on his red fingers and rubbed his arms for warmth. Their hour's wait in the snow had been miserable. "Don't you think it's dark enough now?" he asked while the last rays of light faded from the gray sky.

William nodded, stood up, rubbed his arms and stomped his feet to get his circulation moving. "You ain't scared to go on are you?"

"No way," Hudson declared. The two adventurers mounted up and proceeded cautiously down the road. When they turned up the lane to Fairfield they heard loud noises and saw the house ablaze with bright torchlight.

"Dang it! Looks like our foes are here." William guided his horse into the woods. He tied the horse at the bottom of the hill and the two boys crept through the woods until they could see the front yard. They crouched low in the snow while their eyes adjusted to the light. It appeared that three soldiers were holding at least fifteen horses. Shattering glass and oaths flew like hail, the door opened; several soldiers carried out bags of loot. Another smashed a chair against the front steps. They heaved piles of clothes on the snow and ignited them with a torch. The vindictive laughter of the assailants caused fury to burn in William. "We're going to pick off some of those bastards," he vowed through gritted teeth. Six Federals carrying a torch, filed towards the outbuildings and slave quarters.

"Man alive, they're going after the servants!" Hudson hissed. The soldiers kicked down the doors of two slave cabins amidst the screams of the inhabitants. Dishes smashed, furniture crashed, and the Yankees laughed fiendishly after they thrust a nude old darkie out into the snow. "Dance for us nigger! We hear you people can sure dance!" The shriveled up old man looked like a prune while he moved his feet frantically in the snow. "Faster!" One Yankee fired several shots at the man's feet amidst contemptuous laughter. Finally, the exhausted old fellow slipped and fell in the snow. A spectator kicked him savagely with his boot. Their devilment over, the soldiers paraded back to the house.

"Those sons of bitches will fry in hell for this," William snarled. Suddenly, the two boys became aware of five dark forms moving towards them in the woods. Hudson froze while the blood vessels in his throat throbbed.

"Damn Yankees! Can't believe they'd go after a defenseless old woman!" they heard one of them whisper.

Heaving a sigh of relief, William said softly, "We're Rebels."

The men stopped startled. One slowly crept towards the boys, trying to see them in the sliver of moonlight. "Hudson?" Hans Yager asked shocked. "What in God's name are you doing here, boy?"

"Grandpa?" Hudson whispered. The old man knelt and wrapped his arms around him. They hadn't seen each other since Alex's death. "I'm...gonna kill one of 'em...for Daddy," he stammered, his voice breaking.

"Oh, son, I understand," Yager whispered with moist eyes. "But you're too young...no business being here...does your mother know?"

"I snuck out...had to get away."

The other four men joined them trying to grasp the situation. "My grandson," Hans said, motioning towards Hudson, "her grandson," he indicated William.

"Dang it! Let's see how much damage five old men and two boys can do to those vile creatures," one of the men sputtered.

"I suggest, Hans, that you and I stay here with the boys. The other three of you double back and get in the woods on the other side of the lane. When they ride off we'll hit them from both directions. I think they'll run, but if not we can retreat through the woods," a tall old man said.

"Sounds like a good plan to me," Hans answered. Within a short time, they all lay in position. Hans looked at his grandson lying in the snow beside him with his gun pointed at the horses. Amanda and Marta would have conniption fits if they knew what was happening. He took his hand and ruffled the boy's blonde hair affectionately. They understood each other. The door opened and the boisterous Yankees mounted their horses. "Steady, wait until they start moving," he whispered. Hudson aimed his gun at a big Yankee and kept him in his sights when they rode forward. "Now!" Yager whispered. Shots rang out from both sides of the lane. Hudson squeezed the trigger and watched five Yankees fall to the ground. Sure he had hit the big one, he fell flat on his face when the startled Yankees fired back. Bullets whistled overhead. Hans and the other men opened up on the Federals again and this time they galloped away, still firing. Hans jumped to his feet, bolted into the lane and fired on the retreating soldiers. They returned his fire and he felt a sharp pain in his arm

Hudson dashed towards his grandfather. "Grandpa are you hit?"

Hans winced from the pain. "Don't worry, it's not bad." He grasped his arm.

The others quickly reached the lane and chased the stray horses. William examined the fallen soldiers. Four were dead and one writhed in pain. Hudson, prowling through the bodies, looked at the injured man without pity. He pointed his gun at his head. "No!" William cried as he pushed the gun aside. "You can't shoot an injured man. We'll take him down the road to the Payne's for care."

"They had no mercy for my father," Hudson said, his eyes smoldering. "They hung him. Let me finish this one off."

"Don't do it son." Hans stumbled towards them. "We aren't Barbarians."

"You and the boys go on into the house," a friend said. "We'll take care of things out here."

William groaned at the sad spectacle that confronted them inside the house. Everything that could be carried off was gone and the rest lay in shambles. Doors hung wrenched off the hinges, broken glass covered the floor, splinters and shattered pieces of once beautiful furniture were thrown helter skelter, and the upholstery was cut to pieces. The devilish Yankees had even soaked the upholstery with molasses. William rushed to his small gray-haired grandmother, sobbing in the corner. He pulled the aristocratic lady against him, touching her bleeding ear lobes.

"Ripped my earrings out...wrenched off my rings." She held up her swollen left hand. "Stole my food, brandy, bedclothes, shoes, clothes, every single thing!"

"We shot five of 'em. Retrieved several bags of plunder," William said proudly. "Grandma, why don't you come back to Val Verde with me?"

The little woman pulled away, stood tall, and cried defiantly, "Never! This is my house and I won't let those blue devils run me off!" She leaned towards William and whispered, "They grabbed me by the collar and shook me fiercely, trying to make me tell them where my money was hidden. I wouldn't give in," she said with her blue eyes crinkling. "They didn't get it!"

"Grandma, you're a tough old Rebel," William admitted while Hans stumbled in with the help of a friend. "We've got a wounded fellow."

Hudson picked up a piece of wood and swept the broken glass from in front of the fireplace. Hans stretched out on the floor, then his companion pulled his sleeve away to examine the bleeding wound. Hudson's eyes scanned the room, and he pulled one of the draperies down and tore it into strips. The friend said he thought the bullet had passed through the arm while he wrapped the wound tightly with the drapery strips. William took his Grandmother's arm and guided her upstairs to investigate the damage. Shivering, Hudson gathered pieces of shredded furniture and piled them on the fire, causing the flames to shoot higher. He took off his wet shoes and socks, placed them in front of the fire, and stretched out on the floor beside his grandfather. Hans, obviously in pain, breathed hard and put his good arm around the boy who snuggled against him. They had not seen each other in over two years and had a lot of catching up to do. They talked for hours, purging themselves of their pain over Alex.

Hudson bolted upright when he heard a knock at the door. The other old man, snoring against the wall, suddenly opened his eyes. A voice from outside the door said, "It's Mosby's men. We heard you had some trouble."

Wary, Hudson crept to the door and answered, "Did you know a Ranger by the name of Yager?"

"Yep, Alex. We knew him before that damn Custer hung him."

Hudson opened the door and welcomed the four men. He gave them a brief account of what had transpired and explained who he and his grandfather were. The Rangers expressed their sympathy about Alex and had nothing but the highest praise for him. With angry eyes, Hudson took them aside and whispered to them about the wounded Yankee he desired to kill in revenge. They asked for directions to the Payne's house and promised to finish the scoundrel off for him.

The boy threw some more furniture fragments on the fire and stretched out beside his grandfather again. Hans lectured him about his behavior and made him promise to go home in the morning and face Amanda's wrath. Hudson closed his eyes with a slight smile of malicious triumph on his face. His mother would rant, rave, scream, and punish him, but he had the satisfaction of knowing he was responsible for the death of at least one, and perhaps two Yankees. It had been worth the risk.

Two months later, February 22, 1865: Sadie's kitchen

The flickering pine knot in the metal pan provided sufficient light for Constance to read aloud to the rest of the family. Day after day, night after night of the endless dreary winter, they had found solace by escaping into the imaginary world of books. The extreme cold had rapidly consumed their precious firewood and now they huddled together in the warmth of the kitchen. The modern iron cook stove heated far more efficiently than the fireplaces in the house. Thus, in the most frigid weather they had been forced to eat, live, and sleep in the small kitchen, packed together like sardines. Constance turned the page of Augusta Jane Evans's popular book, *Marcaria,* published last year to send the message of self-reliance and independence to the struggling women of the South.

"Everybody ought to be of some use in this world, but I feel like a bunch of mistletoe, growing on somebody else, and doing nothing," Constance read in a low musical voice. "All who seek true happiness should be employed in some way."

"Humph!" Amanda snorted. "With half the men in the South either dead or wounded, we women have no choice but to be employed. There's nothing to glorify in single life."

"But the message here, Mandy, is that women now have opportunities for self-realization outside of marriage," Constance argued.

David coughed incessantly and Amanda felt the baby kick. She grimaced while her stomach cramped from the wretched rabbit stew she had consumed for supper. "That's easy for you to say since you know your Yankee is safe…he'll return to you," she snapped.

Constance realized her sister had grown jealous of her relationship with Aaron. "I can't assume he's not in danger. He's constantly exposed to diseases and there may be more fighting. He'll be in the middle of it, rescuing the wounded."

"Mommy, I'm sleepy," David whined, leaning against her.

"Yes, I believe we all need rest," Amanda said curtly after she stood up. She and Hudson pushed the trestle table against one wall and lifted the benches on top of it. Sadie and Constance unpiled the palettes and mattresses, spreading them over every inch of the floor, while Billy went outside for wood to fill the stove. They all stretched out and pulled blankets over them and Billy stoked the stove and blew out the pine knot. David crawled into his secure spot under the table still coughing.

Constance rolled over, trying to get comfortable on the straw palette next to Amanda, while her sister tossed and turned. Eight months pregnant, Amanda could find no position on the brick floor conducive to sleep. Constance listened to the coughing and wheezing of both boys as well as Billy's snoring. She didn't feel physically tired, just bored to death of their mundane existence. They lived like caged animals, constantly bickering and fighting, struggling to survive. Attempting to ignore the constant gnawing hunger pangs, she focused on their situation. All but thirty dollars of the precious money had been spent on wood and food. Along with most of the people of the county, they now had to rely on small game, cornmeal, and the few canned goods that remained to stay alive. The heavily hunted animals were beginning to disappear. She feared Sadie had put rats in their soup without telling them. Without salt, the food tasted wretched. Many people had dug up the floors of their smokehouses and boiled the dirt to scoop the salt off the top of the water. She grimaced. That sounded disgusting, but she didn't even have a smokehouse available.

She sighed and rolled to her side. Deserters from Lee's army had filtered back into town reporting that conditions in the trenches around Petersburg were deteriorating. The cadaverous soldiers deplored leaving Marse Robert, but felt compelled to keep their families from starving. Only yesterday old George McDonald had returned looking emaciated and complaining that he could no longer survive on a handful of cornmeal a day in the damp cold trenches. He sobbed when he told her about the plight of Lee's brave men and his fear for the Confederacy. Her hopes had risen when Lincoln and Vice-President Stephens met earlier in the month to discuss a negotiated peace, but rumors now circulated that no agreement had been reached. The South vowed to fight on. Rumors, rumors, rumors! She didn't know what to believe. In December there was a rumor that Mosby had been seriously wounded and passed through the county heading south to recover. Now rumors circulated that he was back in command. And then there were the constant rumors about foreign intervention…the British were moving troops into Canada…the French were occupying Mexico…the Rebels had robbed a bank in Saint Albans, Vermont to finance an invasion from Canada…the Copperheads would revolt. Her mind spun and reeled. She had to focus on something more pleasant if she ever hoped to drift to sleep.

A year ago tonight she had been waltzing in Aaron's strong arms. Had it only been a year? She felt as if it had been ten years since she had touched him. His letters arrived unpredictably. Some came, others never reached her. Frequently it took as long as six weeks for one to be relayed through his sister. His visit home had caused a conflict with his family, except his sister. He reported that his mother, her health stronger now, vowed to disinherit him if he married a Rebel. Unruffled, he reconfirmed his love for her and pledged to flee to her side as soon as the war ended. Her lips turned up in a slight smile of contentment as she dreamed of his touch, the passion of his kisses, the rapture of feeling his fit body against hers. She could endure any hardship as long as she held on to the hope of his return. She understood Amanda's depression. Without that hope there was little reason to live.

A month later, March 22, 1865: Armstrong front bedroom

Constance took a piece of magnolia wood from Hudson's arms and added it to the crackling fire in the front bedroom. Determined that Amanda would have her baby in he warmth of the best bedroom, she had been forced to have Billy cut down the massive tree. She had shed a few tears when the centerpiece of their once beautiful garden crashed to the ground. It seemed as if her whole world was crumbling around her. "Stack those other pieces by the fireplace." She scrutinized Hudson's sullen blue eyes. More communicative following the killing of the Union cavalrymen, he seemed to have released his fury. But last week they received word that Hans Yager had died from complications of his wound. The angry boy once again withdrew. He glanced at his mother and silently left the room.

Constance rushed to her sister's side when she cried out from the labor pain. She took Amanda's bony hand and studied her damp pallid face. The dark circles under her sunken eyes revealed the malnutrition that plagued them all. Amanda breathed loudly with labored breath. Suffering from chest congestion, her body was already weak. Constance gulped for air furiously while she stared at Sadie, her eyes wide in alarm.

"Her water jist broke...pains is closer together...ain't gonna be long," Sadie said with a high strained voice. She grabbed rags to soak up the liquid.

Constance wiped her sister's face. "Hang on, Mandy. Your baby girl is going to be here soon." Constance felt a wave of acid well up in her belly. With no doctors in town, she and Sadie would have to deliver this child. Realizing that they had prepared as best they knew how, she prayed for guidance and strength. Sadie had experience; she knew nothing. Amanda cried out again and her fingers dug into Constance's hand. The cold March wind whistled outside the windows with an eerie effect while the pains and the screams came closer and closer together.

"Push!" Sadie cried. Amanda mustered all her strength again and again but nothing happened.

"One more time, Mandy, push!" Constance pleaded, holding her sister's arms. Fearing Amanda had reached the point of exhaustion she stared at Sadie in desperation.

"Can't...tired," Amanda whispered faintly.

"You's got to Miss Amanda. I see the baby comin'," Sadie yelled.

Amanda screamed and pushed one more time. "Oh dear Lawd," Sadie moaned in numbed horror. "It's comin' feet first!"

"What do we do?" Constance screamed hysterically.

"We's got to help get that baby out or else they both die," Sadie said, her eyes full of fear. "Push, Miss Amanda!" Amanda screamed and exerted all her energy to push again.

"I've got the feet. Miss Constance, you push down on her stomach when she pushes." Constance gulped spastically and tried to do as she had been told. Amanda let out a bloodcurdling scream.

"We're hurting her," Constance pleaded.

"Save...baby," Amanda moaned.

Sadie worked frantically trying to grasp the child. Constance kept applying pressure in waves while Amanda moaned.

"I've almost got her!" Sadie said excited. "One more push!" Amanda mustered all her strength, pushed one more time and then passed out.

Sadie's face registered relief when she held the blood-covered baby up, stuck her finger in her mouth, and then slapped her on her red bottom.

Constance watched paralyzed until the child puckered her prune like face and let out a shrill cry. "Praise God!" she gasped in a broken voice.

She moved to Sadie's side, helped her cut the umbilical cord, and wrap the child. When she looked at the blood-soaked bed her head began to swim. Suddenly, the ceiling, walls, everything swirled in a fog. Sadie grabbed her arm and shoveded her into the rocking chair.

"Sit still. I got enough problems without havin' you faint."

Constance closed her eyes and took deep breaths, grasping the arms of the chair firmly. If she just kept taking deep breaths she would be fine. She cracked her eyelids and saw Sadie frantically trying to mop up all the blood spurting from Amanda. Everything was not fine. She closed her eyes again and tried not to see it. She could not think, could not cope with it, dared not comprehend it. She focused on taking deep breaths and listened to the whimpering child.

After what seemed an eternity, Sadie touched her hand. "How ya doin' Miss Constance?"

Constance slowly cracked her eyes and looked into the sweat-soaked face of her faithful servant. "Sadie, I don't know what I would have done without you. How is she?"

Sadie's dark eyes gave a despairing look, then she shrugged her hands in a helpless gesture. "I ain't no doctor. Done the best I could. She was tore an' done bled a lot. Don't know…she's weak."

Constance felt a dull empty gnawing in her soul. *Please God, let her live. Don' leave me with such responsibility.* She stood slowly until she got her balance, took tiny steps to the bedside and stared down at the wrapped bundle lying beside Amanda. Little stands of auburn hair stuck straight up in a ridge on top of the baby's head like a rooster's comb. She wiped Amanda's face with a cloth, then grasped her hand. "Mandy you have a beautiful daughter. She's got Alex's hair."

Constance continued to massage Amanda's hand and arms and rub her face. "Wake up and look at her."

Amanda forced her eyes upward. Constance picked up the baby and laid her in her mother's arms. Amanda smiled faintly, then whispered ever so softly, "Harriet Stuart Yager," and brushed her lips against the baby's head. Her eyelids drifted downward as she drifted away.

Two days later, March 24, 1865: Constance's bedroom

Constance tossed in her bed and drifted through cobwebs of restless nightmares. She had shadowy visions of the baby nursing at Amanda's breast, no milk coming, Amanda weak, rarely conscious, still bleeding, running a fever. That was all day today. Or was it yesterday? Constance rolled to her back, put her hand over her forehead. She had to sleep, must get rest. If she woke up she would have to face reality. No, couldn't do that. The small whimper, then the loud cry forced her to open her eyes again. She tried to focus in the dim morning light while the rain beat against the window in sheets. Looking at the bassinet beside her bed, she saw a small hand waving in protest. She mustered her strength, pulled the covers back, and tiptoed to the bassinet. So tiny and helpless, little Harriet was red and battle worn from her arduous arrival into the world. Constance felt her wet diaper. She quickly changed it while the little legs flailed in protest. Constance wondered how they would ever keep her in clean diapers with so little cloth available. Cradling the baby in her arms, she sat in the rocking chair, poked the nipple of a bottle

510

f sorghum and water in the hungry baby's mouth. The child sucked energetically while Constance's mind swirled with thoughts of how to keep her alive if Amanda's milk didn't come in or if Amanda…she couldn't face it. After several minutes of sucking the child let out a cry. She reached up and wrapped her fingers tightly around Constance's little finger. Never maternal, Constance found herself overwhelmed with feelings of love and protection for the plucky little creature.

"That's right, little Hattie, hang on tight. I know you're strong. You showed your grit by the way you came into this world. I promise you, you're going to grow up in a far better world than this one." She looked into the baby's hazel eyes with flecks of green.

Constance stood up, slipped her feet into her worn slippers, and shuffled across the hall to Amanda's room, fearful of what she might find. She threw two more pieces of wood into the coals, stirred them, and watched the tongues of darting flame. Cautiously, she approached the bed and laid the baby beside Amanda. She reeled with shock when she felt her sister's burning forehead. Panicking, she leaned over her face and listened for breathing—it was faint and labored. "Mandy, you've got to hang on!" She grasped her hand tightly. "Your children need you. Don't leave me!" she wailed, her voice becoming high and hysterical.

Amanda felt herself basking in the hot summer sun. In the swirling depths of her mind she saw Alex running towards her through the tall, lush fields at the farm. Teenagers, the two of them laughed and collapsed contentedly in each other warm embrace. The sun grew hotter and the light got brighter and brighter, until it became a beautiful intense white light beckoning to her. Alex waved to her from the light, motioned to her to come to him. "Alex…coming!" Her head rolled to the side of the pillow; her eyes stared blankly into space.

"No!" Constance threw herself over her sister. "No, Mandy, don't go." She sobbed violently.

Sadie shuffled into the room breathing heavily, her eyes transfixed with horror. She put her arms on both of Constance's shaking shoulders. Slowly, Constance stood up and threw herself against Sadie, resting her head in her bosom. Unable to fight back her own tears, Sadie tried to console her devastated child. "We done the best we could. At least we saved the baby. She's in glory with the good Lawd now."

Constance struggled to get her breath. "Can't handle this alone…three children…how?"

Sadie stroked her hair. "Sometime we don't have no choices in life. Jist have to do what we have to do."

Constance's vision blurred when she looked into Sadie's stricken face. This woman had served her family faithfully all of her life. It was not a life of her choosing, but she had borne life's many burdens cheerfully and religiously. Could Constance do any less?

"Sadie you're a saint. You give me strength. Please…help me…don't leave."

Sadie attempted a smile through her tears. "I ain't no saint an' I ain't gonna leave ya. Don't know why you's had so much agony, but we's gonna survive together."

Constance's lower lips trembled. "Baby…can't lose her…how?"

Sadie shook her head and held Constance. "Don't know…need wet nurse or milk."

"Maybe if I can focus on keeping her alive…I can make it…one day at a time. Boys…how?"

Sadie sighed and thought for a minute. "Jist git yourself together first. Then ya gotta tell 'em; let 'em see her. Next, we gotta send Hudson to ever'body in town. See if anybody's sucklin' a chile."

When she brought the boys into the room, Constance watched helplessly while David climbed into the bed and snuggled beside his mother. Sobbing, he let his grief flow from him. Hudson's angry eyes showed little emotion. He kissed his mother on the cheek and stalked from the room. Feeling totally inadequate, she had assured both of them of her love and that they would survive together as a family. She would always take care of them, never leave them. What comfort could that be to children who had lost three grandparents and both parents within two and a half years? She rocked Hattie in her arms, praying for a wet nurse.

The dreary rain had stopped by afternoon when Reverend Cole called on Constance. The old priest prayed with her, offered her words of condolence, but no, he didn't know anyone in town nursing a child. Constance felt her primary attention should be to the child's survival. She resolved that she could not handle attempting to get Amanda to the farm and burying her there. It would take a whole day of her time. Even though it depressed her, she would have to bury her at Saint Stephen's with the hope of moving her to the farm later. Reverend Cole promised to attempt to build a casket, but with wood so scarce, he couldn't guarantee it.

Hudson returned and reported that he had gone to every inhabited house in town. There was no one, black or white, nursing a child. The townspeople sent their condolences, and Constance knew they would start flooding into the house shortly. She could not wait. She must find milk for the baby and knew of no source other than John Minor Botts' cows.

Constance pulled her cape tightly around her while the wagon jostled through the ruts and mud puddles. Gaunt, practically bald George McDonald slapped the reins of the Gorrell's horse. Constance felt comfort knowing that everyone wanted to help her solve her desperate situation. They both cocked their heads at the sound of a train coming from the north towards Brandy Station, the first one to arrive in ages. Constance commented that she hoped it brought food. McDonald feared it might be full of Yankee soldiers, coming to take over. They knew the end was near.

"But at least they'll get the telegraph operating again. We'll know what's happening, even if we have to hear their version," she said after the wagon stopped in front of Auburn.

Constance took a deep breath, then knocked on the door. An old man servant greeted them and invited them in when she explained that she was a friend of Mary's. John Minor Botts and Mary joined them shortly. Constance found herself somewhat intimidated by the bushy eyebrows and flowery rhetoric of the father. She understood why Jeb Stuart had so strongly detested the old Unionist windbag. Mary, however, was delighted to see her. McDonald held Constance's hand while she related her tragic situation. Breaking down several times, she finally got the story out. She pulled twenty dollars out of her pocket and offered to buy milk and eggs from them.

Mary, most sympathetic, convinced her father that it was their Christian duty to help. Constance discreetly inquired if they knew of anyone nursing a child. Both looked embarrassed, but said no, they did not know anyone. Constance wondered if the rumor Aaron had told her indicating one of the daughters was with child was true or false. Nevertheless, Botts agreed to sell her two gallons of milk and two dozen eggs a week for one month. He went so far as to offer to have one of his men deliver to her twice a week. Touched by their compassion, Constance regained hope and eagerly returned to town with the food.

Next day, March 25, 1865: Saint Stephen's cemetery

Constance watched the three men push the rough pine box into the muddy red hole while she stood between the two boys, clutching their hands tightly. She had the sensation of floating above in space, observing the surreal scene. She was not a part of it. She was far away looking at it in a fog. Somehow she knew that the box had been constructed from the doors to the carriage house and the people standing around were her friends: the Ashbys, the Gorrells, the Paynes, the Starkes, Mildred Hill, George McDonald, and of course ever faithful Sadie. Off in the distance she heard the familiar scripture, the prayers. Beads of water from the light drizzle formed on the brim of her black hat and dripped in front of her eyes. Her cheeks felt wet. Then she heard the dirt pelting against the pine box. No, couldn't listen, couldn't think about what was in the box. Had to focus on the tiny baby, the baby she must keep alive. Where was she? Oh, yes, Millie Payne had her. She had to talk to God, couldn't think about the red dirt falling on the box.

Dear God, please give me strength. Help me provide for these three children. Don't let that beautiful little girl die. Suddenly, I love and want her in the worst way. She keeps spitting up the milk. May not be keeping enough down to grow. Help me, Lord. Show me what to do. She needs breast milk. Send me a wet nurse. I can't do this alone. Please bring Aaron safely back to me. Make him willing to accept the children. I need him desperately. You know that I love him with all my heart. Only you can provide for us, Lord. I'm starving and helpless.

She felt Sadie's arm on her shoulder. The noise of the falling dirt had stopped. It must be time to go.

Two days later, March 27, 1865: Davis Street

Constance walked towards the depot yawning. The warm sunlight felt good on her tired face. She had been up every two hours for the last several nights feeding the baby. The child took the milk, spit part of it back up, cried and screamed with stomach pains, passed gas. Having heard a train arrive, she decided a walk would do her good. Maybe there would be some news or newspapers or perhaps a cherished letter from Aaron. The Yankee soldiers laughed and talked around the depot. She detested their insolent looks, their arrogant attitude of assumed victory. She noticed a colored woman and four children maneuvering their way through the soldiers towards her. The boy looked familiar.

"Miss Constance," the thin small woman said in a strained voice. "I's so sorry I took your dresses. Please forgive me...let me come back,"

"Selene?" Constance asked with a questioning look.

"Yas'm. We's been in Washington while Joseph went with the cal'vy. We promised we'd meet back at the farm when this terrible war ended. It's gotta end soon. We don't wanna live no where else. Please let us come back," she begged with tears in her eyes.

"But Selene, I have no food...can't take care of you."

"We'll work," Isaac said. "We was starvin' in Washington. Had to beg."

"I had to be a whore to get money for food...had no choice," Selene confessed. Then the bundle in her arms moved and let out a small cry.

Startled, Constance gaped after Selene pulled back the blanket to reveal a honey-skinned mulatto baby. "Couldn't help it, had to get money...hope Joseph don't hate me."

"Selene!" Constance exclaimed, her spirit soaring. "Do you have milk?"

"Yas'm, I got milk," the Negro answered confused.

"God has sent you to me! Come with me!"

Eight days later, April 4, 1865: Armstrong parlor

Granny paced the floor restlessly tamping her cane while Constance rocked the baby and Lucy sat dejected on the sofa. "I refuse to believe what those arrogant soldiers are saying, that Petersburg has fallen," the little lady said defiantly. "I think Lee's marching to take Washington. Defeat would be a calamity like we have never known."

"The thought of all our sacrifices being in vain; of the blood of our men shed for nothing; of the probable seizure and death of our leaders," moaned Lucy. "It's too horrible to think of."[2]

"The continuation of the struggle will only cause us all to starve," Constance said. "We must have the will to survive, to endure their taunts, so that we can pass on our honor and the truth about this war to our children."

"I will never tolerate their sneers, their jibes," Granny declared, sparks shooting from her eyes.

Lucy stood and walked towards her grandmother. "We must be going now so Constance can get the baby to sleep." Turning towards Constance, she smiled. "I'm glad she's doing so much better."

"Thank you. I appreciate your visit. God seems to have answered my prayers."

After they left, Constance tickled Harriet's chin. The baby cooed and closed her eyes contently. The change in her since Selene began nursing her was a miracle. She had gained weight, slept longer, and kept all of her milk down. Amazingly, Selene's baby had been able to tolerate the cow's milk. On top of that, Hudson's spirits had improved now that Isaac was back. The two of them talked and laughed like old times. Then, George McDonald had the good fortune of killing a deer. He had shared the meat with them and for the first time in months, there were no hunger pangs. She loved feeling the baby sleeping happily in her arms. God was looking out for her.

Constance enjoyed the warmth of the late afternoon sun while she raked the glossy magnolia leaves. It was spring, the season of rebirth and hope. She smiled at Selene's Hope, Ruth, and Mary, who picked the persistent jonquils blooming amongst the weeds. Billy heaved the sledgehammer over his shoulders and struck a sharp blow on the splitting wedge, causing the magnolia wood to shatter into several pieces. Isaac and

David tossed pieces of wood to Hudson who stacked them neatly. Hudson actually laughed after Isaac tossed a piece of wood out of his reach, forcing him to lunge for it.

In the background she listened to the chatter of Selene and Sadie, seated in the gazebo feeding the babies. Harriet nursed noisily, greedily at Selene's breast. Not to be outdone, little Moses consumed the bottle of milk from Sadie with great gusto. Selene rattled on about the over 8000 prostitutes in Washington, the starving Negroes looking for work, rampant disease and filth, thousands upon thousands of wounded soldiers, and her homesickness for the farm.

Distracted from her tranquil reverie, Constance noticed a lone Union soldier riding slowly on Cameron Street, staring at them. The few Yankees at the depot had mercifully left the town residents alone. Her pulse quickened when he dismounted and called to her across the fence, "I'm looking for Miss Constance Armstrong."

Her pulse roared in her ears. Had he come to arrest her for being a spy? She licked her dry lips. "I'm Miss Armstrong," she answered in a strained voice.

"I have a telegram for you." He held an envelope over the picket fence.

Constance dropped the rake, took off her gloves, and inched her way through the tall grass to him. "Thank you." She clasped the envelope in her shaking hand. Slowly walking back towards the gazebo, she felt the butterflies fluttering in her stomach. It had to be from or about Aaron. Was it good news or bad news? Sadie gave her a questioning look. She must open it. Taking a deep breath, she ripped open the envelope. Maybe it was over and he was coming to her at last. With clammy palms she unfolded the paper and read:

Miss Armstrong,

    With grief, I inform you that we received a telegram notifying us that Aaron is missing after the Battle of Five Forks, April 1. The 1st Maine cavalry suffered high casualties in an ill-fated charge. Against orders, he rushed on to the battlefield to aid his former comrades. The Rebels countercharged and gained control of the field. He could not be located when his friends searched for him the next day. We must pray without ceasing that he is captured or wounded and will return safely to us. Will keep you informed.

Abby

Constance shuddered as if a bolt of lightning had struck her. Everything began to spin wildly; the darkness closed in, her legs melted away, and she crashed to the ground.

22

Surrender

April 5-24, 1865

I have met with many of the great men of my time, but Lee alone impressed me with the feeling that I was in the presence of a man who was cast in a grander mold and made of a different and finer metal than all other men. He is stamped upon my memory as being apart and superior to all others in every way, a man with whom none I ever knew and few of whom I have read are worthy to be classed. When all the angry feelings aroused by the secession are buried with those that existed when the American Declaration of Independence was written; when Americans can review the history of their last great war with calm impartiality, I believe all will admit that General Lee towered far above all men on either side of the struggle. I believe he will be regarded not only as the most prominent figure of the Confederacy, but as the greatest American of the nineteenth century, whose statue is well worthy to stand on an equal pedestal with that of Washington and whose memory is equally worthy to be enshrined in the hearts of all his countrymen.

Lord Wolseley when commander-in-chief of the armies of Great Britain

---

Next day, April 5, 1865: Constance's bedroom

The baby's shrill cry aroused Constance from her tormented stupor. She struggled to open her eyes to the dawn light, then reality seeped back into her haunted mind. Rolling on her side, her cheek felt the dampness of the tear stained pillow. She realized she was in her own bed, not desperately stumbling through dead and wounded men in search of Aaron. The possibility that he could have been swallowed up in the last gasps of this tragic war had stunned her into oblivion. Little Hattie's cries grew louder, more demanding. Praying for strength, Constance slowly sat up and pulled the covers back. Why did her hip ache so painfully? She pushed her hair out of her face and attempted to focus. Then it came back to her…she had fainted in the yard.

"Miss Constance?" Sadie hurried into the room, her face drawn. Constance gave her a look of mute appeal, her face scarlet and swollen from crying. Sadie sat down beside her, pulled her head against her shoulder. "How ya feelin', chile?"

"Hip's sore," Constance replied in a barely audible tone without emotion.

"That's cause ya took a bad tumble. Now I want ya to listen to me. He ain't dead! I knows it! Ya can't give up hope. If he was wounded or captured, he's gonna survive to come back to ya. He loves ya too much to give up an' die. Trust Sadie."

Constance stared at Sadie with a lost expression. "Need him…can't hang on without him…three children."

"And those chil'en needs ya. Ya can't sit here feeling sorry for yourself all day. That baby needs lovin' an' those boys need schoolin'." Sadie walked to the bassinet and

516

changed the baby. "Now, I want to hear ya talk 'bout hope." She placed the squirming infant in Constance's arms.

Little Hattie blew bubbles and kicked her diminutive legs, then reached up and grabbed at Constance's hair. With the faintest smile, Constance said, "You're right, Sadie. There is still hope. My whole world has crumbled, but I must cling to that tiny ray of hope."

Three days later, April 8, 1865: Armstrong dining room

Unable to concentrate, Constance listened to Hudson's monotonous reading. Her stomach growled. She had little appetite since receiving the telegram about Aaron, but it didn't matter. Lacking enough food for all of them, she knew Selene came first. She tried to focus when Hudson paused and pointed to a word. "Revolution." Her mind slipped back to thoughts of Aaron. It had been over four days and no word. She prayed without ceasing, refusing to give up hope. Rumors abounded that Richmond had been evacuated and the government and army had fled south. Poor old Governor Smith. She prayed for his safety.[i] What would the Yankees do to him and President Davis if they captured them? She had not heard from Frank since before Christmas. Was he still alive?

The knock at the door startled her. Hudson ran to answer it, delighted to have an excuse to escape his studies.

Ashen faced, Millie Payne rushed into the dining room clutching a newspaper. "Constance, I got a Baltimore paper from one of the Yankees eating at the hotel. The terrible rumor is true. Richmond has fallen and Lincoln marched through the streets like a conquering hero."

"How much humiliation must we bear?" Constance grabbed the paper.

"Our men will never stop fighting," Hudson said with blazing eyes. "Mosby will kill Yankees forever."

"Oh, dear God," Constance cried in anguish. "Did you see this? Powell Hill is dead!"

"No!" Millie sank into a chair beside Constance, reading along with her.

"Culpeper's fiercest warrior dead for his country. Will the death toll never stop rising?[ii] Where have they laid him? He should be buried here."

"It doesn't say," Millie said, wiping a tear from her face. "His poor young wife and daughters. Do you suppose they'll come back here?"

"Probably. I doubt that Mildred knows." Constance gave Millie a helpless look, her bottom lip trembling. "I don't have the strength to do it. Will you go to her?"

"I understand." Millie offered Constance a consoling hug. "I'll muster the strength and take this paper to Mildred."

---

[i]When the war ended, Smith surrendered to Federal authorities and returned on parole to Warrenton. He remained robust and active through his writing and speaking until his death at age 90. His body lay in state in Richmond. A cast of his face was made for the statue of him, which was erected on the capital grounds. He was the only governor to be so honored until modern times.

[ii]623,000 Americans died in The Civil War, more than in all other wars combined through Vietnam. Another 471,000 were wounded or crippled. There is no estimate of the civilian deaths in the South.

Three days later, April 11, 1865: The Culpeper Observer

Tears rolled slowly down George McDonald's face while rifle shots rang out from the depot where the damn Yankees celebrated Lee's surrender. He had been there half an hour ago when the train came in with the news and the newspapers. Rummaging through his desk drawer, he found the deed, took it out, dipped his pen in the berry juice and began to write. He heard the rapid footsteps at the door, looked up to see Constance's owlish eyes searching his face for an answer.

"Are we finished?" she asked pensively.

His tears flowed and he struggled to speak. Finally he sobbed, "I would not believe it...told them I could not hear it...that it was false...asked God to take me." She rushed to the chair beside his desk, sat down and clasped his hand. "Lee the greatest general and gentleman...forced to surrender to Grant, the butcher!"

Constance inhaled sharply, could not speak for the lump in her throat. She thought she was empty, could cry no more, but when she heard the inevitable news tears flooded her eyes. "How will we...ever endure their scorn...taunts?"

He squeezed her hand and gave her his handkerchief. "Will the sun ever shine again on our wretched people...ruined country? I would have borne ten times more privations to see our country free from our enemies."

"No army ever fought more bravely...suffered more. We still have our honor...our spirit," she said defiantly through her tears.

McDonald leaned back in his chair and sighed heavily. "I'm fifty-eight years old. I will not endure Yankee rule and tyranny for the rest of my life. I have no family here. I'm originally from Connecticut...could never go back to see their smugness. I've decided to go to Toronto...lots of Rebels there. I'm taking the train north in a short while. The sooner I escape these gloating Yankees, the better."

"No! You can't leave. Who's going to run the newspaper and tell the truth about it all?"

He pushed the deed in front of her. "You are, Miss Armstrong. I'm afraid I've been a bit of a hermit since my wife died. You've been my most loyal friend. I've deeded the building to you, and of course the printing press comes with it."

She shot upright in her chair, blinking with surprise. "Me? Oh, I could never accept such a gift."

"Our money and our property are worthless. No Southerner could buy the building, and I don't want it to go to the Yankees. You'll struggle just to pay the taxes. I hope you can hang on to it and run the paper again."

"But...I don't know...if I have to sell it, I'll send you the money."

"No, you won't," he said firmly. "You won't know where I am. You're going to need all the help you can get to provide for those three children."

Before she could protest further, Granny Ashby scampered into the office and scrutinized their tear stained faces. "It must be true," she squeaked.

"I'm afraid so," Constance murmured. "Now they're going to self-righteously mock us; tell us God was on their side. They were right and we were wrong."

"Balderdash!" Granny pounded her cane on the floor and pulled up a chair next to Constance. "I think God simply weeps when he sees men killing men. Might doesn't make right. This war doesn't prove they were right. All it proves is that a nation with three times more men and horses and more than three-fourths of the manufacturing and railroads can conquer a weaker nation. But it took the fools four long years to do it, because our men fought so valiantly." She tamped her cane for drama.

"We can only feel pride in seeking the rights of our state and upholding the constitution," McDonald agreed.

They heard the whistle of the train. "Oh, I've got to run." McDonald grabbed his carpetbag.

Constance hugged him warmly and kissed him on the cheek. "God be with you. Thank you for your generosity."

He dashed out of the office with Granny gaping. "Where's he going?"

"To Toronto. He refuses to live under Yankee rule."

"I don't blame him. I'd rather live in the Sahara desert than put up with what we're going to have to endure. Trouble is, I'm trapped here. Don't even have money for a train ticket."

"Now they'll grind us under their heels, go for our land...take it away from us," Constance speculated as a muscle flicked angrily in her jaw.

Three days later, April 14, 1865: Armstrong front porch

Half in anticipation, half in dread, Constance watched the tall soldier walk down Coleman Street towards her. She abruptly stopped rocking the chair, her heart jumping in her chest. Gradually, a glazed look of despair spread over her face after she realized he was another emaciated, ragged Confederate. Her head bowed, she slumped back into the chair and cuddled Hattie. All day she had watched in eager anticipation while soldiers drifted back into town. If Aaron had been taken prisoner, surely he had been released by now. She had begun the day with the slight spark of hope that he might return today. Now, at dusk, her expression was grim. She heard Millie Payne and her Yankee laughing across the street on the porch of the Virginia House. She could not look at them, could not stand the pain of seeing them touch. They had been kind to her, visited, offered her hope, but now she felt bereft and desolate.

She pulled her body up and walked towards the door, weak from hunger, sure that her backbone had rubbed a hole in her stomach. Visions of her morning visit from Bettie Browning and Daniel Grimsley, joyfully reunited, passed before her eyes. She saw Bettie's face, blissfully euphoric, announcing their marriage in few days. With humble dignity, Daniel had explained that he was one of the fortunate few who fought in every cavalry battle without ever being wounded.[iii] Grant had allowed them to keep their horses and he must begin spring planting at once. The returning soldiers reported that the railroad only ran to Rapidan Station, forcing them to walk the rest of the way.

Constance entered the hall where the peeling faux marble wallpaper and darkness matched her dull ache of foreboding. She cuddled Hattie softly, desperately needing to touch and love someone. The baby was a Godsend. She must focus on the children and

---

[iii] Grimsley studied law after the war, served in the Virginia Senate for 10 years, and spent 24 years as a judge. He and Bettie had 6 children. The Grimsleys are buried in Fairview Cemetery.

her efforts to provide for them. In work, she found a distraction that helped camouflage the depth of her loneliness.

Next day, April 15, 1865: Armstrong parlor

"She's a beautiful baby," Annie Crittenden Smoot exclaimed leaning over the bassinet.

"We're all just heartsick about Amanda's death," Catherine Crittenden said with a catch in her voice. She put her hand compassionately on Constance's back. "You've got an awesome responsibility."

Constance's eyebrows drew together in an agonized expression. "I feel totally inadequate. Please, won't all of you sit and visit a few minutes. I'm desperate for company."

"For a short spell," Major Charles Crittenden answered, then he maneuvered his stiff, frail body into a chair. "We came to town looking for seeds and potatoes." Annie, her husband Major Jim Smoot, and Catherine made themselves comfortable on the sofa while Constance dropped into the rocking chair.

Constance studied Charles's weathered gaunt face. "Food is a desperate problem. When were you wounded?"

"At Spotsylvania," he answered with a tight grim mouth "Bloodiest battle of the war. I seen them all. Even survived Pickett's charge."[iv]

Constance stared at the badly scarred face of Annie's husband. "Were you at Appomattox, Major Smoot?"

Gripping Annie's hand tightly, he answered, "Yes. It was the most heartbreaking scene I've ever witnessed. Tough, rugged, seasoned soldiers sobbed like babies." His voice fell to a broken whisper. "When Marse Robert told us farewell, said he'd done the best he could for us, wished us well, we all broke down. Couldn't bear the thought of not seeing him again. We all tried to touch him, touch Traveller, pull hairs from Traveller's tail. Poor horse," he said in a forced laugh. "He ain't got much tail left."

Annie caressed his hand. "At least the Yankees showed our men proper respect," she said softly. "Saluted them in silence. That man from Maine, Chamberlain, was in charge."

After an uncomfortable silence, Catherine cleared her throat. "Constance, I regret that our dire straits prevent us from offering you assistance at the moment. When our crops come in, we'll share with you."

Constance fought hard against the tears she refused to let fall. "That's most kind of you. We...we will survive somehow. God will help us."

"What are your prospects?" Charles asked with deep concern.

She tried to keep her fragile control. "I hope that our servant, Joseph, will return. His wife and family are here. Then we'll go to the farm and plant."

They all offered her words of encouragement and praised her fortitude.

After she walked outside to bid them goodbye, she decided to sit a spell in the rocking chair. She closed her eyes and her body absorbed the warmth of the sunshine. The baby

---

[iv] Charles Crittenden entered the Confederate Soldier's Home in Richmond in 1902 suffering from war wounds. He died in 1907 and is buried at the foot of Cedar Mountain not far from the lane he so gallantly defended in August, 1862.

was asleep; it would be fine for her to rest a few minutes. Her spirit felt empty and drained from having to relate the terrible story of Alex and Amanda's deaths, not once, but twice. Fannie and James Barbour had stopped by earlier in the day. Fannie, distraught at the news about Amanda, pledged to help Constance with the children as soon as they got on their feet again. Constance heard the same story over and over again. People were returning, life would resume some degree of normalcy, but for the next few months they would all struggle to survive starvation. Tides of weariness and despair engulfed her until she slowly drifted into a restless stupor. Her mind filled with memories of Aaron, pure and clear. She recalled the ecstasy of being held against his strong body, the tingling warmth of his kiss. Her face burned while she recalled the smoldering passion that he aroused in her.

A male voice interrupted her reverie. Her heart sank when she realized the familiar voice wasn't Aaron's. Instantly awake, her eyes sprang open. She stared at the thin soldier dismounting. He was a bag of bones, but then he had always been that way.

"Frank!" she shouted in utter joy. She bolted from the chair and sprinted down the steps into his arms. They hugged each other with reckless abandon. "Thank God!" she blurted. "Someone I love has survived!" They kissed each other and both seemed to be laughing and crying at the same time.

He stared at her tired, haggard face. "It's great to see you, Connie. You look peaked."

"You're not the picture of health yourself," she retorted with a sad laugh.

He wrapped his arms around her and squeezed her tight. "But, we've both survived. That's a blessing," he muttered in a choking, tired voice.

"Oh, do come in," she said, her voice rising in excitement. "There's so much to tell."

After she introduced him to Hattie, Sadie took the baby to be fed. They settled onto the sofa, Constance explained her desperate situation, and he began his narrative. In January, President Davis had ordered him to go under cover into Washington to determine the climate for a negotiated peace. He had managed to reach the city and establish contacts with Confederate sympathizers without much difficulty. However, he decided to keep moving around in order not to arouse suspicion. With typical reckless abandon, he had moved into a boarding house frequented by Union spies. He figured they would never suspect he would have the audacity to go there. Things went well for a good while, until the proprietress became suspicious of him. Finally, one night at dinner she devised a scheme to expose him. She proposed a toast to President Lincoln. Stringfellow, unable to stoop to such a level, did not drink. When she questioned him, he replied that wine never touched his lips. Craftily, she filled his glass with water and again proposed the toast. In an ill advised show of patriotism, he flung the water across the table and shouted, "Long live Jefferson Davis!"

Dashing into the street, he fled for his life. Shortly thereafter, he was captured and sent to prison. Realizing his days were numbered if they discovered his true identity, he determined to escape. After one failed attempt, he managed to creep past the sleeping guard. A search party soon pursued him, hunting him in the woods like an animal. Only by hiding inside a log, did he escape. After stealing a horse, and traveling twenty-one nights, he had reached Culpeper, hearing in route the terrible news of Lee's surrender.

Her luminous eyes widened in astonishment. "Frank, that's incredible, absolutely incredible."

"I...I feel like I let the Confederacy down. I would have given my life to change the outcome of this war," he admitted, his voice breaking.

She took his bony fingers in hers. "Frank, you couldn't lose the war single-handed any more than you could win it alone."

His sunken eyes glistened with tears. "I know that my information helped us win several battles, but there were two times when I failed miserably. If I hadn't allowed myself to be captured prior to Gettysburg, I could have guided Stuart across the Potomac. The Union army wouldn't have gotten between him and Lee."

"His late arrival did hurt our efforts, but you can't blame yourself."

His face flushed with humiliation. "I had an opportunity to kill Grant. His profile was outlined in front the campfire and all I had to do was pull the trigger." He turned and gave her an imploring look. "I couldn't do it...kept hearing your voice saying, 'Don't give up your life needlessly, Frank.'"

She leaned closer in an instinctive gesture of comfort. "You're not a cold-blooded murderer. Trading your life for his would have accomplished nothing. No man risked his life more frequently for our cause than you. I will hear no more of this foolish talk."

He moved his shoulders in a shrug of resignation. "I feel like I have little to live for. I'm a wanted man with $10,000 on my head. I don't feel safe here. Who knows what type of revenge they'll seek?"

"They're expressing less bitterness than I expected." She picked up the newspaper from the table and laid it in his lap. "They seem ready to welcome us poor Rebels as friends, now that they have whipped us and can return to their money-getting. This paper even suggests that Lee should show himself in the North where he would receive a hero's ovation."

Frank's eyes scanned the paper. "It says they admire his high character, soldierly qualities, and military greatness, and would shower honors on him if he would allow himself to be gazed at." His lips twisted in a mocking smile. "They are used to their coarse-minded heroes who were failures in civilian life, like Grant, Sherman, and the vainglorious Custer and Sheridan. Men who have killed and destroyed to advance their reputations and fortunes."

"You're right. They can't understand a hero with Lee's principles. He would never make a spectacle of himself for money or fame."

The knock on the door caused her spine to become rigid. David raced down the steps and answered it. Breathlessly, she wondered, could it be Aaron? Millie Payne dashed into the room, breathing laboriously, her round face flushed with excitement. Constance's face fell with disappointment. "Millie, please sit down. Whatever is wrong?" Millie's wide eyes darted from one to the other of them in uncertainty. She recognized Stringfellow and the tension in her face relaxed.

"Constance, Frank," she stammered. "I just returned from putting my beau on the train. You won't believe what the Yankees are saying, what came over the telegraph."

Frank leaned forward his eyebrows raised in curiosity. "What, Millie? Tell us!"

"Lincoln," she gasped. "He's dead. Shot in the head at the theatre last night by that actor, John Wilkes Booth!"

Stringfellow took a quick sharp breath and shot up from the sofa like an arrow. "Are you positive?"

"Yes," she panted. "There's no doubt that he's dead and that Booth did it!"

Constance's face paled with shock. "I…I can't shed any tears over the man who caused hundreds of thousands to die. Yet…the violence must stop."

"Booth is a Virginian. I fear their wrath and rage will be hurled against us more fiercely than ever." Stringfellow burned his nervous energy by pacing, running his hands through his hair. He confronted Millie. "You must not tell anyone you saw me here. My life is in danger."

Millie's body stiffened. "No, of course not. I won't tell. I'm afraid the fighting is going to start all over again. I must go." She rushed towards the door.

Constance jumped up and followed her. "Millie, thank you for telling us, and please keep Frank's secret." She gripped Millie's arm firmly. "Tell no one, not even your family."

Millie's facial muscles twitched nervously as she opened the door. "Yes," she whispered and then fled across the street.

Constance hurried back into the parlor, her arms blossoming with goosebumps. "Frank, did you have anything to do with it?"

"No," he said, his skin growing clammy. He pulled her to him and his eyes took on a hunted look. "But I knew Booth. Met him at a safe house for Rebels in Maryland. They'll hunt down anybody connected with him. Reprisal's going to be bloody."

She wrapped her arms around him, attempting to remain calm. "I knew you weren't an assassin. What will you do?"

He stood paralyzed for a few minutes, trying to think. "I've got to flee…to Canada. I know I can make connections with sympathizers along the way."

She tried to find her voice. "I can't believe I've got to let you go so soon…the one person who's dear to me."

"Can we trust Millie?" he asked tensely.

Constance bit her lip nervously. "I think so, but if they find out about the $10,000 bounty, that's enough to tempt anybody."

They froze at the sound of another knock at the door. "My God," Constance said, feeling acid well in her stomach. "Who can that be?"

"Is the bookstore unlocked? Just to be safe, I'm going to slip over there."

"Yes." Constance's face was a mask of terror. "That's a good idea. I'll get the door."

Her knees quaked while she walked cautiously to the door. She opened the door and looked into the face of a tall soldier, but it was not the face she longed to see.

"Good evening, Miss Armstrong," Channing Smith said. "I'm traveling from Richmond back to Colonel Mosby, and I thought I'd pay my respects."

She studied him acutely and then her lips slowly turned up in a smile of relief. "It's good to see you, Mr. Smith. Please come in."

"I've been with Mosby since August," he explained while they walked through the hall. "I'm deeply sorry about your brother-in-law's tragic death."

"Thank you." She maintained her calm and escorted him into the parlor. "If you'll wait for a minute, there's someone here you'll want to see."

Smith shifted nervously from one foot to the other, wondering what was going on. Stringfellow bounded into the room. "Stringfellow, by God! You're a sight for sore eyes." The two scouts threw their arms around each other.

"I know you two have much to discuss. I'll have Sadie prepare a meal for you," Constance told them before she walked out the door.

"You go first." Stringfellow motioned for Smith to sit.

"Mosby sent me to Richmond to see General Lee to inquire if we should continue the fight."

"How's our beloved leader?"

"I found him somber but dignified, dressed in his gray coat with no insignia. He said he must remain true to his parole and could not issue any orders. I then inquired as to what I should do personally. He told me to go home."

Stringfellow nodded, his eyes moist. "Is that what you'll do?"

"Yes, after I report to Colonel Mosby. I suspect he'll disband, but I question if he'll ever formally surrender."

"I envy you. I'm afraid my situation isn't so simple." Stringfellow told him about Lincoln's assassination and his personal dilemma.

At 10 o'clock Constance and Frank stood in the street, attempting to tell each other goodbye. He had slept for three hours and Smith remained upstairs asleep. He cupped her chin in his hand and lifted her face towards his in the moonlight. "You'll get word to mother that I'm safe." She nodded, unable to speak. "I pray that your Aaron returns and makes you the happiest woman on the face of the earth. You're beautiful and brave." He kissed her softly.

She struggled to speak through her constricting throat. "God protect you, big brother. I love you."

He felt her cling tightly to his sparse body. "It's by the grace of God that I've survived this terrible war. He's certainly not going to desert me now. I'm only twenty five. Surely, He must have some useful purpose for my life."[v]

"I know that He does. Listen and He will guide you. Besides, you must return and make me laugh again, and then make Emma your wife."

He pulled away reluctantly and mounted his horse. She rigidly held her tears in check and watched him ride away. This time she felt confident he would return, but that did not ease the permanent sorrow that consumed her. She was one of many women facing the harsh realities of loneliness.

Next day, April 16, 1865, Easter Sunday: Saint Stephen's

Reverend John Cole surveyed his flock, seated before him on rough planks in the severely damaged church. Their despondent eyes looked to him for hope. There were more of them today. People had come back to rebuild their lives: the lucky survivors, the physically maimed, and the mentally maimed. He could deliver the traditional Easter message of hope, hope of a better world to come, release from the agonies of this

---

[v] Stringfellow remained in Canada 2 years. He returned, married his beloved Emma, became an Episcopal minister at age 36, and had six children. He lectured throughout the country about his war experiences to raise money for the Episcopal Church and was the first chaplain at Woodberry Forest School for Boys. At age 57 he accompanied his son to Cuba as a chaplain in the Spanish American War. He died at age 73.

world, and hope of eventual reunion with lost loved ones. But more than that, he felt compelled to help them put the bitterness and hatred behind them. He must preach of reconciliation.

Constance listened intently to his words. "Be ye not overcome by evil, but overcome evil with good." It struck home with her. She looked at the two boys seated on each side of her. How could she make them understand the meaning of those words? She must not allow bitterness to gnaw away at their souls. David leaned his head against her shoulder. His brown eyes looked up at her affectionately after she brushed a wisp of auburn hair from his face. She knew there was hope for him. Hudson sat rigidly upright, his cold unresponsive eyes staring straight ahead. The icy blue eyes that had seen too much revealed an inner pain. He held his mouth tight and rigid. She knew instinctively that he had built a fortress around his soul. How could she ever penetrate it?

Her eyes turned downward to the sleeping girl in her arms, her pink mouth poised in a slight smile of contentment. She was hers to love, cherish, and mold. While Constance basked in the knowledge of her power, a sense of strength came to her. She would fight for a better world for this little girl, a world where women enjoyed the same rights as men. Her courage and determination were like a rock inside her. She vowed to build a new life for all of them.

When the time came for prayer, her long lashes brushed her cheeks and she bared her soul to God:

Dear heavenly Father, help me to release my bitterness as I strive to build a better life for these children in a world where all people, black and white, male and female, enjoy their God given rights. As my darling Aaron said, 'I cannot change the past, I can only hope to change the future.' You heard my cry and sent Selene to save the baby. Hear my cry again. I have more mouths to feed and nothing but a little cornmeal and whatever game we can trap. Before we can build a better world, we must survive the next few months in this one. I need Joseph, and a horse or mule, and of course Aaron, so that we can go to the farm and plant. We must have greens or vegetables soon or we will suffer from scurvy. Every morning I wake up in the hope that I will find Aaron sitting on my doorstep and every night I cry myself to sleep in disappointment. He must be lying somewhere unconscious or too weak to come to me. You see him, Lord. Save him and send him safely to me. He is my hope, my life.

Three days later, April 19, 1865: Davis and East Streets

Constance walked dejected with her head down, returning from her fruitless daily trek to the telegraph office. The creaking wagon wheels caused her to look up at another group of returning refugees. The tall man driving eyed her curiously. "Miss Armstrong?"

He was so much thinner; she had to study his eyes to recognize him. "Yes, Mr. Hill, welcome back," she said to Baptist Hill.

The sad lady in the wagon, seated between the two girls, looked down at her when he stopped the horses. "Constance, I must see my dear Amanda, immediately. I need her."

Constance moved closer and stared into the blue eyes flickering with pain. "Dolly, let me express my deepest sympathy. General Hill was loved and admired by us all." She bit her lip and tried to ago on. "I'm sorry I must tell you…Amanda…died in childbirth last month."

"No!" The blood drained from Dolly's face. She gave Constance an imploring look, her eyes awash with tears. "Please, will you visit me later today? We must talk."

"Yes, I'll come this afternoon. I'll bring her beautiful daughter."

Hattie cooed at Dolly and Mildred. "Amanda wanted a little girl desperately. It seems so tragic that's she's gone," Dolly mused. "But our world overflows with tragedy."

"Amanda told me of your friendship last winter. She treasured you," Constance said.

"And I her." Dolly maneuvered her round pregnant body into a chair.

"Dolly, if you're up to talking about it, I'd like to hear the circumstances of Powell's death," Mildred said.

"He's our own fallen hero," Constance added.

Dolly leaned her head against the back of the chair and sighed. "Perhaps it will do me good to get it all out. Forgive me if I break down."

She crossed her hands over her large abdomen while her eyes stared off in the distance, recalling the painful memories. When it became obvious that the Yankees were attempting to break through their lines at Petersburg, Powell had ridden to the front lines to assess the situation. She had known in her heart that he would rather die than surrender. An hour or so later, she answered the knock at the door to see one of his staff members. "The general is dead!" she'd cried in anguish. Shortly, some soldiers arrived with his body draped over a horse. He had confronted several Yankees, drawn his gun and ordered them to surrender. One had fired a single bullet through his heart, killing him instantly. Powell's nephew, Captain Frank Hill and a courier were designated to escort her and the girls safely to Richmond. They found a dilapidated old army wagon with irregular wheels, laid Powell's body in it and covered his face with a cape. Dolly recalled cradling her girls in her arms and staring at the conspicuous wedding ring on Powell's left hand during the jostling ride towards Richmond.

She had hoped to bury him in Hollywood Cemetery with the other Confederate heroes. It was after dark when they tried to cross the Mayo Bridge into the city. Part of the city glowed in flames and fleeing civilians and wagons obstructed all roads leading out. Unable to penetrate the fleeing tide or chaos, they determined to try to reach the estate of Powell's uncle in Chesterfield County instead. It was the afternoon of the next day before they got there. Her second choice of burial places was Culpeper, beside his parents. However, in the warmth of the day they realized the impracticality of getting his unembalmed remains to Culpeper. They laid him to rest in a coffin and rough case in the cemetery of his uncle's estate without religious ceremony or fanfare.[1]

"I hated to leave him there." Dolly wiped her eyes. "I hope that at some future date he can be brought home to his beloved Culpeper."[vi]

[vi]Anne Powell (A.P.) Hill was born on June 6 in Culpeper. Only one of Hill's daughters survived to adulthood and she never had any children. Thus, there are no direct descendants of A.P. Hill. His loyal veterans, with Dolly's reluctant permission, moved Hill's remains to Hollywood Cemetery in 1867. However, the location did not seem honorable enough for the beloved leader of The Third Corps. Funds were raised, and his body was moved again and is interred beneath the statue of him, which stands at the intersection of Hermitage Road and Laburnum Avenue in Richmond.

"We'll see that it's done eventually," Mildred told her. "I hope that you and the girls will stay and live with us. This is your home now."

"Thank you, Mildred. You've all been most kind to me. I'll stay until the baby is born, because I know Powell would want his child born here. I pray it's a boy so he'll have a namesake."

"But then what will you do?" Constance asked.

"I'm going home to Kentucky to be with Mother. We need each other. I've also lost two brothers."

Hattie let out a demanding cry. Rising to her feet Constance bent over Dolly and embraced her. "I believe Miss Hattie is ready to be fed. Thank you for sharing your story with us. You're a courageous lady."

Dolly held her hand and then released it reluctantly. "So are you Constance. We're both going to face raising three children alone."

Constance entered the back gate, then heard laughter and animated talking emanating from the kitchen. "We's so glad to have ya back!" she overheard Sadie exclaim, and then a man laughed. Her heart pulsed wildly. She ran towards the door. Could it be Aaron? She dashed inside to see Joseph surrounded by his family. Sheathing her inner feelings, she handed the baby to Selene.

"Joseph," she heard herself say, "Thank God you're back. We've been worried."

"It took me a while, Miss Constance, 'cause I could only travel at night. There's all kinds of men driftin' out there, stealin' anything they can get their hands on. I couldn't let nobody steal mah mule," he bragged, his chest swelling with pride.

"Mule!" Constance blurted, her eyes bulging. "How did you get a mule?"

Joseph sat down beside Selene, who nursed Hattie. "Well, now. I figgered as long as I'd served them Yankees, they owed me a mule. How else we gonna plow? So near the end, I procured mahself one an' disappeared into the night. He's hidden in the carriage house."

The children laughed. Constance sat opposite him and the tight lines of her face gradually melted into a smile. "Joseph, I think the good Lord must have inspired you. We desperately need that mule. Now we can go to the farm and plant."

"Yas'm." His face split into a wide grin. He pulled a roll of money from his pocket and laid it on the table. "I hope the good Lawd will forgive me for robbin' dead men, but I knew we'd need some money."

They all leaned forward, gaping at the bills. "How much ya got?" Sadie asked.

"'Round thirty dollars. That oughtta buy us some food an' seeds."

Constance's face flushed with humiliation at the thought of taking charity from her servants. "I...I can't take your money...your charity."

Sadie sauntered over and put her hand on Constance's shoulder. "Now, Miss Constance, we's all the same now. We can give to you like you's given to us. Don't ya argue!"

Constance put her hand on Sadie's. "Thank you," she whispered softly. Looking at Joseph's confident face she asked, "When should we go to the farm?"

"Let me get a good night's sleep tonight. I'll take the mule an' go tomorrow night. Don't want ya'll along if there's any trouble. I've got a rifle. Besides, maybe I can bag a deer."

"And should we walk out there the next morning?"

"Yep. We's all got a pow'ful lotta hard work to do." He lifted Moses from Isaac's lap. Cuddling the child, he mumbled, "Can't believe the mess the damn Yankees done made 'round here."

Next day, April 20, 1865: Armstrong front bedroom

Constance wandered aimlessly into the front bedroom before the dark night grayed into dawn. After another restless night, she must prepare to journey to the farm tomorrow. Unable to think, her mind flooded with memories of the past four years. At almost twenty three, she had seen too much, endured too much, felt like Methuselah. During the past bleak winter she had yearned to write her story of the war but could not due to lack of paper and ink. She vowed to record the truth for future generations. Her face twisted into a scowl when she thought of the whitewashed version the Yankees would put in their history books. They would suddenly turn their war of aggression into a noble effort to help the people of color. She knew better. She had seen their blatant racism. The Negroes would now suffer in worse poverty than slavery, with no efforts made to bring them north or find them jobs

Her eyes focused on the poster bed in this their guest bedroom, the room with the nicest view of the street. Her fingers slowly traced over the smooth mahogany footpost. She drank in the beauty of the intricate quilt made by her grandmother. What a story this bed could tell. It had seen grief. It was the bed John and Amanda had both died in. She moved her hand softly over the quilt, thinking of the many people who had slept there: that young reporter—Townsend, Belle Boyd, Flora Stuart, Governor Bailey of Florida, the redhead and brunette from Richmond, the numerous Yankee soldiers of the winter encampment, dear honorable Robert. But most importantly to her, it was the bed Aaron had recovered in.

As if in a hypnotic state, she walked to the bureau and tenderly touched the chess set on top of it, allowing the heart on Aaron's bracelet to dangle before her. She remembered how they relished challenging each other and laughing together over the chessboard. Next she reached for the volume of *Romeo and Juliet*. Opening it, she tore out a page. She had no paper to leave him a note when they left in the morning. This would be more significant. Dipping her pen in the berry ink, she wrote in the margin, *Dearest Aaron, We are at the farm. I pray that you will come to me. Yours always, Constance.*

She knew that if he did not return, she would never marry another. Love like theirs only came along once in a lifetime to the fortunate few. The children would give her a purpose and she would consume herself with work—the bookstore, the newspaper. But, there would be no joy, no one to share her life with. She turned quickly towards her bedroom, deciding to dress and go to Saint Stephen's. God had heard her cry about Joseph and the mule. She must prostrate herself in prayer for Aaron's return. She refused to give up hope.

Constance stood in the gate of the tumbled down stonewall that surrounded the churchyard, her mind playing tricks on her. There in the street she saw Jeb Stuart, prancing and careening his horse to the excitement of all the ladies gathered to see him. A devout

Episcopalian, he never missed a service when in Culpeper. She walked forward into the churchyard and watched distinguished, gentlemanly General Lee take off his hat before he entered the sanctuary, while John Pelham stood beside her, his blue eyes laughing. She wondered if the worshipers who would stand in this church yard a hundred or two hundred years in the future would know and remember the character of the heroes who had been here before them. She hoped they would.

She felt the morning dew on her feet while she walked slowly towards the door. Entering the sanctuary, she paused to allow her eyes to adjust to the dim light. All but one of the windows had been damaged by the shelling and thus were covered with boards. But the morning sun radiated through the remaining stained glass window. Her eyes fixed on it, she moved forward and fell on her knees in front of the altar. She basked in the beauty of the light, feeling God's presence. Hot tears flooded down her cheeks. Her body slumped until she lay prostrate on the wooden floor. All of her pain and anguish flowed from her. She laid everything in God's hands.

Constance pulled the chain that lifted her watch from her pocket when she emerged into the bright sunlight. Nine o'clock! Could she possibly have been inside the church for two hours? She had been lost in time and space. She stepped into East Street, then saw Lucy striding towards her.

"Constance, wait. It's Granny."

"What?" Constance asked alarmed.

"She died in her sleep last night," Lucy stammered. "She's at peace now. It's those of us left behind who must suffer."

Constance released a deep sigh. "Perhaps it's a blessing. She never could have endured Yankee rule."

"No. I almost believe she willed herself to die. We're destitute. I don't know how we'll support ourselves. Heaven forbid, that we will end up like so many women," Lucy stopped and shuddered, "in the brothels."

Constance's eyebrows flew up. "Don't even talk of it. You can work for me in the bookstore. There is a light at the end of the tunnel."

The lines on Lucy's face relaxed. "Yes, you're right. Will you come to the viewing?"

"Yes, if it's tonight. We're leaving for the farm in the morning. Joseph is back with a mule." Lucy nodded yes and Constance put her arm around her shoulder. "I loved and admired Granny, especially the way she always spoke the truth. If I live that long, I hope I'll be just like her."

Four days later, April 24, 1865: Panorama

Sadie smiled at Hattie and Moses squirming on the blanket beside her on the front porch of Panorama. She inhaled the sweet fragrance of the apple blossoms with Mary tugging on her tattered skirt. Watching the first rays of sunset spread across the sky, she knew it must be almost time to start supper. But, there was no rush today. They would want to work in the field until dark again. Tonight they would enjoy the bounty of the deer Joseph had killed and the fish the boys had caught in the Hazel River. It felt so good to be back on the farm and have her family reunited. Her eyes turned to one of the dangling shutters that rattled in the gentle breeze. After the crops were planted, Joseph would begin repairs on the house and build new cabins for all of his family. It would take time, but they would eventually get life back to normal.

She lifted Mary onto her lap and scanned the hill down the lane. Her eyes fixed on the figure in the distance, a man walking up the lane. Probably just another straggler looking for a handout. They seemed to show up around dinnertime. She watched carefully while the tall soldier came nearer, taking long strides. This man was moving forward with a purpose, not simply ambling along. She stood up with Mary on her hip and picked her way through the tall grass to get a better view. He leaned into the wind, then glanced up to see her. "Sadie," he called in a rich low nasal voice, distinctly Yankee.

She stared wordlessly at him, her heart pounding with excitement. He had a beard, was thinner, but when he took his hat off in salute, she was sure. "Praise the Lawd God Almighty! Lieutenant Ames, you's alive!" she screamed, her voice breaking.

"Only by the grace of God," he admitted with a faint tremor in his voice. His whole face spread into a smile.

Sadie placed Mary on the ground and unable to control herself, she threw her arms around him.

"Aha! I always knew you really liked me," he chuckled while returning her hug.

"She gotta telegram saying ya was missin' over three weeks ago. Ya don't know what it's been like 'round here!" The words gushed from her as she took Mary's hand and they walked towards the porch.

"Is she well?" he asked panicking. "Where is she?"

"They's all way down back workin' in the field. She's wore out. Been through a terrible strain. Nary a bite to eat 'round here. So where in all creation has ya been?"

"I must have been kicked in the head by a horse. About a week later I woke up in the house of an old Confederate couple. Guess since I was in a blue coat without insignia, they thought I was one of them. Trouble is, I was in a fog. Couldn't remember anything. I stayed that way for a couple of weeks. Could talk to them, understand them, but had no memory of who I was or where I came from." The borders of his eyes grew moist. "Then suddenly, miraculously, I woke up on the twenty first, and the clouds had lifted. Everything came back to me clear as a bell, my family, the war, and especially Constance. I knew I had to get here as quickly as possible," he said animated. "I had no money...borrowed some from some Yankees I found at the station and took the train. Train broke down...had to walk a good part of the way."

Sadie sniffled. "It's a miracle." The two of them sat down on the edge of the porch and he glanced at the two babies with questioning eyes. "That's Miss Amanda's baby, Harriet. We calls her Hattie." Sadie looked down and shook her head regretfully. "Miss Amanda died two days after the baby was born."

His expression was like someone who had been struck in the face. "No! My God! Poor Constance! She's been carrying the weight of the world on her shoulders...providing for three children."

"Sure nuff. She needs ya bad."

He smiled down at Hattie, brushed his hand tenderly against her wisps of auburn hair. She blew bubbles and reached towards his hand, finally wrapping her tiny fingers around his thumb. Overwhelmed with emotion, he felt her tugging his heartstrings. It was love at first sight. He picked the infant up and cradled her in his arms.

"This is Moses," Sadie said patting her grandson on the abdomen. "Selene, she had to be a whore to get money for food after Joseph left. That's where he come from."

His brows drew together in an angry frown. "Well, he's a handsome young fellow. Is Joseph back?"

"Yas'r an' he brung a mule."

He stared deep into her ebony eyes. "Do you think she'll marry me now?"

Sadie threw back her head in a hearty laugh. "Well now, I'd say your chances is pow'ful good. She told me this mornin' she was goin' to Petersburg to search for ya tomorrow, if she had to walk the whole way."

His broad smile revealed his joy. "I've waited a long time for this. I want to do it properly. Since you're the only family she has left, I ask you for her hand in marriage."

Sadie sat tall and swelled with pride. "Well, now, I 'preciate that." She became serious and stern. "I know her Momma an' her Daddy would roll over in their graves if they knew she'd married a Yankee. Yas'r, this is a big respons'bility." Her face slowly softened into a smile. "But I know you's one good damn Yankee. Ya has mah permission to marry Miss Constance."

He smiled in relief and touched her hand. "I understand how dearly she loves you. I want you to know you'll always be a cherished and important member of our family."

"We'll get along jist fine, Mista Ames, long as ya remember which one of us was here first," she cackled. "Now, go an' make mah baby the happiest woman on the face of this earth. She's gonna have a conniption fit when she sees ya."

He placed Hattie in her arms and loped around the house, his pulse racing wildly. He thought his heart would jump out of his chest when he caught sight of her, way down the hill, off in the distance, hoeing in the field. He had left her exactly a year ago today. Trying to absorb the whole scene, he rushed to the well and dropped the bucket. He watched Joseph plowing with the mule while Billy[vii] worked behind him with a hoe. Constance, Hudson, and Selene opened up the rows and David and Isaac raked clumps of weeds. One little black girl dropped in the seeds while her sister tagged behind carrying the water bucket. Aaron lifted the dipper of cool water to his lips to help calm the fire raging inside him. Constance looked so small and frail. How could anyone that size possess such an enormous spirit? He longed to enfold her in his protective arms and give her a better life than this.

The blisters on Constance's hands ached each time she pulled the hoe. She chopped the clods of red clay with determination. They had made good progress and had almost the entire garden planted. Her lips turned up slightly at the thought of her visit with Aunt Martha last night. A shadow of her former self, Aunt Martha remained irrepressible. How they had laughed when they compared their lives as spies. Of course Aunt Martha decided to plan a party to welcome everyone back to Rixeyville. So what if there was little to eat? They still had each other.

[vii] Billy Magnum, the unknown Federal soldier injured at Cedar Mountain, was cared for by the citizens of Culpeper until his death in 1913. Many unsuccessful attempts were made to learn his identity.

Since Aunt Martha had agreed to come and help Sadie with the children, Constance remained determined to leave in the morning to go to Petersburg in search of Aaron. She could not, would not, accept the fact that he might be one of the thousands of missing soldiers buried in unmarked graves. There must be another answer.

She paused and rubbed her hands against the throbbing muscles in the small of her back that cramped into knots. Taking her gloves off, she stared at her callused bleeding fingers, pulled the handkerchief from her pocket, wiped the beads of sweat from her face, and blotted the blood on her fingers. She leaned against the hoe allowing her eyes to sweep the horizon. It would be dark soon; they must hurry to finish.

Suddenly her eyes riveted towards the house. She squinted to be sure. Yes, it looked like a man standing by the well. She blinked her eyes several times thinking it was a mirage. Her imagination had been playing tricks on her. No, he was definitely there and she sensed that he was staring back at her. Although she could not see him clearly, his tall height was obvious. She dropped the hoe and gloves and took a few cautious steps forward, feeling the grit through the holes in her shoes. "Aaron?" she whispered incredulously to herself. Trembling, she was afraid to hope again.

He took off his hat and waved it high above his head in a salute to her. Yes! She could see that curly unruly hair she loved so dearly! Her heart exploding with joy, she picked up her skirt and began to run. "Aaron!" she screamed at the top of her lungs.

"Constance!" she heard him call back. He rushed down the hill towards her. Her heart hammering in her chest, she ran faster. When she reached the tall grass she puffed her way up the hill. Slipping, she fell forward and caught herself on her bleeding hand, as her straw hat tumbled to the ground. He charged through the grass towards her, taking long strides. She struggled to get to him, to touch him.

"Aaron!" she screamed again, her legs thrashing wildly. The tears blurred her vision but she hurled herself forward, her chest heaving laboriously. She heard his feet pounding against the earth.

"Constance, I love you!" His athletic body surged towards her. She reached out her arms and leaped into his strong embrace. His mouth covered hers hungrily, setting her aflame. Her fingers became entangled in his hair, caressed the tendons of his neck as he crushed her against him. His tongue explored the recesses of her mouth again and again sending shivers racing through her. Blood pounded in her brain, leapt through her heart while she absorbed the firmness of his lips against hers. He slowly lowered her so that the tips of her toes touched the ground. His moist lips moved over her cheeks, her eyes, her forehead, tasting the salt of her tears of joy.

She ran her fingertips over his beard, caressed his face realizing it, too, was wet. She felt his heart pounding against hers, tried to find her voice. "Love you," she managed to whisper into his ear. He smothered her lips with demanding mastery. Melting, her knees grew weak. She lifted her chin until his eyes probed her very soul. "I surrender my heart to you," she whispered as her lips brushed his. "Now and forever. Marry me."

The tenderness of his gaze told her everything he felt. "Yes, a thousand times yes," he whispered huskily. "You captured my heart a long time ago." They both laughed and cried at the same time, each one trying to consume the other with kisses. The feel of his body against hers lulled her into a blissful euphoria.

"Feared you were dead…where…have you been?" She moved her hands over his powerful shoulders.

"Kicked in the head by a horse." He showered kisses down her slender white neck. "Unconscious...then no memory." His warm lips pressed against the throbbing hollow at the base of her throat. "Suddenly, four days ago, my mind cleared. It all came back to me."

"I knew God would hear my cry." She took his face in her hands. "I prayed for two hours for your return; lay prostrate on the floor of the church." Her fingertips caressed the gold cross around his neck.

His hazel eyes glistened with tears again. "I've thanked God a million times over the last four days for not leaving me like Billy. We've been blessed. He has a purpose for our lives." His large hands explored the soft lines of her back, her waist, her hips.

"I'm afraid I come with a lot of dependents. Are you willing to accept that challenge?"

His lips brushed the top of her head. "I met little Hattie. I'm already smitten." He stood back and looked at the others in the field. They were all frozen in a tableau, watching the touching love scene without a dry eye amongst them. "Know them all..." His fingers caressed her ear lobes. "Care for them all...share your responsibility." He swung her into the circle of his arms, holding her snugly. "Guess I've got a lot to learn about farming."

She buried her face against the corded muscles of his chest. "Joseph is capable of running the farm. I've got a better job for you."

He pulled back and stared into her eyes with his eyebrows raised. "And what would that be?"

"We've got a newspaper to run. Mr. McDonald fled to Canada to avoid living under Yankee rule and gave me the deed to the building."

His face creased into an irresistible smile, then he chuckled. "That's the perfect job for us. Can you imagine how we'll censor each other? One thing's for sure, we'll have to print the truth."

She moved her hands around his firm, narrow waist. "True. As much as I hate to admit it, I believe the good people of Culpeper will accept a Yankee male editor before they'd accept a female one." Her brows moved together in a frown and she stuck her chin out. "I suspect illiterate black men will be given the right to vote while educated women remain powerless. But, that's...another battle to be fought," she sighed with sparks in her eyes.

Delighted to see her fighting spirit back, he threw his head back in a laugh. "My beautiful spirited Rebel! I will support you every step of the way." He hoisted her high above his head, whirling in a circle. "I believe I have loved you since that very first day you defiantly marched out to meet us on almost this exact spot." Slowly, he lowered her until her parted lips met his. She pulsed with desire as her body gradually slid over his to the ground.

"I'm burning up," she said with ragged breath. "Let's go to the well for water."

She felt the movement of his thigh pressed against her hip while they walked up the hill, arms around each other, relishing the excitement of their body contact.

Sadie, not wanting to be caught spying, jumped back around the corner of the house and wiped a tear from her eye. She was ready to join Abraham in paradise now that her dearest child was happy.

Aaron looked down at her thoughtfully. "Constance, we'll run the paper until we get on our feet financially. Then I'll turn it over to you. My ultimate desire is to be a doctor. I'm determined to discover better ways to heal people."

"Aaron, you'd make a wonderful, compassionate doctor!" She dipped into the bucket of water and drank greedily, moving her tongue over her mouth. "If that's your dream, we'll work together until you achieve it." The water didn't quench her raging desire. She tingled while he traced his fingertips lightly up her arms. Suddenly, the touch of his hand was almost unbearable in its tenderness. "Hungry?" She leaned against his firm body.

She felt his moist breath in her hair. "Only for your love."

Looking into his magnetic eyes, she said in her soft sultry southern drawl, "You owe me two hours of back scratching, Yank. Pay up."

His eyes sparkled with merriment and passion. "Does this mean the wily Stringfellow is alive? I know Mosby survives."

"Yes, he was here last week. He's fled to Canada because of the bounty on his head."

He captured her with his eyes. "I look forward to shaking his hand one day and telling him what a helluva swimmer I think he is." He leaned forward placing his muscular arm under her knees and lifted her weightlessly into his arms. "But now I intend to honor my wager," he whispered. He carried her with long, purposeful strides towards the house.

She wrapped her arms around his neck, moved her lips against his ear, and felt their pulses racing in unison. Looking over his shoulder, her eyes drank in the eternal beauty of the blue mountains outlined against the gilt-edged magenta clouds. Miraculously, out of the swirling smoke, death, and devastation of the holocaust, God had sent her this magnificent man from Maine, a man she knew she would love passionately for the rest of her life, a man who would accept her as an equal partner. Life was good again. Floating in a cocoon of euphoria, she heard the thud of his boot on the threshold.

It was over.

Epilogue

The healing hands of time and the staunch determination of Culpeper's citizens returned the county to its former beauty. Today it remains a predominantly rural county with undulating fields and breathtaking mountain vistas. It is, as George Washington said, "a high and pleasant situation," an idyllic spot to while away a weekend or a lifetime. The county boasts over 190 antebellum structures, including the following ones named in this book: Afton, the Ashby's House, Ashland, Auburn, Beauregard, Clover Hill, the Episcopal Rectory, Gourdvine Baptist Church, Greenwood, A. P. Hill's boyhood home, the Hill Mansion, Little Fork Episcopal Church, Madden's Tavern, Redwood, Rose Dale, Rose Hill, Pleasant Hill, Saint Stephen's Episcopal Church, Salubria, Summerduck, Val Verde, the Virginia House Hotel, and Zimmerman's Tavern.

At long last, portions of the Cedar Mountain and Brandy Station battlefields have been preserved for posterity. However, funds are needed to interpret these historical sites for the public and much more needs to be done in the way of preservation. Today, the enemy marching from the north towards Culpeper is urban sprawl. Time is running out. Once lost, these precious fields where our forefathers died can never be regained.

To plan a trip or help with preservation efforts, contact:

The Museum of Culpeper History
Hours & Tours 540-829-1749
Office 540-829-6434 Fax 9698
http://www.culpepermuseum.com

Culpeper County Chamber of Commerce
109 South Commerce Street
Culpeper, Virginia 22701
540-825-8628 Fax 1449
culpepercc@summit.net
www.culpepervachamber.com

The Civil War Preservation Trust
11 Public Square, Suite 200
Hagerstown, Maryland 21740
301-665-1400 Fax 1416
www.civilwar.org

The Brandy Station Foundation
P.O. Box 165
Brandy Station, Virginia 22714
http//www.brandystation.org
703-403-1910

Fact verses fiction

Constance Armstrong is based on Bessie Shackelford, the daughter of Judge Henry Shackelford. The family lived across the street from the Virginia House Hotel as well as at their farmhouse in the country. Bessie and her sisters were described as extraordinary for their era due to their classical education and outspokenness on public issues. incorporated everything I knew about Bessie into Constance's character while striving to weave an entertaining and educational tale.

According to local lore, there was a romance between Bessie and John Pelham. He and Heroes VonBorcke visited her home for two weeks in Feb. 1863 and Pelham died in her home following the Battle of Kelly's Ford as described in this book. However some history buffs maintain that Pelham was secretly engaged to Sally Dandridge of the Bower. Thus, Constance's romance with Pelham is perhaps exaggerated, but it appears several young ladies donned black at the time of his death believing they were his intended. In no way is this story intended to tarnish Pelham's reputation. Since he was admired by many ladies, no one knows whom he would have married had he lived His memory and honor deservedly shine even brighter today as more people learn of his fame, popularity, phenomenal bravery and battle record.

There is no indication that Beckam and Pelham competed for the affection of the same young lady, although they certainly could have because Beckam was a native of the area. A letter Beckam wrote his father shortly before his death indicates he may have been engaged, but the identity of his intended is unknown.

Bessie Shackelford married a Union officer at the end of the war. The details of their romance remain a mystery.

About the author

Richmond native Virginia Beard Morton has lived in Culpeper for over thirty-four years. The Longwood College graduate is a former teacher. She became fascinated with Culpeper's vast Civil War history and decided to tell Culpeper's story to the world. This is her first novel.

In addition, she conducts Civil War Walking Tours of historic downtown Culpeper and narrates tours of the Brandy Station, Cedar Mountain, and Kelly's Ford battlefields by appointment.

A frequent speaker at Civil War Round Tables, civic groups, libraries and book clubs, she was a particapant in a panel discussion on historical fiction at the Virginia Festival of the Book. She joined a panel of Civil War writers at the Mary Washington College President's Book Club, and served as leader of a HistoryAmerica Mississippi Riverboat Cruise focusing on "Women in the Civil War."

She welcomes comments and questions about the book. You may contact her or purchase signed copies of this book at:

www.edgehillbooks.com, vbmorton@edgehillbooks.com
800-431-1579 (orders only), 540-825-9147
Edgehill Books
P.O. Box 1342
Orange, Virginia 22960

Notes

Chapter 2

1. Richmond *Inquirer*, January 1, 1861, p. 2
2. Richmond, *Inquirer,* January 1, 1861, p. 2.
3. Culpeper *Observer*, January 11, 1861. pp. 2-3.
4. Crofts, *Reluctant Confederates*, pp. 267-68, 270-71.
5. Ibid, pp. 13, 15.
6. Ibid, p. 23.
7. Sutherland, *Seasons of War*, pp. 34-5.

Chapter 3

1. Brown, *Stringfellow of the Fourth*, p. 3
2. Ibid, p. 8.
3. Faust, *Mothers of Invention*, p.14
4. Schenck, *Up Came Hill*, p. 8.
5. Brown, *Stringfellow of the Fourth*, pp. 12-15.
6. Sutherland, *Seasons of War*, p. 57.
7. Ibid, p. 58.
8. Faust, *Mothers of Invention*, p. 13.
9. Brown, *Stringfellow of the Fourth*, pp. 43-4.
10. Hammond, *Diary of a Union Lady*, pp. 26, 32.
11. From a lecture given by Stringfellow in Warrenton, Va. 1878.

Chapter 4

1. Brown, *Stringfellow of the Fourth*, pp. 61, 62.
2. Faust, *Mothers of Invention*, p.14.
3. Hassler, *Col. John Pelham, Lee's Boy Artillerist*, p. 26.
4. Ibid, p. 66.
5. Robertson, *General A. P. Hill*, p. 47.

Chapter 5

1. Sutherland, *Seasons of War*, p. 100.
2. Cooke, *Wearing of the Gray*, pp. 12, 13.
3. McGuire, *Diary of a Southern Refugee*, p. 15.
4. Letter from John Pelham to his brother, Samuel, Feb. 26, 1859.
5. Hammond, *Diary of a Union Lady*, pp. 98, 99, 106.
6. *War of the Rebellion*, vol. 12, pt. 2, pp. 50-52.

Chapter 6

1. Richmond *Daily Dispatch*, July 25, 1862.
2. Lee, *Wartime Papers,* pp. 239, 271.
3. Brown, *Stringfellow of the Fourth*, pp. 153-4.
4. Ibid, p. 155.
5. Mcguire, *Diary of a Southern Refugee*, p. 66.
6. Blackford, *Letters from Lee's Army*, p. 99.
7. *Official Record*, XII, pt. 2, p. 214.
8. Townsend, *Campaigns of a Non-combatant*, pp. 248-9.
9. McGuire, *Address*.
10. Krick, *Stonewall Jackson at Cedar Mountain*, p. 51.
11. Neese, *Horse Artillery*, p. 86, SHSP 10:89.
12. Dabney, *Life of Jackson*, p. 501.
13. Blackford, *Letters*, p. 105.
14. Buck, *Gen. Joseph A. Walker*, p. 36.
15. Brown, *Stringfellow of the Fourth*, pp. 155-6.
16. Strother, *A Virginia Yankee in the Civil War*, pp. 77-8.
17. Cooke, *Stonewall Jackson*, p. 265.
18. Strother, *A Virginia Yankee in the Civil War*, p. 80.
19. Claims of Willis Madden, No. 128.
20. Ibid
21. Krick, *Stonewall Jackson at Cedar Mountain*, p. 349.
22. Ibid, p. 350.
23. Townsend, *Campaigns of a Non-Combatant*, p. 270.
24. Ibid, p. 262.

Chapter 7

1. Cooke, *Wearing of the Gray*, p. 196-7.
2. Ibid, p. 158.
3. Milham, *Gallant Pelham*, p. 121.
4. Sutherland, *Seasons of War*, p. 184.
5. Brown, *Stringfellow of the Fourth*, p. 160.
6. Thomas, *Bold Dragoon*, p. 146.
7. Ibid, p. 147.
8. Ibid, p. 147.
9. Davis, *They Called Him Stonewall*, p. 287.

10. Brown, *Stringfellow of the Fourth,* pp. 165-6.

Chapter 8

1. Bartlett, *My Dear Brother,* pp. 23-25.
2. Semmes, *Memoirs of Service Afloat,* p. 61.
3. Tate, *Stonewall Jackson,* p. 241.
4. Ibid, p. 207.
5. Durkin, *John Dooley, Confederate Soldier,* p. 28.
6. McGuire, *Diary of a Southern Refugee,* p. 279.
7. Ibid, p. 279.
8. Hammond, *Diary of a Union Lady,* p. 169.
9. Ibid, p. 171.
10. Ibid, p. 170.

Chapter 9

1. Robertson, *General A. P. Hill,* p. 157.
2. Ibid, p. 157.
3. Hassler, *Col. John Pelham, Lee's Boy Artillerist,* p. 95.
4. Von Borcke, *Memoirs of the Confederate War,* Vol. 2, p. 49.
5. Ibid, p. 55.
6. Davis, *The Gray Fox,* p. 161.
7. Von Borcke, *Memoirs of the Confederate War,* Vol. 2, p. 54.
8. Hammond, *Diary of a Union Lady,* p. 177.
9. Ibid, p. 179.
10. Ibid, p. 184.

Chapter 10

1. Thomas, *Bold Dragoon,* p. 199.
2. Von Borcke, *Memoirs of the Confederate War,* pp. 180-1.
3. Ibid, p. 181.
4. Ibid, p. 181.
5. Constance Carey to Clarence Cary, LOC, March 7, 1863.
6. Gilmor, *Four Years in the Saddle,* p. 66.
7. Milham, *Gallant Pelham,* p. 231.
8. Gilmor, *Four Years in the Saddle,* p. 70.
9. Milham, *Gallant Pelham,* p. 231.
10. Gilmore, *Four Years in the Saddle,* p. 72.
11. Milham, *Gallant Pelham,* p. 233.
12. Ibid, p. 235.

Chapter 11

1. Brown, *Stringfellow of the Fourth,* pp. 172-181.
2. Tate, *Stonewall Jackson,* p. 288.
3. Ibid, p. 289.
4. General Fitzhugh Lee's Chancellorsville Address
5. Von Borcke, *Memoirs of the Confederate War,* p. 258.

Chapter 12

1. Sutherland, *Seasons of War,* pp. 240-1.
2. Brown, *Stringfellow of the Fourth,* p. 198.
3. Gallager, "Brandy Station," pp. 19-20.
4. Sutherland, *Seasons of War,* p. 249.
5. McClellan, *I Rode with Jeb Stuart,* p. 292.
6. Ibid, p. 292.
7. Ibid, p. 292.
8. Brown, *Stringfellow of the Fourth,* pp. 206-7.

Chapter 13

1. Faust, *Mothers of Invention,* p. 183.
2. Ibid, p. 181.
3. Hammond, *Diary of a Union Lady,* p. 246.
4. Ibid, p. 248.
5. Ibid, pp. 249-50.
6. Ibid, pp. 250-1.
7. Ibid, p. 251.
8. Stiles, *Four Years Under Marse Robert,* pp. 203-5.
9. Utley, *Cavalier in Buckskin,* p. 24.
10. Henderson, *The Road to Bristoe Station,* p. 23.
11. Brown, *Stringfellow of the Fourth,* pp. 211-13.
12. Ibid, p. 213.

Chapter 14

1. Cooke, *Wearing of the Gray,* pp. 474-82.
2. Brown, *Stringfellow of the Fourth,* pp. 217-9.

Chapter 15

1. Henderson, *The Road to Bristoe Station,* p. 85-6.
2. Suterhland, *Seasons of War,* p. 190.
3. Wert, *Custer,* p. 117.
4. Sutherland, *Seasons of War,* p. 293.

Henderson, *The Road to Bristoe Station,*
    p. 190.
. Ibid, p. 193.
. Baylor, *Bull Run to Bull Run,* p. 178.
. Hassler, *A. P. Hill,* p. 181.

Chapter 16
. Brown, *Stringfellow of the Fourth,* p.
    224.
. Ibid, pp. 225-6.
. Ibid, pp. 226-7.

Chapter 17
. Brown, *Stringfellow of the Fourth,* pp.
    227-30.
2. Ibid, pp. 230-34.
3. Ibid, pp. 242-3.
4. Ibid, pp. 244-5.

Chapter 18
1. Brown, *Stringfellow of the Fourth,* pp.
    246-7.
2. Ibid, pp. 247-49.
3. Frost, *General Custer's Libbie,* p. 97.
4. Brown, *Stringfellow of the Fourth,* pp.
    250-1.
5. Ibid, pp. 252-5.
6. Schultz, *The Dahlgren Affair,* p. 109.

Chapter 19
1. Barnett, *Touched by Fire,* p. 38.
2. Trout, *They Followed the Plume,* p. 296-7

Chapter 20
1. Madden, *We Were Always Free,* pp. 109-
    10.
2. Perret, *Ulysses S. Grant, Soldier and
    President,* p. 307.
3. Bakeless, *Spies of the Confederacy,* p.
    369.

Chapter 21
1. Hall, *Robt. F. Beckam,* Dec. '91, Blue &
    Gray
2. McDonald, *A Woman's Civil War Diary,*
    p. 222.

Chapter 22
1. Robertson, *General A. P. Hill,* pp.
    319-21.

Avary, Marta Lockett. *A Virginia Girl in The Civil War.* New York, N.Y., 1903.

Bakeless, John. *Spies of the Confederacy.* Philadelphia & New York, 1970.

Bartlett, Catherine Thom. Ed. and comp. *"My Dear Brother" Confederate Chronicle* Richmond, 1952.

Barnett, Louise. *Touched by Fire.* New York, N.Y., 1996.

Baylor, George. *Bull Run to Bull Run.* Washington, D. C., 1983.

Blackford, Charles M. *Letters from Lee's Army.* New York, N.Y., 1947.

Brown, R. Shepard. *Stringfellow of the Fourth.* New York, 1960.

Buck, Lucy Rebecca. *Sad Earth, Sweet Heaven,The Diary of Lucy Rebecca Buck during the War between the States,* Birmingham. Ala., 1973

Buck, Samuel D. "General Joseph A. Walker." *Confederate Veteran* 10 (1902): 32-36.

Calfee, Mrs. Berkeley G. *Confederate History of Culpeper County in the War Between the States.* Culpeper, Va. 1948

Cooke, John Esten. *Stonewall Jackson, A Military Biography.* New York, N.Y., 1866.

Cooke, John Esten. *Wearing of the Gray: Being Personal Portraits, Scenes and Adventures of the War.* Ed. by Philip Van Doren Stern. Bloomington, Ind., 1959.

Crofts, Daniel W. *Reluctant Confederates: Upper South Unionists in the Secession Crisis.* Chapel Hill, N.C., 1989.

Culpeper Historical Society. *Historic Culpeper,* Culpeper, Va., 1974.

Dabney, Robert L. *Life and Campaigns of Lieut.-General Stonewall Jackson.* New York, N.Y., 1866.

Davis, Burke. *Gray Fox: Robert E. Lee and the Civil War.* New York, N.Y., 1981.

Davis, Burke. *They Called Him Stonewall: A Life of Lt. General T.J. Jackson, C.S.A..* New York, N.Y., 1954.

Durkin, Joseph T., S.J. *John Dooley Confederate Soldier, His War Diary.* Georgetown, D.C., 1945.

Faust, Drew Gilpin. *Mothers of Invention: Women of the Slaveholding South in the American Civil War.* Chapel Hill, N.C., 1996.

Frost, Lawrence A. *General Custer's Libbie.* Seattle, Washington

Gallager, Gary W. "Brandy Station: The Civil War's Bloodiest Arena of Mounted Combat." *Blue & Gray,* VII (October 1990), pp. 8-12, 44-53.

Gilmor, Harry. *Four Years in the Saddle.* New York, 1866.

Hackley, Woodford B. *The Little Fork Rangers: A Sketch of Company "D," Fourth Virginia Cavalry.* Richmond, Va. 1927.

Hall, Clark B. "The Battle of Brandy Station." *Civil War Times,* XXIX (May-June 1990), pp. 32-42, 45.

Hall, Clark B. "Robert F. Beckam: The Man Who Commanded Stuart's Horse Artillery After Pelham Fell." *Blue & Gray, IX (December 1991), pp 34-37*

Hall, Clark B. "Season of Change: The Winter Encampment of the Army of the Potomac, December 1, 1863 – May 4, 1864." *Blue & Gray,* VIII (April 1991), pp. 8-22, 48-62.

Hammond, Harold Earl. *Diary of a Union Lady 1861-1865.* New York, 1962.

Hassler, William Woods. *A .P. Hill: Lee's Forgotten General.* Richmond, Va., 1957.

Hassler, William Woods. *Colonel John Pelham, Lee's Boy Artillerist.* Richmond, Va. 1960.

Henderson, William D. *The Road to Bristoe Station: Campaigning with Lee and Meade, August 1 – October 20, 1863.* Lynchburg, Va. 1987.

Jones & Jones, *Historic Culpeper*

Kennedy, James Ronald and Kennedy, Walter Donald. *The South Was Right!* Gretna, La., 1991.

Kidd, J.H. *Riding With Custer: Recollections of a Cavalryman in the Civil War.* Lincoln, Neb. 1997

Krick, Robert K. *Stonewall Jackson at Cedar Mountain.* Chapel Hill, N.C., 1990.

Lee, Robert E., Jr. *Recollections and Letters of General Robert E. Lee.* New York, N.Y., 1904.

Madden, T. O. Jr. *We Were Always Free: The Maddens of Culpeper County, Virginia; A 200-Year Family History.* New York, N. Y., 1992

McCellan, H. B. *I Rode With J.E.B. Stuart.* Bloomington, Ind.

McDonald, Cornelia Peake. *A Woman's Civil War Dairy, with Reminiscences of the War from March 1862.* Madison, Wis. 1992.

McGuire, Hunter Holmes. *Address of Dr. Hunter McGuire...on June 23, 1897.* Lynchburg, Va., *1897.*

McGuire, Judith W. *Diary of a Southern Refugee.* New York, 1972.

Milham, Charles G. *Gallant Pelham American Extraordinary.* Washington, D.C., 1959

Neese, George M. *Three Years in the Confederate Horse Artillery.* New York, N.Y., 1911.

Perret, *Ulysses S. Grant, Soldier and President.* New York, N.Y., 1997.

Robertson, James I., Jr. *General A. P. Hill: The Story of a Confederate Warrior.* New York, 1987.

Rozwenc, Edwin C. *The Causes of The American Civil War,* Boston, Massachussettes, 1961.

Schenck, Martin. *Up Came Hill: The Story of the Light Division and Its Leaders.* Harrisonburg, Va., 1958.

Schultz, Duane. *The Dahlgren Affair.* New York, 1998.

Semmes. *Memoirs of Service Afloat*

Springer, Francis W. *War For What.* Nashville, Tenn., 1990.

Stackpole, Edward J. *From Cedar Mountain to Antietam, August – September, 1862.* Harrisburg, Pa., 1959.

Stiles, Robert. *Four Years Under Marse Rober.* New York & Washington, *1903.*

Strother, David H. *A Virginia Yankee in the Civil War, The Diaries of David H. Strother,* edited by Cecil D. Eby, Jr. Chapel Hill, N.C., 1961.

Sutherland, Daniel E. *Seasons of War, The Ordeal of a Confederate Community, 1861-1865.* New York, 1995.

Tate, Allen. *Stonewall Jackson, The Good Soldier.* Ann Arbor, Michigan, 1957.

Thomas, Emory M. *Bold Dragoon, The Life of J.E.B. Stuart.* New York, N. Y., 1986.

Townsend, George Alfred. *Campaigns of a Non-Combatant.* New York, 1866.

Trout, Robert J. *They Followed the Plume: The Story of J.E.B. Stuart and His Staff.*

Mechanicsburg, Pa., 1993.

Utley, Robert M. *Cavalier in Buckskin.* Oklahoma, 1988.

Von Borcke, Heros. *Memoirs of the Confederate War for Independence.* New York, 1938

Wert, Jeffry D. *Custer: The Controversial Life of George Armstrong Custer.* New York, N.Y., 1996.

Wert, Jeffry D. *Mosby's Rangers.* New York, N.Y., 1990.

War of the Rebellion. Vl. 12, pt 2, pp.50-55.

Newspapers and letters:

Richmond *Inquirer.* Jan. 1, 1861, P. 2.

Culpeper Observer, Janauary 11, 1861, pp. 2-3.

Claims of Willis Madden, No. 128.

Constance Cary to Clarence Cary, March 7, 1863, Library of Congress

General Fitzhugh Lee's Chancellorsville Address

McCellan, G. B., MSS. Letter from A. P. Hill to G. B. McClellan, June 18, 1859